SOMETIMES THE DRAGON WINS

ii

Library of Congress Catalog Number 93-094263
International Standard Book No. 0-9616282-2-7

Published by Van Trees Associates
P. O. Box 2062, Fairborn, OH 45324-8062

Manufactured by BookCrafters, Chelsea, Michigan 48118-0370

PRINTED IN THE UNITED STATES OF AMERICA

Dedicated to the more than nine hundred men, women, and children whose mortal remains have blended with hallowed soil on the banks of the Wabash River where Fort Recovery was erected in late 1793.

BOOKS   BY

ROBERT V. VAN TREES

BANKS   OF   THE   WABASH
ORDINANCE   OF   FREEDOM

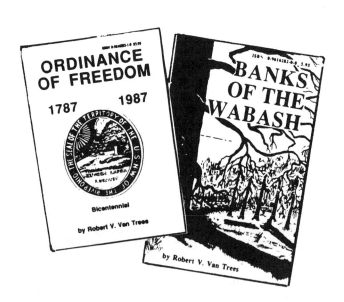

AUTHOR'S NOTE

In writing this story about a young settler's journey from Maryland to the "territory" created by the Ordinance of 1787, and his trials and tribulations as he stubbornly faced the ordeal of frontier life, the author has diligently attempted to remain true to historic and geographic fact.

Born and raised in an area of Ohio which hosted pivotal events crucial to this nation's westward expansion, and stimulated by informative and interesting story-telling by my grandfather years before television erased that fascinating pastime from the family scene, the author has endeavored to "unfold" the pages of this country's "diaper years" history. The incidents referred to in this story did happen, the dates are factual, and most characters lived in the role in which they are portrayed. In an effort to tie together related events, and still provide the reader a smooth-flowing narrative, dialogue has been freely supplemented--but not at the expense of historical accuracy.

Believing an understanding of our progenitor's sacrifices is important to the proper appreciation of our 20th century way of life, the author hopes this narrative will provide the reader an informative picture of frontier life and the brave people who inhabitated the Northwest Territory two hundred years ago.

But no one writes a book without a lot of help and foremost among many whom the author is indebted is my Pennsylvania bride, Marjorie Helen Van Trees, whose patience and assistance never wa vered during the lengthy period of research and writing of this narrative. I also wish to express my appreciation for the knowledgeable assistance provided me by Mrs Virginia Staugler, Fort Recovery Library; Julie M. Overton, Greene County Library, Xenia, OH; Shirley G.M. Iscrupe, Curator of Collections, Fort Ligonier

Association, Ligonier, PA; John P. & Nancy Louella Dolan, Alpharetta, GA; and Lt Col Karl R. Johnson, USAF (Ret), President, 2nd Infantry Reg't Officer's Association, Fairborn, OH.

In traveling from Washington, D.C. to Madison, WI; Lexington, KY to Ann Arbor, MI; and Fort Wayne, IN to Blue Jacket, OK, I never met a librarian or courthouse clerk who was not willing, and able, to help me in locating and retrieving manuscripts and source material from which this book was written. A few of the many correspondents and contacts who aided this effort are listed below with an asterisk indicating those who were particularly helpful in research of the Swearingen and Blue Jacket lineage:

	Austin, Eva (Tolan)	St. Cloud, FL
*	Bailey, Chris H.	Bristol, CT
	Barnhart, Terry A.	OHS, Columbus, OH
	Butler, Stuart L.	NA, Washington, D.C.
*	Chadwick, George C.	Xenia, OH
	Crebbs, Ruthe E.	Steubenville, OH
	Freemyer, Robert L.	Fort Recovery, OH
	Hein, Charles J.	Fort Recovery, OH
	Hiestand, O.S. Jr	Bethesda, MD
	Irelan, William T.	Washington, D.C.
*	Johnson, Louise F.	Round Rock, TX
*	Kincaid, John W.	Norman, OK
	Knapke, Nancy	Fort Recovery, OH
*	Meek, Mrs. Jean	Cardin, OK
	Miller, Anna Louise	Fort Recovery, OH
*	Mize, Leoti Jean	Sarasota, FL
	Seiler, Toni T.	Greenville, OH
*	Spencer, Donna R.	Huntsville, OH
*	Sprenger, Martha	Sioux City, IA
*	Swearengin, Gene	Franklin, OH
*	Swearingen, Richard	Crawfordsville, IN
	Wagner, James J.	Lafayette, IN
*	Williams, Mary Len	Tulsa, OK
*	Wolfe, Nancy C.	Columbus, OH

PREFACE

In the immense virgin wilderness region of the United States later apportioned among the states of Ohio, Indiana, Illinois, Michigan, Wisconsin, and a part of Minnesota, the divergent cultures and varying interests of the pioneer settlers met—one 19th century chronicler called it "America's first real melting pot!" When the French and Indian war ended in 1763, France was forced to cede to Great Britain most of her colonial empire in North America. That same year, 1763, King George III decreed, by royal proclamation, that all land west of the Alleghenies would henceforth be "off limits" to settlers. But German and Dutch settlers paid little attention to this order they could not read and the Scottish and Irish immigrants refused to recognize the decree. Through the compromise efforts by delegates of the thirteen contentious and discordant states, in the summer of 1787 the Continental Congress adopted an historic ordinance which created "The Territory Of The United States Northwest Of The River Ohio." Armed with axe, hunting rifle, and land stakes—and strengthened by unbounded hope—the freedom-loving, land-hungry immigrants trudged across the mountains to challenge the timeless sylvan region beyond the Ohio. It was a vast area which had heretofore only known the presence of abundant game and the silent footsteps of its copper-colored natives.

"Deeds" and "ownership" of the land were words Indians didn't understand. The Shawnees in particular had an infinite reverence for the land. They firmly believed "The Great Manitou" had given them

the right to live and hunt on the land, to protect
it, and become a part of it when they died. Stead-
fast in their heathenish convictions, they believed
Manitou, "The Supreme Being," had created the Shawnees first from his brain with all the wisdom and
knowledge this spirit of good and evil influence
possessed--all of the other Indians descended from
the Shawnees. Having created the favored Shawnees,
Manitou then made the white man from other parts of
his body such as the Americans from his hands and
and the English from his breast. Because they were
inferior to Manitou's favorite red-skinned people,
he had located white men "far away across the great
salt water according to the Shawnee's belief."

But despite their pagan belief Manitou planned
a world divided along such color lines, after the
Continental Congress adopted the Ordinance of 1787,
the "Magna Carta" of American colonial expansion,
the red man's isolated tranquility was doomed. Referring to the historic charter, President Franklin
Roosevelt eloquently stated: "The principles there-
in embodied served as the highway, broad and safe,
over which poured the westward march of our civilization!"

Into this "land of promise" surged the strong
and weak, young and old, rich and poor, artful and
naive, proud and humble, saint and sinner, civilian
and military. Some viewed the untouched wilderness
as posing unknown threats equally as dangerous as
those regions of Europe where mythical dragons had
lived. Pitting their skill against a foe whose way
of life and fighting were foreign to them, the sacrifices of military leaders like Generals Braddock,
Harmar, and St. Clair helped shape the destiny of
the westward march of civilization. But, being human, such "dragon killers" sometimes underestimated
their adversary in the Northwest Territory.

Among the mass of immigrants who rode, walked,
and floated into the Northwest Territory was Jason
Evenstar, twenty-four year old son of Johanne and

Catherine Evenstar. During his childhood Jason had
often listened carefully as visitors to his uncle's
blacksmith shop in Frederick, Maryland spoke of the
"faraway land beyond where the blue haze hangs over
the forested ridges of the Alleghenies" they called
"the Ohio country."

Early in life Jason had been shown a treasured
picture which his uncle said was brought to America
from Germany by his grandfather. Titled "Fighting
The Dragon," it was a copy of a pen-and-ink drawing
by Venetian artist, Jacopo Bellini.   Seated by the
fireplace at his uncle's knee, he often listened to
stories about those lizard-like mythical beasts and
how they were sometimes slain by the brave medieval
knights. According to the folklore of the European
Middle Ages, dragons represented the evil fought by
human beings. Such mythical dragons lived in wild,
remote regions where they often guarded huge caches
of treasures in their caves. Anyone who killed the
blood-thirsty beast became owner of the wealth. In
graphic detail Jason's foster-father had often told
the wide-eyed boy about Saint George, patron saint
of England, who killed a fierce fire-eating dragon
with a lance and rescued a beautiful princess being
held captive by the serpent-like monster.

In his childhood fantasy, Jason often tracked
such dragons to their lair along the Monocacy River
where he killed the fierce winged reptiles, seized
great stores of wealth, and freed lovely maidens in
distress. Having grown to manhood, and prayerfully
dreaming of the country he longed to see beyond the
Alleghenies, Jason's daydreaming sometimes included
imaginative thoughts wherein "the Ohio country" was
a faraway land of wealth and opportunity which must
be freed of dragons.   It never occurred to Jason--
and his uncle never mentioned it--but sometimes the
dragon wins.

C O N T E N T S

THE SEAL OF THE TERRITORY OF THE U.S. N.W. OF THE RIVER OHIO ·

MELIOREM LAPSA
LOCAVIT

CHAPTER ONE

THE GREAT CAT!

Silhouetted against the lengthening shadows of late evening, the settler walked slowly despite the invigorating crispness of the clear night air which typifies southwestern Pennsylvania in early March—1768 was no exception. The widower appeared old for his age—he felt old! Thrusting his mitten-covered hands deep into the pockets of his bearskin coat to ward off a sudden chill, the settler paused facing the western horizon. A tear rolled down his cheek as he recalled another time when his wife had stood beside him and watched a similar dying day—she had poetically described it as: "the Laurel's kiss to the sky's infinity." Now her mortal remains rested in a small grave behind his cabin.

The settler's visit to his brother-in-law's cabin—a stone's throw away from his own—had run a little late but there was no one waiting for him in his lonely abode so after supper he had toasted his toes by the fireplace and talked. Standing in the cold , and savoring a raspberry cobbler his sister-in-law had baked, the settler remembered his wife's good cooking. With the back of his mitten he wiped away an annoying tear and pensively recalled it had been "an eternity" since his wife died—in reality, two years and four months. Shaking his head sadly, he turned his thoughts to his son who was back east along the Monocacy River.

Johanne Evenstar recalled all too well how his irritation with England's detestable Stamp Act had prompted him to move from Maryland. This unpopular

edict, ratified by the British Parliament in March
of 1765, required every document, newspaper, deed,
pamphlet, license--even a college diploma--to have
affixed an infernal British stamp which cost from a
half penny to ten pounds. The opposition had been
immediate and violent as the cry was heard throughout the colonies::
    "Taxation without representation!"
    John Adams, a lawyer from Massachusetts, had
voiced his opposition loudly: "This tax was set on
foot for my ruin as well as that of Americans in
general!"
    Years later, upon being chosen the first Vice
President of the United States, this outspoken man
called this position "the most insignificant office
that ever the invention of man contrived or his imagination ever conceived!"
    Equally outspoken, and an eloquent speaker, in
1765 Patrick Henry stood before Virginia's House of
Burgesses and emphatically warned King George III
of the fearful consequences of the hated Stamp Act.
He concluded his moving remarks declaring: "If this
be treason, make the most of it!"
    Ten years later, on March 23, 1775, this same
statesman would face the members of a Revolutionary
Convention at the St. Johns Church in Richmond and
with great emotion proclaim his unequivocal stand:
"Give me liberty or give me death!"
    Colonial protest against taxation was destined
to prompt calling the First Continental Congress at
Carpenter Hall in Philadelphia during September of
1774 and this subject was foremost in the minds of
those who gathered the next year on May 10th at the
State House for the Second Continental Congress.
    Although the Stamp act was repealed by England
the next year after its passage, the strong-willed
Johanne Evenstar had left Maryland. The burden of
unnecessary taxation was vexing and growing talk of
a "revolution" was of great concern. To escape the
turmoil of the Frederick County area, Johanne had

just loaded up his pregnant wife and belongings and moved west. Beyond Fort Cumberland, at the "Great Crossing" of the Youghiogheny River, Johanne turned his horses north. A few miles beyond "Three Forks" he stopped by a beautiful little stream and, in the summer of 1765, built a small log cabin at the foot of the Laurels. It was here, in this tiny one-room cabin that his son, Jason, was born on November 23, 1765--his wife, Catherine, died the same day.

A group of German Baptists had settled in this same region several years earlier and Johanne soon became friendly with many of them. In a spirit of true friendship, Johanne's neighbors offered understanding sympathy and any help if needed during his time of sorrow. Grateful for their thoughtfulness, but declining all offers of assistance, Johanne insisted on digging the little grave in which he laid his beloved wife to rest. Then, that same winter-- ten years before a group of determined New England citizens faced the British at "the rude bridge that arched the flood" and signaled the beginning of the Revolutionary War--Johanne carried his newborn son back east to the Monocacy Valley in Maryland where his wife's older brother, Frederick, agreed to take care of little Jason.

The trees along the Braddock Road were not yet in leaf a few months later when Johanne and another of wife's brothers, Conrad, returned to the shelter he had carved out of the wilderness at the foot of the Laurels. Laboring from sunrise to sunset, and helped by friendly neighbors, it was only a matter of days until they had erected for Conrad a window- less log cabin not far from Johanne's little cabin. To the delight of Conrad's wife, their cabin had a puncheon floor. After clearing some trees from the land along the river bottom, they planted a little patch of corn, beans and pumpkins in the moist loam and then watched with satisfaction as the fruits of their efforts blossomed. That fall the good earth yielded a bountiful reward for each seed planted.

Shortly after the first frost in the autumn of 1766, Johanne and Conrad took a hunting trip which led them north up the valley to where the west fork of the Kishkemanetas River crossed the Forbes Road. The road had been forged through the forest covered region from Raystown to Fort Pitt during the French and Indian War. As they rested their horses before traveling the twenty miles west to Fort Ligonier, a handsome gentleman hailed them. After a customary exchange of introductory remarks, the trio traveled west together on the John Forbes Road with Johanne and Conrad's new-found acquaintance politely pointing out geographical matters of interest.

They quickly learned this thirty-one year old Scottish born gentleman was on his way from Bedford to Fort Ligonier. As the trio stopped briefly for a drink at a small stream they crossed, Conrad asked the well-mannered gentleman about Fort Ligonier and a report he had heard that it was in a state of "disrepair." Politely, and with no outward show of vanity, the gentleman replied:

"Just this past March I was appointed by Major General Thomas Gage, Commander in Chief of all His Majesty's Forces in North America, as caretaker of Fort Ligonier. The fort is in a somewhat sad state of neglect but it is slowly being repaired. General Gage has been ordered to reduce his military budget and military posts seem to be the first to suffer. But I must say, the land around the Fort is fine-- the soil is rich and healthy. It produces all kinds of grain, hemp and flax. Captain Harry Gordon, a former engineer with General Forbe's army, visited with us recently and he was very optimistic regarding the future of His Majesty's Fort Ligonier."

Affable and energetic, their new found friend explained having had a preference for military life as opposed to "existence" among social equals.

"I was born in Thurso Castle on the northern tip of Scotland and studied the medical arts at the University of Edinburgh. For a brief period I was a surgeon's apprentice but decided to come to North America and fight in the war against the French."

He also explained how, on May 13, 1757, he had purchased an ensign's commission in the 60th Royal Regiment of Foot under the Duke of Cumberland.

"It was my good fortune to come to America in May of 1758 with General Jeffery Amherst's army and serve in the siege against Louisburg."

Pausing for a moment, he then added:

"Torn between purpose and doubt, I resigned my commission in 1762 and then, following some serious head-scratching while I rested on my laurels in the Boston area, I decided to come out here. It was my great pleasure the past several days to visit with, and accompany to Bedford, two missionaries, Charles Beatty and his associate. They were returning back east having visited the Indians along the Muskingum River in the Ohio country."

In the years that followed, Conrad would learn their new-found friend, Arthur St. Clair, had been a British officer in the service of General Wolfe and scaled the heights of Abraham in 1759 helping to wrest Quebec and Canada from France for England. Married on May 15, 1760 at the Trinity Chapel in Boston to Miss Phoebe Bayard--attractive and well educated niece of James Bowdoin, Governor of Massa-chusetts--St. Clair obtained by dowry the handsome sum of 20,000 pounds. Just when, or where, Arthur St. Clair began his life on Pennsylvania's western frontier is a matter of conjecture but his wife re-mained in Boston for some time after his first trip west about 1764. Regardless, St. Clair's integrity and common sense soon earned for him appointment as Commandant of Fort Ligonier.

During the ensuing years Conrad would find St. Clair to be an unselfish man, a wise counselor, and a trusted friend of the Indians whose acquaintance-ship he made. A man of wealth and property, it was plain to see Arthur St. Clair could enjoy the rest of his life in comparative ease. Unfortunately, as

history would record, this would not be his fate in
his adopted country where he was destined to be the
governor of a territory which knew no equal.

But such honor was twenty history-making years
in the future and now, on this crisp night in early
March of 1768, Johanne Evenstar watched spellbound
a silent awe-inspiring streak of light flash across
the star-studded stillness overhead. Marveling at
the wonderment of God's great universe, he recalled
a passage his wife had often quoted from one of her
treasured books, KING RICHARD by Wm Shakespeare:

"I see thy glory, like a shooting star,
Fall to the base earth, from the firmament."

And on this fateful night the brilliant heavenly phenomenon was the last thing Johanne Evenstar
would ever see this side of eternity. The tomahawk
made a sickening sound as it crashed into the young
settler's skull and a kaleidoscope of light flashed
across his mind before blackness obliterated everything. The two shadowy figures could not see the
twitching of the lifeless body as the taller one of
the killers now began cutting away the bloody scalp
while his evil companion removed the dead settler's
clothing. The shooting star had long disappeared
before the wicked pair had finished their loathsome
task and silently vanished in the woods surrounding
two small cabins in Bedford County, Pennsylvania.

Two hundred fifty miles west of where Johanne
Evenstar's lifeless body lay, the robust squall of
Methotasa's newborn child filled the conical pole
and animal skin shelter. Standing just outside the
wigwam, Pucksinwah heard the baby's healthy outcry
as he stoically watched a fiery atmospheric phenomenon made by the white-hot meteor streaking through
a darkened sky overhead. Thoughtfully contemplating
having witnessed the crossing over of msi-pish-wi,
"the great cat," Pucksinwah decided his newborn son
would be called "Tecumtha" (The Panther). It was

the ninth day of March in 1768.

Jason's foster father didn't see the meteoroid silently streak across his cabin along the Monocacy River in Maryland. Comfortably seated in his rocking chair near the fireplace, with his young nephew sprawled across his lap, he rocked slowly and gazed unseeingly at the pen and ink drawing on the wall-- the child's question about the drawing had prompted him to tell Jason a story about the medieval knight who rescued a beautiful princess from a scaly ferocious dragon. Frederick's wife urged him to avoid telling the child such tales before bedtime but the boy's insistence melted his aunt's resistance. The wide-eyed boy had listened attentively as his uncle related the gory details of a brave knight's battle with the fire-breathing winged dragon. Finally, at the firm suggestion of Frederick's wife, the story had ended and little Jason was in slumberland a few moments later. When the boy moved slightly with an involuntary jerk, and muttered a quick painful cry, Frederick pulled Jason close to him and soothingly patted the boy's backside as he said in a low voice coated with a tinge of merriment:

"Jason's after that dragon!"

Conrad found Johanne's lifeless body early the next morning and the nauseous mixture of hate, disgust, desolation, and futility which surged through his body was overwhelming. Although shocked by the dastardly murder, providence gave Conrad the needed strength to wield the mattock and shovel and dig a grave in the partially frozen soil behind Johanne's cabin. Then, as the late afternoon shadows of the Laurels mingled sadly with the barren trees, Conrad buried his brother-in-law beside his wife. Only a shallow depression in the earth evidenced the place where Conrad's younger sister had been laid to rest a little more than two years before.

Dejected and heartsick, Conrad buried with his brother-in-law the newspaper Johanne had wedged behind a muzzleloader which hung on the wall next to

8

Albrecht Durer's engraving of St.Michael
fighting the Dragon of the Apocalypse.

the fireplace.   Dated October 31, 1765, it was the
PENNSYLVANIA JOURNAL AND WEEKLY ADVERTISER, # 1195.
In bold print the headline declared it was William
Bradford's intent to cease publication of the news-
paper because of the Stamp Act:

EXPIRING! IN HOPES OF RESURRECTION TO LIFE AGAIN

Pausing occasionally to brush away tears that
blurred his vision, Conrad slowly filled the little
grave--with the excess dirt he leveled the adjacent
depression. Then, with the sun dropping behind the
Laurels, Conrad and his wife, and their only son,
walked slowly toward their cabin. Nothing was said
as Conrad entered the cabin, sat down in his rocker
by the fireplace, and stared into the flames. Quietly his wife pulled a chair close to his side and
began knitting.   Without being reminded, their ten
year old boy now filled the woodbox in an unusually
quiet manner, pulled in the latch string, and then
stretched out on the puncheon floor at his mother's
feet. Now the deathly silence of the room was only
broken by the sounds of wood crackling in the fireplace.   Despite a nauseous mixture of sympathy and
alarm which filtered into her normally optimistic
mind, Conrad's wife said nothing even when her husband spoke, addressing no one in particular:
    "Two years. Has it really only been two years
since we moved out here?"
    No one said a word---the question did not need
an answer. All too well Conrad's wife recalled the
spring of 1766 when they had joined Johanne for the
arduous trek west from the Monocacy Valley leaving
Jason behind.   Tearfully, Johanne had listened as
his kind brother-in-law had said:
    "Now don't you fret none. Me and maw is gonna
stay right here in Frederick County and we're gonna
see to it Jason gets book larnin'. I plan to teach
that little fellar how to play the fiddle too!"

Now Jason's birth parents were gone. Although saddened by his brother-in-law's tragic death, the long hours of hard work on the frontier left little time for grieving. As if providence somehow shared Conrad's mourning, the earth's bountiful rewards in the autumn of 1768 helped ease the painful memory of Johanne's senseless murder. On the way to Fort Pitt in the summer of 1769 Conrad talked at length with Arthur St. Clair at Fort Ligonier. As he told his friendly acquaintance:

"My sister Catherine and her husband, Johanne, are now at rest in the shadows of the Laurels. May God bless them both."

The two men paused for a moment of respectful silence and then St. Clair softly said:

"So mote it be."

With typical compassion St. Clair asked:

"And their son, Jason?"

"He lives with an older brother of mine along the Monocacy back in Maryland."

While riding together to Fort Pitt, St. Clair told Conrad about having submitted a request to the Governor for the acreage surrounding Fort Ligonier. Later this tract--in excess of five hundred acres--would be known as "The Octagon Tract." An optimist concerning the future of that area of western Pennsylvania, St. Clair said:

"Just last April Simon Eaker applied for three hundred acres of fine land joining Chestnut Ridge and Shelving Rocks on the southwest side of the Loyalhanna Creek. Four days later--seventh of April as I recall--John Grant applied for three hundred acres on Nine Mile Run close to Fort Ligonier--it joins my land. Perhaps you might be interested in a piece of land here yourself Conrad. You could do worse you know."

The "piece of land" St. Clair spoke of was in an area of western Bedford County out of which the county of Westmoreland would be created in February of 1773. It was an area destined to be devastated by the Indian attacks during the early years of the Revolutionary War--desultory raids which ruined St. Clair's property and contributed to the erosion of his wealth.

At Fort Pitt Conrad met several of St. Clair's Indian friends. Although he greeted each one in a polite manner, Conrad could not erase from his mind the senseless killing of his brother-in-law. A man of great perception, St. Clair sensed his friend's feelings and gently admonished him saying:

"Perhaps it was not an Indian who perpetrated that despicable deed. We are always quick to blame them. Some of the trappers rob and murder and the Indians are blamed for it."

In the relatively short time Arthur St. Clair had been in America, he had learned much about his adopted country. A trusted friend of many Indians, he often tried to prevent wanton aggression against them. In the aftermath of one such occurrence, St. Clair explained to Conrad how some of the problems between the white man and Indians had developed:

"One hundred years ago a Frenchman by the name of Robert Cavelier, Sieur de la Salle, discovered the Ohio River and gave to France the valley which was watered by its tributaries. A treaty, made in 1701 with the Iroquois, enabled France to maintain their mastery of the Great Lakes. But about twenty years ago France felt her hold was slipping."

The amiable gentleman paused and a mischievous smile tugged at the corners of his mouth as he continued:

"The Indians preferred to trade with the British--it was just a simple matter of economics. For a muskrat skin the Indian could get drunk--with the French it took a beaver skin to do the same thing!"

The smile gone, St. Clair explained to Conrad how, in 1749, the Marquis de la Galissonier--governor-general of France's vast domain in America--had dispatched Canadian born Captain Pierre Joseph Celoron de Blainville, Knight of the Royal Order of St

Louis, to the Ohio valley. In Celoron's expedition were 8 officer, 6 cadets, 80 Indians, 100 Canad ns of mixed blood, and one chaplain. Members of this expedition were destined for everlasting fame when, in 1847, Henry Wadsworth Longfellow published his romantic poem, "Evangeline." In this tragic story about two young Acadian lovers who were separated during the French and Indian War, Longfellow called the men of this expedition "Coureurs de Bois," the hunters of the woods.

But now, in the summer of 1769, St. Clair continued with his explanation to Conrad:

"Carrying the flag of France, and moving in a southwesterly direction, it took them fifty days to reach the junction of the Allegheny and Monongahela Rivers. At that point Captain Celoron and his men took to their boats and floated down the "La Belle Riviere" as he was wont to call the Ohio River. At the mouth of the major tributaries, Captain Celoron buried a seven by eleven inch lead plate which proclaimed France's renewal of their claim to the land in the Ohio River valley. With great ceremony, the Captain hung tin markers—duplicates of the six engraved plates he buried—on branches of surrounding trees. At the mouth of the Big Miami Celoron turned upsteam and made his way north along that river and then overland to a river which leads east into Lake Erie."

Conrad was impressed and remarked:

"You have an enviable knowledge of the country west of Fort Pitt sir!"

"While an ensign in General Amherst's command, I learned a lot about France's colonial claims."

St. Clair also frankly admitted he had learned much of what he knew from the Indians he befriended after the French and Indian War.

"Remember that old Indian you met this morning Conrad? Well, last year he told me a tale about a party of white men, led by a Frenchman, who stopped at the village of the Twightees along the Big Miami many winters ago. From what he said, there were at least two hundred men in the party that visited the village he called Pickawillany. It certainly could have been Captain Celoron's expedition."

The wilderness village called Pickawillany was located at a point where the Loramie Creek emptied into the Great Miami River. Although demolished in 1752 by a group of French-backed traders and dissident Indians, prior to the devastation Pickawillany had slowly replaced Kekionga as the principal community of anti-French Miami Indians or "Twightees" as the English called them.   Some Indians in that area south and west of Lake Erie persisted in calling themselves "Ta-way," a linguistic form similar to the Algonquin word "tawa" which, in loose translation, meant "the naked Indians."   But regardless of the Indian's preference, by 1750 they were being called "Miamis" by the French and the "Twightees" by the English. It was ironic the French should be the ones to author the name of the Indians who were living in the wilderness area France surrendered to Great Britain.   But that was six years in the past as St. Clair spoke to Conrad in 1769 saying:

"Although Captain Celoron was reportedly quite impressed with British influence in the Ohio River valley, his demeanor must surely have been of great interest to the Indians he met."

Indeed the copper-colored natives that Celoron encountered along his watery road--and particularly at Pickawillany--had been impressed with his visit. Thereafter the Indians kept two flags handy for use as circumstances dictated--the British "Union Jack" and the French "Fleur-De-Lis." Indians in the Ohio valley may have lacked some of the formal education white men possessed, but they were not stupid--they knew which flag to fly!

As Conrad listened, he began to understand how conflicting interests of the French, British, and Indians had caused increasing tension and hostile confrontations after 1750. The nerve-center of the dispute between the French and British had been the control of land drained by the Ohio and the Indians were caught up in the ensuing controversy and eventual war which kept the area west of the Allegheny Mountains in a state of turmoil. Desultory raids, horse stealing, and actions shocking to all humanity, were perpetrated by both sides. The spirited settler's continual movement west merely served to further alarm and infuriate the frustrated Indians.

During a journey to Pittsburgh in early summer of 1770, Conrad had an opportunity to talk with St. Clair and was pleased to learn his acquaintance had been appointed Surveyor for the District of Cumberland. In an unassuming manner St. Clair explained:

"I received that appointment on April 5th and last month, the 23rd of May, it was my pleasure to be appointed Justice of Quarter Sessions and Common Pleas and a member of the Proprietory Council for Cumberland County west of Laurel Hill. It keeps me away from my family far too much but I do enjoy the challenge of my work."

While at Fort Pitt in the fall of 1772, Conrad met a seasoned woodsman who said he was on his way to his sister's home in Hampshire County, Virginia. As he explained:

"My kid sister lives a couple hours ride south and east of Fort Ashby. Had figured on heading up the Monongahela to the mouth of the Cheat and visit with a shirt-tail cousin, Kate Swearingen, and her family. They came out here a couple years back and got some land down there. But, I can stop there on the way back and travel on Braddock's Road would be a treat after all the damn brush I've been through this year north and west of here. This past spring I went up the Beaver River to talk with a Moravian missionary named Reverend David Zeisberger. He had a mission up there and was talking about moving out west to the Ohio country. I heard a trapper say he saw that preacher in early May with a flock of his converts out along a branch of the Muskingum."

History would show David Zeisberger did arrive at the site of Schoenbrunn in the Tuscarawas River valley on May 3, 1772 leading thirty-three Delaware Indian converts. A few miles south of this site an Indian mission was soon built--the Moravians called it "Gnadenhutten." But now, in the summer of 1772, Conrad listened as the frontiersman remarked:

"You got a fine looking horse there mister and I know a few shortcuts to Dunbar's. We could ride together if you're a mind to."

Preferring to return to his home north of Turkey Foot traveling southeast from Fort Pitt to Dunbar's Camp and Great Crossing, Conrad welcomed the opportunity to ride with this frontier woodsman who obviously knew the wilderness roads of the western Pennsylvania country. Riding in trail most of the time, with the woodsman who introduced himself only as "Josh" leading the way, the travelers engaged in little conversation. But around their campfire the first night--and now several miles northeast of the fort located between where Redstone Creek and Dunlap's Creek emptied into the Monongahela--Josh listened politely as Conrad related the poignant story about his brother-in-law's death and then recounted some of the things St. Clair had said regarding the problems in the land beyond the Ohio. Josh's eyes twinkled at the mention of "problems" in the region northwest of the Ohio and then, after a short pause in Conrad's remarks, he shook his head and said:

"Well, its a little like I told Reverend David Jones one night when me and that bible-thumper was heading down the Ohio. He was hell-bent on getting down to the Muskinghum to preach and we was sneaking by some Indians at Mingo Bottom. Like I told him, when that war between France and England ended in 1763, England got Canada and most of the French lands east of the Mississippi. But what most folks don't understand is, Indians wasn't a party to that treaty that divided up the land they live on. That was pretty bitter medicine for Indians to swallow!

That preacher fellar sure found that was true while he was out there in the Ohio country. Said he eye-balled that Shawnee some folks call Blue Jacket."

Pausing in his discourse, the crusty woodsman slowly filled his pipe with a mixture he dug out of an old pouch. Then, as Conrad silently watched and waited, his traveling companion selected a burning stick from the fire and used it to light his pipe. Seemingly lost in the ritual of his undertaking, he slowly sucked the smoke deep into his lungs and then noisily exhaled the sickening sweet smoke. Sensing Conrad's questioning gaze, the rugged fron-tiersman explained that the mixture had been given him by a Delaware Indian he had befriended.

"Found that Indian almost dead along the trail next to Big Whiteley Creek just beyond John Minor's place. He had fallen from his horse and busted his leg. A bobcat would have finished him off if I had not found him when I did. He was real grateful and gave me this mixture he called 'kinnikinick' after I poured some rum down his gullet, set his leg best I could, found his damn horse, and then helped him through the woods to a point along the Ohio across from Chief Logan's camp. It was there we ran into some Delawares who were out looking for him. Last time I saw that rum-soaked red-skin he was calling me 'ne-kah-noh' which means 'my friend.' Anyway, that's how I came by this mixture."

Having inhaled deeply several times, and then coughing spasmodically until tears rolled down his weather-beaten cheeks, Josh wiped his nose with the back of his hand and noisily cleared his throat. Staring intently into the bowl of his pipe, he in-haled sharply a few times and continued his story:

"Three years back a fellar named George Croghan left Fort Pitt with a couple of Englishmen and some Shawnee red-skins--started down the Ohio in canoes. Near the mouth of the Wabash they was jumped by the Kickapoos and a couple of George's party was killed in the skirmish--old George himself took a tomahawk

I heard!   But it didn't stop that cagey old cuss--
he just smoked the calumet and talked his way right
up the Wabash.   I hear tell George got them British
fellars the right to take possession of them French
posts out there.   That old George is slippery as a
snot-covered gun barrel!"

Later Conrad often recalled this trip with the
woodsman. Although many details of their conversations were vague, on three points Conrad's mind was
clear. First, his acquaintance had introduced himself only as "Josh" but later confided his name was
"Joshua." Second, the pipe mixture Josh smoked was
terrible. Third, and regardless of what he preferred to be called or what he smoked, his similie was
atrocious.

Major-General Arthur St. Clair
Drawing from OLD WESTMORELAND (May 1984) published
by   Southwest Pennsylvania Genealogical Services,
Laughlintown, Pennsylvania

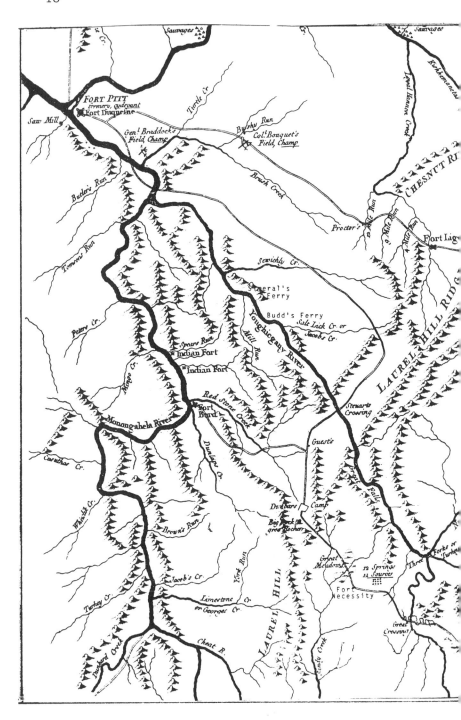

CHAPTER TWO

MAGNA CARTA OF THE NORTHWEST TERRITORY

It was a typically lovely spring day along the Monocacy River when Frederick returned from a visit with his brother in Frederick, Maryland, and called his young nephew to his side. Talk of "revolution" was being heard everywhere in 1774 and his brother Emanuel's blacksmith shop was no exception.

"Jason, my boy! What would you say to a visit with your Uncle Conrad?"

"Oh father, could we? I should like so much to see the Bedford County you speak of!"

The boy's excitement bespoke his approval--he had heard so much about his Uncle Conrad and longed for the day when he could visit with him. Later he would be told the truth about his birth parents but just now was not the right time his foster parents felt. After several weeks of thoughtful delibera-tion, Frederick had concluded a trip west to visit his brother was prudent--talk of "a revolution" was distasteful to him and "the change of pace," as he called it, would be welcome.

As for Jason, those "dragons" he chased on the banks of the Monocacy would have to wait. The days seemed to drag as the lad impatiently waited until everything was ready for their trip. But finally, in early June, Jason and his "father" climbed up on their wagon and "headed out." Pausing only briefly in Hagar's Town to look up an old friend, innkeeper Frederick Rohrer, Jason's uncle drove his team west to Fort Cumberland and then on to a place he called "Great Crossing." It was here the happy youth heard his uncle sing out: "Gee!"

At this command the horses obediently turned right. Jason marveled at the beauty of the verdant country not knowing his birth parents had traveled along this same road the summer before he was born. Watching his nephew's youthful exuberance with each changing vista, Frederick wondered when it would be the right time to tell the boy the truth about his birth parents. At the same moment he also pondered a question which had been tossed his way at Fort Cumberland by a man in a dust-covered wagon:

"How far you going friend?"

"We are turning north at Great Crossing."

Frederick had heard several comments about "a horrible massacre out in the Ohio country" and he pressed the traveler for information.

"Indians west of Pitt are real upset about the butcher job some Virginia fellars did last month on Chief Logan's family. Fellar named Greathouse was the ring leader some say—don't know for sure."

The man related how the past April 28th six or seven disreputable frontier characters had enticed the peaceful Mingo chief's sister, her husband, and five of their red-skinned guards across the Ohio near where the Yellow Creek flows into that river. Although Frederick would have preferred Jason not hear the gory details, the man continued:

"Having filled the guard's stomachs with whiskey, them ruffians slit that squaw's belly open and cut out her bowels! Killed them other Indians too. It was John Connolly's circular, warning folks of a war with the red-skins, that got them fellars riled up I think. But there ain't no cussed reason for a killing like that and its got that whole area west of Pitt on fire—them Indians want revenge! Fellar that told me claimed old Chief Logan was one of the best friends English folks had in the Ohio valley."

Frustrated by this senseless slaughter, Chief Logan had taken up his tomahawk and rode toward the setting sun to confer with the 54 year old Shawnee chief called "Cornstalk" who was known far and wide as an advocate of peace and long time friend of the Moravian Indians. Before heading west, the elderly Mingo chief had declared: "The peace is ended!"

The disappointed would-be-settler who had just returned from Pittsburgh also related to Frederick:

"A friend of mine headed back to Baltimore two days ago. He said he talked with a Captain Thomas Bullit who made a trip down the Ohio last year and went up the Big Miami to a Shawnee village he called Pickawillany. He told my friend he talked with a Shawnee chief called Pucksinwah or something like that. Anyway, Bullit claims them Indians out there are mad as hornets. No place for me friend!"

Hearing their conversation, a man interjected:

"A trapper I met along the river south of Fort Fincastle said it was Michael Cresap who led that posse that killed old Chief Logan's sister!"

Just who led "that posse" would be the subject of controversy two hundred years later but now--and introducing himself as Joe Tomlinson--he continued:

"But it don't make any difference who did it-- or why or when. The fact is its got them red-skins on the warpath--you can be sure of that!"

Fifty miles north and west of where Joe voiced his conviction, an outraged Arthur St. Clair reread his letter addressed to the governor. Praying for relief by the Pennsylvania Assembly, it read:

"Vengeful individuals, both red and white, now wantonly perpetrate crimes that are a disgrace to humanity. I have hired one hundred rangers at my own expense!"

But regardless of who was the real instigator of the mindless slaughter of Logan's sister, or the date of the incident, this unprovoked atrocity--and the peril posed by the Mingo, Shawnee, and Delaware raiding parties--put a damper on the brewing warfare between Virginia and Pennsylvania. It also dampened the spirits of those who were initiating a petition which proposed creation of "Westsylvania."

United against a "common enemy," Lord Dunmore led his troops down the Ohio in October of 1774 and General Andrew Lewis—in a pincer movement—pushed up from the southeast. Along the banks of the Ohio River, at Point Pleasant, Chief Pucksinwah and his warriors made their move. After a series of determined attacks, the Indians suddenly retreated when a report circulated among the warriors saying their Shawnee chief, Pucksinwah, had been fatally wounded and died in his son's arms on the field of battle. Word was sent to the "white invaders"---the Indians would talk peace.

But even this surrender by the Indians was not enough to still the white man's vengeance and Lord Dunmore had to lift his sword against General Lewis whose followers now insisted on "blood!" With such hatred on both sides, and reports of sporadic raids keeping the western frontier in a constant state of alarm, it was just a matter of time until the peace agreement signed by Lord Dunmore and the Indians in 1774 was broken. Adding fuel to the frontier fire, the smoldering embers of the Revolutionary War were being fanned.

And while Lord Dunmore was engaged in his campaign west of Pittsburgh, along the Monocacy Jason chased dragons and his uncle Emanuel told visitors to his blacksmith shop about his brother's journey:

"Frederick was telling me about some gentleman brother Conrad knows at Fort Ligonier named Arthur St. Clair. Conrad said St. Clair is real concerned about the actions of John Connoly out there."

Emanuel's customer indicated he was well aware of the problems created by Lord Dunmore's agent in western Pennsylvania and remarked:

"The English Parliament passed an Act that annexed that entire territory beyond the Ohio as part of the Province of Quebec which was established by the Royal Proclamation of 1763. That's nonsense-- what do they know over there about that land?"

Emanuel recalled that Frederick had said their

brother was impressed with St. Clair's knowledge of
the territory northwest of the Ohio River—it was a
vast area few white men had ever seen.   But, among
these "few" were two men who vowed eternal friendship and became blood brothers along the Muskingum
in the early 1770s. One was a tall muscular youth,
son of Mark and Mary (Miller) Kenton, who was born
April 3, 1755 in Culpepper County, Virginia. Simon
Kenton left Virginia in 1771 erroneously believing
that he had slain his girl friend's suitor, William
Veach. Only three years later (1774) many frontier
settlers were calling this wilderness-wise man "The
Pathfinder." The other frontiersman—a man who had
vowed eternal allegiance to the British—was Simon
Girty (1741-1818). After both his father and step-
father had been killed by Indians, and he was taken
prisoner in 1756, Simon Girty was raised by Senecas
as an adopted son. By 1774 this infamous friend of
Simon Kenton and the Indians was known far and wide
as "The White Savage." Born in 1771 along the Muskingum was a warm friendship which would prove the
wisdom of a later sage remark:
    "War makes strange bed-partners!"
    The trees were bare and snow lay on the slopes
of Laurel Hill and Chestnut Ridge when Conrad made
another of his infrequent trips to Fort Ligonier in
late 1775 and heard it said Judge Richard Henderson
had negotiated a treaty with the Cherokees for the
land south of the Ohio. Conrad's informant added:
    "Trapper I met at Pitt says the Judge plans to
call it Transylvania."
    Although the trapper's report was correct, in
1776 Judge Henderson's treaty was declared illegal.
But, by then, the thirteen colonies were embroiled
in a war with England.
    During that visit to Fort Ligonier Conrad also
learned St. Clair had departed for the east coast.
Discreetly an innkeeper confided:
    "There is a strong possibility he might become
personally involved in the revolution!"

Conrad knew   St. Clair need not offer his service to his adopted country--his wealth was such he certainly could live a life of ease should he be so inclined.   But that was not to be St. Clair's life and when John Hancock, President of the Continental Congress, summoned him to Philadelphia in the final month of 1775, he departed from his home saying:

"I am as close to British Detroit as America's Philadelphia or New York but my allegiance now must be to my adopted country!"

And so, without any hesitation, St. Clair rode his horse to Philadelphia through inclement weather and reported as requested. On January 22, 1776 he was commissioned as a colonel.   He was destined to serve his country in an exemplary manner and earn the confidence and respect of General Washington.

During St. Clair's years of dedicated service to his adopted country, his wife, Phoebe--daughter of Balthazer and Mary (Bowdin) Bayard--was ill much of the time.   Faced with the demands of his service obligations, and the inherent danger of the Indian raids in western Pennsylvania, St. Clair moved his wife and family to eastern Pennsylvania. Throughout the Revolutionary War period, and later during his devoted service as governor of the Territory of the United States Northwest of the River Ohio, St. Clair lived alone during his many far-flung assignments. Willingly, he unselfishly pledged his time and personal wealth in support of such assignments.

Although Conrad had not known St. Clair's convictions concerning "a revolution," there was never a doubt in his mind his acquaintance would be a big assset to any "cause" he chose to support. When he learned St. Clair had left for Philadelphia, Conrad knew it was an obvious move to support his adopted country. It was, as he had heard Joshua say, "time to fish or cut bait!"   From the day "the embattled farmers" drove the British troops from the bridge at Concord, it was just a matter of time until the 13 colonies would declare their independence after

Thomas Paine, on January 10, 1776, fervently stated in his book titled "Common Sense:"

"The time has come for the final separation from England and arms must decide the contest!"

One hundred thousand copies were sold in less than three months--America's first "best seller!"

On July 4, 1776 Richard Henry Lee of Virginia presented the "Declaration of Independence" to the Continental Congress--John Adams seconded it. With his bold signature, John Hancock was the first to sign it. The Revolutionary War ended unofficially at Yorktown on October 19, 1781 with the surrender of Lord Charles Cornwallis and the Treaty of Paris signed in 1783 made it official.

During the Revolutionary War there was continual unrest along both sides of the Ohio as settlers made "reprisal attacks" and then the Indians would launch a revengeful raid--the bloodshed and loss of property on both sides was terrible and the British urged the Indians on. And, the wanton depredation was not limited to the Ohio valley--a stone's throw from Fort Ligonier St. Clair's property was a victim of the Indian's wrath. To protect his wife and children while he was in the service, he moved his family to Pottstown and the "fruits" of his labor suffered materially during the war. As a result of damages to his properties around Fort Ligonier, St. Clair experienced financial adversities from which he would never recover.

While the Revolutionary War held the attention of everyone east of the Appalachians, a twenty-six year old frontiersman from Virginia achieved an important military victory with a minimal expenditure of lead or life. Accompanied by Simon Kenton during the early part of his western campaign, in late summer of 1778 Major George Rogers Clark and 175 of his "Long Knives" took the Kaskaskia settlement on the Mississippi without firing a shot. A few weeks later, nearby Cahokia was taken in a similar manner by Clark's men. Having ordered Kenton to return to

"The Falls," Major Clark then turned his attention to a British stronghold about seventy miles up the Wabash. Weary but determined, in February of 1779 Clark's intrepid troops marched against the fort at Vincennes. It didn't take long to convince the infamous "hair buyer" from Detroit—Governor-General Henry Hamilton—that it would be prudent to hoist a white flag. But, even as Vincennes welcomed Clark and his men—and taunted Hamilton for his alleged practice of buying prisoners, or "live meat" as he called them—about 250 miles northeast Simon Kenton was running the gauntlet as an Indian prisoner.

After the capture of Kaskaskia, Clark had sent Simon Kenton to spy on the Vincennes settlement and then brief Colonel Bowman at "The Falls" regarding their victory along the Mississippi. During a raid in September of 1778 on a Shawnee village along the Little Miami River, Kenton was taken prisoner and suffered harsh treatment—a weaker man would surely not have been able to endure the pain. His "blood brother," Simon Girty—who made his home at Girty's Town along the headwaters of the St. Marys River—persuaded his Indian friends to take their prisoner to Detroit where Kenton managed to escape in 1779. But, having been accepted into the Shawnee tribe as an alternative to death, his escape now made him a "marked man" and the penalty of his recapture was a horrible death at the stake.

Nor was Simon Kenton the only frontier fighter to suffer imprisonment by the Indians. In February of 1778 Daniel Boone was captured by Blue Jacket. Like Kenton, Boone had quite a "reputation" and the Indians heaped painful vulgarities upon him before he escaped four months after being captured. Boone returned to fighting Indians knowing full well that he was a marked man. Upon hearing of Kenton's escape, Blue Jacket wrathfully said to Simon Girty:

"Does not the white man's word mean a thing?"

Girty listened to this meaningful innuendo but did not reply to Blue Jacket whose grimace signaled his seething hate for both Boone and Kenton.

And "hate" was not an ingrained feeling unique to the red man--a common expression, heard wherever the western frontier was discussed, was:

"The only good Indian is a dead Indian!"

Such animosity precluded meaningful reasoning between the men of different colored skins before, during, and after the Revolutionary War.

After George Rogers Clark's "victory" against the Indian villages along the Little Miami and Mad Rivers in August of 1780, the Indians had initiated a series of reprisals which included attacks on the boats coming down the Ohio. Canoes were upset and flatboats boarded and mutilated corpses were seen floating down the river in ever-increasing numbers. In April of 1781, a short distance upstream from Limestone, 40 or 50 Indians ambushed a party of settlers and left 12 women, 16 men, and 8 children lifeless and scalped along the banks of the Ohio.

Jason Evenstar was only sixteen when news came to Frederick, Maryland saying 27 women, 35 men, and 34 boys had been brutally murdered on March 7, 1782 at a place west of Fort Pitt called "Gnadenhutten." Stopping briefly to have his horse's shoe repaired in the blacksmith shop where Jason worked as an apprentice, the courier from Fort Pitt commented:

"Gnadenhutten is out in the Ohio country south of Fort Laurens along the Tuscarawas River--General McIntosh built that fort in 1778."

The courier said the incident was being called "The Moravian Massacre" and Colonel Williamson was the officer-in-charge when 98 red-skinned religious converts were bludgeoned to death with a mallet and their "death house" torched. As the courier said:

"Those Indians embraced the religion Reverend Zeisberger taught out there for the past ten years. According to a story told by the only ones who got away--two boys about fourteen years old--those condemned Indians prayed all night."

In both boisterous frontier meetings, and the

sedate halls of government bureaucracy, there were
those who called this senseless slaughter "a great
victory over the red savages!" In retrospect, the
Indian's reaction was not a surprise--and it wasn't
long in surfacing when Colonel William Crawford and
Colonel David Williamson led 480 soldiers west from
Mingo Bottom with their orders to: "Finish what has
been started!"

There were no provisions for taking prisoners
and the army chanted as they marched:

"Take no prisoners! Kill! Kill! Kill!"

But, as the army marched west in early June of
1782, they found the Indian villages along the way
abandoned. The exuberance and shouting gave way to
an ominous silence as they neared the headwaters of
the Sandusky River where they encamped. Then, just
before sunset, Simon Girty walked into the encampment carrying a flag of truce and warning Crawford
of the Indian's avowed vengeance. Dissension, fear
of ambush--and open insubordination by Crawford's
second-in-command (Williamson)--resulted in a disorderly retreat. With the army in confused flight,
the Indians quickly captured Crawford. Infuriated
because Williamson had eluded them, it was not surprising Chief Pipe decreed Crawford would be burned
at the stake. On June 13th, 1782 Doctor Knight--an
army surgeon whose life was spared--and Simon Girty
stood helpless along the Tymochtee Creek and watched as Crawford was slowly put to death in the most
horrifying manner the vengeful mind could contrive.

Years later, and long after the Indians ceased
to be a menace, some historians would say "torture"
was an ingrained part of the red man's being even
before the white man's "encroachment." These same
historians would declare life for the Indians was a
never-ending struggle for survival and the constant
fear and hatred of other tribes hung over the head
of each like the sword of Damocles. Arrival of the
white immigrants in North America only added to the
red man's hate. Thus, whether in a frontier cabin

or around some campfire before, during, and after
the Revolutionary War, it was not uncommon to hear
stories about the Indian's satanic torture and the
pleasure they seemed to derive from inflicting pain
upon their prisoners. In 1649 Father Jean de Bre-
beuf, a Jesuit missionary living among the Iroquois
and Hurons, was subjected to having his fingernails
ripped off, boiling water poured on his naked body,
a collar of red-hot hatchets tied around his neck,
and a belt of birch bark--filled with pitch and re-
sin--set afire around his waist. The Indians even
cut flesh from his skin and devoured it before his
eyes. For the coup de grace they cut out his heart
and ate it--and drank his blood.

And now, in 1782--while the bloody attacks and
counter-attacks continued in the Ohio valley--Jason
listened to the courier's story about the massacre
at Gnadenhutten as he helped his uncle Emanuel nail
a new shoe on the speaker's horse. Before leaving,
the courier remarked:

"Jason, you've really grown this past year. I
swear it seems ages since I first met you and Frederick near Cumberland--that was in '74 wasn't it?"

"That is correct sir--you have a good memory."

An impish smile betrayed the courier's feigned
seriousness as he said:

"As I recall you had big plans to hunt dragons
in the Laurels near your uncle's place--find any?"

Now it was Jason's turn at pretense. Without
so much as a telltale smile, he politely replied:

"Just two sir. But they were small ones and I
did not find a blessed farthing in.their caves!"

The little smile on the courier's face changed
to a grin as he laughingly said:

"That's good Jason--that's good! You're going
to get along fine in this world--got to have a good
sense of humor. By the way, there's a lot of dragons west of Fort Pitt and if you ever have a mind
to go looking for them, stop by and see me!"

Even as the courier continued his way east, in

that region west of Fort Pitt which he referred to, the atrocities and reprisals increased and the British encouraged the copper-colored natives in their depredations.   As for the Ohio, it was a nightmare for settlers who dared use this water highway.

Along the banks of the Mad River east of Pick-awillany, an old Indian shook his head slowly as he stared at his devastated village. Standing quietly nearby, a man wearing a dirty red coat said nothing even as the Indian turned to Simon Girty and said:

"Red man not understand how great and powerful British red-coats with big guns are beaten by pale-faces of thirteen fires!"

The two Revolutionary War veterans who greeted a man on horseback along the Rappahannock River in Virginia could have answered the question--they had been at Valley Forge during what future historians would call the "Winter of Despair." Now, with 1783 not yet five months old, the men listened carefully to the traveler who carried news of interest.

"Them Congress fellars finally agreed to give Virginia some of that land north of the Ohio--gonna use it fer settling veteran service claims I heard! They call it "Virginia Military Lands."

Although this compromise between the dissonant states did solve one problem, there were only a few delegates in the Continental Congress who seemed to pay any attention to the fact Indians lived in that area which was to be divided by the white invaders. While congressmen had deliberated this legislation, and the bloody attacks and counter-attacks continued in the Ohio valley, across the Atlantic in Paris delegates from England and the United States wrestled with terms of the peace.   During negotiations in November of 1782 John Adams had wisely insisted the western boundary of the ceded territory be the Mississippi River and not the Ohio River as England preferred.   Then, and despite the fact the wording in the final agreement remained nebulous concerning the British concession to abandon fortifications at

Detroit and Niagara, the Treaty of Paris was signed
on September 3, 1783.

After the war ended there was a great deal of
talk, and some legislation, regarding the territory
which had been "won." But the vast wilderness area
northwest of the Ohio was far away and overlapping
claims by some of the states merely served to muddy
the water. In an attempt to provide some guidance
regarding settlement of the wilderness region, Congress passed the Ordinance of 1784 but it failed to
achieve the desired intent. The Ordinance of 1785
was equally unsuccessful although this charter did
include provisions for the rectangular survey which
was employed later that same year by men who began
surveying the Seven Ranges west of the Ohio River.

"Better git out there and stake out your claim
Conrad--fellars in the employ of General Tupper are
doing survey work beyond the Ohio."

The comment was made by an old acquaintance of
Jason's uncle who hailed him in the summer of 1786
at Stewart's Crossing along the Youghiogheny.

"Josh! You old son of a gun--haven't seen you
in a coon's age. How've you been?"

"Tolerable--a little saddle weary but I got no
complaints. You still over at Turkey Foot?"

"That I am," replied Conrad.

Josh still reeked of woodsmoke and body odor--
and was still smoking the same sickening sweet mixture he called "kinnikinick." In reminiscing about
the years gone by, the end of the war, and the continuing frontier atrocities, Conrad again mentioned
his brother-in-law's tragic death in 1768. In turn
Joshua related the misfortunes of his "cousin."

"Being you're from back in Maryland, you might
have heard tell of old "Maryland Van" Swearingen--
married Elizabeth Walker. They did live at Hagar's
Town and a nephew of his had a ferry at Shepherdstown years back--folks thereabouts used to call him
'Thomas of the Ferry.' Ever hear of him?"

Conrad nodded and Joshua continued:

"Anyhow, Maryland Van's son, John, married a shirt-tail cousin of mine, Catherine Stull. Maybe I told you before John and Kate had a flock of kids when they came out here sixteen years ago. Anyway, them cussed Indian raids got so damn bad down there along the Cheat that John and his neighbors built themselves a fort—calls it Swearingen's Fort."

The old woodsman glanced unseeingly toward the sun-drenched Laurels and added:

"John had big plans but he took sick and died the early part of August last year."

"I am truly sorry to hear that" said Conrad.

Conrad's misty-eyed acquaintance continued:

"That ain't all. One of Kate's boys she named Marmaduke was took prisoner by Indians one day when he was fetchin' the cows in. Folks thereabouts say they was Shawnee but no one knows for sure. Kate told me a few weeks back she ain't heard a blessed word about Duke. I 'spect them Indians might have adopted that lad if'n he warn't done in runnin' the gantlet!"

History would show Josh's speculation was not the result of smoking too much kinnikinick. On the other hand, some of the alleged "facts" concerning Marmaduke Swearingen's disappearance by sensationalists many years later would give rise to the conjecture they might be smoking something—maybe they had found some of Josh's kinnikinick!

In early 1787 a proposed charter was introduced in Congress concerning government of the western frontier territory and sale of land in that region. Some provisions of the proposed ordinance were controversial and it was "referred to committee." Not having any real champion, the charter became bogged down in committee. But, while most state delegates were focusing their attention on Philadelphia where a "constitution" was being drafted, in New York one of Virginia's representatives, Richard Henry Lee—Chairman of the Committee—urged the members of his committee to consider some "compromise changes" to the proposed "Ordinance of 1787" which promised to settle, once and for all, the irksome problems concerning the wilderness area across the Alleghenies. With mixed reactions committeemen read Article III:

"The utmost good faith shall always be observed toward the Indians; their land and property shall never be taken from them without their consent; and in their property rights, and liberty they shall never be invaded or disturbed, unless in just and lawful wars authorized by Congress; but laws founded in justice and humanity shall; from time to time be made, for preventing wrongs being done to them, and for preserving peace and friendship with them."

Those who drafted this Article, and members of Congress who read and adopted this charter on July 13, 1787, meant well. Subsequent events indicated everyone did not read this Article--or at least pay any attention to it. At Lexington, in Virginia's District of Kentucky, Robert Patterson read this provision and voiced mixed expletives not repeated in the presence of ladies. Another frustrated and irate frontiersman declared his convictions saying:

"Them damn redskins sneak over here and steal us blind but we ain't allowed to chase them savages back across the Ohio--that ain't right!"

And while the frustrated settlers of the Ohio valley pondered their plight in the fall of 1787, and some legislators in New York City congratulated each other on having "selected" one of their own to be governor of the Northwest Territory, in the Monocacy Valley Jason Evenstar enjoyed a huge piece of the cake his foster mother baked for his birthday-- his 22nd. To himself he thought:

"Perhaps I will visit Uncle Conrad next year!"

Despite the unrest in the Ohio valley in early 1788, John May obtained approval from the Virginia Legislature for a settlement at Limestone Point he planned to call "Maysville." That same year Daniel Boone resigned his job as sheriff of Fayette County in Kentucky. On the opposite side of the Ohio, and

upstream, Arthur St. Clair arrived at Fort Harmar
on July 9, 1788 and looked across the Muskingum at
the new settlement which was called "Marietta." An
Indian scout in the nearby woods watched every move
he made.

Meantime, as the frontier warfare blazed along
the Ohio, Tecumseh and his older brother rode south
to visit the Cherokee tribes. Each carried a vivid
memory of how Moluntha, the elderly Shawnee chief,
had been killed in cold blood in 1786 by Major Hugh
McGary. After British Captain William Caldwell led
an Indian raid against Bryant's Station in Kentucky
on Aug. 15, 1782, thirty year old Colonel John Todd
had led 182 Kentuckians in pursuit of the raiders
with Daniel Boone as their scout. Four days later
they caught up with the retreating raiders and--at
Hugh McGary's ill-advised urging--launched a disastrous attack in which 72 Kentuckians were killed.
A relief force of 470 men, led by Benjamin Logan,
arrived too late. Major McGary had never forgotten
this incident and now the Indians would not forget
his senseless murder of Chief Moluntha.

Although not all future historians would agree
as to the year of his death, some would say it was
during this journey south that Tecumseh's brother,
Cheeseekau, was killed and over his prostrate body
the future Shawnee leader vowed to unite all of the
Indians and drive the white invader from their land
west of the mountains.

But even as Tecumseh voiced his avowed intent,
travel on the Ohio was increasing and Indian scouts
monitored this "invasion" with growing alarm. From
his strategic location about 20 miles upstream from
the mouth of the Scioto River, a blue-jacketed figure watched a flotilla of boats float down the Ohio
and his eyes seethed with hate. Jutting out over
this water highway--in an area of limestone and ore
which would host 100 furnaces only 38 years later--
"Hanging Rock" towered majestically over the northern shore. From this advantageous site Blue Jacket

and his Shawnee cohorts could watch the river traffic and spring their trap when it was opportune.

Although years of involvement with the Shawnee nation's activities had made Blue Jacket a respected and widely known member of their tribe, and his prowess was a subject of conversation among cohorts and white wilderness travelers alike, he sometimes made an error in judgment--not often, but occasionally. On one such occasion, in April of 1788, this Shawnee failed to reckon with his adversary's "lead bird" which flew farther than he anticipated and it almost cost him his life at "Hanging Rock." And, a month later he was captured by a raiding party from south of the Ohio and taken back across that river to Maysville. It was here the cunning Blue Jacket managed to escape and then made his way back to his village where he was named "War Chief."

A nip of autumn was in the air in 1788 when a group of settlers gathered at Maysville to discuss plans for settlements downstream. Among this group were Benjamin Stites, Robert Patterson, Jacob Piat, Israel Ludlow, Matthias Denman, and the frustrated John Cleves Symmes who bitterly complained:

"Gentlemen, October is upon us! Soon the snow will fly! I have asked Governor St. Clair time and time again for a military escort but none has been provided. Unfortunately, I have no alternative--my party will have to wait until an escort arrives!"

The talk of a military escort prompted Captain Piat to inquire of Robert Patterson the whereabouts of Daniel Boone. The man who had built a stockade at Lexington in 1780 replied:

"He went up the Big Sandy to see his son Jesse and then plans to go out west. Old Daniel's on the back side of fifty-three now you know!"

The "old" frontiersman he referred to was born November 2, 1734 in Bucks County, Pennsylvania. He and Benjamin Kelly had been captured by Indians on February 7, 1778 but Boone escaped---Kelly remained a prisoner until 1783. Boone was destined to die

36

in Missouri on September 26, 1820 and twenty-five years later his mortal remains would be returned to Kentucky for reinternment on September 13, 1845.

"And Simon Kenton, where is he?

Patterson smiled as he again replied to Piat:

"Oh, he's around someplace. Claims he aims to stay put for a spell now. He's a top notch man and the best shot on the river in my book!"

John Cleves Symmes said nothing--he was thinking about what this delay was costing him. As fate would decree, it was going to be the latter part of January 1789 before John Cleves Symmes and his party shoved off from the dock at Maysville.

That year--and a month of back-breaking travel east of where Symmes led his settlers ashore a few miles downstream from Losantiville--in New York the fledgling nation's first president was inaugurated April 30, 1789. And in early December of that same year Mary O'Donnell and Jason Evenstar were married at the bride's home in Baltimore.

"Religion, morality, and knowledge, being necessary to good government and the happiness of mankind, schools and the means of education shall forever be encouraged."   Article III, Ordinance of 1787

CHAPTER THREE

ENCOUNTER AT GREAT CROSSING

The year was 1791 and it was February. Smoke from the little log cabin curled lazily up past the snow-covered trees and blended with the low hanging clouds in the afternoon sky. Although the wind was bone-chilling in southwestern Pennsylvania, the open arms of his wife, and the warmth of the crackling fireplace, soon made him forget the discomfort of a four-day hunting trip.

Standing in front of the fireplace, he briskly rubbed his weather-chapped hands together. Just 25 years of age, he was in life's springtime and the world was sunshine, happiness, and opportunity—each morning offered a new challenge. Without saying a word, he politely moved aside slightly as his wife came close to adjust the iron crane holding a steaming pot of bean soup. Coupled with the acrid odor of wood smoke, and the tempting smell of bean soup, he sensed the delicate fragrance of a perfume his wife had brought back from Baltimore—a present from her mother. This night he stared quietly into the fireplace and watched the multicolored flames which licked the logs and helped light the interior of the windowless cabin.

After extending his arms to their full length, and yawning, he linked his fingers behind his head and slowly raised his eyes to where a pewter plate hung above the fireplace. Busy preparing the evening meal, his wife bent over to select a piece of firewood from the wooden firebox half expecting his usual gentle pat on her backside—none came.

Relishing thoughts of how nice it was to have
her husband home again, she did not comprehend the
full meaning of what he had said. She now quickly
straightened up--the piece of firewood was still in
her hands. Stunned and rejecting what she had just
heard as untrue, she turned to face the man she had
taken "for better or worse." Speechless for what
seemed an eternity, she finally said:
"You want to move where?"
He wasn't really surprised with his wife's reaction and, looking directly into a pair of lovely
brown eyes, he unhesitatingly repeated:
"How would you feel about us moving out to the
Northwest Territory?"
His wife stared at him in disbelief--her heart
beat rapidly. She blinked her eyes quickly to hold
back the tears and her chin quivered as she said:
"Jason Evenstar! Pray tell whatever put such
a crazy thought in your head?"
He said nothing. He had obviously said enough
to get his wife's attention. Now he listened.
"We have been married only a little more than
a year. I reluctantly moved out here with you away
from the comforts of my home in Baltimore. I gave
up my work in a new school and left my family and
friends back east just like the good wife I hope to
be. Now you waltz in here after a hunting trip and
give me a peck on the cheek and have the audacity
to calmly ask me how I feel about us moving further
out into this no-man's land. And to the Northwest
Territory no less! You must be joking!"
But he wasn't joking and he did not reply--and
his austere silence only served to pour salt in the
wound he had opened with his question. She choked
down an overwhelming impulse to scream and then,
biting off a sarcastic comment, she continued:
"You are really serious about this dumb fool
notion, aren't you?"
Jason merely nodded his head as he watched his
wife's small hands clasp and unclasp. He could see

her breasts pulsating rapidly against the doeskin garment she wore--she had made it from the skin of a deer he caught. His silent but meaningful action strained her homespun qualities and now she watched unbelievingly as he calmly picked up a powder-horn, hung it on the deer antlers next to the fireplace, and then leisurely uncoiled in the rocker which he had made. A nauseous feeling of helplessness swept over her body as she breathed rapidly. Still holding the piece of firewood, for a moment she had an urge to throw it at her tormentor. With noticeable control she said in measured tones:

"I just do not understand you Jason. Nothing would do but we move out here to this God-forsaken land where you were born. Where your parents--God rest their souls--are buried. We just up and leave a civilized place where I could have taught school and you could have worked--or attended Washington College at Chestertown like you talked about. But no, my dear husband just had to move out here where his parents died---died before they had a chance to live!"

Jason remembered the story well--his uncle had often told him stories of how his parents moved to Turkeyfoot in 1765. "Patience" had not been one of his father's virtues either! But his hard work and unshakeable convictions had not been sufficient to conquer the "frontier dragons" and, as Jason's kind uncle Frederick had said:

"It was indeed unfortunate your father did not live to see the day when the 13 colonies adopted an eloquent statement declaring their independence."

Jason would not, could not, forget that 4th of July in 1776---the day the Declaration of Independence was signed and York, Pennsylvania was selected as headquarters for the Continental Congress while it drafted the Articles of Confederation. But this was not the reason Jason would always remember that date--it was the day he learned the truth about his birth parents.

He was only in his tenth year at the time but he noticed with perplexed interest that his sister was having her birthday party less than five months after his--children learned about the facts of life early on the farm. And so one evening Jason's aunt and uncle gently explained how his parents had died in Bedford County and professed their love for him. As his aunt tenderly said:

"It is as if you were truly one of our own."

So that was it--the boy had always harbored an intuitive feeling he was an adopted son. Although Frederick and his wife always treated him as if he were one of their own, the sensitive youth had not been able to erase from his mind a strange feeling that somehow he did not "belong." Along the banks of the Monocacy River that afternoon Jason cried as if his little heart would surely break and then, as the sun was sinking behind John's Mountain, the lad dried his tears and slowly walked back toward home. With his proud chin thrust forward defiantly, Jason vowed he would never cry again.

In the years to come, Jason spent a great deal of time alone. Although he enjoyed hunting and became an excellent shot, the happiest hours of his childhood were those spent in the fanciful pursuit of dragons along the nearby river--not a single one of the ferocious beasts ever managed to best him in their deadly contest. And, as Jason grew older, he worked hard to excel. Whether serving as a blacksmith's apprentice or in his studies, he surpassed everyone's expectations and his tutors praised his progress. But even as he worked and studied, Jason could not escape thinking he had been "given away." One thought persisted: "My father deserted me."

An inmature attitude perhaps, but it was something to be reckoned with. His kind-hearted uncle Frederick tried to explain how his parents had been victims of circumstances over which they had little control and, despite the fact the boy had been left with them, his father loved him and his mother had died giving him life. But in spite of his aunt and uncle's understanding, affection, and well-intended explanations, Jason seemed unable to dispel his ingrained feeling of rejection. In private Frederick and his wife often talked about Jason's fierce independence and the boy's uncle would try and quiet his wife's concern by saying:

"He's a lot like his dad--proud and stubborn!"

A handsome young man, it was inevitable Jason would gain the admiration of young ladies with whom he came in contact at church or in Frederick where he worked and studied. Although Mary O'Donnel was the only girl Jason ever became interested in, and the one he married, during their courtship even she occasionally found his obstinacy and independence a matter of concern and mentioned it to Conrad's wife who counseled:

"Don't fret dear. He will break to the traces once you get him hitched up!"

Although Mary candidly admitted there was some doubt she could ever have a meaningful relationship with such a stubborn and independent person, slowly she began to understand the man she would marry.

"I love you Jason Evenstar. There is nothing more important in this world than love and when you start loving yourself, you love everybody!"

Although he listened, Jason found it difficult to talk about his feelings. And, despite the fact Jason knew he loved Mary, there was a reluctance on his part to even say so. Mary hoped their marriage would bring some peace of mind to her sensitive and restless husband and prayed their move to the place where he was born would somehow help him "find himself" as she put it. And here, in Turkeyfoot Township, Jason's association with his father's brother seemed to have helped---for a while Mary thought he had found what he was searching for. Now he wanted to move again! To herself she admitted:

"I don't know about you Jason--perhaps I don't understand you after all."

It appeared pointless to remind Jason they had been in this cabin less than a year, this was where he was born, and it was here the mortal remains of his parents rested. They were already hundreds of miles from Baltimore and now Jason actually wanted to move even further out into the wilderness. Fear and desperation made Mary want to cry but she tried to appear calm as she continued to plead her case:

"Jason, you know I was not real happy about us moving out here. But, now we are here and it seems the least you could do would be to stick around for a while. Uncle Conrad and his wife live only a few miles away in Westmoreland County, their son lives not twenty miles from here, and you was the one who talked your uncle Emanuel into moving out here last summer. It seems you would want to stay here! But no, now my dear husband wants to move! Jason, that doesn't make any sense to me!"

Jason knew his wife well enough to know he had his work cut out for him if she was to agree to any move. Before he could offer a rebuttal, she added:

"You could make a good living for us right here in Bedford County--you have never even touched that blacksmith equipment we hauled way out here. Uncle Emanuel always spoke so well of your work while you were an apprentice in his blacksmith shop and uncle Frederick has often said he thought you would make a fine surveyor."

Mary paused but when Jason offered no comment, she continued. But now there was a little tinge of exasperation in her voice:

"This is not fair Jason--your wife is entitled to know what you have on your mind! You just walk in here out of the cold and casually ask your wife how she feels about moving way out to the Northwest Territory. Pray tell dear Jason, what in the world are we going to do out there?"

Mary's parents were of Irish ancestry and she too had the "courage of her own convictions" as she often reminded her husband when he would accuse her of being "stubborn" or "set in her ways."

"Finished?"

Jason's matter-of-fact calmness and his single word question only served to further irritate Mary. She wanted to cry and pound his head with her fists but she merely nodded. Her thin-lipped grimace hid clenched teeth. With exaggerated care Mary put the piece of firewood back in the box and then stepped back in order to see her husband's face. Only then did she give him her terse reply :

"Yes! I am finished--for now at least!"

"Mary O'Donnell Evenstar, you know very well I love you."

To herself she thought:

"Oh no, here comes the sweet talk!"

But aloud she declared flatly without a smile:

"Don't be patronizing Jason--forget that sugar and spice routine. Just tell ME what YOU have decided WE are going to do!"

Mary wasn't being nice----she didn't intend to. With her pretty little jaw jutting forth defiantly, Jason's wife stood with her hands on her hips. She sounded bitter but had made up her mind she was not going to let Jason see her cry. She swallowed hard to keep from calling him "a big bully." As if Mary had not interrupted with her fervent tirade, Jason continued:

"As I was saying, I do love you Mary--and in my own way I love those parents of mine who are buried here. In my heart, I appreciate what they both did for me even though I never knew either of them. It may be hard for you to understand, but I feel I owe them something--and I owe you so much."

Jason paused, glanced at the fire, and then he looked at his wife as he added:

"That probably does not make much sense to you but what I'm saying is I have my own life to live."

"You are absolutely correct Jason, it does not make any sense--not to me at least! I want to live my life too you know."

Absorbed in his own thought's, Mary's clipped retort created no visible change in Jason's facial expression or the tone of his voice as he said:

"Please Mary, I am aware of my responsibility to care for you—and our children when they come."

Mary's response was immediate and rather curt:

"Fat chance with all this moving around—and I am not certain we should have children anyway!"

There—that should bring him to his feet. But it didn't and she quickly added:

"I would probably end up having your son in a wagon, or some lean-to in the woods—God only knows where! Maybe while you were out chasing some coons or bears or God only knows what!"

Every word was tinged with desperation. Jason waited for her to stop talking and then said:

"Mary, please. I beg you not to use the name of our God in your anger."

Beneath that shock of reddish-brown hair his dark eyes were deadly serious and Mary knew it.

"I am truly sorry Jason but.....well, you just make me so angry I could scream."

"Now Mary, please hear me out. I have thought about this move a lot—given it much consideration. Give me some credit, please. Who do you think you married—an irresponsible, self-centered idiot?"

"That's close enough to start with!"

The muscles twitched in her husband's face and he rhythmically drummed the arm of his rocker with an index finger. All too well she knew the meaning of that tattoo—his mind was made up. Despite her frustration, Mary had a great respect for Jason and although he was stubborn, he was a good man and she would listen. Without saying a word, Mary now drew a straight-back chair close to her husband's rocker and seated herself. After an awkward silence Jason cleared his throat and began:

"Well, the other day Hank and I ran into these settlers down on the Braddock Road—names were Dawson and Parker as I recall. They were camped right

west of where Braddock Road crosses the south fork
of the Youghiogheny. It was close to where we left
the road and turned north last year, remember?

To herself Mary thought:

"Remember? Last year? Seems like ten years!"

Aloud she replied pertly:

"Oh, I remember the place Jason--that is where
the Wilkins turned east when they so kindly took me
back to Baltimore last summer."

Jason glanced at his wife. He had not missed
her insinuation. The snide reference to that trip
she had made back to Baltimore by herself broke his
trend of thought. Jason quietly studied his wife's
unwavering look of determination before saying:

"Please Mary--please? Those men said Captain
Piatt is out there--remember him? That just could
be the officer your father always talked about--the
one he said was on General Washington's staff. And
he also said Captain Piatt was a member of that Society of Cincinnati. Uncle Conrad said Arthur St.
Clair was a charter member of that society."

"Parker? Piatt? St. Clair? Jason, you have
me completely confused!"

"Never mind--main thing is the men we met said
Captain Piatt sent word back east there is a great
need for carpenters, surveyors, and blacksmiths out
there. And think of it Mary, good farming land at
only sixty-six cents an acre out there!"

Jason was bubbling! Mary interrupted saying:

"Out there! That is all very good Jason but I
fail to understand what any Captain Piatt, Dawson,
Parker, or St. Clair has to do with us here."

Deep inside she felt a gnawing ache--a growing
tightness. All too well she knew what it had to do
with them--she just hated to admit it. But she did
not intend to resign herself to such a fate without
a "fight!" What was it her husband was now saying:

"Mary, don't you understand? There is a need
for blacksmiths out there and Parker confided to me
he feels certain we can buy land out there for only

one dollar an acre."

"Whoa! One moment please Jason. A moment ago I distinctly heard you say land *out theʌe* was selling for only sixty-six cents an acre."

Had she found a flaw in his plans? Mary knew she was grasping at straws but anything to dampen her husband's interest in moving--anything!

"It *waʌ* sixty-six and two-thirds cents an acre until November of 1788 and then John Symmes raised the price to one dollar an acre. Mike thinks some of our neighbors would be interested in moving."

Jason's enthusiasm was almost contagious. But Mary wasn't buying any of it--not yet anway.

"Think of it Mary, out there they are going to need carpenters and......"

Jason's wife interrupted saying:

"I know--and surveyors and blacksmiths!"

Mary managed a half-hearted smile as she somewhat sarcastically added:

"It would appear practically everyone is going to move to the Northwest Territory."

Her sardonic remark never phased Jason.

"Well, perhaps not everyone. Just those with vision--those who are interested in being a part of a new civilization where a man can feel needed."

Every now and then Mary's husband made remarks which were best left unsaid--Mary knew this was one of them but she decided to ignore the comment. But Jason's enthusiasm was something Mary knew she must reckon with. From the recesses of her mind she recalled reading in a Baltimore paper something about a man who had traveled west in 1787 and returned to New Jersey quite optimistic regarding the potential of the land he had seen. In a subsequent petition to Congress, this man declared it was his desire to purchase one million acres of land in the Northwest Territory which he said would be sold to settlers. And, during a visit with her father by a businessman from Philadelphia, Mary overheard them discussing this "land in the Ohio valley." Her father's

visitor had said one of the major obstacles to any
"business development" was a "problem with the red-
skins." Mary was not particulary interested in the
Northwest Territory then and was not really interested now. However, with Jason chomping at the bit
and ready to move, Mary searched her mind carefully
for recollections which might be of some assistance
in her deliberation.

Mary had been only sixteen when the Treaty of
Paris was signed in 1783 at the Hotel d'York in the
rue Jacob of that French city. Benjamin Franklin,
John Jay, John Adams, and Henry Laurens had signed
for the United States while England was represented
by David Hartley, British Commissioner. The treaty
had been finalized after Lord Cornwallis surrendered at Yorktown and officially ended the Revolutionary War. Just one month after Franklin returned to
America in September of 1785, Mary accompanied her
father when he visited this chief negotiator of the
peace talks. Mary politely curtsied to the old man
with the gray hair and then listened as he told her
father about Paris:

"Parisians have the art of making themselves
beloved by strangers."

Mary also recalled how Franklin told about an
incident on October 15, 1783 when Francois Pilatre
de Rozier and Francois Marquis d'Arlandes had taken
off in their smoke-filled hot-air balloon:

"That balloon--a Montgolfiere they called it--
took off that day from the Chateau de la Muette in
the western part of Paris and, blown by prevailing
winds, crossed the Seine River and landed at Butte-
aux Cailles only twenty-five minutes later."

With mild enthusiasm Franklin added:

"I can see a practical application for these.
Imagine, if you will, five thousand balloons---each
holding two men. Ten thousand men descending from
the clouds could do an infinite amount of damage.
The first of December that same year I saw Jacques
Charles fly an improved model of the balloon."

Among other things, Mary's father and the distinguished statesman talked about the recent war.
After September 21, 1784 Philadelphia boasted of
having a daily newspaper and the reporter covering
Franklin's return from Paris quoted him as saying:

"There hardly ever existed such a thing as a
bad peace or a good war.   An army is a devouring
monster!"

Franklin would have been "flabbergasted" if he
could have seen a Philadelphia daily newspaper 200
years later which editorialized a proposed Department of Defense budget of $292.1 billion dollars.
In the exacting "science" of government budgeting,
the decimal point imparts a note of grotesque pre-
cision to a quantity beyond imagination.   But, as a
popular news media personality would observe in the
late 20th century:

"With all the commas in a twelve digit number,
who is watching decimals!"

But that would be more than 200 years in the
future as Mary pondered the past in 1791 and said:

"Symmes? John Symmes? I do recall reading an
item about your Pied Piper of the Woods in the Baltimore paper two years ago---December 12th, 1787 it
was. I remember the date because it was that issue
which editorialized Delaware being the first state
to ratify the Constitution that week on the 7th and
I saved it for school."

Although "mental telepathy" would not be coined by F.W. Myers until 1882, Mary had a feeling her
husband must have read her mind as he said smugly;

"I remember the 12th of December in 1789--that
was the Saturday Mrs. O'Donnel's daughter promised
to love, honor and obey yours truly."

"I know Jason--and when we moved out here last
spring I thought you would be happy to settle down
and forget this urge to be on the edge of the great
beyond as your father did. What did it get him?"

She could have bitten her tongue and added:

"I am truly sorry Jason--I meant no disrespect

for your father. Forgive me please."

"I understand. He did what he thought was the right thing. Someplace I read a man should stretch his wings--seek the farthest reaches of his world."

Even as he spoke Jason was studying his lovely wife's face. Flames bathed her soft pinkish skin with an orange glow and her reddish-brown hair hung in loose waves on her shoulders. She was beautiful and he did love her. Jason understood her trepidation---his own mother may have been equally fearful of frontier life. But the opportunities of life on the frontier was a powerful tonic for a man and the young man had given a great deal of thought to this move. It was Mary who broke the silence saying:

"It would appear there has been a lot of talk between the men about moving---it certainly is nice of you gentlemen to finally tell the women."

Mary's remark had all the overtones of sarcasm and Jason stared at her a moment before he replied:

"Mary, my love. Several of the men hereabouts see great opportunity in this. I admit, some of us have been talking about this ever since Hank was at Fort Pitt last fall and met some settlers who were going down the river to that Symme's Purchase area. It did not seem right to get the women all riled up about moving until we learned more about this."

Jason spoke calmly and hoped Mary would understand, but he soon learned there was still a lot of fight in his spunky Irish bride.

"So now you and good old Hank Weiser go hunting, meet some other nomads, and you two men decide it is time to pack up and move. If it were summer, I would swear the heat had made you daft!"

"That is not fair Mary. Most of the men that I have talked with believe the Northwest Territory offers tremendous opportunity. Personally, I see a good chance to use the trade and education my aunt and uncle sacrificed for. They always said it was their fervent hope we would have a better life than my parents. This is a young country, a new nation, and that land out there is one of the fruits of the revolution. Now it is just begging for settlers!"

Mary eyed Jason carefully--he was sincere!

"John Symmes should employ you to sell land my dear husband. You certainly picked up a real gift of gab during your association with George Mason."

For the first time since her husband broached the subject of moving, Mary allowed herself an insincere laugh.

"It isn't funny Mary. A lot of brave men laid down their lives for our independence---your father certainly did his bit. Now it is our turn to make sure their sacrifices were not in vain. I believe the opportunity of a lifetime is waiting for us out there--it is up to us to reach out and grab it!"

Mary brought her lips together tightly--if her husband used that word "opportunity" one more time she was going to scream. After a pause she said:

"You have been chasing too many dragons! They say the Irish are the ones with the blarney but you certainly picked up more than your share at cousin Emanuel's blacksmith shop. I am not saying you are wrong, I am just saying you have a way with words."

With that she arose and began to stir the bean soup. As she slowly stirred the thick substance in the black pot, she could feel her husband's eyes on her. As Mary moved the crane, she remembered how proud Jason had been when he told her he made it in the blacksmith shop. Jason was a good man and Mary knew he loved her as much as life itself. But despite his many virtues, living with Jason was a real challenge. Still, she knew him well enough to know he had made up his mind to move. Slowly she picked up a piece of wood and carefully placed it in the fire as Jason spoke:

"In my cousin's blacksmith shop in Frederick I heard many stories about the Ohio valley and it always sounded quite interesting."

"I know. You told me."

Mary tried to sound indifferent but Jason paid

no attention to her slight and continued talking:

"Parson Weems was of the opinion it offered a tremendous opportunity."

Mary clenched her teeth--Jason did not see the wry smile that crossed her face as he used the word "opportunity" again. Realizing it was obviously a hopeless situation, Mary shrugged her shoulders and went about her work as Jason added:

"While my uncle was helping to survey a boundary line up north of Quirauk Mountain--before I was born--he worked with some man named Rittenhouse who later, in 1769, measured the earth's distance from the sun. Five years ago this same man came up with an idea for using what he called 'spider lines' on the focus of telescopes. A smart man! My point is this Mary, way back when I was just a twinkle in my father's eye Rittenhouse told my uncle a man could make a fortune in the Ohio valley if he had a mind to take advantage of opportunities out there."

The man Jason referred to, Pennsylvania born David Rittenhouse, had indeed helped Charles Mason and Jeremiah Dixon perform a survey of the boundary between Pennsylvania and Maryland during the period from 1763 to 1767. But his "credentials," as presented by her husband, did not impress Mary and she muttered under her breath:

"We better get out there quick!"

Jason never even noticed her facetious sarcasm as he quietly studied the tiny wisps of steam which periodically emerged from the bubbling pot of soup. Mary glanced at Jason--quiet and manly strength had replaced the boyishness of the person she married a little more than a year before. Lines of character had already started to etch themselves in Jason's face and his gaze could be penetrating. The jut of her husband's chin betrayed his stubborn independence. One of the German Baptist ladies confided:

"Your husband's whole carriage is one of self-assurance."

Nodding, Mary thanked her for the compliment--

to herself she thought:

"Self-assurance? He is a hard-head!"

As she stirred the soup again, Mary turned and caught her husband's eyes--they were thoughtful and serious. This night there was a look in his eyes Mary had never seen before. And, as Mary looked at her husband's eager face, she thought:

"I cannot figure out this restless urge to move --is it discontent? With me? With himself? Jason my love, I have tried so hard to understand you."

Deep in thought, Jason was turning over in his mind what he and his friendly neighbor, Hank, heard at Great Crossing. They had agreed it was best not to say anything to their wives about some comments Parker had made concerning General Josiah Harmar's unsuccessful campaign against the Indians only four months ago in October of 1790.

"No need gittin' the women folks all riled up" Hank had remarked.

Thoughtfully countering what Jason now thought might be an objection in the making, he looked into his wife's troubled eyes and said:

"We have a good life together Mary, and I need you. There is nothing we cannot work out together. That Ohio country needs men like me and I certainly need my wife with me. It is my firm belief that we should move--that our fortune lies in the Northwest Territory."

He could not hide an impish smile as he added:

"Your dearly beloved is going to slay a couple of dragons out there!"

Mary shook her head slowly in meaningful fash- ion and moved to where she could give her husband a kiss on the top of his head as she said:

"I love you, but I swear some of that stubborn salesmanship of George Mason must have rubbed off on you while you were working down there in Fairfax County."

Mary referred to a sixty-one year old Virginia gentleman who came out of retirement in 1786 and, as a member of the Virginia Assembly, had refused to sign the proposed Federal Constitution in 1787. He insisted it should include a "Bill of Rights" to clarify controversial points and declared: "Gentlemen, what you propose will not safeguard individual rights!"

There was heated debate at the Constitutional Convention but finally 39 of the 55 delegates signed the proposed Constitution on September 17, 1787. Sent to the states for ratification, Delaware was the first to ratify it and six months later, on the 21st of June in 1788, New Hampshire did likewise as the ninth state. The law was supreme!

But, on the heels of ratification, ten amendments to the Constitution had been the subject of spirited debate. The one which prompted the most heated debate was Amendment Two:

"A well-regulated Militia, being necessary to the security of a free State, the right of the people to keep and bear Arms, shall not be infringed."

Supporters of this amendment vehemently argued it was necessary to preclude the Congress from disarming a State's militia--this "right" would still be provoking argument in the twilight years of the 20th century. Virginia adamantly refused to ratify the Constitution until the first ten amendments had been formally proposed to Congress on September 25, 1789. Virginia's George Mason was instrumental in framing these "changes" which protected individuals from the unjust acts of government--they are called "The Bill of Rights."

Mason had been an out-spoken sponsor of George Rogers Clark's expeditions to the Ohio valley. His acquaintance with that area was a delight to Jason when the young man had been employed by Mason for a short time at the suggestion of Parson Locke Weems. The minister had been on one of his preaching trips when he was delayed in Frederick, Maryland for some repairs to his wagon. Weems had been impressed not only with the young blacksmith's work, but Jason's

ability to play the violin.   A willing listener to
Parson Weem's many stories, it was only natural the
young man would endear himself to the friendly man.

A firm believer in education, George Mason encouraged Jason in his educational endeavors.   Mason
had been tutored and studied law under John Mercer,
his legal guardian.   Enchanted with the region west
of the mountains, Jason had listened spellbound to
the stories about the western frontier which George
Rogers Clark reported in his letters to Mason.   The
Virginia born Clark always proclaimed his belief in
the future of Virginia's western lands and said:

"If a country is not worth protecting, then it
is not worth claiming!"

With a mixture of pride and amusement, the old
Virginia statesman had told Jason how Clark and his
intrepid Pennsylvania and Virginia volunteers--"Big
Knives" as some called them--had captured Kaskaskia
on July 4, 1778 "without firing a shot!" The audacity of Clark and his men had won the admiration of
frontiersmen as well as Virginia statesmen.   Justly
pleased with Clark's accomplishments, Mason proudly
told his wide-eyed listener:

"Then Clark sent Simon Kenton, Elisha Beatty,
and Shadrach Bond to spy on Vincennes while he just
walked into Cahokia and took over--not a shot fired
there either! He had sent Father Pierre Gibault, a
scholarly vicar at Kaskaskia, to Vincennes and he
returned saying the Indians along the Wabash wanted
to smoke the peace pipe.   He also said inhabitants
of Vincennes were ready to swear allegiance to our
new nation."

Based on the good news, Clark had sent Captain
Leonard Helm to take command at Vincennes.   But, in
the autumn of 1778, British General Henry Hamilton
left Detroit and marched southwest along the Wabash
River recruiting warriors and inflaming the Indians
with hate for the American soldiers.   At Vincennes,
Hamilton quickly raised the British flag over Fort
Sackville. When a report of this coup reached his

ears at Kaskaskia, Clark dispatched a gunboat and six cannons by the river route and he marched overland with one hundred and thirty of his men. Mason had summarized Clark's campaign saying:

"After a rendezvous with the gunboat, Clark's men launched an attack and Fort Sackville hoisted a white flag on February 25, 1779. Old General Henry Hamilton was now Clark's prisoner!"

Although George Rogers Clark was subsequently appointed a general himself, this frontier leader-- one who had spent his own money to feed and pay his men--was destined to die poverty-stricken in 1818. But, in 1791, the 39 year old Clark was a "frontier idol" of Jason Evenstar who told his wife:

"George Mason said General Clark was quite excited about the opportunities out there! We do not have any real reason for staying here--and we could buy some land in the Northwest Territory. Perhaps I could have my own blacksmith shop--or even try my hand at a little survey work. By the way dear, how about something to eat--your husband is starved. I tell you, that campfire cooking is for the birds!"

She wanted to say, "You had better get used to it!" But she thought better of it and filled their bowls with steaming soup. Jason took a seat at the home-made table and waited for Mary. After placing a plate of corn bread in front of him, she sat down and said:

"Please say grace Jason."

During their evening meal Jason told her about his hunting trip. Although Mary listened politely, her mind was in a whirl--not so much thinking about the future as the past. Despite the fact she had heard talk about the "Northwest Territory" and the legislation which created it, she was not about to admit it to her husband. Mary and her lady friends had talked about the Ohio country--they had already sensed their husband's interest. Mary had told one neighbor lady about a stop she made during her trip in early June of 1787 to see her aunt in New York.

"While stopping for a brief visit with my dear cousin in Philadelphia, she and her husband took me to a concert for the benefit of Alexander Reinagle, a refined musician from London. In attendance that evening was General George Washington."

The following day, June 13th, the Philadelphia newspaper carried a report indicating this Virginia delegate to the Constitutional Convention had commented after the concert:

"Reinagle has a sweetness of manner in the way he touches the pianoforte."

Seeing the renowned Washington at the concert, Mary's cousin related a story of how this man had, in 1756, been a candidate for election to the House of Burgesses opposing tippling houses and general drunkenness. In the 1756 election, he was defeated by Thomas "Of the Ferry" Swearingen. But, Washington turned the tables on his opponent and won the 1758 election by a wide margin.

Travelers seldom forgot the 96 mile coach trip from Philadelphia to New York City on the old Post Road--it took a day and a half. It also cost six dollars and that did not include a night's lodging.

"Things were so expensive" Mary thought.

There were a number of inns and taverns along the way where an occasional stop helped break the monotony of the journey. Although the swaying and jolting of the coach was disconcerting much of the time, most travelers did manage to engage in light conversation. While waiting for the coach to leave the Philadelphia station, Mary learned one of her traveling companions was Mary Nickols, operator of the "Conestoga Wagon Inn" which was located between Fourth and Fifth Streets in the city whose name, in Greek, means "brotherly love." Back home again in Baltimore, and relating the details of her journey, she had told her parents about having been informed "Conestoga" was the name of an old Indian tribe. A knowledgeable man, her father had countered saying:

"It is also the name of a little river not far

from Lancaster. As for that inn your traveling co-
panion operates, it is only a small dirty room in a
small tavern frequented by common countrymen. Personally, I prefer John Stein's place nearby at 434
Market Street--he calls it THE BLACK BEAR INN."
        Recalling her father's comments, Mary Evenstar
smiled and muttered to herself:
        "My Irish father certainly gets around!"
        Jason glanced at his wife across the table and
said:
        "Did you say something dear?"
        "It was nothing Jason--I was just thinking out
loud. What do they call it out here--cabin fever?"
        Continuing to eat, Mary mused over the fact it
had been only four years ago that she was seated in
her aunt Margaret's home in New York City listening
to the story of how a Dutchman, Peter Minuit, landed there in May of 1625 and bought the island for a
paltry sum of sixty dollars. "He called it Nieuw
Amsterdam" her aunt related for the umpteenth time.
Mary had been there on July 13, 1787 when Congress
passed an ordinance which created the "Territory of
the United States Northwest of the River Ohio." It
was in the newspaper but Mary paid little attention
to the article since, as she mentioned to her aunt:
        "I have no intention of ever living there!"
        But, as fate would decree, only two and a half
years later Mary would be bumping her way westward
in a "springless" Conestoga. Now tonight, in 1791,
her eyes swept around their little cabin in western
Pennsylvania and Mary recalled what her aunt said:
        "Only 18 representatives from 8 states cast a
vote for this ordinance. Delegates from Maryland,
Connecticut, New Hampshire, Pennsylvania, and Rhode
Island were not present. Even the President of the
Continental Congress, Arthur St. Clair, was absent.
Virginia's representative, William Grayson, sat in
the president's chair when the vote was taken. Our
representative, Abraham Yates, cast the only 'naye'
vote. I fail to understand his reasoning, or lack

of it perhaps. The United States must do something about that Ohio country--Yates should be tarred and feathered!"

On this night in early February of 1791 it was Mary Evenstar's prayerful wish all of those who had voted for the ORDINANCE OF 1787 had been tarred and feathered and rode out of town on a rail. Erasing this malicious thought from her mind, Mary recalled stopping in Philadelphia during her return trip and hearing her cousin's husband relate how he had had the recent pleasure of being a guest in the home of eighty-one year old Benjamin Franklin.

"As I recall it was Friday evening, July 13th. Reverend Manasseh Cutler and I accompanied Elbridge Gerry, along with a few other members of Congress, to Doctor Franklin's home on Market Street between Second and Third Streets. The doctor was attired in ordinary Quaker dress--not the regal bearing one might expect of a person who had spent years in the royal courts of Europe. Being a preacher, teacher, lawyer, physician, and botanist, Doctor Cutler soon fell into a long conversation with Doctor Franklin. The following day Doctor Cutler was invited to join James Madison, Alexander Hamilton--and a few other delegates to the Constitution Convention--when they visted John Bartram's botanical gardens on the west bank of the Schuylkill. I understand those gentlemen were not only quite impressed with the doctor's knowledge of botany, but they were also interested in hearing about his recent visit to New York where he reportedly suggested some changes to legislation being drafted regarding that wilderness country beyond the mountains. As you probably are aware, the ordinance was adopted."

The commentary he provided was informative but Mary was no more interested in Manasseh Cutler than she had been when her aunt had told her about this "teacher-preacher." She was more interested in the young man her cousin had introduced her to--twenty-two year old John Young. Mary was fascinated with an account he gave concerning a lecture he recently heard by a James Glen at Bell's Book Shop. Enroute from London back to British Guiana, Glen had talked about the teachings of the Swedish mystic and philosopher, Emanuel Swedenborg. Francis Bailey, an elder in the Presbyterian Church, and publisher of THE FREEMAN'S JOURNAL during the Revolutionary War, had formed a reading group which included such personages as Benjamin Franklin and William Morris. As John had confided to Mary:

"They say such religious teachings are fanning the flames of a stirring emotional revivalism north of here in Massachusetts!"

The religious doctrines of Swedenborg which he told Mary about in 1787 were those Johnny Appleseed would advocate during his seed-planting sojourns in the region her husband was now interested in. This was one part of her trip Mary had never shared with the man she had taken "for better or worse."

"Jason, do you remember my aunt Margaret--the one in New York City?"

"You mean the one with the gold toothpicks you used to tell me about?"

Jason smiled broadly and Mary frowned--it was true her dowager aunt was quite well off.

"Shame on you--she was very nice to me. Well, she had this friend, Manasseh Cutler, who came from Massachusetts to New York while I was there. As I recall it was on July 5th and she said he stayed at the Plow and Harrow Tavern in the Bowery. She said he was in town to, as she put it, 'ride herd on the Ohio Company's interests' in some land speculations west of Pittsburgh. My cousin's husband said this Reverend Cutler was in Philadelphia just eight days later. Do you think the John Symmes you talk about has anything to do with what he was doing?"

Jason was elated--his wife was expressing some interest in the Northwest Territory! He replied:

"As I understand the Ordinance of 1787, it was adopted about two weeks before a group of men from

Boston--the Ohio Company of Associates--submitted a petition to buy land. July 27th sticks in my mind. There was an item in the Baltimore paper which said General Rufus Putnam, Nathan Dane, and the preacher you mentioned were the three men mostly responsible for moving the Northwest Territory land legislation through Congress. The newspaper said the ordinance guaranteed freedom of religion, prohibited slavery, encouraged education, and provided a plan for the government of that territory. The writer called it 'The Magna Carta of the Northwest!'"

In the two hundred years following adoption of this ordinance, some historians would express doubt whether a nation, composed of thirteen contentious states, could have survived long without it. The colonies along the eastern seaboard were a discordant group, jealous of their "sovereignty," and the government provided by the loose Articles of Confederation was not capable of lasting performance. The "common bond" provided by this agreement would probably have failed had not the Ordinance of 1787 been enacted. Inextricably drawn together by the common interest of drafting legislation for government of the area northwest of the Ohio, the resultant "Magna Carta" Jason spoke of heralded the birth of a model of government unique among those of all mankind. It included six articles of compact which insured the most cherished principles of individual rights and freedom.

Mary had listened to her husband carefully--it was obvious he had been doing a lot of reading and talking with his friends. Trying not to appear too interested, Mary remarked:

"It appears to me the same gentlemen who were involved in the enactment of that Ordinance of 1787 were also interested in that company's petition for land."

Mary was right. As agent for the Ohio Company of Associates, on July 5, 1787 Manasseh Cutler had voiced a forceful appeal before members of Congress

for 1,500,000 acres of land "in the Ohio country."
He had an enviable faculty for securing the cooperation of State representatives and was a genius at
suggesting provisions for the land contract he proposed. When the Scioto Company, another land spec-
lator, requested him to be their agent, Cutler saw
the advantage of a combined purchase. On behalf of
several petitions he represented, Cutler eventually
obtained approximately 5,000,000 acres of land for
$3,500,000 in Continental Certificates.

Cutler also recognized the propriety of having
the President of the Congress, Arthur St. Clair, as
governor of the new territory. During his lobbying
efforts, he also tactfully suggested Major Winthrop
Sargent be appointed as Secretary of the Northwest
Territory and General Samuel H. Parsons be named as
one of three judges. Both men were veterans of the
Revolutionary War and college graduates. Manasseh
Cutler was not only knowledgeable and alert, he was
thorough! St. Clair was appointed to the office of
governor on October 5, 1787.

Three years four months later, Jason searched
his mind for a response to his wife's observation:

"I believe you are right dear. Those same men
who pushed that ordinance through Congress followed
up with their petition to purchase land under it's
provisions--aggressive men I would say!"

Aggressive? Mary had other choice adjectives
she could have used to describe the proponents of
the legislation which appeared to be a contributing
factor to her domestic problem. Restraining an impulse to heap verbal abuse on those associated with
promulgation of the Ordinance of 1787, she said:

"That General Putnam you mentioned, and Manasseh Cutler, they were officers of that Ohio Company
of Associates. Right?"

Jason was pleased with his wife's assimilation
of what he had related and the information she had
recalled from reading the newspaper. He replied:

"That is my understanding. Officer, director,

agent, or shareholder. Most of the principals were Revolutionary War officers it appears. Some of the shareholders went out there three years ago and are living at the mouth of the Muskingum River on land they purchased. There was some talk about it when we came through Fort Cumberland last year."

Mary thought for a moment and then remarked:

"Did they travel through Fort Cumberland?"

"Probably traveled west along the General John Forbes Road north of here. That Parker we met down at Great Crossing said General Putnam's party built flatboats below Stewart's crossing and floated down the Ohio to the Muskingum River."

"And pray tell where is the Stewart's Crossing you mentioned?"

Jason smiled as he replied:

"It is just across the Laurels on the Youghiogheny River. The Muskingum is down the Ohio but I am not certain how far. Parker told us the settlement called Marietta at the mouth of the Muskingum is really growing!"

As Jason was speaking he got up from his chair and stepped over to the home-made corner cupboard-- Mary watched silently. While reaching for a box on the top shelf he said:

"Six or seven years ago Parson Weems mentioned something about an Ohio Company but that cannot be the one we are talking about. I am confused."

"It is more confusing than amusing!"

Mary had to laugh at her own feeble attempt at humor. Jason glanced at her and a smile tugged at the corners of his mouth as he again seated himself and began sorting through some papers.

Parson Weems had referred to the Ohio Company formed in 1747 by a group of London merchants and wealthy Virginians. Among them were Augustine and Lawrence Washington, George Washington's brothers. King George gave the group a grant of 200,000 acres in an effort to colonize the Ohio River valley and the interests of this land undertaking were later transferred to the Walpole Company. The Ohio Company of Associates was a new business venture whose "roots" stemmed from the Ordinance of 1787. As she now watched Jason digging through some papers, Mary thought to herself:

"I'll bet Reverend Cutler was not one of those settlers who floated down the Ohio on a raft! Aunt Margaret described him as a shrewd individual who enjoyed the finer things in life."

She would have been surprised to know the Yale graduate she referred to had left Massachusetts on July 22, 1788 for the Ohio country driving a sulky. Joined by Major Peter Oliver and Major Ephraim Kendall, the trio had crossed the river at Harrisburg August 3rd, crossed the Youghiogheny River six days later, and then boarded a flatboat at Cox's Fort on the Ohio. Finally, on August 19th—751 miles from the Ipswich hamlet in Massachusetts—Cutler and his companions reached Marietta. Later Reverend Cutler described the new settlement as "an infant country bursting at the seams!" Less optimistic persons on the eastern seaboard referred to Marietta as "Cutler's Indian Heaven" and others called it "Putnam's Paradise." But Cutler had long ago returned to the east coast when Jason triumphantly held up a newspaper clipping saying:

"Here it is! For the life of me I do not know why I saved this."

Mary's response was instantaneous:

"Please, Jason. I was not born yesterday!"

Ignoring her remark, Jason turned his chair to obtain the benefit of the light from the fireplace and began to read aloud:

"The Ohio Company of Associates was awarded a contract by the government on October 27, 1787 for a huge tract of land in the Territory of the United States Northwest of the River Ohio. Samuel Osgood and Arthur Lee signed the contract on behalf of the Board of Treasury and Manasseh Cutler and Winthrop Sargent were signatories for the Ohio Company."

Mary now recalled having seen that clipping in a spelling book she had brought along. Apparently her husband had removed it last September while she was back in Baltimore. To herself she concluded:

"Probably wanted to show it to Hank."

She now silently watched Jason as he carefully examined several other newspaper clippings which he had folded neatly and placed in the box. Jason had built the cupboard in the corner and put the box on the top shelf. They had an unwritten understanding regarding the privacy of each other's personal belongings and she had always considered this box her husband's property. In spite of her silence, Mary missed nothing as Jason occasionally read excerpts from his precious clippings. Suddenly she said:

"Them what has, gets! That's what my dear old father always told me."

Jason glanced at his smiling wife as a puzzled look crossed his face. "What on earth is she talking about" he thought. Sensing her husband's bewilderment, Mary explained:

"That company you were reading about a moment ago--the one you said paid one-half of the purchase price as a down payment. Somehow I doubt they will ever pay the government another pound, shilling, or farthing on the rest of that debt!"

Mary's father was a merchant in Baltimore and she had been raised in a family where commerce and politics were familiar topics of conversation. Her observation was strangely prophetic. Although the Ohio Company of Associates had contemplated raising $1,000,000 in $1,000, shares and purchase 1,500,000 acres of land, only 822 shares were subscribed for. When the final settlement was made on May 20, 1792, the company would be short of funds and it would be necessary to reduce the purchase to 1,064,285 acres with the stipulation 214,285 acres were to be sold to those with Army warrants and 100,000 acres would be offered settlers at no cost provided they settle the land under terms established by Congress. That settlement would also provide that one section in each township was to be reserved for the support of schools; one section to be reserved for religious purposes; and three sections were to be set aside for future disposal by Congress. 46,080 acres were to be reserved to support an institution of higher learning.

Her husband's comments and clippings had been enlightening but Mary still had questions:

"I still fail to understand what that company has to do with your thinking about buying land from John Symmes. And what about the free land that was for settlers? Is that land just for Revolutionary War veterans? My cousin said the Ordinance of 1787 was merely a land speculation scheme cooked up by a few high-ranking officers of the war! It appears I do not understand all this."

"Please dear--one thing at a time. I remember Parson Weems once saying 'man has always had more questions than answers.' I suppose that old cliche applies to the ladies as well."

Jason laughed. He was delighted that Mary had even expressed an interest in this undertaking.

"Your cousin could be right Mary. However, as I understand it, the Ohio Company of Associates and the Marietta settlement, and the land being offered for sale by John Symmes, are two different kettles of fish--one moment please."

Jason selected a newspaper clipping and turned slightly to take advantage of the light from the fireplace as he exclaimed:

"Yes, here it is! Says here the settlement at the mouth of the Muskingum was founded by members of the Ohio Company of Associates who landed there April 7, 1788 and named that settlement in honor of Queen Marie Antoinette of France."

To herself Mary thought, "Now where on earth did he get that?"

Then she remembered the newspapers she brought back from Baltimore last fall. Jason had gleaned a

number of articles from these--one was an editorial
concerning the naming of "Marietta." As the writer
reminded the reader, ever since February 6, 1778--
when France formally recognized the independence of
the fledgling nation in the "Treaties of Alliance &
Commerce," sent a fleet under Admiral d'Estaing to
help the colonists, and French soldiers joined the
fight for freedom--there had been numerous acts of
respect for France and her people. It was Mary who
interrupted Jason's reading with:

"I wonder why those settlers did not name that
settlement Ross after Betsy Ross--or something like
that?"

Jason frowned slightly and continued reading:

"The region around the mouth of the Muskingum
River was once a part of a vast district claimed by
France and called Louisiana. Prior to 1763, France
had colonial claims on three sides of land claimed
by England's Atlantic seaboard colonies--it was inevitable the two countries would be embroiled in a
war. Thus, in 1763, France surrendered to England
the vast majority of her American colonial empire.
Twenty years later--by another treaty concluded in
Paris--England ceded to the fledgling United States
her possessions east of the Mississippi."

The writer said nothing about the fact the Indians were not a party to either of these treaties
negotiated by white men. He also failed to mention
the region along the Ohio had become less peaceful
as it became the field for rivalry of possession
between frustrated Indians and white settlers. Old
antipathies, coupled with the settlers never-ending
encroachment north of the Ohio, had earned the area
a distasteful reputation---some called it "the dark
and bloody ground!" None of Jason's clippings said
anything about this and his wife's eyes sparkled in
the glow from the fireplace as she said:

"You are just a bundle of information tonight.
You never told me you saved all those clippings."

Jason smiled mischievously as he quipped:

"You never asked me! I keep them in this box with all of your old love letters."

He quickly closed the lid of the small wooden box and his wife exlaimed with mock surprise:

"You mean you still have those letters?"

"Certainly. We are going to use them to start a big fire when we get in our new cabin--the one in the Northwest Territory."

Jason ducked as his wife leaned over and made a playful swipe at his head.

"Missed!"

With this exclamation Jason arose and returned the box to the cupboard. Mary sat quietly gazing into the depths of the fire as she pondered various aspects of this undertaking her husband appeared to be dead set on. And there was no purpose in brooding over the matter. As her husband reseated himself in his rocker, Mary arose from her chair.

"Would La Salle like a cup of hot tea? I have saved some for just the right occasion and this may be it. Best we enjoy the comforts of our home here while we can."

Her bittersweet words would be recalled in the future months as prophetic. But this night Jason's confidence overshadowed any gloom and doom talk.

"You really know how to hurt a man! You are a crepe hangar Mary Evenstar but I love you. And you may fix me some tea. Please?"

Jason edged his rocker close to the fireplace. The fire had a soothing effect--particularly to one who had been out hunting for four days in the cold, and blustery, bone-numbing wind that sweeps off the Laurels in the winter. Now, as Mary prepared their tea, Jason turned over in his mind the things they had discussed. Despite his having heard and read a lot about the Northwest Territory, there was much he did not understand.

It was difficult to understand the government was practically bankrupt at the end of the Revolutionary War and could not pay the veterans who had served faithfully and at great personal sacrifice. Some of the fiscal-minded congressmen envisioned an opportunity to liquidate these obligations through the sale of land in the Northwest Territory. These men remembered how, in those hectic days just after the signing of the Declaration of Independence, the Congress had given some thought to the undeveloped land in the Ohio country and agreed, "for services rendered," a Colonel should be given 500 acres, a Lieutenant Colonel 450 acres, and so on down to the "backbone of the army," the Private, who was to receive 100 acres. Since both responsibilities and rewards come with "rank," in 1776 the Congress also enacted legislation authorizing a Major General to receive 1100 acres (later this was elevated to 2400 acres) and a Brigadier General 800 acres.

Searching the deep recesses of his mind for an answer to questions which plagued Jason's thoughts, he recalled something George Mason had said:

"When the war was over, and as a result of the earlier action by Congress, in June of 1783 General Rufus Putnam submitted a petition to Congress which proposed the allocation of land in the Ohio country to veterans. He also sent a personal letter to his friend, General Washington, requesting his support. That petition outlined the area south of Lake Erie and north of the Ohio River, and suggested reservation of land for schools and the ministry. He sent another letter to General Washington the following April inquiring as to the status of that petition. Having both an interest in the welfare of veterans, and strong feelings regarding the potential of that land beyond the Ohio River, General Washington used his personal influence to move this action through Congress but, unfortunately, what Putnam called the "Army Plan" became bogged down in committee."

In late January of 1786 General Putnam, aided by General Benjamin Tupper, issued an invitation to all those interested in forming an "Ohio Company of Associates" to gather at THE BUNCH OF GRAPES TAVERN in Boston on March 1, 1786. General Putnam was not only active in formation of the company, he led the first settlers to the mouth of the Muskingum. Only seven days after pushing off from what Putnam called "Sumrill's Ferry" in his diary, on April 7, 1788 they stepped ashore across the river from Fort Harmar. "Doers" in every sense of the word, they soon cleared more than 100 acres and planted corn. Putnam, a surveyor, quickly laid out the settlement in eight acre plots. During the digging operations at Marietta, a lead plate was unearthed which had been buried by Captain Celoron in 1749--a fine marker it was, but they needed lead for bullets more than artifacts out of the past.

Officers? Soldiers? Many of the settlers at Marietta were veterans who had known the absence of customary necessities and comforts. They could more properly be called farmers, carpenters, surveyors, boat builders, lawyers and blacksmiths--men who had united their efforts in a common undertaking.

"I say there La Salle--wake up! Here is your tea--drink it while it is hot."

Mary's voice brought Jason back to reality in a hurry--the fire felt so good and he had dozed off after supper. He savored the cup of steaming fluid Mary had laced with honey and the fragrance erased the memory of the jerk he had eaten last evening along the Youghiogheny. Mary seated herself and now watched the steam rise from her cup as she said:

"While you were away I had the opportunity to visit with cousin Frederick and his family over in Milford Township. The Wilkins were driving over to see their new grandson and asked me to ride along. Your cousin was curing venison."

Mary had been fascinated learning how the venison was cured "Indian fashion" by cutting the meat into thin strips and placing them on a framework of sticks over a bed of live coals. Conrad's only son told her he 'jerked' the venison. Jason explained:

"Those strips are called 'jerk' Mary--they are

what Hank and I eat when we are hunting."

The somewhat puzzled look on Mary's face faded slowly into a smile as she quipped: "Whatever!"

To herself she thought: "Smarty! I will wager you or your cousin Frederick do not know how to embroider a garmet, crochet, or operate a mule!"

Mary had learned a lot the past year. Now she sipped her tea and listened as Jason spoke:

"I have been thinking about what we were talking about before supper—you asked what John Symmes had to do with the Ohio Company of Associates. The way I figure it out is this. Some frontiersman saw a piece of favorable land in the Ohio country along the Miami and he told Symmes about it. Then, like the newspaper says, in 1787 John Symmes petitioned congress for land west of that tract which Manasseh Cutler asked for. That land Symmes is offering for sale is downstream from the Marietta settlement."

Jason took a little sip of tea—it was hot and just the way he liked it. With a telltale smile of satisfaction he added: "How about that?"

He had covered a lot of territory in his brief summary. Shaking her head slowly, Mary replied:

"You are so smart Jason. You have been thinking about this for a long time but it has caught me off guard. I'll have to think about it some more."

Although Jason's conclusion was the epitome of brevity, it was accurate. Major Benjamin Stites, a native of New Jersey and a capable militia officer, lived in a cabin on Ten Mile Creek in southwestern Pennsylvania not far from old Fort Brownsville. At home in the wilderness, in early 1787 Stites floated down the Monongahela and Ohio on a flatboat with his load of flour, whiskey, and trading goods. Being unable to dispose of his goods along the river, at Limestone Point he traveled inland five miles to a little settlement called Washington. Here Stites became involved in an Indian chase which led across the Ohio and on north to an Indian village located along the banks of the Little Miami. At this point he decided to quit the chase and headed back south. On his return trip Stites passed through the region between the two Miami rivers and here the idea of a "Miami Purchase" was born. Stites then headed east to Trenton, New Jersey and talked with John Symmes.

Symmes, a 45 year old New Jersey congressman, was impressed with Stites' story. Along with five companions, Symmes departed early in the summer of 1787 to see for himself the "land of opportunity." Sufficiently impressed, Symmes returned and quickly initiated a petition to congress on August 29, 1787 which eventually resulted in what came to be known as "The Symmes Purchase." The petition referred to a congressional resolution of July 27, 1787 regarding the petition of Manasseh Cutler, Esquire, agent for the Ohio Company of Associates, and requested a grant of acreage on the same terms except for the place and quantity of land. The area described in this petition envisioned a grant of 600,000 acres. Frustrated by the lack of any favorable action, on October 2, 1787 John Cleves Symmes, et al submitted a second petition which was, for all practical purposes, merely a clarification of his first request. Three weeks later, on October 23rd, Congress passed legislation which authorized the Board of Treasury to contract for sale of land in the new territory where the tracts were less than one million acres. As Jonathan Dayton explained to Symmes: "It is the government paper mill that takes so long!"

It would not be any different 200 years later. But now, in 1791, Mary's mind was in a whirl--something her father had said flashed across her mind.

"You know Jason, about a week or so before we were married, my father came back from Philadelphia saying he heard something about 'Miami Lands' being for sale. Being busy with our wedding plans, I was not at all interested in the Northwest Territory at the time. And, frankly, I am not really interested in it now. Just thought I would mention it dear."

Impatient to get on with his business venture,

and believing he had the "green light" for his land undertaking, on November 26, 1787 John Symmes had released "To The General Public" a brochure titled: "Terms of Sale and Settlement of Miami Lands." The advertisement announced land was for sale at sixty-six and two-thirds cents an acre until November 1st of 1788. The land warrants which were to be issued stated the buyer would be charged an extra one cent per acre to defray survey expenses and one farthing per acre for printing and miscellaneous costs. The sale agreement indicated buyers had to settle their purchase within two years or forfeit a part of the cost. On December 17, 1787 Benjamin Stites bought a 640 acre "Miami Land Warrant"--the first one sold by Symmes. As the primary motivator of the "Miami Purchase," Stites was given a covenant for 10,000 acres at five shillings per acre.

Jason gave only a fleeting thought to Mary's facetious comment--he was turning over in his mind what she had said about the "Miami Lands." Staring thoughtfully into his empty cup, he muttered:

"Yes sir, that's it! The John Symmes purchase is a different land undertaking than the one Cutler is involved with."

Like her husband, Mary had savored her tea and watched the patterns which danced in the fireplace. It was good to have her husband home at night for a change. She had heard Jason's muttering but enough was enough for one day and she simply said:

"Care for more tea Jason?"

"No thank you--that was excellent. Certainly does beat that bark and hot water Hank makes!"

Jason made a wry face and then his face clouded up as he soberly added:

"Listen to that wind howl--its not a fit night out for man or beast. Glad I'm home!"

Jason and Mary had no way of knowing that even as they enjoyed the warmth of their fireplace, John Cleves Symmes and his settlers were celebrating the second anniversary of their arrival at North Bend.

Late in July of 1788 Symmes and his party had left New Jersey with fourteen wagons pulled by four horses each. Sixty people, including his wife and family, made up the entourage. Stites had already left the east coast with a party but agreed to wait at Limestone Point until Symmes arrived. When John Symmes reached Devon's Ferry on the Monongahela, he sent his horses overland to Wheeling and the rest of the group boarded a flatboat. After stopping at Pittsburgh for two days, they reunited at Wheeling and continued downstream. Symmes reached Limestone in late September where, much to his aversion, circumstances then forced him to stay several months. At Fort Pitt, and again at Marietta, Symmes voiced his urgent need for a military escort to safeguard against the Indian menace.

And while the indignant Symmes waited for his escort, the settlers with him grew impatient—they wanted to see the land they had purchased. And the feeling against Symmes intensified when Stites took off downstream on November 28, 1788 with a party of surveyors, a sergeant, and 18 soldiers. This group went ashore at what became Columbia and immediately began building a blockhouse—it was the nucleus of the first settlement in the "Miami Purchase." Two weeks later, on December 12, 1788, Symmes' military escort arrived—Captain William Kearsey and his 45 soldiers were all set to go. But now it was Symmes who had problems which delayed travel.

And so, as Symmes sat in Limestone and chewed his fingernails, at Fort Harmar Governor St. Clair was conducting negotiations with Indian sachems who had gathered there at his personal invitation—many were Indians he had known for years. On January 9, 1789 the governor signed a treaty with sachems from various Wyandot, Delaware, Ottawa, Chippewa, Sac, and Potawatomie villages. These peace negotiations reaffirmed the treaty which had been signed in 1785 at Fort McIntosh. The governor concluded the talks declaring it was his fervent hope this treaty would ease unrest and stem the growing hostilities which plagued the vast territory he governed.

Although St. Clair had sent a runner to carry his personal invitation to Captain Joseph Brant, he and his Mohawks would not attend the peace talks at Fort Harmar. And significant by their absence, the sachems of the powerful Miami and Shawnee villages did not attend. But St. Clair optimistically said: "The treaty signed at Fort Harmar is a start!"

The governor had not advised John Symmes about the peace talks. However, anticipating a favorable agreement, he had sent Captain Kearsey downstream. Then, awaiting favorable weather, Symmes was forced to subsist Kearsey's detachment when provisions at Limestone were costing two or three times more than the price at Lexington 60 miles away. Reeling from the expense of buying a house at Limestone for his family, it was a blow to Symmes' ego when word came up the river saying cabins were already being built at Columbia. While bemoaning his fate, he received several urgent pleas from Stites to "come on down!" Symmes was livid!

And, adding insult to injury, Robert Patterson of Lexington was the next to move downstream to the "Miami Lands." On December 24th Colonel Patterson and his party of Kentucky and eastern settlers took off from Limestone and moved 69 miles down the Ohio through ice-infested waters to a point opposite the mouth of the Licking River. On the 28th they landed at "Yeatman's Cove" and began surveying what was called "Losantiville." Word of this second settlement was soon relayed upstream to where the founder of "Symmes' Purchase" sat on his "laurels" fuming.

Finally, with Captain Kearsey's men providing a military escort, the Symmes party pushed off from Limestone January 29, 1789. After stopping briefly at Columbia and Losantiville, shortly after noon on February 2nd the members of this party went ashore. With a hastily erected lean-to to provide shelter, and a huge fire to keep them warm, the Symmes party huddled together along the banks of the Ohio River. Then, with the sun slowly sinking behind the rim of the wooded horizon, and a bone-chilling wind sweepin down from a high ridge behind him, Symmes looked across the ice-infested Ohio toward Virginia's Kentucky District and firmly declared to himself:

"Here on this bend we will build a city!"

Three hundred miles east of that north bend in the trouble-plagued river, Mary Evenstar looked intently down at her husband's upturned face.

"Good to have you home Jason," she said.

Jason stretched his arms and yawned. Watching his wife as she stepped toward the bed he asked:

"You ready for bed already?"

Without any reply Mary kneeled, pulled a small black case from beneath the bed, and then replied:

"How about a little tune maestro?"

The violin served to pass away many an evening on the lonely frontier and Jason was a fine fiddle player. Uncle Frederick claimed Johanne had been a "gifted fiddle player" and Uncle Conrad was always agreeable to "saw a few tunes" when asked. "Playing the fiddle runs in the family," Conrad always said. During the past year here in Turkey Foot, Jason had often been asked to play his fiddle after a barn or cabin raising--or, like last fall when they joined their friends at the Wilkins for a corn-husking and taffy-pull party. As Mary said one day:

"Regardless of the get-together, if a fiddler is present the day usually ends up with a dance."

Like their ever-present gun, the violin was an indispensable part of rural life 200 years ago.

Jason unsnapped the worn wooden case and carefully removed the aged violin from its velvet-lined resting place. His foster father once told him his grandfather had brought that violin to America from Germany. It had been Johanne's request his brother teach Jason to play the violin. Frederick not only honored his younger brother's request, he had given the violin to Jason when the boy was sixteen.

76

With loving care Jason now carefully drew the
bow strings through a notch in a worn piece of resin as his wife watched every move with interest and
admiration--she did not say a word. Finally he was
ready and Mary's eyes sparkled as the sound of his
"tuning up" broke the silence. Having made a final
adjustment, Jason tucked the violin under his chin
and began playing a mirthful ditty which Mary soon
recognized and began to sing:

> *"Drink and be merry, merry boyes;*
> *Let all your delight be in Hymens joyes.*
> *Joy to Hymen now the day is come,*
> *About the merry Maypole take a Roome."*

"Oh, that was fun Jason!" With an impish grin
Mary added: "By the way dear, did you know 'Hymen'
was the ancient Greek god of marriage? He probably
didn't know what 'jerk' was either."
Jason feigned a frown, shook his head slowly,
and said: "I don't know about you Mary--but you do
have a lovely voice."
Now Jason made just a slight adjustment on one
of the four strings by tightening one of the wooden
pegs. When the sound was to his satisfaction, he
drew the bow back and forth across the strings several times. Now he adjusted the frog on the bottom
of the old bow. It would be years before anyone in
America would see the bow developed by a Frenchman,
Francois Tourte--he would lengthen the bow, reverse
its curve, and make it lighter and more slender and
graceful than the one Jason used. But now, on this
early February night in 1791, the one hundred fifty
horsehair threads of Jason's bow produced pleasing
sounds which filled his wife's heart with happiness
and made her forget for a moment her worries about
him wanting to move to the Northwest Territory.
"Remember that English ballad--the one written
by Seaborn Cotton? You know, the minister's son."
Mary looked puzzled and Jason quickly added:

"He was born at sea--the son of Reverend John Cotton. Parson Weems told me about him."

Parson Weems had told him many stories during his visits to Frederick. Always a welcome visitor, the preacher enjoyed listening to Jason play. Some of the local composers made up tunes and harmonized them as Jason played during the evening hours.   It was Parson Weems who suggested Jason should prepare a book of tunes and remarked:

"The country is hungry for books Jason!"

Despite the well-meaning suggestion, there was never time for the undertaking. Although Jason had an ear for music, he had no talent for reading what he called "those chicken tracks."   Content to play from memory, Jason enjoyed the happiness his violin playing brought to others.

"Jason, I remember a song which is sung to the tune of 'Franklin Is Fled Away.' It is called 'Two Faithful Lovers.' Do you remember it?"

After "sawing" a few notes, Jason recalled the song. As he began to play, Mary sang:

"You loyal lovers all that hear this ditty,
Sigh and lament my fall, let's move you to
pity;
She lies now in the deep, in everlasting
sleep,
And left me here to weep in great distress."

Jason rested his violin on his knee and looked at his wife with a pained expression--a mischievous smile spread across his face as he remarked:

"It is a pretty tune and your singing is beautiful--but the words give me the shivers."

To herself Mary thought about how sensitive he was. Aloud she laughingly pleaded:

"All right, you select something."

Mary was always enraptured with her husband's playing and now Jason looked intently at his wife's sparkling eyes and petal soft face as it reflected

the glow of the fireplace. Softly he said:
"You're mighty pretty Mrs. Evenstar."
"Go on!   You fiddle players are all alike. I
bet you and Hank tell that to all of the girls you
meet on your hunting trips!"
Jason feigned shocked surprise at her quip--he
knew that she knew it was quite unlikely they would
ever run into any women on their hunting sojourns.
There wasn't much night life in the Laurels! Carefully cradling the fingerboard in his left hand and
tucking the tailpiece of the violin under his chin,
Jason played several tunes he had learned from his
uncle Emanuel who told him:
"Sellinger's Round and Green Sleeves have been
around for more than a hundred years I suppose."
Jason paused and studied the fire. Mary broke
the silence saying: "Yes? What is on your mind?"
"Oh, I'm sorry. I was was just thinking about
something Parson Weems told me.   Did you ever hear
of Mother Ann Lee?"
"Certainly. Our minister told us about her in
one of his sermons. As I recall, she and eight of
her followers came to America from England in 1774,
settled along the Hudson River, and she went to her
eternal reward several years ago--1784 I believe it
was. He said Ann Lee had an unhappy marriage, bore
and lost four children, and converted to the Shaker
religion whose members believe in sharing community
property and observe a doctrine of celibacy."
The orange glow from the fireplace helped hide
the redness of Jason's face. Parson Weems had told
the sensitive young man all about "celibacy."
"Why Jason, I do believe you are blushing! It
was Mother Ann Lee who looked upon sexual relations
as the root of all evil and imposed that silly rule
of celibacy among Shakers. Our minister was always
frank in his sermons concerning this religious sect
and said he was of the opinion they would be unable
to maintain their membership since they did not believe in having children."

"That was not what I was referring to Mary! I was talking about something Parson Weems said about the Shakers trembling and chanting wordless songs."

Mary interrupted saying:

"Small wonder!   Universal brotherhood, peace, love, and nonviolence may be fine religious princi- ples, but, any sect which advocates the practice of not marrying and celibacy leaves much to be desired in my humble opinion! By the way, did Parson Weems tell you her father was a blacksmith?"

Jason had been watching his wife and now said:

"One is never in doubt as to the Irish opinion on any issue! But, as I was saying before I was so rudely interrupted by my Irish bride, it was my un- derstanding Mother Ann Lee was supposed to have re- vealed by inspiration a system of musical notation which designates notes of the musical scale by the first seven letters of the alphabet beginning with 'A' for middle 'C'."

"I am not certain about that but those are the 'little chicken scratches' you refuse to learn any- thing about Jason!"

"Mary, I cannot read music--and I am not about to take the time to learn!"

Jason smiled broadly as he added:

"By the way, Parson Weems told me those Shaker folks depend on conversions and adoptions to main- tain their membership."

Not intending to allow her husband to have the final word on the subject, Mary hastily declared:

"It does not sound very practical to me--and I believe it is contrary to the teachings of the Good Book. But I am happy to hear they do not object to music. And speaking of music, how about a tune?"

Jason carefully twisted one of the pegs on his violin as he drew the bow across the strings. Mary was about to suggest a tune when her husband said:

"I knew a family of Moravians who lived on the east fork of the Monocacy--they were from Georgia I heard. My uncle said Moravians were partial to the

trombone. He told me a story once about a party of
Indians who were all set to attack a settlement one
night during the French and Indian War. Well, when
the Indians heard one of the Moravians play a trombone sounding the death of a brethern, they thought
the sound must be the voice of the Great Spirit and
decided not to attack Calypso Island."

Mary listened politely and then said: "Interesting dear—now will you please play your fiddle?"

Music had always shared an important niche in
Jason's life—he spent many hours with his violin
along the Monocacy. Among the several books he had
packed was "The Turtle-Taube," a hymn book of some
750 songs written in 1746.   He also brought along
his treasured "Bay Psalm Book" given him by Parson
Weems. This 9th Edition had been printed in 1698
and contained "Low Dutch," "York," and one of his
wife's favorite songs, "119th Psalm Tune."

The Evenstars were not alone in their love of
music on the frontier—music was "a partner" in the
life of settlers whose life was coupled with strenuous labor, imminent danger, and their ever-present
companion, loneliness.   But music appreciation was
not limited to frontier life. Jason would not forget one visitor to his uncle's blacksmith shop who
said Thomas Jefferson and Patrick Henry often played violin duets. While waiting for his horse to be
shod, the Irish gentleman also said it was Benjamin
Franklin who had invented the Glassychord.   With a
twinkle in his eye, and the brogue of a true son of
Erin, he had added: "Sure and that would be back in
1761 when ye were a wee gleam in yer father's eye!"

And now, on this cold February night in 1791,
that Irishman's only daughter shared with Jason the
warmth of a fireplace in their log cabin nestled in
the purple shadows of Laurel Hill. From a chest at
the foot of their bed, Mary carried to her chair a
copy of "Harmonica Sacra" and a book titled "Select
Hymns For Use Of Christians." Jason remarked:

"Now Mary, you know I cannot read that music—

those chicken scratches mean nothing to me!"

She was fully aware of this "weakness" in her husband's musical ability and, ignoring his rebuke, Mary nonchalantly seated herself again and began to leaf through a hymn book. Having located what she was looking for, Mary glanced at Jason saying:

"I know you cannot read music Jason. And I am also painfully aware you refuse to learn how."

Politely, but firmly, she added:

"You are just set in your ways dear. However, I feel certain you can play this hymn. Please?"

Written by Charles Wesley before she was born, "Jesus, Lover Of My Soul" was Mary's favorite hymn. Having purchased the hymnal in Philadelphia, one of Mary's friends played it for them several times in Baltimore and Jason was able to play it from memory ever since. Without further prompting, Jason began to play this song and Mary sang in a voice he said "would surely make the angels envious."

After that Jason carefully laid the violin in the red velvet-lined case, gently replaced the bow, snapped the lid shut, and returned the case to its place beneath their bed. This done, they silently prepared for bed. As Jason now tended the fire and made certain the latch string was pulled in, Mary slipped into her flannel night gown--she was in bed before her husband had removed his deerskin hunting shirt. With the help of Hank's wife, Mary had made his hunting shirt. Because Jason said the deerskin was cold and hard to care for when wet, she made an inner shirt for him out of some linsey-woolsey she purchased during her visit to Baltimore last year. Beneath his deerskin trousers, Jason wore underwear made of this same part-linen and part-wool homemade cloth.

Standing in front of the fireplace clothed in his underwear, Jason toasted himself on both sides. The fire felt good. Bewitching flames in the fire-place cast weird patterns on the walls and restless shadows danced eerily across the puncheon floor. A

little reluctant to leave the penetrating warmth of
the fire, he watched his wife making shadowy images
on the wall with her hands. Suddenly Jason gave up
his warm post and obliterated the image of a rabbit
on the wall with his own shadow as he lunged at the
bed, kicked off his deerskin moccasins, and eagerly
began working his way through the heavy blankets to
the waiting arms of his wife who squealed with delight. Sensing the subtle fragrance of his wife's
perfume, and feeling the stimulating warmth of her
body, Jason tenderly kissed Mary's cheek, her forehead, and finally her lips. A surge of passion engulfed Jason's body as he quickly wrapped his arms
around his wife and pulled her warm and tender body
close to him. Instinctively Mary slipped her arms
around her husband and gently massaged his back as
they kissed. Mary offered no resistance as Jason's
ardor increased and willingly responded when he was
ready. Then, as they made passionate love, she allowed the fantasies and physical sensations of her
sexual warmth to kaleidoscope across her mind without censorship.

Finally exhausted, and breathing heavily, they
lay for a long time without saying a word. The only
light in the room came from the fireplace and Mary
could see her husband's profile silhouetted against
the orange and yellow glow--he was handsome and she
loved him dearly.

Outside, the cold and blustery winds from off
the Laurels whistled around·the little cabin and a
sleet peppered the clapboard roof persistently. It
failed to drown the mournful wails of a maurauding
pack of wolves however. Mary shivered slightly and
nestled close to Jason. Inside their tiny one-room
cabin, cuddled in the arms of her husband, she felt
safe and secure and knew full well she would follow
Jason to the end of the earth if necesary.

CHAPTER FOUR

"DON'T FORGET YOUR FIDDLE!"

Mary was up and around long before her husband and had her husband's favorite hoecake and sorghum on the table when she awakened him.

"Come on sleepy head, we have a lot of packing to do!"

The little cabin was her first home away from home after they were married. In here they worked, ate, and slept. Describing the place to her before she moved to Turkey Foot Township, Jason quipped:

"It has one room and a path!"

In the long evenings of the past winter, Jason had whittled several utensils, molded bullets, and made a rocking chair. The iron crane Jason brought along was fastened to the side of the fireplace and extended out over the fire so kettles could be hung in the best position--the crane could also be drawn out over the hearth so Mary could tend the kettles. Jason took pride in the things he made both in the cabin and outside. From his boyhood experience and training Jason quickly learned all of the frontier jobs men must do. Mary Evenstar also soon learned what it was like to be a frontier wife far removed from the comforts of life in Baltimore. As she now prepared breakfast, she was thinking:

"We are together and together we will stay!"

Turning to watch Jason slip into his shirt and trousers, Mary frowned as she touched the side of her face. With an impish smile she said:

"I would be obliged if you would take a moment after breakfast and remove that four-day stubble of yours. This is not the Sabbath--and we do not have Blue Laws here!"

She referred to a history book Jason purchased in Baltimore shortly after they were married. When she had admonished him about shaving before he went to church, Jason had jokingly called her attention to one of the forty-five "Blue Laws Of The New Haven Colony" listed in the history book.*

"No one shall travel, sweep house, make beds, cook victuals, cut hair, or shave on the Sabbath."

Mary had carefully read each of the Blue Laws and felt it was opportune to remind Jason of one of them when he returned from his hunting trip:

"Married persons must live together, or be imprisoned!"

Jason had intended to shave--his beard was beginning to itch. A smile tugged at the corners of his mouth as he saluted smartly and replied:

"Yes mam!"

Now he glanced at the blackened kettle hanging over the fire--Mary was preparing one of his favorite dishes, "potpie." The lid was gently moving up periodically allowing a puff of steam to escape and the delicious odor permeated the room. He sniffed, smiled, and leaned over slightly to move the handle of the spider which rested on the hearth. The spider had been a gift from his wife's parents--it was something like a frying pan with a long handle and legs for use over an open fire. Although Jason did not mention it, he sensed his wife was a little too cheerful this morning. As for Mary, in spite of a brave attempt to be of good cheer, there was an air of pensive disbelief in her manner and deep inside she was repeating over and over:

"Am I dreaming? Is it really possible we are going to move farther out in this wilderness?"

* "A General History of Connecticut" by Samuel Peters (1781)

Brushing by Jason on the way to the fireplace, he caught her eye and said: "I love you Mary."

"Go on! You just smell that potpie. But mind you dear one, not a bite until noon."

Returning to the table where Jason was seated, she gave her husband a kiss on the top of his head.

"Remember, no strudel mit der stubble!"

"I said I would shave--right after breakfast-- and a little stroll in the morning air."

It was just twelve steps to the outhouse Jason had built behind their cabin.

From a small copper kettle on the hearth, Mary filled a cup with an amber fluid and carried it to Jason. He put his nose into the steam saying:

"What is this?"

Mary replied with a smile: "Sassafras tea."

"Sassafras tea? What is it for and where did you get it?"

"Mrs. Keeling gave it to me. She says this is good 'spring tonic.' You are going to need all of the tonic you can get before we get packed!"

She smoothed her apron and smiled mischievouly as Jason remarked:

"I do believe my Baltimore bride is more riled up about this move than I am."

Deep inside Jason was happy she was showing an interest in the move. Mary replied:

"Well, someone had better be giving thought to what we are taking along--be a little late to think about it after we are sitting in some lean-to along the Mississippi River!"

"Oh for heaven's sake Mary, cut out that crepe hanging--its the Ohio, not the Mississippi! And we have not fared badly so far, have we? We are both young and we have a lot to look forward to."

"That my dear husband is the understatement of the year. We will probably both be a lot smarter before folks hereabouts have the maple sugaring-off parties next year. Our good neighbors have told me so much about them and I was looking forward to the parties this spring. I don't suppose they have any maple trees out in your Northwest Territory."

"Mary, now stop it please! You know very well you're just trying to get me riled up. Your womanly ways of trying to change my mind will not work!"

He was serious and Mary knew it. But quick as it had surfaced, Jason's reprimand was over and he added with sheepish smile:

"And besides, I feel confident there are maple trees in the Northwest Territory--there must be."

Mary said nothing--she was thinking:

"Well, you can't blame a girl for trying!"

Deciding silence was the best policy just now, a wave of nostalgia swept over Mary and she fought down an urge to cry. This was her home and she did hate to move. While washing dishes she thought:

"Men do not think about things like that--they are just like that hard-headed husband of mine!"

As she went about her work Mary knew Jason was watching her. He had backed up to the fire and was rubbing his buttocks. Nothing was said for a long time until she broke the silence saying:

"I just could not sleep last night!"

"Yes, I know.

Mary glanced at her husband--he was smiling in a knowing sort of way. She felt a sudden rush of heat to her cheeks and quickly commented:

"Don't be crude. You know what I mean."

"Certainly do dear--certainly do."

Jason gave Mary a kiss on the cheek and patted her on the back side. Remembering the fragrance of her perfume and nearness last night, Jason suddenly pulled his wife into his arms and kissed her.

"Jason!"

Mary feigned indignation and opposition to his amorous attention but deep inside she loved him for it. Free from his arms, she quickly remarked:

"I swear you are positively indecent since you have been hanging around with Hank. Maybe a little morning air will cool thee down--we need firewood."

Mary's mischievous smile betrayed her attempt to be stern. Then, as Jason dutifully grabbed his gun and started out the door, she muttered:

"Is it possible we have been married only one year and two months! So much has happened.

They had been married in Baltimore and travel- ed northeast on the Post Road to Philadelphia. Two fun-filled weeks in the Quaker City, with all their expenses paid, had been her Aunt Margaret's wedding present. It was a wonderful time and everyone was talking about the nation's first president, cabinet appointments, and the "Indian problem in the North- west Territory." Those two precious weeks had gone by quickly and they returned to Baltimore and began preparing for their trek to Bedford County. Jason had visited with his uncle Conrad during the summer of 1789 and returned saying he had been told:

"This land rightfully belongs to you Jason. I already staked out a few acres west of here and got a cabin almost built. Our son Frederick is all set on his place over in Milford Township and I've been just itching for an excuse to move to Westmoreland. Be a real blessing if you took over here--I'll give you a deed to this land one year from the day that you move here. Be nice having you boys so close."

Without discussing his plans with his intended wife--and working from sunup to sundown--Jason cut the timber and put up his cabin on the same ground where his father had built his wilderness home just twenty-four years before. Returning to Frederick, and then on to Baltimore, Jason proudly announced:

"I have a beautiful piece of land and a cabin in Bedford County--they await our arrival!"

This was Jason's way of a proposal to Mary and she had accepted. Eagerly he explained:

"I plan to use my uncle's old cabin for a barn and build a lean-to on the side for horses. Cousin Frederick is going to let me have a riding horse--a beautiful black gelding with a white stocking fore- foot and a matching star on its forehead."

He was so excited and Mary was so much in love with him. By coach they had traveled west to Frederick, Maryland where they looked around for a new Conestoga--a wagon made by German settlers. One of the men who worked in a wagon shop told them:

"Them Conestogas are named after those Indians who live in the upper Chesapeake Bay country."

The Conestoga Jason and Mary selected had been made by James Rudy northeast of Frederick in York, Pennsylvania. They had looked at the "farm- type" and the "freighter" model with its two boxes before finally selecting the nine-bow variety which Jason decided best suited their needs. Then they spent a week buying furniture, supplies, and selecting the horses for their journey. Jason appeared to be so knowledgeable of what they would need and Mary admired his business-like manner. She thought:

"My Irish father was right--Jason would be an excellent 'partner' for him in his business. Well, maybe after he gets this 'live on my parent's land' idea out of his head, he may be willing to consider my father's offer."

Mary had a lot to learn about her new husband, her new Conestoga and her new way of life. After staying with Jason's foster parents for a few days, they headed west. In spite of the rough road, the excitement of the travel made the time pass quickly and soon they reached Fort Cumberland. Continuing west on the Braddock Road, they finally reached the "Great Crossing." Here Jason turned north and followed the river road to the "Turkeyfoot" area which was so named because of the confluence of a trio of rivers in the headwaters region of the Youghiogheny River. Jason had seemed so confident and Mary felt no cause for any alarm along the way. And finally, about noon one day, they pulled into a clearing and Jason proudly declared:

"Well, this is it--we are home!"

He was proud of his accomplishment--it was not a big cabin but it was home. Mary's "first" home!

Nearby stood Conrad's old cabin--the one Jason said would be their barn. Several squirrels had already taken "squatter's rights" in the rafters of Jason's cabin but hurriedly exited as the new tenants open- ed the door and sunshine flooded the interior.

With her husband's help, Mary immediately hung a pewter plate above the mantle--it was a treasured gift from her girl-friend in Philadelphia. A blue homemade rug--given them by Mary's cousin in Balti- more--was placed on the puncheon floor. Two yellow candlesticks which Mary had purchased in Frederick were placed on the wooden table Jason had made last summer. Several wooden pegs in the wall served to hold their clothes and a set of deer antlers which were given them by Uncle Frederick. Jason's bullet pouch and an engraved powder horn were hung on the antlers. Three guns were propped against the wall by the fireplace and Mary eyed these with a certain misgiving. Two were guns which Jason had purchased in Philadelphia and one was a trusty flintlock that Conrad made and had given to his nephew. This gun was Jason's pride and joy.

The joy of unpacking boxes, putting her things away, and getting their home in order occupied most of Mary's time the first month or so. It was all so new and she was busy all of the time. Jason was also busy clearing land, planting corn, beans, and pumpkins--and remodeling the barn where Conrad had lived. They were both exhausted when evening came but neither complained.

Conrad and his wife, and cousin Frederick, all came to visit soon after they arrived. True to his word, Frederick brought along the black horse with the star on its forehead--Jason had the horse's new home ready. The Evenstar's neighbors were friendly and always ready and willing to help if needed. At church service on Sunday Jason and Mary were always greeted warmly by old and new friends. Hospitality was simple and heartfelt--the latch string on their cabin door was always out during the daytime. Some

of their neighbors kept a barrel of whiskey stored
away for use during house-warmings and other merry-
making gatherings. Jason's wife had little time to
think about anything the first several months--from
early morning until dark she was busy. And most of
the time her husband was within sight of the door.

Then one day one of the foes which plagued the
frontier came "knocking" at the door. Actually it
didn't "knock," this insidious thing just "seeped"
in. It was just as if one day Mary finished washing dishes and there "it" was--that unwelcome, but
all too common frontier guest, "loneliness."

Now, six months later, Mary silently watched
her husband shave and a cold chill coarsed through
her body as she recalled that overwhelming homesick
feeling. Jason spent most of his time outside--he
never had time to be lonely. But it was different
with a woman whose daily chores kept her inside the
cabin so much of the time. Although Mary did not
complain, Jason did notice his wife grew sullen as
the days passed and finally refused to sing during
the church services she had always enjoyed so much.
Mary's wistful smile was a story in itself and even
Hank bluntly inquired about her health:

"Your wife been having morning sickness Jason?
She might just be a bit homesick you know."

Jason understood what it was like to be "homesick." Then, as he pondered what to do, providence
stepped in and offered a helping hand.

"We are planning a trip back east to Frederick
and thought you and Mary might like to join us."

The Wilkins family was going to Maryland for a
visit with relatives and there was always room in a
Conestoga for friends. Being an understanding man,
Jason encouraged his wife to accompany the Wilkins.

"You could take the coach from Frederick on in
to Baltimore. The visit with your parents would do
you a world of good!"

But Jason insisted he must remain behind.

"I have too much to do here. Before you know

it, you will be there and back. You will come back
won't you?"

"Of course silly! It would be nice if you did
come along but I understand. The Wilkins have kids
who will watch things while they are away. I would
very much like to go however--you understand, don't
you Jason?"

Jason had never even considered the thought of
denying his wife this opportunity to see her mother
and father. He took Mary in his arms and held her
as she cried softly.

"Come on now, let us be of cheerful thoughts--
this trip is just what you need! Before the leaves
fall you will be back. And by the way, perhaps you
will bring back some tea and coffee--all right?"

Mary realized his cheerful enthusiasm was for
her benefit. With her tiny handkerchief she wiped
her eyes, blew her nose, and looked at Jason.

"All right, I'll go--if you are certain you do
not mind my going."

Mary wrinkled up her little nose and smiled in
a mischievous way as Jason jokingly admonished:

"You just stay out of trouble and do not allow
any of those city slickers to steal my best girl!"

"I love you Jason Evenstar and don't you worry
about anyone stealing me away--you are stuck! Like
the preacher man said: "Till death us do part."

Mary threw her arms around her husband and for
the first time in weeks he once again saw that old
familiar "sparkle" in her eyes. He would miss her
but it was best she go. In his heart he was thankful providence had made it so opportune.

Two weeks afer Mary departed the minister must
have been reading Jason's mind when he mentioned in
his Sunday sermon how "time moves on leaden wings."
But Jason's days were filled with hard work--when
he was not clearing timber or working in the field,
he chinked and daubed the cracks of his cabin with
a mixture of clay, grass, and mud so the room would
be warmer when the cold winds of winter came. Each

night Jason prayed his wife was safe and would soon return--life without his wife was a torment and his heart ached at night as he lay alone in the cabin.

The rolling hills around the log cabin offered a beautiful vista but Jason hardly noticed nature's handiwork as he stood currying his horse one autumn day. His wife had been away a little more than one month--and the trees were putting on their colorful autumn apparel--when he heard the Wilkin's wagon in the distance. Just as she promised, Mary was back "before the trees shed their leaves!" Lifted from the wagon by her waiting husband, Mary "dissolved" into Jason's "welcome home" embrace. Her tiny body trembled and she clung to her husband tightly for a long time as she tearfully said:

"I missed you so much darling."

"And I missed you too. Don't cry now, we will do our traveling together from now on."

Having unloaded Mary's things, and understand- ably anxious to get home, the Wilkins bid Jason and his wife goodbye and were on their way. Inside the cabin, Mary now went around examining every item as if to be certain it was exactly where she had left it--they were. Jason sat in his chair and laughed as his happy wife showed him all the "pretties" she had brought back. "Grace" before their evening meal included special thanks for Mary's safe return and later, as they sat by the fireplace, Jason enjoyed a cup of the coffee she had brought back for him.

A beautiful Indian summer passed quickly after Mary's return and then one day winter rushed in and brushed fall aside. And as the days grew shorter, Jason spent more time in the cabin. While his wife knitted, he whittled--a wooden basket, four knives, and four forks evidenced the skill of his endeavors and Mary made a sweater which she gave her husband for Christmas. And now, February had brought Jason back from a hunting trip asking Mary:

"How would you feel about us pulling up stakes here and moving west to the Northwest Territory?"

Jason heard his hunting partner's wagon coming down the road early the following morning. Hank's beaming face was like that of a little child seeing a Christmas tree for the first time--eager anticipation was written all over it. As Hank drew near, Jason opened the door and walked briskly toward him waving his hand.

"Mornin' Jason. Well, how'd it go with you?"

Hank was not long in coming to the point--that was the purpose of this early morning visit. Jason expected the question and was about to ask the same of him. Yesterday they agreed the time had come to broach the subject of moving. Hank had four children--ages four, seven, ten and fourteen--and he had frankly admitted he expected "some difficulty with with Sarah and the kids!" Glancing quickly toward the door of his cabin, Jason replied confidently:

"Oh, Mary is a bit skittish but I believe she is coming around--how did things go over your way?"

Hank shifted his big chaw of tobacco from one cheek to the other, let go with a stream of tobacco juice on the other side of the wagon, and wiped his mouth with the back of a weather-chapped hand.

"Can't say maw and the kids was too happy."

Hank grinned revealing a missing tooth in the middle of an upper row of tobacco stained teeth.

"Maw's worried 'bout the kids more'n anything. Old lady Bridge is of the same mind I guess--Barney says they ain't movin'. But Dave and Noah is riled up and rarin' to go. Of course, old Noah's got ten kids--that might be a catch. On the other hand old Dave's only got one kid and she's almost six. Barney's old lady keeps harpin' to maw 'bout her kids gittin' book larnin'. Shucks, like I told maw last night, I didn't git no book larnin' but her and the kids got a warm cabin, clothes on their back, and I keep food on the table. Thet ain't too bad!"

A robust individual with a jovial manner and a heart of gold if he liked you, Hank would willingly share his last piece of bread. And, as Jason had

learned last year at Fort Ligonier when a braggart
aroused Hank's anger, his six-foot three, 230 pound
friend was able to take care of himself if need be.
Now Jason remarked:

"Well, you must admit the ladies have a point.
The opportunity for education is something to think
about where children are concerned."

Jason believed education was important and was
impressed when he learned the "Articles of Compact"
in the Ordinance of 1787 had addressed this matter.
His friend Hank had different priorities and said:

"Yeah, I s'pose so Jason. The old man kept us
kids so busy we never had time for book larnin'--we
had to work to eat! Sarah says 'times have changed
and kids need book larnin' nowdays.' Might be, but
like I tell her, let's cross thet damn bridge when
git to it. Dave's chompin' at the bit and may head
on out even if no one else goes. There's jes a lot
to jaw over but sometimes a fellar's gotta take the
bull by the horns and do what he thinks is right!"

Hank was of German lineage--a hard working man
who loved his freedom and didn't care for politics.
In spite of his coarse remarks on occasion, he was
God-fearing and honest--the latch string was always
out at the Weisers. Anything Hank lacked in social
graces he made up ten fold in being a true friend.

Invited inside, Hank dismounted and followed
Jason. Mary was courteous and quickly began fixing
their friend a cup of sassafras tea.   Hank glanced
around nervously for a spittoon and then remembered
Mary did not approve of such a thing in her cabin--
she did not approve of chewing tobacco. Hank never
said a word--he just disappeared through the door.
Having disposed of his cud, Hank spit, cleared his
throat, wiped his chin, and rejoined Jason near the
fireplace on a three-legged stool.

Jason and Hank talked while Mary fixed the tea
but she never missed a word. In a few minutes Mary
handed their guest a cup of the steaming beverage
and then watched as he sipped it noisily. Dropping

easily into the small rocking chair she had brought back from Baltimore, Mary said nothing as the burly man enjoyed his tea and Jason made small talk about their recent hunting trip. Turning slightly toward Mary, Hank nodded his head approvingly as he said:

"Thet wer mighty good Mary! Right nippy this mornin' and thet takes off the chill. Thank you."

"And thank you. Jason and I enjoyed ours."

Without delay Mary came quickly to the point:

"It is my understanding you 'coureurs de bois' ran into two settlers who were moving to the Northwest Territory and now you believe we should follow some Pied Piper to that Indian infested country!"

Bewildered by Mary's sudden verbal lambasting, Hank glanced at Jason who quickly interjected:

"Now Mary, let us not be uppity! Don't worry Hank, my teacher-bride called us 'men of the woods' in French--I think."

Hank may not have been able to translate what Mary said in French but he understood what she said in English. It was plain to see Jason's wife was a little "out of sorts" as he called it. He also was not stupid and followed up Jason's comment saying:

"I don't rightly know any of thet French Mary. Not too good with English either. Only thing I do know in ferin talk is a couple German cuss words."

The broad grin on Hank's face was infectious--it quickly broke the tension. Jason looked at Mary and laughed and she shook her head slowly as a big smile crossed her face. Hank continued:

"But you're right Mary--them settler folks was a fixin' to go up to Pitt, git a flatboat, and skedaddle down the Ohio. Warn't they Jason?"

Jason merely nodded and Hank added:

"Thet feller Dawson had a whole mess of kids--they was huddled up in thet Conestoga like a kitten to a warm rock! Maw is worried 'bout our kids but shucks, like I told her, if thet Dawson fellar can make it, we shore can."

He thought it might be a good idea to tell her

about Dawson's children in case the women discussed this matter--Jason knew they would. Mary knew they had and she probed.

"Then you and Sarah agree on this move."

Her comment sounded more like a statement than a question and Hank glanced at Jason before saying:

"Oh shore!"

His exclamation was the epitome of confidence and he added quickly:

"Maw's over talking with the Dolans now. Dave Jones thinks we could get four or five families together if'n we was a mind to go--right Jason?"

What Hank may have lacked in "book larnin'" he more than made up with enthusiasm, knowledge of the woods, and pure grit. As Mary once told Jason:

"You just have to like that affable character. He sort of reminds me of a big bear with the heart of a pussy cat! His bark is worse than his bite."

Jason had seen his friend in action and he was confident Hank could be rough if circumstances ever required it. But now he sat quietly as Mary probed with the skill of a surgeon regarding Hank's motive for wanting to move. Although Jason felt sorry for his friend at first, he soon found out Hank was a capable conversationalist concerning this undertaking. He knew that mountainous area of southwestern Pennsylvania like the back of his hand and it was a comfort to Mary knowing Jason was with Hank during their hunting sojourns. Convinced her husband had told her all there was to tell about the meeting at Great Crossing, Mary's "assault" slackened.

"Tell me Hank, if--and remember I said if--we decide to move, where would we get passage down the Ohio River to that country you speak of so glibly?"

This question was one the men had discussed on several occasions, and one which Hank had wrestled with. Placing his cup in Mary's outstretched hand, Hank wiped his mouth with his huge hand--he missed his "chew." Hank thoughtfully studied the fire for a moment, glanced at Jason, and then replied:

"Well, off hand Mary, I got a gut feelin' that tells me Pitt might be best. But, gittin' there is a whole different bucket of worms!"

"And what pray tell do you mean by that?"

"Like I've told Jason, there's several ways to look at it. What I mean is this. We could head up north through the valley east of the Laurels n' hit Forbes Road west of Stony Creek--'bout twenty-five miles this side of Fort Ligonier."

At the mention of "Ligonier," Jason remembered the time last summer when he and his uncle had rode to Fort Ligonier and learned Conrad's acquaintance had just gone down the Ohio to Marietta. St. Clair had been back east on business and stopped briefly at his home. In poor health, his wife had remained in western Pennsylvania ever since her husband had been appointed governor of the Northwest Territory. Hank's voice interrupted Jason's thoughts.

"Once you git on thet Forbes Road, the biggest worry in gittin' to Pitt would be them pesky little streams thet lead into them big criks called Loyal Hannon and Brush. In the spring them freshets can be pretty damn nasty! 'Scuse my French Mary!"

Jason smothered an involuntary burst of laughter prompted by Hank's apologetic remark. But Hank never cracked a smile and Mary paid no attention to the apology as she quickly asked:

"Then you are not in favor of that way?"

Deadly serious, Hank scratched his head as he thoughtfully replied:

"Can't rightly say I am Mary. It might be all right once you git on thet Forbes Road."

Hank studied the back of his hand and rubbed it with his thumb as he pondered his next words.

"Lot of travel on thet road up north but seems to me the farther south a fellar stays this time of year the better off he is."

Jason nodded and interjected:

"My thinking exactly Hank. The trail down to the three forks of the Youghiogheny and on to Great

Crossing is real good."

Jason had become well acquainted with the area at the southern end of Laurel Hill Ridge. Now Hank picked up saying:

"And at the Crossin' we hit Braddock's Road!"

Hank glanced at Mary and politely queried:

"You know where Great Crossin' is don't you?"

Mary nodded dejectedly as Hank continued:

"We can travel west through the Great Meadows, past Big Rock, and on to Dunbar's Camp. Thet would be the place for decision time."

Jason and Mary looked puzzled--Mary asked:

"What do you mean Hank?"

Hank stroked his chin and his eyes twinkled as he responded with a broad smile:

"Well, a bit north of Dunbar's Camp, we either head west, cross Redstone Crik, and try to catch us a ride down the Monongahela at old Fort Burd, or we head on north and cross the Youghiogheny at Stewart Crossin'. We'd have to ford Sewichly Crik and Jacob's Crik but thet way leads to a place a tad below where the Monongahela and Youghogheny come together upstream from Pitt. Be a longer way but we'd stand a fair chance a meetin' folks comin' west on Forbes Road. Seems like we'd have a better chance gittin' a ride at Pitt too. But, its six of one and half a dozen of the other."

Mary shrugged her shoulders and asked:

"Which way is the easiest Hank?"

"To be real honest, there ain't no _easy_ way-- them freshets can be buggers in the spring. Me and Jason heard them fellars at the Crossin' talk about shovin' off down the Monongahela somewheres between the Redstone and Dunlap Criks. One of them told us he knew some of them Revolutionary War fellars that pushed off downstream at Alexander Simeral's Ferry* two years ago this spring--they was heading for the mouth of the Muskingum."

* Formerly Robbstown until 1835, now West Newton, Pennsylvania

Mary held up her hand saying:

"Whoa! One moment please. Where is Alexander Simeral's Ferry--and the Muskingum?"

"Sorry Mary. Simeral's Ferry is northwest of here on the Youghiogheny--'bout fifteen miles downstream from Stewart's Crossin'. And the Muskingum, its way out in the Ohio country. Fellar named Tom Hutchins I met at Fort Pitt--a geographer he said-- claims the Muskingum valley is the best part of the western country. Said he'd been out surveyin' what he called the "Seven Ranges.""

It was Jason who now said:

"I do not recall you mentioning anything about Simeral's Ferry. I learn something new every time we get together. It seems both trails offer advantages and disadvantages."

"Mostly disadvantages!"

Mary made the remark as she arose and now took Hank's empty cup to the table. Jason watched Mary until she turned to see what his reaction had been. Only then did he speak:

"You just had to do that, didn't you? You had to throw a little cold water on our enthusiasm."

With a saucy grimace she replied:

"No comment."

"You'll have to excuse my child bride Hank!"

Jason smiled in a halfhearted manner. Just as he began to think she was becoming interested, she had to make a remark like that. Hank quickly said:

"Heck Jason, I git the same thing at my house. Women folk jest ain't fer movin'--never are. But I told maw last night we'd been sittin' here so long we'd best move 'fore we git rusty! And speakin' of movin', I best be gittin' home. Sarah will be back and I got some 'honey dos' I ain't done--its always 'honey do this and honey do thet' over at my place. I figger we oughta be in the saddle 'bout the first of April if'n we is a mind to go, but I'll jaw with you later Jason. Thanks fer thet tea Mary--it were mighty good!"

And with that, Hank was gone. Jason then went out to cut some firewood while Mary busied herself about the windowless cabin thinking:

"Be nice when it gets warm and we can have the door open. Perhaps a little sunshine in this cabin would make it more cheerful."

It wasn't exactly "open door" type weather but nature was on their side and a welcome thaw came to Turkeyfoot Township in early March. Along with the warmer weather, the pace quickened as those who had decided to move made their preparations. It was to be expected some members of the family would not be overjoyed at the thought of moving but, over a period of weeks, each became resigned to the fact that "travel" was in their future and pitched in to help with the many tasks which had to be done. Although agreeable at first, Jonathan Dolan decided he would not be moving--his wife threatened to return to her parent's home on the east coast and take their two children with her. Of Irish lineage, he said:

"Shore and be jasus, thet cussed woman is real set in her ways. For a fact, she's scared to death of red-skins and we'd be movin' south to Charleston if she had her way. But shore as St. Patrick himself was once a slave in Ireland, when it comes to the color of a man's skin, there's more blacks than white folks down in South Carolina."

The last two weeks of March in 1790 were busy days for Jason--the pace was feverish. Kindly old Mr. Keeling agreed to purchase from Conrad the farm which adjoined his on the south. One of the oldest settlers in the area, Mr. Keeling had a rugged face with "character" lines indicative of self-reliance, changeless purpose, and years of out-of-doors work. But, as he told the Evenstars:

"Me and maw's made our last move. We'll just have to leave that new frontier to you folks."

One warm day Mr. Keeling came over and silently watched Jason work on a marker he was making for his parent's grave. Painstakingly Jason carved the names of his parents, and a short verse he made up, on a short length of plank similar to that used for the puncheon floor of his cabin. It read:

     "JOHANNE AND CATHERINE EVENSTAR

     The Lord took both these folks away
     Their days on earth were few.
     Beneath this willow tree they rest
     Two souls their first born never knew."

Old Mr. Keeling helped Jason put the marker up when it was finished. And then, as if on cue, the sun came out from behind a fleecy cloud and bathed the area with its warm rays. Mr. Keeling remarked:

"Thet war real thoughtful of ye Jason. I knew yer folks well--mighty good people. They was taken awful young--not yet thirty as I recollect. I well remember that winter when yer pap toted you back to the Monocacy--some never figured he'd come back but I did. I been here since sixty and I've seen folks come and go--I can pick them what's got a heart for frontier livin' and yer pap was one of the best. I was shore happy when he came back and fetched along yer uncle. Now Conrad's moved over to Westmoreland and yer a fixin' to go. Won't be long 'fore other folks'll be headin' west too I suppose."

He paused, adjusted his coonskin cap, and then thoughtfully continued:

"Come summer, I reckon to put up a stone fence around this spot here and use if fer a bury'n place if'n ye don' mind Jason. Maw 'n me talked 'bout we would like to be buried here when our time comes."

Jason nodded his assent saying:

"That would be nice. Thank you."

The old man scratched the side of his head and a tear trickled down his cheek as he said:

"Maybe you and Mary will git back up this way after you've sittl'd down out whar yer goin'."

Deep in their hearts both men knew the chances

of "getting back up this way" would be mighty slim but it was a nice thought and made them feel better just to think of the possibility. Jason gave the marker a final tap with his sledge and said:

"Maybe Mr. Keeling. You just never know."

Together they slowly walked toward the cabin. Jason remembered the often heard story of how Moses had gone from the wilderness to Mount Sinai and returned with the Decalogue "written with the finger of God" on two tablets of stone. In silence Jason pondered the 20th Chapter of the Book of Exodus and the teachings of the verse which reads: "Honor thy father and thy mother, that thy days may be long upon the land which the Lord thy God giveth thee."

The young man often wished he had been given a chance to know his parents—maybe things would have been different had his father kept him here on this land. Perhaps, but in the past year Jason had come to realize that he too might have met the same fate as his father who undoubtedly meant well in what he did. His thoughts were broken as Mr. Keeling said:

"Afternoon Mary—you're lookin' fit."

The friendly old man removed his cap as he and Jason approached where Mary stood and then followed her into the cabin. Seating himself on one of the homemade rockers, he slowly said:

"Told maw ye young folks got the movin' fever. Heerd lots of talk the pas' year 'bout folks movin' out to thet Meskingum valley—some even further Dan Storms tells me. Last summer, over on the Monongahela, Dan heerd some fellar name of Ben Stites took some settler folks downstream—took 'em way on past thet Meskingum. Dan's got a fancy to go west someday. But like I was tellin' Jason, me and maw is a gittin' on—we ain't interested in movin' again."

The old man ran his weather-beaten hand slowly through a shock of salt and pepper hair—more salt than pepper. Pensively Mary thought:

"I am not interested in moving either but what can I do!"

Aloud she said: "What is it with these German settlers Mr. Keeling--sometimes they act as if they drank too much hard cider when they get to talking about the Northwest Territory."

Jason looked at her sharply but said nothing-- he continued with his whittling. He had used his razor-sharp knife to make cheese hoops and a wooden dipper but Mary had no idea what he was making now. Both politely waited for Mr. Keeling's reply.

"Don't jes rightly know Mary--German folks always been strong on gittin' land. But there's some Scotch, Irish, and English settlers movin' out into thet Ohio country. Three years ago come April some fellars from Massachusetts got together over across the Laurels. Yer uncle Conrad and me met up with a couple of them fellars in the woods north of Budd's Ferry on the Youghiogheny thet spring--Oliver Dodge and Amos Porter as I recollect. We didn' jaw long after one fellar said they had some kinda sickness in their party which might be smallpox. Me n' old Conrad gave thet bunch a wide berth."

Jason stopped whittling and listened carefully as the elderly man continued:

"I heerd later on--over near Brownsville along Redstone Crik--there was forty-eight in thet party. Irishman called Joe Tomlinson told me them fellars built themselves five boats and then the whole kit and kaboodle headed down the river in early April-- said they named one boat 'Union Galley.' Can't say for sure but them fellars might 'a been the soljers Dan Storms heerd was gonna sittle on some land thet some Massachusetts officers got from the givernment three years back. My old bones warn't fit fer gun totin' in the war so I 'spose I couldn't git any of thet land if'n I was a mind to. And I ain't!"

Mary glanced at Jason and an insincere smile spread across her face. Jason paid no attention to her--he was thinking about what the old man said.

"It is quite an undertaking Mr. Keeling. But, I remember my uncle once told me, "Anything that is worth having is worth working for!"

Mr. Keeling cupped his hand to his ear saying:
"What's thet you say son?"

As Jason repeated his words, he didn't see his
wife's little grimace or the tip of her tongue dart
out as she made a snoot at him. Jason also added:

"Only took seven days to get to the Muskingum
as I understand. There were more than a hundred of
those settlers who went out to the Ohio valley that
year according to the folks Hank and I met down on
Braddock's Road the other day."

"Oh, is that a fact. Must be really somethin'
to git the interest of so many folks.   Wish me and
maw was thirty years younger—but we ain't."

Mr. Keeling showed a keen interest in what his
young friend knew about the Northwest Territory and
they continued to talk. Stories about the settlers
moving west had been told and retold until some of
the facts were blown out of proportion.   Conducted
by Major Haffield White, the vanguard of twenty-two
members of the Ohio Company of Associates had left
Ipswich, Massachusetts on December 3, 1787. Driven
by their determined interest, this "section" of the
expedition reached Simeral's Ferry* on the banks of
the Youghiogheny River January 21, 1788. Here they
paused to build boats and await arrival of the rest
of the expedition. According to his diary, General
Rufus Putnam departed Rutland, Massachusetts on the
last day of December in 1787 intending to join the
second party which left Massachusetts on January 1,
1788 led by Colonel Ebenezer Sproat.   Pushing forward in inclement weather, this second "section" of
the expedition reached Homels Town on January 24th.
It was here General Putnam joined them and together
they moved forward across Swartara Creek, abandoned

* Near here, according to a West Newton, PA newspaper account
published in 1940, Sewickley Old Town was a Shawnee settlement
where, in 1731, the Hatawekela clan, under Aqueloma, settled at
the mouth of the Big Sewickley (or Sewichly) Creek.

wagons and built sleds when deep snow threatened to
halt travel at the Kittatinny Mountains, and forged
their way over difficult mountainous terrain until
finally, on February 14, 1788, the twenty-six brave
men reached Simeral's Ferry.   Although their first
"section" had arrived three weeks earlier, sickness
had delayed the anticipated boat-building.

Now, three years later, Jason's attention was
drawn to the sound of a wagon coming up the trail.
Followed closely by his wife and Mr. Keeling, Jason
went outside and saw a neighbor, Jacob Morningstar,
approaching. After the Evenstars had greeted their
friend and suggested he dismount, Mr. Keeling said:

"Afternoon Jacob. Yer a lookin' mighty fit."

Not until he had cautiously alighted did Jacob
turn toward his old friend and energetically reply:

"And I feel fit! Beautiful day, good friends,
and in good health--couldn't ask for much more. As
my wife said this morning, 'Life is a gift sent to
us every sunrise.'"

Mary and Jason had soon become acquainted with
Jacob after they arrived.   It had been Mr. Keeling
who observed they had a "morningstar" in the neigh-
borhood and good-naturedly said: "Its real fittin'
we have an 'evenin' star' here in Turkeyfoot too!"
Everyone agreed Jason and Mary's name fit the bill.

And now today Jacob motioned for the Evenstars
to look in his wagon. With pride he pointed out an
adz, a frow, an awl, and a maul. With sincere pride
Jacob explained:

"You'll be needing these I figure--getting too
old to use them myself. Time for me and my friend
here to let young folks take the reins.   That iron
piece with the beveled edge and wooden handle is a
frow. That adz there is used to dress wood--smooth
the flat sides of split logs. You'll be a wantin'
that awl for making your moccasins. I reckon they
got deer out there in that Northwest Territory!"

The friendly man grinned and continued:

"And I'd be mighty proud if you would use that

old wooden maul to drive your first land stakes out there Jason. Me and maw figured the least we could do for such nice friends was to pass these along to you. We're sure gonna miss you young folks."

"Thank you Mr. Morningstar--we're not so young anymore you know." Jason paused and then quickly added: "I was twenty-five last November!"

Both of Jason's friendly neighbors remembered the year Jason was born and the subsequent death of his father. Mr. Keeling rubbed his chin and said:

"Shecks Jason, I got boots older than that!"

As the men unloaded the gifts and talked about the planned move, Jason told them what he had heard and read about the "land of opportunity." Listening carefully, the eyes of the older men reflected the excitement they felt--like old war horses who once again smelled the smoke of battle. They could talk of the adventure but both knew they would not move again--they were destined to be buried here in the shadows of the Laurels. As Mr. Morningstar now prepared to leave, Mary said:

"We will certainly miss our good friends here. You have all be so good to us and we appreciate the friendship you have shown."

"Me and my wife sure have enjoyed your singing in church Mary. I was real partial to that one you sang last Sunday, remember?"

Mary remembered the song which Mr. Morningstar referred to. It was one written by Isaac Watts, an English clergyman, titled "Oh God, Our Help In Ages Past." Several had commented concerning the words of the last verse:

> "O God, our help in ages past,
> Our hope for years to come.
> Be Thou our guide while life shall last,
> And our eternal home."

There was a lump in Jacob Morningstar's throat and his eyes were moist as he picked up the reins, cleared his throat, and said:

"Well, I must be getting back now. The missus is fixing a big batch of corn bread and bean soup-- she knows my weakness!"

"I'll ride a spell with ye if'n ye don't mind Jacob."

The trail would take Jacob past the lane leading to Mr. Keeling's place and he decided to avail himself of an opportunity. As he quipped:

"Save some wear 'n tear on these old legs."

Slowly he climbed up on the seat beside Jacob who said in parting:

"We wish you folks God speed and good fortune in your venture. May the Lord be with you always."

As the wagon pulled away both men raised their hand in a farewell motion.

It was like that--everyone offered assistance and shared.   From neighbors came dried pumpkin and fruit, homemade yeast cakes, apple butter, sorghum, and several sacks of the ever-needed corn meal used in some form for almost every meal--pone, hoecake, cornbread, mush, or johnnycake. All one needed was corn meal, salt, and water--the way it was cooked made the difference. Corn pone--bread usually made without milk or eggs--had little pieces of sliced bacon mixed in it and was baked in the hot ashes of a fireplace. Hoecake was cooked on a hot griddle-- when baked on a smooth board before a fire it was called "johnnycake." Gifts of corn meal would come in real handy during their journey.

A few days before Jason and Mary were ready to leave, Conrad and his wife paid them a last visit. They brought along a spinning wheel and explained:

"This one's fitted with a single spindle which is driven by the rotation of that large wheel which is spun by hand. You will get the hang of it in no time Mary" said Conrad's wife confidently.

It sounded pretty complicated to Mary but she graciously accepted the gift and Conrad remarked:

"This belonged to Jason's mother, Catherine--I

know my sister would want you to have it."

Tears came to Mary's eyes and Jason swallowed hard. Mary broke the awkward silence saying:

"Thank you--it is a most cherished gift and we will always treasure it."

That evening Conrad talked at length about his sister and brother-in-law:

"Johanne and Catherine lived here in a lean-to for quite a spell. Your father finally got enough logs cut and then several of the German Baptists in these parts helped him with the cabin raising. Put his cabin on the same spot where you built. Nothing would do but I build my cabin close to him when we came out here with him in the spring of 1766 but I wasn't with him when he really needed me."

Conrad shook his head sadly--everyone knew the story. After a short pause, Conrad related how he and Johanne first met Arthur St. Clair:

"He was a tall and dignified gentleman with a light complexion, reddish-brown hair, and blue-grey eyes."

"He lived around Ligonier then?"

"That he did Jason. He was a surveyor for the Penn family, a Justice of Peace, Recorder of Deeds, and Judge of the Probate Court. We met him shortly after his cousin, General Gage, appointed him Commandant of Fort Ligonier in 1767. Although he was reported to be a personal friend of King George, he was given the appointment as a reward for military services rendered the British. St. Clair had quite a knowledge of the French language and came to know a number of Indians in western Pennsylvania. It is not surprising this friendly and knowledgeable gentleman was chosen as governor of the Ohio country."

It was obvious Conrad had the greatest respect for the man he had known at Fort Ligonier, one of the wilderness outposts built by Brigadier General John Forbes in 1758 along an old Indian trail used in early days by English fur traders trafficking with Indians in the Ohio valley. Cutting their way through mountainous wilderness terrain to seize the French-held Fort Dusquesne, John Forbes and his men cleared the way for what was to become the "Glades Trail" or Forbes Road as it was more commonly known in later years. Conrad took a keen interest in the commentary offered by Jason regarding the Ordinance of 1787 and asked him to explain what it said about the slavery issue.

"It says slavery and involuntary servitude are forbidden. They cannot be introduced in the Northwest Territory to compete with honest free labor. Why do you ask?"

"Well, I know for a fact that on the first day of July in 1788--when St. Clair was preparing to go out to Fort Harmar--he purchased a couple slaves by the names of Ben and Bill from the estate of Thomas Gailbreath--cost him 165 pounds as I recall. Have no idea what ever became of them. He probably kept them at his place near Fort Ligonier. His wife did not accompany him--she had been in poor health for a long time and could not travel."

Regardless of the purpose of his purchase, age or circumstances prompted a change of heart by St. Clair. In later years at Cincinnati he declared:

"Let them say what they will about republicanism, a man who is willing to entail slavery upon any party of God's creation is no friend to the rational happiness of any, and had he the power would as readily enslave his neighbors as the poor black that he has torn from his country and his fields."

"You say St. Clair left his wife at Ligonier?"

Mary's question to Conrad caused Jason to look at his wife sharply. She quickly added:

"And does this fine gentleman you always speak so highly of have a large family?"

If Conrad did catch Mary's veiled inference he gave no indication of it as he replied:

"He has seven children if my memory serves me correctly. He was married the same day we were--on May 14th in 1760. I won't forget that date!"

110

"And you better not" said Conrad's wife.
Again Mary repeated her question:
"You say he left his wife behind at Ligonier?"
In a rather irritated tone Jason interjected:
"Yes Mary, St. Clair left his wife at Ligonier
when he went to the Northwest Territory."
Jason had noted the not-so-subtle inference of
Mary's question. Overlooking, or ignoring Jason's
retort, Conrad picked up the conversation saying:
"Well, St. Clair had no choice really. Phoebe
just could not make the journey."
His comment gave no indication he had noticed
the brief exchange of "barbs." Mary smiled mischievously and avoided Jason's eyes as he probed:
"You did say Arthur St. Clair returned to duty
in the military after my father and you met him?"
"Oh my yes. When John Hancock, President of
the Continental Congress at that time, summoned him
in December of 1775, he saddled up and rode down to
Philadelphia where he was appointed a Colonel. The
next year, in August, he was appointed a Brigadier
General and the following February he was promoted
to Major General. A fine military record I'd say."
"Now he is the first governor of the Northwest
Territory--what a responsibility!"
Jason's exclamation was quickly followed by a
further testimony of St. Clair's prowess by Conrad:
"Although St. Clair is a man with the manners,
tastes, and usual beliefs of upper class folks--and
is a gentleman of affluence at heart--he has taken
on the enormous burdens of frontier administration
at a time of life when most men of his age would be
seeking the comfort of home and their easy chair."
Impressed with Conrad's remarks, Jason said:
"For his age Governor St. Clair certainly must
get around. Rides a horse a lot I suppose."
Conrad had nothing but praise for the frontier
leader and remarked:
"I recall hearing him say he could make twenty
miles an hour over a hundred mile journey! Travels

a lot by horseback even now I understand."

It was late when Conrad finally suggested they "hit the hay" knowing tomorrow he and his wife must bid the Evenstars goodbye. Before leaving the next day Conrad revealed his piece de resistance saying:

"I wanted to give you something you could use. Brother Frederick spoke highly of your apprentice training and I thought you ought to have this forge and anvil. Your father used it and I know he would be happy knowing it was in your hands. Might come in handy where you folks are going."

"Indeed it will! Thank you very much."

Conrad's wife also had a little something very special for Mary--a book written by John Bunyan.

"Mary, I know how much you enjoy reading and I want you to have 'The Pilgrim's Progress.' It was given me long ago by Johanne's wife before she came out here. Written more than one hundred years ago, it is the story of a man named Christian who crosses a river and journeys to heaven. The story has a beautiful religious message."

Mary smiled as she thought to herself:

"I remember the story about John Bunyan. His wife led him to religion and he spent twelve years in prison after being jailed in 1660 as a preacher. Perhaps I could interest my husband in the ministry after we make this journey down the Ohio."

Jason was happy to see Mary smiling--he had no way of knowing what she was really thinking. Jason was very pleased with his aunt and uncle's thoughtfulness and generosity. The book, the old spinning wheel, the forge and anvil--all were treasures from the past his parents had touched. A little wave of nostalgia swept over Jason and he silently walked around the corner of the cabin to where his parents were buried under the weeping willow tree. Everone understood and continued their conversation until her returned. Conrad was explaining how he planned to visit the Monocacy Valley the coming summer:

"We are getting on in years and we both agree

it is best we do it now before we can't make it."

"Go on now" said Mary.   "You folks will still
be traveling these trails for years to come."

Everyone knew Mary's prognostication was not a
likelihood but it was nice to hear anyway.   Conrad
added a bit of his home-spun philosophy.

"Way I figure it is this. When I'm sitting in
in my old rocking chair I want to be thinking about
things I've done, not things I wish I'd done!"

Everyone joined in polite laughter and Jason
remarked:

"Lot of truth in what you say."

But all good things must come to an end and so
it was with Conrad's visit.   Saying he intended to
stop for a visit with his son, Frederick, in nearby
Milford Township, the kindly man prefaced his farewell with one of his witticisms:

"Well, we better git to gittin'!   We know you
got lots of packing to do.   Seems like it was only
yesterday we packed up and headed west. Don't know
what I'd have done without my wife here. And I am
not certain where we might have ended up if Johanne
hadn't run across a bunch of German Baptists headed
up to this neck of the woods--he always spoke of it
as 'the benevolent guidance of God' but some of the
things that have happened sure left me wondering."

Everyone stood in silence not knowing what to
say. It was Conrad's wife who finally said:

"Well, you gonna stand here and jaw all day or
are we going? Our son will be worrying about us."

"As they say, there's a time for stayin' and a
time for gittin' and now is the time to git!"

Conrad tried to be cheerful but his heart just
wasn't in it. He didn't like the thought of having
to leave but it was time to go. The ladies embraced and Jason shook his uncle's hand warmly. Jason,
like his uncle, wasn't one to make a show of affection in public. The "goodbyes" said, the Evenstars
quietly watched Conrad's wagon until it was out of
sight. Back in their cabin Mary said:

"Your uncle Conrad is a lot like your father--your uncle Frederick I mean. He's a rather private person but very nice. I like him."

"I know what you mean. You know Mary, I never saw either one of my uncles cry--or Emanuel either. They must cry sometimes--when alone perhaps."

To herself Mary thought, "Runs in the family!" She knew her husband often sought the solace of his parent's grave for meditation--she always respected his privacy during such moments.

That evening Jason removed his violin from its case and played a few songs--none were lively tunes and he stared into the dancing flames as he "sawed" away mechanically. Mary listened and prayed Jason would find what he was looking for in the Northwest Territory but in her heart she firmly believed his peace of mind would not come with "moving." There was something deeply rooted in his own inner feelings and their moving was not going to solve it.

As Jason played his violin and stared into the fireplace, two hundred miles east Arthur St. Clair talked with President Washington. Although plagued by the effects of exposure and exhaustion which the elderly man experienced during his long and arduous trip from Cincinnati to Philadelphia, the governor pleaded with the president to appoint him commander of the army and approve his plan for a summer campaign against the troublesome Indians in the wake of General Harmar's unsuccessful expedition to the Miami villages in October of 1790. After St. Clair had taken his leave, the fifty-nine year old president sat by his fireplace gazing thoughtfully into the flames as he mused over the enormity of the job before him. As he had told his secretary this day:

"Never has a government been born with more burdens on its infant shoulders!"

Two months later Jason marveled at the sunrise and recalled the words of Jacob Morningstar's wife: "Life is a gift sent to us every sunrise!" Spring was in the air and the robins had returned from the south. Flowers had started to poke their heads up through the leaves and dogwood and rebud checkered the hills of Turkeyfoot Township with their shades of red, pink, and white.   Another annual "ice age" was over.

The last several days of March had been hectic ones at the Evenstar farm but "the day" had finally arrived--"time to head out" as Hank had eagerly declared. Everyone agreed the three-family entourage would meet at Jason's place and drive on south from there.   And so, with April still wearing its first diaper, Jason and Mary arose before the sun was up, loaded the last of their belongings in the red and blue Conestoga, hitched up the horses, and tied the cow to one side of the back of the wagon--the black gelding, the gift from cousin Frederick was tied to the opposite side. Jason and Mary were ready.

For Mary it did not seem possible it had been only a year since they had left Maryland in their Conestoga.   It was such a sturdy wagon and served well to move their possessions. Their Conestoga's floor was curved up at the end making it almost impossible for their belongings to fall out--even on the roughest roads.   And the shape of the body was such the Conestoga would float and could be used as a boat if necessary. As Jason said with a laugh:

"A boat is what we may need if Hank is right and we run into any freshets!"

"It is no laughing matter Jason. I pray we do not run into such trouble--trouble we don't need!"

The Evenstars had prayed their trip would be a safe one.   Now as they hurried about checking this and that and doing all sorts of last minute things, Jason said: "I'll give Star and Molly a drink."

The white star on the black gelding's head had prompted its name.   The cow had been named "Molly Pitcher" by its former owner, Hank Weiser. Waiting for the cow to drink, Jason said in a soft voice:

"Molly, you have a long walk ahead of you."

Meantime Mary was busy checking to be certain they had packed everything.   Aloud she said: "Let me see now...corn meal, hominy blocks, iron kettle, tin grater, spinning wheel, hoe...." She continued to enumerate the myriad of items they had carefully loaded in the wagon. Mary had watched her husband make their hominy blocks--a short log had been used and hollowed out to form a bowl. Shelled corn was cracked into small pieces using a wooden hammer and then reduced to meal. Jason was handy making such things as that. Impatiently Jason now said:

"For heaven's sake Mary, we have checked every item a dozen times!"

Although he pretended to be annoyed by Mary's repeated checking of their belongings, deep inside Jason was proud of her and pleased she had taken an interest in this move. Actually , Mary had become fascinated by the preparations for their move. The three families joined together to butcher several cattle and these were dressed, quartered, and salted down in huge barrels. A quantity of venison had also been smoked and packed away for their journey. Everyone was well stocked with basic necessities-- corn meal, flour, and salt. As the wide-eyed young lady who had promised to love, honor, and obey--and fry Jason's johnnycake--admonished with a smile:

"One cannot be too careful you know!"

But Mary never dreamed her marital commitment was to be performed beyond the boundaries of Maryland and now she thoughtfully pondered her plight:

"Here I am miles from Baltimore checking over our belongings and fixing to move farther away--to some Northwest Territory my husband raves about. I must be out of my ever lovin' Irish mind!"

"A farthing for my pretty bride's thoughts."

Jason's offer jarred Mary back to reality and, with a generous smile and saucy wave of her hand, she gave Jason a quick glance and a prompt retort:

"Cheapskate--your wife's thoughts this morning are worth much more than a farthing. And besides, it is too early to start an argument."

With that Mary walked back into the cabin and

Jason followed. Shaking his head slowly he muttered to himself:

"Women. I'll never understand them."

With the sun barely peeking over the ridge to the east, and the Laurels to the west bathed in a rose-colored morning mist, the Evenstars prepared to eat their last breakfast in the cabin which Mary called her "first home away from home."

The Keelings had insisted on providing "all of the fixin's for breakfast" and promised to clean up after the Evenstars were gone. They arrived shortly after Jason and Mary were up and now Mrs Keeling had a hearty meal ready and waiting for them. Mary and Jason were enjoying the last of their breakfast when Mary suddenly said:

"Listen! I think I hear a wagon coming."

Old Mr. Keeling cupped his hand over his ear--he had been partially deaf for years. Jason wasn't surprised his wife had heard a wagon--she had very sensitive hearing. Jason finally confirmed Mary's report and Mr. Keeling said:

"Ye jes go 'head with your eatin'--I'll have me a look-see. Ye young folks will be needin' them victuals 'fore the day's done."

Excited as a small child on Christmas morning, he quickly returned exclaiming:

"They's comin' Jason--they's comin'! Hank and Dave is comin' down the trail!"

Breakfast finished, Mary scurried around doing those last minute things one does before embarking on a journey. As she paused by the fireplace, mentally reviewing a "must do" list, Mrs. Keeling gave her a little bundle. Later Mary would learn it was some candles, a bar of perfumed soap, and a dainty handkerchief which the elderly lady had made. She also gave Mary a horn comb which her husband made. The dear old lady's eyes were moist as she said:

"Think of us when you use these Mary."

"Thank you dear friend--thank you so much. We will think of you and your husband often. We want to thank you folks for all you have done--we are so grateful and fortunate to have such good friends."

Mary's voice quavered and now the tears flowed freely. She had wanted so much to appear brave but it was no use. As Mary dabbed at her cheeks with a handkerchief, Mrs. Keeling consoled her saying:

"There now dear, I know exactly how you feel. Me and paw has done our share of packin' and movin' in our time. Its an unpleasant chore for us women but in no time you'll meet a lot of new folks where you're headin'. Just don't you be forgettin' your old friends here in Turkey Foot."

Jason and Mr. Keeling were waiting by the Conestoga as their wives finally emerged from the cabin and slowly walked toward them. After the women had embraced, Jason helped Mary into the wagon and then shook hands with the Keelings saying:

"Thank you. Thank you both for everything."

Jason turned and climbed up into the Conestoga and seated himself by his tearful wife. Trying his best to appear cheerful, old Mr. Keeling looked up at the young couple and voiced an Irish blessing:

"May the road rise up to meet you and the wind be always at your back and may the Lord hold you in the hollow of His hand. Goodbye dear friends."

Jason could say nothing--there was nothing to say. And even if there was, the lump in his throat was so big he could not speak. Without any further adieu, he turned to the horses and exclaimed:

"Gitty ap!"

The horses promptly obeyed Jason's command and the wagon moved forward--they were on their way!

By now the other wagons were near and everyone was waving. From Hank's lead wagon came the sound of his excited children's laughter drifting across the ever-narrowing space which separated them. And as the gap closed, Jason shouted:

"Morning everyone! We should make Three Forks before noon and be down where Braddock Road crosses the south branch by nightfall--make camp near Great Crossing! In the morning we will head for Dunbar's Camp! Is that agreeable?"

"Lead the way friend!"

Hank grinned as he shouted his agreement and his wife, Sarah, smiled as she waved. Everyone was familiar with the trail to Great Crossing--that was the easy part!   Still, Jason's brief enthusiastic synopsis was followed by a chorus of cheers signifying their approval--they were ready to head out! To the east the early morning mist made a glory on the mountains as Jason picked up the reins, glanced at Mary, and exclaimed: "Let's get rolling!"

Jason chirped the horses and the wagon started to move. In trail the three families headed south leaving Turkey Foot Township behind. The Evenstars were silent as the wagon bumped along and only once did Mary turn and look back along the side of the Conestoga toward their cabin. Through tearful eyes she could see the Keelings still waving. She never looked back again.

From behind his wagon Jason could hear the excited screams of Hank's children. Glancing to his right he saw a big bird swooping low into the field beside a small stream nearby--moments later it disappeared behind the curtain of foilage which marked the western boundary of what had been Jason's farm. Now it belonged to Mr. Keeling and Jason had all of the proceeds from its sale in his coat pocket. His uncle insisted Johanne had been the first to stake out the land and although the property had been recorded in Conrad's name, it rightfully belonged to Jason. Like Jason, Conrad was set in his ways too. Thoughtfully reflecting on his uncle's generosity, the young man thought:

"Uncle Conrad didn't have to give us the money but it certainly will be helpful in getting a start in the Northwest Territory."

Jason's gaze lifted to the distant Laurel Hill Ridge, now bathed by a pinkish-gold as the sun rose steadily in the east. A big bank of fleecy clouds, tinged with the same pinkish-gold, towered majestically above the mountain range. Suddenly the first two verses of Psalm 121 flashed across his mind: "I will lift up mine eyes unto the hills, from whence cometh my help. My help cometh from the Lord which made heaven and earth."

With his eyes riveted on the beautiful clouds, Jason muttered half-aloud: "Somebody up there must be looking out for us."

Reaching into a pocket, Jason pulled out a red handkerchief and blew his nose noisily. Mary turned her head slightly and looked at her husband.

"I heard that—and you are right. Somebody up there is looking out for you and you dragon slayers need all the help you can get."

Mary intended her remark to be cheerful but it didn't come out that way and she choked down an impulse to cry. Through misty eyes she stared at her husband—he looked so strong and lean and his face was locked in an attitude of determination. All of a sudden Jason sensed his wife's penetrating gaze and he remarked:

"Now don't you be worrying yourself sick Mary, everything will work out just fine. Remember what the minister said last Sunday, 'Live your life one day at a time.'"

Mary also remembered something her father was always saying: "Live each day as if it may be your last because it just might be!"

Her fleeting recollection was interrupted when Jason added:

"Remember that old Athenian writer named Sophocles? Didn't he once say 'One must wait until the evening to see how the day has been.'"

Mary wanted to say "that was said four hundred years before the birth of Christ" but such a retort seemed useless. Instead Mary said in a low voice:

"You are so brave Jason."

After a short pause--and never taking his eyes from the bumpy trail--Jason said:

"I'm not brave Mary. I am scared to death."

She patted Jason's arm, glanced at the Laurels in the distance, and then--unable to suppress the urge to cry--Mary's little shoulders shook and she cried as if her heart would break. When Jason gently pulled her close to his side, she bravely wiped away the tears with a little lace handkerchief--the same one she carried the day they left Baltimore a year ago.

Mustering up a feminine display of bravado before she burst into tears again, Mary turned to her husband and asked half-heartedly:

"Did you bring your fiddle?"

121

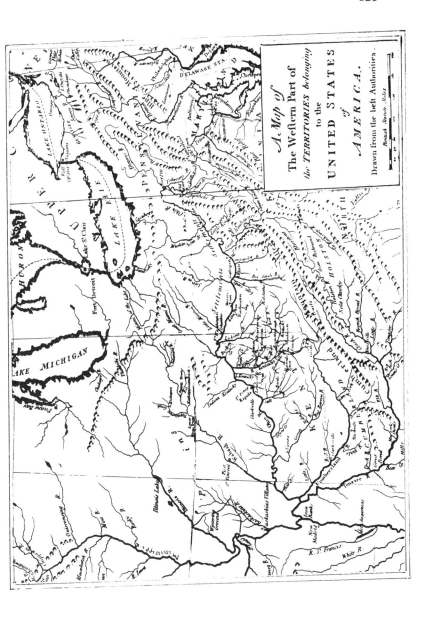

MAP

SHOWING FRENCH OCCUPATION OF THE
OHIO VALLEY: TAKEN FROM M. ROBERT'S
ATLAS UNIVERSEL, PARIS 1755. BASED ON
CHRISTOPHER GIST'S SURVEYS MADE 1751.
DRAWN EXPRESSLY FOR THIS
WORK BY JOHN G. RUPLE, C.E.

From "History of Washington County,
Pennsylvania" by Boyd Crumrine 1882

CHAPTER FIVE

PROUD-PIED APRIL

Spring came early in 1791 and April brought warmer air and all the familiar signs of that time of year in southwestern Pennsylvania. The air was calm and sweet with the scent of dawn as the three wagons rolled along. Some trees were donning their foilage and the red bud, hawthorn and dogwood trees were already in bloom. A variety of trees dotted the hillsides. Tiny wisps of cotton drifted slowly across the azure canopy and flirted with the majestic peaks as the morning sun soon drenched everything. Suddenly Mary exclaimed:

"Isn't it beautiful Jason?"

Quiet for a long time, Mary's voice broke the silence and Jason nodded happily as he said:

"The Lord is smiling on our undertaking."

By mid-morning the Evenstars were in a fairly light-hearted mood as Mary pointed out with delight the beautiful vistas along the trail which followed a winding creek bed. Joyfully she remarked:

"If my memory serves me right, it was William Shakespeare who penned something about April. Let me think." After a short pause Mary began reciting a Shakespearean sonnet:

"When proud-pied April, dressed in all his trim,
Hath put a spirit of youth in everything."

"Bravo! My pretty school teacher bride has not

forgotten her book larnin'."

Both laughed at Jason's use of the word often used by Hank Weiser.

It was late in the afternoon when they arrived at Great Crossing and a hasty conference concluded this was the place to make camp. Mary looked long- ingly to the east and then reluctantly allowed her gaze to turn away from the road which led toward Fort Cumberland and on to Baltimore. Jason had been watching Mary and noticed the sad and pensive look which crossed his wife's face. Suddenly aware Jason was watching her, Mary managed a half-hearted smile as her husband asked:

"Regrets?"

Jason's one-word questions and answers annoyed Mary but to this one she quickly replied:

"As my dear old father always said, 'Regret is a fathomless bottom of quicksand, nothing to build on, just something to flounder in!'"

"Glory be," said Jason, "I will have to ponder that bit of wisdom for a while. Meantime, I better feed the horses and old Molly."

Around the campfire that evening Hank explain- ed how tomorrow they would travel through a region he called "Great Meadows" and said it was the place where Fort Necessity had been built in 1754 by men of Lt. Col. George Washington's command.

"The French had control of a strategic spot up north of here where the Monongahela and Allegheny Rivers meet--the place where Fort Pitt now stands. Colonel Washington led a small force of Virginians, not more than 160, against the French in 1754. The story goes that on May 27th Washington killed Sieur de Jumonville and Ensign Joseph Coulon de Villiers during a surprise attack on a party of French sol- diers. Then, the following July 3rd, Captain Louis Coulon de Villiers, a brother of the slain officer, attack Fort Necessity with 500 French soldiers and 400 Indians."

What Hank may have lacked in formal education,

he more than made up with his knowledge of history. When Hank paused, Mary urged him to continue.

"Well, some officer I talked with at Fort Pitt told me the terms of surrender which Washington was forced to sign admitted to the assassination of the two Frenchmen who were supposed to have been on a diplomatic mission when killed. He also said them surrender papers was written in French."

Glancing at Mary and smiling, Hank added:

"Washington should a had you along with him as an interpreter Mary."

Almeretta Jones interrupted a ripple of polite laughter asking: "What happened to that fort Hank?"

"Oh, the French and Indians tore it down after Washington surrendered," replied Hank. "We'll pass there tomorrow. Some remains of that old fort can still be seen along a little weed-grown stream that winds through Great Meadows."

Now it was Jason who inquired: "Wasn't George Washington with General Braddock?"

"That he was," replied Hank. "He resigned his commission after the Fort Necessity incident but he served as a volunteer aide to that British general. The French had showed no intent to leave this area which the British claimed, so the French and Indian war started. Your uncle Conrad said he talked with some old fellar up at Pitt a while back who claimed he was at Braddock's defeat with two wagoners that he called Henry Prescutt and Michael Stoner."

Jason had listened carefully and now remarked:

"Uncle Conrad told me Colonel Washington's report to Governor Dinwiddie said 'the British troops broke and ran like sheep before the hounds!"

General Braddock had been appointed commander of British forces in America and planned to capture Fort Duquesne as the first move in his campaign. He was joined in 1755 by Virginia troops at Alexandria and added Washington to his staff at Fort Frederick soon thereafter. A veteran of wilderness service, Washington warned Braddock against exposing his men to an Indian ambush as they marched west from Fort Cumberland along the trail Washington had marked on his prior expedition. At the mouth of Turtle Creek, when only a few miles southeast of Fort Dusquesne, the advance guard was attack by French soldiers and Indians on July 5, 1755. The British, confused by the Indians way of fighting from behind trees, were soundly defeated. As Hank related:

"General Braddock was mortally wounded in that battle and died a few days later--July 14th. More than half his soldiers, and most of his officers, were killed. Although Washington led the survivors to safety, 714 men fell in the massacre that day."

"I heard it was one of Braddock's own men that shot him," said Dave. "Fellar by the name of Thomas Fawcett. Think that's true Hank?"

"I've heard that said too Dave but I can't say for sure. A lot of wild stories always get started after such a battle--some true and some made up."

Jason recalled a story he had heard a visitor to his cousin's blacksmith shop relate and said:

"A Virginian who came to our blacksmith shop a couple years ago told of Phillipe Francois Rastel, Sieur de Rocheblare who was with the French at that battle. Later, in 1778, he switched his allegiance and was the British commander at Kaskaskia when he was awakened late one night by George Rogers Clark who informed him his fort had been taken without a single shot. Imagine his surprise!"

Now it was Dave who spoke up saying:

"Back home my father said he once heard an old one-legged British officer in a Philadelphia tavern say he was with Braddock. Father said the man complained bitterly about Indians sniping at them from behind trees--told everyone it was an infamous way of carrying on a war!"

"May have been," said Hank thoughtfully. "But its like me and Jason here talked about last winter up on Laurel Ridge when some fellar we met told us about General Harmar's army being waylaid last fall

out in the Ohio country by what he called 'them red
skinned dragons.' There ain't no rules in war, the
idea is to win! And you can call them Indians what
you please, but like old Braddock and Harmar found
out the hard way--sometimes the dragon wins! Right
Jason?"

Jason sheepishly replied: "Right Hank."

He had glanced at his wife when Hank mentioned
General Harmar's unsuccessful campaign. Assimilat-
ing the significance of Hank's remark regarding the
country where they planned to make their new home,
Mary directed a piercing gaze at her husband as she
muttered to herself:

"You never mentioned that Jason Evenstar!"

Even as Jason and his friends talked about the
defeat of Braddock that evening in early 1791, several hundred miles to the west, on the banks of the
Little Miami, an elderly Indian chief spoke of his
fervent hate for the "white invader." It was Catahecassa, or "Black Hoof" of the Shawnee nation, and
in 1791 he was sixty-five years of age. Thirty-six
years earlier he had participated in Braddock's defeat and he still carried his hate for white men.

Late the next afternoon Jason's party reached
a small stream Hank called "Sandy Crik." "It flows
into the Cheat River down south of here," explained
Hank. Pausing to allow their horses to drink from
the beautiful stream, Jason remarked to his wife:

"Just think of it Mary, here is where Washington surrendered back in 1754 and so many of General
Braddock's expedition were killed the next year!"

"I would rather not think of it at all, if you
do not mind Jason."

That evening as they made camp and he unhitch-
ed his horses, Jason thought about the courage and
fortitude it took for soldiers to forge their way
through the wilderness 36 years before. "Took a lot
of courage, resolution, and faith," declared Jason
half aloud.

"Talking to yourself Jason?"

Jason had not noticed Hank's approach but now quickly replied:

"I always like to talk with a man who has good sense Hank." As Hank laughed, Jason added: "Think we can make Dunbar's Camp tomorrow?"

"Tell you better when we get to Great Rock!"

Late the next afternoon at Dunbar's Camp, Hank and Jason talked with a seedy old man who told them he had just come overland from Fort Henry along the Ohio. Deep lines were etched in the elderly man's rugged weather-beaten face and he smelled of smoke, horses, and body odor. Jason realized bathing was not a frequent occurence on the wilderness frontier but this was ridiculous. From somewhere out of the old man's smoke-stained beard came a brusque reply to Jason's question about travel west.

"Left the Ohio myself just a week ago--trails a damn sight better than when them Iroquois claimed that country along the Ohio as their home. I came down Ten Mile Crik from south of Washington--crossed the Monongahela upstream from Red Stone Crik."

The look on Jason's youthful face mirrored his ignorance regarding the geographical points the old man had mentioned. Politely explaining his lack of knowledge concerning the land to the west, and just what their destination was, the old man's manner of speaking softened--he understood. Introducing himself only as "Josh," he explained the Red Stone and Dunlap creeks flowed into the Monongahela from the east--where Fort Burd had been built 40 miles above Fort Pitt.

"And there, young man, at the end of the trail leading from Braddocks's Road, is a point of embarkation--a gate to that land of the setting sun that all you settlers are hell bent for!"

Ignoring the pessimistic remark Jason asked:

"Think we could make it overland to the Ohio?"

Eyeing Jason carefully the old man replied:

"Can't say I'd even try young man--trail's all right for shank's mare but with wagons and women, I say forget it!   Man by name of Wilson keeps a damn good tavern at Washington if you're foolish enough to go that way. There's three stores there--run by fellars named Blakeny, Cunningham, and Metrick. Do a damn good business I'm told."

Hank glanced at Jason saying: ""I think we're better off stickin' to our plan of heading on up to the river below Pitt."

"Sounds like you got a pretty damn good head a sittin' on them shoulders," said the old man. "How far'd you folks come up Braddock's Road?"

"Just since Great Crossing," replied Hank. "We been livin' north of there. You familiar with that country?"

"Yep.   Been roaming these hills for years. I was with that smart-assed English general that got his drawers taken down way back in '55. I was just a damn snot-nosed kid then but I sure learned fast. Daniel Boone and John Finley from Reading, Pennsylvania was there too. Them two fellars was together when Boone blazed that path through the Cumberland Gap a few years back. Fellar name of Montour saved my ass--John or Andrew, I forget which. We called him Monty. He was a little rash I guess--drank too much some said. But he was a damn good interpreter and could read and write English. Old Monty served with Washington, Braddock, and General Forbes--knew all of 'em. And like I said, he sure as hell helped me git out of that ambush back down the road. I guess you folks heard all about that though."

Jason nodded--he didn't care for the old man's coarse language but it was obvious he knew the land they were heading for and he listened carefully as the traveler provided some further counsel concerning their undertaking. Fortunately the women and children were out of earshot and could not hear the liberal use of expletives interwoven in his informative discourse which included:

"You're from up north of Great Crossing, huh? Ever hear tell of a fellar up that way by the name of Conrad? I forget his last name--mind ain't what it used to be I guess. Anyway, he lived in Turkey-foot as I recollect."

It was Jason who now eagerly injected:

"I have an uncle by that name. He moved over to Westmoreland County not long ago."

The old man eyed Jason carefully and a look of disbelief spread across his face.

"You must be the lad Conrad told me about--his brother's boy! Your pap was done in by the Indians some time before I met your uncle. You was just a little tyke then!"

Rubbing his bearded chin, and smiling from ear to ear for the first time, the old man chortled:

"Well I'll be horn-swoggled--sure is something running into you after all these years."

Thoughtfully the old man added: "And you say you're headin' out to the Ohio country, huh? Maybe you'll meet up with my cousin Kate's boy, Marmaduke Swearingen--some Shawnees took him its said. Could be Duke took a fancy to livin' with them--and then maybe he's dead, who knows. Only thing for sure is his maw ain't heard a thing about his whereabouts."

The old man's eyes were misty as he glanced at the distant hills and thoughtfully added:

"But like Kate says, 'hope springs etenal,' so if you do happen to run across Duke, I'd be obliged if you'd tell him his maw is worried about him. Be good to know what happened to him."

After taking their leave of the old man, Jason and his friends discussed their alternatives. Hank summarized the situation saying: "Well, just north of here we gotta make a decision. The trail across Stewart's Crossing and on north on the east side of the Youghiogheny is used by more wagons but I'll go along with what you two fellars want to do."

Hank had made the trip to Pittsburgh only five months before and had traveled the road he suggested. Jason looked at Dave and said:

"I agree with Hank. Majority being two out of

three, it looks like we head for Stewart's Crossing and on north--is that agreeable Dave?"

With a big smile, Dave replied:

"I suppose the longer way would be much better if it would offer more chances of us finding a ride downstream."

With the Laurels lining the eastern horizon on their right, and Hank taking the "point," Jason and his party doubled back in a northeasterly direction and crossed the ever-widening Youghiogheny River at Stewart's Crossing. And each new day spawned a new experience as they rolled along in their springless creaking wagons which occasionally mired down in the soft ground. On one occasion a huge tree had fallen across the road and had to be removed before they could move ahead. At Salt Creek--or "Jacob's Crik" as Hank called it--the turbulent water swept into Dave's wagon bed when he attempted to ford the shallow stream. As the lead wagon that morning, he had chosen to try and cross the shallow creek downstream from the regular crossing. After leading Dave's team of horses to safety, Hank and Jason led their horses through the clear, cool water, picking their way carefully over the slippery rocks.

Exhausted by their vigorous efforts in fording the stream, they made camp early that day. Pushing into the surrounding woods in search of game, Jason and Hank returned soon. As Hank confided to Jason:

"Maybe I'm just a might jittery, but there's a few tell-tale signs of Indians around here!"

That night, at Hank's suggestion, the men took turns in maintaining a careful watch and the children were admonished to refrain from loud talk.

The sun was approaching its zenith the following day when Jason saw Hank raise his arm signaling everyone to stop. Up ahead Jason could see a wagon coming south toward them. As the Conestoga drew up abreast of Hank's wagon, Jason heard Hank call out:

"Howdy friend! How's the road ahead?"

"Not too bad," was the unenthusiastic reply of

the disheartened driver. "Where you folks headed?"

"Headin' for the Ohio country!" Hank's answer reflected the epitome of confidence. "We're hoping to get a ride down the river at Pittsburgh."

Countering Hank's optimism with unmistakable pessimism, the southbound driver unenthusiastically said: "Good luck! Hope you have better luck than me and maw."

The discouraged traveler then tossed more cold water on the hopes of Jason and Mary who were within earshot of the conversation.

"We came down the Monongahela headin' for that Ohio country but got side tracked. Me and maw came out to this God forsaken country from down south of Cumberland to Dunkard Creek seven years this spring and last fall my neighbor talked me into moving out to the Ohio country. Turned out he knew less about boats than I did--and that sure ain't much! Well, we shoved off from down south at Rice's Landing and got caught crossways in the current at the junction of the Youghiogheny--lost every thing we had. Darn near drown too! Good thing maw here had our cash stashed away in her corset! But now all our money is gone and maw's pregnant so we've decided to head back east. Frontier life ain't for us I guess!"

Hoping to terminate the flood of discouraging words, Hank interrupted saying:

"I guess they're building a lot of boats these days over on the Monongahela."

"Oh yes. There's John Minor on Big Whiteley, John Armstrong at Muddy Creek, and there's a boat builder at the mouth of Ten Mile Creek. We had our boat built at Rice's Landing. Just takes money!"

"We figured it might be better if we tried to get a ride up near Pitt." Hank's countering remark evoked no change in the disheartened man's attitude and he replied:

"Wouldn't bet on it friend--we didn't have any luck. We might have been better off if we'd stayed on Dunkard Creek, but the Indians are a troublesome

lot. Couple of years ago they killed a neighbor of
ours--fellar named Bryant. Them red-skinned devils
burned down his cabin, killed and scalped his kids,
and took his wife. Luckily, she got away from them
Indians. Poor woman went back east."

Bidding the discouraged traveler goodbye, Hank
shifted his "chaw" of tobacco to the other cheek,
ejected a stream of tobacco juice toward a big rock
beside the road, and snapped a rein smartly against
the rump of his horses.

As the disgruntled man's wagon passed Jason's,
Mary nodded politely to his wife--she was at least
seven months pregnant and her hands remained clasp-
ed over her stomach. From under the rim of a faded
blue bonnet Mary saw a haggard face which momentarily flashed a half-hearted smile as the two wagons
passed. Only Mary knew what they had in common.

Undaunted by the discouraged traveler's words,
Jason and his party continued on and, several days
later, Hank said they were only a few miles south
of the Forbes Road and a place where Colonel Henry
Bouquet was surprised by an Indian attack in 1764.
As Hank explained:

"Born in Switzerland, and only thirty-nine at
the time, Bouquet was with General John Forbes back
in 1758 when they marched against Fort Duquesne and
ended France's control of the Forks. But six years
later, while marching to Fort Pitt, Indians attack
Bouquet just north of here at Bushy Run and he lost
104 men. He died of yellow fever the next year."

Late in the afternoon the following day, Jason
heard Hank let out a yell. Standing on the seat of
his wagon, Hank waved his hat and grinned from ear
to ear as he pointed ahead. Pulling abreast of his
friend's wagon, Jason could see through the trees a
ribbon of bluish-green which was the Monongahela a
few miles downstream from its confluence with the
Youghiogheny.

Although excited at the prospect of getting to
the river, discretion dictated they make camp where

they were and move on the next day. The excitement
around the campfire that night was invigorating--it
strengthened the hope and faith of each man, woman,
and child. Falling asleep was difficult that night
and Jason lay for a long time thinking about their
next move. Sensing his restlessness, Mary cuddled
closer to him saying: "The dragons will wait until
morning Jason--go to sleep!"

Awake before sunrise, and with breakfast over,
they slowly worked their way down the winding road
to the river where others, like themselves, looked
for passage downstream. Some waited impatiently in
their tent or wagon while other frustrated settlers
traded everything they had for a ride down the Ohio
River. Tents and lean-tos could be seen everywhere
interspersed with an assortment of wagons, horses,
cows, dogs, trunks, boxes, bales, chairs, kettles,
pots, tubs, and people. While sober-faced parents
discussed their "options," and their next move, the
children dashed hither and yon among the wagons and
tents completely oblivious of the dangers which lay
ahead of them. Noncommittal faces watched Jason's
party pass--some nodded and smiled but most watched
indifferently as they rolled by.

At the ferry dock Jason spied a "Notice Board"
which travelers used for "writ by hand" messages
advertising a need for passage space or announcing
their availability to work as a blacksmith, carpenter, or other such service. Having taken the lead
this day, Jason pulled up, gingerly jumped down off
his wagon, and made his way to the board. Scanning
the board carefully, Jason could not find a single
notice offering passage downstream. One weather-
worn, and undated, message caught his eye--it read:
"Seeking passage to Symme's Country," and was signed: "William Rittenhouse."

He remembered the name and wondered how long
that message had been on the board. Later he would
learn Rittenhouse arranged passage down the Ohio on
a flatboat. But now, and not knowing exactly where

they were going, Jason led his party down a winding muddy road looking for a place to make camp.

"Hey mister, got an ark lined up?"

The question was hurled at Jason by one of two men standing beside the road leading away from the dock area. Their clothing was similar to that of some others--the trousers and hunting shirt made of deerskin, a shirt open at the neck, and a wide belt which held the shirt snugly in place. Tucked under the belt of the man who had hailed Jason was a long ugly-looking knife which glinted in the sunlight. His companion had a tomahawk tied to his belt. The rugged-faced individual who shouted to Jason had an ugly scar beneath his right eye, the sight of which gave Mary goose flesh and she gripped her husband's arm in fright. Cocked jauntily on his head was an old badly worn Revolutionary War cap with a turkey feather threaded through two holes in the crown.

"It looks silly," thought Mary.

Sheer fright precluded her from saying a word but she heard Jason politely reply:

"No, we do not. But we are looking for a ride downstream however."

"Well, good luck! Sure hope you dudes brought along plenty of money--you're gonna need it!"

As both men now laughed loudly, the one with a feather in his cap pulled a bottle from somewhere inside his shirt and handed it to his companion who took a big swig and then returned it to his cohort who did likewise. Wiping his tobacco-stained chin with the back of his hand, he rebuked his companion with an insincere remark:

"Now that warn't called for Walt--you gotta be nice to fancy Dans wantin' to git downstream!"

He winked at Mary and grinned and she quickly turned her head and whispered to Jason: "Those men are crude! Can we move on?"

Both men roared with laughter as Jason chirped his horses into action. Although their coarse remarks continued as Dave's wagon went by, they grew silent as Hank pulled abreast of them—it was quite obvious they wanted no part of him. Mary would see many such men in the months ahead—greedy, uncouth, and ill-mannered men.

It was a strange mixture that gathered on the banks of the Monongahela in the spring of 1791—the young and old, strong and infirm, novice and woods-wise, rich and poor, optimist and pessimist, saint and sinner, the educated and those who had not seen the inside of a schoolhouse. From cities along the eastern coast, from the hills and valleys of Penn-sylvania and Virginia, from every nook and corner of the thirteen states, would-be settlers surged westward toward "the promised land." And among the clamoring migrants many languages could be heard—German, French, Irish, Scotch, English, and Dutch.

It didn't take Jason and his entourage long to realize the "warning" his antagonist had voiced was true. But, although "plenty of money" was indeed a necessary ingredient, so was a builder who could be trusted to build them a flatboat—or an "ark" as it was sometimes called. Hank's boy had a fitting de-scription:

"It looks like a big floating box!"

And box-like they were—crude but serviceable. Although the river craft were not built for beauty, they were in demand. But optimistic, and hoping to find a ride with someone else—or an alternative to river travel—Jason and his friends set out to look for such an arrangement. In their fruitless quest they soon learned overland travel was not a viable option—huge trees had to be felled every few rods to permit the passage of wagons and there were only a few open spaces according to those who appeared to be knowledgeable and trustworthy. As one said:

"Nothing but mile after mile of impenetrable forest—freshets clear up some of the river bottom trails but in the spring you can't depend on them."

This discouraging bit of information came from a carpenter who had given up the thought of moving downstream and had set up a business along the road repairing wagons. Near where the carpenter was now engaged in repairing a broken wheel, an assortment of traders, soldiers, explorers, and well-mannered gentlemen talked with several rough-talking men of the wilderness who offered their service as guides. Despite their diligent search, securing passage for a party of three families and their belongings was next to impossible. It was a bit discouraging but, as Jason optimistically remarked:

"It is just a fact of life we must face!"

During their unsuccessful quest, as with women who remained with the wagons guarding their belongings, on all sides they were met with a battery of mixed emotions. Fortified by an unquenchable faith, some stuck out the wait in crowded camps which soon became a quagmire as the April showers added to the misery and discomfort. Some just gave up and each day a few of the beaten and dejected packed up and headed east--their hopes and dreams of the promised land torn asunder by the bitter facts of reality.

And while Jason was away, Mary became friendly with a lady whose husband had parked his Conestoga next to them--they had a family-type wagon and were also headed downstream. In practically no time the two women were engaged in a long conversation--with Mary this was not a difficult task but in this lady she met her match.

"It took us twenty days to come from Carlisle. I never saw such roads. Thank heaven we stopped at Fort Bedford and Fort Ligonier to shake loose our stoved-up bones. But I met the nicest lady at Fort Ligonier, Phoebe St. Clair--she is the wife of the governor of the Northwest Territory you know. Such a lovely person but in very poor health. She confided that her husband was back in Philadelphia on urgent business at the time."

Mary mentioned her husband's father and uncle had come to know Arthur St. Clair and that she had only recently learned that Phoebe St. Clair had not accompanied her husband to Marietta. Upon hearing of Mary's relatively short journey from Turkeyfoot, the woman exclaimed:

"Dear me, you are indeed fortunate you did not have as far to come as we did! My husband thought for certain we would break our panes!"

"Your what? Your panes! What panes?"

There was understandable puzzlement in Mary's voice, and on her face. The woman laughed politely and explained:

"That husband of mine bought twenty-four glass window panes from Henry Stiegel at Lancaster. He's got a place nearby in Manheim where he makes them. Someone told my husband he would need them for our cabin and he decided to bring along several to sell when we get to where we are going."

Mary thought of their windowless cabin and her husband's explanation for not having such an opening. She decided this was neither the time nor the place to discuss such an unpleasant subject and besides, her friend was already talking about something else.

"My husband talked over our plans to move with several men before we started and they suggested we arrange to have a boat built here at Pittsburgh before we left Philadelphia. A good thing we did!"

She paused for a deep breath and Mary quickly seized the opportunity to say:

"You are indeed fortunate. My husband and his friends are looking for a ride but so far they have found nothing. But sitting here beats bumping over Braddock's Road. By the way, how far did you folks travel each day on the John Forbes Road?"

"Generally about fifteen miles on a good day-- it varied. Depended on a number of things. There were six wagons in our party so all in all we had a lot of reasons for delays."

She shrugged her shoulders, smiled, and heaved a big sigh as she continued:

"We came from Philadelphia by way of Carlisle.

Carlisle--that's a story in itself. My husband did some nosing about and learned there is some private stock company trying to get money together to build a surface road twenty-four feet wide from Philadelphia to Lancaster! Won't that be something?"

Mary was about to make a comment when the lady quickly added:

"That road will cost over one hundred thousand dollars my husband says. A great deal of money but we can use that road. That John Forbes Road is all right but we have so much more travel now than when it was opened twenty-three years ago. And now with this opening of the Northwest Territory, there will be so much more travel. By the way dear, what did you say your name was?"

"I didn't say but it's Mary--Mary Evenstar. My husband's name is Jason. It seems to me that every person I meet opens or ends their conversation with two words--Northwest Territory!"

"Glad to meet you Mary. My name is Rachel. I know what you mean about this talk of the Northwest Territory. Isaac--that's my husband--says this new territory offers us the opportunity of a lifetime!"

"Nice making your acquaintance Rachel. As for the Northwest Territory being the 'opportunity of a lifetime,' those are the exact words Jason uses and frankly I am sick of that trite expression!"

Rachel fairly beamed as she laughingly replied to Mary's fervent outburst:

"I see--you didn't want to come either!"

The road from Philadelphia to Lancaster which Rachel mentioned--the Lancaster Pike--was destined to open in 1797. The sixty-two mile highway would cost $465,000--even then estimates for a government project were exceeded by actual construction costs. 193 years later taxpayers would still be complaining about the same under-estimations of government project costs.

"I am from Baltimore myself. Jason and I came out through Fort Cumberland and lived the past year along the north branch of the Youghiogheny River."

"Lord All Mighty woman, and now you are moving again? I told Isaac just last night, I swear when we stop this time I'm never going to move again! I think there should be a law saying a woman has only got to make one of these pilgrimages with her man."

Somewhat dejectedly Mary picked up on Rachel's commentary saying:

"When I left Baltimore with Jason I thought it would be my only move. That first move was a rough one but now here we are moving again--or at least I think we are moving. I do pray Jason returns soon with some good news."

Despite an occasional tinge of bitterness, her comments exuded mature confidence and Rachel quickly remarked:

"You can tell that man of yours for me that he has a very good wife. I can tell. Not every woman in the world would put up with all the bouncing and jerking around just to get someplace where she will have all the inconveniences of frontier life. Lord knows you already know more about it than me but so far this doesn't look like any picnic."

An insincere smile crossed Rachel's face and Mary shrugged her shoulders saying:

"We just never know what married life is going to bring do we?"

Rachel extended both of her arms with upturned palms and a mischievous smile flooded her face when she remarked:

"Bless you Mary Evenstar. As I always tell my husband, I took him for better or worse but I swear he's worse than I took him for!"

Both laughed and Mary glanced around as if to be certain their husbands were not listening. What she saw was Dave's wife walking toward them. Mary introduced the ladies and after talking for a while Almeretta mentioned having heard someone speak of a trail far to the south. Rachel quickly said:

"A friend of ours told Isaac a woodsman by the

name of Daniel Boone opened up what he called 'The Wilderness Trail.' It was my understanding he took his wife, Jemima Boone, across that trail in 1775-- brave woman! Isaac said the wilderness road starts in Virginia, crosses the Powell Mountains, and then snakes through the Cumberland Gap into the central part of the Kentucky District."

Almeretta interrupted saying:

"You seem quite knowledgeable of that southern trail--had you considered traveling that way?"

"Heavens yes! We talked about going south but Isaac thought we would be better off this way. The southern way is supposed to be rocky, mountainous, and infested with Indians--it's three hundred miles through dangerous wilderness we were told. Like I told my husband, that kind of burden I do not need. Isaac picked this northern route because he said it was shorter and it can't be more dangerous."

Rachel quickly glanced at Mary and then looked back at Dave's wife as she added:

"Can it?"

Difficult and dangerous as it was across the road Rachel talked about, by 1800 more than 200,000 settlers would traverse "The Wilderness Trail" into Kentucky. The Indians called the road "Quasioto" which meant, "mountains where deer are plenty." In 1791 there were also "plenty of Indians" in those same mountains!"

As with the women, there was much talk around the wagon camp among the restless men. With unused energy and time on their hands--and surrounded by a seemingly hopeless situation--some drank their "Old Monongahela" and became boisterous during the long evening hours. In hopeful desperation a few talked about taking an overland trail but in the end they agreed it would be too hazardous for family travel and it would take too long even if they did manage to get through. As one man declared:

"I'm gonna float down or I ain't gonna go!"

Frustrated as he was, the man had not lost his

sense of humor. After taking a big swig of whiskey he added:

"There are old trail-breakers and there's bold trail-breakers, but there ain't no old, bold trail breakers!"

There was an element of wisdom in this drunken logic. Everyone wanted to get out to the Northwest Territory and the most logical route appeared to be down the "cussed and discussed" Ohio. A few of the migrants had made arrangements in advance for their passage but the majority were like Jason who had to confess to his wife:

"It did not occur to me we should make advance downstream travel plans. Hank and me both thought we could easily obtain passage."

But finding passage on the flatboat of someone who had made advance plans was next to impossible-- their ark was loaded with the migrant's plunder and left precious little room for those who did get on board to stand, sit, or sleep. There was seldom an opportunity for "passengers" and there were always soldiers looking for a ride downstream if space was available. Around their campfire that night Jason and his friends talked over the thought a return to Turkeyfoot might be in order but this alternative was quickly shelved as Jason zealously declared:

"We are not whipped yet!"

All did agree their chances of obtaining passage together was practically nil. Faced with this discouraging conclusion, Jason glanced at his wife and then summarized their position saying:

"If we cannot buy passage then we should think about having an ark built. I suggest that tomorrow we talk with some boat builders."

There was really no other choice so all agreed to the suggestion and said goodnight. As Jason now walked slowly toward his Conestoga with Mary clinging to his arm, he was jubilant and an overwhelming feeling of new hope coursed through his body. Mary said nothing as Jason talked about the idea of them building an ark. To herself she thought:

"That is quite an undertaking! I wonder if it
is the right time to advise Jason of my undertaking
--our undertaking that is."

Jason could not see the smile that spread over
his wife's face as she thought:

"Perchance the thought of being a father would
change my husband's mind about going downstream!"

Mary decided the time was not opportune--Jason
was simply bubbling over with the thought of building an ark. Hank gathered his family together and
talked over this suggestion while Dave did likewise
with his wife. All around them they could hear the
sounds of frustration occasioned by indecision concerning this same alternative, the lack of money,
a change of mind regarding the whole idea of moving
downstream. From nearby campfires, covered wagons,
tents, and lean-tos came the sound of children crying, women shouting, and the cursing of discouraged
men who lashed out at everything and everybody in
their despair. And for those who turned to whiskey
when things got rough, there was never any shortage
of "Old Monogahela" on the banks of its namesake.

To the north of the camp area lay the bustling
frontier town of Pittsburgh which had grown up at
this strategic location. Carpenters, blacksmiths,
and masons were needed everywhere and many of the
migrants changed their travel plans and remained at
"The Forks."   There were several boat builders who
advertised their availability "at a price." Wilson
and Wallace offered an assortment of "merchandise
from Philadelphia" including axes, wagoner's tools,
forges, and so forth. Pittsburgh was a "boom town"
area and with it came the good and bad, the honest
and dishonest, the poor and wealthy, the ambitious
and laggard, the temperate and intemperate. It was
a bizarre collection of humanity that "worked" the
the eastern shore of the Monongahela River just below "The Forks" in the spring of 1791.

Knowing dawn would usher in another busy day,

Jason and his wife retired early in their Conestoga
and lay listening to the sounds around them. Jason
was mindful of the danger from his restless neighbors and kept his rifle near his side, primed and
ready to fire. His powder horn and shot pouch were
a short reach away. Tonight the Evenstars lay for
a long time listening to the sounds of the campers
around them. Although his wife was unusually quiet
tonight, Jason did not encourage her to talk. Mary
knew Jason had many things on his mind. From somewhere across the road a baby cried and a man cursed
loudly. Moments later they heard what sounded like
a bottle being broken over the rim of a wagon wheel
and then a woman's high-pitched scream was stifled.
Just behind their Conestoga they now heard the sobs
of a woman and vulgar language of a man who sounded
as if he had consumed a great deal of liquor. When
the quarrelsome couple suddenly bumped against the
side of the Evenstar's Conestoga, Jason sat up and
reached for his rifle. After unleashing a torrent
of vulgar verbal abuse against the wagon which had
the audacity to get in his way, the sound of the
drunken man's voice and sobs of his companion faded
into the night.

Mary shuddered with fright and whispered:

"Jason, what are we doing here? We must have
taken leave of our senses!"

Jason said nothing--there was nothing he could
say. Drawing his trembling wife close to his side,
Jason lay quietly staring into the semi-darkness of
the Conestoga's interior. The light from the campfire made grotesque figures on the wagon canvas and
Jason could feel his wife relax--minutes later she
was asleep.

With the disturbing sounds outside their wagon
now quieted, Jason's thoughts turned to the contemplated undertaking. If they built an ark, then the
trip downstream posed the next obstacle--the hidden
rocks, sand bars, treacherous currents, and "Indian
menace" everyone spoke of. Flatboat pilots were in

demand, expensive, and good ones hard to come by it
was said. Thoughtfully he pondered the situation:

"These matters must be given careful attention
but tomorrow is a new day and we will find a way."

The eternal optimist kissed his sleeping wife
and then he fell asleep.

Jason did not know how long he had been asleep
but all of a sudden he was wide awake--maybe it had
been the rustle of the canvas as the rear curtains
of the Conestoga slowly parted. With the glow from
the campfire providing an orange-yellow background,
Jason saw a silhouetted figure with an unmistakable
Revolutionary War cap on his head--a turkey feather
protruded from the crest. He could hear his wife's
deep breathing and was certain she was asleep as he
carefully moved his hand to his gun. He could hear
his own pulse pounding. Suddenly he felt his wife
nudge him ever so slightly and she placed her tiny
index finger on his mouth--she was awake! Jason's
eyes never moved from the silhouette and the parted
curtains quickly dissolved any cobwebs which might
have lingered in his mind. The silhouette remained
motionless for what seemed an eternity not knowing
he was just a move away from his maker. From somewhere nearby a dog barked and the rustle of canvas
was again heard as the silhouette disappeared.

Quietly Jason worked his way toward the rear
curtains and carefully peered through the opening--
light from the campfire revealed no movement within
his field of vision. After a long time he returned
to his wife's side and tried to sleep. Near morning he did manage to fall asleep but the shouts of
an inconsiderate traveler soon awakened him and he
climbed out of the Conestoga and seated himself on
a log by the dying fire where he muttered:

"Oh well, the fire needed some wood anyway."

Jason was seated by the fire when Mary emerged
from their Conestoga and began preparing breakfast.
Across the road a wagon pulled away with the driver
shouting obscene vulgarities which left no doubt he

had given up and decided to go back east:

"The hell with Putnam's Paradise and Cutler's Indian Haven--I'm gonna go back to God's country in Connecticut!"

The disgruntled man was still shouting obscenities when his wagon disappeared down the road.

With breakfast over Jason and his friends took off toward the river where they hoped to talk with some boat builders. All had agreed they could, if at all possible, assist with some of the work and hopefully save part of the cost of the undertaking. Shared labor and shared cost seemed to be a viable solution if they could find the right builder. From others they had learned a flatboat would cost about four dollars a foot and Jason figured they would be needing a sixty-five foot craft at least. But, as Jason proposed:

"We are ready to negotiate and compromise. Is that agreeable to everyone?"

The first builder they met was a rather coarse talking individual--one who chewed tobacco and spit profusely disregarding where the stream of brownish fluid splattered. He told them:

"Ah kin make ye a damn good Kentucke boat. Ah been buildin' the bastards since '83. Used to make a damn sixty footer ark fer thirty-five dollars but times have changed and everythings gone up."

The man spat into the fire as if to punctuate a point. Now the boat builder wisp his hat into a roll and slapped his arm with a resounding wallop. Looking at the smashed insect he grinned and said:

"Take thet ye little bastard!"

The coarse individual flicked the insect from his arm and sent a stream of juice toward the spot where it landed--some of the brown juice splattered Jason's shoes. That did it! Jason said they would look around.

"We will advise you of our decision."

Once again the boat builder let go a stream of juice aimed at a bug which was working its way over

a split oak log--it was a direct hit! The smell of
whiskey on the boat builder's breath only served to
convince them to look elsewhere. As they prepared
to take their leave the boat builder warned them:

"You eastern dudes ain't gonna find no better
deal than ah can give ye!"

Discussing the cost of building a flatboat, or
a "Kaintuck" as another builder called it, was both
interesting and mind-boggling. In 1785 the Continental Congress had established the decimal system
with dollars as the unit and the following year had
provided for the issue of the gold eagle and a half
eagle. People were slow to give up the pound, the
shilling, and the pence.   The dollar was equal to
six shillings.   Jason's knowledge of the coversion
was a great help in negotiation. Late in the day a
builder told them:

"I'll build you an ark for four dollars a foot
and find a good pilot to get you down to Limestone.
You can work it out with the pilot to take you down
farther if that be your liking."

The bald-headed boat builder--a man of obvious
tremendous strength and standing at least six foot
five--was both cordial and willing to provide them
a boat but was not overly optimistic concerning the
interest they expressed in going beyond Limestone.

"Word coming back from downstream says most of
the folks don't go farther than Limestone Point but
its up to you.   We make all sizes of boats--twelve
to twenty feet wide and twenty to one hundred feet
long.   Make keel boats too--but they're only seven
to ten feet wide and forty to eighty feet long most
times.   Good for poling upstream but it seems to me
what you folks need is an ark."

The builder's business-like approach impressed
Jason--he and his friends thought this was the most
honest builder they had encountered. And they were
right--to a point.   What the man failed to mention
was that about one-fourth of the boats which left
Pittsburgh did not reach their destination. It was

Dave who asked:

"Limestone Point? Where's that?"

"About 70 or 80 miles this side of them Miami lands you mentioned--call it Maysville now. Like I told you though, I am agreeable to find you a pilot who will take you down as far as Maysville--then it would be up to you. Some pilots are familiar with the river all the way to The Falls--others are not. Could be the one I find would be agreeable to take you all the way to wherever you aim to go."

None of them dreamed that on October 11, 1811 the "New Orleans" would be steaming downstream from Pittsburgh and arriving at Cincinnati just two days later--it would be the first steamboat on the Ohio. But that would be 20 years in the future and now it was the boat builder who optimistically added:

"Anyhow, by the time you get to Limestone, you fellars will be able to steer her yourself."

The boat builder obviously had more confidence in their ability than any of them felt just now but they were impressed with him as a man. Nine inches shorter than the speaker, Dave had been admiring the boat builder's physique but could not resist a broad smile as he glanced up at the man's glistening bald pate and thought:

"Sure, you don't have to worry about that last seventy or eighty miles--we do! Not only that, the Indians probably wouldn't want a hairless scalp."

Accustomed to having people make remarks about his baldness, Dave's glance and his big smile had not gone unnoticed by the builder. With a knowing grin he quickly addressed Dave's unspoken thought:

"Don't worry mister, my lack of hair has nothing to do with me building boats! As my old father used to say: 'God is great, God is fair, some folks He gave brains, the other He gave hair.'"

Thoroughly nonplussed, Dave glanced at Jason who laughingly said:

"Don't look at me Dave--he was talking to you, right Hank?"

Jason's smile faded as he quickly added:

"As for what we do after reaching Maysville, I guess we will just cross that bridge when we get to it. Just getting that far downstream far outweighs the alternative of hanging around here or returning to Turkeyfoot."

Now it was Hank who grinned as he said: "Right Jason."

The trio now listened carefully to the brawny boatbuilder who proudly commented:

"I've built keel boats and arks and I think I know my business. If you three will put a shoulder to the wheel and cut the timber upstream, it should not take more than three weeks at the outside. You can take her down the river and sell the planks and probably get back a fourth of your investment. Ben Stites said some folks use the wood from their arks to make their cabins. Its up to you."

"Captain Stites?" asked Hank.

"Major Stites we call him—he's carrying that rank now I think. He's the chap from up the Monongahela who went down the Ohio a few years back and got John Symmes all riled up about the 'Miami Land' you folks seem interested in."

This builder was obviously knowledgeable about pioneer settler travel and the water highway which led to the Ohio River valley. Confidently he said:

"But you gentlemen give it some thought. I am not trying to push you but I have several prospects out trying to line up some settlers like yourselves so they can afford one of my one-way arks. Quicker you decide, the quicker we can get going. But I do appreciate you stopping by and talking with me."

The logic of what this builder said made sense to Hank and Jason—he obviously had a wealth of experience gained from dealing with problems posed by various travelers. As Dave said after they left:

"Now that old boy knows his business!"

Around their campfire that night the three men talked over the builder's proposition and the women

listened closely to what was said. Finally it was
Jason who summed up the situation saying:

"We are unable to obtain passage on someone's
flatboat, and pushing west on a wilderness trail is
not advisable. So what do we do? I for one am not
going back to Turkeyfoot!"

Each man nodded as Jason looked at his friends
in turn. Hearing no suggestion, Jason said:

"Then let us build our own flatboat. I figure
it would cost each of us eighty-eight dollars if we
build a sixty-six footer, twenty-two feet wide. We
should get back about twenty-five dollars each when
we dismantle our ark."

Although Jason was the one who quickly fathom-
ed the arithmetic of the undertaking, each readily
understood the need of eighty-eight dollars apiece.
Hard cash was in short supply in any frontier area
and western Pennsylvania was no exception in 1791.
"Trade in kind" was used by most and the fact Jason
and his companions had some "hard cash" put them in
a good bargaining position.

Having concluded they should consider building
their own ark, the men began discussing the details
of such an undertaking. The last builder they had
talked with said the ark he proposed would be rec-
tangular with the hull built of timbers ten inches
square--the hull would be caulked to minimize leak-
age. The entire deck was to be enclosed with four
inch stout oak planks flush with the sides and fastened with wooden pins to the wooden timber frame.
To the front of the cabin area wooden sides would
protect the animals from gun fire. The top of the
cabin would be covered and a door in the side would
allow wagons to be loaded. Three trap doors in the
roof of the cabin would allow smoke to escape. And
as the last builder had wisely suggested:

"You will be needing a fire for cooking and to
keep you warm."

With varying degrees of interest and emotion,
coupled with occasional whispers, the women and the

children listened carefully. Jason used a piece of burned stick to make a crude drawing of an ark on a piece of board and explained:

"It would be a bit crowded, but it will not be forever. True, they are roughly made, and its like Hank's boy said, 'they look like a box!' The main thing is, they float, provide shelter, and give us protection against Indians if necessary."

Jason paused as a ripple of excited whispers passed among the women and children. It was Dave's wife who now asked:

"Do you really think we will see any Indians?"

Looking her straight in the eye Jason replied:

"The last builder we talked with—a good one I believe—said he did not think we would experience any problem with the Indians but it is something we must think about."

Sober-faced, Jason waited until another flurry of whispers subsided—then he continued.

"Our ark would have several long oars for use if necessary, and a sweep is used for steering if I understand correctly—right Hank?"

Hank nodded.

"With a pilot who knows the river, we minimize the danger of our ark being grounded or swept into treacherous currents."

"Then we will have an experienced pilot?" The query was from Hank's wife.

"Yep," replied Hank when Jason glanced at him. "Like Jason says, the last builder we jawboned with seemed honest and said he'd get us a good one."

Mary had listened as Jason explained away each question and his enthusiasm seemed to grow as the evening hours passed. She was proud of her husband and his capabilities but she thought to herself:

"My dear husband—you could sell life boats to a camel driver in the desert. You have hardly ever seen a boat and here you are telling us all about them."

The men had previously talked about trying to

obtain passage on someone else's boat. But if they
built their own ark, Dave thought he would like to
reconsider selling his horses. It was Hank who now
offered some thoughts on the matter.

"I talked with a man who claimed he was out in
that country below Limestone, and he told me I'd be
better off to sell my horses and take oxen down the
river. Said them cussed Indians will steal horses,
but won't touch oxen."

Later Hank would learn this man had not been
further west than Pittsburgh. "Advice" was readily
available along the Monongahela River that spring--
not necessarily "good advice," but free anyway. On
one occasion Hank and his son ran into a talkative
camper who bragged about having been in the southwestern Pennsylvania country "for two months!" His
knowledge of the perils of river travel was without
end. Afterward Hank's son told Jason of the meeting and said of the man's story:

"It was a windy!"

But now on this April night, Jason turned over
in his mind what Hank said about Indians not stealing oxen and remarked:

"A good point Hank--it is food for thought. I
talked with Mary about us trading our Conestoga for
a smaller wagon and she thought it made good sense.
We could sell it, or make a good trade with someone
wanting to go back east. We do not need all of our
horses either. But one thing is certain however, I
am keeping Star! And my wife of course!"

Involved in her conversation with Dave's wife,
Mary missed some of Jason's remark. But just for a
brief moment her eyes lighted up mischievously when
she heard Jason mention "someone wanting to go back
east!" She had to restrain herself from saying:

"I'll go along and show them the way to Baltimore!"

But she didn't have the heart to pour water on
her husband's "glow."

Having the largest family, Hank was hesitant

about selling anything--his wife also believed they
should keep everything they had brought with them.
Dave decided he would sell his horses but keep his
wagon--he heard horses could be bought downstream.

And so it went until the men finally agreed to
plan on taking three wagons, four horses, two milk
cows, the sheep, and all the furniture and farming
implements they had brought. Now all that remained
to do was select a builder and build an ark!

There was also the matter of sharing the cost
of the undertaking. After much head-scratching and
husband-wife talk, Jason proposed he would be willing to bear one half of the cost of building an ark
with the understanding it would be his to dismantle
and dispose of when they reached their destination.
As he explained:

"It would mean a cash outlay by Mary and me of
one hundred and thirty-two dollars provided our ark
cost two hundred and sixty-four dollars. Hank and
Dave would each pay sixty-six dollars. Using that
boat builder's estimate of a one fourth return for
dismantled planks, then I could realize a return of
sixty-six dollars. The cost to each of us that way
would be sixty-six dollars."

Suggesting each family might wish to talk more
about the matter in private, and they could get together in the morning, Jason and his wife walked to
their Conestoga and the others did likewise. Jason
optimistically remarked to Mary:

"Now all we must do is select a good builder--
and agree on a fair cost."

With Hank and Dave agreeing to shake hands on
Jason's proposal, the three men departed early the
next morning to talk with the builder they believed
had appeared trustworthy.

"Like I told you gentlemen yesterday, your ark
should be ready for sailing inside of three weeks.
She might look a bit clumsy but I can assure you it
will be serviceable.   No windows--just a few peep-
holes you can use if the Delawares get after you!"

It was Hank who replied sharply:

"That ain't so funny from what I've heard!"

"No, it isn't funny Mr. Weiser--and I offer my apology for that remark. I know what you folks are up against and I aim to make you a good ark to protect you and your families and your belongings. I too was headed for the Ohio valley when I came out here from Massachusetts. But we like it here and I plan to make this our home. And again I apologize for my ill-advised remark gentlemen."

Hank nodded acknowledgement of the apology and the builder continued--he understood their concern:

"I'd like to put a narrow walkway on one side of the deck cabin. It would cut down a bit on the cabin space but it has advantages--I'll explain as we go along. I sort of keep the plans up here!"

The builder smiled and tapped the side of his head with an index finger. As they headed back to camp that afternoon, Jason remarked:

"I think we have commissioned a good builder."

The following two weeks were busy ones and the atmosphere among the three families was better than the past few days of anticipation. Jason sold all of his horses except "Star" and traded his Conestoga for a smaller wagon and two oxen--he was to keep the Conestoga until the ark was ready. The Weisers held onto their wagons as long as possible and then lived in a half-faced camp Hank and his son erected close to Jason's rig. Before selling his wagon, he went into the woods and returned with a big load of clapboards which he used in making his lean-to and declared his intent to take these boards downstream with them. With plenty to spare, Hank shared these clapboards with Dave who traded his Conestoga for a small wagon similar to Jason's.

The Weiser children bent some nearby saplings and lashed them together. This framework was then covered with some hides they had brought along. It provided the children an excellent shelter against the spring chill and a campfire was kept burning in front of their refuge all of the time.

The various camps which blossomed on the banks of the Monongahela River in the spring of 1791 were tableaus of strong contrast ranging from refined camp-life to unbridled depravity. Loud cursing and use of strong drink seemed to be more common among the discontented settlers who were "waiting" or had given up hope. Jason kept a watchful eye open for the man who wore a Revolutionary War cap with the turkey feather in it.

Word soon spread that Jason and his companions were having an ark built and settlers besieged them seeking passage. But, as Jason politely explained, with three families and their belongings, their ark would be filled. One settler tearfully related how he had spent everything he had to get to Pittsburgh and was willing to work his way down the Ohio.

"Me and my wife and our four kids came all the way from Harrisburg to Pitt on a Conestoga--cost me a hundred dollars and we only made fifteen miles a day. Now I ain't got enough money to go back east and I can't find passage downstream. I don't know what we're gonna do."

Liquor had made the man even more distraught and he might have fallen had Jason not assisted him when he grabbed the wheel of the Conestoga. Jason sympathetically explained:

"I am indeed sorry we cannot be of assistance, but, like you, we too have our problems."

His words fell on deaf ears and the frustrated settler continued to bemoan his fate repeating over and over again his plight. It was Mary who finally came to Jason's aid as she called him over to where she talked with Dave's wife. The settler staggered away and was soon heard relating his sad story at a nearby campfire.

"Thanks Mary, you saved my life," said Jason.

In reply she waved a newspaper toward him.

"What have you got?"

Smiling mischievously, Mary replied:

"The PITTSBURGH GAZETTE. It has been published here since 1786--did you know that?"

Jason shook his head and his wife continued:

"Dave's wife saw where a store in Pittsburgh
have bifocals and she plans to get a pair before we
leave."

"Bifocals?"

A look of puzzlement on his face, Jason looked
at each of the women in turn. Mary explained:

"Yes, bifocals Jason. The paper says Benjamin
Franklin invented the bifocal lens in 1780. Almeretta thinks she needs a pair. You mean you haven't
heard of them--smart as you are!"

Mary smiled as she gazed at Jason in mock surprise. In her mind she recalled Franklin had been
in Europe from 1778 to 1785 and wondered if he had
invented them while in Paris. Mary dismissed this
trivia from her mind as Jason remarked:

"Haven't had any need of any kind of glasses I
guess--probably why I haven't heard of them. That
is one advantage of playing the fiddle by ear--you
don't need bifocals to see the chicken scratches!"

As Jason now examined the paper Mary said:

"We had a great time looking around the stores
in Pittsburgh. It is truly amazing the things they
have out here. We plan to do some more looking before we go downstream. You don't mind do you?"

Mary's happiness was almost childlike and her
husband was happy to see her smiling and laughing.
With a little laugh he remarked:

"That is good--you ladies do a lot of looking,
and little buying!"

"Oh Jason," Mary quickly remarked with just a
trace of a pout, "You know very well I do not spend
money foolishly."

"I know you don't. I was just kidding."

Jason now glanced at Dave's wife and asked:

"Where's that man of yours?"

"Oh, he and Hank went over to see some settler
about trading guns. I do swear that man will be the

death of me yet--him and his guns!"

Almeretta now pointed across the deeply rutted road to where Jason caught a glimpse of his friend. Jason too was interested in guns and longed for the day when he would have time to make one of his own. As he started across the road, Mary called to him:

"You hurry back now, our evening meal will be ready soon!"

Jason disappeared around the end of a Conestoga across the street but soon returned accompanied by Hank and Dave, the proud owner of a new gun. He beamed as he showed his wife his new possession and exclaimed: "She's a real gem dandy!"

Although Dave was happy that night, there were others not far away who were not. Darkness always seems to bring out the worst in frustrated men and there were a number of those within a stone's throw from where Dave, Hank, and Jason camped this night. Anxious to get passage downstream, or smarting from the sting of defeat and preparing to go back east, some unhappy men loitered around campfires "licking their wounds." Across the road from where Mary and Jason thoughtfully gazed into the smoldering embers of their campfire, another campfire burned brightly and around it sat a number of men who passed around a jug of whiskey. Feelings ran high and one of the men ripped off a string of obscenities as he reacted to something said by a man who had arrived from back east just that day:

"S'pose you think 'cause you wuz a bootlicker fer General Washington you'll be somethin' special out west now he's president! He's gitting twenty-five thousand a year now but the only damn thing we are gonna git at Fort Washington is more of what we got at Valley Forge!"

There was a flurry of obscenities and then the same voice was heard saying:

"The Indians chased that general out west back down to the Ohio with his tail between his legs and now Congress wants us to go out there and whip them red-assed heathens. Hell man, I never got a cussed thing from the last war but a damn piece of lead in my leg and some worthless Continentals!"

Mary whispered to Jason, "Did you hear that?"

He really did not have a choice but replied:

"I heard--he is probably talking about General Harmar but I think we would be well advised to wait until we get our word from a more reliable source."

Jason was about to make a further comment when they heard another boisterous outburst quieted as a loud voice exclaimed:

"You're full of crap Max--all you do is bitch! Sure, they gave us Continental Certificates but the lead you keep crying about is in your ass, not your leg! The government was short-sighted in discharging all of its army men after the war but that's no reason why the president can't call on us veterans to insure the freedom of the Northwest Territory we won!"

It was obviously the one called "Max" who now quickly replied in a surly voice:

"Well, well, aren't you the patriotic one! We won it--now we gotta go fight for it again---right? That's a lot of crap George! And don't give me any horse manure about all that free and equal crap out in the Northwest Territory. You see the same type of bastards on every damn froniter--and they're all runnin' from somethin'! And they ain't never gonna satisfy their damn urge to move--see what's on the other side of the hill! It ain't land or freedom-- they's just unhappy with themselves and they gotta make everybody else unhappy runnin' around like a fool chicken with his head chopped off! Whole damn camp here is full of 'em--they just can't sit still anyplace very long!"

A conciliatroy voice was now heard to remark:

"I suppose you got a point Max. Seems most of these settler fellars have stopped someplace before looking for something that maybe doesn't even exist on this side of the Pearly Gates. Last year it was

Will's Creek*, before that Hagar's Town, and before
that Lancaster or some other frontier town.   Guess
we ain't much better though when you get right down
to it--we're all just sittin' here on our rear ends
waitin' to go someplace but I ain't sure where."

The drunken logic, or the lack of it, prompted
a burst of laughter followed by a youthful high-
pitched voice saying:

"I think you're full of something--you and Max
neither one know what the hell you're talking about
it seems. What in the hell are you two doing here?
Are you a couple of them discontented bastards that
Max talks about?"

Once again Max's unmistakable surly voice was
heard to say:

"Listen you young snot-nose--I know damn well
what I'm doing here. Sure wasn't gonna sit around
on my ass in Trenton and marry that split-tail that
said I knocked her up! How the hell did I know she
was gonna take serious what I poked at her in fun!"

Over the roar of raucous laughter that flooded
the night air Max was heard to add:

"I'm gonna go downstream, whip those damn red-
skins, make a pile of money, and then come back to
Pitt and screw it all away!"

Once again the roar of laughter was punctuated
by two or three men who applauded the drunken man's
intentions.   Over the mutterings of those who now
clamored for a chance at the jug of whiskey, the
youthful voice was heard saying:

"Big deal Max! I still think its a good thing
we had all those pioneers who came to this country
or we wouldn't have had the opportunity to come out
here. They didn't just sit in the comfort of their
homes--they went out and made a life for themselves
on the frontier."

The speaker's voice bespoke his youth and the
latter part of his remark was lost in a barrage of

* Cumberland, MD

profanity from Max:

"Now look here you young bastard, I didn't see your peach-fuzz face at Valley Forge--you ain't dry behind the ears and you're trying to tell me? I've been farther around the rim of a piss-pot a lookin' for the old handle than you've been away from your mamma's knee!"

There was some commotion and loud cursing and then Max's drunken voice was again heard:

"I really think its about time someone whipped your ass--stand up! I'm gonna learn you something right now kid!"

Now Jason and Mary heard a booming voice over the shouting of those who anticipated a fight and were already taking sides and encouraging the would be participants.

"All right Max, that's enough! And if there's any ass-whipping to be done, I'm your big--you got to take me first!"

There were angry mutterings but the booming voice of authority prevailed.   After a few moments of silence, the antagonist was heard saying:

"Look here Jim, this ain't none of your business!"

Although Max's voice now did not seem to be as defiant as before, liquor had bolstered his courage and he did not appreciate being humiliated in front of his drinking buddies.   But before he could say anthing more, Jim bellowed:

"Well I'm gonna make it my business unless you sit down and shut up!   I'm getting sick and tired of this fighting among ourselves everytime somebody gets his nose bent out of shape.   There's gonna be plenty of time to fight later on. Who gives a damn what brought us out here--we're here ain't we?"

The night held its breath as the seconds ticked away.   Suddenly the awkward silence was broken as a different voice was heard--one liberally laced with Old Monongahela:

"I got it Jim--we're all here because we ain't

all there!"

Stupid as it was, the remark broke the tension and loud raucous laughter filled the night air. As the laughter faded, Jim's booming voice exclaimed:

"All right you fellars, tell you what. Let's all go up toward Pitt and see if we can rassle up a couple ladies of the night and give them the pleassure of our company. It beats hell out of sittin' around here chewing each other's ass out!"

The shouts and commotion from around the campfire indicated agreement with the suggestion. In a slow drawling voice someone injected:

"Understand there's a pair of red-heads at the tavern up the way--came downstream from New Store a couple days ago way I heard it!"

"I'll carry that damn jug if'n you don't mind snot-nose!"

The voice was obviously that of the one called Max and he had directed his remark to the young man who had aroused his anger. Jim's voice now quickly stabbed the night air:

"Max! Now I'm telling you for the last time-- lay off damn it, or you and me is gonna settle this thing right now!"

Mary gripped her husband's arm--it was deathly silent for at least ten or fifteen seconds and then Max's surly voice was heard to say:

"No need gittin' all riled up Jim--just gimmie a drink of that whiskey and let's git up the road!"

Led by a six-foot seven broad-shouldered man, five figures now appeared from behind the Conestoga parked across the road. Momentarily silhouetted against the orange glow of the campfire, Jason saw that one carried a jug--he had what appeared to be a long feather protruding from his cap. Laughing and shouting obscenities to others along the road, the noisy group disappeared in the wood smoke and evening river mist. It was Mary who then said:

"Good riddance! Did you ever hear such filthy language? Perhaps now we can get some sleep!"

After rising to place a piece of wood on their fire, Jason looked at his wife and said:

"Loneliness, frustration, and whiskey make men do funny things--that was mostly whiskey talk."

From behind Jason's Conestoga a baby began to cry and a woman's shrill voice broke the stillness:

"Charlie, fetch some wood for this damn fire!"

It had been a busy day and the Evenstars felt the need for a good night's rest. Having taken refuge in their canvas covered wagon, Jason moved his rifle to a position where it was instantly ready, kissed his wife, and muttered:

"Good night dear."

"Jason, can we talk?"

"Can't it wait until morning Mary," Jason replied wearily. "I am really bushed."

Although Mary believed the subject she planned to discuss with her husband would probably make him "wide awake," she decided this was perhaps not the best time. Giving Jason a quick kiss on his cheek, Mary merely said:

"Good night Jason."

Tonight Mary lay for a long time contemplating what she had heard that day. Not only had the loud profane language by the drunken men across the road been unnerving, earlier in the day Mary had heard a woman tell of an incident which occurred along the Forbes Road a few days before. The woman said she had been attack by one of the drivers in the wagon train and she had killed him. The inevitable riffraff that pour into any new country--contaminating the air with their boisterous profanity and actions which shocked the sensibilities of peace-loving and well-intentioned settlers--made travel on the wilderness roads dangerous. Life in the crowded camps along the Monongahela in the spring of 1791 had its share of risks too. Mary edged closer to Jason and sighed--finally she fell asleep.

While Jason and his friends labored to build a flatboat, the women stood guard over their precious

belongings--all of their earthly possessions were
with them. And each day brought more settlers down
the road often passing a wagon loaded with the disappointed souls heading back east.

Meantime, work proceeded without incident and
the ark began to take shape. The boat builder used
timber which was on hand and directed the effort to
replace it. Trees were felled upstream and floated
down to the boat yard. With tremendous energy and
vitality, Jason and his companions spent long hours
each day either cutting timber or placing the wood
where it could be quickly handled by the craftsmen.
Although a blacksmith shop stood nearby, it was not
used much since the ark was constructed of wood and
fastened together with wooden pins. Besides, iron
was expensive.

It was necessary to build the ark with the top
side down and then turn it over before being floated. Turning the flatboat over was a tremendous job
and accomplished by carefully raising one side with
long poles as levers until it stood on its side and
then it was lowered gradually, using shorter poles,
until the bottom was on the ground. As the ark was
turned, "ways" were laid on the inclined slope that
led down to the river. Then the craft was held in
place by ropes until the launching.

Six foot upright timbers were fastened to the
gunwales and hewn planks were pinned to these using
wooden pins. The seams, or cracks between the logs,
were filled with oakum--old rope driven in with a
hammer. Finishing touches included a stock fence
in front of the cabin, scuttle holes or trap doors
in the roof, and a fireplace in the stern.   Elated
with the progress on the ark, Jason told his wife:

"It has all the comforts of home--and you will
like the fireplace!

Jason explained how a layer of dirt was spread
over a four by six foot area with stones laid over
that. With youthful enthusiasm he said: "The fireplace is six feet wide and walled inside with stone

and clay. The stone chimney tapers off so that it is about three feet square at the top--it is built with what they call 'cat and clay.'"

In the nearby blacksmith shop Jason fashioned what he said were "pot rambles." Justifiably proud of his effort, he explained to Mary:

"These are used to suspend pots and kettles in the fireplace--useful for cooking, and making soup. We plan to keep a fire in the fireplace all of the time--just getting one started with flint and steel isn't an easy task you know!"

His comment was prompted by Mary's pessimistic question about "starting a fire each day." Matches were a luxury not available in 1791. After hearing Jason's comments, his wife remarked:

"Mr. Franklin told my father a group of French chemists invented some type of glass fire-producing device in 1780 while he was Minister to France. It is unfortunate we do not have any of those."

Jason pondered his wife's comment for a moment and replied:

"I know what you are talking about. I heard a tradesman who stopped at my uncle's blacksmith shop say something about a sealed glass tube device made in France--called it a 'phosphoric candle' as I re-call. It contained a piece of phosphorous tipped paper that ignited when exposed to air according to him. He said it was a rather dangerous device."

They had no way of knowing it would be almost four decades before an early kind of friction match was invented by Sir William Congreve (1772-1828) and, in 1827, John Walker--an English pharmacist--would manufacture and sell what he was destined to call "congreves."

But, just south of Pittsburgh in the spring of 1791, Jason summed up the "fire" situation saying:

"As I said, we will just keep a fire going all of the time."

Although their bodies ached at night from such back-breaking work as swinging a broad axe all day or wielding an adz--an axe-like tool used to dress wood--no one complained. And despite an occasional April shower which plagued their efforts, their ark slowly began to take shape. Jason and his friends took renewed spirit each morning when they surveyed the accomplishments of the previous day. Two weeks and five days from the day the work started, their builder advised them one afternoon:

"Tomorrow we'll see if she will float!"

And, just as he promised, early the next morning the lines holding the ark in place were cut and the huge flatboat slipped into the Monongahela with a tremendous splash. Standing on the bank with his arms akimbo and a big grin on his face, the builder proudly proclaimed:

"There she be gentlemen! Now we'll just add a few finishing touches and you'll be on your way."

With the ark now afloat, that evening everyone in Jason's party assembled along the river bank and surveyed what Hank called "our pride and joy!" As they viewed the immense box-like craft, each person mentally conjectured just where the wagons, horses, cattle, oxen, furniture, provisions, and themselves would be located. Laughingly, Almeretta voiced her observation:

"Anyway you look at it, it looks to me like we are going to be mighty crowded!"

On this point everyone agreed but such a minor negative factor did not dampen the men's optimistic enthusiasm--particularly Jason who was elated with the progress.

"You are probably right Almeretta--but it will not be for long. Before you know it we will all be downstream and soon forget being crowded together a few days on our ark."

As Jason, Hank, and Dave labored from dawn until dark helping with those "finishing touches" the builder had promised, their wives put in even more hours as they cooked, washed clothes, and performed their household tasks. Although no one complained, the ladies missed the few conveniences they had enjoyed back in Turkeyfoot. And, with no children of her own to help her, the daily chore of milking the cow fell on Mary's shoulders. One day Rachel came over to visit while Mary was milking.

"Please have a seat Rachel--I will be finished milking Molly Pitcher in a minute."

"What a name for a lowly cow!"

Having voiced obvious disapproval of the cow's name, Rachel seated herself on a nearby tree stump and watched Mary rhythmically pulling the teats of their cow. She had become quite adept at this task the past year and never missed a "squeeze" when she replied politely but firmly:

"Good as any I suppose. Old Molly here knows she is an important member of our family."

Mary decided to ignore the term "lowly"--Molly was a fine cow. She did explain the name saying:

"The name was our neighbor Hank's idea--he has one he calls Betsy Ross. That's her over there."

Mary nodded in the direction where Hank's cow stood chewing her cud. Shaking her head in disbelief, Rachel exclaimed:

"Sakes alive! What names to give cows of all creatures on earth--it is positively sacrilegious. Why do you know I am acquainted with Betsy Ross who lives back home in Philadelphia? Elizabeth--that's her given name--is the daughter of Samuel Griscom, a fine Quaker carpenter. She eloped with John Ross in 1773 but he was killed shortly thereafter."

Pausing slightly, Rachel added: "The last time I saw her she was a seamstress on Arch Street."

Glancing sideways quickly at Rachel, but never missing a "squeeze," Mary indifferently replied:

"Oh, is that so?"

Rachel paid no attention to Mary's brief reply and lack of interest. Taking a deep breath and exhaling somewhat noisily to insure Mary was aware of her contempt, Rachel continued:

"As for Molly Pitcher, she's from Trenton, New

Jersey. She was employed as a servant in Carlisle
at the home of Colonel Irvine--a friend of theirs.
While there she met and married William Hays."

Hoping to change the subject, Mary quickly interjected: "Hank did mention something about how he
came to name his cows. But frankly Rachel, I never
was much interested in any cow's pedigree."

Rachel paid little attention to Mary's lack of
interest and continued her commentary:

"Molly Pitcher's real name is Mary Ludwig--did
you know that?"

"You don't say."

Mary voiced her reply in mock surprise but did
not take her eyes off her work.   Molly swished her
tail and looked back along her side with utter disdain as Rachel rambled on:

"Shortly after William and Mary were married,
he joined the First Pennsylvania Artillery and was
at Valley Forge that terrible winter.   Then, during
the Battle of Monmouth on June 28th in 1778, Mary
carried water in a pitcher from a nearby spring to
her husband and other thirsty soldiers--that's how
she got the name 'Molly Pitcher!' When her husband
was wounded, she volunteered to take his place."

Mary patted Molly on the side saying:

"I guess you didn't know you carry the name of
a Revolutionary War heroine?"

Again Molly turned her head, eyed both ladies
with sad brown eyes, and continued chewing her cud.
Rachel now glanced around and lowered her voice as
she continued talking:

"I would not want you to repeat this but I met
a woman in Harrisburg on our way out here who told
me she was a close friend of Colonel Irvine. Well,
he told her William Hays died several years ago and
it was being said thereabouts that George McCauly
and William's widow were now quite friendly--if you
know what I mean."

Mary arose from her milking stool and covered
her lips with her hand in mock surprise--she had no

interest in such gossip and merely replied:

"Like I said, Hank named our cow and we bought
her from him--the name came with her."

Anxious to avoid any further conversation regarding such idle gossip, Mary added:

"Molly did not seem to mind the trip here--she
should enjoy the ride downstream. Be more pleasant
than traipsing along behind a wagon I would think."

Apparently Rachel got the message--she did not
mention Betsy Ross or Mary Ludwig again. In taking
her leave Rachel remarked:

"Well, I see Isaac is back--better see what he
is up to. We plan to leave just as soon as he gets
the name of our ark painted on the side. He thinks
'The Exodus' would be a suitable name."

Several days after Isaac and Rachel departed,
and with only minor "finishing touches" remaining,
the ark builder told Jason they could begin loading
their precious cargo.   With utmost care everything
was put on board and lashed down in accordance with
the builder's instructions. The animals were to be
quartered forward in the fenced-in pen outside the
cabin--high walls on each side provided protection
against Indian lead or arrows should they be attack
downstream.   Canvas wagon covers and blankets were
used to provide some privacy for the cabin sleeping
spaces. Their fireplace was located at the rear of
the cabin and a door nearby led to a narrow walkway
along the port side.

A six foot area aft of the cabin afforded room
for the pilot to man the huge sweep.   Everyone was
naturally interested in who would be their pilot--
they did not have long to wait.   True to his word,
the builder came on board one afternoon saying:

"Gentlemen, I would like you to meet Tom May--
one of the best pilots on the river!"

Tom was a friendly person--his wind-roughened
cheeks and calloused hands bespoke his familiarity
with out-of-door life and hard work. He wore buck-
skins with fringing, deerskin moccasins, and an old

flop-brimmed frontier hat which almost concealed an abundance of graying hair and crow's feet on either side of deep-set ice-blue eyes. An English dragoon pistol was shoved behind a leather belt and a hunting knife hung at his side. Tom was an interesting study of frontier manhood and, as they were soon to discover, he knew his business.

"As my friend here says, I just got back a few days ago. We had a much smaller boat last time and ran into some nasty weather. The men and boys were quartered in the bow while the women and the little children slept near the stern where we kept a fire. Wasn't very comfortable and they were real happy to see Marietta. With such a fine ark, and only three families, our journey should be an enjoyable one."

Tom explained to the men how he would need the help of everyone to keep a sharp lookout for trees, limbs, and submerged rocks and logs. He said they would stop periodically along the way to take on a load of firewood for the fireplace and added:

"There isn't a lot for you to do along the way if all goes well. It can be a rather pleasant trip if we don't run into trouble. Big thing is to keep your eyes open at all times and I mean everyone! I also suggest you try and keep yourself protected at all times as much you can. Make sure you tell your wife and the children that--its important! A pesky Indian hidden along the shore can cause us a lot of trouble if we aren't careful--and don't forget it!"

When Dave suggested they fly a flag on the bow everyone was in agreement and Jason offered to provide one which had been given him by Parson Weems-- it had thirteen alternate red and white stripes and a circle of thirteen white stars on a blue field. The Standard of the United States had originated as the result of a resolution submitted by the Marine Committee of the Second Continental Congress on the 14th of June 1777 at Philadelphia. The proposed flag had thirteen red and white stripes and a white star for each of the original colonies but the flag

of 1777 had no "official" arrangement for the stars
in the field of blue. With everyone in agreement
their ark should carry a flag, Jason volunteered:

"Parson Weems said the Minutemen from Bedford
carried a flag at Concord, Massachusetts April 19th
in 1775--said it had a silver arm with a sword on a
red field and displayed the Latin words 'vince aut
morire.' My school-teacher bride says that means:
'conquer or die.'"

Tom May had been studying Jason and now said:

"That would be just before Washington went to
Boston from Philadelphia in June to take charge of
the army wouldn't it Mr. Evenstar?"

Jason nodded agreement and replied:

"That it would--and please call me Jason."

Dave had listened carefully and now said:

"My father told me they hoisted the Stars and
Stripes in Easton, Pennsylvania on July 8th of 1776
when the signing of the Declaration of Independence
was announced."

Jason was turning Dave's comment over in his
mind when Tom May interjected politely:

"I well remember that after the Declaration of
Independence some folks considered it inappropriate
to fly the Continental Colors with its thirteen red
and white stripes and the British flag in the upper
corner. It is my understanding that a variation of
the thirteen red and white stripes and the thirteen
stars first flew in a land battle on August 16th of
1777 when the troops under John Stark fought in the
Battle of Bennington on New York's northern border.
I've also heard it said our flag received its first
salute from another country on the 14th of February
in 1778 when John Paul Jones sailed the RANGER into
Quiberon Bay at Nantes, France. A gentleman from
Boston was among my last group of passengers and he
told me the stars and strips flew aboard a ship out
of Boston, the COLUMBIA, which traveled around the
world. He told me it sailed September 30th in 1787
and returned the 10th of last August last year."

From the recesses of his mind, Jason recalled having read where the study of the history of flags was called "vexillology." As his teacher-bride had explained:

"As I recall, 'vexillum' is a Latin word which means a square flag or banner carried by troops."

Jason was intrigued by Tom May's comments and had listened carefully. He concluded this man was not only a good pilot, but was also a knowledgeable individual. His trend of thought was broken as the boat pilot pushed his hat back, scratched his graying head, and continued his commentary:

"Of course, our first standard may have been the Cambridge, or Grand Union, Flag, which had the British flag in the corner. It was first unfurled January 1st in 1776 at Prospect Hill in Somerville, Massachusetts. General Washington was there that day I've been told. I do know for a fact troops of the Third Regiment, during the Battle of Cowpens in January of 1781, carried a flag of thirteen red and white stripes with a blue canton which contained twelve stars in a circle and another star right in the center--my brother was there and saw it!"

But even Tom May had no way of knowing in 1791 that Congress would, only a couple of years later, have under consideration a proposal the flag of the United States have 15 stars after Vermont (in 1791) and Kentucky (in 1792) were granted statehood. On April 4, 1818, and in accordance with a proposal by Captain Samuel Chester Reid, U. S. Navy, Congress was destined to approve legislation which set the number of stripes at thirteen--seven red and six white. A white star on a field of blue was to represent each state.

That evening the Evenstars stood arm in arm on the bow of their "home on the water" and watched as Hank and his boys loaded the last of their belongings. With the builder's permission, everyone had agreed they should start sleeping on board the ark. But, as Jason observed:

"With everyone so steamed up about us finally getting on board, it might be difficult to get much sleep tonight." And to his wife Jason said:

"I was happy to see you and Tom hit it off so well. Everyone seems to agree we have ourselves a real good pilot. He seems to know his business."

"Lord, I hope so!"

"Mary," said Jason softly, "please do not use the Lord's name in jest."

"Whose jesting?" replied Mary quickly. "I was never more serious in my life!"

Momentarily taken aback by Mary's candid reply to his admonishment, a big smile spread across his face as Jason exclaimed:

"Touche! I told Tom this afternoon all about my child bride's wit."

Without a moment's hesitation Mary once again replied quickly:

"And by any chance did you tell Tom your bride was pregnant?"

Jason was dumfounded--he took a step backward and might have fallen overboard if his wife had not seized his arm. After what seemed an eternity, the father-to-be finally muttered:

"Surely you jest."

Mary looked intently into Jason's stunned face and softly replied:

"Dear husband--believe me. As I said a minute ago, I was never more serious in my life!"

Again Jason muttered:

"You mean I am going to be a father? When?"

With a beautiful smile on her face she replied in a coquettish manner:

"Oh, I would say we should have a little guest for Christmas. Would that be convenient sir?"

Scratching the side of his face, Jason's eyes reflected the bewilderment which was racing through his mind as he stammered:

"But...but when? I...I don't remember...I..."

"Jason, my dear, please do not worry your head about when or anything else! I will do the counting--you just get us downstream and find us a lean-to. Trust me Jason, I will do the rest."

Obviously nonplussed, and ignoring his wife's terse remarks, Jason finally managed to blurt out:

"Me, a father! That's wonderful. But, do you think--should we--what about.....?"

"Jason, for crying out loud--my having a child does not change a thing. I am going to be a mother and you are going to be a father--that is it! What is of importance right now is getting downstream to this Northwest Territory you keep raving about--you have enough to worry about just finding us a place to live. I suggest we should turn our thoughts to river travel right now."

Captivated by his wife's calmness and wisdom, Jason merely nodded and then suddenly exclaimed:

"I'm going to be a father! I must tell Hank!"

The father-to-be jumped off the boat and found Hank a short distance away engaged in conversation with a well-dressed gentleman. Eagerly Jason said:

"Pardon me gentlemen but I have some fantastic news. Hank, I'm going to be a father!"

With an unusually sober face, Hank congratulated his friend and then quickly added:

"This gentleman just arrived from Philadelphia and he's got some news that's of interest to us."

Hank paused, deftly moved his chew of tobacco from one cheek to the other, and continued:

"This here's my friend I told you about, Jason Evenstar. I'd be beholdin' to you mister if you'd tell Jason what the army is gonna do out west!"

Jason's broad smile faded as the man said:

"I was just telling your friend here that last month congress approved a plan to increase the size of the army and authorized the money for Arthur St. Clair to lead an expedition against those troublesome Indians this summer. He has been appointed a

major general and given command of the army. As I
told Hank a moment ago, the governor is a friend of
the president and both Washington and congress need
someone they can trust who has a personal knowledge
of that country beyond the Ohio."

"And you say congress authorized the money for
a campaign against the Indians?" Jason paused and
quickly added: "This summer?"

"Right you are friend. After General Harmar's
unsuccessful expedition last fall the governor went
back east and convinced the president and congress
he had a plan that would put an end to the troublesome Indian problem. So even as we talk, back east
troops are being enlisted in cities and surrounding
communities. Some states have even been instructed
to furnish levies to fill the ranks of the army. A
gentleman I met in the inn at Frederick on my way
here, a Captain Van Swearingen from Berkeley County
in the Commonwealth of Virginia, confided St. Clair
was indeed authorized to call on the state militia
if enough troops cannot be raised any other way!"

In bidding Hank and Jason goodbye, the gentleman from Philadelphia wished them success in their
undertaking but said in parting:

"That Indian problem has been a burr under the
government's saddle for a long time and everyone is
praying St. Clair has the answer. Its unfortunate,
but I'm painfully afraid you folks are heading into
an all-out war against the Indians in the Northwest
Territory."

CHAPTER SIX

LA BELLE RIVIERE

All eleven members of Jason's three family entourage stood silently on the deck of their ark and
watched as Dave hoisted the United States flag over
the bow. Each felt a shiver of prideful emotion as
the red, white, and blue standard unfurled and then
rippled in the morning breeze. It was Tuesday, the
10th day of May in 1791.

Coming on board just before dawn, Tom May told
Jason he heard a detachment of soldiers had arrived
at Fort Pitt two days earlier--they were headed for
Fort Washington. The pilot also said he heard some
of Virginia's militiamen had been ordered to muster
at Fort Pitt. These reports added credence to what
Jason and Hank had been told and immediately after
the early morning flag raising ceremony, Jason suggested everyone join in a prayer. It would be more
than a century before the "Pledge of Allegiance" by
Frances Bellamy was first publicized in 1892.

Several of their new-found friends, who either
still hoped for passage or awaited completion of an
ark, watched quietly as Tom prepared to "push off"
into the morning mist which still clung tenaciously
to the river. With the ropes that had held the ark
captive now loosened, and everyone on shore waving
and voicing polite cheers, the cumbersome flatboat
drifted slowly away from its mooring place. Standing on the bow Jason acknowledged several greetings
and best wishes for a safe journey before he caught

sight of two bearded ruffians standing on the river bank downstream from where the ark had been moored. As both rowdies now gestured with an upraised index finger, the boisterous one with a turkey feather in his Revolutionary War cap yelled to Jason:

"Hang on to your hair dude!"

The mist had surrendered to the sunshine by the time the ark reached a point above where a fort sat majestically on a spit of land jutting into the confluence of the two rivers which melted together to spawn the Ohio River. Jason and Hank stood on the stern and watched in fascination as Tom wielded the sweep to steer the huge craft down the Monongahela. Pointing up toward the fort Tom said:

"Old Fort Pitt has seen a lot of folks pass by here this past year. Easy to see why Colonel Henry Bouquet picked this place for a fort in 1763--its a strategic location."

"Wonder who the first white man was that stood up there and looked down on these three rivers?"

Jason did not direct his question to anyone in particular but it was Tom who replied:

"Well, Sieur de Robert La Salle is supposed to have been the first white man to pass down the Ohio in 1669 but I can't swear he ever stood up there on that point! Some Frenchman by the name of Captain Celeron de Blainville came down through these parts in the middle of 1749."

"Who built the first fort here?"

"Let's see. In order to answer that, allow me to explain a few things Jason. About the time that French captain was floating down the Ohio, the Virginia and Pennsylvania legislatures were beginning to get itchy about France taking over control of the rich fur trade west of Fort Pitt so they sent three traders out here to talk with the Indians. There was an Irishman name of George Croghan, some three-quarter Indian by the name of Andrew Montour, and a frontiersman who knew the Indians real well--man by the name of Christopher Gist."

Tom paused as he carefully adjusted the sweep. That taken care of, he continued:

"Anyway, those three men met with sachems from a number of Indian tribes--the Delawares, Wyandots, Shawnee, Miamis--and they all smoked the calumet at Logstown just downstream about eighteen miles. The Indians agreed to trade with the English in friendship. That done some men of wealth in England and a few Virginia businessmen formed the Ohio Company aiming to colonize the western land along the Ohio. By the way gentlemen, two of those charter members of the company were half-brothers of our president. A provision of their charter said they had to build a fort in this region and have one hundred settlers living nearby within seven years."

Jason interrupted saying:

"Pardon me Tom. I was just thinking--a moment ago you mentioned someone named Montour. Along the trail we met an old codger who said he knew someone by that name. Said they were at General Braddock's defeat. Also said that Montour drank quite a bit."

Tom smiled as he replied:

"Well, he was three-quarter Indian and they've got quite a reputation of liking the stuff--and not being able to hold their liquor either! However, I heard it said Christopher Gist and that half-breed conducted the first Protestant services in the Ohio country. He couldn't have been all bad!"

Hank grinned as he said:

"That fellar Montour might have been in charge of the wine for communion!"

The expression on Hank's face clouded when he saw Jason frown and he quickly added:

"Sorry, go ahead with your story Tom."

"Like I said a moment ago, the French had sent Captain Celeron down through here and then Governor General Duquesne of Canada ordered some forts to be built south of Lake Ontario and Lake Erie--he knew it was just a matter of time before there was going to be a fight over the Ohio country. Then in 1753,

Governor Dinwiddie dispatched Major Washington out here with his interpreter, Christopher Gist. After spending five days at Logstown, Washington sent the commandant at Fort Le Boeuf north of here a message saying French encroachment on England's land would not be tolerated."

Hank interrupted saying:

"Pretty big talk for a young major!"

"You got to remember Hank, these were colonial troops and it wasn't just Virginia and Pennsylvania talking--it was England! Anyhow, in 1754 Captain William Trent and thirty soldiers came out here and started to built a fort up there."

Tom waved his hand toward Fort Pitt and added:

"The same summer Governor Dinwiddie dispatched George Washington with some troops and they marched to Great Meadows and began building Fort Necessity. When the French received word that some diplomatic figure had been assassinated, they moved quickly."

By now the ark was abreast of Fort Pitt and it was Hank who pointed toward it saying:

"Didn't Fort Duquesne used to sit up there?"

"That's right Hank. It didn't take the French long to take Captain Trent and his men prisoners up there. Then, after only nine hours of attack, they took Fort Necessity which was as yet not completed. The French did allow Washington the "honors of war" to retreat but that was the start of the French and Indian War."

Tom adjusted the sweep and then continued:

"After completely destroying Fort Necessity in July of 1754, the French returned here and finished the fort up there which Captain Trent had started-- they called it Fort Duquesne. Four years later, in 1758, Prime Minister William Pitt of Great Britain breathed some new life into the British cause over here and his troops stormed Louisburg, Crown Point, Niagara, Quebec, and in November of that same year General John Forbes took this strategic location."

"That was sort of the beginning of the end for

the French influence in this area, right?"

Jason's remark brought a quick reply from Tom:

"Pretty much, Jason. It was only natural this site would be called Fort Pitt after General Forbes captured the point here. An Ottawa chief, Pontiac, captured some key forts to the west of here in 1763 but Fort Pitt held. Pontiac fought on the side of the French at Braddock's Defeat and was quite taken with them because they treated him better than the English he called 'white dogs with red coats!' But the British had the upper-hand and by terms of the Treaty of Paris in 1763 England got Canada and most of the French possessions east of the Mississippi."

Jason studied Tom's face thoughtfully and then asked:

"How did the Indians feel about England taking over this land out here—apparently they were not a party to that Treaty of Paris you mentioned?"

"You are right—not a single red man sat in on making that treaty. However, the British were very anxious to calm the Indian fears and the same year, 1763, England published its Royal Proclamation Line decree which forbid the colonies making land grants or authorizing settlements west of the Alleghenies. But land speculators, frontiersmen, and capitalists paid no attention to it. Along with others, George Washington himself staked out choice land tracts in the Ohio valley. With their homes in the Ohio valley, it was only natural the Indians resented this encroachment. To make matters even worse, in 1768 the Iroquois made a treaty giving the white man the Indian's sacred land south of the Ohio River."

"Sounds like trouble to me!"

Emerging from the cabin, Mary had heard Tom's last few words and succinctly declared her feelings regarding the complex issue being discussed. Jason turned to his wife and quickly explained:

"We've been listening to Tom here tell us all about the history of that fort up there."

Jason pointed as he spoke and Mary remarked:

"We ladies thought you might have fallen overboard. Thought I best be looking for you!"

It was Tom May who now explained:

"Along with my story-telling, I've been teaching your husband and Hank how to operate the sweep.
I'll be needing their help along the way."

"Tom was telling us how that fort up there was
taken from the French in 1758 by General Forbes."

As he spoke, Jason moved to where he could put
his arm around his wife. Tom May now politely cor-
rected Jason saying:

"General Forbes with the aid of Washington. I
failed to mention he was there in 1758 with Forbes.
The Frenchmen burned their garrison the day before
so the British had to build a new fort--took almost
two years but then the British commanded this point
here. Although some Indians did manage to overrun
this point in 1763 while General Henry Bouquet was
back east and Captain Simon Ecuyer had been left in
command, when the general got word about the attack
on Fort Pitt, he quickly organized a relief force
at Carlisle and hurried back leading 460 regulars.
On July 27th, at Bushy Run near Fort Ligonier, the
Indians almost repeated the 1755 ambush of General
Braddock. It was the 10th of August before General
Bouquet was able to get to Fort Pitt."

Like Hank and Jason, Mary was impressed with
Tom May's knowledge of what he called "the forks."
They also admired the skill with which he now carefully maneuvered the huge ark into the swirling and
tricky waters of that junction. Mary asked Tom:

"How long has Pittsburgh been up there?"

"It was laid out in 1764. It was only natural
a settlement would spring up around the fort."

"And the British? When did they leave?"

"They abandoned Fort Pitt in 1772. By the way
Mrs. Evenstar, downstream you'll be hearing about a
frontiersman who was here at Pitt back then--one of
the best marksmen anyone ever seen. It was said he
could outshoot the best soldier and had one of the

finest guns hereabouts--name was Simon Kenton. Its
said he made his first trip down the Ohio in 1771."

As everyone stood watching the slowly changing
river scenery, Tom suddenly sang out:

"And so my friends, away we go,
Down the beautiful O-hi-o!"

Cold shivers ran up Mary's spine--they were on
their way down the Ohio. She moved closer to Jason
and they watched Pittsburgh blend into the horizon
as Tom provided a commentary:

"Shawnees call it 'Eagle River'--Kiskepilasepe
in their language. Wyandots say 'O-he-zu' meaning
great, grand, and fair to look upon. The Iroquois
use about the same name, 'O-he-you.' Means a great
and beautiful river. The French call it "La Belle
Riviere.' But regardless of which name you choose,
we are on our way and it is a thousand miles to the
Mississippi!"

The pilot laughed good naturedly. Although he
had never gone beyond "The Falls," Tom had made the
trip down the Ohio a number of times and understood
the apprehension most felt in embarking upon such a
river journey. Snuggled close in the crook of her
husband's arm, Mary rolled that word "Kis-ke-pi-la-
sepe" around on her tongue. She had decided to use
"Ohio" when she heard Hank exclaim:

"We seem to be moving north!"

"A good observation" said Tom. "This old Ohio
flows north and a little west for about twenty-five
miles and then turns west about the same distance--
after that we travel mostly south for several days.
But, its downhill all the way."

Although Tom May never cracked a smile, he did
wink at Jason. It took Hank a moment to catch on
to the pilot's remark and then all enjoyed a hearty
laugh. Such remarks helped ease the tension. Tom
was carefully watching his passengers and their reaction to each word, changing vista, and new sound.

Knowing his passengers was part of his job.

Jason and Mary now carefully made their way to a place immediately in front of the stock fence and marveled at the ever-changing vistas which greeted them at each bend of the river. On the slopes--the ones which occasionally opened to the wooded ridges high above--the ground was alive with the fruits of an early spring. Here and there they could see the blood root of the poppy family, the herbal ginseng, the shield-shaped leaves of the May apple, and many other herbs and flowers which were fully two weeks ahead of the season. The pure and untouched beauty of virgin forests, straining to unleash their foilage, prompted squeals of delight from the children and silent adoration by adults.

Before the sun was overhead everyone had made a pilgrimage to the stern of the ark and watched in fascination as the pilot moved the sweep skillfully guiding the huge river craft around large rocks and dangerous submerged logs. When Dave and his wife visited the stern, Almeretta remarked:

"Mr. May, it is just amazing how you manage to steer this big thing!"

"As I told your husband, I've been doing this for quite a spell. And by the way, we are going to be living in rather close quarters for a while so I suggest we drop the formalities--just call me Tom."

"And please call me Alma. Dave said you might prefer using given names."

"Works out a lot better! And by the way Alma, Dave says you brought along some books to read."

"Oh yes. A busy mind is a happy mind I always say Mr. May--I mean, Tom. I brought along my Bible and a 1733 copy of POOR RICHARD'S ALMANACK. There are many good maxims in it--I particularly like the one, 'God helps them that help themselves!'"

"A good rule of conduct," said Tom. "As I recall, Benjamin Franklin published his almanacs from 1732 to 1757 under the pen name of Richard Saunders --started his publication the year I was born."

"Come now Tom, I would not have thought you to be a man of that age."

To herself Almeretta conceded the pilot was in excellent physical condition and quite intelligent. Tom interrupted her trend of thought saying:

"Thank you. I owe it all to good clean living and a wee bit of Old Monongahela now and then. For medicinal purposes only of course!"

Tom looked at Almeretta seriously, glanced at her husband and winked, and then an infectious grin spread across his face as Dave's wife replied:

"Of course."

She herself had been known, on occasion—but, sometimes on no occasion at all—to partake of one or two spoonfuls of spirits in a cup of hot water. Strictly for "medicinal purposes" of course.

"By the way, speaking of almanacs, Alma," said Tom, "did you know the present Gregorian calendar lost eleven days and fourteen seconds?"

A puzzled look swept over Almeretta's face as she glanced at her husband and then somewhat doubtfully and haltingly replied:

"Why no, I didn't. How did that happen Tom?"

"Back in the days of Julius Ceasar most people used the lunar calendar but they had to add a month every few years so it would fit the solar year. In 46 B.C. Ceasar decreed the year was to be $365\frac{1}{4}$ days and the Julian calendar came into being—that's how leap year got started. In 1582 Pope Gregory XIII came up with the Gregorian calendar and got rid of the accumulated error by proclaiming the day after October 4th would be October 15th. On the 2nd of September in 1752 England decreed her empire would use the Gregorian calendar with the next day being September 14th under the Julian calendar. We lost eleven days! And because today's calendar is now off 26 seconds each year, it requires a correction every 3300 years. That gives us a lot of time just to figure where we will put that day when the year 4882 rolls around. Don't you agree?"

Again Tom's feigned look of seriousness slowly
faded into a broad smile as he watched Dave's wife
contemplate the trivia he had offered. Glancing at
her husband and seeing a big grin on his face, Alma
suddenly realized Tom had been "putting her on" and
she joined him in polite laughter. Actually, Alma
had not been as interested in Tom's story about the
calendar as she was in the revelation of the age of
their pilot--he didn't look to be 59 years of age!

"As I said before, you certainly do carry your
age well. But tell me, doesn't your wife take any
exception to your being away on trips so long?"

Although somewhat personal, it was a straight-
forward question deserving a straight-forward reply
and Tom did not hesitate with his response.

"I am a widower myself. I lost my wife twelve
years ago--cholera the doctor said. So it does not
make a lot of difference how long the trips take--
nothing at Pittsburgh for me except my sister and
her family."

"I am truly sorry. I didn't mean to pry."

"Don't be sorry--and you weren't prying.   You
will find we learn a lot about each other on these
trips and you'd have found out sooner or later."

During the ensuing conversation, Tom explained
how he made his first trip down the Ohio:

"It was in the fall of 1779 and I went all the
way down to The Falls--some call it Clarksville. A
lot of water has gone down the Ohio since then!"

Thomas May was a man among men and had earned
a reputation of being honest and trustworthy. Dave
and Almeretta concluded they were fortunate to have
him as their pilot.

"I would imagine you have had many close calls
during your travels," said Almeretta. "Just staying
alive out here seems to be a matter of chance."

Dave winced--his wife's remark was pessimistic
to say the least. Although her comment did not require an answer, Tom felt it begged for a reply and
he chose his words carefully when he spoke:

"You mentioned having a copy of POOR RICHARD'S ALMANACK and it reminded me of one of those general truths which came from Franklin's pen. Perhaps you have heard of Solomon's maxim, 'A wise man carries his longevity in his hands.' Of that maxim, Doctor Franklin said: 'The element of chance enters into all things much less than we believe!' Rather sage observation it seems to me."

Almeretta was taken a little aback by this bit of philosphy and admitted she would need to ponder this adage before further comment. To herself she also admitted Tom May was both charming and a know-ledgeable conversationalist. Their little informal chat was now abruptly interrupted by the appearance of Hank, his wife, and their daughter. Although he and his wife had only caught the last part of Tom's comment, they were not interested in POOR RICHARD'S ALMANACK or the Gregorian calendar and could care less about philosophy. Thanking Tom for explaining the operation of the sweep, and the comments he had offered, Dave and Alma excused themselves and head-ed along the narrow walkway to the cabin where Dave commented to Jason:

"We sure got ourselves a good pilot!"

The sun climbed steadily as the huge flatboat drifted along with the current. Birds flitted from tree to tree and seemed to provide an escort as the ark glided silently along the ever-widening river. The multi-colored birds made the wilderness around them vocal with their melody and the vivid sunlight scattered golden sparks on the water around them. It was past mid-day, and they were now twenty miles downstream from Fort Pitt, when Tom May pointed out a site where he said John Gibson ran a trading post in 1771. Tom called it Logstown and added:

"Used to be an old Shawnee village here where the Shenango empties into the Ohio. An old Indian trail crossed the river here. By the way, this is the northernmost point of the Ohio River."

The occupants of the ark had no way of knowing

that thirteen turbulent months hence General Wayne, the Scotch-Irish hero of Stony Point, would arrive at this very place in June of 1792. An audacious and adroit politician, and having been selected by President George Washington to command the nation's "military force," Wayne would recruit 2,500 men and organize his army as a "Legion." Recruiting troops along the way, Wayne's expedition would descend the Ohio in 1793 and prepare to march against those who had defeated his predecessor--a man who in April of 1791 stopped briefly at his home near Fort Ligonier while hastening back to Fort Washington from urgent meetings in Philadelphia. And now, even as Tom was maneuvering the ark past Logstown, at Fort Pitt St. Clair was preparing to move down the Ohio River.

With a growing respect for Hank's "wilderness savvy," as Tom called it, the pilot remarked:

"And now we head west Hank! How about keeping your weather-eye open on the bow for any submerged rocks or logs!"

"Aye, aye Captain!"

With Hank up forward, Jason joined Tom on the stern and was there when Hank called out:

"Big rock dead ahead!"

Instinctively Tom threw his weight against the handle of the sweep and the ark narrowly missed the submerged rock. As they passed this obstacle Jason uttered a deep sigh of relief saying:

"Shades of Saint George!"

"You mean the dragon killer?"

Jason was slightly startled by Tom's quick reply and said:

"What do you mean?"

Having maneuvered the ark safely away from the submerged rock, Tom replied:

"Saint George! Wasn't he the patron saint of England who slew a ferocious dragon with his lance and saved the king's daughter? Settler heading for Kentucky last year told me some sculptor from Italy by the name of Donatello carved a marble statue of

Saint George."

Jason shook his head in disbelief--was there a single thing that Tom was not conversant about? In reply Jason merely asked:

"Do you believe in dragons Tom?"

Tom eyed Jason for a moment before answering.

"Well, that's a hard question to answer Jason. Let me put it this way--the way I read Chapter 3 of Genesis, God ordained there would be eternal enmity between serpents, or dragons, and human beings. We all face a few dragons in our lifetime it seems."

Jason listened carefully to what Tom said. In all seriousness he now remarked:

"I chased a lot of dragons along the Monocacy when I was young."

Anxious to steer away from such a serious discussion, Tom smiled as he laughingly asked:

"Catch any? How about the fair maidens being held captive by them fire-eating reptiles? Did you free any?"

Now it was Jason who smiled broadly and said:

"Freed a few I guess!"

Intending to close out the subject, Tom looked Jason squarely in the eye as he counseled:

"To square off with the dragon now and then is just part of life I suppose, but remember one thing son, sometimes that old dragon wins!"

Although Jason did not mention this portion of their conversation, he did tell Mary that Tom said it was from Logstown in 1753 that George Washington had dispatched a message to Fort LeBoeuf demanding the French "cease and desist" encroachment against British lands. And now, in early May of 1791 , the same man was thinking about his former comrade-in-arms, Arthur St. Clair, who had dutifully headed back to Fort Washington to lead a summer campaign against the troublesome Indians.

Standing inside the fenced-in stock enclosure, Jason and Mary watched the passing vistas unmindful they drifted ever closer to an area where no season or day or hour was without peril. The Indians were past masters of wilderness hit-and-run strategy and could move in deadly silence through the very woods where Jason and his companions planned to live--the outlandish Northwest Territory which lay just ahead of them. Now the melancholy wail of a dove drifted to their ears and from somewhere close in the near-by woods the gobble of a turkey could be heard. It was only natural Jason felt an urge to shoulder his rifle but he remembered Tom had admonished against indiscriminate shooting. Mary exclaimed softly:

"It is positively breath taking Jason!"

Along the nearby shore they could see blossoming snowy dogwood which mingled in harmony with the redbud and beautiful white flowers of the vexatious thorn. Purple, white, and red cup-shaped anemones were just emerging and mingled with the soft grass and wild gravevines adding a pleasing perfume which filled the air with an intoxicating fragrance. All around them was a freshness and a newness which was excitingly beautiful. Jason now whispered to Mary:

"Look, over there!

His whisper was accompanied by an index finger pointing to where a clumsy bear moved, reluctantly, away from the river bank and into the tall grass at the edge of the woods. Now the bear raised erect and watched the passing ark with an attitude of unconcern. Having satisfied his curiousity, the bear lumbered away and disappeared in the underbrush and trees where dozens of parakeets could be seen deckout in the rich plummage of gold and green. Paying only slight attention to the passing ark, the birds of the virgin forest busily went on with their work of preparing for their own future.

A few minutes later the Evenstars caught sight of several timid deer moving across a meadow by the river. Although watchfully pausing occasionally to rest, or cautiously feeding, they seemed unmindful of the huge ark passing by so close. Suddenly they gracefully bounded off into the cover of the nearby trees as the deer sensed danger. Just ahead of the ark Mary now caught sight of a huge male deer which was standing by the river taking a drink. Sensing their noiseless approach from upwind, the buck now raised his stately head, carefully looked over the approaching intruder, and then retreated springing over logs and bushes with a single bound and easily out-distancing any real or imagined pursuers. With the exception of the understandable apprehension of Indians who might be lurking in the deep shadows of the primeval forest around them, this was indeed an earthly paradise.

"Work time! I need some help!"

Tom's call brought three men and Hank's boy to the stern quickly. Tom explained:

"Got a shallow ahead we got to go through so a couple of you grab a pole and be ready just in case we run into any trouble. Just walk along the walkway and push. Good idea putting that walkway along the side of the cabin!"

Jason and Hank each grabbed a pole and stood ready near the bow awaiting further commands. Dave also awaited Tom's orders. Several minutes passed before Tom gave them the all clear signal saying:

"Guess that old sand bar has shifted--we won't have to pole her through after all. Thanks gentlemen--and you too young man--for being ready. Takes all of us to crew this ark.   Hank, that young man of yours would make a fine sailor--you want to be a sailor?"

The bashful lad shrugged his shoulders, looked at his dad, and shook his head. Life on a boat did not appeal to him.

Throughout the day Tom explained the operation of the ark and pointed out the dangers of the ever-moving river. He cautioned the men it would be not only necessary to maintain a watch during the daytime, but at night as well. Despite their appreciation for nature's wonders, and the pristine beauty of constantly changing vistas, the air was leaden with danger and insecurity. The fear of an Indian attack, captivity, torture, and massacre hung like a pall over the ark. They could overlook the hardships of moving and river travel but not the menace posed by the red-skinned natives that dogged their footsteps.

Fingers of light pointed where the ark drifted into the setting sun as Tom maneuvered the ark into midstream. With the last glow of sunset spreading over the river like rich butter smeared on homemade bread, and the last drop of daylight leaching from the western sky, Tom called out to Hank:

"Drop the anchor!"

Sheltered by the stock fence, Jason stood near Star and watched the dying sun fade into the hills. His thoughts were miles away when Tom spoke to him:

"Well Jason my boy, what do you think?"

"This is really something! As Dave said, it is indeed unfortunate the Indian threat must spoil what otherwise would be a wonderful sojourn."

They watched a broad-winged hawk circling near the shoreline. The bird's customary silent flight was periodically punctuated by a high-pitched whistling and then it circled in silence again.

"Not very fond of us poaching on its territory this evening," remarked Tom.

Suddenly the hawk made a lightning swift dive. The winged predator's sharp eyesight had enabled it to spot its prey and now the hawk rose triumphantly holding a frog in its vice-like grip. Silently the victor now headed for its nest high in an oak tree silhouetted against an orange sky. With the aerial coup now ended, Tom stretched, pushed his old flop-brimmed hat back, and slowly shook his head. Jason could see the firm set of his jaw as Tom said:

"As you say Jason, it is most unfortunate this Indian menace must plague our travel. However, as you realize I'm sure, in one way we have brought it upon ourselves. Some of the early settlers in this area found the natives quite friendly."

Jason pondered Tom's remark and replied:

"Are you saying it was our greed for land that brought about the Indian problem out here?"

"Probably--that and the British and French who used the Indian's frustrations to their own selfish advantage!"

Even in the vanishing light Jason could see in Tom's eyes the disgust he had for the greediness of the white men he had escorted down the Ohio. Looking toward the narrow band of orange on the western horizon, Tom slowly asked:

"Jason, did you ever hear of a preacher by the name of David Zeisberger and his followers?"

"Cannot say I have Tom. Why?"

"Well, he was a Christian missionary--a leader of some Moravian Brethern who came out to this Ohio country from Pennsylvania and founded a little log cabin community about fifty miles or so ahead where you saw the sun go down. The chief of the Delaware Indians in that area was White Eyes and he welcomed that missionary with open arms I've been told."

Tom's gaze remained fixed on the purple sky in the west as he continued:

"Those Moravians built their first settlement out here and called it Schoenbrunn--means beautiful spring in German. The church held five hundred and they were called to worship by the first bell ever heard in the Ohio country. Not far away they built another settlements--called it Gnadenhutten."

"I have heard the name," said Jason. "Please go on."

"Wouldn't surprise me you had--the incident at Gnadenhutten nine years ago set a lot of tongues to wagging! For years the Delawares out here tried to remain friends with the French and British--and with other Indians too. But, in 1781, the British rangers and some Wyandots forced those peace-loving Delawares who lived near Schoenbrunn to move west to the Sandusky River--those Indians barely existed that winter. When their food supply began to run low, the British allowed a hundred and fifty of the Moravian Indians to come back and gather their un-harvested crops. Then, in early March of 1782, at Gnadenhutten--just south of Schoenbrunn, ninety-six of those Christian Delaware Indians were savagely beaten to death and their death-house was torched. It is said 35 men, 27 women, and 34 children were murdered that night. Two little boys were the only ones who escaped the slaughter which white ruffians then hailed as a 'great victory.'"

"That is absolutely horrible Tom--who on earth would order such a carnage?"

"It was said General Daniel Brodhead ordered a hundred soldiers from Fort Pitt under Colonel David Williamson with instructions to 'teach the Delaware Indians a lesson.' That shameful incident was what happened. According to a story I heard it was some officer named Captain Charles Builderback who did a lot of the killing--those boys who escaped told the story I heard."

Both men were silent for a moment before Jason finally spoke:

"Now that you tell the story, I recall hearing someone mention that massacre. Such an awful thing must have really stirred up the Indians!"

"Naturally. And, only a few months after that Gnadenhutten incident, Colonel William Crawford and that same Colonel Williamson were ordered out from Fort Pitt to 'finish the job' as one fellar told me later. Same fellar said about 480 of them soldiers marched west out of Fort Pitt shouting 'Kill! Kill! Take no prisoners!'"

Jason shook his head slowly as Tom continued:

"Well, the Indians were waiting and in June it was not surprising they put that army to rout along the Sandusky. I understand Colonel Williamson made it back safely but Colonel Crawford was burned at the stake--he died a horrible death according to an eye witness who later escaped. It was the Indian's turn for revenge."

"Where did you say Gnadenhutten was?"

"Not more than fifty miles due west from where the Ohio bends south downstream. We ought to reach that point by high noon tomorrow the Lord willing!"

Jason said nothing as Tom now removed his hat, scratched his graying head, and added:

"Its a real shame son--such senseless killings are bound to be followed by cruel retaliation! And the British, they are always fanning the flames of the Indian's hate and frustration. Some missionary folks tried to bring Christianity to the Indians in this country out here but they got all caught up in the bitterness of the settlers moving west and the Revolutionary War. You were a little too young for that one I guess."

"You are right--just a little young in 1776."

"You was fortunate. I was at Valley Forge the winter of 1777 and it was miserable I can tell you. Had it not been for General Washington we might all have gone home--maybe lost the war!"

After an awkward pause Jason broke the silence saying:

"I understand things were mighty rough for you men that winter. Hank was in that war you know."

"That's what I hear. Suppose he told you that General George had quite a temper. But I will say this for him, he was a fair man--treated all of the men justly. Yes sir, things were bad that winter-- you never forget something like that I suppose."

"I heard Hank and some other veterans talking back along the Monongahela about their service that winter--one called it 'The Winter of Despair.'"

"Describes it pretty well Jason--couple of bad years I don't look back on fondly."

Tom said nothing for a long time--he seemed to be lost in his thoughts and Jason remained silent. At long last the pilot cleared his throat and said:

"Lost my missus a short time after that winter at Valley Forge. Took a ball in the leg at German-town when we were chasing General Howe. So cussed foggy that morning you couldn't see—not sure if it was an enemy ball or one of ours that did me in!"

Tom smiled weakly and added:

"Anyway, that wound never did heal right and I was discharged in the spring of 1778. My wife died in June after that."

"I am truly sorry to hear that Tom."

"Never will forget that day Jason. Just after the missus died we had a solar eclipse—turned the noon into night. Coming so soon after my wife died it was real frightening. Guess the Lord was trying to tell me something but I never figured out what."

Although Jason said nothing, something Tom had said earlier flashed across his mind:

"Sometimes the dragon wins!"

Once again an awkward silence was broken when Tom remarked:

"Dave and his wife were telling me about meeting that settler over north of Stewart's Crossing—one from down on Dunkard Creek."

Jason nodded and Tom continued:

"Well, I didn't want to say any thing in front of the ladies but coming back to Pittsburgh from my last trip downstream I came back overland from Fort Henry and at Washington it was being said an Indian party wiped out a family name of Bozarth on Dunkard Creek a couple years ago. Story was the father and three kids were killed but his missus got away."

Jason didn't say a word—he remembered hearing that discouraged settler they met mention the name of that family living on Dunkard Creek. From somewhere nearby the hoot of an owl broke the stillness and from far away a wolf's wailing cry sent shivers up Jason's back. Tom broke the silence saying:

"Speaking of Indians taking kids reminds me of a story told about old John Moore in Virginia who had two of his daughters captured during the French and Indian War—the one he called Margaret was only nine years old at the time. When the war was over and both sides agreed to release prisoners, Peggy—

that's what they called her--came back home saying
she had married a Shawnee chief by the name of Blue
Jacket and had given birth to a half-blood son that
she called Joseph.* She was also pregnant again and
had another half-blood she named Nancy. Folks down
in Virginia didn't doubt she came home pregnant but
there wasn't any proof the father was anyone but an
Indian--he sure wasn't a white man if both her kids
were half-bloods."

Jason was pondering what Tom had said when his
wife's voice beckoned:

"How about a little food for you hard-working
gentlemen--or should I say 'gentleman?' You do not
appear to have earned your salt today Jason!"

Needing no prodding, and hungry as a couple of
bears, both men now carefully made their way toward
the stern along the narrow walkway as Jason said:

"That woman of mine does not appreciate me."

"I heard that remark Jason Evenstar!"

Mary tried to sound stern but the love in her
voice betrayed her--she knew full well that he knew
she appreciated him. It was Tom who now cheerfully
interjected:

"She called us 'gentlemen' Jason--I'd say your
wife is a fine judge of character! And the mention
of food sure is music to my ears."

Tom rubbed his hands together briskly as they
entered the cabin door and exclaimed:

"I'm hungry--my old backbone's rubbing my belt
buckle and I'm drier than an old maid's lips!"

As Tom and Jason entered the cabin, Dave picked up his gun and quickly exited--he had the first
night watch. Hank's eldest son had cared for the
animals and then, having enjoyed some hot foot, had
taken a seat beside his brothers near the fireplace

---

* A property deed, signed at Fort Wayne October 2, 1810
  granted to "Joseph Moore, a (Shawnee) half-breed, land
  along the Miami River.

where they talked about the events of the day. It had been an exciting day and the women and children quickly sought refuge in their respective sleeping quarters. Hank remarked as he prepared to join his wife and children:

"This river travel makes a fellar tired!"

Seated quietly by the fire in Jason's homemade rocker, and puffing on an old pipe, Tom watched the orange and yellow flames dance in the fireplace and the wavering shadows they cast on the blankets and walls of the cabin. Although the old pilot had put in a busy day and was rather sleepy, the inviting warmth of the fire made him a bit reluctant to seek his sleeping quarters. With everyone except Dave and Tom now asleep—and the silence broken only by occasional snoring, the sound of a horse stamping, and the crackling of the wood in the fireplace—the old pilot dozed off. Suddenly Tom's little nap was interrupted as Dave whispered:

"Everybody asleep in there?"

Tom was instantly wide awake and instinctively glanced toward the cabin doorway where Dave stood bathed in the yellow glow from the fireplace. In a low voice like rolling thunder Tom exclaimed:

"Dave, for God's sake, get out of that light! You're a sitting duck silhouetted in that doorway—best way I know to make Alma a widow. You can die soon enough out here without making yourself a sacrificial lamb!"

Having said this, Tom quietly moved to where a blanket over a pile of pine needles offered a most welcome retreat from the day's labor. Although he was nonplussed by Tom's stern rebuke, Dave realized the admonishment was for his own good. And it was a warning he turned over in his mind many times as he moved carefully around the deck the remainder of his watch.

Jason had the midnight watch and "slept like a log" as his uncle Conrad often used to say. It was a rather strange sensation sleeping on the boat but

the gentle undulation was soothing and the sound of
heavy breathing did not disturb him. From just in
front of the cabin the horse's hooves made muffled
thuds as they stamped the floor which had been covered with several inches of earth--riding on a boat
was a strange sensation for the animals too. Jason
slept soundly and never stirred until Dave awakened
him saying:

"Sorry Jason, your turn in the barrel! Everything is quiet as a mouse in church."

Without a word Jason gathered up his rifle and
pouch and then checked to be certain his knife was
in the sheath on his boot. Dave waited until his
relief had disappeared through the doorway into the
quarter-moon darkness and then he quickly retired.

Adjusting to the darkness, Jason now carefully
made his way to the stern and relieved himself into
the water below. Except for the incessant croaking
of frogs, and an occasional night bird sweeping low
over the trespassing flatboat, the silence was only
broken by the sound of water gently lapping around
the hull. On both sides of the river a seemingly
impenetrable wall of black velvet rose to where it
blended with a million eyes of the night. Now and
then the hooting of an owl or the mournful cry of a
nightbird pierced the stillness.

Keeping a sharp lookout, Jason moved about the
ark avoiding making any sound which might alarm the
others. Like waiting for the drip-drip of sap from
a sugar maple to fill a bucket, the minutes passed.
Entering the animal enclosure, in the semi-darkness
Jason could see the cows standing silently and the
sheep huddled together in the little area which had
been partitioned off for them. Except for the usual
sounds of that time of early morning, it was quiet.
As he now stepped to where he could pat Star's head
and allow the animal to nuzzle his hand, from somewhere far away the cry of a wolf broke the still of
the night and sent a surge of loneliness and isolation through his body. Star also heard the wolf's

lonesome wail. As the nervous horse now jerked its
head away from his hand, Jason said in a low voice:
"Easy. Easy there boy."
"That you Jason?"
Jason recognized Hank's voice and whispered:
"Its me Hank--over here in the stock pen."
"Figured it was. I'll take over now. You can
still ketch a few winks before sunup."
With breakfast over, everyone assembled around
the fireplace for Sunday worship service. With the
first rays of sunshine streaming through the open
trap doors, and Tom standing watch just outside the
doorway keeping a sharp lookout for any Indians who
might be lurking along the shore, Jason led them in
a prayer of thanks for the bountiful blessings be-
stowed upon them. Hank's youngest child asked him
to be sure and include a special thanks to the Lord
for their ark--he did. As Jason played his violin,
Mary sang a hymn and then everyone joined together
in singing another beautiful hymn. Dave now read a
short passage from the Bible and then concluded the
service with the fourth verse of the 23rd Psalm:
"Yea, though I walk through the valley of the
shadow of death, I will fear no evil........"
In spite of everyone's belief in the sanctity
of the Sabbath, all things being considered, it was
agreed travel this Sunday would be advisable. With
the morning service concluded, Tom ordered Hank to
"hoist the anchor!" As if voicing agreement travel
on this Sabbath would not violate God's will, birds
kept the woods alive with their melodious tunes.
Occasionally the huge ark would drift close to
the river bank as Tom expertly steered around some
hidden danger. Now and then the gobble of a turkey
or rumbling of a partridge along the shore could be
heard. Jason noticed Tom avoided overhanging trees
and any nearby dense underbrush which might conceal
some animal or an Indian--such pitfalls their pilot
avoided like the plague. As Dave watched the pilot
carefully moving the sweep, he pointed to the shore

nearby saying:

"Sure looks peaceful enough!"

Tom smiled but his face clouded as he replied:

"From here--yes! Shame such an earthly bit of paradise also contains so many hidden dangers--the deadly copperhead, the coiled rattlesnake, and then of course, the Indians with their guns and bows and arrows.   Trails through that wilderness over there can be dangerous beyond your wildest imagination."

Tom paused and pulled on his old pipe noisily. He looked at his pipe thoughtfully and then glanced at Dave. Almost as an apology Tom added:

"Don't mean to paint a bad picture of this old country out here--just suggesting we must be mighty careful. No substitute for caution you know!   For example, and something a lot of settler folks learn to their sorrow, those bears like we saw yesterday aren't afraid of a man--they may attack in the face of danger to them. Don't know any better I guess."

The changing vistas provided a relief from the humdrum of just drifting with the current. Now and then the pilot pointed out various landmarks to men on deck and the women and children inside the cabin were occasionally permitted to cautiously peer from the trap door. Strategically located holes between the side timbers also enabled insiders to watch the passing vistas. Inside, and aided by the brilliant sunshine streaming through the open trap doors--and carefully placing her rocker to avoid being direct- ly in front of the open doorway, Mary read to the children from a book she recently purchased.

"This is a collection of verses, poems, little ditties, and songs from William Shakespeare's plays --it is called 'Mother Goose's Melody.' The store- keeper in Pittsburgh from whom I obtained this book last week said it was first printed in 1768 by the John Newberry publishing house in England. This is a reprint by an American publisher, Isaiah Thomas. It was printed only five years ago in 1786."

Having listened carefully as Mary read "Little

Tom Tucker," Hank's daughter asked:

"Who is Mother Goose?"

"I have heard many answers to that question my dear. One of my teachers said she was the Queen of Sheba who lived in Biblical times but my father was of the opinion she was the mother of Charlemagne, a great military leader of the Holy Roman Empire who lived a thousand years ago. In our library in Baltimore there was a book titled "Histories or Tales of Past Times, With Morals." It had an interesting engraving on the cover showing an old woman sitting by the fireplace telling stories to some children-- just like you."

Glancing at Sarah and Almeretta, Mary added:

"Of course the storyteller was much older than yours you understand."

Mary smiled pleasantly and continued:

"In any case, a small sign on the wall in that engraving read 'Contes de Ma Mere L'oye.' That is French. Translated in our language it means 'Tales of Mother Goose.' Originally written in French by Charles Perrault, it was translated into English in 1729 by Robert Samber. I always did enjoy reading the story of Red Riding Hood, Sleeping Beauty, and Cinderella in that book."

As the spellbound children seated on the floor listened, Mary looked at her book after saying:

"Now children, let us see which one of you can give me the answer to this riddle:

> What runs all day and never walks,
> Sometimes murmurs but never talks;
> It has a bed but never sleeps,
> It has a mouth but never eats!"

Absorbed in her reading, Mary failed to notice Jason and Tom quietly enter the cabin. Giving Mary their undivided attention, and now pleading for the answer, the children paid little attention to Jason when he added his request for the answer saying:

"We give up--what is the answer?"

Glancing up, Mary saw the smiling faces of Tom and Jason standing just inside the doorway. With a mischievous smile, she now politely ignored Jason's question and her eyes sparkled as they slowly swept over the upturned faces impatiently waiting for her to give the answer. With a tinge of seriousness in her voice, she ended the suspense saying:

"A river! A river like the one we are on now. It never walks--runs day and night. The river does have a bed, but it never stops to sleep. Our pilot says the Ohio river has a mouth far away downstream but it never eats. And if we listen carefully, you can hear the river murmur. But, unlike some people I know, the river never, never talks."

The last few words were obviously intended for Jason's ears and Mary glanced at her husband as she wrinkled up her nose, gave him a polite snoot, and then smiled broadly. It was Jason who then said:

"Touche Mrs. Evenstar!"

Moments before, and standing on the stern, Tom had pointed to where the Beaver Creek emptied into the Ohio and Jason had suggested the pilot repeat a story for the children he related. With the answer to the riddle no longer a mystery, Jason explained to Mary and the children the purpose of this sudden intrusion. Pointing his index finger ominously in the direction of the shore, Tom began:

"As I was just telling Jason, last year I tied up here to take on some wood and two boys--nine and eleven they were--jumped off to play. Quicker than a wink some Indians snatched them boys and took off into the woods right over there."

Once again Tom pointed toward the north shore and one of Hank's boys stepped over to the wall and stared for a moment through a crack at that shoreline with awe stricken eyes. Not a sound was heard as Tom added:

"We took off after those Indians but it was so late in the day we couldn't follow the red-skinned

rascals very far--had to come back and wait for it
to come daylight. Well now, don't you know those
boys waited until the Indians were sound asleep and
then they sneaked away! Took themselves a tomahawk
and gun and found their way back to this very spot
where we was still tied up. Like I told Jason, the
boys were mighty smart--and lucky too."

Urged to tell "another story," Tom obliged by
telling how five Linn brothers had been captured by
an Indian war party.

"At the Indian's village those white boys were
forced to run between two rows of Indian children
who tried to knock them down. When one of the Linn
brothers lashed out and struck one of the offending
Indian boys, the older Indian braves did not interfere. The Indians have their own code of fair play
and those Linn boys punched their way to victory in
that uneven free-for-all. Their courage and fighting ability so impressed the Indians that the tribe
adopted every single one of the Linn brothers!"

None of Jason's party knew if these stories he
told were true, but the children did not stray from
their boat the rest of the journey downstream. And
occasionally during the months ahead they were destined to hear others relate the same stories--maybe
it really did happen just the way Tom said.

That afternoon Jason carefully ushered Mary up
the narrow walkway and they entered the boarded-in
stock enclosure. Because of Mary's "condition," he
suggested to their pilot she needed some sunshine--
Tom agreed. Seated on two short up-ended pieces of
log, and with the enclosure door propped open, Mary
enjoyed the panoramic view. As their ark finished
drifting through a long sweeping curve, Jason took
notice of the fact the sun was now to their right
whereas it had been almost in front of them. While
pondering the change, a voice behind them was heard
saying:

"Out that way about fifty miles is that place
I was telling you about yesterday Jason."

Both turned to see Tom sitting on top of their cabin looking down at them.

"What are you doing up there? And who—who is steering this ark?"

Jason's somewhat startled questions brought a big smile to Tom's face and he slowly replied:

"We're out of gunshot from the shore Jason and your friend Hank handles that sweep like a veteran pilot. Don't worry, I'm keeping a weather eye open for Indians. But, like I said, Schoenbrunn if over that way.

Tom pointed toward where the sun was suspended halfway in the western sky. With a puzzled look on her face, Mary looked at Tom and then back at her husband. In a questionable manner she asked Jason:

"Shoenbrunn? Did I hear him correctly?"

Mary recalled having read about Schoenbrunn in Vienna, Austria—a beautiful palace with 1400 rooms built in the late 1600s by the emperor of the Holy Roman Empire, Leopold I. He had hoped this "summer residence" would outshine all of the royal palaces in Europe and even eclipse the Palace of Versailles which King Louis XIV of France had built at a cost of more than $160,000,000. Marie-Antoinette, born in 1755, spent her childhood in Schoenbrunn and, as fate would ironically decree, was the last queen of France to live at Versailles. From here she was to be taken to the guillotine in 1793. But now in the spring of 1791, Mary could not understand why these men would be talking about Schoenbrunn.

"Yes Mary, Schoenbrunn. Last evening Tom told me about some Moravian Indians who lived just south of Schoenbrunn—place he called Gnadenhutten."

"Oh yes. One of the ladies in camp back along the Monongahela talked about a senseless slaying in some village south of Fort Laurens—I do believe it was the one you mentioned. She said it provoked a great deal of unrest in that area. But that is far away from where we are going—is it not Jason?

As Mary talked, Tom climbed down from where he

was seated and carefully made his way through the animal enclosure to where the Evenstars were seated in the sunshine. He understood the look of anguish on Mary's face and saw no purpose in repeating that depressing story wherein Colonel William Crawford--a friend of George Washington since 1747 when they worked together surveying lands of Lord Fairfax in the Shenandoah Valley--had marched west from Mingo Bottom in 1782 and passed through the area south of where Fort Laurens had stood. That march had taken him through Gnadenhutten where the "senseless slaying" Mary mentioned had taken place. The fort she referred to--one designed by a lieutenant from Fort Pitt, the Chevalier de Cambray-Digny--was the only Revolutionary War fort erected in the Ohio country. Erected during the winter of 1778-79, Fort Laurens had been quickly destroyed by British and Indian attacks led by Sir Henry Hamilton and the renegades Simon Girty, Alexander McKee, and Matthew Elliott. Lt. Colonel Daniel Brodhead, Colonel John Gibson's successor, had found it advisable to withdraw from Fort Laurens in August of 1779 and was anxious for an opportunity to seize the initiative against the Indians. The meaningless massacre at Gnadenhutten had been hailed as "the first step!"

Tom would never forget the Indian's revengeful ambush of Colonel Crawford and Colonel Williamson's command on June 4, 1782 about 60 miles southeast of where the Maumee empties into Lake Erie. There, in the Indian way of fighting from the cover of trees, Captain William Caldwell's woods-wise force of 100 British Rangers, and about 200 Delaware and Wyandot Indians, soon put the army to rout and took several prisoners. Called by the Indians "Sauganash" which meant "The Englishman," Captain Caldwell had at his side McKee, Elliott, and Girty. Probably fearing a similar fate should they try to intervene, none of of these renegades could save Colonel Crawford from the Indian's revengeful hate.

Jason did not answer Mary's question directly.

He concluded it might be better not to say anything about the proximity of Schoenbrunn to "where we are going." By way of an answer he did say:

"Mary, please do not be concerned--you should not be getting yourself all worked up just now. We both realize that British colonial ambitions in the Ohio country have been a problem for years but with the arrival of so many new settlers out here in the Northwest Territory, I feel confident everything is bound to be better."

Tom listened to Jason's optimistic comment and said nothing--he knew it would not be appropriate just now to mention they would soon be passing the mouth of Yellow Creek. But Mary was still thinking about the poor Indians who had been savagely killed at the place called Schoenbrunn. Realizing Jason's commentary was evasive, Mary decided on a different approach. Looking at Tom she said:

"Tell me, were those Moravians the first white folks to move out to this country?"

Tom glanced at Jason and then back to Mary as he replied:

"Heavens no, settlers have been coming out to this Ohio country for years. A few here and a few there. Then there was Mary Harris--she is said to have been the first white woman to live out here!"

The insincere grin on Tom's face prompted Mary to say:

"All right Tom, please do not tease--you know very well I am anxious to learn more about the Mary Harris you mentioned."

Realizing Mary was eagerly waiting to hear his reply, Tom glanced at Jason mischievously, studied the back of his hand a moment, and then said:

"Well, its like this Mary. About forty--maybe fifty years ago--the Indians raided a settlement up in Massachusetts called Deerfield. Old timers call it the 'Deerfield Massacre.' The Delawares carried away a ten year old girl by the name of Mary Harris and brought her out here to the Ohio country where, sometime before 1750, she married Eagle Feather, a Delaware chief."

"That is it?" Somehow Mary expected more.

"That's it! That's all I know Mary. She was, according to what I have been told, the <u>first</u> white woman out here. There's been several stories about white women prisoners marrying Indians out here but the one about Mary Harris must be the first."

Mary glanced at Jason. She was contemplating asking Tom about the story they had heard regarding Margaret Moore when Tom said:

"But, back to your question about the settlers coming out here on their own. The Indian unrest--provoked of course by the British and French before them--hasn't made it easy for anyone to get a foot-hold in the country west of here."

Tom paused. He had chosen his words carefully avoiding any mention of the fact it was right here, in late April of 1774, that the Mingo Chief Logan's pregnant sister, her husband, and their guards, had been savagely murdered. Tom's thoughtful pause was interrupted when Mary exclaimed:

"What pray tell is that?"

Mary had spotted a blockhouse among the trees at the mouth of a stream. Tom hesitated and looked at Jason before he replied:

"That's an old blockhouse on Yellow Creek near where old Chief Logan of the Mingos lived some time ago. He was friendly with the white man then."

Attempting to change the subject, Tom said:

"Downstream a ways is Mingo Botton--might drop anchor there this evening. As early as 1766 there were about sixty families in a little settlement at Mingo Bottom--only white settlement on the Ohio be-tween Pennsylvania and The Falls at the time. Some Iroquois lived there back in 1750 I understand. It was probably here at Yellow Creek, or down below at Mingo Junction, that Reverend Zeisberger took leave of the Ohio and headed west to Schoenbrunn."

Tom wasn't certain he had laid Mary's question

to rest--she still had a perplexed look on her face and appeared to be deep in thought. Still, perhaps his many faceted commentary had steered the conversation away from that atrocity along the Tuscarawas on March 7, 1782. Jason had talked with him about Mary's "condition" so Tom felt it was inappropriate to mention anything concerning that unfortunate incident which occurred here nineteen years ago. As Mary now said something about "the beautiful shoreline," Tom smiled as Jason gave him a quick knowing look. Unbeknown to Mary, her husband drew in a big breath and gave a quiet sigh of relief.

Everything was going just fine until suddenly Dave called down from where he had seated himself on the edge of the cabin roof:

"Hey Tom! Wasn't it someplace along here that some fellar named Greathouse and a gang of ruffians butchered old Chief Logan's pregnant sister and her husband?"

Tom looked at Jason and Jason looked at Mary. Mary looked straight into the old pilot's surprised face as she quickly remarked:

"You did not mention that Thomas!"

Tom knew he was in trouble and he cleared his throat before saying:

"Well Mary, its like this--I'm not certain who it was that did that dastardly deed Dave's talking about. Daniel Greathouse has been accused of being involved in that atrocity but there are folks hereabouts who swear he is not to blame. There is also the story that Captain Michael Cresap had a hand in that unwarranted killing and Chief Logan had Major Robinson write a letter to him asking why he would do such a terrible thing."

Tom was referring to a letter reported to have been written by Major William Robinson on July 21st following that dreadful incident. Tom added:

"And who can say what prompted Major Robinson to write that letter for Chief Logan? Indians can be very persuasive at times!"

Tom glanced at Jason and then continued:

"Cresap just may have been involved in another senseless incident downstream at Captina about that same time, but many folks around here say he wasn't even near Yellow Creek at the time and shouldn't be blamed for killing Logan's family. Matter of fact, a lot of folks hereabouts blame the Virginia governor's agent, John Connolly! He was spreading a lot of hate and discontent in southwestern Pennsylvania about then--caused so much dissension St. Clair had him arrested just a few months before that dreadful incident. But, with all his Tory friends, Connolly was quickly released on bail."

Indeed, the normally affable Arthur St. Clair, representative of the proprietors of Pennsylvania in the west, had been so angered by Connolly's continued unscrupulous conduct asserting that the land in western Pennsylvania was a part of Virginia, he ordered the rabble rouser be arrested January 25th, 1774. Tom's commentary prompted Mary to interrupt politely:

"St. Clair? Arthur St. Clair? Jason's uncle Conrad always spoke so highly of him. I presume we are talking about the same person."

"We are," replied Tom. "St. Clair is not only a gentleman and a scholar, he will be an excellent governor for this new territory. But, he does have his work cut out for him!"

Tom paused thoughtfully and then added:

"Oh yes, as I was saying a moment ago, there's always a lot of finger-pointing and tongue-wagging after such senseless killings as this one at Yellow Creek and the one over at Gnadenhutten--everyone is quick to lay the blame on someone. There are those who say David Williamson should not be censured for that grisly affair at Gnadenhutten. The colonel, a young militia officer, had a number of those in his command who had seen their wife and children killed or captured by Indians--seen their homes looted and burned! Although it is said the colonel was not in favor of killing the Indians, he was caught between a rock and a hard place. He put the matter up to a vote and he lost."

"You mean the Indians lost!"

Mary's hasty remark brought a little smile to Tom's face and he cheerfully replied:

"Perhaps that is a better way to put it. Your husband told me you were a school teacher and I had to be careful with my words."

The smile on Tom's face faded as continued:

"As I told Jason yesterday, I don't approve of killing any human being, red or white! What I hope you understand is this Mary, out here there's been a lot of hard feelings, bitterness, and frustration on both sides and no law to protect the settlers or the Indians from the unjust acts of the other. The injured party is generally quick to lash out at the other party--all they can think of is striking back at someone! It is also unfortunate that for years there has been this feeling by a few on both sides that extermination of the other is the only road to a lasting peace--that feeling must change!"

Tom looked at Jason who nodded and then turned to Mary smiling broadly as he said:

"Excuse me folks. I think it best I get off my soapbox and take a turn at the sweep. Hank may think I fell overboard. Come on Dave!"

Motioning for Dave to follow, Tom headed for the stern thinking to himself:

"Dave's question may have been inopportune but its high time these folks understand how things are out here in this country."

With Tom now steering the ark, and Hank's boy watching carefully every movement of the huge sweep as they drifted by a narrow shoal of sand along the shore, the pilot suddenly pointed his finger toward the west where a blockhouse stood half-hidden among the trees.

"Look over there! That's Fort Steuben--named it in honor of that German who came over to help us in 1777. Remember General von Steuben Hank?"

"Sure do! Some men didn't care much for that discipline but General Washington sure knew what he was doing when he put him in charge of training us dunderheads!"

"Good thing he was on our side," Tom added.

Hank's son glanced toward his father and then turned to Tom saying:

"Why did they build a fort way out here?"

"Well son, Congress passed a Land Ordinance in 1785 which said the land out here would be surveyed using the rectangular survey method. You take your dad and me, we were raised thinking land boundaries were always measured using metes and bounds."

"And tomahawk rights," interjected Hank with a chuckle. "Takes book larnin' now! My Sarah is set on Will here and the others gittin' book larnin'."

"Reading, writing, and arithmetic! Dad always said a man should get all of the education he could because it was one thing no person could ever take away from him. It opens a lot of doors," said Tom.

Hank grinned as he drawled:

"I've opened up a lot of doors with a big club or these fists! But I know what you're trying to say--I don't need a tree to fall on me. My wife is always singing the same tune."

Although Hank's boy looked a bit puzzled, Tom understood. Turning to the young man, he said:

"Back to your question Will. In the summer of 1785 the United States sent General Benjamin Tupper out here to start work on surveying the land northwest of the Ohio. General Rufus Putnam was offered the job, but he deferred to his good friend Tupper, saying he had an interest in land north of Rutland, Massachusetts that needed his attention. Impressed with the potential of this area, Tupper rushed back to Rutland in January of 1786 where he and Putnam put together a plan for buying and selling land out here and formed an Ohio Company of Associates--some of those shareholders are at Marietta now. As for

Fort Steuben over there, General Tupper's surveyors and woodsmen built it. Men like James Foulks, John Cuppy, Isaac Miller, James Downing, and others too, were working out of there five years ago surveying what is called 'The Seven Ranges.' One surveyor, a man named Israel Ludlow, said the weather out here, and the Indians, make survey work in this country a real challenge!

Hank's son thanked Tom for his commentary and then the pilot said:

"Knowing the river is an important part of the a pilot's job but keeping this ark afloat is everyone's job--yours and mine. There's more to it than just steering! Those who watch for sunken logs and sand bars and fallen trees are an important part of getting any boat this size downstream safely."

The men took turns maintaining a sharp lookout for Indians and the hidden dangers of a river whose treacherous swirling waters could be unforgiving of carelessness or a mistake. Even Hank's eldest son took his turn and was proud of his responsibility. But, as Tom cautioned Will:

"Our lives are in your hands young man!"

But regardless of task assignments, Tom always seemed to be somewhere in the background carefully watching over his charges. As Dave complained to Jason when they were alone in the stock enclosure:

"Alma says he's like an old setting hen!"

Although Jason did not care for this demeaning remark, he said nothing. After all, everyone else appeared to appreciate Tom's alert watchfulness.

On the third evening of their journey, Tom ordered the anchor dropped opposite Fort Henry. That night, after their evening meal, the ark passengers listened as Tom told how the Iroquois had given up all land southeast of that point in 1768 for 10,000 British pounds paid by the Penn family. Tom said:

"But even though the confederacy of Iroquois-- the Six Nations--supposedly gave up the land southeast of here, settlers were repeatedly plagued with

Indian raids. But those Germans, Dutch, Scotch and Irish would not leave.   A stubborn lot they were-- especially the Irish!"

With a twinkle in his eye, Tom glanced at Mary and winked. She had apologized to him for being "a wee bit curt" as she put it. He continued:

"As I said, they were a stubborn lot and even boldly informed the king back in 1771 they wanted a separate government. The Revolutionary War did put a quietus to their clamor but they fought hard for the cause. Several Indian parties, led by British officers, came into this area between 1777 and 1782 but they couldn't chase these settlers out."

Fiercely independent, the area Tom referred to would be the State of West Virginia in 1863 but not before a bitter political fight in 1861 when people proposed their region should be called the state of "Kanawha." Having lighted his pipe, Tom added:

"It was back about 1770 when twenty-three year old Ebenezer Zane founded a settlement here--called it Wheeling. This was a strategic point because of its advantages for trade with the interior so they built a fort here. In the beginning they called it Fort Fincastle but in 1776 it was renamed in honor of Virginia's governor, Patrick Henry."

Dave's wife now interrupted with a question:

"Was Ebenezer Zane related to Betty Zane?"

"Brother is all," replied Tom. His smile faded as he thoughtfully added: "But seriously, the woman you mentioned might have helped save that fort over there in early September of 1782 when Captain Bradt led British soldiers, the Girtys, and some Indians against Fort Henry. Colonel Zane had built a house about sixty yards from the fort and resolved he was not going to leave that house until the end if need be. According to a story told me by a woodsman who had been down south in Abbs' Valley digging ginseng and was heading up to Pittsburgh when he got caught in that attack, the men in the colonel's house ran short of powder and some woman volunteered to dash

over to the fort and carry back eight or ten pounds
of the precious gunpowder--said it was Betty Zane."

Ginseng , a perennial plant with three to five
leaves, has a long, fleshy root which can be dried
and ground into a powder. This herb is used medic-
inally in many foreign countries as a cure for various illnesses. Woodsmen who harvested ginseng for
export to China found a ready market in Pittsburgh.
Ginseng's medicinal use was not on Almeretta's mind
as she sharply commented:

"Whoever that man was, he must have been chewing that ginseng root! Dave and me heard that same
story in Hagars Town last year but as I recall, the
woman's name was Molly Scott, not Betty Zane!"

Tom looked at Dave's wife attentively as she
added in a pedantic manner:

"Well, the tavern keeper said he was told that
story by someone who was there at the time."

Without hesitation Tom courteously said:

"That tavern keeper might be right Alma--I was
not there.   But it is just one of the many stories
you hear about border warfare here and the names do
get a little mixed up.   But I'll do my best to get
the name of that brave woman straightened out in my
head the next time I pass through Wheeling."

With the same self-satisfied look on her face,
Almeretta now remarked:

"And those Girty brothers--we heard no mention
of them."

Tom scratched the side of his head and studied
Alma's face for a moment before replying:

"Well, its like this. I'll admit the names of
of those Girty brothers--Simon, George, and James--
do seem to be connected with every incident in the
Ohio country. They were taken prisoners by Indians
in 1756 when kids and James was raised by Shawnees,
George by Delawares, and Simon--the renegade called
'The White Savage'--grew up among the Senecas tribe
and worked for the British before the war. Its not
surprising the Girtys brothers have thrown in with

the Indians and British.   Anyway, their names seem
to crop up everytime something bad happens out here
in this country.   I heard the Girtys were among the
British and Indians when they stormed Fort Henry in
1777 and 1782 but I can't be certain.   Some of what
I tell you is what has been told to me and I am the
first to admit it."

Glancing at Jason and then at Mary, Tom added:

"Like I was saying this afternoon, it is often
difficult to separate truth from fiction and I do
appreciate questions concerning anything I say."

Two hundred years later a knowledgeable person
would voice a sage observation concerning "truth."
Calling truth a "demure lady," he would say "people
must want her, and seek her out."

"What was all that talk this afternoon about a
ferry back upstream?"

Dave's question pertained to something Tom had
mentioned to Hank. As Tom now explained:

"That was Martin's Ferry.   As I told Hank, it
just may be the oldest white settlement in the Ohio
country."

The comment brought a mild look of surprise to
Dave's face who quickly exclaimed:

"I thought Marietta was the first settlement?"

"It was and it wasn't! Marietta was the first
white settlement in the Ohio country <u>after</u> that Ordinance of 1787 created this vast 'Territory Of The
United States Northwest Of The River Ohio' as it is
officially called. However, years ago enterprising
pioneers of western Pennsylvania and Virginia had
crossed this Ohio and started small settlements out
west of here a long time before those fellars from
Massachusetts and Connecticut floated downstream to
the mouth of the Muskingum. Friend of mine at Fort
Pitt told me there were more settlers living in the
Ohio country in 1785 than there were at Marietta in
1789 but the majority have been driven out by the
government soldiers who claim they are trespassers.
They've tried to band together and resist what they

feel is government interference but they have been unsuccessful."

Tom took a few puffs on his pipe and added:

"Many of those who peacefully retired to lands south or east of the Ohio are now heading back--and others too! There's just something in the blood of some people that makes them want to be right on the edge of the frontier!"

He was right--the restless pioneer settlers of those "diaper years" of this country's early growth were always found in advance of the westward movement. Industrious, thrifty, and intelligent, more than one-third of Pennsylvania's population in 1776 were of German and Swiss descent. Scattered among the remaining populace were the land-hungry Scotch, Dutch, and Irish. All thirsted for frontier land-- and the freedom they could enjoy there.

Jason and the others now watched Tom as he re-lighted his pipe with a flaming splinter of wood he extracted carefully from the fireplace. Finally he commented:

"I've been bringing a lot of settlers down the Ohio these past few years--mighty interesting folks I must say. I always learn so much from them--more probably than they learn from me! One thing I have noticed is that most folks talk about the 'freedom' they hope to find out here in this country."

Tom carefully examined the tobacco in his pipe and took several puffs as Dave now enthusiastically interjected:

"That's what got me and Alma here all fired up about this country--freedom! We heard it said the Northwest Territory offered more freedoms than any-place in America--freedom of religion, the right of a trial by jury, freedom from slavery, and....well, you know what I mean."

Everyone appeared to be waiting for Tom to say something. After thoughtfully searching the faces of those around him, Tom looked at Dave and said:

"I know what you mean. Its the same feeling a

lot of folks have as they push across the mountains and head for this country out here."

Tom's eyes were dead serious as they now swept across his audience before continuing:

"But, and I beg you good people not take any offense at my observation, isn't it interesting how many of those who seek freedom see nothing wrong in curtailing the freedom of others."

There was complete silence before Dave's wife commented rather smugly:

"Appears our good pilot has a soft spot in his heart for the Indians! Life on this river road do that to a man out here? No offense intended Tom."

Regardless of how Alma had intended her remark to be taken, no one was amused. Even Dave quickly nudged his wife saying:

"Oh, hush up Alma! You don't know what you're talking about."

Looking her squarely in the eye, Tom said:

"Its all right Almaretta--no offense taken. I think I mentioned the other day that people seem to speak their mind on these trips--the farther we go down this river road, the better acquainted we will become. As for your comment, please do not mistake heartfelt respect for the rights of another human being to be that of an 'Indian lover' as some might think you are implying. That would indeed be very unfortunate I assure you!"

The message in the old pilot's eyes was unmistakeable and everyone, including Almaretta, understood what he meant. Dave glanced quickly at Hank and Jason but said nothing. Gentleman that he was, Tom now broke the tension as he pointed a pipe stem toward the eastern bank of the river saying:

"Speaking of going down this river road, a few years ago I brought a settler down from Pittsburgh who planted some peach trees over by Fort Henry. I saw him a couple weeks ago and he said those trees were doing just fine."

Glancing at Mary, Tom said seriously:

"And by the way Mary, I don't want you to be a
worrying--there are scads of sugar maple trees out
here in this country!"

Tom grinned. Jason had mentioned to him about
Mary's subtle effort to delay their departure saying she hoped they might be in Turkeyfoot for maple
sugar time. Mary blushed as she quickly exclaimed:

"Jason Evenstar! You didn't?"

"Appears I did," replied Jason casually.

Jason had been quietly pondering their pilot's
many-faceted commentary and now remarked:

"Tom, I remember my uncle Conrad telling me he
and my father once met a frustrated Indian at Fort
Ligonier who was complaining about the treaty which
ended that French and Indian War in 1763."

"Doesn't surprise me--Indians were not a party
to that Treaty of Paris whereby France gave England
the land here where the red man lived. As one old
chief put it, 'king three thousand miles away gives
another king our land!' And George Rogers Clark--a
fine officer during the war--had this idea the Delawares were divided and the Shawnees weren't united
in support of England. So, he thought if he could
drive the British from western posts, Indians could
be awed into submission or bribed into neutrality--
or friendship. Now we have another Treaty of Paris
signed in 1783 which gives the land out here to the
United States. Although that treaty did officially
end the war with England, it only added to the red
man's frustration. Once again the Indians were not
a party to a treaty which gave the colonists a vast
piece of land which so far they have been unable to
occupy, govern, or protect. A treaty was signed at
Fort Harmar six years ago which reinforced the one
signed at Fort McIntosh but it hasn't brought peace
to this country. And, in spite of those treaties,
the British have not vacated all of their forts out
here and the Indians still pound the war drum. The
Indians aren't the only ones who are frustrated!"

For a moment Jason thought about what Tom had

said and then he posed another question:

"You said a few minutes ago the Iroquois sold land in 1768 to the Penn family--did that have anything to do with that treaty uncle Conrad said was signed at Fort Stanwix a few years ago?"

"Well, yes and no Jason. You see, in spite of the terms of that so-called purchase, and Dunmore's Treaty in 1774, Indians continued raiding settlers in this area. And, although they failed to capture Fort Henry in 1777 or 1782, maddened by successes elsewhere, the Indians struck all along the eastern shore of the Ohio from Wheeling downstream to Point Pleasant keeping the whole area in a constant state of alarm. Finally, after treaty talks in August of 1784, sachems from the Delaware, Wyandot, Chippewa, and Ottawa tribes ceded to the United States their land in the Ohio country. Then, in October of that same year, the Six Nation Iroquois confederacy put their mark on a treaty at Fort Stanwix which ceded to the government their land west of the boundaries of Pennsylvania and New York."

"What about the Shawnee tribes you spoke of?"

Tom shook his head slowly and gave a moment of serious thought to Jason's question before saying:

"As you observed, the Shawnee sachems were not a party to that treaty and hostilities have continued. Four years ago this July, as I remember, old man Bevans and his son, John, and two of his girls, were murdered and scalped near Harry Clark's blockhouse just south of Wheeling. There's been quite a few such senseless incidents in the past couple of years hereabouts. Like I told you yesterday or the day before Jason, Mr. Bozarth was murdered by some Indians over on Dunkard's Creek just two years ago. Fort Harmar was built out here to sort of drive the final nail in the red man's coffin but hostilities have not ended. I hate to say it but the truth is, this so-called 'Indian problem' has not been put to rest out here!"

Tom's eyes swept across the sober faces of his

listeners--no one said a word. As the old pilot's eyes met those of Alma's he added:

"What is really unfortunate is that so many of you good people come out to the Northwest Territory looking for opportunity and become victims of something over which you have no control. Out here in this country the only sure thing about tomorrow is, it will arrive."

Jason evaded his wife's tearful eyes. It was Sarah who broke the awkward silence saying:

"Its been a busy day. Perhaps a good night's rest will make things look brighter tomorrow."

During the morning of the fourth day Tom earned everyone's unqualified praise when he skillfully maneuvered the ark through rock filled rapids. The women and children intuitively grabbed for anything in sight to keep from being thrown around the cabin and the watchmen on deck secured themselves with a piece of rope. With the rapids behind them, twelve miles downstream from Wheeling Tom pointed to where Graves Creek emptied into the Ohio and told about a couple from Switzerland who had said last fall this land along the river here reminded them of home.

"They were about ready to have me pull ashore so they could stay here. Said they heard at Pittsburgh that Joseph Tomlinson settled at Grave Creek a few years ago. I suggested they might be wise to go on down to Limestone Point--for now anyway!

Jason was about to say that he recalled having heard a man named Joe Tomlinson talk with his uncle when he was a boy, but he decided not to mention it just now. Although only eight and a half years of age at the time, the man's words about red-skins on the warpath in 1774 were still clear in his mind.

That night Tom appeared rather unexpectedly in the stock enclosure having first given Dave a warning of his approach. With his three-hour watch now almost over, Dave had seated himself on the edge of the cabin roof above the stock enclosure. Quietly, but firmly, Tom warned him:

"Dave, you are silhouetted against the glow of the light coming out of that open trap door. You'd make a good target for an Indian."

With a burst of adrenalin coursing through his body, Dave quickly climbed down from the cabin roof and then whispered:

"Sorry about that Tom, I just forgot."

"I understand" said Tom. "But don't forget in the future, one moment of carelessness can earn you an early grave young man."

"Thanks Tom. I'll be more careful."

When Jason came out on deck for his watch just before midnight, Dave informed him about Tom's admonishment. As his weary colleague now disappeared through the doorway of the cabin, Jason studied the bank of threatening clouds on the western horizon and muttered to himself:

"That Tom must sleep with one eye open!"

The fifth day of river travel Jason was jarred out of his sleep by an ominous roll of thunder. As he stepped from the cabin he was greeted by an awesome flash of lightning that ripped open the black curtain of sky overhead like a polished blade and let through the first drops of the coming storm. A few minutes later, and accompanied by an occasional blue-white flash of lightning , a persistent dreary and clammy rain enveloped the ark. With the river wind-lashed, choppy, and threatening, Tom said the ark would remain anchored in midstream. But he did order two men to maintain a sharp lookout on deck-- one on the bow and the other at the stern.

Although the morning hours passed slowly, near noon the menacing black clouds rolled away, the sun came out, and Tom ordered Hank to "hoist anchor!" Then, with the evening meal over, the atmosphere in the cabin was suddenly sparked with expectation as Tom announced:

"Well folks, I think the rising sun will bring us good weather and tomorrow, the Lord willing, we are going to see Marietta."

CHAPTER SEVEN

STRANGERS IN A STRANGE LAND

Near mid-afternoon of the sixth day--the fifth day of May in 1791--the ark drifted around a sweeping bend in the Ohio and everyone was overjoyed to see a pentagon-shaped fort just ahead nestled among trees on the west side of the Muskingum. Hugging the north shore of the Ohio, Tom called for the men to stand ready to "pole" the boat up a stream which flowed past Fort Harmar. Although it seemed to be an eternity, a few minutes later Jason caught sight of the cabins through the trees on the east bank of the Muskingum and shouted:

"There she is! Marietta!"

Only two years before in New York City, George Washington had been sworn in as the first president of the United States. Of Mariettas he had said:

"No colony in America was ever settled under circumstances more favorable. There never were any people better able to promote the welfare of the community!"

Francis Thierry*, an immigrant whose bakehouse was located between Fort Harmar and the river, was

* Francis Thierry (1765-1832), a baker and confectioner from Paris arrived Marietta in 1790 (pg 322, PIONEER HISTORY by S.P. Hildreth) and married Frances Bowen Blake in 1814 (HISTORY OF WSAHINGTON CO., OH 1881). His grt grt grandson, Ralph Williams and his wife, Dorothy, lived in Fort Recovery, OH when the village commemorated the 150th anniversary of St. Clair's defeat.

the first to greet them.   He had been fishing along
the west bank of the Muskingum and waved happily as
they poled   up the river.   Several settlers quickly
gathered at the dock and obligingly assisted Tom in
securing the ark. Among them was a   distinguished
looking gentleman who greeted the pilot saying:

"Tom old friend, welcome back to Marietta--you
are a sight for sore eyes! How have you been?"

They were soon to learn that the speaker was a
judge of the   Northwest Territory--Rufus Putnam had
been appointed in March of 1790 after Samuel Holden
Parsons had   drown the previous November.   Referred
to as   "General Putnam," the judge enthusiastically
exclaimed as the Evenstars stepped ashore:

"Welcome to Marietta folks.   Been three years
since our party of forty-seven made that right-hand
turn up the Muskingum   on April 7th.   Had a forty-
eighth man,   Colonel Return Meigs, Sr., but he came
overland on horseback and arrived five days later."

General Putnam explained how they had been met
by a group of   Delawares who quickly accepted their
expected presents and then a feast celebrated their
arrival. But those in the general's party were men
of purpose and they soon turned to the work at hand
and   began cutting trees, building cabins, breaking
the soil, planting seed, and laying out the settlement. In spite of the   seeming friendliness of the
Indians who first met them, the settlers decided to
erect a   row of large pointed pickets on the north
and east side of the settlement to guard against an
unexpected hostile encroachment. As Reverend Story
explained after he was introduced by Rufus Putnam:

"Praying for the best, but preparing ourselves
should the worst befall us, our fortification called Campus Martius will ensure safety for those who
live at Marietta. I have been here two years--left
Massachusetts in the spring of 1789 and arrived in
late April. The day after I arrived a gentleman by
the name of William Rittenhouse stopped here. As I
recall, he was heading for the John Symmes land you

mentioned as your destination. Captain John Dodge and Major Haffield White talked with him about the Symmes' undertaking."

Coupled with the friendly greetings and polite interest in their destination, everyone was anxious for any news from back east. Explaining that they had been living in Bedford County, Jason apologized for not being able to provide any news other than a few tidbits they had picked up while their ark was being built. Mary courteously offered to share her copy of THE PITTSBURGH GAZETTE and everyone eagerly examined it. On a tree nearby Dave spotted a piece of paper with large letters and asked:

"What's that?"

General Putnam quickly offered a reply to what he thought was Dave's question:

"Well sir, that's a buckeye tree. Indians out here call it 'hetuck' and I am told that means 'eye of the buck.' Indeed, the nut of that buckeye tree does look like the eye of a buck--both in color and in shape. They grow in abundance here and we use a lot of them to make our cabins."

Although the early settler adopted the English meaning, it would be 1840--the year General William Harrison came out of retirement to be a Whig candidate for the presidency--before the "first-born" of the Northwest Territory began being referred to as "The Buckeye State." In THE WESTERN STATESMAN, a vintage newspaper of Lawrenceburg, Indiana, a poem titled "The Buckeye Tree" would proclaim:

> *"They say the buckeye leaves expand*
> *Five-fingered as an open hand,*
> *Of love and brotherhood the sign*
> *Be welcome! What is mine is thine!"*

Although written years later, the words of the poem described the genuine welcome Jason felt among these Marietta settlers. Everyone was friendly and offered not only words of encouragement but several suggested they consider making Marietta their home. In this same spirit of cordiality, the man standing at General Putnam's elbow interjected:

"Speaking of trees, you folks should have seen the look on Reverend Cutler's face in August of '88 when we showed him a black walnut tree not far from here which has a diameter of thirteen feet--an old sycamore nearby measures forty-four feet in circumference!"

Like the others, Dave was quite impressed with this information but what he was referring to was a piece of paper on the tree titled: "Marietta Code." Pointing to the placard, Dave repeated his query:

"And the poster on that buckeye tree?"

Without hesitation Rufus Putnam replied:

"Oh that! Those are the rules! Governor St. Clair arrived here the 9th of July in 1788 and one of his first tasks was to make a list of good laws for the territory and set up a system of law courts out here. Our governor established the first civil government west of the Alleghenies. From the first day he arrived, the governor has always maintained that 'every society must have rules!' The Marietta Code is our rules!"

Far removed from necessary approval authority, and plagued by Congress dragging its feet, it would be 1795 before a body of laws for use in the Northwest Territory (Maxwell's Code) were destined to be printed by William Maxwell at Cincinnati.

Reverend Story interjected:

"And they are good rules too. A number of the people heading downstream have decided to stay here with us. John and William James arrived last year. Joseph Utter and his family--Joe Rogers and Sherman Waterman--they all joined us last year."

The friendly minister had no way of knowing it would be only a year before Joseph Rogers would be killed and Sherman Waterman would suffer the same fate in 1794. Reverend Story continued:

"Some, like Captain McCurdy and his wife, and

Colonel Israel Putnam, Jr. and his family, arrived
in the summer of 1788. There's the colonel's boys
over there."

The speaker pointed his index finger to where
the Evenstars saw Aaron Waldo and Israel Putnam III
talking with Hank and his wife. Reverend Story introduced them to Colonel Robert Oliver who, after
the customary amenities, turned to his companion as
he said:

"Colonel Sproat, I would like you to meet Mary
and Jason Evenstar from Bedford County. Folks, its
a pleasure to introduce our good sheriff, Ebenezer
Sproat!"

With a friendly smile for the ladies, and firm
handshake for the men, the sheriff greeted Mary and
Jason and then each member of the arriving party in
turn. Not only had he been the sheriff since early
September of 1788, Ebenezer Sproat was a businessman as well. Less than a year after he arrived he
began talking with Thomas Stanley about starting a
mill. Unfortunately Indian hostilities and a flood
were destined to interrupt this venture. But now,
as Reverend Story and the Evenstars strolled away
from the ark, the affable minister remarked:

"Several men, Colonel Oliver, Major White, and
Captain Dodge, were talking about building a flour
mill on Wolf Creek near here when I arrived. This
place is really growing and a mill is needed."

The minister also mentioned that many of those
settlers who arrived with Putnam were members of a
travelling lodge of Free and Accepted Masons which
had been chartered in Massachusetts in 1775. With
a tinge of righteousness in his voice he added:

"Both our governor and Colonel Putnam are members of the Masonic Lodge."

Jason recalled his uncle having mentioned that
St. Clair and George Washington were both Masons--
he never said anything other than that. His trend
of thought was interrupted as Reverend Story said:

"I mentioned that William Rittenhouse stopped

here. You folks will probably hear John Symmes and
his entourage stopped here the 27th of August three
years ago while Reverend Cutler was here. You may
want to talk with Paul Fearing while you are here
if you are interested in that Symmes land venture--
Fearing is a lawyer."

"You say Reverend Cutler was here?"

The note of excitement in Mary's voice brought
a smile to Reverend Story's face as he replied:

"Oh yes, he wanted to see for himself what the
doubters back east were calling 'Putnam's Paradise'
and 'Cutler's Indian Haven!' He departed Ipswitch
on July 21st, arrived here August 19th, departed on
the 9th of September, and was back in Ipswitch the
19th of October three years ago. A busy schedule--
and a fortuitous one for Edward Moulton who was bit
by a copperhead snake on August 26th while Doctor
Cutler was here. I remember the date very well--it
was the day after Major Cushing's first child died
in spite of the doctor's presence."

Mary glanced at Jason and the wan smile which
crossed her face was a story in itself. Quick to
change the subject, Jason said:

"And you will be staying here as a minister?"

Reverend Story smiled as he replied:

"Probably. I preach here the first three Sun-
days of the month and on the fourth Sabbath I visit
the Belpre settlement twelve miles downstream. Our
folks here are largely of English Protestant stock
whereas those upstream between the mouth of Yellow
Creek and Wheeling immigrated from Pennsylvania and
Virginia."

The first church at Marietta was Congregation-
al--thirty of their thirty-one members were of that
denomination in New England. The tract of land referred to north of Wheeling was an area where many
white "squatters" had settled. In years to come it
would be divided between Jefferson and Columbiana
counties in Ohio. Reverend Story's commentary was
now interrupted as they met another of Marietta's

settlers who was introduced as Benjamin Stone. The
friendly settler requested they call him "Ben" and
inquired concerning any news they might have picked
up at Pittsburgh regarding St. Clair's visit to see
President Washington about "the Indian problem."

"The governor is a close friend of the president you know," said Ben. "He was at Washington's
side when he was inaugurated."

Handsomely dressed and wearing the steel hilt-
ed dress sword which Richard Stanup had spent hours
polishing before the president-elect had left for
New York City, George Washington had proceeded from
his quarters on Cherry Street to the Federal Building at Broad and Hall Street. Here, in an emotional
ringing voice, the president of the United States
delivered his acceptance speech before an assembly
of well-wishers and curious on-lookers. Later he
and the vice-president-elect, John Adams, and his
party of followers, journeyed to St. Paul's Church
on Broadway where the president knelt in prayer and
asked for heavenly guidance in his new undertaking.
Officers who had served with Washington during the
war were given recogniton by being invited to stand
near him during the dignified ceremonies and Arthur
St. Clair was present for the inauguration and the
reception. There had been whispered talk heard at
the reception that St. Clair was being urged to run
for governor of Pennsylvania against Major General
Thomas Mifflin--both men were active members of the
Federalist Party. St. Clair's comment had been:

"I have taken the matter under advisement."

And, in taking the helm of the fledgling ship
of state, Washington said to the plump Henry Knox,
his Secretary of War:

"I face an ocean of difficulties, without the
competency of political skills, abilities, and the
inclination which is necessary to manage the helm!"

Acutely aware everything he said and did would
affect history, President Washington soberly added:

"I walk on untrodden ground--there is scarcely

a part of my conduct which may not hereafter be drawn into precedent."

At the mention of George Washington's name by Benjamin Stone, Jason remembered he had been chosen president by all electors who voted--seventy-three being eligible and sixty-nine present casting their vote. John Adams was elected vice-president with thirty-four votes. His trend of thought was broken as Ben continued:

"A courier passed through here early this week saying the president and congress have approved St. Clair's plan to lead a military expedition against the Indians and we could expect a large number of soldiers to pass through here soon on their way to Fort Washington."

Jason decided it was not appropriate to repeat what Tom had heard at Fort Pitt so he said nothing.

It was late-afternoon when Tom May found Jason and introduced Major Doughty from Fort Harmar. Tom knew everyone it seemed. Upon learning of Jason's destination, the major said he planned to travel to Fort Washington soon and indicated the governor was very anxious that a strong military presence be established in that area. He also said St. Clair had stopped at Marietta the past winter on his way back east for meetings concerning the "Indian problem."

"Does Governor St. Clair know John Symmes?"

Jason's question brought a broad smile to the major's face but it faded as he replied:

"Oh, indeed the governor knows Mr. Symmes very well--they have a long acquaintanceship!"

The major glanced at Tom May and then quickly turned his attention to Mary when she remarked:

"I have heard this John Cleves Symmes is a man of action. And, as I understand it, he has repeatedly asked the governor for military protection for his settlers. Is that correct?"

"Yes mam! Not only did he 'ask,' in military parlance you could say he has frequently 'enjoined' the governor to do so with great haste!"

Doughty smiled as he made the remark. In 1784 he had commanded a detachment which came downstream and built Fort Harmar. A capable officer, he was respected by superior and subordinate alike. Major Doughty was anxious to have the governor considered in a favorable light and now in a more serious mood politely explained:

"Governor St. Clair is very much interested in the welfare of all people of this great territory I assure you. It was my honor to escort him down the Ohio from Fort Pitt three years ago. We arrived on the 9th of July and the troops at Fort Harmar gave him a thirteen gun salute! On July 15th the folks here at Marietta formally received him and the guns at Fort Harmar accorded him a fourteen gun salute!"

Now Major Doughty detailed how the territorial government had been inaugurated and the governor, a secretary, and three judges had been inducted into office. Having listened carefully, Jason said:

"That must have been some day! Benjamin Stone told us the governor is back east now."

Once again the major glanced at Tom May before he replied seriously:

"That is correct. The governor is back east-- he had some matters of both an official and private nature requiring his attention. As you may or may not be aware, the governor is a personal friend of the president and will undoubtedly see him."

Although the major was aware that a communique had been delivered to the commandant at Fort Harmar advising him the governor would be leading a summer campaign northwest from Fort Washington, the "spit and polish" officer was not at liberty to reveal the details of such a privileged message. Doughty had no way of knowing that even as he talked with the Evenstars, in Philadelphia President Washington watched his faithful valet, Richard Stanup, polish his boots and recalled his last words to his friend whose plan for a summer expedition he had approved;

"Beware of a surprise!"

It was an ambitious plan and he had confidence
in the recommendations of an officer who had served
him so well during the Revolutionary war.   Despite
this "confidence," Washington had a gnawing feeling
of concern about the reluctance of his Secretary of
War to whole-heartedly approve St. Clair's "plan,"
the idiosyncracies of a somewhat devious Secretary
of State, and the luke-warm cooperation being given
the undertaking by the Secretary of Treasury. The
American historian , Samuel Eliot Morison, who died
in 1976, would write of this person who died with
his century on December 14, 1799 with Richard Stanup standing tearfully at the foot of his bed:

"Washington wisely used the qualities of able
men while ignoring their faults."

Thus he had listened to his old friend, Arthur
St. Clair, and concluded the offer to lead an expedition against the Indians was an unselfish gesture
by a man whose judgment he trusted.

And now, in early May of 1791, only two months
after congress sanctioned St. Clair's "plan," Jason
mentioned to Major Doughty having seen the Marietta
Code on a buckeye tree and it prompted a commentary
regarding law and order:

"It will take a little time, but law must come
to this territory if it is to grow and prosper as
we know it will." But, as the major sadly added:

"We lost one of our respected judges two years
ago this past winter, General James Mitchel Varnum.
He died the 10th of January. He was a graduate of
Brown University and a fine officer. He had arrived
the previous summer on June 5th along with a party
of forty settlers which included James Owen and his
wife, Mary. She was the first woman settler here."

General Varnum's untimely passing was not only
a great personal loss to St. Clair but it also had
a negative impact on his plan to establish a set of
laws for the territory. The governor's "timetable"
experienced another reversal the same year when the
second territorial judge, General Samuel Holden

Parsons drown on November 17th. This fine officer, a major general during the war and a highly touted candidate for governorship of the Northwest Territory, had accompanied St. Clair to Fort Harmar in the summer of 1788.

Shaking his head slowly, the major added:

"Loss of these judges was a severe blow to the governor's plans. A tireless worker, the governor began establishing a system of courts as soon as he arrived. Return J. Meigs was appointed Clerk of Common Pleas Court, Rufus Putnam was appointed Probate Judge, and Colonel Sproat was named sheriff--you met him I believe?"

"We did," said Jason. "He appears to be a fine man for the job."

"That he is," remarked Major Doughty. "And the first court held in this territory was that of the Court of Common Pleas held right here the 2nd day of September 1788 in that northwest blockhouse over there. Reverend Cutler was in Marietta and was the guest speaker that day."

Voiced with obvious pride, the major's comment brought a look of mild surprise to Mary's face and she politely interrupted saying:

"Pardon me but someone else mentioned Reverend Cutler had visited here that summer--would that be Manasseh Cutler from Massachusetts?"

"That he is," replied Major Doughty. "Begging your pardon mam, are you acquainted with him?"

Doughty's query reflected his keen interest in the possibility the Evenstars might be acquainted with Reverend Cutler. Mary explained:

"No, not personally. My aunt in New York City is acquainted with him and my cousin was introduced to Reverend Cutler in Philadelphia four years ago."

As Mary provided her brief explanation, Major Doughty mentally recalled the day Reverend Cutler and Captain Heart's city lots were surveyed August 25, 1788--that same night Major Cushing's child had died. He also recalled how Cutler had gone up the

Muskingum to visit Virgin's Bottom and Wiseman's Bottom on the 29th of August in company with Rufus Putnam and upon their return had dined with Colonel Battele the last day of the month. He remembered Cutler's lengthy speech but now politely remarked:

"As I said a moment ago, Reverend Cutler was a guest speaker and he provided us a good account of how the Ohio Company of Associates came into being and purchased land out here."

"The land around Marietta." said Jason. "Am I correct?"

"Well, almost," replied Doughty with a smile. "In May of 1787 General Parsons had been trying to get legislation passed which would enable the Ohio Company of Associates to buy a million and a half acres here but he had not been successful. So the company requested Reverend Cutler to provide some lobbying effort. On July 13th congress adopted the ordinance which enabled purchase of land out here."

Major Doughty did not mention Arthur St. Clair was President of Congress at the time and agreed to support Cutler's lobbying effort with the tacit understanding he would be appointed governor of the territory to be created by the proposed ordinance. He also did not say St. Clair was absent on the day 18 representatives of 8 states passed the Ordinance of 1787 with one dissenting vote. William Grayson from Virginia was the acting president that day.

But he did explain how William Duer, Secretary of the Treasury Board, and some New York City speculators and Revolutionary War veterans, had formed the Scioto Company. This company proposed to buy 4,900,000 acres west of the Ohio Company's land at sixty-six cents an acre with payment to be made two years after completion of a land survey by Thomas Hutchins. The various principals involved in these land ventures realized that by combining the two purchase requests, it would make a more attractive "package" for congress to consider.

Attractive it was, but the Scioto Company was

in trouble from the start and William Duer was destined to die in prison in 1799. As Doughty said:

"You may have heard the Scioto Company has experienced some difficulties--particularly with the undertaking downstream at Gallipolis."

Jason and his wife exchanged glances and then Mary inquired:

"We heard nothing about it--what happened?"

Choosing his words carefully, Doughty related how a Scioto Company's representative, Joel Barlow, was sent to France to sell acreage. There he teamed up with an unscrupulous individual named William Playfair and they duped hundreds of the citizens of Paris into purchasing land for which they could not convey proper title. As one of the dejected French 500 had politely declared:

"That smooth talking rascal did us in!"

Another Frenchman who had been taken in by Mr. Playfair's sales pitch was more vehement:

"He was a lying son of bitch!"

It sounded different in French but the meaning was the same in any language. The artists, dressmakers, dance teachers, and other emigrants found frontier life difficult and many moved on to other places more suited to their disposition.

"The matter has been a source of embarrassment to the government," said Doughty. "Imagine, if you will, five hundred poor souls landing at Alexandria and being told their title to land out here is just worthless. But undaunted, those immigrants crossed the mountains and came down the Ohio last summer in six Kentucky flatboats. General Putman hired forty men to build two long rows of houses down the river and in October last year most of those French immigrants began their life anew opposite the mouth of the Great Kanawha--they have named their settlement Gallipolis. Some of them, like Jean Pierre, Joseph Utter and his family, the Tyrons, Pierre Venard, and our baker, Francis Thierry--who decided to ply his trade here--stayed at Marietta. Others went on down the Ohio to Maysville and Cincinnati. There's room for everybody out here and with General Putnam and George Turner having been appointed to fill the vacancies of Judge Parsons and Varnum, the governor will be able to establish a body of laws for this territory."

The major concluded with an air of confidence and finality that bordered on the dramatic but he was obviously well informed and the Evenstars were thoroughly impressed. Sheriff Sproat had walked up to where they stood just as the major finished his final remark and added:

"And we get this cussed Indian problem put to rest!"

With a knowing wink at Sheriff Sproat, and an engaging smile for the Evenstars, Major Doughty now excused himself saying:

"And I believe our governor has a plan to put that matter to rest sir! Even now he may be on his way back down the Ohio with plans for a summer campaign. I just saw a courier heading to Fort Harmar so I better get back across the river. Please excuse me folks."

From communiques Doughty knew St. Clair was on his way downstream even as they spoke.

Although the kind-hearted Sheriff Sproat urged everyone to accept offers of lodging, Jason and his friends declined but did take their evening meal as guests of various settlers--Jason and Mary ate with the Utter family. In bidding their friendly host goodnight, or "bonsoir" as Joseph proudly proclaimed, Mary whispered to a very surprised Mrs. Utter:

"Merci, nous avons trouve' le repas tres bon."

"Il n'y a pas de quoi," Mrs. utter replied as the look of surprise faded into a big smile.

On the way back to the ark Jason queried Mary about what she and Mrs. Utter had said.

"I merely thanked her and said we enjoyed the meal very much. She said we were welcome. Anthing else sir!"

Somewhat nonplussed, Jason muttered:

"I must have missed school that day."

It had been a busy day and everyone decided to retire early--for the first time since leaving Turkeyfoot most felt "an unusual sense of security" as Dave's wife said. They would have felt a lot less secure had they known that even as they talked two Indians had watched every move they had made from a nearby point of vantage. But they didn't know they were being watched and Dave's wife remarked:

"Here we are, at least a hundred miles out in this Northwest Territory and for the first time in weeks I feel we can get a good night's rest!"

"I can understand that Alma," said her husband quickly. "The presence of the military and being a stone's throw from Fort Harmar and Marietta makes a person feel much better."

Jason said nothing--he listened. Tom had told him it would now be advisable if they waited for at least one other boat before continuing downstream.

"There's some safety in numbers," Tom said.

Jason did not doubt Tom knew what he was doing and did not question the wisdom of his decision. A short time after returning to the ark Jason said:

"Well, early to bed and early to rise!"

Having the second watch, Jason planned to get some sleep before his "time in the barrel" as Hank called it. While on a hunting trip last year Jason had asked Hank what was meant by that expression-- when Hank explained Jason was sorry he asked. Tom had said a watch would be maintained throughout the night regardless of where they anchored and tonight would be no exception despite the proximity of Fort Harmar. Tonight each man would have his customary "turn in the barrel."

Before going to sleep this night, Mary thought to herself she would write to her aunt the next day and tell her about her minister friend from Ipswich visiting Marietta. Recalling Reverend Story's kind remarks about the successful lobbying effort of the minister, Mary was thankful for Cutler's reported strong stand on the need of a provision for education and a ban against slavery in the country where she planned to live. Lost in her thoughts, Jason's wife fell asleep and did not awaken when he quietly left her side at midnight.

The "midnight watch" was always a lonely time and now, standing on the bow looking at the several campfires scattered through the settlement, Jason thought about Marietta's brief history. The first of two parties heading for the Ohio country had departed Danvers, Massachusetts Dec. 1, 1787. After being joined on the banks of the Youghiogheny River by General Putnam leading the second party, the 48 men built three log canoes, a small flatboat, and a larger one 12 by 50 foot which they finally called "The Mayflower." Tom May had told Jason it carried 50 tons. The settlers hoisted anchor at Alexander Simeral's Ferry on April 1, 1788 and six days later tied up opposite the fort which Jason could now see silhouetted against the western sky. Three years later Jason and his companions had taken the same number of days to drift downstream to Marietta.

Although at first those first pioneer settlers from the New England States called their settlement "Adelphia," it was soon agreed they would honor the country which helped them during the Revolutionary War. As Reverend Story had told him, more than 130 settlers arrived at Marietta by the end of 1788, an estimated 150 more came in 1789, and by 1790 there were 80 log homes in the settlement.

With his "graveyard watch" finally over, Jason disappeared into the bowels of the ark and lost no time in snuggling up to his wife's side and falling asleep. It was Tom who gently shook his shoulder a few hours later and inquired:

"I say there young man, do you intend to sleep your life away?"

Jason was instantly awake and asking what time it was.

"Time?   Why its time to get up," replied Tom. "Your bride has a man-sized breakfast waiting."

Again Tom was right--beside the fireplace Mary had a plate of fried mush and sorghum which Jason devoured quickly.   Saying he had "slept like a log after my middle-of-the-night-watch," Jason thanked Tom for awakening him.   Jokingly Tom said:

"That was Mary's idea.   I do believe your wife is anxious to see more of Marietta."

"No more than me," said Jason.   "Let's go!"

The three walked into the settlement followed by Alma and Dave Jones--the Weisers decided to stay on board since the children were still asleep.   The first person they met was Major Coburn, one of the original settlers.   With justifiable pride Coburn recalled there were 15 families in Marietta only a year after they first arrived.   Coburn introduced them to Majors Goodale and Cushing who also voiced enthusiastic pride in their accomplishments.   Major Cushing swept his arm around in prideful gesture as he remarked:

"Little more than three years and now look at our settlement.   You folks must meet General Tupper and Winthrop Sargent--he is Secretary of the North-west Territory you know.   Getting to be so many of us and everyday more come down the Ohio!"

In late 1789 an officer at Fort Harmar had in-cluded in his official report: "Not less than one hundred people pass the mouth of the Muskingum each day heading downstream."

Earlier, in a letter written December 9, 1787, General Harmar had written to his superior officer:

"Since June of 1787 I have observed 146 boats containing 3,196 souls; 1,381 horses; 171 cattle; 245 sheep, 24 hogs; and 165 wagons on their way to Kentucky."

Earlier Harmar had reported: "177 boats; 2,689 souls; 1,333 horses; 766 cattle; and 102 wagons passed Fort Harmar from October 10, 1786 to May 12, 1787." A statistic-minded historian later reported

238

the population of Virginia's District of Kentucky in 1790 was 73,677.

"Understand you folks met Major Doughty," said Coburn. "A fine chap! He directed construction of Fort Harmar and then, in August two years ago, the major took officers Ferguson, Strong, Drury, Pratt, Kingsbury, and Ensign Hartshorn with him, and built Fort Washington downstream. Major Doughty will be going back to Fort Washington soon I understand."

As Mary listened to Coburn comment on the many improvements at Marietta she thought to herself:

"Doesn't seem possible it was but three months ago that Jason read those newspaper clippings about this place--now here I am!" Aloud she exclaimed:

"I don't believe it!"

Jason glanced at Mary and a puzzled expression crossed his face as he said:

"You don't believe what Mary?"

"Nothing Jason--I was just thinking out loud."

A little embarrassed and anxious to change the subject, Mary quickly added:

"Forget it--don't mind me. By the way major, did I see a cabin across the Ohio yesterday?"

Smiling, Major Coburn pointed his index finger toward the south and replied:

"You've got sharp eyes Mrs. Evenstar. That's Virginia land over there--she surrendered her claim to land north of the Ohio in 1784. That cabin you see is part of the settlement Major Isaac Williams started four years ago...he called it Williamstown! Six years ago Isaac's father-in-law, Joe Tomlinson, staked out some land upstream along Grave's Creek. Joe's daughter, Rebecca, had married John Martin but he was killed by Indians and Isaac married the widow in 1775. Isaac and Rebecca came downstream and settled across there on March 25th in 1787."

Coburn might have added that Captain Stone and Cutler went across the Ohio to visit Isaac Williams on Aug. 22, 1788 while the doctor was at Marietta.

Justifiably proud of their growing settlement,

one of the settlers standing nearby remarked:

"Can you believe it folks, there were no white settlers in this region northwest of the Ohio three years ago except the ones here at Marietta!"

Jason glanced at Tom but said nothing--the man added enthusiastically:

"It is our hope to call this country Ohio!"

Jason made a mental note that there must be a lot of misinformation being unintentionally passed along and he would be well advised to listen carefully to any stories he heard about this Northwest Territory where he planned to live. His meditation was now interrupted as Tom introduced Isaac Pierce, John Nisewonger, and a man whose name someone had mentioned yesterday--Return Jonathan Meigs, Jr.

"This gentleman graduated from Yale and is the Clerk of the Court of Common Pleas. His father was one of the first settlers here. Folks around here speak highly of this young man."

"That's quite an introduction to live up to my friend," said the affable Meigs. "Or live down!"

Those engaged in easy conversation this day in Marietta had no way of knowing it would be this man who would be elected governor of Ohio in 1812. As they talked Tom greeted a man who approached them:

"Good morning--I mean bonjour Mr. Thierry! Je vous pre'sente Mr. and Mrs. Evenstar."

"Bonjour, m'appelle Francis," said Mr. Thierry with a big smile. "Il fait un temps superbe."

"Comment allez-vous," said Mary quickly in an engaging voice. "And indeed, as you say, it is a beautiful day!"

A surprised look crossed Mr. Thierry's face as he quickly asked:

"Je vous que vous parlez francais--pouvez vous comprende ce que je dis?"

Tom glanced at Jason and Mary held everyone's attention as she replied without hesitation: "Oui, en effet. Parlez plus lentement, s'il vous plait. Parlez-vous anglais?"

"Un peu, mais mal, je crains."

It was Dave who now quickly interjected: "All right you two--what are you talking about?"

With a smile Mary said: "He asked if I spoke French and if I could understand him. I told him I indeed could but asked him to speak a little slower please. I then asked him if he spoke English. He said, 'A little, but quite poorly, I'm afraid.'"

With Mary's interpretive assistance, the group now engaged in a lively exchange with Mr. Thierry concerning his journey across the Atlantic and west to Marietta. Not to be completely outdone by Mary, Jason haltingly injected:

"Les Etats-Unis sont un grand pays!"

Francis Thierry looked at Jason in a quizzical manner and then glanced at Mary who explained:

"My husband is trying to say the United States is a very big country. Comprendre?"

"Oui! Vous avez raison. J'aime le pays."

The look on Jason's face prompted Mary to say with a polite laugh: "Mr. Thierry said you're right and he likes the country. Use English dear--he can understand that better than your French!"

Thierry now excused himself saying he must get back across the river and tend to his baking. The friendly Frenchman promised to bring the Evenstars some of his bake goods before they departed.

Having stepped to one side to warmly shake the hand of an obvious long-time acquaintance, Tom then rejoined the group saying:

"Folks, I would like to have you meet a friend of mine, Lieutenant Ebenezer Denny."

During the ensuing conversation there was some mention of John Symmes having landed at Marietta on his way downstream in 1788.

"Tied up right over there on August 27th if my memory serves me right," said Denny. "It was just a week after Reverend Cutler arrived as I recall. Do any of you folks know John Symmes?"

"No," replied Jason. "But we have heard a lot

about him however and hope to make his acquaintance in the near future."

"If you are interested in purchasing land west of Cincinnati you will undoubtedly meet John Cleves Symmes. John, and his daughter, Polly, spent a few days here in the summer of 1788 and there was a lot of talk with General Harmar about insuring a strong military presence in the area between the two Miami rivers downstream."

Denny made no mention of any meetings between Symmes and St. Clair and Jason thought it might be imprudent to ask. Dave did say:

"A gentleman we spoke with yesterday said the Symmes party was delayed for some time in 1788 down the river at--Limestone Point, is that it?"

Denny glanced at Tom May and smiled as he said politely, "Limestone Point or Maysville. And yes, they were delayed for quite a while--several months in fact. A detachment was dispatched downstream in December to provide an escort for the Symmes party but they did not get away until the last of January 1789 and went ashore just below Losantiville--now Cincinnati--the 2nd day of February."

A little cloud of concern crossed Denny's face as he added:

"Mr. Symmes is quite naturally concerned about having a strong military presence in his area."

Mary frowned and Jason, noting her expression, remarked:

"I cannot blame him. As possible settlers in that area, we also are very much interested in the military protection afforded settlers."

Jason was not alone in this concern and Arthur St. Clair was not permitted a waking moment when he was not reminded of the settler's nagging concern about "military protection." During 1789 alone no less than 20,000 people had floated down the Ohio-- that was a lot of "concerned" settlers.

Tom May had listened carefully to the exchange of comments and then commented:

"It seems the governor is doing all he can to provide military protection within the limit of his resources--we don't have a very big army."

"Spoken like a tried and true Federalist Tom," said Denny with a smiling nod of approval. "You are correct on both counts. The governor has found the Indians out here both tedious and troublesome--it's been a matter of concern to him and General Harmar. Both expected there might be some dissention among the Indians which would make negotiations difficult but the governor thought his past acquaintance with the sachems of the Six Nations would help."

Ironically, Fort Harmar had been built in 1785 in an effort to deter the white settler's intrusion in the area northwest of the Ohio. Then, in 1788, it protected the first legal settlement under the provisions of the Ordinance of 1787. As Washington had optimistically concluded:

"The country is large enough to contain us all and I have very little doubt the Indians would compromise for a part of it."

"But "compromise" and land ownership" were not words which most Indians understood. "Freedom" and a "free spirit" had long characterized the natives of the land which the white invader now wanted to "own." The basis for the Indian's simple existence was nature and the land was not something that anyone "owned." During the 1784 negotiatons at Fort Stanwix, Captain Joseph Brant of the Mohawk nation succinctly stated the Indian's convictions concerning the 1783 Treaty of Paris:

"How can the British cede to America what is not theirs to give?"

But being a practical person, and not favoring a destructive war, Joseph Brant had finally agreed to a compromise solution whereby the white man was to be given a portion of the land northwest of the Ohio River. Accordingly, and anticipating a treaty could be negotiated with the Indians in the wilderness north of Fort Harmar, St. Clair ordered Ensign

Nathan McDowell to proceed up the Muskinghum River on June 13, 1788 to build a council house. But the smoke from the cannon which greeted the governor's arrival had not dispersed when word came down the river saying twelve Chippewas had attack the block-house McDowell had constructed. Resenting this un-provoked hostility, St. Clair sent a communique to the Indians saying treaty negotiations would now be conducted at Fort Harmar.

But Captain Joseph Brant was beginning to have misgivings regarding the Indians sharing the land—he had concluded the red man's way of life was in jeopardy. In a terse message to St. Clair, he told St. Clair he wouldn't attend any conference at Fort Harmar in the winter of 1788-89.

As Ebenezer Denny paused Jason asked:

"What about those treaties with the Indians we have heard about?"

Denny glanced at Tom May and then replied:

"Well, there's a lot of Indians out here—many different tribes. The negotiations which St. Clair started here on December 15, 1788 couldn't really be counted as a general meeting but on January 11th of 1789 twenty-seven chiefs did sign two treaties. They renewed the Treaty of Fort Stanwix which was concluded in October of 1784 and signed by Richard Butler, Arthur Lee, and Oliver Wolcott for the gov-ernment. Chief Cornplanter, the Seneca leader, and Mohawk Chiefs Joseph Brant and Aaron Hill, were the principals for the Six Nations back then."

"What about the treaty my uncle Conrad told me was signed at Fort McIntosh several years ago?"

Denny shook his head slowly as he replied:

"Well Mr. Evenstar, the negotiations governor St. Clair concluded on January 11th two years ago reconfirmed that Treaty of Fort McIntosh which was signed four years earlier on January 21, 1785."

Anticipating the expected white man's rewards, a number of Indians did show up for the negotiation conference at Fort Harmar but most were only minor village chiefs without authority to represent their nation. Indians who did attend were from the Fox, Sac, Potawatomie, Chippewa, Ottawa, and the Seneca tribes. Of those who did attend, a few spurned the gifts offered them--but only a few! Significant by their absence were the Delawares and Shawnees. The governor was well aware sachems from these nations were not present but chose to ignore this important fact. Speaking to his secretary, Winthrop Sargent, St. Clair had said: "It is a start!"

In his comments Ebenezer Denny did not mention that Joseph Brant and his Mohawks were not at Fort Harmar nor the fact the Iroquois tribal sachem had countered the invitation suggesting St. Clair meet him at Duncan's Falls north of Marietta. But fearing a plot, St. Clair dispatched a courier urging the Mohawk chief to reconsider his invitation and-- as a popular 20th century television game-show star would say 200 years later: "Come on down! We will talk here."

But Joseph Brant, also known as Thayendanega, would not come to Fort Harmar. Around the Shawnee campfires he had heard about "treaty talks" in the winter of 1785 at the white man's Fort Finney near the mouth of the Big Miami. Delaware Chief Wingenund had been sent by Richard Butler on the 28th of December in 1785 to the Shawnee villages inviting them to Fort Finney. Arriving on January 14, 1786, Chief Kekewepellethy, known as "Tame Hawk," was not so tame as he boldly declared: "This land is ours!"

Speaking just as boldly, Richard Butler said: "Peace or war! Take your choice!"

The assembled Indians felt they had no choice and agreed to sign a treaty on February 1, 1786 as many of the Shawnee warriors got drunk on the white man's rum.

This incident may have contributed to some of the Shawnee warrior's unbridled hatred during what was later the Indians's "surprise" attack along the banks of the Wabash River in the fall of 1791.

But now, on this 6th day of May in 1791, Mary listened to Ebenezer Denny's remarks and then said:

"I feel fairly certain you can understand our position. We have precious little idea of what it will be like farther out in this Ohio country which you speak of but we certainly will be looking forward to having the army around in case the Indians are as unfriendly as we have been led to believe."

The understanding officer explained how Symmes had been provided an escort and replacement troops had been dispatched to that area where they landed after the escort had continued on downstream to The Falls. Mary recalled Tom had explained "The Falls" was a place where the Ohio dropped about 25 feet in a mile and that George Rogers Clark had taken some troops there about ten years ago. Mary's thoughts were abruptly broken when they heard shouting from near the ark and saw two flatboats similar to their own ark heading for shore. As everyone prepared to head for their ark Denny took his leave saying:

"Well, I must get back over to Fort Harmar. I will be heading back downstream to Fort Washington tomorrow and perhaps we shall meet again soon. It was a pleasure to make your acquaintance."

With that Denny took off in the direction of a log cabin Tom said belonged to General Putnam. As Tom now led the little procession back toward their docking area, Jason glanced at his wife--she had a worried look on her face. Mary had sensed from the recent conversation that the availability of sufficient military personnel in "the Miami lands" was a testy issue--she was right!

Mary could not know they were in the center of a geographical area history would remember as the unwelcome host of one of mankind's longest and most ruthless conflicts. Future years would see scores of books and dramas written about love, hate, hope, frustration, attacks, reprisals, anguish, massacre, vengeance, despair, anger, death, victory, defeat--the inhumanity of man against his fellow man during

the diaper years of this nation's history. Offers
by the British "hair buyer" at Detroit were matched
by the colonial government announcing a "bounty of
ten pounds for the scalp of every hostile Indian
taken." There was one problem--the black hair of a
"hostile" Indian looked the same as the black hair
of a "friendly" Indian and there were many greedy
white encroachers who openly declared:
"The only good Indian is a dead Indian!"
Many Europeans called the Indians "cruel" and
branded the red man's kind of warfare as "savage."
Indeed it was a different kind of warfare Europeans
faced but that in itself did not make it "savage."
Unlike the white man who wanted to rule the land,
most of the Indian raids were the quick hit and run
strikes intened to scare the white man away.
King George III of England had hoped his Royal
Proclamation Line of 1763 would check the settler's
westward drive beyond the demarcating Alleghenies
and the Indians would be "Christianized" and become
law-abiding loyal subjects--he was a dreamer! The
settlers were dreamers too and the westward impetus
was strong. And so as the "squatters" marked the
trees with their tomahawks and built their cabins
beyond the Allegheny Mountains, the frontier burned
and bled in a conflict of unmeasurable savagery and
persistence. The Revolutionary War had ended with
the Treaty of Paris but this man-made paper instrument in 1783 only changed the boundaries as far as
the fledgling United States was concerned--it did
not end the conflict between the copper-colored natives and the land-hungry white invaders.
There was little sympathy for the Indians who
had lived here since time immemorial and "paleface"
encroachers indiscriminately violated time-honored
taboos and traditions. The white man plied the un-
educated Indians with whiskey and rum and dazzled
their childish fantasy with combs, mirrors, thread,
needles, buttons, beads, dyes, and similar trivial
things. To buy the white man's trinkets the Indian

willingly made the same agreement as Johannes Faust did with Mephistopheles--he sold his very soul.

Water had been the Indian's only beverage but in just a few short years they eagerly traded skins for the white man's rum and their villages became riddled with social diseases. The sturdy warrior became a miserable, puny, and besotted wretch ready to barter his horse, wife, children--or himself-- for a gulp of liquor.

The old mores and traditions of Indians were thus shattered and their morals were increasingly debased and corrupted by the growing dependence on their greedy opponents. But there were some of the older and wiser sachems who saw the hand-writing in the ashes of their burned villages and devastated fields and in the frustrated faces and the hateful vengeance of their dwindling numbers who gathered around their campfires. These wrinkled and graying leaders who proclaimed:

"The white invader must be driven out of this land!"

And so the undeclared wilderness warfare raged on and in early May of 1791, from a hidden point of vantage, a pair of hate-filled eyes watched Tom May and his charges greet the occupants of the two arks which had just docked at Marietta. The skin of the hidden man was copper-colored and courageous black eyes burned in his expressionless faces. He would watch and wait for the boats to leave.

All along the Ohio--and deep in the country to the south of the river highway--Indians watched and waited for reprisal attacks. Aware of the attacks, Tom talked with the pilots of the other arks and it was agreed they would all move on downstream in the morning. One of the pilots, a novice who admitted this was only his third trip down the Ohio, said:

"I took an ark down to Maysville last fall and one of the passengers was a settler from Lexington who came down the Ohio two years ago this month and had gone back east to get his family. He said they had several boats in their party when some Indians attack them downstream near Hanging Rock. Said the Indians captured Captain Builderback and his wife-- killed Builderback he heard."

Tom nodded--he had heard the story. Remember- ing Captain Builderback was one of those who burned the Indians at Gnadenhutten, the raiding party was said to have systematically cut off his nose, ears, thumbs, and genitals. Another prisoner who escaped later said a geyser of blood erupted as a tomahawk hit Builderback squarely between the eyes and ended his life. His wife was forced to watch but fainted before the tortuous ordeal was over.

"I say Tom, have you seen Charles Greene this morning?"

The question came from a lean, well-built man with a friendly smile and professional manner. Tom introduced him as Paul Fearing and said he had not seen the man in question. Having acknowledged the introduction, Fearing explained:

"I hate to rush away but I must find Charles. He and Isaac Pierce, and Winthrop Sargent, invento- ried General Varnum's estate January 24th two years ago and I have some papers he must sign before the courier heads for Fort Pitt--they need these papers back east. But you folks are in real good hands-- Tom here knows everyone in our growing community."

They didn't need to be told Tom knew everyone, they were convinced. As Paul Fearing politely took his leave, Tom remarked:

"Charles Greene--you folks met him yesterday I believe. By the way, here comes someone else that we talked with yesterday."

As the interval narrowed Tom enthusiastically exclaimed in an Irish brogue:

"Top of the mornin' to you Major Coburn! Good to see you up and about."

"And a good morning it is Thomas--good morning Mr. and Mrs. Evenstar. I hope you folks had a good night's rest."

"We did, thank you."

"Well now, I see we have some more travelers," said Major Coburn.

"Came in this morning," said Tom. "Come along and I'll introduce you. Please excuse us folks."

And with that Tom and the major walked over to where the new arrivals now talked with the Weisers. There were a number of children on the two arriving flatboats and the youngsters were getting acquaint- ed. Soon the Evenstars could hear Coburn extolling the merits of Marietta:

"There were forty-eight in the first party and eighty-nine souls arrived later that year. Fifty of our settlers in 1788 were veterans of the war."

"Sir!"

Jason turned quickly to where a young soldier stood. Although Jason was a bit awed by the snappy salute and salutation, Mary smiled politely at the pomp and circumstance as Jason said:

"Yes soldier, what is it?"

"Mr. Evenstar sir! Major Doughty extends his compliments and requests the pleasure of your com- pany and those in your party at a get-together over at Fort Harmar this evening with supper to begin at five-thirty. May I inform him he can expect you?"

Jason glanced at Mary and she nodded. She was rather amused by her husband's embarrassment--the soldier had caught him off guard. Having recovered his composure, Jason replied:

"Please convey our regards to Major Doughty-- and inform him that we would be honored to join him this evening. And thank you for your service."

"And sir! Major Doughty also requests you do him the honor of bringing along your fiddle. Sorry sir, I mean your violin."

Without waiting for further comment, the youth touched his cap smartly, turned on a heel sharply, and retreated with dispatch.

"What a fine young man," remarked Mary.

At the first opportunity Jason advised Tom and

250

other members of their ark about Doughty's invitation. Then, shortly after midday, Mary and Jason joined Tom on the roof of their cabin and heard him explain how artillery in the corner bastions of the two-story fort across the Muskingum could sweep the land approaches. As they looked at the formidable log stockade, Jason caught sight of a canoe which had just slipped away from the shoreline below Fort Harmar and was heading swiftly across the river in an easterly direction. Tom saw the canoe too.

"That's the courier Paul Fearing told us would be heading upstream," said Tom.

While they watched the canoe gliding silently away, Tom told the Evenstars how General Putnam had brought a large tent to Marietta:

"It was one he had taken from British General John Burgoyne at Saratoga back in 1777. He used it as his headquarters when he first arrived. He has certainly proved to be a wise and capable leader in this new territory. I've heard General Washington considered him the best engineer in the army at one time!"

Called by some future historians as "Father Of Ohio," Putnam was destined to be appointed in 1796 as Surveyor General of the United States--it was an office befitting a man of his capabilities. There were thousands of acres in the vast wilderness territory created by the Ordinance of 1787 that had to be surveyed and divided into 1 mile square sections with 36 sections making a township. The payment for purchased land was generally contingent upon a proof of a valid survey.

Not only did the Ordinance of 1787 provide for formation of "States," which of itself necessitated valid surveys, that ordinance also included a vital provision regarding education:

"Religion, morality, and knowledge, being necessary to good government and the happiness of mankind, schools and the means of education shall forever be encouraged."

Years after this ordinance was adopted, Chief Justice Salmon Portland Chase (1808-1873)--American statesman, jurist, governor of Ohio (1856-1860) and one-time Secretary of the Treasury--declared:

"Never, probably, in the history of the world, did a measure of legislation so accurately fulfill, and yet so mightily exceed, the anticipation of its legislators."

With regard to "the means of education," this far-sighted Ordinance of 1787 provided that Section 16 of each township in the new territory would be earmarked for the support of public schools. After 1795 "education" would receive increasing attention but on this day in early May of 1791, in the cabin below where Tom and the Evenstars stood, it was the topic of a warm discussion by the Weisers. It was only natural the matter of educating their children would come up when women got together and today had been no exception. A mother on one of the arriving flatboats had broached the matter of her children's education and now Mrs. Weiser discussed the subject with her husband.

On the roof above the Evenstars and Tom watched the courier disappear around the tree-lined bend and then Mary broke the silence muttering:

"We would never make it."

Turning to his wife, Jason asked:

"Never make what?"

Aglow with mischievous amusement Mary replied:

"I would wager you could not paddle us back up the Ohio to Pittsburgh in a canoe!"

For a moment Jason just stared at his wife and then he glanced at Tom who was smiling from ear to ear. With a grin Jason remarked:

"The Indians do it--but their squaws do all of the paddling upstream I am told. So, if we do head back upstream, you will be doing all the paddling!"

"Forget it," said Mary. "You aren't an Indian and I am not your squaw! And I never did care much for that story of how the warriors make their wives

252

do all the work while they sit on their....horses."

As Mary then stepped to the trap door and disappeared into the bowels of the ark, Tom bent over laughing as he said: "Jason, your wife's a jewel!"

During their ensuing conversation about river travel, Jason recalled a story he had heard several years ago about James Rumsey who ran a steamboat with a power pump on the Potomac River:

"I heard it said in the blacksmith shop George Washington encouraged Rumsey in that undertaking. I read in a newspaper Mary brought back from Baltimore the first steamboat was built by John Fitch in 1786 as an experiment--said he actually operated it at three miles per hour on the Delaware River the 22nd day of August in 1787."

Tom told Jason he heard Virginia, Delaware,and Pennsylvania had given John Fitch "river rights" in 1790 to operate a steamboat between Philadelphia and Trenton, New Jersey. Neither knew it would be 1811 before a wood-burning side-wheeler steamboat, the "New Orleans," would travel the Ohio River. In May of 1791 Jason was only thinking:

"It would be nice to have a steamboat on the Ohio but how would you get it by "The Falls" downstream which Tom told us about?"

Neither Jason or Tom could know a one hundred ton vessel, built close to where they stood, would make it's maiden voyage downstream past Cincinnati, "The Falls," and on to New Orleans ten years later.

But a lot of water--some running crimson with the lifeblood of the first intrepid settlers of the fledgling nation's Northwest Territory--would flow down the Ohio before the birth of the next century.

Now, in early May of 1791, Johanne Evenstar's "first born" disappeared through the trap door and left Tom May thinking about the next leg of their downstream journey--a "shipyard" where he now stood was the farthest thing from his mind.

CHAPTER EIGHT

THE FIDDLE PLAYER

The evening of May 6th was one Mary and Jason would long remember. The gentle breeze carried the fragrant smell of spring flowers across the clearing and into Fort Harmar. The Evenstars and their companions had taken their evening meal at the fort and now prepared for the music get-together Doughty planned. The energetic settlers, with their strong arms and willing hearts, not only leveled the wilderness lands and cultivated the soil but needed no encouragement following a hard day's work to dance and sing when the occasion arose. The soldiers and settlers alike looked forward to such an evening of entertainment.

Major Doughty made certain everyone in attendance was acquainted with members of Jason's party and informed the waiting assembly it had been Tom May who confided "a fiddler" was among this load of settlers headed downstream. The major then politely encouraged Jason to favor them with his playing and he replied: "It would be my pleasure."

Jason opened his old worn violin case and went through the routine of preparing his bow and tuning up as everyone watched with eager expectation. As Jason applied a small block of resin to the strings of the bow, it was Tom who said:

"Major, perhaps we can encourage or friend to play 'The Battle Of The Kegs!'"

Tom referred to a poem by Francis Hopkinson, a
signer of the Declaration of Independence and a New
Jersey delegate to the Continental Congress. While
the Revolutionary War was in process this poem was
set to music and became popular among both miltiary
and civilian funsters. The composer asked congress
in 1781 to reimburse him for his service during the
design of the American flag but the request was not
approved in spite of the fact no one could uncover
any valid proof Mrs. Betsey Ross had made the flag
in June of 1776 at the request of her uncle George
Ross, Robert Morris, and George Washington.

Reverend Story had also been invited for the
evening festivities and commented he had a friend,
Charles Wilson Peale, who knew Francis Hopkinson.

"Charles told me Hopkinson wrote a pamphlet he
titled 'The History Of A New Roof' and last October
wrote a letter to Thomas Jefferson informing him he
had just composed 'Six Easy And Simple Songs For
The Harpsichord' which he intended to dedicate to
George Washington. A prolific fellow, Charles said
just before I left back east Hopkinson had recently added a new song and now intended to call it the
'Seven Songs.' Dear me, by the time it is published it may be the 'Eight Songs' you know!"

Everyone enjoyed Reverend Story's remarks, and
having now finished preparing his violin, Jason sat
quitely awaiting his turn. With a ripple of polite
laughter when the minister finished his commentary,
Doughty turned to Jason saying:

"Mr. Evenstar, we await your pleasure."

Jason prefaced his playing by saying: "I feel
certain most of you are familiar with the song that
Tom mentioned so those who know the words please
join in the singing."

The confines of Fort Harmar reverberated with
the music as Jason first played the melody and then
the assembly joined in with the words of the song.
Although the flute, flageolet, and haut-boy--or the
"oboe" as some called it--were in general use after

1700, the violin was a popular instrument on the
frontier and Jason played it well. He followed his
playing of Tom's request with "Two Faithful Lovers"
and the snappy toe-tapping "Sellinger's Round." An
enthusiastic round of applause was then followed by
unanimous encouragement by all for Jason to: "Play
another song!"

As everyone became quiet, Jason responded by a
suggestion his wife might be encouraged to sing her
favorite song, "Jesus Lover Of My Soul."

Mary fairly beamed as Jason began to play and
at the right moment she began to sing. A hush fell
over the place as her voice drifted throughout the
fort, over the pallisades, and into the clear night
and wilderness beyond. A reverent silence cloaked
the assembly as she finished and she suggested that
everyone join in another stanza. Her voice blended
with those of the others as smoothly as the nearby
waters of the Muskingum flowed into the Ohio River.
And the strains of that beautiful song also drifted
to the ears of some who were not welcome guests at
Fort Harmar. In the nearby wilderness two Indians
listened with awesome wonder to the melodious sound
coming from the hated white man's fort.

As the song concluded Reverend Story arose and
said sadly: "The gentleman who wrote that beautiful
song was Charles Wesley. Born in 1707, he lived a
full life. Only recently I learned he passed away.
May the Good Lord bless his soul."

It was as if one they all said: "Amen."

Jason rested his violin on his left knee as he
remarked: "I had not heard that. Perhaps my bride
will favor us with another song or two?"

After a warm round of encouragement, Mary sang
"King Henry's Lady," the zestful "Oh, Blow The Candles Out," and concluded with a plaintive Old World
ballad--a story of love and war which was always a
favorite with her father. Again encouraged to sing
"one more," Mary sang "The Pastoral Elegy" which
relates mournfully of Sweet Corydon "asleep in the

clay." Hearing this song many years later may have contributed to Governor William Harrison's decision to name Indiana's first capital "Corydon."

Like the Puritans, frontier settlers sincerely enjoyed their music and song books such as "Select Hymns For Use Of Christians" and "Harmonica Sacra" were treasured items in the home of those fortunate enough to own them.

But on this night in early May of 1791 several lusty voices were now heard as Jason played and all sang the popular "Green Sleeves. This was followed by Jason playing a spirited Irish jig. Then, after a medley of spiritual songs, the young man concluded his playing for the evening and Reverend Story led everyone in prayer.

As Jason carefully put his violin back in its worn case, Mary whispered in her husband's ear:

"I am so proud of you!"

General Putnam had been introduced to everyone and he now remarked:

"My, what an ear for music you young folks do have. And if we have any Indians lurking out there in the woods, they must surely be thinking we have the pleasure of having an angel in our midst!"

He was right--two copper-colored natives had listened attentively in the nearby wilderness.

Mary blushed as Major Doughty spoke glowingly of her singing and the expertise with which Jason handled the violin. "On behalf of everyone, please allow me to say we certainly appreciate both of you providing us such fine entertainment. We are not often favored by the violin playing and singing of such a talented couple. You will be a most welcome addition to any settlement out here--and a popular one I might add. Perhaps we shall meet again downstream--I do hope so."

"And we want to thank you for your hospitality while we were here," said Jason.

Mary's eyes sparkled as she remarked: "It was quite thoughtful of you to invite us to Fort Harmar major--and kind of you to be so complimentary."

Justifiably proud, Mary turned to her husband and softly said: "Jason my dear, if I did not know you better, I would believe you are blushing!"

She purposely made the remark just loud enough so those near them could hear and everyone politely laughed. Jason quickly commented: "Must be wind-burn--this river travel makes my face sore."

One settler, Joshua Shipman, and his wife, expressed their appreciation saying:

"Me and the missus really enjoyed your playing and your wife's singing--such a beautiful voice. I met your friend, Hank, last fall back at Simeral's Ferry."

He came out to Marietta in 1789 and went back east to accompany Charles and Sybil Shipman west in October of 1790. Now Shipman's wife shyly said:

"We don't have too many musicians out here and the Indian's drum is not a welcome sound."

Indians had only two types of native musical instruments--pipe and percussion. Their pipelike instrument or flute, was in reality a kind of flag-elot blown at the end instead of the side--it was about 18 to 24 inches in length and pierced with 3 or 6 holes. Love songs were played on the flute as a form of courtship. Percussion instruments consisted of drums and various kinds of rattles. The water drum was made by filling a keg part way with water and covering the head with an animal skin. The pitch was changed by wetting the skin or scraping it dry. Indians had different sizes of these. They also covered hollow logs with untanned deer skins and played these with a curved wooden stick. The Iroquois used rattles made from dried gourds, steer horns, and carpaces of turtles--a stick being pushed through the head and neck to form a handle.

And love was not foreign to the Indian's feelings--songs implying deep devotion and romance were often heard in the virgin wilderness by wary frontiersmen. With only its four tones, the melody of

258

the "Women's Dance" was voiced in a unique nasal
tone: "Ka non wi yo ka non wi yo he ya a!"

White men who heard the "weird savage rhythmic
arrangement," as they called it, did not know what
all the strange sounds meant. But a copper-colored
brave knew what it meant and so did the object of
his affection. A century and a half later most of
the Indians would be gone from lands drained by the
Ohio River and the more refined and civilized youth
of that enlightened era would be articulating their
romantic feelings with "music" like "Boogie Woogie
Bugle Boy" and "What's New Pussycat!"

It was only natural that Reverend Story would
be most vocal in his enthusiastic approval of Jason
and Mary's entertainment and told how the frontier
settlers had always enjoyed music: "The Puritans
had violins, played harps, and really enjoyed their
psalm singing more than eighty years ago. I recall
reading how someone tried to get a law passed about
1675 prohibiting the playing of any kind of musical
instrument except the drum, trumpet, and jewsharp.
You might have been in trouble with your violin in
those days Jason!"

Everyone laughed at the remark as he added:

"But lest anyone think the Puritans singing of
psalms was dull and solemn, it is only necessary to
read William Shakespeare's 'Winter's Tale' wherein
we find a character says: 'One Puritan amongst them
sings psalms to hornpipes!'"

Those who heard the minister smiled and Mary
nodded politely as he cited the passage from a play
which she remembered as a Shakespearean mixture of
romance, melodrama, and near-tragedy. She was very
familiar with the works of the English poet and had
brought with her a copy of "Hamlet" and "The Taming
Of The Shrew." The latter had been a present from
Jason who knew her appreciation for the writings of
Shakespeare. Mary wasn't at all certain she really
appreciated the veiled inference however. As Story
bid them goodnight, Mary reminded him of a passage

from HAMLET which read:
> *"There's a divinity that shapes our ends,*
> *Rough-hew them how we will!"*

Some of the settlers encouraged all of them to remain in Marietta but the Evenstars and the other members of their party politely declined. As they took leave of their host at Fort Harmar, Jason said to everyone:

"You folks ever get down our way, drop in and see us--the latch string will always be out!"

To herself Mary thought: "Who ever heard of a latch string on a lean-to!"

Without incident they were then escorted back across the Muskingum to their ark by soldiers from Fort Harmar. Later, as Mary stood by the fireplace on their ark, she remarked wistfully:

"Everyone was so nice. I rather wish we were going to stay here."

Jason looked at his wife as she stood quietly in the glow of the fireplace--her eyes were misty. He picked up the Bible which lay on the table near the fireplace and began thumbing through the pages. Although Jason remembered the passage his uncle had often said was in The Good Book, *"There's a time to stay and a time to go,"* that was not the one he was searching for. The one he was looking for, and the one he read to Mary, was:

> *"To everything there is a season and a time to every purpose under the heavens."*

She said nothing after Jason read the passage. She also remembered what Jason's uncle had said but then he was always quoting passages from the Bible and Mary was not certain some were not taken out of context. Quietly she listened as her husband read from Chapter 3 of Ecclesiastes--the first verse. A moment later Jason's eyes dropped down to the verse number seven and he read to himself:

> *"A time to keep silence, and a time to speak!"*

The young man silently vowed he should listen more and speak less.

Mary was not at all sure the passage Jason had read was appropriate so she merely said:

"Good night Jason."

Then, in the close confines of the ark cabin, where food, body odor, woodsmoke, and the smell of animals were on permanent parade, she fell asleep.

Jason had drawn the last watch and he was forward on the bow when the rounded hills to the east became outlined by the rosy glow of a new day. The morning hush was broken only by birds singing and the gentle lapping of small waves against the side of their ark. But the sounds of the awakening wilderness were soon joined by a chorus of new sounds as they prepared to leave.

Several settlers gathered on shore to bid them farewell as Tom maneuvered the big clumsy ark back into the mainstream of the Ohio with the other two boats following close behind--it was the birth of a new day and they were again on their way. And from the hills which lined the northern shore of their water highway came the ominous throbbing of a drum. Tom heard it--but said nothing. He knew a message was being sent downstream announcing their coming!

As demonstrated by the Boy Scouts of Ohio dur- the sesquicentennial celebration of the "Ordinance of 1787," Indians had a remarkably expedient system of long-range communication using drums and signal-fire smoke.

River travel was devoid of strenuous labor for all practical purposes--the ever watchful eye was the most important thing. Occasionally the men did work up a sweat manning the long poles under Tom's expert direction but not often. The ark drifted on downstream at about four or five miles an hour with a constant watch maintained over the water in their path and Tom's keen eyes alertly sweeping the shore on either side.

Meantime the huge wooden steering sweep moved to and fro at the stern as Tom expertly avoided the treacherous sand bars and floating debris. Now two hours downstream they experienced their first cause for alarm as everyone felt a nerve shaking crunch accompanied by a terrifying grinding groan. On the bow Dave had shouted a warning but it was too late. Suddenly the huge ark swung sideways in the treacherous current and then listed dangerously as it ground its way up and over some submerged obstacle. Ominous groans came from deep inside the wooden ark as it grated over the underwater peril and then came down with a resounding slap that made everyone cringe. Inside the cabin Mary murmured a fervent prayer and clung on for dear life. From his place on the stern, Tom quickly signaled the craft behind of the danger and then brought the bow of their ark around deftly.

But the ark weathered the incident and everyone began to breathe easier as everyone joined in a minute check for any damage. A kettle of soup had upset in the fireplace and one of the Weiser children miraculously escaped falling overboard. It was Mary who suffered a nasty fall which left her with a bloody nose and a black and blue eye. Now three months enceinte, Mary's fall was of real concern to Sarah Weiser who was quite knowledgeable concerning such matters and she strongly advised Jason's wife get a lot of rest.

"You just stay in bed--me and Alma will do the work that needs doing here."

Although Jason was naturally worried, his wife assured him she would be all right and urged him to go out and help Tom. Reluctantly he left the cabin and found Hank talking with their pilot who said:

"That was quite a bump in the road back there! But this still beats overland wagon travel through the wilderness north of here!"

Actually there was no wilderness wagon travel where Tom pointed and he knew it. And neither Tom, Hank, or Jason had any way of knowing it was going to be another six years before "Zane's Trace" would be open for wilderness travel across southern Ohio.

As they stood talking on the stern of the ark
a cloud of something almost obliterated the sun and
Dave exclaimed: "My God, what on earth is that?"

"Passenger pigeons," replied Tom promptly. He
could understand Dave's anxiety and added: "Lot of
them out here--plump and tasty and mighty fine eating. You can get two or three with one ball!"

Fifteen miles down the river from Marietta Tom
pointed out the mouth of the Little Kanawha River
to the south. Using the stem of his pipe to point
towards the northern shore, the old pilot added:

"Little settlement over there is called Belpre
or Bell Prairie. Offered Reverend Story a ride but
tomorrow wasn't the right Sabbath for him to preach
down here."

An hour later the ark drifted around a bend in
the river and ahead of them was a large island. It
would be a decade before that island would host the
estate of Harman Blennerhassett. Since the island
was within the bounds of Virginia, Blennerhassett
would have slaves and his estate would be a center
of social life in 1805 when Aaron Burr made a trip
down the Ohio. The Federalists at Marietta would
treat with contempt the man who tied Thomas Jefferson for the presidency in 1800 but Burr would find
Blennerhassett's hospitality a welcome haven. And
although later both of these men would be tried for
treason, both would be acquitted.

Scanning the south shoreline, Hank pointed out
to Tom a canoe working its way tediously upstream
near the island. Tom looked carefully and said:

"Courier out of Maysville probably. Its close
to a hundred and ninety miles upstream to the forks
of the Ohio--got a lot of paddling ahead of him!"

It was the terrified scream of Sarah, and the
quick shot by Jason, that saved little Ella Morning
from being kidnapped or possibly killed and scalped
a short time later. Just above the mouth of the
Hocking River, Tom and the other pilots had tied up
at one of the river islands to take on wood for the

fireplaces--it was a place Tom often stopped.

The Weiser children had taken serious heed of Tom's admonishment and remained on the ark while the men gathered wood to replenish their supply and Jason maintained a sharp lookout for Indians. Two of the children from the flatboat behind Tom's had ventured on shore and playfully romped along the narrow shoreline about fifty yards from the working party. Ella had lingered a little longer after her mother cautioned against straying too far away and now her long blond curls danced in the sunlight as she skipped along the shore in a zigzag course.

Suddenly, as her mother watched in paralyzing horror, a copper-skinned young man dashed from the underbrush and bore down on the unsuspecting girl. Standing on the stern of their boat Sarah witnessed the frightening scene unfold and then her terror-stricken scream split the afternoon air. The other men did not have time to look before Jason whirled and a ball from his gun was on the way. When they did look they saw the would-be-kidnapper running for the nearby woods clutching his shattered and bleeding elbow.

Everyone's supply of firewood had fortunately been fairly well replenished so no time was lost in getting back into the mainstream of the river. Not a sign was seen of any other Indians.

Beside the fireplace that night the wide-eyed Weiser children watched Jason with a sort of "hero" worship and listened attentively when he voiced his praise for Sarah's warning scream which resulted in his life-saving action.

"Had it not been for your mother, I might not have got off a shot and that little girl might be a prisoner on her way to some Indian camp--or something worse!"

The kidnaping and incarceration of any human--be they white, red, black, brown, or yellow--is an emotional experience for eveyone but particularly traumatic for the parents of a boy or girl. It was unfortunate that children of frontier parents--both red and white--were all too often the victims of a kidnaping. It was the regular practice of Seneca Indians of "adopting" into their tribe a captive to fill the place of a slain relative. This night Tom told of such an incident north of Fort Pitt:

"Happened along the banks of Plum Creek up the Allegheny south of Kittanning at the home of John Lytle--he moved there from Carlisle. The place had been an old abandoned Delaware village where Chief Running Fox and his Delawares killed the brother of Seneca Chief Cornplanter before they all decided to move west. By the way, Chief Cornplanter's Indian name was 'War hoy on eh th'--it means Big White Man and I'm told he was just that, big! I don't know know about the white part."

Tom glanced at Hank and smiled as he withdrew a flaming stick from the fireplace and proceeded to light his pipe. Everyone waited quietly for him to continue. Finally he said:

"Cornplanter knew the Delawares had moved and he vowed vengeance against the white man who moved there. So on September 17th in 1779 the chief just kidnapped Sarah Lytle and her three little children right out of their home. Along the way back to old Cornplanter's village up on the headwaters of the Allegheny River, one of his men unmercifully bashed the head of Sarah's little three month old daughter against a tree--just because it began to cry."

Mary felt sick to her stomach but said nothing and breathed deeply as Tom continued:

"Old John Lytle went half daft looking for his family and on the last day of October he finally up and paid a ransom and obtained the release of Sarah and their son Harrison. But Chief Cornplanter just arbitrarily gave nine year old Eleanor Lytle to his mother to replace the younger brother who had been killed by the Delawares. John Lytle did everything he could to secure the release of his daughter--he even sought the help of the British colonel at Fort

Niagara, John Johnson. Then, the tenth day of May
the following year, this so-called adopted daughter
declined a ransom offer saying she was not about to
leave Chief Cornplanter."

Tom again paused. Having listened attentively
and being all caught up in the story, one of Hank's
children just beat Dave's wife in asking:

"What happened Mr. May? Did she get away?"

"Well, you know how children are—that little
girl took a real liking to her Indian mother and a
big brother who gave her an Indian name which meant
'ship under full sail.' In spite of her insistence
on staying with the Indians, a meeting was arranged
for November 23rd in 1783 wherein it was agreed old
Cornplanter would bring his "sister" to Fort George
opposite Fort Niagara to see if the girl wanted to
return to her parents. As I was told, when Eleanor
Lytle faced her folks she rushed into her parent's
arms and old Chief Cornplanter departed with tears
streaming down his rugged face."

Everyone encouraged Tom to "tell another one"
and he obliged by relating how he had heard about a
young man named Marmaduke Swearingen who folks said
had reportedly been taken prisoner by some Shawnee
Indians several years back.

"Happened about fifty miles up the Monongahela
from Fort Pitt I heard. A fellar I took downstream
last fall said Marmaduke just disappeared—said his
family have never heard a word from him."

Hank's wide-eyed daughter injected: "Maybe he
was adopted Mr. May. Could he have been?"

Looking into her eyes, Tom replied soberly:

"At his age? Rather doubtful I think but then
who knows—he'd have to agree to have all his white
blood washed out and live by the Indian ways. Some
say the Shawnees had a black runaway slave boy from
Virginia who underwent this adoption ritual—became
quite a warrior. He was killed at Boonesborough in
1778 according to a story I heard down at Limestone
Point a few years ago—said his name was Ceasar."

The next day being the Sabbath, a brief morning devotional service was conducted in the cabin. Tom had informed the other pilots they wouldn't be hoisting anchor until after such service. They too planned a service--the Morning family in the second boat were particularly grateful for an opportunity to join with others in voicing their thanks that day. Then, with worship services over, the pilots hoisted anchor drifted "pretty much in a southerly direction," as Jason observed.

"Right you are," said Tom. "But before the sun reaches its zenith, we'll turn in a westerly direction and head north by west. We've got some rapids to maneuver through this afternoon and I'm gonna be needing you fellars on the poles!"

"Just say the word," replied Jason.

Curtained by a background of rolling hills, the grandeur and untouched loveliness of the broad sweeping curves of their river highway provided an ever-changing panorama. Arms akimbo, Jason stood watching the trees, vines, flowers, and grasses on the shore. Everywhere he looked the virgin land stretched without limit. His trend of thinking was interrupted when he heard Hank exclaim:

"This level bottom land sure would be mighty good for Indian corn!"

Others had marveled at these same vistas as they drifted with the current down the Ohio River. A curious conglomeration, the countless explorers, traders, merchants, surveyors, ministers, doctors, soldiers, statesmen--rich men and poor men alike-- surged downstream searching for something that in many cases ended up being a stump-dotted piece of "new ground" in the middle of an Indian-infested forest miles from their nearest neighbor. In this virgin country Jason and his friends were destined to melt together with the liars, cheaters, thieves, and drunkards who also flooded the new territory.

But lest anyone think these immigrants would give any thought to delaying their westward sojourn because of the "Indian menace," the reader has but to remember these brash and sensitive, skilled and unskilled, brave and meek, saint and sinner, home- makers and home wreckers, had their "roots" in the dispossessed of Europe. From France, England, and other countries of Europe, had come the war-weary, over-taxed, victims of unfair penal laws, orphans, bastards, and those who sought to escape religious persecution.....refugees who braved ocean perils on ill-fitted ships just to get to America. They were not timid people who came down the Ohio. And King George II had the temerity to believe he could stem the westward movement of such people as these!

That afternoon, shortly after Tom steered the ark around a long bend and through what appeared to be a 180 degrees change of direction, the old pilot ordered each man to "grab a pole!" Then, as he had predicted, Tom carefully maneuvered the huge craft through some rock infested waters. Later, with his gun cradled in the crook of his left arm and watch- ing the sun dropping low in the western sky, Jason heard the pilot order Hank to "drop the anchor!" A few minutes later Tom told Jason and Hank::

"With good weather, tomorrow we will pass the mouth of the Great Kanawha."

A light rain fell early in the evening but the skies cleared near midnight and a slice of the moon peeked over the hills along the eastern shore. As usual, the men took their turn in maintaining a sharp lookout all night. As Tom admonished:

"These beautiful primeval woods, as some call them, are infested with wild beasts and marauding Indians--we must be very cautious!"

The importance of the watch was proven in the wee hours of the morning that night when, close to three o'clock, the anchor came loose and their ark started drifting toward shore. Dave had the watch and immediately alerted Tom. He then assisted Tom in maneuvering the ark back into midstream where a spare anchor was dropped. Fortunately, that slice of moon in the black velvet overhead had been a big help to Dave--he had observed that they were drifting away from the other boats. Tom showed Dave the severed anchor rope saying:

"That's why I carry a spare--an Indian cut our anchor line hoping we would drift onto those rocks over there. Good work Dave!"

The sun was just climbing over the rim of the hills when Tom pointed out to Hank and Jason the rocks along the shore which could have spelled disaster had it not been for Dave's alertness. During breakfast everyone expressed their appreciation to Dave after Tom told them what had happened. Then, to ease the tension, Tom said:

"You know folks, I just remembered something. Just east of here, and up a little creek at a place called "Burning Bush," an old trapper back in 1775 saw some bubbles rising to the top of the water and he said them bubbles actually burned!"

Prior to the old trapper's observation, French missionaries had reported seeing "pillars of fire." And, in 1775, George Washington saw what he called "a burning spring" during his wilderness trip south of the Ohio River. But now, in early May of 1791, Mrs. Weiser glanced at her husband and then said:

"Thomas, that wouldn't be a windy would it?"

"On my honor Sarah, that's the way I heard it said," replied Tom. "Them bubbles actually burned!"

Thirty-eight years later, and in the same area Tom referred to, James Wilson brought in the first natural gas well in the United States while drilling for salt not far from Charleston.

After having ordered Hank to raise the anchor, and then drifting for a while, Tom turned the sweep over to Hank and went forward to where Jason stood watching the Weiser boys clean out the animal pen. Engaged in casual talk, Tom suddenly said:

"Pardon me Jason, just thought you might like to know Point Pleasant is right ahead on the port side--Fort Randolph too. I stopped there last fall and talked to Colonel Thomas Lewis--he was warning folks to steer clear of the north side of the Ohio. Said Colonel Henry Lee, from Mason County, reported about seventy Indians were camped north of Hanging Rock--that's downstream about fifty miles."

It was a strategic location where the Indians watched the river for boats. Using 50 foot canoes they would overtake the unwary boats, rob and kill the occupants, and burn the boats. As Tom said:

"At Wheeling last month a courier heading for Fort Pitt reported thirty settlers had been robbed and killed in March near Hanging Rock. We'll give that northern shore a wide berth!"

Word had spread like wild-fire concerning this multiple-murder and it was not uncommon to see the wreckage of some ill-fated boat or a bloated corpse caught in the low-hanging trees along the shore.

Shaking his head in disbelief, Jason said:

"Please don't mention that to my wife Tom."

Avoiding further referral to that terrible incident, Tom seized the moment to relate how this area had been witness to several occurrences which had provoked the anger of both the Indians and the settlers. He related how Dr. John Connolly, agent for the Virginia governor, Lord Dunmore, had issued a proclamation to settlers southwest of Fort Pitt advising them to "arm and fight" if the Indians did continue their raids in violation of what he called the "Iroquois Agreement of 1768." Tom continued his commentary saying:

"In 1774 Lord Dunmore led his right wing from Pittsburgh southwest through the wilderness staying on the north side of the Ohio. From the southeast, General Andrew Lewis led four hundred militiamen from Virginia northwest along the Kanawha to Point Pleasant. But them Shawnees knew General Lewis was coming and old Chief Pucksinwah and Cornstalk went out to meet him. Reinforced by warriors from the Delaware, Mingo, and Wyandot villages, Pucksinwah led his warriors across the Ohio just upstream from here and, at first light on the 10th of October, he led an attack on the white man's camp."

Future historians would say Indian personages such as Red Hawk, Red Eagle, and Blue Jacket took part in this battle at Point Pleasant.

"I suppose the Indians figured they would just finish off General Lewis and then attack Dunmore," said Jason as Tom paused to examine his pipe. "And you say that battle took place right over there?"

"That's right," replied Tom.

On the heels of this affirmation, Dave's voice was heard from the bow where he stood pointing to the shore "on the port side" as Tom called it. An opening in the tree line signaled the entrance of a large stream.

"That's the Great Kanawha," said Tom. "Jason, maybe you would like to help the women and children take a peek through the trapdoor--it's safe here in midstream. Then you might relieve Hank back on the sweep--he's probably bushed by now."

Later, as Tom stood with Hank in front of the stock fence, the old pilot said:

"Been chatting with Jason about Lord Dunmore's campaign and the battle at Point Pleasant."

Hank tossed his cud of tobacco into the river, wiped his mouth, and said:

"Some fellar I talked with a couple years back told me Colonel Benjamin Wilson and Captain Stuart from Virginia was at that skirmish and both claimed there was a lot of Indians got killed."

Tom looked at Hank thoughtfully and replied:

"Indians take their dead from the battlefield so it is hard to get a true count. I've heard some say the Indians thought they were on the verge of a victory but withdrew when old Chief Pucksinwah was killed or wounded. The fact is, they did withdraw, crossed the Ohio, and made camp north of here. And there, on October 27th in 1774, the Indians signed a peace treaty at Camp Charlotte with Lord Dunmore. It was hailed by the white man as a great victory!"

With Chief Pucksinwah mortally wounded on the field of battle, the Indians had sent word to Lord Dunmore saying they wanted to smoke the peace pipe. But then the Virginia "Long Knives," who had 75 KIA and 140 wounded, had to be threatened by Dunmore to prevent mass slaughter of Indians who had laid down their tomahawks admitting defeat. Although the Indian's loss is unknown, the Shawnee chief mortally wounded that bloody day was the father of Tecumseh.

"You've sure got a good handle on that battle Tom, but there's one thing that sticks in my craw." Hank paused for a moment and added: "I've heard it said Dunmore knew about the Indian's plan to attack General Lewis but he didn't say nothing 'cause he hoped to let them kill off a few of them southern volunteers and then his British soldiers would rush in and save the day. Think that's so Tom?"

Tom studied Hank's face for a long time--what could he say. He had heard the same story also but was not about to add any credence to the report.

"Well, I don't know Hank. War stories have a way of getting twisted out of shape. But what I do know is the treaty signed at Camp Charlotte said the Shawnees agreed to give up their old hunting grounds south of the Ohio, the white man agreed to stay south of the Ohio, and the Indians agreed not to bother boats on this river."

Although Chief Cornstalk said he would comply with the terms of the treaty, the settlers did not stay south of the Ohio and the Indians reacted as one might expect. Back and forth across the river the killing and stealing and reprisal attacks continued. One woman called 'Mad Ann' Bailey, widow of Richard Trotter who was killed during the Point Pleasant battle, became a frontier scout vowing to drive the Indians out of the country. As Tom said:

"I've been told "Mad Ann" Bailey once traveled one hundred miles through the Indian country to get some ammunition for a besieged fort. I can't swear to the truth of the story, and only mention it just to show the continued hate and reprisal attacks which have continued after Dunmore's War supposedly put an end to the trouble out here."

The old pilot studied the shore thoughtfully before he added:

"The other night I was telling you about that kidnapping above Fort Pitt, remember?"

Hank nodded as he placed a chew in his mouth--he remembered.

"Well, there's also been a lot of talk about another murder and kidnapping up the Kanawha in May of 1778. Couple of Moredock McKenzie's daughters, Margaret and Elizabeth, were kidnapped by a Shawnee raiding party. Some say it was Cheesekau, Pucksinwah's son, who paddled his canoe past Fort Randolph and did the dastardly deed himself--killed poor old McKenzie's wife and his twenty year old son in cold blood, burned his cabin to the ground, and carried away his two little girls."

Tom had no way of knowing those two girls were taken north to a Shawnee village where their "white blood" had been washed away and they were made members of Chief Black Fish's family and "sisters" of his ten year old foster son, Tecumseh. It would be 1797 before McKenzie was to find his daughters who escaped their captors on October 17th, 1786 during a reprisal raid led by General Benjamin Logan along the banks of the Little Miami. Riding with General Logan was Colonel Thomas Kennedy, Simon Kenton, and Captain Hugh McGary. Kenton remembered the village well--it had been here that he was held captive and the Indians remembered how the brave white man had endured their severe punishment. Although most of the Shawnee warriors were away that day, the looks of surprise on those who were there quickly changed to fear when Kenton rode into their midst.

One of Logan's men had been dispatched to the Indian village carrying a white flag but was tomahawked and scalped. When Kennedy saw his friend's dead body, his slashing tomahawk soon left six of the defenseless squaws dead while others cowered in fear screaming: "Mat tah tshi!"

You did not need to be a Shawnee linguist to know the terror-stricken squaws were pleading:

"Don't kill us!"

Left behind with the women and children, one proud elderly wrinkled and gray-haired Shawnee was held for questioning--it was old Chief Moluntha who Captain Hugh McGary remembered as one of those who had viciously cut them to ribbons at Blue Licks on August 19, 1782. Without mercy, McGary had buried a tomahawk in the surrendered chief's skull. Court martialed for this brutal murder five months later, McGary was acquitted on March 21, 1787.

Despite General Logan's strong disapproval of the cold-blooded killing, he kidnapped and carried home a young red-skinned twelve year old boy the Indians called "Spemica Lawba." Adopted by General Logan, this young man reluctantly returned to his Shawnee home in 1787 during a prisoner exchange.

As for McKenzie's daughters, they escaped into the wilderness in 1786 during Logan's raid and made their way north to where John Kinzie's trading post stood at the head of the Maumee River--John married Margaret McKenzie the next year. Also located here at the head of the Maumee was the principal village of the Miamis--the place General Harmar's men looted and burned in October of 1790 only seven months before Hank asked their sober-faced pilot:

"What about that murder of old Chief Cornstalk Tom? I heard a lot of talk about that at Pitt."

Tom pointed his index finger saying:

"Happened right over there at Fort Randolph on July 2nd 1778--a senseless and cowardly act! Chief Cornstalk, his son, and another sub-chief, came to that fort over there in good faith and asked to see Captain Arbuckle. Old Cornstalk wanted to warn him about the Shawnee's plan to join the British. But, and without the slightest provocation, those three Indians--unarmed and defenseless--were murdered!"

Years later, in his "Monuments To Historical Indian Chiefs and The Ohio Indians," Colonel Edward Livingston Taylor stated succinctly:

"It always has been, and always will be, considered one of the most inexcusable and unfortunate murders in the history of our contact with the red race!"

An historian, and the nation's 26th president, Theodore Roosevelt is reported to have said: "There was no record of any more infamous deed!"

But on the deck of the flatboat drifting down the Ohio in May of 1791, Tom shook his head sadly saying with a measure of disgust:

"Word of that killing spread across the whole frontier like a plague! After Cornstalk's murder, most of the Indians--except those few Christianized Delawares--sided with the British. I told you what happened to those Delawares at Gnadenhutten!"

Instinctively, Tom suddenly turned his head in the direction of the northern shore and placed his cupped hand over his ear--Hank heard it too. From far away came a muffled throbbing sound like someone pounding on a hollow log. Standing on the bow, Dave heard the pulsating beat too and called out to their old pilot:

"Hey Tom, what's that?"

Careful not to alarm anyone inside the cabin, Tom said in a low but distinct voice:

"That's a drum Dave--an Indian sending word to his partners downstream that some boats are coming. Sounds like there might be some more boats behind us. That's good....safety in numbers you know!"

Although resting quietly on her bed inside the cabin, and not taking part in the children's noisy activities near the fireplace, Mary had heard most of the conversation between Hank and Tom--enough to bring tears to her eyes and she thought to herself:

"What on earth are we getting ourselves into?"

Her thoughts were abruptly interrupted as she heard her husband on the stern shout:

"Look over there Tom!"

Glancing towards the stern where Jason manned the sweep, Tom saw his protege holding the tiller and pointing a finger toward the north shore. Tom stepped quickly to the stern and looked where Jason pointed and then said with a smile:

"That's Gallipolis over there--that settlement Major Doughty was telling you about. The buildings are way back in the woods. What you see looks like a boat unloading along the shore."

Hank had followed Tom to the stern and heard his comment. Now Hank said:

"That fellar Thierry at Marietta said he was told there was gonna be 'a teeming metropolis' out here. Ain't just sure what one of them is supposed to be but that over there sure don't look like one! That baker fellar said a Joel or Joseph Barlow, and some guy named Playfair, told him 'custard grows on trees and candles can be picked up in the swamp out here.' Now that's a real 'windy' for you if I ever heard one."

Indeed Barlow had engaged a nefarious huckster in France named William Playfair and the so-called "Compagnie Du Scioto" provided the toiling denizens of Paris with a brochure which proclaimed:

"The beautiful land abounds in excellent fish of a vast size and there are noble forests with some trees which spontaneously produce sugar--there is a plant which yields ready made candles. And you will find venison in plenty, the pursuit of which is uninterrupted by wolves, lions, foxes, or tigers. A couple of swine will multiply themselves a hundred fold in two or three years without taking any care of them. The climate of Ohio is wholesome and delightful and frost, even in the winter, is almost unknown!"

The pronunciamento promised: "There are no taxes to pay and no military service to be performed!"

Small wonder five hundred French emigrants had quickly packed up their belongings and took off for

the "fabulous Gallipolis along La Belle Riviere" as
the glib-tongued salesman in Paris called it. Born
in 1810 at Bethel, Connecticut--the son of a tavern
keeper--Phineas T. Barnum--a famous showman--would
be remembered as often saying during his lifetime:
"People like to be humbugged!" And it would also be
more than a century after Francis Thierry and his
companions swallowed Playfair's sales pitch before
the Brooklyn Bridge--erected by John A. Roebling in
1883--would be sold by William Playfair's likeness
to a similar trusting and unsuspecting buyer. The
good people of France had no corner on naivete.

"I thought we'd spot some sign of them fellars
at Gallipolis," said Hank. "I 'spose the Indians in
this neck of the woods ain't real happy having that
settlement over there--or any other place out here
for that matter probably."

There was some merit in his remark--settlement
of the land by the British and French had left the
Indians with mixed emotions at first.   The British
in "their New England" had treated the Indians with
a measure of respect and settled on their purchased
land to plant corn. But the French in "their New
France" treated the Indian with disrespect and went
about exploiting the land and building their forts.
Strategically it was a smart move by the French and
the Indians did find the forts valuable for use as
a warehouse or trading post.

But treaties between the French and British in
1763--and the British and United States in 1783--
made the Indians concerned that no consideration
was being given to the red man's interests. In the
area which would later become Ohio, the Wyandots in
the Sandusky Bay region, and the Delawares on the
headwaters of the Muskingum, were separated by a
boundary running from Lake Erie to the Scioto River
established by terms of the McIntosh Treaty which
was signed January 21,1785. These two nations were
flanked by the fierce Miamis and the uncompromising
Shawnees who allied themselves with both the French

and British to "hold back the white invader." The old adage, "war makes strange bedfellows," was certainly a truism in the Northwest Territory.

Incited by "hell-hounds" like renegades Simon Girty and Alexander McKee, the Indian threat deterred but did not stop the development of settlements along the Ohio River. In 1788, at Detroit, another renegade--Matthew Elliott--agreed to service under British Lieutenant Governor Henry Hamiliton saying he would keep the the Indians aroused in their hate of the white invader. And so, the entire Northwest Territory was a seething bed of hate and discontent as Jason and his companion's ark drifted around the southernmost point of their downstream journey this Sunday afternoon, May 8th in 1791.

Inside the cabin Mary decided she would sit up for a while--the smell of bean soup simmering in a pot made her sick to her stomach. The next morning she intended to insist on Tom allowing her to step outside and get some fresh air, weather permitting of course. While contemplating the possibility she heard their pilot just outside the cabin door say:

"That's the Big Sandy on our port side Jason-- now we drift north by west. We've got to watch out for tricky currents and swirls along here--they can be treacherous and carry you into that north shore before you know it. Or, against those rocks on the south shore. Either way it could spell trouble and trouble we don't need! I figure we'll drop anchor soon just ahead out from the south shore and across from Raccoon River--good fishing there!"

Tom addressed the last part of his comment to Hank who came walking back from the bow.

"That'd be on the port side going downstream," said Hank with a big smile. "Right Tom?"

"You got the picture fellar--you're gonna earn your sailor duds before we get to Maysville! A man learns fast out here in this country if he wants to stay alive!"

The half-smile on Jason's face faded quickly--

the throb of a drum on the north shore sent shivers up his spine. Observing the look of anxiety on his young friend's face, Tom remarked:

"Probably some Indian up on Hanging Rock downstream a ways. With their drums and smoke signals, Indians talk back and forth pretty good."

Having dropped anchor and taken the necessary precautions to secure the ark for the night, Jason and Tom leaned against the stock fence and talked:

"Been meaning to ask you something Tom," said Jason. "Ever hear of a man named Hinton who fell in this river and drown about twelve years ago? Uncle Conrad said Hinton was with a party of settlers."

Tom studied for a moment and replied:

"Winter of '79 as I recall. He was with that party that went down to The Falls--the Van Meters, Haycrafts, Helms, and a fellar named John Vertrees. Vertrees was one of Clark's 'Long Knives' I heard-- got himself some land south of The Falls and was a judge at Elizabethtown couple years ago."

"But what about Hinton?"

"Like I said Jason, David Hinton--that was his name I'm pretty sure--was with that party. He fell off the boat and drown someplace right along here. Now that I think about it, Dave married Van Meter's daughter, Mary. Last time I went down to The Falls I heard it said widow Hinton had married Major Bill Chenoweth."

"At Pittsburgh we heard a party of settlers in 1779 or 1780 had more than sixty boats and over one thousand men, women, and children." Jason shook his head in disbelief and added with a smile: "That is a lot of boats--and people!"

Tom pushed his hat back and scratched his head thoughtfully before remarking:

"Like I told Dave this afternoon, there's some safety in numbers. I think you're right about that big party but there were several of those that went downstream back about then. That party Hinton was in had sixty-three boats and, if I remember right,

General Lytle was with them. Hard to keep track of the thousands who have come down this river but one I do remember clear as day was George Rogers Clark when he headed downstream in May of 1778--went all the way down to The Falls and landed at Corn Island and then went out to Kaskaskia on the Mississippi."

"Clark has made quite a name for himself out here in this country, hasn't he?"

"That he has Jason," replied Tom. "That place down at The Falls is now called Clarksville! Named it for him you know. Clark's a good man!"

"Hank met an officer at Fort Pitt last summer who said Clark likes his whiskey--that true Tom?"

"I've heard that too Jason but I can't say for sure. Might be a pretty good idea to find out what he drinks and give all the troops a ration!"

When the time came for Hank to take the watch at four in the morning, Dave told him he thought he had seen some Indians sneaking along in the shadows along the south shore. Dave also complained about an occasional strong smell of dead fish carried to his nostrils by an infrequent breeze from the west. Hank dismissed the complaint telling Dave they must expect such odors on a river boat.

Less than a mile away, along the south shore-- and well hidden from anyone's view--several Indians watched and waited. They had decided it was unwise to attack the three boats just offshore--they would wait for a boat to come drifting downstream alone. They had noticed some of the boats now carried men who seemed to fire an unusual number of their "lead birds" while heading downstream during the daylight hours--a few wore uniforms.

Although he kept a sharp lookout, Hank did not see a soul until Jason came on deck at first light. The impatient bleating of a sheep, and the stomping of the horse's restless feet on the strange earthen cushion beneath them, had awakened Jason. Emerging from the cabin, Jason stretched and yawned and said to Hank:

"Looks like it is going to be a beautiful day. The river is smooth as silk and the sky's not red!"

Hank's rather unusual silence, and the puzzled look on his face, prompted Jason to add cheerfully:

"Red sky at night, sailor's delight. Red sky in the morning, sailor take warning!"

In a dry manner Hank said, "You better go back to bed Jason, it's way too early for that! On the other hand, look over there Jason!"

Hank pointed toward the south shore and added:

"See those cussed lights over there—down near the water? See 'em flicker? What are they?"

As his friend rubbed his eyes and studied the mysterious glittering phenomena, Hank repeated what Dave had said. At long last Jason remarked:

"I can't make it out Hank—they seem to be reflecting the light. See, there's more of them now as it gets brighter. What did Tom say?"

"What did Tom say about what?" It was Tom and after being informed of the sighting he said:

"Looks to me like little mirrors. But what in heaven's name would they be doing over there? They could be pieces of metal—maybe glass. It beats me but I do know one thing—we ain't about to go over there and find out! That might be an Indian trick! But what I really came out here for was to tell you breakfast is ready. I'll stay out here on deck and watch while you two go eat. I want to hoist anchor pretty soon."

With breakfast over, and all hands on deck, it was Tom who called out: "Hoist the anchor!" He had called to the other pilots suggesting they drift in tandem staying close together. The river was like a sheet of smoky glass and only an occasional fish leaping into the air disturbed the mirror-like surface when it ended its brief airborne journey with a splash. With Tom manning the sweep and remaining twenty or thirty yards distant from the overhanging shrubs and trees along the southern shore, the huge flatboat began to move with the current.

Once again the distant muffled throb of a drum was heard as Jason reluctantly followed Mary out of the cabin--the Indians knew they were moving again. Just as she vowed the day before, Mary asked Tom to allow her to get "a breath of fresh air" and he had approved her request provided Jason stay beside her and she not stay outside too long. With Jason next to her, Mary now stood by the stock fence drinking in the morning sunshine and enjoying the fresh air. Although Jason said he would feel more comfortable if they stood between the fence and their wagon, Mary pooh-poohed the suggestion saying:

"I want to watch the water and hear the ripple of the little waves against the boat. Listen dear, isn't that soothing?"

What Jason heard suddenly was Hank on the bow when he shouted:

"Hard right Tom--submerged tree dead ahead!"

Although Tom leaned heavily against the tiller in an effort to avoid the underwater danger, it was too late and the prow of the boat began pushing its way through the branches and embedded debris with a loud grating sound. Then, as the ark shuddered and rode over the trunk of the submerged tree, Mary saw the swollen face of a bloated corpse caught in some branches and wreckage just below the surface of the water. A fraction of a heartbeat later she saw the length of wreckage on which had been painted:

"The Exodus."

As Mary screamed, and then her body went limp in Jason's arms, he saw the sickening sight too before it disappeared along the side of the ark. In disbelief Jason muttered:

"Good grief--that was Isaac and Rachel's boat! Those flashing lights we saw this morning must have been pieces of the glass panes Isaac was carrying!"

Dave helped carry Mary into the cabin and then took the sweep at Tom's request. Inside the cabin Tom then stood helplessly beside Jason and watched as Sarah tried to soothe Mary who was wringing her hands and sobbing softly. Huddled in the corner as they watched quietly, the wide-eyed children didn't make a sound. Unable to be of any assistance, Alma sat near the fireplace and sewed. Like everyone on the boat, Alma could hear the pulsating sound of an Indian drum. Just beyond the forward wall of their cabin the horses stomped the dirt-covered planking restlessly and Star whinnied nervously--the animals had caught the same scent Dave had complained about early that morning.

The tense silence in the close confines of the cabin was abruptly broken when Hank bellowed:

"Tom! Get up here, quick!"

Responding as quickly as his legs would allow, and followed closely by Jason, Tom had not reached the bow when he saw what Hank was pointing to. Ten yards off the port side the partially burned wreckage of an ark similar to their own was caught on a sand bar which had formed just off the south shore. Three badly decomposed stark-naked bodies could be seen among the wreckage and another bloated corpse floated a few feet behind with a piece of rope tied around the poor soul's neck and the other end fastened to the boat--all had been scalped. The stench was sickening and Jason felt a wave of nausea sweep though his body as they drifted by the wreckage.

"Is there nothing we can do?" Jason asked Tom.

"Not that I can think of. It's too late for those unfortunate souls and we'd really be sticking our necks out if we tried to take them off and bury them. The Indians may be just waiting for somebody to try something like that."

Although Tom had quickly shouted to the boats behind about the horrifying sight, and signaled for them to steer right, several occupants of the other boats saw the wreckage. The pilot of the third ark would later say the corpse in the water was that of a man who had been disemboweled and a stake driven through his body.

Taking the sweep, and dragging their anchor to

slow them down, Tom signaled to the boats behind to drift closer. At Tom's suggestion, the three boats were lashed together in tandem. Then, staying left of midstream, the three-boat flotilla floated downstream with what Tom called "Hanging Rock" rearing its ugly head on the north shore. The "rock" stood in an area of limestone and ore which would be host to more than 100 furnaces only 38 years later. But now, in 1791, Tom scratched his head and thought to himself:

"I wonder if the Indians will be sending out a canoe to intercept us?"

Admonished by Tom to avoid unnecessary noise, the trio of arks drifted silently with the current. At Tom's request, Jason stood by Dave on the stern. Carefully hidden behind a wagon on the bow of the lead boat, with a gun cradled in the crook of their left arm and ready for quick use if necessary, Hank and Tom kept a sharp eye on the sun-drenched overhanging rocks that frowned down on the river. And as they watched and waited, inside the cabin Sarah prayed, Alma sewed, and Mary dried her tears—Jason had to help Tom and she knew it. Meantime, Sarah's children strained their eyes peeking through cracks trying to catch a glimpse of the "Hanging Rock" Tom talked about.

Suddenly the three-ark flotilla was swept by a wave of simultaneous gasps, excited talking, and finger pointing. The flurry of excitement had been prompted by the sudden appearance of an Indian high on top of Hanging Rock. Tall and erect, the Indian had a black and white feather hanging from the left side of his head—in his right hand he held a long spear. He wore buckskin leggings with little beads that glistened in the morning sunlight and his arms were bare to the shoulder except for a wide band of silver around each arm. He also wore a jacket with the sleeves cut out—it was blue.

As everyone watched transfixed with a mixture of horror and fascination, a shot suddenly rang out

and the tell-tale puff of smoke showed it came from
the second boat. Close on the heels of this shot a
loud cheer arose quickly from the same ark when the
figure on Hanging Rock reeled about clutching his
arm and disappeared.

It all happened so quickly and having seen the
Indian apparently hit by a ball, Jason was shocked,
stunned, and a little bit frightened. What he felt
within himself, he then saw reflected in the cold
gray eyes of Tom May who had heard the shot and now
came bounding back to the stern shouting:

"What in the hell are you doing?   Do you want
to get us all killed with your damn trigger-happy
shooting? That Indian wasn't doing us a damn speck
of harm--for everyone's sake I hope you didn't kill
him! You should be horse-whipped and one more damn
senseless shot like that and I'll do it!"

It was the first off-color word Jason recalled
having heard Tom utter but he understood the anger
and frustration he felt. Having drifted downstream
away from the dangereous Hanging Rock area, the old
pilot apologized to everyone for his outburst. But
everyone, including the women, assured him they had
taken no offense and they felt he was right in admonishing the guilty party for the thoughtless act.

Long before the sun had reached its zenith the
blue-jacketed Indian rode north from Hanging Rock.
He admonished himself for his own stupidity--he had
heard Tecumseh report some of the white man's "lead
birds" would carry that far now.   Although he had
suffered only a minor flesh wound, he knew the shot
came from one of those long and ungainly small bore
guns made by some Pennsylvania gunsmith according
to what Tecumseh had heard near Fort Washington.

With Hanging Rock now behind them, and the sun
climbing toward its zenith, Tom maneuvered the boat
into midstream saying the lack of rain that spring
had made the river shallow in spots along the south
shore--this accounted for the sand bar on which the
wreckage had hung up. Although they didn't see any

more dead bodies in the river, they did see several pieces of boat wreckage.

Just before noon on that 9th of May, Tom called Jason and Hank to the stern and said:

"Around that bend up ahead is the mouth of the Scioto River--some tricky currents there and I want Jason on the bow. Hank, I'd like to have you keep a sharp eye on that north shore."

He said nothing about a Shawnee Indian village said to be located about 35 miles up the Scioto or a report he heard at Marietta concerning three boat attacks downstream from Hanging Rock. He did add:

"We'll plan to drop anchor early today near an island in midstream about thirty-five miles ahead. Be touch and go trying to make Maysville before the sun sets. The other pilots want to try and make it but I don't recommend it. Better safe than sorry! One of the other pilots got his dander up by what I said this morning--but so be it. My way I know we will be at Maysville in the morning.   In the meantime, how about taking a turn on the sweep Hank?"

Hank's response was instantaneous: "Aye, aye sir! Ensign Weiser at your service!"

Tom glanced at Jason as he laughingly said:

"I'll make a sailor out of him yet!"

With Hank on the sweep, and Dave watching the bow, Tom seated himself beside the stock fence and was smoking his pipe when Jason remarked:

"Our boat builder told us some of the settlers head inland at Limestone--mentioned some place that he called Blue Licks. He said folks get their salt there. Do you know where that is Tom?

"Limestone, Maysville--same place! That's the county seat of Mason County now. By the way, they named that county for old George Mason. Blue Licks is about fifteen miles south of Maysville along the Licking River. And yes, some people do get salt at Blue Licks. I've heard you got to boil 840 gallons of water to get just one bushel of salt. Speaking of Blue Licks, a skirmish there in 1782 is said to have been the last battle of the Revolutionary War. But in a way, that battle was a kind of victory for the Shawnee Indians over some over-zealous Kentucky volunteers who rode into an Indian trap there."

As Tom related, a Shawnee raiding party led by Chief Blackfish had attack Bryan's Station in mid-August of 1782. But then, after a three day siege, they started home. Aroused by the exhortations of Captain Hugh McGary, and led by Colonel John Todd, 170 frustrated frontiersmen from Fayette County engaged in foolhardy wilderness pursuit and fell into the Indian's trap on the north side of the Licking River at a salt producing site called "Blue Licks." There, on August 19th, 250 Indians pounced on their pursuers killing 66, wounding 12, and taking 4 home as their prisoners. Tom concluded by saying:

"Colonel Robert Patterson was wounded in that Battle of Blue Licks and later said Aaron Reynolds saved his life. Friend of mine, Peter Scholl, took a ball in the face that day but he came out of it alive. Daniel Boone's son, Israel, was taken prisoner that day!"

Jason had listened carefully but now a puzzled look crossed his face as he said:

"Our boat builder said Daniel Boone was taken prisoner in the battle at Blue Licks--that right?"

"Right place, wrong time Jason! Several years before that battle I was talking about, on February 7th or 8th in 1778, some Indians surprised a party of salt boilers at the same place during a snowstorm and captured a lot of them--Daniel Boone was one of them. There were others as I recall: Joseph Jackson, Ansel Goodman, Bill Hancock, Richard Wade, Bartlett Searcy--twenty-seven of them. Boone later managed to escape, and so did some of the others it has been said, but I can't say who did get away."

"Sounds as if there has been a lot of back and forth across the river fighting," said Jason. "You hit me, I hit you, and then you hit me!"

"Well, that's one way to look at it. Reprisal

raids have been a way of life out here for years. I remember nine years ago on November 4th in 1782-- Daniel Boone's 48th birthday--when 1500 Kentuckians gathered at the mouth of the Licking and next day headed north on one of those reprisal raids. Boone wanted them to hold off on that chase but they were cocked and primed and ready to go! Among them were Captain Richard Chenoweth, Anthony Jenkins, George Shortridge, John Torrence, three of the Galloways-- James, John, and William--and Captain Eli Cleveland from Fayette County, the Quartermaster. That's all I remember of that party right now."

Tom studied his pipe a moment and added:

"Oh yes, Captain William McCrakin was wounded in that raid--died later back here along the Ohio. But like Colonel John Bowman did in July of 1779-- and later Ben Logan's party did in October of 1786, those 1500 men sacked and burned a Shawnee village along the Little Miami called 'Oldtown'--some call it 'Old Chillicothe.' Still not satisfied, some of that party pushed north a little ways and destroyed Peter Laramie's Store."

When Tom paused, Jason interjected:

"And then it was the Indian's turn I suppose!"

"Of course," replied Tom with a half-hearted smile. "They had to have their revenge you know."

The sun was still two hours high when Tom told Jason to drop the anchor. Anchored upstream from a small island in the middle of the river, Tom caught everyone by surprise when he suggested those inside the cabin come out on the bow and wave goodbye to the other two boats proceeding on downstream. With Jason at her side, Mary enjoyed the late afternoon sunshine but was quite agreeable when Tom said:

"All right, everyone back to the cabin! Dave, you take the watch and I'll relieve you as soon as I grab a bite. I hope everyone gets a good night's sleep--we have a big day ahead of us tomorrow!"

It was a magnificent sunset and one Hank's boy would never forget. During their evening meal Tom

suggested   Hank's eldest son might like to join him
for the six to nine watch. Will was elated and Tom
carefully briefed him regarding his responsibility.
Tom also said there would be two men on each watch
that night and he volunteered to share the midnight
to three turn with Jason.

Although the night passed without incident, no
one slept soundly--missing were the snores and any
heavy breathing.   Everything was quiet until about
five-thirty when Hank sensed a pungent aroma wafted
along by a negligible southeast wind--Dave smelled
it too. In the distance they could hear the sound
of a violin. Always seeming to be around when they
needed him, Tom now emerged from the cabin, sniffed
the air, pointed upstream, and calmly said:

"Someone's bringing a load of pigs downstream!
Must be carrying a fiddle player!"

Holding his nose with thumb and forefinger,
Dave quipped: "Man, that's a stinking job--must be
lonely too. The pilot might be serenading the pigs
Tom. Maybe we ought to call Jason--he could play a
duet with that fellar!"

"I heard that David," said Jason as he stepped
from the cabin. He added cheerfully: "And you just
leave us fiddle players alone!"

Seeing Tom near the stock fence, Jason added:
"Top of the morning to you captain!"

Ten minutes later the source of the aroma came
drifting down the river. When abreast of them, Tom
called out: "Where you headed friend?"

The sound of the violin abruptly stopped and a
deep voice boomed a reply: "The Falls!"

The brief reply was still echoing against the
hills along the river when the scraping of a violin
was again heard. And with that sound the boat load
of pigs was swallowed up in the morning mist.

Dave yawned and then said: "You play a better
fiddle Jason--and we don't have to put up with that
smell either!"

CHAPTER NINE

MAYSVILLE

"Where you folks headed?"

The question came from a man at Maysville who wore a well-exhausted floppy hat pulled down over a mass of long bushy hair. From beneath the rim two friendly blue eyes topped a broad grin and parted lips showed a set of stained teeth minus two. His coarse gray linsey shirt was anchored to his waist by a knotted strand of rawhide and he wore a pair of ungainly ankle high rudely made brogans. In his left hand he clutched the barrel of a short large-bore flintlock. Without waiting for a reply the stranger added:

"I'm looking for passage down to the Miamis—aim to get me some land. Name's Hagan—Pat Hagan!"

With that the stranger extended his weather-beaten hand toward Jason and in a few moments there was no stranger. Although Jason took an immediate liking to him, he explained politely they had a full load but would certainly keep him in mind if any unexpected change prompted such consideration. Pat thanked him and remarked:

"Out here things do take on unexpected changes of color in spite of the best well aimed plans!"

Jason had no way of knowing just how prophetic those words were. Pat added:

"Appreciate you bein' so straight forward with me Mister Evenstar—it's Jason ain't it?"

Jason nodded as Pat continued:

"Me and maw came up from Lexington. Colonel

Patterson down there speaks mighty high of the land between them Miami rivers."

Jason asked, "Have you been here long?"

"Nope! Couple days--but that's long enough to hear a mess of tales about that fellar Symmes. The folks here got real acquainted with him a couple of years back 'fore he went downstream. Got himself a place he calls Miami City I heard. Where you folks aimin' to go?"

Pat wasn't being nosey, just a friendly person and Jason understood. As they talked Pat had been eyeing Jason's gun and finally remarked:

"That's a mighty fine gun you got there Jason. Can't say I ever seen one just like it!"

Jason explained that the forty inch octagonal barrel flintlock rifle was made in Pennsylvania by his uncle and he was very proud of it. The grained curly maple stock was handsomely decorated with the butt plate, triggerguard, and patch box being made of brass. The workmanship of the lock assembly was the finest. Pat looked admiringly at the matched maple forepiece which cradled the barrel and pointed to the distinctive curve behind the trigger guard saying: "Never saw one just like that!"

With pride Jason told Pat the curve on the underside of the stock was a trademark of his uncle Conrad's guns and the shot pouch and finely wrought brass powder flask he carried were gifts from that uncle who now lived in Westmoreland County.

"And that uncle's nephew is a mighty fine shot with that gun I'm here to tell you!"

Jason and Pat turned to find Tom wearing a big grin--he had been listening to their conversation.

"Pat, this is our pilot, Tom May--best one on the river! Tom, meet Pat Hagan."

As they shook hands briskly, Tom noticed Pat's hand was covered with calluses.

"Glad to make you acquaintance Mister Hagan."

"It Pat, just call me Pat."

Pat grinned and looked at Tom saying:

"Heard a lot of good things said about you and by more than just Jason here--real good to know you Mister May."

"Just call me Tom--I ain't long on formalities once we get the hand shaking over. Right Jason?"

Jason nodded his agreement as Tom added:

"Been here at Maysville long Pat?"

"Nope. Was telling Jason here we just came up from Lexington--headin' for that Miami country down the river. Colonel Patterson told me he thought it was a good idea to get a parcel of land down there. Jason here told me you folks just tied up--run into any trouble down below Hanging Rock?"

Tom cringed--he had an inkling of what Pat was referring to. At Marietta Samuel Cushing had mentioned several incidents which had just happened in March near Hanging Rock. Still fresh in Tom's mind was an incident on March 20th the year before. On that day Charles Johnson, John May, Peggy and Dolly Fleming, and Mr. Skyles had been ambushed near the mouth of the Scioto River. Dolly had been killed, John May taken prisoner, and Skyles was wounded.

When Tom said nothing, Pat Hagan began his unsolicited and vivid commentary:

"Jim Ireland and Neil Washburn came downstream about six weeks ago saying Colonel Thomas Lewis was now warning folks stopping at Point Pleasant not to put in on the Ohio side. This past March 18th some discharged servicemen from Fort Washington got waylaid near the mouth of the Scioto. Twenty-one were walking along the shore and fourteen were on a boat loaded with their baggage and provisions when they were attack--only three got away! On March 22nd, John May and his party of twelve men and two women pushed off from Fort Randolph and the Indians killed them at about the same place. Then, according to Colonel Lewis, the day after John May pushed off, a party of sixteen shoved off from Point Pleasant and they were killed and scalped near the mouth of the Scioto--fellar named Greathouse was in that party."

John May, a wealthy land owner, had been captured previously but was released when he promised
to leave the country--the Indians had not forgotten
the broken promise. And now, only two months after
these three incidents, Jason looked at Tom--the old
pilot had not mentioned these incidents. Considering the possibility Tom had not heard about the incidents, Jason turned his attention to Pat saying:

"Pat, you mentioned a man named Greathouse was
with that last party--could that have been Daniel
Greathouse? Years ago I heard someone say he was
involved in a killing at Yellow Creek?"

"That wasn't Daniel," replied Pat. "But I know
what you're talking about. Friend of mine told me
Colonel William Crawford wrote to George Washington
back in May of 1774 saying Daniel Greathouse was in
the party that killed Logan's sister at Yellow Crik
but Daniel died about 1778 so he couldn't have been
the one them Indians tortured and killed this past
March. It was Daniel's younger brother, Jonathan--
about twenty-five years old and not married. They
had a sister, Susanna, who married her cousin--Van
Swearingen. He's a son of John and Kate Swearingen
who lived along the Cheat River back your way. Van
fought in the Revolutionary War and had a brother
named Marmaduke who came up missing some time ago--
some say he might have been captured by Indians!"

Tom listened to every word--Major Cushing had
not provided the details Pat mentioned. Anxious to
change the subject, Tom now said:

"Pat, you mentioned Colonel Patterson a moment
ago--do you know him very well?"

"Not real good," replied Pat. "I talked with
him a few times. I've heard it said he shoved off
right here in some broad horns three years ago come
December--ice was thicker than fleas on a hound-dog
I heard! Took a lot of gumption to cut them grape-
vines. That old river can be pretty nasty when its
a mind to. Folks say the colonel's party landed on
December 28th at a place called Yeatman's Cove and

called the settlement that sprung up there Losantiville. But its now called Cincinnati, right Tom?"

Tom nodded and Jason interjected quickly:

"By the way Pat, would you happen to know how
they came up with that name Losantiville?"

"Fellar by the name of John Filson made it up
I heard." Pat chuckled as he added: "He made it up
out of several words from other languages they say.
That language stuff ain't my strong suit but I hear
that John Filson was a teacher--a smart fellar."

On a more serious note Pat continued:

"Filson came up missin' while downstream with
John Symmes and some others in '88. He just up and
disappeared--a bear or some Indian got him I guess!
Anyway, he's gone. And that's about all I can tell
you Jason."

"Thank you Pat."

Glancing at Tom, Jason added:

"Tom, I was just about to inform Pat our plans
are a little bit up in the air from here on."

Jason shrugged his shoulders and looked again
at Pat as he remarked: "We have no firm arrangement
with our pilot beyond Limestone--or Maysville."

Now it was Tom May's turn to mention something
which had been on his mind--particularly the past
few days as they neared Maysville:

"Since you brought it up Jason, I want to tell
you I've been thinking about that very thing and if
it's all right with you and the others, I'd sort of
like to go on downstream with you until you find a
place to light!"

Although said seriously, the old pilot's face
then lighted up in hopeful expectation. A look of
relief spread across Jason's face as Tom said:

"No big hurry getting back to Pitt--I may even
go all the way down to The Falls!"

Pat listened politely as Jason quickly said:

"Well, I know I speak for everyone when I say
how pleased we are you will be staying on with us
Tom--and we will make it right with you. I'll go

and tell the others--they will be happy to hear the good news. And Pat, I will talk with them concerning your interest. You understand don't you?"

"Sure do Jason--thanks."

Pat and Tom smiled as they watched Jason climb on board the ark and disappear through the door.

"Good news!" said Jason. "Tom is going to stay on with us downstream!"

Almaretta folded her hands and glanced upwards as she said: "Thank heavens! I was so worried we might have to steer this thing ourselves!"

Jason looked at Alma with mock surprise.

"You mean you do not believe Hank, Dave, and I could handle this ark ourselves?"

With a pained look Alma glanced first at Mary and then at Jason as she said apologetically:

"Oh no, Jason! It is just that I know we will all feel much safer--I mean it will be better--oh, you know what I mean Mary!"

Mary put her arm around her frustrated friend and said: "We know what you mean and I know Jason and the others will feel much safer with Tom as our pilot. There is no substitute for experience, particularly in an emergency--right Jason?"

"Couldn't have said it better myself. And now that we have that settled, would Mrs. Evenstar care to join me for a little stroll around Maysville? I dare say we might hear what folks are saying about the Miami Lands. Do you feel up to it?"

Jason glanced at Alma and winked as he added:

"A close look at Maysville will give you something to write to your aunt in New York about."

The Weiser family had already gone ashore and Dave had agreed to watch the ark until someone came back. Ignoring Jason's facetious remark Mary said:

"Be good to set foot on terra firma--I can use the fresh air! Be ready in a moment!"

Long before the Evenstars returned they would learn that the stories being heard around Maysville about the "Miami Lands" proved the wisdom of an old adage which proclaims: "A lie will travel a league while the truth is getting its boots on!"

Everywhere the Evenstars looked they could see settlers in varying degrees of frontier dress, uniformed soldiers, seedy looking trappers, and river hucksters. After all of the stories about Indians, Mary was surprised to see several on the streets of Maysville. Her feelings ran the gamut of delight, fright, and amazement as they slowly made their way through the conglomeration of humanity hearing people talking about "buying, selling, and trading."

Some sought arrangements whereby they might be able to "trade" with the wilderness Indians--it was a well known fact the white man's baubles dazzled the Indians and liquor made them an easy target for the sharp trader. But the Indians were not stupid, as some white men learned to their own sorrow.

One such person, Francois La Ferte, found his crooked dealing to be a two bladed sword when he traded his phony silver jewelry to some Indians for their furs. The next year La Ferte found the sacks of maple sugar he received from some Indians, in a trade for guns, turned out to have several inches of fine maple sugar on top but beneath it was nothing but sand--the crooked trader went bankrupt.

Only a block from their ark the Evenstars were accosted by a thick set, bearded individual in his forties who smiled from his nose down--his bloodshot eyes didn't smile. With him was a big woman--not a pretty person--with a streak of gray in her jet black hair. Her piercing eyes were arched with heavy brows and the gleaming teeth she showed when they first spoke soon vanished during the ensuing conversation. Upon being told the Evenstars would be continuing downstream, the man loudly declared:

"It is suicide for anyone to go to that Miami country--you can't trust John Symmes! But here in Kentucky I have a fine piece of land just south of here and it can be yours for practically nothing."

Now the woman put her face close to Mary's and

spoke in a voice that everyone around could hear:

"My dear, you certainly aren't going to go any farther downstream are you? Of course it isn't any of my business but......"

She never had a chance to finish--Mary cut her off quickly saying:

"No, it really is not any of your business, is it! And now we will bid you good day!"

Without another word Mary and Jason continued on their way. In leaving the startled couple Jason and Mary heard the woman say: "Well, did you ever!"

Proceeding on their way, Jason chuckled as he said to his wife: "You certainly told her!"

"She had a lot of nerve," said Mary. "And it is not any of her business what we do!"

Although proud of his spunky wife, Jason would have preferred Mary not hear other adverse comments which drifted to their ears as they walked:

"I hear that Miami country is depopulated--the inhabitants have been killed and those settlers who did escape the tomahawk have fled!"

"Better go down to the Falls--forget the Miami country. You will most certainly be destroyed by those red savages in Symmes' slaughter house!"

And so it went as Jason and Mary walked, look-ed, and listened. Hand in hand they slowly walked around the frontier village where the rich and poor dreamed alike. Some greeted them as if they lived there but after their initial encounter, they were careful about joining anyone in conversation. Two individuals did politely inquire if they might be the ones who tied up that morning. The affirmative reply brought the inevitable questions about "news from back east." It was an unquenchable thirst that plagued the frontier.

Although the clothing varied, most of the mi-grants could be identified by their plain durable clothing. Here and there one saw a dress from back east, or someone who had just arrived wearing what Tom called "his Philadelphia best," but fancy goods

which inflated the vanity and depleted the pocket-
book, were in short supply in Maysville. Sabbath,
weekday, and holiday dress quickly disappeared west
of the Alleghenies where "survival" was the primary
item of concern. On every hand were men dressed in
their hunting outfit consisting of shirt and pants
made of deerhide, the ever-present hunting knife in
the belt, and a fur hat with a raccoon tail hanging
down the back. Some wore hats made of splinters
rolled in buffalo wool and sewed together with deer
sinews or buckskin whang. A few wore Revolutionary
War uniform apparel mixed with a buckskin shirt and
leggings--not a very "military" sight but serviceable. Hide moccasins could be seen everywhere worn
by women and men alike. Mary noticed most of the
women wore the familiar frontier dress--sunbonnets
and dresses made of linsey wool--most had been made
with their own hands. Beneath most of the women's
outer garments were underwear made of dressed doe
skin.

Jason's wife had been a little shaken by their
first encounter and now she walked close to him and
he patted her arm in an understanding manner. The
fear of captivity, torture, and massacre hung like
a pall over this advance guard of civilization but
such gloom and doom talk had not slowed the influx
of settlers and Jason Evenstar had made up his mind
the pessimism of the disheartened would never deter
him. But such adverse comments did nothing to help
promote the sale of land north of the Ohio or quiet
the trepidations of prospective settlers in 1791.
And before the sun set that day, the Evenstars were
destined to learn the trepidations of one family--
coupled with other personal interests--would prompt
them to say they would "unload at Maysville."

At an inn across the street from a store where
they purchased some supplies Mary needed, the Evenstars met a newly wed couple from Virginia. As the
well-dressed and well-mannered young man explained:

"We embarked from a point where the Red Stone

Creek empties into the Monongahela. We are waiting for repairs to be made on our boat and then we will continue on to Cincinnati."

When Jason learned the couple had not stopped at Marietta, he said: "Mary and I had the good fortune of meeting a number of those who were charter members of the Ohio Company of Associates. Are you familiar with it?"

The question brought a smile to the faces of the couple and the young man's eyes lighted up with keen interest as he replied:

"Oh yes. I had a distant relative by the name of Christopher Gist who was employed to explore the Ohio valley by the <u>original</u> Ohio Company. Mother told me he left Virginia on October 31st in 1750."

Now it was Jason whose eyes glistened with excited interest as he inquired quizzically:

"The original Ohio Company?"

"Quite so," said the young man. "Early in 1749 a grand scheme to colonize this western country was conceived by a few prominent men of Virginia among whom were Augustine and Lawrence Washington, elder half-brothers of our president. Christopher Gist served as an interpreter for George Washington back in the early 1750s in the Ohio valley. As an agent for the Ohio Company, Gist and two companions--one named George Croghan and another of mixed blood he called Montour--left the mouth of the Muskingum in February of 1751 and reached the principal village of the Twight-wees Indians on February 17th."

"The what Indians?" said Jason.

Jason's puzzled query brought a smile to the young man's face and he politely explained:

"The British call them 'Twight-wees' while the French call them 'Miamis.' As I understand, they migrated from the Pacific coast years ago. But regardless of what you call them--and 'Miamis' is the preferred name today I understand--they're the ones who put General Harmar's army to rout last fall and vow to chase all white men from that country."

Jason listened carefully.   When the young man
paused Jason optimistically interjected:
"But Christopher Gist spoke highly of the land
he saw, did he not?"
"Indeed he did. His journal indicates buffalo
graze near the mouth of a river* which empties into
the Big Miami and he said there was nothing wanting
but cultivation to make it a delightful country."
It was Mary who now interrupted saying:
"But there were, and still are, Indians there!
Right?"
Jason frowned but the young man said quickly:
"You are quite right Mrs. Evenstar--his report
mentioned there were many Indians in that country."
The two women exchanged meaningful glances and
then both laughed insincerely--each a bit reluctant
to show her own true emotions. Breaking a somewhat
awkward silence, Jason said:
"I wonder how our president became interested
in joining the military in the first place?   Uncle
Conrad always said Washington was a man of means."
It was the young man's wife who now injected:
"He also married well. Daniel Custis left his
widow Martha a sizeable estate."
Appearing a little uncomfortable by his wife's
comment, the young man added: "The president could
have lived quite comfortably at Mount Vernon had he
not answered his country's call when needed."
Again the young man's wife interrupted saying:
"If Sally Fairfax had stayed at nearby Belvoir
a little longer Martha would have been very glad to
see George go off to war. Will Fairfax took Sally
away to England just in time your mother told me."
The young man rebuked his wife sharply with a
single word: "Rowena!"
Without explaining that George William Fairfax
and his wife, residents of Mount Vernon's neighbor-
ing estate, had moved to England just as the winds

* The Mad River

of revolution swept Virginia, the young man cleared
his throat and attempted to answer Jason's query:

"Lawrence Washington was the Adjutant General
of Virginia and died of tuberculosis in 1752. This
half-brother of the president was very influential
when he was seeking a commission in the Virginia
Militia. But George did serve the governor well so
I have been told."

Again the young man's wife interrupted with:

"Now John, you know very well your mother told
us Governor Dinwiddie was not at all pleased when
George surrendered his command at Fort Necessity
and signed those papers admitting to the assassination of a French diplomat. Your mother often said
the governor blamed him for starting the French and
Indian War."

"Yes dear," said the young man politely. "But
that is water down the Potomac and I am certain our
friends are not interested in what my mother said."

As the foursome walked toward the river Jason
said: "I understand Arthur St. Clair was a personal
friend of President Washington during the war."

"Indeed he was and it is not surprising he was
picked as governor of this territory out here," replied the young man. "Federalists stick together!"

They talked and walked and fortunately did not
encounter any of the "spreaders of hate and discontent" as John called them. Upon reaching the river
landing they said their goodbyes and then Jason and
Mary watched the newlyweds walk hand in hand down
the bank toward their boat.

"Nice couple," remarked Mary.

As they stood watching John and Rowena walk up
the gangplank and disappear into their cabin, Jason
thought about the diverse comments they had heard
this day and mentioned it to Mary saying they sort
of reminded him of an adage his uncle often used:

"Two men looked out between the bars, one saw
mud, the other saw stars."

Mary studied for a moment and then replied:

"Your uncle had one for every occasion Jason. I also recall another one he used: 'Everybody hears a different drummer!'"

In her mind Mary was turning over and over the comment she heard as they walked regarding a Thomas Ridout who had been ambushed and taken prisoner on March 21st in 1788 just below Limestone. Her trend of thought was broken as she watched Jason pick up a stone and send it skipping across the river. He recalled how he had enjoyed doing that as a little boy playing along the Monocacy. Now thinking about what his wife had just said, Jason remarked:

"Uncle Conrad and Uncle Frederick both used to say that Mary. Took it from a passage in the Bible I think. They had a lot of those old sayings."

Mary's face reflected the mischief she felt as she now said: "Like that one: 'There is a time to to stay and a time to go.'"

Happy his wife appeared to be in a much better frame of mind, Jason feigned seriousness but a tiny smile tugged at his mouth as he said: "That's right Mary, your husband learned that while he was still skipping stones across the Monocacy. And now dear, it's time to go on board and give Dave and Alma an opportunity to look around Maysville."

That evening the Weisers surprised everyone by announcing their intention of leaving the ark and buying some land in Kentucky.

"We met the nicest couple who have a farm for sale southwest of here on the road to Lexington--it is about forty miles they said." Sarah glanced at her husband and added: "He said it was about half-way to an old frontier fort that was built in 1774. Called it Fort Harrod didn't he Hank?"

"Yep," replied Hank. "First settlement out in these parts he said. But that fort's a fur piece on the other side of Lexington I'm told. Lexington is about fifteen miles from his place he said."

His wife enthusiastically added:

"They are heading back east and paw and me can

302

buy the property right we believe--right Hank?"

"Looks that way. He said its got mighty good buildings, cleared land, and there's schooling not fur off where the kids can get some education--be a big worry off my mind. Them folks are agreeable to selling us a Conestoga, a wagon, and three horses."

Hank sensed what he knew was his friend's keen disappointment and apologetically explained:

"Me and maw's been real worried about the kids gittin' an education even before we left. Now this just sorta pops right in our lap. Maw kinda thinks it's the work of the Almighty."

Sarah Weiser solemnly nodded her agreement and the children listened in non-committal silence--the parents made the decisions. Jason remained silent as Dave and Alma voiced their reaction to Sarah and Hank's change of plans. Finally, they ran out of words and Hank glanced at Jason with a look of expectation. Soberly Jason said:

"Of course we all hate to see you folks leave us. But we understand and you have our best wishes for good fortune and happiness in your new home."

Jason knew he spoke for everyone. In the days just ahead he would come to know lives on the frontier were often changed by the turn of a card, the silent flight of an arrow, the course of the deadly "lead birds," fire, floods, and even the direction of the wind. Two centuries later such events would be called "the fickle finger of fate!"

Sleep didn't come easy for anyone that night--Jason himself lay for a long time just watching the flickering shadows on the ceiling of the cabin made by the flames in the fireplace. Mary sensed his restlessness, patted his arm, and softly said:

"Go to sleep Jason--everything will work out!"

But he didn't sleep and actually felt a little sense of relief when Dave touched his shoulder--it was his turn to take the "watch." On deck he leaned against the stock pen and thought about Hank--he was a good friend and Jason was going to miss him.

But thoughtful minutes became hours and finally on the eastern horizon Jason watched the pinkish
glow grow brighter and heard a rooster crow--there
was no way to stop the inevitable.

Thus, after breakfast, Jason and Dave began to
unload the Weiser's livestock and belongings while
Hank and Sarah finalized an agreement to purchase a
farm, two wagons, and three horses--they were back
at the ark shortly after noon. That afternoon they
began to load the Conestoga. Everything they owned
was either in or tied to the wagon except the cow--
Betsy Ross had to walk behind. Inside their wagons
they would carry four sheep, a plow, Hank's tools,
and all their household belongings. And somewhere
among the several trunks and various boxes, the two
youngest boys would ride while their sister sat between Hank and Sarah on the front seat. Will would
drive the second wagon.

Despite Hank's repeated cheerful reassurances
to his wife and children, and the friends they must
now leave behind, there was a tightness in the air
that evening as everyone sat around the fireplace.
Jason thought Hank was a little more talkative than
usual and listened quietly when Hank said:

"That community around Lexington has grown the
past twelve years according to the folks we bought
from--they cleared the land we're a fixing' to live
on. The innkeeper has seen that place and he told
me and maw we got ourselves a steal. Sure hope maw
and the kids will be happy down there."

Jason listened to Hank praise the merits of a
place he had never seen and the muscles twitched in
his face--he would never say anything to discourage
Hank and Sarah but to himself he thought:

"Such blind faith! But on the other hand, who
am I to say anyone is wrong in following a pathway
prompted by the courage of their own convictions--
aren't we all?"

Although Jason considered suggesting Hank take
a look at the property first, he decided the Weiser

family had probably thought about this alternative. To himself he concluded: "The children's education is undoubtedly foremost in the mind of Hank and his wife--particularly his wife!"

Early the next morning Hank began making final preparations for their departure. As Dave and Will finished loading the clapboards Hank had cut along the Monongahela, Jason offered to help his friend hitch up the horses--it gave them a last chance for a word in private. Sounding almost like an apology Hank said briefly: "I know you understand Jason."

Jason nodded as he replied: "You know I do."

Playfully cuffing his friend on the shoulder, Jason added: "You have your family to think about-- and your children's education. I understand Hank."

Jason took a deep breath and added quickly:

"And you folks will not be that far away--less than a hundred miles Tom says."

While waiting for Hank and Sarah to return the previous day Tom had told Jason how John Symmes was supposed to have arrived at Limestone Point by the 15th of September in 1788 and attend a meeting that day to lay out a road from Lexington to the mouth of the Licking River.

"But it was held a week later, " explained the old pilot. "And present that day were John Symmes, Robert Patterson, Matthias Denman, Benjamin Stites, Israel Ludlow, John Filson and about sixty others. Then they embarked on an exploratory trip and spent several days looking over that land along the north side of the Ohio. I've been told Ludlow and Denman had already started to survey some land in the area now called Cincinnati. I also heard it said Symmes and Filson went upstream a few miles to explore the region along the Big Miami."

Tom shook his head and soberly added: "During that exploratory trip John Filson disappeared--they don't know what happened to him."

The wilderness swallowed Filson up without any trace of his intrusion--the unfenced, unmarked, and

unspoiled country silently claimed another victim.
It had been planned Filson would be one of the surveyors and his disappearance delayed the project
until a replacement could be found. Israel Ludlow
stepped in as a partner, surveyor and general agent
of the Losantiville land venture since John Filson
had invested no money as yet. And now, two years
and eight months later, Jason said to Hank:

"By now they must have a pretty good road from
Lexington to the mouth of the Licking River. After
all the traveling we done in the Laurels, a hundred
miles of wilderness won't make us strangers!"

Somehow his comment did not come out as cheerful as Jason intended. Hank wiped a tear from his
cheek with the back of his hand and swallowed hard.
But he did not say a word--just looked at Jason for
a long time and then turned quickly to check something on the harness that needed no attention.

Mary and Alma stood with Sarah and listened as
she too apologetically explained:

"The kids need more than a Testament and Dilworth's Speller to teach them. Me and paw want our
kids to have a better education than we got."

Mary put her arm around Sarah and said: "You
have got to do what you think is best. Our prayers
will be with you and your family Sarah."

With the sun perched on the eastern horizon,
and his wife seated by their daughter on the front
seat, Hank stepped to the rear of the Conestoga to
check--for the fourth time--a rope which tied Betsy
to the wagon. Hank stared quietly for a moment at
the excited children who were now getting situated
among the boxes, trunks, and sheep. Stepping back
to eye his Conestoga, Hank said in a choked voice:

"I'd say we got quite a load! Ready Will?"

Hank Weiser tried to appear cheerful but there
were tears in his eyes as he gave their cow a quick
pat on the rump and quipped:

"Sorry Betsy, but you gotta walk."

Jason remembered having asked Hank once why he

named his cows Molly Pitcher and Betsy Ross and he had replied: "They gotta have names don't they?"

Jason also recalled having asked Hank: "Why do you always answer a question with a question?"

Without hesitation Hank had said: "Why not?"

That's the kind of a man he was--a good friend and a true companion and Jason would miss him. But Jason understood the Weiser's reasoning. The price of learning was a persistent individual effort on the frontier and one had to admire Hank and Sarah's interest and unselfish devotion to their children's needs. Conditions on the frontier precluded public instruction--made it inefficient and inadequate. Common interests would eventually provide for an education system but this was 1791 and proximity to available teachers was of vital interest to Sarah. Jason silently thanked the Lord that he had been privileged to know Hank the past year--he had been almost like a father to him.

It was a sad parting--just a few days ago they had talked of life as neighbors in the Territory of the United States Northwest of the Ohio River and now they were saying their goodbyes. Of course all wished the Weisers good fortune in this changed undertaking but each was saddened to see them depart. Even Tom had grown very fond of the Weiser children and blew his nose noisly to cover the removal of a tear that trickled down his weathern-beaten cheek.

Finally taking his place on the Conestoga next to his wife and daughter, Hank Weiser looked at his friends and declared:

"Well, we'll be seeing you nice folks. And if things don't pan out we can always give old Betsy a little more exercise and hunt you up!"

And with that Hank and his family drove away.

Standing on the porch of the inn Pat Hagan saw the Weisers drive by and he took off at a fast pace for the dock area where he found Jason talking with Tom and Dave. Jason greeted Pat saying: "You're a lucky man Pat--somebody up there must like you!"

Pat grinned from ear to ear as he exclaimed:

"Even a blind pig roots up an acorn every now and then!"

Jason had discussed his intention with Tom and Dave and they interposed no objection. Accordingly Jason now explained their proposition:

"We are in agreement you can travel with us if you pay our pilot for his service from here on--you just make your peace with Tom here and get your belongings on board. We'll shove off tomorrow!"

"Sounds fair to me and I'm much obliged to you and Dave--and Tom."

In quick succession Pat and Tom shook hands on the ark pilot's fee and then Hagan took off saying:

"I'll get the missus and our wagon and be back this afternoon."

That evening, with the Hagans on board and the evening meal over, Jason was encouraged to play his violin. Despite all attempts to be cheerful, there was an unshakeable air of sadness in the air--maybe it was the absence of the children's voices and the clapping when a lively reel was played. And Mary's voice did not have its usual sparkle when she was finally persuaded to sing. Even Tom had mentioned to Jason that Mary had been unusually quiet during the evening meal.

Jason drew the nine to twelve "watch" and Mary joined him on the stern saying: "I am not sleepy."

Together they stood and looked out across the waters of the river--a sliver of moonlight provided just enough light to add a shimmering effect on the dark water. It was Jason who then said:

"All right Mary, what is it with you tonight?"

As if waiting for his question Mary replied:

"I will be perfectly honest with you Jason--I have this premonition about the place we are going, wherever that is. I cannot put my finger on it but I have this--well, a funny feeling!"

Even in the dim light Jason could see the look of frustration on his wife's face and he sensed the

feeling of helplessness that engulfed her feelings.
It had been there ever since the Weisers said they
were leaving.   Mary shrugged her shoulders, turned
the palms of her small hands upwards, and in a very
plaintive voice said:

"I do not know what it is--but you asked."

"Probably has something to do with the Weisers
leaving unexpectedly--it was a real surprise.   And
the uncertainty of what lies ahead is of concern to
you I'm sure--normal feeling for women I suppose."

Jason paused for a moment and continued:

"Men too I guess.   But you know that if I felt
there was any danger downstream we could not handle
together, I would unload right here.   But I believe
with all my heart Mary that there is an opportunity
just waiting for us downstream and we should take a
hack at it!"

Mary would have preferred the "opportunity" he
had been offered in her father's employment and the
home her father had said was theirs for the asking.
But Jason, in his own hard-headed way, was asking
her to understand and be a part of his dreams.   She
did understand but her heart was not in this undertaking.   To herself she thought:

"Perhaps he is right--and the unexpected parting by the Weisers certainly does have something to
do with the way I feel."

Being the good wife she was, Mary now managed
a half smile which she hoped Jason could see in the
dim light.   He saw it but knew it was not sincere.
When Jason put his arms around her, Mary reached up
and gave him a little kiss.   Then she said:

"I don't care what anyone says Jason, you play
a mighty good fiddle!"

Although there was a touch of mischievousness
in her voice, and the faint light betrayed a half-
hearted smile, Jason recognized his wife was trying
to impress him with her bravado and he feigned mock
disgust as he exclaimed softly:

"I play a good fiddle? What kind of a teacher

talks like that? You mean I play the violin well."

"Whatever!" said Mary pertly.

Mary knew Jason was smiling and had that know-ing look she often saw on his face. Now she pulled away from him in a movement of feigned surprise as he reached around and gave her a playful pat on the back side.

"Jason! What if someone saw you?"

"Have mighty good eyesight I would say!"

"Shame on you."

Jason put his arm around her shoulder again and pulled her close to him as he said:

"You started it!"

"Then I will end it!"

Jason could not see her pursed lips revealed a half smile but he sensed his wife did not find his amour as objectionable as she let on.

"Don't be so puritanical Mary."

"I am not being puritanical--just practical!"

Jason thought for a moment and then laughingly remarked:

"If I remember that Shakespeare you gave me to read--the Twelth Night I believe--there was a pass-age which read: 'Dost thou think, because thou art virtuous, there shall be no more cakes and ale!'"

Jason thought some spirited conversation with his wife might help her escape the mood she was in. Without a moment of hesitation Mary replied:

"Very good my dear husband. And as long as we are discussing William Shakespeare, may I call your attention to a passage from the Merchant of Venice which reads: 'The devil can cite Scripture for his purpose!'"

"Touche!" said Jason. "You're not only pretty but smart. Wish I had had a pretty school teacher like you."

In the faint light she couldn't see the adora-tion in her husband's eyes but Mary could feel it. Jason could see his wife's little chin thrust for-ward--proud and independent and so afraid of what lay downstream. He watched the night breeze ripple the edge of her bonnet and thought to himself:

"Maybe my wife is the smart one."

Aloud he said:

"I love you Mary O'Donnell Evenstar!"

"Go on, you are just saying that--I have heard stories about you sailors!"

Despite the faintness of the light, Jason knew the corners of Mary's mouth revealed a smiling face and that old familiar sparkle must be in her eyes. He pulled her close and kissed her and then said:

"That's my girl--everything is going to be all right. You just wait and see."

The mood was abruptly broken by Tom's voice:

"Jason! Everything all right?"

Somewhat startled, Jason and Mary looked up to where Tom crouched on the roof of the cabin--he was silhouetted against the sky. Jason replied softly:

"Everything is just fine Tom."

"Didn't hear you walking," said Tom. "I just thought something might be wrong."

Good old Tom--he was always on his toes. With quiet assurance Jason said softly: "Everything is just fine Tom--get some sleep."

And with that Jason kissed his wife on the top of her bonneted head.

"Fresh! You sailors are all alike. It is time for a nice girl like me to get a little sleep--good night sailor boy!"

Assisted by Jason, Mary now carefully made her way around the corner and disappeared through the cabin door leaving her husband alone with the darkness of night. Then listening to Jason's footsteps as he walked slowly to the bow Mary closed her eyes and fell asleep.

CHAPTER TEN

FRIDAY THE 13TH

"Friday the 13th--up and at 'em!" Joining Pat for the three to six "watch," Tom had been awake a long time when he roused Jason from a deep sleep at six o'clock. "We got an early morning mist hanging over the Ohio but by the time we have breakfast and get Pat's wagon loaded it should be burned off."

But the mist did not burn off and a persistent drizzle starting about noon prompted Tom to suggest they delay their departure until the next day. All night long the dreary rain continued and threatened to delay the Saturday morning departure until about ten o'clock and then the skies cleared and Tom gave Dave the signal to "hoist anchor." And then, standing on the bow with his feet wide apart and bracing himself with his gun, Jason kept a sharp eye on the river ahead while enjoying the fragrance of the May flowers that dotted the banks of the river. While admiring the constantly changing view, he suddenly saw a herd of buffalo feeding in a meadow along the north bank and remembered what the young Virginian had said about Christopher Gist's report of buffalo in the region.

The huge beasts did not take flight as the ark silently drifted by. Jason and his companions had no way of knowing the thundering herds of buffalo would all have disappeared from that area only ten years later--the same would be true of the stately elk they often saw along the Ohio.

Not far from where Jason stood on the bow, Pat and Dave leaned against the fenced-in stock enclosure talking and enjoying the sunshine. Quite unexpectedly Pat suddenly said:

"You know Dave, I used to know a guide down at Fort Harrod everyone called 'Buffalo!'"

Dave seriously studied one of the monstrous beasts and then casually replied with all the innocence of a naive foil: "Is that so Pat--because he was so big and strong I suppose."

"Naw! It was because he had a great big head covered with long dirty hair, had a little ass and a snotty nose!"

Pat slapped his leg repeatedly and roared with laughter as Dave looked at him and said:

"That's terrible Pat, just terrible!"

Jason agreed with Dave and chose to ignore the crude remark. Walking back to where Tom manned the sweep, Jason thought to himself

"They are indeed abominable creatures but they are God's creation."

"What's all the laughing up front?" asked Tom.

"Oh, that's Pat. We have ourselves a clown on board it seems." Jason refused to pass along Pat's tasteless remark and Tom did not press the issue.

Late that afternoon Tom informed everyone:

"We will drop anchor today well offshore a few miles upstream from the mouth of the Little Miami--current is real tricky where the Miami comes in and there's an island along the north shore we want to steer clear of. I'll need every man on a pole when we put in at Columbia tomorrow morning."

The sunrise heralded the birth of a beautiful day and, it being the Sabbath, everyone gathered in front of the stock fence on the bow of the deck and listened as Jason read the first verse of the 19th Psalm: "The heavens declare the glory of God; and the firmament sheweth his handiwork."

Together everyone then repeated the 23rd Psalm while Tom stood guard on the stern maintaining his customary vigilance. With the short service over, and in accordance with his prior agreement with the passengers, Tom ordered the anchor lifted.

Carefully maneuvering the huge river craft to avoid any hidden sand bars, Tom allowed the ark to drift with the current as he hugged the north shore line with affection--he knew the river. With Jason and Pat on either side of the bow intently watching the water ahead, and Dave having gone in the cabin with the women, everyone was suddenly surprised as Tom on the stern sang out:

"Jason! Pat! Dave! Look sharp--boat bearing down on us astern!"

Jason and Pat took cover quickly as Dave raced out on deck with his gun and crouched beside Tom on the stern saying: "What is it Tom?"

Moments later the pilot again called out:

"No alarm fellars--it's the governor's boat!"

With mixed feelings of wonder, reverence, and respect the men then watched as Arthur St. Clair's flag-bedecked boat passed them in midstream on the port side. As Jason observed, a number of men were manning oars on the relatively swift river craft.

Then, with the adrenalin still racing through Jason's veins, another ripple of excitement swept his body when he spotted several Columbia settlers, three soldiers, and an Indian standing on the north bank watching Tom skillfully guide the big ark into shore. As the women now stood wide-eyed with mixed emotions by the stock pen looking at the settlement they had heard so much about, Jason and Dave stood on the bow, and Pat on the stern, waiting for Tom's orders. A shiver of excitment swept over Jason as he heard the sound of the people on shore shouting.

Along with their shouted greetings, two grape-vines were tossed from the bank to waiting hands on the ark. Then, with the ark secure, everyone began making their way ashore where a customary exchange of greetings was quickly followed by the answering of questions. News from back east was a priceless

commodity and of course information about their new
surroundings was eagerly sought by the travelers.
It was Sunday, the 15th of May in 1791.

Despite all of the "doom and gloom" talk heard
at Maysville, settlers still continued downstream
and many stopped at Columbia--a few stayed. And
the continuing influx was more than a mere interest
in the fertile land, the flowing rivers, and cheap
acreage--the very character of these immigrants and
their industry was the key. Energetic, bold, and
imaginative by birthright, they brought to this new
frontier various levels of education and a variety
of capabilities. They were veterans of the spirit
which had prompted the Declaration of Independence
or children of those individualists and the untamed
Northwest Territory was a "stepping-stone" to the
needs of these restless pioneers.

It was to be expected most women would not be
as enthusiastic as the men. As Alma Jones said:

"I don't know what I expected really. Somehow
I thought there might be more--well, more cabins or
something!"

She sounded a little disappointed as her eyes
made a 180 degree survey of the three sides of the
clearing before them where the wilderness provided
a solid backdrop. On a more optimistic note Pat's
wife said haltingly:

"Well, they've been here only three and a half
years you know--and look what they've done!"

Mary had her eyes glued on the Indian with the
feather stuck in the band around his head. She had
expected to see a tall and muscular copper-colored
person with a beautiful feathered head dress. But
instead, the man before her looked a bit emaciated
and his features were those of an old man. He had
a blanket draped over his shoulders and a breech-
clout covered his buttocks. There was a tightening
of his expression as he watched them disembark--as
if he were containing only with great effort a vast
dislike for them. Mary thought to herself:

"Perhaps it is my imagination but he certainly does not smile much."

Mary had no way of knowing but this Indian was in his advanced years and the Columbia settlers had taken him in only a few weeks before when he was at death's door.

But any disappointnment or misgivings that any person in Jason's party may have had was dispelled by the personable greetings of Columbia's settlers. Even the old Indian raised his arm in his customary greeting and said in a guttural voice: "How!"

As they talked, Jason's eyes swept the budding green parapet in front of which stood log buildings evidencing the toiling back-breaking efforts by the determined settlers. Jason thought to himself:

"Just think of it! Right here Benjamin Stites drove his stake three years ago last November!"

Nearby Jason overheard someone telling Dave:

"Well, I can tell you Mr. Jones, Major Stites got the first, or one of the first at least, Miami Land Warrants issued by John Symmes. He got it the 17th of December in 1787 and it was for six hundred and forty acres--one thirty-sixth of a township his warrant called for. The major also got some other purchase rights too and Symmes agreed to take John Carpenter into his East Jersey Company. This whole thing was Ben's idea in the first place you know."

Jason was overwhelmed by the thought of this undertaking that he had read and heard about. Here he stood with the loveliness of all of the works of nature spread so lavishly and beautifully about him and his wife. Once again Jason shook his head and marveled at the vision of men like Benjamin Stites and John Symmes. Now he too would be a part of the great undertaking of which historians of the future would say:

"Bred to free thought and courageous actions, bold and energetic and ever mindful of the dangers and hardships, the rugged optimists came to this region, looked at the new frontier, and tackled it knowing the forest must be leveled, crops had to be planted, and blockhouses built--and, of course, the Indians had to be subdued."

And on this day as Jason stood in Columbia and breathed in the beauty of the surrounding vistas, he had no way of knowing that years later men--and women too--would be "taking off and landing" in a marvel of the 20th Century at Lunken Airport. 150 years later the "fly boys" of W.W. II would call it "Sunken Lunken" and sweat out bad weather arrivals and departures from this valley.

Jason was abruptly jarred from his thoughts by a friendly voice he had not heard before:

"Hello Tom, good to see you again. Go all the way back to Pitt this time?"

Jason turned and saw the speaker shaking hands with Tom. Now he listened as Tom replied:

"Sure did--second trip this year Ben."

In turn, Tom then introduced his passengers to Benjamin Stites.

"These are the Evenstars Ben--this pretty young lady is Mary Evenstar."

Mary extended her tiny hand and the frontier pioneer warmly but gently engulfed it in his huge weather-beaten grip saying:

"Welcome to Columbia!"

As Jason shook hands with the affable pioneer Stites remarked:

"You have a good grip Mr. Evenstar--you'll be needing that out here!"

Stites keen eyes swept Jason's upright frame and he added:

"You'll like it out here--Jason isn't it?"

"Jason it is--glad to make your acquaintance. My wife and I feel we should do some looking before making up our minds on a place to live. She thinks we all hear a different drummer and what may be all right for one might not be to another's liking."

Stites smiled and looked directly into Mary's eyes as he spoke:

"I'd say your wife has a good outlook--and she
certainly knows her Bible."

Mary demurely lowered her eyes but then looked
at Stites again as Tom introduced Pat Hagan and his
wife. Although the major politely said nothing, he
could not help but notice Pat's two missing teeth
when he smiling said:

"Glad to meet you! Me and Kate joined up with
these folks at Maysville--they came downstream from
Pittsburgh and kindly gave us a ride."

Jason briefly related their travel experience
and then Stites said:

"So you considered putting in at old Fort Burd
huh. That's near where we launched our broad horns
in the summer of '88--tied up at Limestone Point in
July. We had an agreement to build a settlement at
the mouth of the Little Miami so 'the faithful,' as
we call them, pushed off from Limestone the 16th of
November and twenty-six of us landed here the 18th.
We had a sergeant and eighteen troops as a military
escort but three of us preceded the party in canoes
as scouts--Daniel Shoemaker, my brother Hezekiah,
and myself. Daniel went downstream to Losantiville
later--I mean Cincinnati! My other brother Elijah,
John Hanson, James Bailey, and Mister Cox were with
us when we landed here.".

Stites paused for a moment and added: "Brother
Hezekiah was the first one to step ashore. Then we
said a prayer and started to build a blockhouse--we
finished it the twenty-fourth of November!"

"Just before the bad weather started!"

Ben Stites turned and saw Tom May grinning.

"You're right you old rascal. We'd been waiting at Limestone for weeks and Symmes was up to his
ears in delays--cost him a pretty farthing too!

Tom shrugged his shoulders saying: "So I have
heard. By the way Ben, is Bill Woods around? Like
to have the Evenstars meet him."

He referred to a settler from Milford Township
in Bedford County, Pennsylvania that Tom had met in

Pittsburgh. Woods had come out to Columbia in the spring of 1789, cleared some ground, built a cabin, put in a little crop, and then went back to get his family. As he had told Tom: "I don't want to burn all of my bridges behind me."

"I believe he's down at Cincinnati--that's his place up there," replied Stites.

Stites waved his arm toward the forest clothed hills to the northwest where a cabin stood and some stumps had been burned off. Mary was still looking when Tom said:

"As I recall Ben, Edmund Buston and Owen Owens came to Columbia about the same time as Bill. When did Jacob White get out here?"

"Can't say off the top of my head Tom--been so many settle here. Colonel Brown, Major Gam, Major Kilby, Captain Flinn, Judge Goforth, Judge Foster, John Reiley, Ben Randolph, John Gano, Reverend John Smith---we're getting to be quite a settlement!"

Ben Stites paused, looked at the Evenstars and Hagans, and grinned as he said:

"A moment ago Tom was kidding me about getting our blockhouse built before bad weather set in and it reminded me of how high our spirits were the day we finished and some of us began shooting our guns to celebrate. Well, within forty-eight hours Simon Kenton* and some men came down from Maysville--they had a report our place was under siege!"

Appearing slightly puzzled, Jason said: "Then Mister Symmes followed you downstream--right?"

"That's one way to put it," said Stites with a smile. "As Tom probably told you, John has himself a settlement at the north bend of the Ohio. But he didn't get away from Maysville for two months after we landed here. By then we were up to our eyeballs in water. In late January the Symmes party stayed here overnight but left the next morning. However, we learned a lesson from that flood and John found

* Simon Kenton (1755-1836) son of Mark Kenton & Mary Miller

out a thing or two about this river too as a result of our unfortunate experience."

Stites smiled grimly as he recalled the freshet that had sent everyone scurrying to high ground as flood waters engulfed many of the cabins at Columbia. Glancing toward the river Stites said:

"Some of the spring freshets can be real nasty but we learn from experience and now we build our cabins on higher ground--we get smarter every day! But the bottom land around here is fertile--Indians have been cultivating a lot of this bottom land for many years and some of it is like an ash heap--particularly the piece we call 'Turkey Bottom.'"

The fertile river bottom lands of the southwestern region of what was to become the State of Ohio in 1803 had long been cultivated by the Indian tribes and the Mound Builders before them. Much of the bottom lands of the Symmes' Miami Purchase was as mellow as Stites said. "Turkey Bottom," a mile and a half above the mouth of the Little Miami furnished, along with some smaller lots near Columbia, all the corn that settlement needed the first year with some to spare for nearby Losantiville.

"Some of that bottom land up the Little Miami is mighty fertile folks--all it needs is a hoe and some seed.!"

Mary's face was impassive as she now listened to Jason say: "Sounds interesting but we planned to go further downstream." Pat Hagan said nothing.

Proud of his settler's accomplishments, Stites remarked candidly: "I am aware of the stories circulating around Maysville about what we have done--and haven't done. Truth is the Indians were quite anxious to meet Symmes and I sent several messages back upstream urging him to come downstream at his earliest convenience--I told him about the Indian's concern too. But, by the time Captain Kearsey got to Maysville, the river was less favorable. That river can be troublesome in the winter, right Tom?"

Tom nodded his agreement and Stites continued:

"Captain Kearsey arrived December 12th in 1788 with forty-five troops but the weather was against an immediate departure from Limestone. A sergeant and twelve soldiers did join one party that shoved off but river ice forced them to abort their downstream venture here at Columbia. We have had a lot of boats stop here that were bound for Losantiville and Miami City--John calls it North Bend now!"

Jason thought it was opportune to now say:

"Pat here told us someone at Losantiville, or Cincinnati, was giving away lots there."

Stites glanced at Pat and then eyed Jason very thoughtfully as he replied:

"Oh, that was a couple years ago--right after Colonel Patterson, Matthias Denman, and John Filson formed a partnership. They got their land warrant from John Symmes same as I did. Too bad about poor John Filson--we have no idea what happened to him."

Jason interrupted saying: "Excuse me major, I have not heard much about that Matthias Denman."

"You will if you stop at Cincinnati," said Ben with a grin. "Denman was one of the Massachusetts Minutemen. With Filson gone, Israel Ludlow joined up with Patterson and Denman as a partner. Ludlow is a young man about your age Jason. They've been selling lots since Patterson made a survey in early January of '89. But now that you mention it, there was an announcement in the KENTUCKY GAZETTE about 'donation lots' but that was several months before we even landed here. That was Bob Patterson's land promotion plan."

In the September 6, 1788 issue of the KENTUCKY GAZETTE Colonel Robert Patterson announced 30 half acre in-lots and four acre out-lots would be given to settlers who agreed to become residents of what became Losantiville. Each recipient of a "donation lot" had to agree to pay a dollar and a half survey and deed fee for each lot; become a resident before April 1, 1789; plant and tend two crops successively; and build a one and a half story house not less than 25 feet square. Proclaiming "the local and natural advantages speak of its future prosperity," the advertisement also announced a plan to meet at Lexington on September 15, 1788 to make a plan for a road to the mouth of the Licking."

Justifiably proud, Stites now said: "I got my warrant for ten thousand acres from John himself at Brunswick, New Jersey. By the way Jason, Tom tells me you are a blacksmith--we sure could use you here in our growing community!"

It was Mary who now rather unexpectedly said:

"I have a question major. Why do those people at Maysville insist on throwing cold water on our dream of settling in this land north of the Ohio?"

It was a question he often heard--one that had bothered Alma and Pat Hagan's wife too. Ben Stites thought carefully before he replied:

"Well Mrs. Evenstar, opinions are like noses--everybody's got one! But you asked me for mine and here it is. To start with, there's a lot of folks over there in the Kentucky District that have been out here a long time looking longingly at this area across the river and some object to what they think are some Revolutionary officers from back east coming out here and grabbing this 'prize land' as they call it. But the plain fact is the Ohio Company of Associates and John Symmes got in there first after the Ordinance of 1787 was adopted and filed their petitions for land grants which were approved. Its just a simple case of good business!"

A smile tugged at the corners of Major Stites' mouth as he added: "John Symmes sold the land down the river just opposite the mouth of the Licking to Matthias Denman and he formed a partnership with Patterson and Filson from Kentucky. Again, that is just good business in my opinion. It's really that simple. That answer your question Mrs. Evenstar?"

"It certainly helps. And I thank you for your candid opinion. One more question please--what is the situation with regard to the Indians out here?"

322

The major glanced at Jason and then looked at
Mary thoughtfully--it was not an easy question for
him to answer. Finally Stites did say:

"In all honesty I admit we've had our problems
here and I understand your concern--it is a concern
we all share. But somehow we must put this issue
to rest if we are to enjoy the fruits of our labor.
Two years ago this spring we had some horses stolen
here and Captain James Flinn and Lieutenant Bailey
chased those thieving Indians up north about eighty
miles. Them Indians took Flinn prisoner but he got
away--we got our horses back too!"

Stites shook his head as if trying to rid his
mind of a bad dream and continued:

"Some of us believe the Indians don't want any
trouble but they just have not learned the white
man's way of doing things--or we theirs for that
matter. And Indians can't handle 'Autumn Leaves.'"

A puzzled look crossed Mary's face and quickly
she asked: "Autumn Leaves? What have autumn leaves
to do with our relations with the Indians?"

A broad grin spread across the major's face as
he replied: "Men here call the 'fire water' we get
across in Kentucky 'Autumn Leaves'---two drinks and
you fall on the ground!"

Stites paused as everyone chuckled and added:

"I think it's a cousin of that Old Monongahela
Tom carries for snake bites. But whatever you call
it, the Indians cannot handle it and when they get
too much of it their love of the white man's horses
is more than they can handle. We both have a whole
lot to learn before we can live together in peace."

The frontier pioneer looked at Mary for a long
time before he concluded saying:

"I'm not certain I have answered your question
Mrs. Evenstar--but it's the best I can do."

Mary liked what she saw in the frontiersman's
eyes and she said:

"Again I want to thank you for being so candid
in answering my questions."

Stites now stepped back politely and excused himself saying: "I know I leave you folks in good hands-- Tom here knows everybody at Columbia."

Tom had already recognized someone he knew and hailed him saying:

"Come over here John--I want you to meet these folks from back in Pennsylvania. Mary and Jason, I want you to meet John Gano!"

Of course none of them could know John S. Gano would be a witness to the land purchase payment of $10,652.23 to John Cleves Symmes by Benjamin Stites in Cincinnati on February 8, 1793. With the intro- duction over, John said to Tom:

"And where are you taking these nice folks?"

"To see John Symmes maybe--what have you heard lately from down that way?"

"Old John is still yelling at the governor for military protection! John never got over having to subsist Captain Kearsey's troops at Maysville. And he had to buy a house there too--cost him a bundle! He was mad as a hornet at the governor and General Harmar. Remember when Captain Kearsey and his men went on down to The Falls after they escorted John and his party to that north bend in the Ohio?   The captain didn't see eye to eye with John on where he should locate. And then that Ensign Luce went down there and built a blockhouse--he couldn't keep John happy either. I heard John has been writing to his friends back east complaining about the governor-- he sure is a burr under St. Clair's saddle. By the way, did you happen to see St. Clair's boat heading downstream this morning?   It's said he is going to lead an expedition against those pesky Indians this summer--that should make John happy!"

Gano paused as if to catch his breath and Tom seized the opportunity to ask:

"Have you seen Benjamin Randolph today?"

"Saw him in church this morning. There he is, over there with Oliver Spencer and that fellar with your party, Dave Jones. Hey Ben, come over here!"

Obediently the tall muscular red-faced settler quickly made his way to where John Gano talked with the Evenstars and Hagans. When Tom made the introductions, Randolph's smile revealed a missing front tooth. As he shook hands with Pat he said:

"I see you ran into the same fellar I did!"

Not to be outdone, Pat replied quickly:

"Yeah, but he got two of my teeth."

When the laughter subsided Tom May said:

"Ben, I remember when you came out here from New Jersey a couple years ago and then went back to talk with your Revolutionary War friends."

A little embarrassed, Randolph replied: "Well, I was concerned that Congress would not give Symmes title to all of this land between the two Miamis as they told him they would do. It was discouraging to anyone wanting a clear title to his land.

A report had circulated saying Congress wanted to put the eastern boundary of Symmes' purchase 20 miles due north from the mouth of the Little Miami and establish a boundary line on the north side 20 miles upstream from the Great Miami River.

The look of concern that silently passed among the visitors did not go unnoticed by Gano. Hoping to pour some oil on the troubled waters occasioned by Randolph's comment, Gano injected:

"I am certain Symmes will get the matter ironed out soon. Major Stites has submitted an idea to Symmes about the region north of here where the Mad River empties into the Big Miami--he plans to build a settlement there and call it Venice!"

Those who gathered at Columbia that day had no way of knowing history would record Stite's "dream" was doomed to failure because of "title" problems-- and a fear of Indian harrassment. It would be five years before the first cabin was built at the mouth of the deep channeled Mad River where overhanging branches almost met overhead. Only the most daring optimist could envision the possibility of future river boats stemming the muddy current of the Great

Miami but this was Stite's dream as early as 1789.

Indeed that eastern boundary line controversy was finally settled in favor of John Symmes' land interests--but not before the land owners along the Little Miami had experienced a lot of distress and Stites' "dream" was shattered.

As history would record, the problems with the Indians were pacified a few turbulent years later and the favorable site at the confluence of the Mad and Great Miami was acquired by a company composed of such personages as Governor Arthur St. Clair, U. S. Representative Jonathan Dayton, Colonel (Brevet General) James Wilkinson and Colonel Israel Ludlow. Although this consortium would negotiate with John Cleves Symmes for the desirable tract of land, they would finally have to purchase it from the government when Symmes' 1794 patent did not include that area. Nine year old Mary Van Cleve and Catherine Thompson would be the first to step ashore in early April of 1795 at a place later to be called Dayton.

But in May of 1791, and on the heels of Gano's optimistic remark, Randolph said: "I already had my seed in when I left for New Jersey and that fall my one acre plot yielded a hundred bushels of corn per acre--not bad for the first year!"

Later Oliver M. Spencer, another of the early residents of that Columbia area, reported his nine acres of rich bottom land produced 963 bushels of corn the first season.

But those men of courage and vision who tilled the soil of the "Miami Purchase" were not the first to recognize the unrealized value of the Ohio River valley lands. The Earl of Hillsborough, attached to the North American Department, dispatched this expectation in 1770 before the area was settled:

"No part of North America will require less encouragement for the production of naval stores and raw materials for manufactories in Europe than the country of Ohio!"

In spite of the kind offers of lodging, Jason

and his friends politely refused saying they had to "take their turn standing watch" on the ark but did attend church service in the blockhouse that Sunday evening. Later around the fireplace they discussed what they had seen and heard at Columbia that day. The Hagans were concerned about the talk of Indians who prowled around near the cabins and occasionally "pick off settlers who dare to till their fields."

Although several had mentioned words of praise for the mellow soil of "Turkey Bottom," no one said anything about how James Seward from New Jersey had been left grief stricken after an Indian killed his 15 year old son, John, and captured his other son, 21 year old Obadiah, in that choice bottom land on September 20, 1789. A few weeks later he learned the Indians, in a fit of anger, had killed Obadiah along the trail.

"Far too often burning, looting, and slaughter follows some Indians' seemingly friendly visit here we heard someone say." No one said a word as Pat's wife paused for a moment and then added: "I don't think we would be safe here--I would rather go back to Lexington. Cincinnati might be better."

Dave chimed in saying: "It don't feel right to me--I don't think Columbia is our cup of tea!"

Alma sat with pursed lips nodding--she had had misgivings about leaving Pennsylvania in the first place and said so. Jason thoughtfully listened to the comments, glanced at his wife, and then said:

"Apparently none of us feel this is the place we are looking for so let's push off tomorrow morning. Tom says it shouldn't take us more than three hours to reach Cincinnati--right Tom?"

The old pilot had been sitting quietly by the fireplace listening to their conversation--he had heard many such conversations. Tapping his pipe on the upended log beside him, Tom said:

"You folks are the doctor. We can push off in the morning as soon as you are ready!"

CHAPTER ELEVEN

LOSANTIVILLE, A BUSY PLACE

An eerie symphony accompanied the rising sun--
the sound of birds and the metallic ring of axes.
As Tom and Jason enjoyed their fried mush and sorghum molasses with their early morning visitor, Ben
Stites, Mary handed each a steaming cup of coffee--
she had purchased it in Maysville. While they then
enjoyed their coffee, and Tom said they would hoist
anchor soon, Stites said:

"I hoped you might settle here Jason--not only
do we need a blacksmith but I believe you have what
it takes out here. I have a liberal arrangement
with John which entitles me to locate ten thousand
acres in the Miami Purchase around the mouth of the
Little Miami and I need good settlers. I know that
there's some concern about the United States Board
of Treasury's refusal to recognize the Little Miami
as the eastern boundary but I feel that matter will
be settled soon."

He sounded sincere but Jason was also sincere
when he replied:

"Thank you sir. I appreciate your confidence
but we have discussed the matter and have agreed to
continue downstream. Perhaps our paths will cross
again--I hope so. Meantime, you have our very best
wishes for success in this undertaking."

Then, with Stites and several others standing
on shore watching, Tom ordered Pat to raise the anchor and the ark slowly drifted away from the shore

out into the ribbon of gleaming gold. The air was fresh with the fragrance of spring and Tom remarked to Jason who stood beside him carefully holding his rifle and looking at the northern shore line.

"Sure is a beautiful morning Jason, and we are away early. Good way to start the week!"

A stone's throw away on the northern bank they could see the new foilage alive with birds of every hue building their nests. Jason said to himself:

"They are not much different than us--they too are making a 'nest' in the Northwest Territory and preparing for the future ahead."

His trend of thought was broken when he heard his wife call out from the cabin door:

"Jason, could I have a word with thee!"

"Certainly," replied Jason. "I suppose Tom can handle this ark without me."

Jason laughed and said to Tom:

"My master summons--call if you need me!"

Rounding the corner of the cabin Jason listened as his wife asked:

"Any regrets about not staying in Columbia?"

"None at all. Lot to be said for it but like Pat said, it just didn't feel right. Their loss is someone else's gain!"

"My, aren't you the conceited one. But, there is a time to stay and a time to go!"

Jason merely looked at his wife with a feigned scornful scowl as he said:

"It seems to me I have heard that old Biblical quotation before young lady. You know, when we get to Cincinnati I am going to trade you off!"

Despite his pretended displeasure, Jason was inwardly happy to see Mary in such a good mood. In reply to his remark she quipped:

"For what? A squaw?"

Dave had been making his way down the walkway beside the cabin and could not help overhearing the last part of their conversation and now exclaimed:

"Them squaws do a lot of work Jason!"

Mary glanced at Dave and with scornful disdain said: "You men--I think both of you spent too much time in the woods with Hank!" She winked at Jason and then retreated into the cabin as he remarked:

"Women have got to have the last word!"

Moments later, standing on the stern with Tom, Jason studied the southern horizon and reflected on what Major Stites had said about how the people of Kentucky felt regarding "the rich prize just across the Ohio." As if reading his mind Tom said:

"That Israel Ludlow Stites mentioned is from Kentucky--served under General Scott." Staring at the swirling waters behind the ark the pilot added: "And that Matthias Denman he talked about is a land speculator who obtained warrants for land out here opposite the mouth of the Licking in 1787 but fail-ed to enter them before Symmes got approval for his purchase from Congress and the Board of Treasury. Denman planned to lay out a town and start a ferry across to the south shore. Good spot too--right on the trail between Detroit and Kentucky."

"Nothing upstream before Maysville I suppose," said Jason.

"Right!" replied Tom. "After Denman realized what had happened, he bought the land from Symmes in January of 1788--more than six hundred acres in the area where Cincinnati now is. In August of '88 Denman came out here and formed a partnership--sold two-thirds of his interest to Robert Patterson and John Filson for twenty pounds in Virginia money. Abe McConnel and Henry Owen witnessed the deed."

Waving his hand toward the north, and then the south, Tom continued: "Been a lot of bloodshed out here along this river since '78."

That was the year vengeful Indians attack Fort Boonesborough, Major Clark captured Kaskaskia and then marched against Fort Sackville at Vincennes, and Chief Black Fish's warriors "surprised" a party of their pursuers at Blue Licks. It was the year the Shawnee tribes split and 4000 headed west while

3000 remained on the banks of the Mad, Great Miami, and Little Miami under the leadership of the forty-nine year old Chief Black Hoof (Catahecassa). 1778 was also the year Daniel Boone was held prisoner by Shawnee Indians along the Little Miami and ten year old Tecumseh heard Simon Kenton condemned to death at the stake. It was only one of several years the commander of Fort Detroit, Henry Hamilton, offered $50 for a white man's scalp and $100 for every live white prisoner. 1778 was just one more year of the continuing hate and vengeance, bloodshed and tears, attacks and reprisals, and unrest that plagued the Ohio frontier. Now, in May of 1791, Tom May pointed his finger at the south shore saying to Jason:

"Right up there back in '79 Colonel Rogers and seventy of his seventy-nine troops were killed--ran into an Indian 'surprise!' Major Benham was with Rogers and was badly wounded--only managed to stay alive by hiding under a fallen tree. He suffered for several days before he ran into another wounded comrade and they helped each other stay alive until a passing boat picked them up and took them down to The Falls. Lucky they got away with their scalps!"

This incident occurred at a place which would later be called Dayton, Kentucky. Near here, that same year, Colonel John Bowman (1738-1784) led 296 Kentucky mounted volunteers across the Ohio and on north to old Chillicothe on the banks of the Little Miami where, on May 29th, they were unsuccessful in an attack on Chief Black Fish's village. 'Big Ben' Logan was second-in-command and Captain Harrod and William Whitley served as scouts during this raid. Whitley, from Crab Orchard, was destined to die on the banks of the Thames during the War of 1812.

Jason had listened carefully and now inquired: "Tom, did General Clark cross here?"

"Several times," replied Tom. "Since you call him 'general,' you are probably talking about 1782. Flushed with success downstream, Clark was wearing stars by then when he took one thousand and fifty

men across the Ohio and landed where Cincinnati now
is. He had built two blockhouses there in August
of 1780 but the Indians had destroyed them--thought
they were obnoxious. But in 1782 Clark led his men
up to the mouth of the Mad and north along the Big
Miami where he set up his headquarters about three
miles north of where the Loramie empties into that
river. Clark was bent on destroying all the Indian
villages where the St. Marys and St. Joseph rivers
meet. But although his men burned the Old Loramie
Post, they didn't go any farther north."

"Pat said some Shawnee chief was killed during
one raid," said Jason. "Was that the one?"

"No, not that one--been so many it's real easy
to get mixed up. The one Pat was talking about was
the one led by General Logan after Little Turtle's
made a daring raid south of the Ohio and kidnapped
a red-headed lad named William Wells.*   Well, that
really stirred up a hornet's nest and them settlers
were itching to retaliate when they rode north!"

From Logan's Station, about thirty-five miles
south of Lexington, Benjamin Logan had sent out the
word for volunteers to join him at Limestone Point
in late September of 1786. Of the 780 volunteers
who showed up, 500 brought their own horses, guns,
ammunition, and 50 cows for food--the settlers were
determined to put an end to those Indian raids from
villages north of Limestone Point. In a concerted
action, General George Rogers Clark planned to raid
the Miami Indian's villages along the Wabash River.

As Tom related, on September 29, 1786 Logan's
volunteers crossed the Ohio and marched north. Although one of Logan's guides, a man of mixed-blood
named Willis Chadley, deserted southeast of present
day Xenia, Ohio in his attempt to warn the Indians,
their approach was undetected. Finding the village
called "Old Chillicothe" (Oldtown) still devastated

---

* Little Turtle called this adopted son "Apekonit," or
  "wild carrot."

332

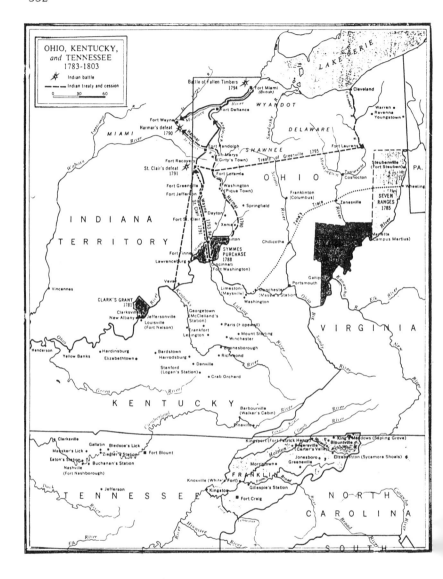

by the desultory raid led by George Rogers Clark on November 10th four years before, Logan continued on north along the Mad River to the Shawnee villages on the Wapatomica Trail near where West Liberty, OH stands today. Tom concluded his commentary saying:

"Unaware of General Logan's approach, and upon hearing General Clark intended to march against the Miamis in the Wabash country, most of those Shawnee warriors had rode west to help their neighbor fight a common enemy."

And that's how it was in October of 1786 when Logan's "raiders" stormed the Shawnee villages with Colonel Robert Patterson on the left flank, Colonel Thomas Kennedy on the right flank, and the general in the center followed by such men as Colonel James Trotter, Major McGary, Captains Samuel Scott, William Irwin, and Stucker, Daniel Boone, Simon Kenton, John Arnold, Benjamin Proctor, Richard Singleton, Lewis Wetzel, Robert Caldwell, and sixteen year old William Lytle. As Tom May told Jason:

"I was told they completely destroyed eight of the Mac-o-chee villages, burned their corn fields, killed twenty warriors, and took seventy prisoners. Among those prisoners was an old Shawnee chief named Moluntha, his three wives, and their children."

Tom paused and then thoughtfully added:

"Among those prisoners was a little Indian boy that Logan took back to Kentucky and adopted. The Indians called that boy 'Spemica Lawba.'"

Contrary to what some historical stories would have the reader believe, research by 20th century chroniclers such as Mary McClintock, Wapakoneta, OH ("Logan Made Local History," WAPAKONETA DAILY NEWS, Feb 15, 1966) and history-minded George C. Chadwick from Xenia, OH ("General Benjamin Logan's Kentucky Long-Knives," XENIA DAILY GAZETTE, May 23, 1986) indicates General Logan named this adopted Indian boy "James," not "Johnny" Logan.

During the desultory devastation Captain Irwin was killed and Colonel Kennedy, emotionally drained by the Indian's continual raids, cleaved a cowering squaw's skull as she and six other squaws screamed: "Mat-tah-tshi!"* Simon Kenton had been a prisoner of these Indians and returned with a vengeance--he would get his "pound of flesh" for the punishment he had suffered. When Captain Hugh McGary learned that one of the prisoners was the old Shawnee chief who had ambushed his friends at Blue Licks in 1778, he buried a tomahawk in Chief Moluntha's skull.

Although McGary was tried by court-martial for the dastardly deed at Bardstown on March 20, 1787-- not at Harrodsburg on November 11, 1786 as declared "fact" by a 20th century writer--he was acquitted.

Pensively Tom May nodded at the north shore as he slowly said: "Seeing those high bluffs up there reminds me of the spring of 1780 and the fourteenth day of April--that was my wife's birthday. But she was gone by then, God bless her soul."

The old pilot swallowed hard and fought off an urge to cry. Glancing at Jason, Tom said: "Excuse me, an old memory got the best of me."

"I understand," said Jason and Tom continued:

"As I started to say, around the bend up ahead we spotted some Indians on that north shore. They were clearly visible--just sitting up there on that bluff big as all get out. Some scout probably seen us drifting down the river and thought we might be intending to land on that side."

Tom paused and leaned into the sweep to keep the ark from drifting too close to the north shore.

"Come on Tom, what happened?" said Jason.

"Nothing," replied Tom. "They just watched us and we kept a sharp eye on them too. This area has always been a crossing place and the Indians keep a close watch on it most of the time."

Tom did not know what they saw was a scouting party for Henry Byrd, a British officer from Fort Detroit. In May of 1780 Byrd, under orders of the

* Do not kill us!

commander at Fort Detroit, Major Arent Schuyler De
Peyster, marched toward the settlements in Kentucky
with his scarlet coated Eighth Regiment and seventy
five green-coated Canadian militiamen. With him on
this march were Thomas, James and Simon Girty, and
Alexander McKee--four white renegades who had found
the red man's cause tailored to their fiendish interests. Byrd had brought with them four pieces of
artillery--an impressive sight to Indians. Marching south in 1780 they passed through the Shawnee
village along the Little Miami which would later be
known as "Old Town." Along his line of march Byrd
was joined by a number of revengeful Indians and by
the time he was ready to cross the Ohio his "force"
approximated 600 men. In June of 1780 Henry Byrd's
followers launched a successful attack on Ruddell's
Station and twelve year old Stephen Ruddell, along
with 400 others, was taken prisoner by the Indians.
Called Simanatha, or "The Big Fish," Stephen became
a friend of an Indian boy his own age, Tecumseh.

But then the Kentucky settlers sought revenge
and on August 16, 1780 the Shawnee village on the
Little Miami was devastated. After this raid the
old Shawnee chief, Catahecassa, looked at the ruins
of his village and the ravaged fields and began to
speak of peace. But the desultory raids back and
forth across the Ohio had continued and now, in May
of 1791, the Indians carefully watched boats coming
downstream. High above the river, and concealed by
overhanging trees, an Indian watched Tom and Jason
standing on the stern of their boat as they drifted
by. There did not appear to be any soldiers on the
boat and he relayed this observation to Tecumseh.

After drifting around a long bend in the Ohio,
Tom shouted to Dave and Pat on the bow:

"Keep a sharp eye on that starboard side men--
Cincinnati is right ahead!"

His announcement brought the women out of the
cabin and everyone strained their eyes "looking."
Carefully maneuvering the sweep, Tom headed the ark

toward shore and a landing place at the foot of the
settlement. From the shore came a friendly shout:
"Grab a line and we'll pull you in!"
On the bow Pat grabbed a rope that came hurl-
ing through the air--simultaneously another one was
thrown to the stern and Jason pulled it in. With
Tom calling out orders, the ark was soon secure and
a bearded man on shore called out to the pilot:
"Tom! You old son of a gun--how ya' been?"
"Right tolerable Rube, how 'bout you?"
A slight grimace crossed Rube's face and then
faded into a smile as he rubbed his hands together
briskly and replied:
"Well, 'cept for rheumatism I'm in pretty fair
shape for an old man! Sun is oiling up these bones
but I'm hoping you fetched some Old Monongahela for
your old friend! I been fixing that ramp for you--
gonna cost you though!"
Tom laughed heartily as he looked at those who
were slowly working their way down the crude wooden
gang plank. With a grin Tom remarked:
"I figured as much! I think we might be able
to find a wee bit of oil for your old bones soon as
I have some spare time."
Tom walked off the ramp, wrung the hand of his
old acquaintance and then introduced his passengers
in turn. With a huge smile that displayed two rows
of stained teeth, Rube told Tom's passengers:
"Tom and me's been through a lot of doors!"
After a flurry of greetings, Tom led the group
up twenty steps which had been cut in the hillside.
Upon reaching the top of the steps, Jason surveyed
the sloping ground ahead which led into a clearing.
He had no way of knowing he stood at the foot of
what would someday be Sycamore Street in the city
some would nickname "The Paris of America." Up the
hill on the right he could see the top of a fortification he knew must be Fort Washington.
Two men now approached the group and one said:
"Welcome to Cincinnati folks! My name is Bob

Patterson and this is my partner, Israel Ludlow."

With a smile of recognition, Patterson glanced at Tom and quickly added: "Welcome back Tom--good to see you again! Have a good trip?"

"Good trip Bob--and I am traveling with a fine bunch of folks I want you to meet."

Tom introduced each in turn ending with Jason:

"And these are the Evenstars--Mary and Jason."

Jason shook hands with each of the men and his wife curtsied politely. Colonel Patterson's charm reminded her of a gentleman from Richmond, Virginia that visited her father in Baltimore--he had an engaging smile. Mary listened as Patterson spoke:

"It's nice of you folks to bring Tom here back down the river with you--we miss him!"

Tom quickly commented: "I never traveled with nicer people colonel--they're all anxious to settle out here in this country." Tom paused and quickly added: "I'm not speaking out of turn am I Jason?"

"Not at all," replied Jason. "We are going to unload that ark someplace--just looking for a place that feels right!"

Mary beamed--she was proud of her husband and it showed. She put her arm through the crook of his elbow and gave him a playful nudge as Patterson remarked:

"I am certain you and your charming wife--and your friends--will find Cincinnati to your liking."

Colonel Patterson had built a stockade at Lexington in March of 1780 when other stations such as Bryant's, Martin's, McAfee's, and Ruddell's were in being--he knew that part of the country. His sharp eyes swept the group and settled on Pat Hagan:

"What did you say you name was--have we met?"

"Pat Hagan. We talked briefly several times at Lexington last summer."

Patterson studied Pat's face thoughtfully and then said: "Oh certainly, now I remember you. And again welcome to Cincinnati and I hope you stay."

"We're thinking about it. By the way colonel,

where did that name ' Losantiville' come from?"

Patterson smiled, glanced at Ludlow, and said:

"I hear that question often. As you may know, my partner, John Filson, mysteriously disappeared three years ago but one of his last earthly doings was to name this settlement. As I understand, John coined the name out of several words--the 'L' being for Licking, the 'os' is Latin for mouth I believe, 'anti' means opposite, and 'ville' is French for town. Did I miss anything Israel?"

Ludlow grinned and replied: "He knows foreign language is not my strong suit. At Maysville a man informed me it was 'Losantiburg' in the Articles of Agreement that John signed with Matthias Denman and the colonel here. He also said it was spelled that way in the KENTUCKY GAZETTE published in September of 1788--the one that announced lots would be given away. A man can learn a lot just walking down the streets of Maysville these days!"

Patterson joined everyone in polite laughter and then in a business-like tone of voice remarked:

"Regardless of what anyone says, this list of our pioneer settlers reads 'Losantiville!'"

Jason looked at the paper on which were listed the names of the three partners followed by Isaac Freeman, Henry Bechtle, Noah Badgely, Samuel Blackburn, Thaddeus Bruen, Robert Caldwell, James and Matthew Campbell, James Carpenter, William Connell, James and Benjamin Dumont, Matthew Fowler, Luther Kitchell, Henry Lindsey, David McClever, James McConnell, William McMillan, Elijah Martin, Evan Shelby, James Monson, Samuel Mooney, John Porter, Jesse and Richard Stewart, Joe Thorton, Scott Traverse, John Vance, Isaac Van Meter, Isaac Tuttle, Joel Williams, Sylvester White, Ephraim Kibbey, Thomas Gizzel, Frank Hardesty, Captain Henry, Mr. Davidson, and Mr. Fulton.

Near the bottom of the page Jason saw the name "Daniel Shoemaker" followed by "Columbia."

The young man's interest in the list had not gone unnoticed and Robert Patterson asked him if he were looking for anyone in particular.

"My friend and I met two settlers named Dawson and Parker on Braddock's road last January," Jason explained. "Thought they might have settled here."

Patterson looked at Jason intently as he said:

"Last January? They wouldn't be on that list. They might have stopped at Marietta, Maysville, or gone on down to North Bend. Some pass by here and go on down to The Falls too."

Jason did not see Alma Jones nudge her husband but Mary did. Jason now explained to Patterson how the Weisers had left them intending to settle north and east of Lexington. Colonel Patterson said:

"Some of the most beautiful country you could ask for is northeast of Lexington. You folks would not be far from them if you decide to settle here-- overland it is less than a hundred miles. You can also use the Licking if you are so inclined--river travel may not be so appealing after your last few weeks but soon you'll only remember the good things and forget the bad ones."

Mary listened--she wasn't nearly as optimistic about having very many "happy recollections" of the trip downstream and simply looked foward to setting up housekeeping as soon as possible. Somewhere!

"We have our growing pains here but sitting on our hands and crying will not solve them. Governor St. Clair is painfully aware of the Indian menace and anxious to establish a strong military presence in this area which will not only discourage harass- ment but will encourage settlement. This is, as my English friend would put it, 'a sticky wicket!'"

Jason sensed the frustration Patterson and his partners must feel and hastened to explain that the Weiser's principal reason for their change of plans was the "education of the children" matter. Jason said they had heard many favorable reports concern- ing what had been accomplished and added:

"Much of the gloom and doom commments we heard are not worthy of repeating. My uncle always said crepe hangars can be found on the doorstep of every undertaking. But, as my wife often remarks, 'every person hears a different drummer.' Right Mary?"

His wife nodded and Patterson remarked:

"Your wife is not only pretty, it sounds as if she is very wise. Don't you agree Israel?"

"Could not have said it better myself Bob, and perhaps we can entice them to make their home right here in Cincinnati."

A natural born salesman, Israel Ludlow added:

"We are a growing community folks and there is great opportunity here!"

Mary glanced at Jason and an insincere smile crossed her face—Ludlow had used "that word!"

Warm and friendly, he had an energetic quality about him that Jason found delightful. Like Jason, Ludlow was born in 1765 and his survey work in the Northwest Territory was destined to be a remembered part of its rich history. He had been appointed by the United States Surveyor General Thomas Hutchins to survey both the land contracted for by Symmes as well as the land acquired by the Ohio Company of Associates. However, obtaining military protection for the wilderness effort was a continuing problem. It was Ludlow who now broached the subject of surveying as he said:

"Tom informed me you have some experience as a surveyor?"

Jason related how his uncle had said he helped Charles Mason and Jeremiah Dixon in 1767 when they were surveying the Mason-Dixon line north of where Jason lived as a boy along the Monocacy and added:

"Uncle Frederick worked with a man named David Rittenhouse as I recall—been a long time. Anyway, what I know I learned from my uncle."

Ludlow listened politely and remarked:

"If you're acquainted with a thirty-three foot surveyor's chain, an eight inch compass mounted on a Jacob Staff, and can handle your rifle as good as Tom says, we can put you to work. Survey work out here pays seven or eight shillings a mile--you earn it. When do you want to start work Jason?

Jason recalled his Uncle Conrad had once told him about visiting Captain Hutchins at Fort Pitt in 1786 when the surveyor opened an office there. The geographer was author of a system of surveying that Conrad had explained to Jason. Conrad had told him Hutchins had made explorations in the Ohio valley and mentioned this Miami River region.

"It is a small world in some respects," Jason thought to himself. Aloud he said cheerfully:

"I am certain I could hold up my end of survey work but I had thought about starting a blacksmith shop....where we decide to settle of course."

Mary was inwardly happy to hear him say that. Ludlow's mention of the need for use of a gun had conjectured up a distasteful picture of men working in the Indian infested wilderness. A good salesman learns to read what is in the eyes of his customer, as well as hearing what the prospect says. Ludlow saw the fear in Mary's eyes and quickly said:

"There is a lot of survey work to do here with all of the settlers moving in and establishing land claims. Mrs. Evenstar, are you aware surveying is a very old art? It originated in Egypt."

They had no way of knowing this man would pass away in 1804 at a relatively young age. But before Israel Ludlow died he would survey a large part of the Treaty of Greene Ville Line and many other land grants employing the old English "metes and bounds" method wherein natural features such as boulders, rivers, and large oak, elm, and chestnut trees were used as survey monuments. It would be the early 1800s before the third president, Thomas Jefferson, would encourage a wide use of the replacement "rec-tangular survey system" using range and base lines and establishing "checkerboard" townships six miles square and containing 640 acres.

With the Hagans and Jones having been engaged in conversation by other settlers, Robert Patterson directed his remarks to the Evenstars: "We've got all of Section Eighteen and a fractional portion of Section Seventeen here in Township Four." Pointing toward the river Patterson added: "Israel started to survey this tract just as soon as we landed down there at Yeatman's Cove on December 28th. We spent that first night beneath those beech trees next to that little beaver pond--mighty cold that night!"

"Is that where the Symmes party landed?" asked Mary politely.

"Right you are Mrs. Evenstar." With a note of pride in his voice, Patterson added: "But he didn't get here until the end of January--five weeks after we landed. John stayed two days and pulled anchor on Monday morning, second day of February."

Looking across the river toward Kentucky, the colonel continued:

"I am fortunate to have such knowledgeable and hard-working partners. Speaking of partners, here comes my other one, Matthias Denman."

After being introduced to everyone, this third partner remarked:

"Sorry I couldn't get here sooner--I have been with the governor...or perhaps I should say General St. Clair. He just returned from the east where he was appointed a Major General, given command of the army, and was authorized to lead a campaign against those troublesome Indians this summer. Said he has the backing of congress and the president. I don't wish to appear overly optimistic but I believe this is a turning point for our community!"

On March 21,1791 the Secretary of War provided Arthur St. Clair with instructions which started as follows: "The President of the U. S. having, by and with the advise and consent of the Senate, appointed you a major general in the service of the U. S., and of consequence invested you with the chief command of the troops to be employed upon the frontier during the ensuing campaign, it is proper that you should be possessed of the views of the Government respecting the objects of your command."

A rather wordy communique, Henry Knox detailed the intent and objectives of a 1791 summer campaign against the Indians. A loyal and obedient officer, St. Clair could be trusted to carry out his orders exactly as given.

In Cincinnati in mid-May, Patterson and Ludlow were elated. Turning to Jason, Patterson said:

"Well, that's a step in the right direction!"

"It sounds encouraging," said Jason. "I trust it is all right if I tell my companions--this could influence our decision on where we settle."

"Certainly, I understand," said Patterson. "I imagine you have many things to talk over. In the meantime, perhaps you and your wife would join Mrs. Patterson and me for the evening meal?"

Jason glanced at his beaming wife and replied:

"We would be honored colonel--and thank you."

"Good, then shall we say five-thirty? I will tell Mrs. Patterson to expect you. By the way, I understand you play the fiddle and I am anxious to hear you. May I take the liberty of asking you to bring along your violin and permit me the privilege of telling our neighbors to gather in front of our cabin for a little music this evening?"

Jason could not refuse such a pleasant request and replied: "It would be my pleasure--thank you."

Bob Patterson and Denman now politely excused themselves and Ludlow seized the opportunity to introduce the Evenstars to a man who had come to this settlement determined to operate a ferry across the Ohio, Joel Williams. A jovial, but business-minded person, Joel informed Jason salt cost six dollars a pound, coffee was a dollar a pound, and corn from Columbia last fall brought two shillings a bushel.

"Pork costs twenty-five shillings per hundred but there's plenty of wild meat around," said Joel. "Tom probably told you folks 'Old Monongahela' from

344

down in Kentucky costs twenty-five cents a gallon."
With a smile he glanced at Mary saying: "And plain
calico that comes down the river costs you a dollar
a yard!"

To some newcomers the monetary exchange on the
frontier was often confusing. Spanish dollars, cut
into quarters and eighths, were not frequently used
any longer by 1791. The troops at Fort Washington
were paid, when they were paid, in Federal money--
usually bills of the Old Bank of the United States,
a three dollar note.

As Joel continued his commentary, Mary's eyes
surveyed the surrounding area. All around them the
woods was alive with the sound of ringing axes and
bon fires could be seen everywhere she looked. The
advocates of "clean air" and "save the tree" issues
who picketed streets of Cincinnati 200 years later
would have had apoplexy had they seen the wanton
felling of the trees and clouds of billowing smoke
that afternoon in 1791. To herself, Mary thought:

"What tremendous things these people have done
in such a short time."

Mary's admiration was well placed--without an
iron will and indomitable resolution they could not
have accomplished what they did so quickly. A few
had spent their personal fortunes in the service of
their country and were left with nothing but their
willing hands, stout hearts, and an unconquerable
supply of energy. Many settlers were veterans of
the recent war who had cut their teeth on hardships
and privations--some remembered the terrible winter
at Valley Forge! The brave and toilsome accomplishments of the first settlers at Losantiville rightly
deserve a lasting place in the historical annals of
the Northwest Territory.

Looking across the Ohio that afternoon, Ludlow
related how Captain Celoron had learned the name of
the river that lay before them:

"The Seneca Indians north of Fort Pitt thought
the Allegheny and Ohio were one river--they called

it 'O-hee-yuh,' the beautiful river.* Joncaire, a Frenchman taken prisoner by the Senecas, called the river 'O-hee-o.' According to a letter Washington sent to Governor Dinwiddie in 1753, he was taken to task by Joncaire about his pronunciation of 'Ohio' during his visit to Venango."

"A visitor to my uncle's blacksmith shop said early geographers thought the Ohio was a tributary of the Wabash River," said Jason.

"An interesting thought," said Ludlow. "By the way Jason, speaking of rivers, a few of us are riding northwest toward the Big Miami in the morning-- would you care to join us?"

Jason glanced at Mary quickly--the glow on his face spoke for itself. And the frown on his wife's face also needed no interpretation. But before she could throw cold water on the matter, Jason said:

"It would be an opportunity to exercise Star-- he would like that!" Jason's eyes were begging as he added: "You wouldn't mind too much would you?"

In spite of her misgivings, Mary could not refuse his request and she replied:

"If you must Jason. As you say, it would give Star some exercise and my feet could use the rest."

"Then it's settled," said Ludlow.

His similar offer to Dave and Pat fell on deaf ears. Alma was adamant Dave was not going to leave her alone--and besides, they had made plans to meet Captain Jacob White (1759-1849) and his wife in the morning. A native of Redstone, Pennsylvania, Jacob White and Joanna Mounts were married in New Jersey October 25, 1780 and came to Losantiville in 1789. Destined to locate Section One in Springfield Township on July 23, 1792, Captain White was proprietor of White's Station. As the captain explained:

"Our cabin is about seven or eight miles north of here. Andrew Goble and David Flinn built their cabins near me. And, in keeping with John Symmes'

* "Craig's Olden Times" (1845) Pittsburgh

encouragement, some of us have established stations for refuge in case of an Indian attack. The first one was Dunlap's Station about seventeen miles up the Big Miami; the second was Ludlow's Station five miles north of here along Mill Creek; and the third was Covalt's Station ten miles north of Columbia."

He said nothing about an Indian attack at Dunlap's Station on Sunday, January 9, 1791. Close on the heels of a five inch snow, 250 Indians led by Blue Jacket had suddenly appeared near the gate of the three sided stockade where Captain Kingsbury's detachment of 35 soldiers were garrisoned. John S. Wallace, Cunningham, Sloane, and Abner Hunt were outside the station and spotted the Indian raiding party. As the wounded Sloane and terrified Wallace rode for their lives to the station, the Indians killed Cunningham and captured Hunt. Then, as the nearby settlers huddled together in fear inside the wilderness station, Hunt was tortured and burned to death right in front of his companion's eyes as the Indians demanded the station surrender. With Abner Hunt dead, and the garrison having only 24 rounds of ammunition, the women cast their pewter plates and spoons into bullets and a soldier rode to Fort Washington for help. Young Benjamin Van Cleve was among the party that quickly came to the station's rescue and the tiny fortification held. On January 11th the Indians withdrew.

Now four months later, in mid-May of 1791, Pat Hagan also declined Ludlow's invitation saying his wife preferred they continue on downstream. As for Mary, she looked forward to the chance for a day of rest and back at the ark that afternoon Tom assured her she would be completely safe.

Everyone had been invited to enjoy the evening meal with someone in Cincinnati and at five o'clock they all headed up the slope. Always thinking, Tom had arranged for someone to guard their ark and now as he walked with the Evenstars, Jason remarked:

"I wonder how Colonel Patterson knew I played

the fiddle? Did you tell him Tom?"

Without answering directly Tom said: "Perhaps you forgot Major Doughty was coming down this way."

Laced with friendly hospitality, their evening meal with the Pattersons was simple but delightful. Afterwards the colonel and Jason took a little turn about the settlement before it was time for "entertainment." The mid-May evening was warm and before sunset the settlers began to gather in front of the Patterson cabin--word had passed a "fiddler" was in their midst. Seated a comfortable distance from a big fire intended to light the area, Jason took his seat on a log and removed his violin from its case.

As at Marietta, Jason started off with "Battle of the Kegs" and everyone quickly joined in singing this lively song. After listening to Jason play a few tunes, Israel Ludlow politely requested he play a dance tune and Jason nodded--he knew how much the settlers enjoyed three or four handed reels, square sets, and jigs. Commencing with a square four, the dancers were soon "jigging it off" as Jason played. Colonel Patterson then urged Jason's wife to favor them with a song and she sang her favorite, "Jesus Lover Of My Soul." Although asked to "sing another song," Jason realized his wife was tired and said:

"Dear friends--the hour grows late and we have had a busy day. Mary and I really appreciate your hospitality but as my wife likes to say, 'there's a time to stay and time to go,' and now it is time we must go. Thank you for a most memorable evening!"

Walking slowly back down the slope to the ark, a lonely night bird swooped low over the Evenstars and headed across the river. The inky darkness hid the steep forested hills around the settlement and Mary wondered if some Indian might not be somewhere up in that black void watching them.

Jason took the first watch that night and Mary lay for a long time listening to the water burbling around the hull--the rhythmic pattern was soothing. Pat's unmistakable snoring, and the rich smell of animals blended unpleasantly with the odor of dead fish, tobacco smoke, unclean bodies, and unwashed clothing made Jason's wife long for the day their river travel would end. Listening to her husband's footsteps as he moved slowly up and down the narrow walkway, Mary fell asleep.

Looking up to where the upper portion of Fort Washington was outlined against a starry sky, Jason recalled Colonel Patterson's remarks about General Harmar's arrival at that stockade with 300 regulars in January of 1790. Only six months earlier Major Doughty, accompanied by Captain David Strong, had arrived and started construction of that fort which now stood on the horizon high above the river. The gray-haired man who poured over some papers in that fort, Arthur St. Clair, had commented upon arriving at Fort Washington:

"It is five hundred miles up the Ohio to Fort Pitt and fatiguing to send my reports by canoes and boats each month. Therefore, my dispatches will be sent to Danville, Kentucky and forwarded through the wilderness to Richmond, Virginia where they will be deposited in the post office as the most expeditious conveyance."

At daybreak the next morning Tom helped Jason get Star off the ark and he was waiting when Ludlow rode down the slope. Already Jason could hear the sounds of those who toiled to lay the foundations of a city which had started to bloom around him---a metropolis that would someday boast the nickname, "The Queen City."

In front of the gate to Fort Washington Jason was introduced to several settlers including Joseph Cutter, A. W. Pryor, John Van Cleve, James Miller, Daniel Bates, Enos Terry, and Thomas Goudy. Goudy, the first lawyer in Cincinnati, had come from Pennsylvania in 1789 and was destined to marry Sarah Wallace in 1793. Tom Goudy, along with some of the other settlers, had build a blockhouse in that area north of Cincinnati later called the "Cumminsville area" but now simply known as "Ludlow's Station." Here, where Israel Ludlow had entered land warrants on March 9, 1790, a blockhouse which had been built would be offered to St. Clair as a "staging area" for his forthcoming campaign. But the first three settlers Jason met that morning were destined for an early grave--they would be dead within a month. Joseph Cutter was destined to be killed by Indians four days later, May 21st, while with Van Cleve in a field near Cincinnati. Only a few days later, on June 1st, an Indian would kill Van Cleve--Benjamin Van Cleve's father. Pryor was destined to be slain in June by Indians not far from Cincinnati while he was hunting with two other settlers.

Sitting astride their horses waiting for their military escort, Ludlow and the settlers paid scant attention to an Indian who stood close to the gate watching as Star nervously pawed the air. With a mixture of hate, envy, and admiration, the copper-skinned Indian took special note of Jason's horse--it was the finest horse he had ever seen. When an officer, Lieutenant Hartshorne, came riding out of the fort followed by eight soldiers, an Indian took a quick step back and allowed them to pass.

Ludlow's party then proceeded north along Mill Creek five miles to Mill Creek Station--or Ludlow's Station--where they talked awhile with Abner Boston and then rode west up a valley. Jason marveled at the virgin woods--oak, beech, hickory, walnut, ash, elm, poplar, sycamore, butternut, cherry, cotton-wood, and buckeye trees. Occasionally a startled bird would sweep out of its shelter in a tree as it angrily protested their presence. From somewhere up the steep ridges on either side dislodged rocks sometimes rolled down noisly through the underbrush signaling the movement of some wilderness predator. At one point Ludlow silently pointed up to a ledge high above them saying: "Look right--look up!"

High above them Jason saw a huge bear watching them with seeming unconcern. As they watched, the brownish-black bear suddenly turned and disappeared in the undergrowth and rocks. Jason muttered:

"I would wager that bear's legs are shorter on one side from climbing around these hills!"

Following an Indian trail, they worked their way up a hill with the azure blue sky above often blocked from sight by overhanging tree branches. In spite of Jason's familiarity with the wooded trails of Pennsylvania, the Indian menace here plagued his thoughts and he rode close behind Ludlow. Each man cradled his gun in his arms carefully with a finger always near the trigger. Onward and upward they rode with the arched green roof overhead checkered with stabs of sunlight. The sun was directly overhead when suddenly through an opening in front of them Jason saw a promise of light and then the "Big Miami River" country lay below. The beauty of the rolling wilderness sea stretching endlessly to the northern horizon, and the lush blossoming green of the fertile valley, was breath-taking. A profound stillness filled the earth and sky and Jason felt infinitely small. Overcome with a mixed feeling of wonder and reverence, Jason whispered verse 24 of the 104th Psalm:

"Oh Lord, how manifold are thy works! In wisdom hast thou made them all: the earth is full of thy riches!"

Ludlow sensed Jason's feelings and remarked: "Beautiful, is it not?"

But here in these beautiful surroundings, some found a feeling of isolation and loneliness hard to shake off—it had made many stout hearts turn back to the abodes of comfort and companionship they had left east of the Alleghenies. Overhearing Ludlow's remark, one soldier declared:

"Beautiful? No neighbors! Only thing you got to worry about here are copperheads, rattlesnakes, and those hellish red savages!"

Ignoring the soldier's comment, Ludlow glanced at Jason and said reassuringly:

"Being alert is a rule of life out here!"

Pointing his finger toward the Great Miami in the distance, Ludlow added:

"Along that river is some of the best soil it has ever been my good fortune to see. Should yield a great harvest. John Symmes wrote to his business colleague back east stating that land is positively worth a silver dollar an acre!"

He neglected to mention how many of those rich and mellow fields were surrounded by the wilderness where the dreaded Indians roamed at will ready to kill and scalp anyone who dared till the rich soil.

"Indians around here probably never laid eyes on a white man until Captain Celoron buried a lead plate below Fort Hill and called that river you see in the distance 'Riviere a la Roche'--that's French for Rock River John Filson told me. Personally, I prefer 'Big Miami!'"

Standing on the ridge they had no way of knowing a few eventful years later Kentucky "squatters" would aggravate St. Clair as they came up the Great Miami and settled on those bottom lands after the Treaty of Greene Ville in 1795. In that same river area Ludlow pointed to, Billy Jones was destined to be appointed as a Whitewater Township schoolmaster in 1799 with the Testament and a copy of Dilworth's Speller as his primary teaching tools. That same year settlers on the north side of the Great Miami would sign a petition which read:

PETITION TO CONGRESS - From inhabitants northwest of the Miami River. We are apprehensive that by the mode of sale, and the scarcity of cash experienced by us that all our endeavors will be frustrated and we shall be deprived of the enjoyment of those improvements we have made hereon and hereby involved in distress and ruin. We therefore humbly petition your Honors.

One of the petitioners who would sign this was Emanuel Vantrees, an early settler and surveyor who was destined to survey a 2,000 acre tract of land on the north side of the Great Miami for Jeremiah Butterfield et al in 1801. Although "worlds apart" in a manner of speaking, a Massachusetts born poet, John Greenleaf Whittier (1807-1892), would say of "The Miamese:"

> *"I hear the tread of pioneers*
> *Of Nations yet to be*
> *The first low wash of waves, where soon*
> *Shall roll a human sea.*
> *The elements of empire are here*
> *Are plastic yet and warm*
> *And the chaos of a mighty world*
> *Is rounding into form."*

But all that was in the future and the Symmes' "Miami Purchase" area--and the entire region north-west of Cincinnati--would be the unwitting witness to a lot of bloodshed before that Quaker poet was even born. And, in May of 1791, as Ludlow's party started back to Cincinnati, everyone was mindful of the danger that lay around them. Snaking their way back down through the virgin woods, everyone kept a sharp eye open for the deadly copperheads--it could lay silently coiled among the leaves and strike its victim without warning. At least a rattlesnake was generous with the warning noise of its rattle--it apprised the hunter of danger. But the fearful and insidious Indian who crawled through the underbrush and noiselessly tracked his quarry from behind the trees in the trackless wilderness was a disturbing menace--his deadly arrow and fatal bullet brought fear to the heart of the most seasoned settler.

The hills west of Cincinnati were silhouetted by the orange sky when Jason emerged from the woods near where the Mill Creek emptied into the Ohio--it had been an enlightening day and it was destined to

be an evening full of surprises. He had not reached the ark before he was met by Dave who exclaimed:

"Well, me and maw are unloading!   We got ourselves a place to board and room while I go take a
look at some land with Captain White."

"That's fine," said Jason as he dismounted and
led Star toward the ark.   "There's some mighty fine
land up north of here.   How about Pat?"

"Pat's going on downstream!"

Jason recognized the voice--it was Pat's wife.
Pat now came walking down the ramp saying:

"We've decided to go on downstream--my wife's
got a sister at Elizabethtown she hasn't seen in a
coon's age!   She came out here about twelve years
ago with General William Lytle's party--sixty-three
boats in that party she said.   Maybe we should have
gone there in the first place--but we didn't!   Anyway, things are going to get pretty lively around
here I hear.   Two loads of soldiers landed here today and there's more on the way one of them said."

On the ark Jason listened as the women told of
the day's events.   It was Alma who adamantly said:

"No way are we gonna go to that Miami City--or
North Bend--whatever you call it!   That woman where
we plan to stay told me a relative of hers, Captain
Matson, brought his wife and their four sons downstream with Symmes' party.   When they visited here
last October, Mrs. Matson told her a settler by the
name of Carter was murdered last year at North Bend
by an Indian in sight of Daniel Howell's door!"

Daniel Gideon Howell came west from New Jersey
in the fall of 1789 with his newlywed wife, Eunice
(Keen), and his father-in-law, Captain James Keen.
Daniel Howell sent a letter to the widow's brother,
Jacob Parkhurst, telling of Stephen Carter's murder
in April of 1790 but he too was destined to be dead
a few months later.

Pausing only to catch her breath, Alma added:
"As if it wasn't bad enough to have somone murdered
in their front yard, Eunice Howell was pregnant at

the time and then she lost her husband the sixth of
July last year."

Mary had been listening very carefully and now
asked quickly:

"What about the baby Alma?"

"Baby was born the first of August--first baby
born at North Bend."

Mary glanced at her husband but he never took
his eyes off Alma as she continued:

"She named her son Daniel Gideon Howell."

Later Alma would learn this widow, Eunice Keen
Howell, married William Rittenhouse in 1791. After
building a grist mill near North Bend, Rittenhouse
was destined to cut a wilderness road to a place he
would call "Mount Nebo"--the name of the mountain
from which Moses saw the "Promised Land." Undoubtedly he was inspired by Chapter 34 of Deuteronomy--
the first verse reads:

*"And Moses went up from the plains
of Moab unto the mountain of Nebo,.."*

Jason now turned and searched his wife's eyes.
Finally he thoughtfully said:

"I haven't had the opportunity to talk with my
bride as yet, but if she has no objections, we will
unload here too!"

A mixture of relief, resignation, and anxiety
spread across Mary's face--she would be quite happy
to get off the ark but she prayed her husband would
not say he planned to go with Dave. Perhaps Jason
was reading his wife's mind because he added:

"I am thinking very strongly of opening my own
blacksmith shop here! Mr. Ludlow feels there would
be a lot of work here now with so many settlers and
soldiers arriving--said he will introduce me to St.
Clair at the governor's earliest convenience."

Mary's eyes sparkled--she was so proud of her
husband! Life in Cincinnati would not be the same
as living in Baltimore but it beat Turkeyfoot and

what she had heard of North Bend.   Although Symmes
did have his problems, he still dreamed of building
a future metropolis the likes of which Pittsburgh
would be envious. Even as Jason made his decision,
the silver-tongued "Pied Piper of the Miami Wilderness" was telling a future settler at North Bend:

"Beyond those trees I can see church spires
and the smoke from hundreds of homes. I can hear
the sound of businesses--a mill grinding corn and a
saw mill cutting timber for new buildings."

But in the meantime at Cincinnati, and prefac-
ing his remarks saying he had this day met a young
man from North Bend named James Silver, Dave said:

"He came out here with Symmes' first party and
said their military escort leader, Captain Kearsey,
took exception to where Symmes wanted to go ashore.
Kearsey preferred the bottom land where Fort Finney
had stood.   Silver said all of them had very vivid
recollections of those Columbia cabins being under
water and supported Symmes' preference to land on a
higher piece of land. Anyway, Captain Kearsey took
his soldiers on downstream leaving them without any
military protection. Ensign Luce brought 18 troops
down to North Bend in March and build a blockhouse
Silver said. Then, only two months later--the 19th
of May as I recall--Ensign Luce and eight soldiers
were going upstream in a boat to the mouth of Muddy
Creek when some Indians attack them. Jim said John
R. Mills was killed and five others were wounded."

James Silver, an early settler destined to become a "judge," married John Symmes' niece, Betsey
(Elizabeth) Thompson June 12, 1789. Dave added:

"That attack on Ensign Luce really had those
settlers at North Bend upset--and it was worse when
Luce decided to move his troops back upstream that
winter. Left without any military protection, John
Symmes was furious according to Silver."

It was Alma who now injected: "The woman where
we plan to stay said it wasn't any fear of Indians
that caused Ensign Luce to move--said he had an eye

356

for the ladies and just followed a married woman by
the name of Strong whose husband decided they would
move upstream to here from a little settlement down
below North Bend."

Slightly nonplussed by his wife's repeating of
what he accepted as a "rumor," Dave quickly added:

"Alma, I have told you I would rather you did
not repeat that story. She was not at all positive
that woman's name was Strong. However, she did say
Ensign Luce resigned from the military service last
year--the first of May I believe--and Captain Brice
Virgin took his place."

Growing like a mushroom where Fort Finney had
been "wiped out" by the April flood in 1786, "Sugar
Camp" was a riverside settlement where some settler
lived with his beautiful wife before deciding to go
upstream in the winter of 1789. Although the move
may have been prompted by many things, it was left
for posterity to say this "moving incident" played
a part in the fate of the "metropolis" that Symmes
envisoned would someday be the envy of Pittsburgh.
A story by one chronicler* would romantically com-
pare the incident with that of the captivating wife
of King Menelaus of Sparta, Helen, who was literally "carried away" by her eager paramour, Paris, son
of King Priam of Troy. As narrated by Virgil, the
Roman poet whose "Aeneid" tells of the legendary
Troy, the "wife-napping" of the beautiful Spartan
queen prompted the history-changing ten year siege
of Troy. In a similar way according to this story,
the charms of this attractive "Sugar Camp" Helen of
Troy contributed to the transfer of the commercial
emporium of Ohio from North Bend to Cincinnati.

But the Sugar Camp settlement's femme couverte
and Ensign Luce had barely departed when, on December 21st, 1789, an Indian tomahawked John Hiller's
son about a half-mile from North Bend while the boy
was rounding up their livestock in the bottom land.

* "Cincinnati Beginnings" by Francis W. Miller (1880)

And, only five days later, Andrew Vaneman and James Lafferty were shot in the back and scalped while on a hunting trip across the river in Kentucky. John Dunlop found the two settlers and buried them.

Disregarding her husband's admonition, Dave's wife repeated another story she had heard:

"I know it ain't polite to repeat stories Dave, but that woman where we're aiming to stay also told me some settler by the name of Carter was killed by an Indian last year in his own yard at North Bend. She said Carter's neighbor--man named Daniel Howell as I recall--told her himself he had written to the widow Carter's brother back east telling him about the murder so it must be the truth!"

In Daniel Howell's letter to Carter's 18 year old brother-in-law, Jacob Parkhurst, he stated:

"On April 23rd last, an Indian shot Stephen in the breast, cut his throat, and scalped him."

Although Daniel Howell died July 6th, 1790, in September of that year Jacob Parkhurst, accompanied by Captain Virgin, visited his sister at North Bend and found a debilitating illness had left her bald.

As a "coup de grace" Alma added something else she had been told: "Not only did that poor Eunice Howell lose her husband last July, she had two sisters, Elizabeth and Sibel Keen, who came down sick with the fever and died last summer at North Bend! I certainly am glad we're going to stay here--there is a very good doctor here I was told."

An early physician in the Cincinnati area was Doctor John Hole (1755-1813) who came downstream to Losantiville in 1789, moved to Kentucky in 1790, and then returned to Cincinnati in 1790. Work as a wilderness doctor was not a money-making profession in those days--a house call was only 25¢.

"There's a big difference in the Marietta plan and Symmes' method of settling this area it seems," remarked Dave quickly hoping to change the subject. "At Marietta they allow settlers to settle as they please on that New England plan of staying together in villages to guard against the Indians. But here between the two Miami rivers, Symmes allows a land purchaser to choose his own ground. Then if ten or twelve settlers want to go together and build themselves a station, so be it. I like it here!"

Pat's wife said sarcastically:

"Well, its like this--you can do as you please but we are going on downstream! And that is that."

But regardless of what everyone planned to do, there was still the necessity of guarding their belongings and this night Jason volunteered to stand the first watch. Emboldened by their success over Harmar's army in October of 1790, the Indians had made several harassing attacks on Fort Washington. In spite of the loss of three soldiers during these attacks, the fort had held and several Indians were captured. But the danger was real and everyone was keeping their guard up. And now, with a curtain of deepening purple silhouetting the hills across the Ohio, and only the sound of the birds breaking the stillness, the Evenstars stood in the shadow of the wagon on the bow of the ark as Mary remarked rather pensively:

"I just cannot help thinking about that Eunice Howell having the first child born at North Bend."

Jason recalled that Major Doughty had told him about an enlisted man at Fort Harmar, David Blake, who married Martha Daggett back east in 1785. His daughter, Sarah, was the first white child born at Marietta. Drawing Mary close to him, Jason said:

"We may not have the first child born here but he will be the best in the Northwest Territory, you can bet on that!"

"Oh, its 'he' is it?" said Mary with an impish smile. "I was thinking about a girl! By the way, speaking of children, Tom was telling me this morning there is a flatboat tied to a tree a little way from here where Benjamin Griffith has been teaching school since last year."

In the midst of physical necessities, and of

that progress necessary to the settler's existence, schools, churches, and social institutions were always in the settler's thoughts. Mary continued:

"Tom says last year's census showed there were 2000 people living between the Little Miami and the Big Miami rivers."

Most of those 2000 people lived in that region with unquenchable hopes which fired the souls of those hearty settlers surrounded by prospects of virgin soil, an abundance of natural resources, and the uninhabited wilderness--well, not really "uninhabited!" That was the problem.

Taken only seven years after the Revolutionary War ended, and while the region north of Cincinnati was inhabited by Miamis and Shawnees, the young nation counted its people in 1790 for the first time. As might be expected, most people (3,929,214) lived along the eastern coast--Virginia was the most populous (619,737), and New York was the largest city (33,000). The 1790 census asked only six questions and women's names were not recorded--they did not count it seemed. When it came to cooking, baking, sewing, weaving, making beds, baby tending, and any garden making they counted all right but officially they were like the mother of ten who, when asked by the census taker what she did, replied: "I have no occupation."

Staring thoughtfully at the hills across the river, and turning over in his mind what Mary had said, Jason had no way of knowing a steamboat, the "New Orleans," would dock October 13th in 1811 at Cincinnati only two days out of Pittsburgh. But that was 20 years in the future and he now listened as Mary recited the opening lines of Thomas Gray's "Elegy Written In A Country Churchyard:"

"The curfew tolls the knell of parting day,
The lowing herd winds slowly oer the lea,
The weary plowman homeward plods his weary way
And leaves a world of darkness unto me."

"That is beautiful--written by an English poet named Gray as I recall." With a little laugh Jason added: "I didn't hear the bell toll but that world of darkness fits. I think you had better go inside dear--this damp night air is no good for you and my son!"

Pausing at the cabin door to kiss her husband, Mary whispered in Jason's ear:

"Like I said, your son may be a girl!"

Mary was asleep when Jason joined her when his watch was over. And he never stirred when his wife arose early the following morning and began to make his breakfast. With breakfast over, and having fed Star and his oxen, Jason began to help Dave unload. With his travel plans up in the air, Pat started up the slope in search of "a ride" down to Louisville. With Dave's belongings unloaded, and then standing by the stock enclosure gently nuzzling Star's nose, Jason heard Tom say:

"You'll have to talk with Jason Evenstar--he's up on the bow by the stock pen I believe."

Quickly moving to where he had a clear view of the stern, Jason saw a short, solid, individual of about 40 years of age with large brown eyes and a shock of red hair streaked with gray. In quick order the visitor introduced himself, suggested Jason call him "Red," and declared he was seeking passage downstream to "the falls of the Ohio." Sensing the man was in a hurry, Jason quickly and candidly told the visitor he did not anticipate he would continue downstream and anticipated dismantling his ark and using the timber to build a cabin. The red-haired man's eyes lighted up as he exclaimed:

"I have a cabin on a piece of land that I have leased--perhaps I could interest you in a trade!"

Although such a thought had never entered his mind, Jason was quick to realize the possibilities of such a "trade" and he excused himself saying he would discuss the matter with his wife.

"A cabin already built," said Mary eagerly, "I

think that would be delightful! But, let us take a look at it first. Where is it?"

Along with Tom May, the Evenstars joined "Red" in his wagon and started up the slope and through the settlement toward the cabin their driver talked about: "Folks here built forty cabins last summer. Mine needs a little work but she's liveable. I got puncheon floors made of split timber that I hewed smooth with a broad axe. I used clay and grass for mortar and covered the window opening with greased paper. Ordered me some window panes from back east but they ain't here yet!"

Jason glanced at Mary who winced as she remembered Rachel and Isaac. And she was still thinking about them when "Red" announced:

"Well folks, there she is! It ain't a vine-covered cottage but she'll keep you warm and dry!"

It was a typical frontier cabin about 18 by 24 feet in size and built of logs 12 to 18 inches in diameter. A number of unused logs still lay behind the cabin and deep ruts showed where they had been dragged out of the nearby wilderness. Jason made a mental note he could use these to build his black-smith shop and a lean-to for the sheep and Molly. It was not a two-story frame house like Mary's back in Baltimore but Jason had one advantage--his wife had lived in a frontier cabin. Although Jason knew how to put up a cabin, he listened carefully as the red-headed settler explained:

"We used hand-spikes and skid-poles to raise the logs and notched them with an axe--rafters hold the logs together at the top. Took a heap of sweat to cut and smooth them rived ash and oak clapboards or 'shakes' I guess folks call them. I used wooden pins instead of nails and metal hinges--they're too expensive out here and finding a good blacksmith is pretty hard these days."

Jason glanced at his wife and then at Tom who said with a smile: "Looks like you are needed here Jason!"

Engrossed in his unpleasant chore of disposing of something he had put a lot of blood, sweat, and tears into, the red-haired man paid no attention to Tom's remark and continued:

"That latch string is passed through a gimlet-hole in the door--you pull that in at night!"

Opening the door and pointing to the puncheon floor, he explained: "I left a couple boards loose for a cellar." Jerking a thumb upward, the red-head added: "There's a little loft up there too."

To the right of the door a puncheon table projected from the wall. Another table, made of split slab, had 4 crude hickory sapling legs set in auger holes. Two three legged stools stood by the fire-place along with two upended logs he pointed to and said: "Them block chairs go with the cabin."

Not particularly thrilled with this pronouncement, Mary eyed the bed in the corner--it was crude but typical. The outside rail was a pole stuck in the wall a foot above the floor and the loose end held up by a forked leg driven into an auger hole in the puncheon floor. As "Red" explained:

"Its got crosspoles and clapboards laid from the side to the wall and a couple deer hides spread over a thick matting of grass. I'll leave them and you can use corn husks and leaves this fall."

The red-headed settler had no idea that region was destined for a corn blight that summer--another of the unexpected "reversals" that summer of 1791. But by then "Red" would be in Louisville. As they prepared to leave the cabin the red-head said:

"There's a two-holer out back!"

Convinced that further argument with his wife concerning remaining in Cincinnati was useless, the red-haired settler was open to any reasonable offer and a simple trade of his cabin for Jason's ark was quickly concluded. Shaking hands, Jason said:

"I will remove our belongings tomorrow and the ark will be yours Friday--is that agreeable?"

"Done! My wife is already packed and staying

with a neighbor--she'll be tickled to death."

Back at the ark Jason broke the news to Dave--
he had his belongings loaded on his small wagon and
had arranged for a team of horses to pull it to the
place where he and Alma planned to board. Although
reluctant to leave behind the "fruit" of his labor,
the red-haired man faced the inevitable with forced
amiability and soon concluded an agreement with Tom
to continue on as the pilot. Of course Pat was delighted with this unexpected opportunity to obtain
transportation on down the river and quickly shook
hands with "Red" concerning passage for the Hagans.

Invited to join Israel Ludlow for the evening
repast, the Evenstars enjoyed a meal of wild turkey
eggs fried in oppossum fat and then Jason discussed
with their host his plan to open a blacksmith shop.
Congratulating the Evenstars on their decision, the
youthful Ludlow remarked:

"Somehow I thought you might decide to settle
here and I have taken the liberty of making you an
appointment with Governor St. Clair tomorrow afternoon. I trust this meets with your approval?"

Having unloaded the majority of his belongings
the following morning, at one o'clock Jason rode up
the slope and joined Israel Ludlow in front of Fort
Washington. Built of hewed timber, and a perfect
square two stories high with 18' by 24' blockhouses
at the angles, the stockade in 1791 had barracks on
all four sides and a 30' by 60' council house in
the center. An 18' by 24' building located between
the east and west walls housed military stores and
Indian goods. A magazine had been built along the
north curtain. It was an imposing structure.

Waiting at the gate for the sentry to admit
them, Star suddenly reared nervously when an Indian
standing nearby tried to pat the beast's nose. The
look of admiration for the horse was unmistakeable
and his hate for the white owner was also apparent.
But not a word was said--Tecumseh was there to observe who, and what, entered Fort Washington. His

was a watching and waiting game just now.

Born in 1768, and only eleven at the time, all too well Tecumseh remembered that time 12 years ago when the Shawnee nation was split and 4000 of their members had headed west toward the Father of Waters to live on land across the Mississippi offered them by the Spanish. 3000 Shawnees had remained in 1779 with elderly Chief Black Fish as their leader and Shemento (Black Snake) as their War Chief. It was the year Running Fox declared: "The white men are here to stay!" But now in 1791, and after General Harmar's army had been put to rout, the Miami Chief Little Turtle said the Indians must drive the hated white man back beyond the Ohio and Blue Jacket, the Shawnee War Chief, agreed.

But Governor St. Clair had other plans and in early March had briefed the president and congress regarding a proposal to build a chain of wilderness forts from Fort Washington to the very heart of the Miami Indian villages at Kekionga. Although Secretary Knox did not share the governor's optimism, he did not interpose any objection--he remembered the French had envisioned a similar plan of building a chain of fortifications and trading posts from the St. Lawrence River to the Gulf of Mexico. For his summer campaign St. Clair had estimated the need of 4000 rations per day after leaving Fort Washington. Although the office of Quartermaster General had been abolished in 1785, it was reinstated and Hodgdon, the appointee, was ordered to Fort Washington under General St. Clair's direct command. Hodgdon was given $20,000 by the Secretary of War and promised more if needed and approved by St. Clair. Although directed to proceed west as soon as supplies had been arranged for at Philadelphia, Hodgdon was still in Philadelphia at the end of May and only a "direct order" by Knox prompted him to move to Fort Pitt where he tarried until late August in 1791.

St. Clair's office was in a blockhouse at Fort Washington and in an anteroom on the 19th of May in

1791 Ludlow and Jason "cooled their heels." Those who knew Winthrop Sargent said he was in the habit of making everyone wait—it was to impress visitors with his importance. Declared by some to be "overbearing and an overpaid stuffed shirt," Sargent was called "The Ruler" by some settlers from Kentucky. On the other hand, Secretary Sargent was reportedly "shocked by the boisterous, intemperate, and noisy settlers from Kentucky," and endeared himself to no one by saying he "abhorred their use of profane language and utter contempt for local regulations!"

The antithesis of the back-slapping and jovial politician, this prim and reserved Harvard graduate was an uncompromising aristocratic Federalist who believed the rich, wise, and good administered for the benefit of those deemed incapable. Four years later, in 1795, the Secretary would complain to his friend Tom Pickering, the new Secretary of War:

"The people of Hamilton and Washington counties seem not to have intended to live under the same government. Some of the settlers in Hamilton County are indolent and extremely debauched!"

The exact opposite of the open, frank, and accessible St. Clair, Sargent craved the respect due his office but did not get it from the settlers of the Cincinnati area who were a different breed from the industrious who settled at Marietta. The carefree and light-hearted settlers from Kentucky liked to dance and fiddle—they crossed the Ohio lightly laden with very little sense of destination believing moving was just a natural part of life. Thus, it was inevitable the high bred Virginians and condescending sharp traders from the New England area would clash with settlers from the District of Kentucky and North Carolina. It was a real "melting pot" and prompted Sargent to say in a letter to his colleague back east: "The people here are decidedly inferior to the select colony at Marietta!"

With this attitude, it was understandable the secretary would be disliked by many of the settlers unaccustomed to the pomp and ceremony acceptable at Marietta. But although he may have lacked tact and prudence, Sargent had distinguished himself in the eyes of his superiors during the Revolutionary War and was held in high esteem by his New England contemporaries. And regardless of what he was called, the Ordinance of 1787 specifically stated the secretary was to be in total charge during the absence of the governor—an awesome responsibility!

Confounding their governing and administration problems, St. Clair and Sargent were weeks removed from the president and congress with only a copy of the Ordinance of 1787 to guide their contemplations in a wilderness area where a "body of laws" was yet to be adopted by a far-off congress. Selection by his congressional colleagues to be governor was "an honorarium" forced upon him according to St. Clair. But being a dedicated public servant, and hoping to eradicate the public's memory of his surrender at Fort Ticonderoga, he plunged headlong into the task before him. But, in addition to his normal duties as governor, he had to keep a rein on the ambitious Indians—it was dangerous and tiring not to mention the vexation caused by John Symmes' cries for more military protection right in his own "front yard." Keeping tabs on his many faceted job, and trying to keep everyone happy, took a toll of his seeming unending supply of energy.

And all this for a paltry salary of $1,500 per year—the secretary received only $750 for the same period. Under such circumstances, the fledgling nation was fortunate to have St. Clair as governor of the "fruit of the revolution." But, as Benjamin Franklin wisely observed on one occasion:

"Much of the strength and efficiency of any government in procuring and securing happiness to the people depends on the general opinion of the goodness of the government, as well as the wisdom and integrity of its governor."

History would not be kind to Arthur St. Clair.

Under slightly different circumstances, the elderly man now seated beneath a placard on the wall of the blockhouse at Fort Washington might have been seated in the president's chair. The placard read:

"COMIT YI VARK TO GOD!"

Just outside the door to his office Lieutenant Colonel Winthrop Sargent explained to Israel Ludlow and Jason that the rank had been given him by Major General St. Clair who was now authorized to commission up to and including the rank of full colonel. Sargent also informed them he was now the "Adjutant General of the Army." As they now proferred their congratulations, an officer wearing the rank of a brigadier general and deep in thought emerged from St. Clair's office and disappeared through the door of the blockhouse—General Scott had just received his "marching orders."

As a part of the government's "strategy," and a prelude to St. Clair's summer campaign, Colonel Thomas Proctor had been dispatched by Henry Knox on a "peace mission" to that region below British held Fort Niagara. When the colonel and Captain Michael Gabriel Houdin arrived at Cornplanter's village on April 6, 1791 they learned the Indian chief was at Fort Franklin in fear of his life. From the 27th of April until May 21st Proctor remained at Buffalo Creek trying to obtain support for the government's peace overtures and even the Mohawk chief, Captain Brant, rode west seeking support for peace. Later, Captain Brant sent a letter to Sir John Johnson advising him he "could not withdraw from a conference at the foot of the Maumee Rapids without incurring the displeasure of all the nations in this quarter" and he "felt obliged to join them in the defense of their country."

Meantime, unaware of what Colonel Proctor was doing, and with the incongruity of the Indians and white men living in close proximity hanging around his neck like a millstone, St. Clair sent a letter to the British commander at Fort Niagara, Colonel

Andrevo Gordon, asking him to join an an expedition
against the western Indians. Thus, on one hand the
U.S. government was talking of "peace" while on the
other hand there was talk of "war!" No wonder the
Indians were confused and inclined toward war.

And, in accordance with an approved plan for a
summer campaign against the troublesome Indians, at
Fort Washington St. Clair ordered General Scott's
mounted Kentucky Militia to proceed May 23rd northwest on a feint intended to throw the Miami Indians
along the Wabash off guard. Glancing at the roster
Scott had given him, St. Clair randomly noted the
names of such Kentucky Militia officers as Colonel
Hardin, Colonel John Campbell from Louisville, Lt.
Colonel Commandant Wilkinson, Major Barbee, Captain
Asheton, Captain McCoy, Captain William Price, and
those in King's and Logan's companies. To himself
St. Clair muttered:

"Where in the hell is Colonel Proctor!"

Although Secretary Knox had ordered Proctor to
advise St. Clair the results of his "peace" mission
not later than May 15th, Proctor not only failed to
do so, he simply ignored Knox's edict to proceed on
to Fort Washington not later than May 5th and headed back to Philadelphia on May 21st and leaving St.
Clair in the dark as to the results of his efforts.

Obviously pleased with the congratulations his
visitors had proferred, Sargent said to Jason:

"Major Doughty certainly speaks very highly of
you Mister Evenstar. Do I understand your uncle is
a personal acquaintance of the governor?"

Framed in the doorway a well-groomed two-star
general now said in a kindly voice: "He certainly
is! I have known old Conrad since before the war--
and this young man's father too." Pausing briefly
to look Jason over he added with a smile: You certainly favor your father young man!"

"Thank you sir," said Jason. "My uncle always
said I do. But, as you probably know, I never knew
my father."

Not desirous of further referral to the tragic
incident, St. Clair politely but firmly said:
"Israel, you and our young friend grab a chair
and let me hear him say what his plans are!"
The first thing that caught Jason's eye was a
placard hanging on the wall of St. Clair's office--
it was his family coat of arms bearing the inscription: "Comit Yi Vark To God!" It was inspirational
but the problems St. Clair faced were monumental!
Jason realized the general's time was valuable
and, after briefly stating he had left his uncle in
good health, he succinctly outlined his reasons for
leaving Turkeyfoot. As Ludlow had suggested, Jason
also mentioned he had been an apprentice blacksmith
back in Maryland, intended to pursue this craft at
Cincinnati, and was available should his services
be needed.
"Word certainly gets around!" said the general
with a twinkle in his eye. "You not only look like
your father, you sound like him--he was a determined young man too." In a more serious tone of voice
the affable officer continued:
"As Israel may have told you, I intend to lead
an expedition this summer and put an end to this
problem with the Indians. They have killed four of
our soldiers in attacks on this very fort this last
year and continue to harass those settlers who come
down the Ohio. We cannot, and I will not, tolerate
that! General Harmar's campaign last fall was not
a total success but I intend to put an end to this
menace once and for all!"
At best Harmar's "success" was like Pyrrhus,
King of Espirus in Greece, who is reported to have
declared in 279 B. C. after the battle of Asculum
against the Romans wherein he lost most of his men,
"Another such victory and I shall be ruined!"
Josiah Harmar, like General St. Clair in 1791,
was a victim of a miserly system that relied on the
militia in time of a national emergency. After the
preliminary peace treaty was ratified by the United

States April 15th, 1783, the following November 2nd Congress ordered the army disbanded. This in spite of the fact Washington had considered it advisable to retain a regiment of infantry and two battalions of artillery after the end of hostilities. When he said goodbye to his officers at Fraunces Tavern on December 4, 1783, and returned his commission a few days later, the 51 year old Washington—a respected military leader who had scoffed at the idea of setting up a monarchy with him as king—admonished the congress: "No militia will ever acquire the habits necessary to resist a regular force!"

When the final peace treaty was signed September 3rd, 1783, Congress was plagued by suspicion of any centralized authority backed by a large standing army. Believing a well regulated militia could protect the nation, on June 2, 1784 a resolution by congress stated: "Standing armies in time of peace are inconsistent with the principles of republican government, dangerous to the liberties of a free people, and generally converted into destructive engines for establishing despotism!"

But the congress did call on the states of New Jersey, New York, Connecticut, and Pennsylvania to provide 700 men for twelve months to guard stores at West Point and to the garrison western forts—a proportional number of officers were to be provided also. Privates were to receive $6.67 a month. The quota was never filled!

When the congress created the War Department on August 7, 1789 as one of the executive branches, with the president as commander-in-chief, Brigadier General by brevet (i.e. higher rank without higher pay) Josiah Harmar was appointed commander of the U. S. Army on September 29, 1789—an army consisting of 672 men scattered across the entire country.

After moving his headquarters from Fort Harmar to Fort Washington in early 1790, and under orders from Henry Knox, in the fall of 1790 Harmar led 320 regulars from Pennsylvania and New Jersey, and 1133 drafted militia from Pennsylvania and Virginia's District of Kentucky, toward the heart of the Miami tribal lands. With flags flying, drums beating, and the disorderly militiamen shouting, four companies of Kentucky mounted riflemen, one Pennsylvania and three Kentucky infantry battalions, and one company of artillery with a six-pounder, four brass three-pounders, and a 5½ inch howitzer, the expeditionary force moved ten miles a day--it gave the Indians an ample opportunity to fade into the wilderness. It was also the fifth time a force of "white raiders" had marched north to destroy Indian villages.

Colonel Hardin led the militia away from Fort Washington on September 26, 1790 and General Harmar followed with his "regulars" five day later. They followed the same wilderness route along the Little Miami northeast that George Rogers Clark had used in 1782. West of present-day Springfield, Ohio the expedition took up a northwest line of march toward Girty's Town where St. Marys, Ohio now stands.

General Harmar's march was not only plagued by complaints about a shortage of guns, hatchets, axes and camp utensils, the commissary was grossly inadequate and soldiers had back pay due them. Coupled with such problems, a planned flank attack by Major Hamtramck was aborted. In his dispatch of July 15, 1790 Harmar advised Hamtramck 300 militiamen from Kentucky would arrive at Fort Knox in time to march up the Wabash from Vincennes on September 25th. The militia not only failed to arrive until the 29th of September, upon reaching Vermillion along the banks of the Wabash on October 10th they found the Indian village had been deserted. Unnerved by this unexpected turn of events, the militiamen threatened to desert and Hamtramck had no choice but to return to Fort Knox.

With no knowledge of the failure of this planned feint, Harmar had marched on to Kekionga where, on October 17th, he found the Miami Indian villages abandoned. Here, where Fort Wayne now stands, the undisciplined militiamen not only burned and sacked the villages but senselessly destroyed the Indian's corn, beans, and hay and the fine orchards they had tended for years. This wanton destruction of their food supply infuriated the Indians and only served to unite them against the white man.

Watching the devastation, and just waiting for a favorable opportunity, on October 19th 150 Miamis put Colonel John Hardin's detachment to rout northwest of Kekionga along the Eel River. Then, three days later, it was Little Turtle who seized the initiative when Harmar--having concluded his army had accomplished its mission and had started his return march--dispatched a party of 340 vindictive militia and 60 regulars back toward the smoldering villages hoping to catch returning Indians off guard and inflict the coup d'etat. But it was the vengeful men of Major Wyllys', Fontaine's, Hall's and McMillen's command who were caught "napping" and Little Turtle closed the "jaws" of an Indian trap which sent them running for their lives. Major John Wyllys, a regular army officer who was killed, had a premonition of misfortune and had openly declared he expected to have problems with the militia who broke and ran at the first sound of war whoops. A Revolutionary War veteran, Captain Joseph Ashton, declared in his post battle report "Lieutenant Ebenezer Frothingham died bravely shouting to his men, 'Escape for yourself!'" But there was no "escape" for 183 officers and men who were killed in the early morning ambush and, as Lieutenant Ebenezer Denny reported, "31 men were wounded!" Captain Jonathan Heart's optimistic report of Harmar's expedition stated: "We have entirely destroyed that nest of Miami murderers!"

Even St. Clair's November 6, 1790 dispatch to the Secretary of War was encouraging: "The Indians have been delivered a terrible stroke and did not harass the army on the return march!"

Now, only six months later--and even as Israel Ludlow and Jason conversed with St. Clair at Fort

Washington--Harmar impatiently awaited a "board of inquiry" that he had requested to clear his name of charges of intemperance, brutality, and "failure of command." Although Harmar's expedition had proved an army could penetrate the wilderness, cut roads, and subsist, in the absence of achieving a complete victory against the Indians, there were a number of charges, counter-charges, and "finger pointing," as government officials--and the Kentucky militiamen-- licked the wounds of adversity.

Meantime, the Indians, flushed with a sense of having driven the "white invader" back to the Ohio, increased their attacks on isolated cabins, wilderness settlements, and river craft. But to some of the older sachems, burning the Miami villages was a psychological loss--they now knew their wilderness villages were vulnerable and could be reached in previously unchallenged territory. For the young braves however, the ambush of Harmar's troops only whetted their appetite for war and, flushed with what they called "victory," they cried out against those who counseled peace saying: "We shall put out the fire of every pale-face on the Indian shore!"

Despite his optimistic report of November 6th, and with the tragic news of the Jan. 2nd, 1791 "Big Bottom Massacre" north of Marietta still ringing in his ears, St. Clair had hurried east with his plan to put an end to this "Indian problem" that plagued his governorship and it had been approved.

President Washington had already received an urgent letter from the well-respected Judge Putnam saying Asa and Eleazar Bullard had miraculously escaped the massacre at Big Bottom wherein 11 men and a woman were killed. Saying the Indians had left a war club and this meant war, Putnam concluded with: "We have only 20 troops at Fort Harmar and only 287 poorly armed men at Marietta capable of bearing arms. We are a ruined people unless help is sent."

By express courier Judge Symmes' sent a letter to his business colleague, Jonathan Dayton, asking:

"Is it a matter of no moment to the United States whether we are saved or destroyed by savages?"

Only a few days before Dayton had received another dispatch in which Symmes complained about St. Clair's recent decision regarding the east boundary of the Miami Purchase. Branding the governor's decisions "dictatorial," Symmes stated: "Every person must admit the governor has treated me and settlers of this area in a most cruel manner!"

With news of the January frontier atrocities, and letters from influential settlers now circulating among members of Congress, some questioned the leadership of a nation that could not put an end to the problem. Sensing the growing concern, and worried over the growing problem with Creek Indians in Georgia, Knox had advised Washington:

"Something must be done! Unless some decisive measures are now undertaken to terminate the mutual hostilities north of the Ohio they will probably become general. We must establish a strong fort at the confluence of the St. Marys and St. Joseph rivers. And our military force must be enlarged!"

Tactfully reminding the president that Article 3 of the Ordinance of 1787 states: "The utmost good faith shall always be observed toward the Indians," statesman and postmaster general Timothy Pickering (1745-1829) cautioned him saying: "The Indians must be treated with humanity and understanding."

Small wonder most in the government's growing bureaucracy listened with somber expectation when St. Clair rode into Philadelphia with his "plan" to end the vexatious Indian problem. Although it did involve cutting a road through more than 150 miles of unchartered wilderness from Fort Washington to the headwaters of the Miami-of-the-lake (the Maumee River), building forts, training and equipping and subsisting troops, and minimal reliance on militia, such a devastating stroke delivered by a formidable force, seemed to be a logical way to end what some referred to as "the troublesome Indian problem."

But such an expensive proposal was not without its opposition and one congressman declared: "The government is ill-equipped to raise either enough money or the manpower for such a large army made up entirely of regulars!"

But, by typical government committee action, a compromise vote finally authorized a "mixed force" of regulars, 2000 special six month levies, and the militia. On March 4th, 1791 congress appropriated $300,000 for the campaign and the Senate confirmed St. Clair's nomination as Major General. Congress also authorized a second regiment of 912 regulars and ordered Maryland, Virginia, and New Jersey to each raise one battalion of levies and Pennsylvania to provide two. The president was also authorized to call up the 2000 levies for 6 months of service. The militiamen from Pennsylvania, Virginia, and the Kentucky District were to provide their own horses, arms, and provisions. Kentucky was to provide any troops necessary to bring St. Clair's expeditionary force up to 4,000 effectives.

It sounded good but later, in the aftermath of the 1791 fiasco, many "Monday-morning quarterbacks" would say it was unfortunate the president did not take into account the age of his trusted friend or recognize the increased burden he had placed on the shoulders of this faithful officer.

And now, two and a half months later, and more than 500 miles west of Philadelphia--and burdened greatly with family problems and a constitutional weakness that hampered his efficiency--fifty-seven year old Arthur St. Clair took time out of his busy schedule to talk with Jason and Israel Ludlow. It was typical of this unselfish patriot who now said:

"Rest assured I will advise Major Ferguson of your capabilities and availability Jason."

At the stockade gate Star again reared when an Indian loitering near the entrance stepped from the shadow of the palisade--it was the same Indian who tried to pat Star's nose earlier.

Back at the foot of the slope Jason found Pat and "Red" loading boxes belonging to the new owner. As the red-haired settler explained:

"Your missus said it would be all right to put them boxes on the bow Jason."

Now it was Mary who exclaimed: "I have everything we will need for our last night on this ark. I am ready to move into our new home tomorrow!"

The sun was still perched on the eastern horizon when "Red" came driving down the slope--seated by his side was his wife beaming from ear to ear. With Tom and Pat's help, Jason had already unloaded the rest of his belongings and said to "Red:"

"Well, she is all yours!"

"And we left the latch string out for you!"

An hour later Dave showed up offering to help but by then they were almost finished and Tom was supervising tying down a wagon. By mid-morning the pilot said the ark was "ship-shape" and they would "cast off" just as soon as the new owner was ready. This was the moment Jason knew must come sooner or later and now he faced the old pilot with a lump in his throat as they shook hands and Jason said:

"Well Tom, we certainly thank you for bringing us downstream safely and don't be a stranger--we'll leave that latch string out for you!"

Minutes later Jason let go of the rope tied to bow and Dave did the same on the stern. Then while Pat hauled in the anchor, Tom called out to his old friend who had come down to see him off:

"See you again Rube! You take good care of my friends and keep those old joints oiled!"

As the current slowly moved the ark into midstream, Tom looked wistfully at Jason and Mary who were waving goodbye. As the ark reached midstream, Jason pointed upsteam and said to Mary and Dave:

"Look! There are some more settlers arriving. Busy place this Cincinnati!"

CHAPTER TWELVE

ST. CLAIR'S EXPEDITION

There was an unusual tinge of anticipation and excitement in the air as Jason began unloading the boxes, Mary's steamer trunk, the spider, crane, and andirons. Two of their new neighbors came over and asked if they had heard "General St. Clair is going to lead an expedition against the Indians!" Since the governor had returned on the 15th of May rumors had been circulating about "an army of 4,000 troops marching against that nest of villany where Little Turtle's Miami villages are."

Under Mary's watchful eye, Jason unpacked each box. Happily his wife carefully examined each item as if she had never seen it before--her treasured copy of Charles Wesley's "Bay Psalm Book," Samuel Johnson's "Dictionary of the English Language," and two books by William Shakespeare. Meantime, Jason made an ingenious contraption, suspended from overhead rafters, to protect the corn meal they brought from Pennsylvania. On Sunday, they went to church.

Early the following morning Jason began building his blacksmith shop behind the cabin using the logs "Red" had left at the rear of the lot. On the south side of his shop, Jason added a partially enclosed lean-to for the oxen, sheep, and cow. Mary was delighted to hear their cow had a roof over her head--Molly's milk provided a valuable supplement to their diet.

Deciding not to move north to White's Station, Dave helped Jason when not working as a surveyor's helper. Alma was not pleased with Dave being away in "that Indian-infested wilderness" as she called it. But, as Dave remarked one day while they were working on a split-rail fence around Jason's lot:

"I'm not aiming to be a surveyor's helper forever but it does help keep the wolf from the door!"

The two young settlers got "a big charge" out of laying the shakes they brought from Pennsylvania over the northeast corner of the shop--that was the corner where Jason decided to stable Star.

Working from first light until darkness forced him inside, and with a blacksmith's services in demand, Jason shoed horses, fashioned hinges, chains, and other items. And he was shoeing a horse on the 13th of June when Dave walked in the shop saying:

"Captain John Armstrong just came downstream-- said he led 76 men to Fort Pitt from Philadelphia. Left them there to be uniformed according to Israel Ludlow. By the way, Israel tells me that there are about 20 families living in some settlement called South Bend about nine miles downstream. Thought I would ride over that way and take a look at a piece of river bottom land--care to join me?"

The settlement Dave referred to had been laid out by John Symmes' brother, Timothy. Only a few miles upstream from North Bend, this settlement was destined to later be called "Anderson's Ferry."

Anxious to see the Ohio River bottom land west of Cincinnati, Jason quickly concluded Star needed a little exercise and he would join Dave. On their return trip Jason spied a wounded Indian along the densely wooded trail who would surely have been devoured had not the young settler quickly shot the menacing bobcat. During a rare moment when he was caught off guard while pulling out a piece of dried venison from the pouch he carried, the Indian had been attack by the huge beast. Later Jason was to learn the Indian had just returned from across the

Ohio in Kentucky where he had been searching for an Indian boy taken by a white officer during a raid on their village five years ago. He said the boy's name was "Spemica Lawba!" Exhausted from the trip, the Indian had momentarily dropped his guard---an error which all too often proved fatal in the wilderness. Jason recalled hearing the boy's name in one of Tom May's stories but he said nothing.

Tired and badly wounded, the Indian offered no great objection to being seated behind Jason on his horse--Dave removed the Indian's knife and tomahawk however. Back at the Evenstar's cabin, where Mary carefully attended the scar-faced Indian's wounds, Jason decided "their Indian patient" could sleep in the blacksmith shop until he recuperated.

Through careful analysis of the Indian's sign language and guttural expressions, Jason learned it was a white officer's sword that caused the hideous scar on his left cheek "ten or eleven winters ago." Jason also learned "tsi" was this Indian's word for kill, "peshwa" was a bobcat or wildcat, "persotum" was a squaw, and the wind from the south was called "Shawondasee." But he was having difficulty trying to decipher "ne-kah-no" when Ben Thomas visited the blacksmith shop one day and explained:

"He says you are his friend Jason!"

Ben Thomas, a resident of North Bend, had gone downstream in the spring of 1789 leaving his family at Pittsburgh. Later, that same year, Ben returned to Pittsburgh and brought his wife and two children downstream. Recently he had gone down the Ohio and gathered a load of salt which he brought to Cincinnati on June 22nd.

"Landed yesterday and walked up from the river with Captain Zebulon Pike, a veteran of the Revolutionary War I knew back east. He had just arrived here too. Told me he led seventy-three recruits to Fort Pitt from New Jersey but left them there to be uniformed and equipped."

Regarding the salt he had gathered at Big Bone

Lick, Ben explained: "It's about twenty miles below
the mouth of the Big Miami. Deer, buffalo, and the
Indians have been coming there for years. Ebenezer
Denny, an army lieutenant, made several trips down
there from Fort Finney in 1786."

Jason's "patient" never tired of watching him
fashion horseshoes, hoops, hinges, and other things
from iron. And as he watched in fascination, Jason
learned of a place he said was the "Shawnee Lookout
Point." In broken guttural words, the Indian slowly explained it was a place at the mouth of the Big
Miami where Shawnee sachems often went to meditate
and talk with "Manitou, the great spirit." He also
told Jason about "beargrass" that grew in the river
bottom land, was harvested in the fall, its bulbous
roots dried on smooth boards, and then pounded into
a kind of flour from which bread could be made.

Attending the Indian's wounds on Sunday after
church, Mary began singing a hymn written by Isaac
Watts (1674-1748), an English clergyman:

"Alas! and did my Saviour bleed,
And did my Sovereign die,
Would He devote that sacred head
For such a worm as I."

Emotionally aroused, the Indian explained that
he knew the song--it was the hymn he learned from a
missionary, Reverend David Jones, in 1773 while a
boy living along the Scioto. His eyes sparkled as
he sang, in his own Shawnee language,* the hymn:

"Na-peache mi ce ta ha
Che na mo si ti we
Ma ci ke na mis wa la ti
Mi ti na ta pi ni."

*   Pg 184, "Transactions of the Kansas State Historical
     Society, 1905-1906 Vol. IX" Topeka, KS

Slowly, but resolutely, and using a mixture of his guttural language and that of Mary's, the scar-faced Indian said his people prayed and fasted, did not believe in heaven or hell, and Manitou was the great spirit! "The moon is our mother, the sun our father--not the white man in Philadelphia the pale face calls 'Great White Father.' Manitou rules the universe! Manitou put the white man far across the great waters but the white man was not content with his land and now comes to divide the land here with his stakes. The great spirit knows no boundaries--nor will his red people!"

Mary said nothing--what could she say? Standing nearby, Jason heard most of what had been said but also said nothing. The subject of the Indian's belief never came up again and, two days later--and having sufficiently regained his strength--Mary and Jason's "patient" bid them goodbye and disappeared in the nearby wilderness.

At church service on Sunday Jason and Mary had met John Whistler and his family. He was a veteran of the Revolutionary War---on the other side! When released after the war, he had lived in Hagerstown, Maryland until hearing St. Clair needed men for his expedition against the Indians. With no hesitation at all, he had moved his family west to Cincinnati and offered his service to St. Clair on June 2nd.

Well aware of the value of a woman's contribution to the success of a frontier undertaking, that Sunday the minister read a few verses from Proverbs 31 pertaining to the words of King Lemuel regarding the properties of a good wife:

"She seeketh wool, and flax, and worketh willingly with her hands. She layeth her hand to the spindle and her hands hold the distaff. She riseth also while it is yet night, and giveth meat to her household, and a portion to her maidens."

Mary and John Whistler's wife, Ann, became instant friends--she was pregnant too! Mary confided she was "expecting in December!" Both ladies were

pleasantly surprised when the minister took each by
the hand after church and said in German:

"Ehret die Frauen! Sie flechten und weben,
Himmlische rosen in's irdische Leben!" He quickly
translated: "Honor women! They entwine and weave,
heavenly roses in our earthly life!"

The friendly minister then hastened to explain
this was from a poem* written by his good friend in
Germany, Johann Christopher Friedrick Von Schiller.
"Born in 1759, he has always had a burning ambition
to write and left his post as an army surgeon nine
years ago to devote all of his time to writing."

The day the Indian left, John Whistler and his
twelve year old son, William, visited Jason's shop.
The veteran's observations were of natural interest
and Jason listened carefully when John said:

"You know Jason, that major that arrived last
week is pretty sharp--he might have hit the nail on
the head!"

The U.S. First Infantry regular he referred to
was Major David Ziegler, a person given to speaking
his own mind. Arriving June 20th, along with Major
William Ferguson, Ziegler looked over the equipment
and supplies available for a wilderness expedition
and adamantly declared: "Samuel Hodgdon is unfit to
be Quartermaster General!"

Standing with St. Clair near the gates of Fort
Washington a few days later, and watching a ragtag
group of arriving recruits, Ziegler remarked: "What
a motely bunch---some of them are almost naked! It
was my understanding recruits and levies were to be
uniformed and equipped at Fort Pitt!"

"That was the plan," replied St. Clair. Eter-
nally optimistic, he added: "They do look a little
rough around the edges, but a few weeks among the
old regulars will make a big difference in them!"

Engaged a few feet away repairing a loose shoe
on St. Clair's horse, Jason heard the conversation.

* "Wurde der Frauen" by Schiller

To himself he thought: "What 'old' regulars?" He
also remembered an old cliche his uncle often used:
"You can't make a silk purse out of a pig's ear!"

Among the group of recruits that shuffled into
Fort Washington that morning Jason saw the boisterous "Max" he had seen along the Monongahela. A few
steps behind this loudmouthed braggart was another
person he recognized, the bearded ruffian who first
hailed him south of Pittsburgh along the river--he
still wore the dirty old Revolutionary War hat with
the feather stuck in the crown.

The tardy arrival of his "effectives" was of
growing concern to St. Clair and he pondered what
Captain Pike had said concerning the retention of
recruits and levies at Fort Pitt in accordance with
"General Butler's orders!" A short delay to equip
and uniform troops was understandable but they were
intended for St. Clair's expedition and a delay at
Fort Pitt had not been envisioned by St. Clair.

Contrary to the original campaign plan agreed
on in March of 1791, and without consultation with
or advisement of St. Clair, General Butler ordered
part of St. Clair's troops be held at Fort Pitt for
defense of western Pennsylvania against any Indian
attack. Although Secretary Knox had authorized the
delay, St. Clair had not been advised.

Anxiously awaiting the arrival of his expected
"effectives," St. Clair saw July 10th come and go.
Poorly equipped, and untrained, the idle levies and
recruits that had arrived spent far too much time
roaming the streets of Cincinnati and reports of
their drinking and use of profane language were of
increasing concern. Compounding his problems, St.
Clair was advised there was an increasing number of
cases of a contagious epidemic disease in that area
and the doctor at Fort Washington warned all troops
against drinking water from wells in Cincinnati.

Sauntering out the gate at Fort Washington the
following day, the bearded ruffian with the feather
in his hat nudged his cohort saying: "Now don't you

be fergettin' what the doctor told us Max--don't be drinkin' no water! It'll kill you he said!"

"Don't intend to," replied Max with a coarse burst of laughter. "Water's fer washin' yer socks! Fer drinkin' you can't beat Old Monongahela or them Kentucky corn squeezins!"

The bearded ruffian let go a stream of tobacco juice and then remarked: "Old doc says whiskey will kill you but you know, you see more old drunks than old doctors!"

But while they joked about the medicinal value of whiskey, on the opposite side of the Cincinnati settlement Mary Evenstar was deathly sick. And she was no better on July 15th when 298 regulars of the U. S. First Infantry arrrived at Fort Washington-- five days after St. Clair's planned departure date. The brief euphoria that accompanied the arrival of the First Infantry quickly faded as a devastating plague swept through the settlement leaving entire families dead in its wake. Although Jason did not fall victim to the plague, for almost two weeks he lived in mortal fear for Mary's life as alternating waves of debilitating dysentery, vomiting, and high fever swept through her frail body. Exhausted, and emotionally drained, Mary lost her baby.

As the doctor ordered, Jason removed and burn- ed the bed and bed clothes, boiled their clothing outside in a big kettle, and used soap and scalding water to wash each pot, pan, knife, fork, and dish. Slowly--ever so slowly--Mary regained her strength.

Ten days later, on August 1st, Tom May sudden- ly appeared on the Evenstar's doorstep. Although still pale and weak, and suffering severe bouts of depression, the old pilot's appearance was just the medicine Mary needed. Through tears Mary told him about the loss of her baby and Tom comforted her as he would have his own daughter. Then, arm in arm, they walked back to the blacksmith shop where they found Jason shoeing a horse for Captain Matson, Sr. from North Bend. Thoroughly impressed with the work of the young blacksmith, Matson had just remarked:

"I swear Jason, you are the best farrier along the Ohio from Pittsburgh to North Bend!"

Standing in the doorway to the shop, Tom said: "And on downstream to Louisville I might add!"

"Tom!" exclaimed Jason. "You are a sight for sore eyes--high time you were getting back down the river to see us! I just made a new calendar on the wall over there with a hot iron this morning!"

Across town St. Clair did not need a calendar to remind him July was history and his campaign was three weeks behind schedule. Leading a contingent of Maryland levies, Major Henry Gaither had reported to St. Clair on July 28th indicating his troops had reluctantly agreed their "six months period of service" was to start the day they arrived at Fort Washington and not the day they left home. Most of the levies were not as agreeable--they insisted the "six months period" started the day they left home. It was an administrative faux pas that would plague the entire campaign--and beyond.

An express communique received by St. Clair on July 31st indicated 1,574 troops were still enroute to Fort Washington. A reassessment of his predicament indicated he could realistically expect 3,257 effectives, including 820 Kentucky militiamen, for his expedition. But here again he was doomed to be disappointed when only half this number of Kentucky militiamen would show up 60 days later and a number of those would turn around and go home. As for the six month levies, few knew a thing about wilderness warfare--some had yet to use a razor! The recruits were a different problem--drunks, riffraff, and the dregs of a society far removed from the realities of frontier life. Indeed they were a sorry lot but St. Clair hopefully declared:

"Some field training will whip them into shape I am certain."!"

Early the morning of August 1st, and suffering from a recurrent attack of gout, St. Clair met with

Colonel (brevet Brigadier General) James Wilkinson, whose 525 mounted volunteers from Kentucky awaited the order to strike the Eel River villages (Ke-na-pa-corn-aqua) along the Wabash River. Among these volunteers were Thomas Allen, James M'Dowell, James Brown, William M'Millin, John E. King, Jos. M'Faul, Samuel Patterson, Joseph Jones, John Peoples, Benjamin Gibbs, John Arnold, and Richard Bartlett--the latter two had participated in Colonel Scott's late May campaign. This was to be the second of planned diversionary raids and this date St. Clair approved Wilkinson's immediate departure.

This same day St. Clair also directed the contractor to scour the Kentucky region for the cattle and horses he had requisitioned for his expedition. Colonel William Duer, a Revolutionary War veteran, and friend of both the President and the Secretary of War, had been appointed contractor in January of 1791. He had been charged with furnishing the 4000 rations per day St. Clair stated would be required for his campaign. In March St. Clair had indicated the success of his expedition hinged to a great extent on Duer's performance. Duer had commissioned another Revolutionary War officer, Captain Richard Benham, to procure the horses. Captain Benham, in turn, hired several young men including his 18 year old nephew, Benjamin Van Cleve, and Messrs. Sloane, Irwin, Stebbins, and Curtner, to help him. William Duer was destined to be imprisoned in 1792 for bond speculation and die, seven years later, in prison.

In an effort to improve communications, a post rider now departed Philadelphia for Fort Washington each Friday and Henry Knox took this opportunity to provide St.Clair with frequent reminders concerning the necessity to march from Fort Washington as soon as possible. In a recent communique, the Secretary "enjoined" St. Clair to "proceed forward with great haste;" assured him of "President Washington's continued interest in your campaign," and prodded him with his closing nudge: "The president is anxiously awaiting word of your progress."

In St. Clair's August 2nd letter to Henry Knox he pointedly, but diplomatically noted that neither his second-in-command or the Quartermaster General had put in an appearance at Fort Washington as yet.

The untrained and undisciplined troops who had "put in their appearance" posed a problem too! The general recognized there was a growing restlessness among the troops crowded into Fort Washington and allowing them to aimlessly roam the streets of Cincinnati was asking for trouble. Colonel Sargent's remark concerning an increase in the use of profane language reminded St. Clair of the time in New York City in July of 1776 when General Washington faced a somewhat similar situation and issued a General Order reading:

> "The General is sorry to be informed that the foolish and wicked practice of profane cursing and swearing, a vice heretofore little known in an American army, is growing in fashion. He hopes the officers will, by example as well as influence, endeavor to check it, and that both they and the men will reflect, that we can have little hope of the blessing of Heaven on our arms, if we insult it by our impiety and folly. Added to this, it is a vice so mean and low, without any temptation, that every man of sense and character detests and despises it."

Early on Saturday morning, August 6th, General St. Clair met with his officers. In spite of some well-supported objections by officers who cited the shortages of supplies, equipment, and manpower, St. Clair decided they would vacate Fort Washington the following morning leaving only a small garrison of soldiers to forward supplies and arriving troops.

Thus, on August 7th, 1791, immediately following church service, the army marched out the gate with flags flying and drums beating. It was an impressive sight despite the unmilitary appearance of many troops and their marching cadence left much to be desired. Among the recruits Jason saw the character with that absurd feather in his hat and "Max" who was wildly waving at everyone along the street. But finally the army disappeared in a cloud of dust and that afternoon St. Clair dispatched an express courier with a brief communique reporting: "My army is proceeding from Fort Washington."

It is a fetish of dedicated officers that they keep their superiors advised of minute details--and St. Clair was a dedicated officer whose friendship with President Washington he held in high regard. But this message was a little like the "itsy-bitsy, teeny-weeny, polka dot bikini" soldiers would sing about, and ogle, a century and a half later....what it revealed was not as interesting as what it concealed! St. Clair had no intention of marching his army more than six miles--just to Ludlow's Station.

Abner Boston had a cabin at this location that he offered for General St. Clair's comfort and use. The proximity to Fort Washington also made it very attractive.   Here fresh pasture was available, the supply of liquor could be controlled, and his army could receive some sorely needed in-field training. Standing in front of the cabin early on the morning of August 8th, St. Clair heard the staccato beat of drums--his troops were already learning the meaning of "troop beating" which signaled attack, retreat, parade, and other commands not particularly suited to wilderness type warfare. And in the surrounding wilderness copper-colored scouts watched every move St. Clair and his officers made.   Late that afternoon they saw a courier head south carrying another communique reading: "My army is now involved in extensive in-field training."

That same day, and about sixteen miles west of Ludlow's Station, young William Fuller disappeared while working on a fish dam for Captain Matson near the mouth of the Great Miami River. A settler from North Bend concluded "the Indians probably took the lad" and John Clawson from Columbia said it reminded him of the time, two years before, when Indians had killed John Seward's son near the mouth of the Little Miami and he carried the lifeless boy home.

With the army gone on Monday, August 8th, Dave came by the blacksmith shop suggesting he and Jason "wet a line" in the creek the scar faced Indian had called "Mah-ke-te-wah." Local residents called the nearby stream "Mill Creek." Having heard some good reports about fishing in that stream, Jason quickly decided "a mess of fish would be a welcome repast!" Thus, a short time later, and with the horses tied to a nearby tree, they began working their way down the stream keeping an eye open for wolves, bobcats, snakes, and Indians. But Jason failed to see the copperhead coiled among the rocks until it was too late. Quick as a flash, the reptile sunk its fangs into Jason's leg a few inches above the knee.

Pausing only long enough to kill the three and a half foot long snake, Dave quickly slit open the leg of Jason's trousers with his long-bladed Barlow knife; used his handkerchief as a tourniquet above the fang marks; made two quick incisions over the wound; and proceeded to try and suck out the snake venom with his mouth. Realizing he should get his friend home as soon as possible, Dave helped Jason mount Star and they started for home. Although not fully recovered herself, Mary helped Dave get Jason inside--already he was weak and pale and complained of being sick to his stomach.

Well meaning neighbors suggested giving Jason rock fern boiled in milk and a poultice of the same plant was placed on the wound. But in spite of all they did, Jason carried a high fever and Mary feared for his life. Then, in their darkest hour, the scar faced Indian suddenly appeared on the doorstep holding what he called a "Mad Stone" and asked Mary to boil the rock in sweet milk. That done, the Indian carefully applied the mysterious rock directly to Jason's swollen and discolored leg. Only twelve hours later, Jason's fever began to drop and he was able to take some hot soup.

Crouched near the doorstep, the Indian remained near Jason until he was again on his feet—then the Indian again disappeared in the nearby woods.

Intending to dispatch his communique the next morning, on August 18th Secretary Knox prepared a message for St. Clair saying Joseph Miller, an east coast gunpowder manufacturer, had conducted several tests concerning complaints about the gunpowder he sold the government. Miller advised the Secretary his tests indicated the gunpowder was useable. In June at Fort Pitt Major William Ferguson had tested the gunpowder in a howitzer and claimed it was not suitable for field use. "Survivors" of the battle less than 80 days in the future would indicate they had "defective gunpowder." The "investigation" in the aftermath of the early November encounter would conclude: "Gunpowder shipping and storage problems contributed to the failures!" But long before the "investigation" was ended, Major Ferguson's mortal remains would be forever mixed with the snow, soil, and defective gunpowder on the banks of the Wabash.

On August 21st Colonel James Wilkinson led his Kentucky militiamen across the river at Louisville having completed a 450 mile desultory flanking raid against the Indian villages along the Wabash. Not only had mounted volunteers destroyed the Eel River villages, burned 430 acres of corn, and captured a number of Indians for interrogation, they had also devastated Quiatenon and taken more prisoners. The wilderness raids by Scott and Wilkinson proved that special forces could indeed penetrate the Indian's "home court" and return with minimum casualties.

Elated by the success of Wilkinson's flanking raids, and that of Scott earlier, St. Clair was understandably frustrated he was unable to initiate a "coup d'etat" against the heart of the Miami Indian villages as planned--the necessary men and supplies still had not arrived!   Pondering his predicament, St. Clair remarked to his aide-de-camp, Viscount de Malartie: "It is unfortunate General Harmar's campaign last fall was not preceded by such successful raids. But, although these raids have achieved the desired result, I should not at all be surprised if they did not force those Wabash Indians to move upstream and join Little Turtle!"

He was referring to an incident involving the refusal by 330 of the Kentucky militia to support a planned flanking raid along the Wabash led by Major Hamtramck in September of 1790.   The intent was to draw some of the Miami warriors away from Kekionga but it never materialized and Harmar's campaign had suffered accordingly.

Monday morning, August 22nd, Jason was working on a pair of horseshoes when he heard someone say: "Do you know what you're doing?"

The voice was a familiar one and Jason glanced up quickly to see Hank silhouetted in the doorway.

"Hank Weiser, you old Kentucky dirt farmer," exclaimed Jason. "How on earth did you get here?"

"Just drifted down the Licking to your front door! Sarah's happy as a pig in slop, and the kids are busy hoeing corn, so thought I'd jes mosey over and see you folks."

During the ensuing conversation Jason told his friend about Mary's illness and her losing the baby last month. After expressing his profound feelings of sorrow, Hank inquired: "Seen Dave lately?"

Jason was still explaining what had happened since they parted at Maysville when Dave walked in. Seated on short upended pieces of log Hank and Dave talked and watched Jason finish the horseshoes he had been working on. That done, the blacksmith sat down and joined the conversation.   Failing to hear an occasional "ring" of the anvil, Mary walked back to the shop and found the three old friends engaged in reminiscing. After the customary greeting, Mary politely injected:

"Hank, I presume Jason told you Tom stopped to see us a few weeks ago? He brought us some coffee from Pittsburgh--would you gentlemen like a cup?"

"Does a bear like honey?" said Hank with a big smile. "Sure beats my bark tea, right Jason?"

Not only did Hank enjoy the coffee, he readily accepted Jason's invitation to stay with them. The evening meal included "snaps" (green string beans) and fresh peas and Hank remarked: "I like to eat my peas with sorghum. It makes 'em taste funny but it helps keep 'em on my knife!"

After their evening meal, Jason and Hank took a seat in the shade at the corner of the cabin. It was also a place where Hank could enjoy his chew of tobacco just beyond Mary's line of view. Jason had known Hank long enough to know when something was on his friend's mind but he waited until he said:

"Jason, what do you know about this expedition St. Clair is fixing to lead up north?"

Jason explained he had talked with St. Clair, worked on occasion for Major Ferguson, and was acquainted with a number of those who would be going. "There's a shortage of men--seasoned troops I mean. St. Clair even offered me a commission--you know he must be hurting! Why do you ask?"

"Well, I got a neighbor down in Kentucky who was with General Harmar last fall--didn't care much for him! Said Harmar drank a lot. Told me the old general had some Kentucky preacher's son tied to a cannon and given six lashes for a breach of discipline. Claimed Harmar didn't have authority to do that. Fact is Jason, I ain't heard any militiamen down my way say anything good about Harmar. But my neighbor does tell me he never saw any better river bottom land than what's up north! Me and him went over to Bardstown a couple of weeks back to see his friend who was also with Harmar last fall. He said the same thing about that bottom land up north and wants to tag along with St. Clair.

Hank scratched his chin and added:

"Seems everybody you talk to from Lexington to Bardstown are interested in St. Clair's expedition. We met an old fellar at Bardstown name of John Ash, one of the earliest settlers in that area. He said a Shawnee hunting party took his ten year old son and the lad's little sister in May of 1780--boy's name was George. * Said he heard the girl had been killed but George was living with them Shawnees up north of an Indian village he called Pickawillany. John said he's got another boy just turned nineteen who is determined to join St. Clair's army and see if he can find his brother up north."

Jason recalled the day when that old codger at Dunbar's Camp had said his cousin's boy, Marmaduke, had disappeared along the Cheat and might be living among the Indians. Jason was about to remind Hank of that story when his friend continued:

"My neighbor's got another friend name of Ezra Axton he says plans to tag along with St. Clair and

---

* According to "A Sketch of George Ash" by The Western Traveler, first published in THE CINCINNATI CHRONICLE and later, November 19, 1829, appearing in THE EATON REGISTER (No. 10, Vol 1) and THE PIQUA DAILY CALL, Piqua, Ohio (February 21, 1951), George Ash was with the Indians when "St. Clair came at us in 1791" and "my brother, a member of St. Clair's command, was left on the field of action." A story of fratricide involving Marmaduke (Duke) Swearingen alias Blue Jacket, and Charles Van Swearingen, may have its "roots" in this sketch and a controversial genealogical commentary written by Thomas Jefferson Larsh (1809-1883) of Eaton, OH titled "Blue Jacket, Famous Shawnee Chief" published in TRANSACTIONS OF THE KANSAS STATE HISTORICAL SOCIETY 1907-08. Larsh worked as an apprentice (1824) and later (1850) was editor of the WEEKLY REGISTER in Eaton, Ohio.

stake out a piece of that bottom land up along what
he calls the 'Miami of the lake river.' Says Axton
aims to take his family too. You think the general
will get away this summer Jason?"

Jason studied his friend's face for a moment--
Hank was serious about this undertaking. "I don't
know," replied Jason. "All of the troops St. Clair
expected have not arrived and Fort Washington looks
like a manufactory. Harness makers, wheelwrights,
gunsmiths, and other artificers are working day and
night but St. Clair still needs carpenters to make
and repair gun carriages for the artillery, coopers
to make kegs for ammuntion, and...."

"And blacksmiths," said Hank dryly.

"As a matter of fact, St. Clair asked me if I
would be interested in going along as a farrier if
I did not want to join the army--and I do not. But
frankly Hank, with Mary being sick, the snake bite,
and my work, I have not given it much thought."

Mary had pulled her chair close to the doorway
where she could enjoy the evening breeze--she heard
the latter part of the conversation and was pleased
with her husband's comment. As Harry M. Strickler
asserted in his 1924 publication: "A woman's scent
of danger is keener than that of the male!"*

But regardless of her intuition, Mary was very
surprised the next morning when Alma and Dave came
by saying they had decided to go back to Kentucky
with Hank, and on to Lexington. As Alma said:

"We've been talking about it for some time and
now that I am in a family way I think it is best we
go back home!"

Taken by surprise, Mary said with an astonish-
ed look on her face: "Oh, I didn't know!"

"I didn't either" replied Alma with a sardonic
smile. "You folks been having enough problems so I
didn't think it was right to say anything. I guess
it was the joy of getting off the ark that did it."

* "Massanutten, Settled By The Pennsylvania Pilgrim" (1924)

"I sold everything last night," said Dave with a shrug of his shoulders. "I figure we'll go down through that Cumberland Gap and double back northeast to Philadelphia. Frontier life just ain't our cup of tea I guess. And besides--it will be better for Alma when her time comes."

Dave could have bitten his tongue--some things are better left unspoken--this was one of them. He glanced at Mary and then at Jason as he said: "I'm sorry Mary, and Jason--but you know what I mean."

"I understand Dave," said Mary. "And you have our best wishes for a safe journey of course."

That evening, sitting outside their doorway as darkness closed in around them, Mary glanced at her husband and said: "Ironic, is it not Jason, all of our friends have gone south of the Ohio River. Are we being realistic in this undertaking?"

Jason didn't reply--he was thinking about what Hank said regarding "that rich river bottom land up north." Mary did not repeat her query--his silence was her answer. But early the following morning he had cause for reflection on her question when Jason found his sheep had been killed during the night by wolves and, worst of all, his black gelding was not in the blacksmith shop--Star had been stolen!

Waves of frustration, anger, and grief coursed through Jason's body--he was dumbfounded. Although he had once vowed never to cry, he was on the verge of tears when another settler down the street came storming into the blacksmith shop exclaiming:

"Them damn Indians stole my best wagon horse! Aside from the fact a good wagon horse brings sixty to a hundred dollars, I don't see why them thieving bastards can't keep their hands off our horses! Do you suppose that scar-faced Indian you had hanging around here had anything to do with it?"

Jason took a deep breath, looked the angry man in the eyes, and said with noticeable restraint:

"Absolutely not! I would bet my life on it!"

Jason then explained that he had also suffered

a terrible loss during the night--someone had taken Star and all his sheep had been killed. Moved by Jason's emphatic defense of the scar-faced Indian, and with understanding sympathy, the settter said:

"Well, as my father used to say, 'misery loves company.' Seems we're both in the same boat. I am lucky in one way. I'd have lost another horse if I hadn't spotted that cussed redskin in a blue jacket leading another horse away when I was on my way out to the privy at first light. I'd have dropped that redskin too if I hadn't been afraid of shooting one of my other horses. Its always something out here, Indians, bobcats, wolves, snakes!" With a hint of a smile he added: "There may even be a few of them dragons you used to chase back in Maryland!"

Jason had told him on one occasion how much he had enjoyed chasing dragons along the Monocacy when a boy. But now Jason remarked seriously: "Indians, snakes, wolves, bobcats--they were all put on earth by God too you know." An impish smile crossed his face as he added: "Dragons too I suppose."

Lieutenant Colonel William Darke marched into Fort Washington on August 29th with a contingent of Virginia levies. Although his men were ordered to proceed on to Ludlow's Station, Darke was ordered to remain at Fort Washington as a member of General Harmar's special board of inquiry. There were not a sufficient number of officers of suitable rank to sit on a court-martial for Harmar.

A text book soldier, Harmar lived by Prussian Baron Von Steuben's 1779 Military Manual. Left an orphan at only three years of age, he was reared by a Quaker aunt and educated in a Society of Friends school. In October of 1784 he married Sarah Jenkins of Philadelphia. Appointed General-In-Chief of the Army as Washington's replacement, and promoted from Lieutenant Colonel to General, Harmar vehemently opposed the use of state militia troops. It was a resentment which plagued his fall campaign in 1790 and would hinder St. Clair's effectiveness in 1791.

Adamant that untrained militia hindered, not helped, his expedition--and spurred into defensive action by degrading rumors concerning his reported intemperance and treatment of militia personnel in the fall of 1790, Harmar demanded a trial by court-martial to prove his conduct and leadership were above reproach.

Undoubtedly contributing to the general's lack of success in 1790 was his failure to stem a wanton destruction of the Indian's food supply. As a 20th century humanistic psychologist would say: "Hunger is a dominant drive!" * Destruction of the Indian's food supply merely served to unite them against the "white invaders" and the ferocious vigor of their punishment inflicted on St. Clair's expedition in 1791 was in no small way the result of the hate and vengeance prompted by Harmar's 1790 campaign.

But now, sixty-seven days before Little Turtle and his warriors would reap their vengeance, on the 29th of August St. Clair prepared to return to Fort Washington and subsequent trip to Kentucky for more troops--his third trip since May. Before departing the Ludlow Station camp, he ordered Major Hamtramck to lead a detachment forward to the Miami River as soon as the surveyor (Mr. Ganoe) laid out a route.

"Open a road as you advance so the artillery can be moved up fast as soon as the horses arrive."

Riding to Fort Washington St. Clair thought of that day, February 11th in 1777, when he had first been appointed a major general. He also remembered his selection to be President of Congress in 1787-- the highest office in the land at the time--and his later nomination to be governor of Pennsylvania. And now here he was: 57 years old; far removed from his children and chronically ill wife; plagued by recurrent attacks of debilitating gout worsened by exposure; concerned over personal financial matters occasioned in part by his absence; and frustrated

---

* "Motivation and Personality" by Abraham H. Maslow (1954)

over the tardiness of expected troops and supplies
promised by his "colleagues" back east. Although
Quartermaster General Samuel Hodgdon--a colonel in
the Continental Army who now received the pay and
allowances of lieutenant colonel but not the rank--
had quartermaster experience during the war and was
a merchant in Philadelphia, he lacked the necessary
talent for quick improvisation. William Knox, the
quartermaster's incompetent assistant--a brother of
the Secretary of War--was of little help. Delaying
his departure from Philadelphia until June 4th, the
quartermaster general spent an inordinate amount of
time procuring 15 axes, 18 broadaxes, 12 hammers,
and 24 handsaws in his penny-pinching procurements.
Hodgdon forwarded to St. Clair useless leg splints,
ill-fitting pack saddles, tents that leaked, knap
sacks and shabby clothes of poor quality, and shoes
that quickly wore out.

It is to be expected military commanders will
spend a lot of time on supply problems but St Clair
had more than his share of such problems in 1791.
Samuel Hodgdon, a political appointee, was directed
by the Secretary of War "to act entirely under St.
Clair's orders, in all respects." But he stayed in
Philadelphia until the early part of June, remained
at Pittsburgh until the latter part of August, and
did not show up in Cincinnati until September 7th.
Thus, in trying to remedy his many supply problems,
St. Clair was, in effect, his own quartermaster.

Nine months later, on May 8, 1792, Representative Thomas Fitzsimons of Pennsylvania would state:
"The delays consequent upon the gross and various
mismanagements and neglects in the quartermaster's
and contractor's departments were particularly to
blame for St. Clair's logistical failures."

St. Clair was also destined to learn the wisdom of Napoleon Bonaparte's later declaration: "An
army marches on its stomach!" Signed October 28th,
1790 by Theodosius Fowler, a New York merchant, the
unclear government contract was intended to provide

food for the soldiers. But, drawn up months before St. Clair's campaign was approved, the contract was not clear concerning responsibility for movement of the food supplies. The contract did say a "ration" consisted of one pound of flour or bread, one pound of beef or twelve ounces of pork, salt, and whiskey or rum. The cost was to be 5.28 cents per ration at Pittsburgh, 6.83 cents at Cincinnati, and 15.28 cents per ration after troops moved away from Fort Washington. Fowler, in a letter to the War Department dated April 7, 1791, stated he transferred the contract to William Duer on January 3rd, 1791. The date of this letter was later declared questionable and by March of 1792 William Duer—a close friend and business associate of Secretary Henry Knox who admitted he had recognized Duer as "the contractor" during the 1791 campaign—was in debtor's prison.

Victim of a miserable manpower and logistical supply system, and far removed from a president and congress who had approved the frontier undertaking, and appropriated $312,686.20 for expenses the first year, confident of reimbursement St. Clair expended personal funds to help outfit and subsist his expedition—expenditures which would contribute to his financial ruin in the years to come. To cover some expenses incurred in the negotiations with Indians in 1789, and promised reimbursement by Secretary of the Treasury Alexander Hamilton, the governor signed a note for $7,042 to James O'Hara never doubting the U.S. government would honor the pledge. Almost two decades later—after St. Clair had been "fired" as governor in 1802 and Hamilton was fatally wounded in a gun duel with Aaron Burr on July 11, 1804—his request for reimbursement was destined to fall on deaf ears. Unable to obtain any reimbursement for this obligation, St. Clair would be forced to sell personal property in 1808 at a tremendous loss to satisfy the indebtedness.

But such financial adversity was 17 years in the future as St. Clair, on September 1, 1791, was advised of an immediate procurement problem--Israel Ludlow advised him that whereas 800 horses had been requisitioned, he had only been able to procure 650 pack horses with the money ($17,500) he was given.

While St. Clair bemoaned the negligence of the quartermaster and tardiness of his expected troops, Ebenezer Denny was pondering the thought of joining the expedition--he concluded he would talk with his good friend, General Harmar, first. At Fort Harmar in August of 1788, John Symmes' daughter had been fascinated by Lieutenant Denny's story about being at Yorktown October 19th, 1781 when Cornwallis surrendered. As the lieutenant related: "On six-hole fifes and rope tension drums, the scarlet uniformed British band began playing 'The World Turned Upside Down' when Brigadier Charles O'Hara, acting on behalf of Cornwallis, handed over his sword to Major General Benjamin Lincoln."

But now in September of 1791 as Denny pondered his options, another veteran of the Revolutionary War--enroute to join St. Clair--penned a letter to his friend back home in Connecticut. In Major Jonathan Heart's letter dated September 2nd, 1791, the frontier-wise regular army officer stated pessimistically: "Our numbers may be sufficient were they disciplined but it grows late." He didn't know how late it was--his days on earth were numbered.

No one knew better than St. Clair the lateness of the season as he rode to Lexington the first of September carrying a brace of horsemen's pistols on the cantle of his saddle. High overhead he watched a skein of ducks winging southward and he urged his horse into a faster gait. While his aide obtained lodging at widow Curtner's rooming house on Western Street, St. Clair quickly began making arrangements to draft 1,150 Kentucky militiamen secretly expecting only 750 would show up the 25th of September. He thought the militia could quickly catch the slow moving army and perhaps he could draft the militiamen into the infantry rather than have a separate detachment of mounted volunteers.

To say there was some confusion concerning the status of militia officers under the new constitutional government would be an understatement. District of Kentucky officials understood mounted men were under the direct command of their own officers who received sixty-six and two-thirds cents a day and footmen would receive three dollars a month and be under martial law. It was the same "confusion" that plagued Harmar's campaign and was destined to hinder the effectiveness of St. Clair's expedition. Although St. Clair did obtain a verbal promise of support during his September trip to Lexington, the citizen-soldier controversy was far from settled.

When St. Clair's August 8th report arrived at the "seat" of the government, this news of the army departing Fort Washington was quickly embellished by Secretary Knox who advised President Washington: "St. Clair, with 2300 troops, is now forging ahead toward the projected goal." It sounded encouraging and Secretary of State Thomas Jefferson confided to his political friends: "We shall give the Indians a thorough drubbing this summer." However, before 1791 ended, Jefferson would learn St. Clair was the "drubee," not the "drubor!"

When St. Clair returned to Fort Washington an early August communique from Secretary Knox awaited his attention. It advised him the $5\frac{1}{2}$ inch howitzer shells he anxiously awaited wouldn't arrive in time for the expedition but this letter, and another one dated August 11, 1791, urged St. Clair to "proceed forward as soon as possible." Adding insult to injury, the pompous Secretary Knox's addendum stated: "The president continues anxious that you commence your operations at the earliest moment!"

Avoiding any rebuttal to such goading, in his communique dated September 4th St. Clair offered an estimate of his adversary's strength: "I expect my army will face a force of 1,000 to 1,500 Indians."

While Jason Evenstar was helping to shape into

kettles sheet iron sent downstream from Pittsburgh, at Marietta on September 4, 1791 Lieutenant Daniel Bradley from Connecticut met Captain Joseph Shaylor who, like himself, was leading a party of troops to Fort Washington. Bradley had departed Connecticut August 1st and arrived at Pittsburgh 23 days later. In his group were Peter C. Davis, John Dowling, and Dennis Dogan. Deciding to continue on downstream with Major Jonathan Heart, at first light September 5th the three officers and their charges pushed off at Marietta. Approaching the mouth of the Kanawha, Heart told his companions: "Just one year ago, the 26th of September as I recall, the governor wrote a letter to Secretary Knox advising him some protection would be necessary for the settlement forming near the Kanawha." *   Passing Point Pleasant, Heart explained this was where Chief Pucksinwha had been killed October 10, 1774 during Lord Dunmore's War. The knowledgeable major--a graduate of Yale, former Connecticut schoolteacher, and veteran of the Revolutionary War--frowned as he added: "A treaty was signed after the war but the promises of the treaty soon disappeared as snow might before the burning sun and blood lust soon replaced reason out here."

A century and a half later Charles De Gaulle, French general and statesman, would dryly declare: "Treaties are like roses and young girls, they last while they last!"

At Fort Randolph on September 7th, Major Heart heard Colonel Thomas Lee say Colonel Henry Lee of Mason County reported 70 Indians were harassing the boats passing Hanging Rock. That same day, but 125 miles west, Major Hamtramck's detachment began cutting a wilderness road north from the encampment at Ludlow's Station. The difficulty of building that stretch of road to the river was a harbinger of the problems that lay ahead. Major Ziegler later said: "The march north was slow and provisions short. We

* Pg 195 "St. Clair Papers" Vol 2 W. H. Smith (1882)

didn't reach the Great Miami until September 15th."

According to an entry in the diary maintained by Lieutenant James Stephenson from Virginia: "It took 12 oxen to pull a wagon up a hill."

On September 7th Major General Richard Butler arrived at Fort Washington--almost two months after St. Clair had expected to march northwest. After a perfunctory greeting St. Clair enjoined his second-in-command to convene as soon as possible the board of inquiry Harmar awaited and added tartly:

"As the ranking officer, you will be president of the board of course. The other two members of the board, Lieutenant Colonel Darke and Lieutenant Colonel Gibson, have been waiting for your arrival. As soon as you complete your inquiry, the adjutant will arrange to have you escorted to the encampment and I will brief you on our line of march."

Although none of the members of the board were "regulars," General Butler had served with credit in the Pennsylvania Line during the Revolutionary War and later as an Indian agent. St. Clair's sharp inference regarding his ill-advised delay of troops at Fort Pitt was countered by Butler's equally curt reply: "The Secretary of War's orders were to hold necessary troops in western Pennsylvania to protect the frontier settlers and I acted accordingly."

As General Butler took his leave, the adjutant ushered into St. Clair's office an Indian scout who reported Little Turtle had summoned representatives of the Miami Indian confederation to meet with him in early September at Kekionga. Advising St. Clair Canada East and Canada West had been united August 24, 1791, and would now be called "The Province of Canada," the scout said John Graves Simcoe, a Lieutenant Governor of Canada, had ordered construction of a fort at the rapids on the Miami-of-the-lake which Indians were calling "Fort Miami." St. Clair frowned--British troops in such a location could be expected to support the Indians.

During St. Clair's visit along the Mississippi

404

in 1790 he had learned about a portage between the Miami-of-the-lake (the Maumee River) and the Wabash River which facilitated water travel from Lake Erie to the Ohio River. But those who paddled canoes on the Wabash in 1791 had no way of knowing that river with its frogs, snakes, mosquitoes, and pestilence would someday be treated romantically in literature and feated in the song a youthful swain would sing, 145 years later, in the shadow of the recently constructed fort on the banks of that river: "Oh the moonlight's bright tonight along the Wabash....."

And during the bicentennial anniversary of St. Clair's ill-fated expedition, a native of southern Illinois would publish an account of his 500 mile canoe trip down the Wabash River with his grandson. As this narrative would indicate, the origin of the Wabash River is four miles south of where St. Clair camped on its banks November 3rd, 1791 believing it to be the St. Marys River. The general should have had a copy of "Ouabache Adventure."*

Standing beside the door leading to his office in the bastion at Fort Washington on September 7th, St. Clair recalled the words of the Chinese strategist, Sun Tzu, shown him by Knox: "There has never been a protracted war from which a country has ever benefited. What is essential in war is victory, not prolonged operations."

And while he was pondering this comment, Major Ferguson and Jason Evenstar approached where he was standing. After their customary greeting, Ferguson informed St.Clair the guns ordered from Springfield had finally arrived but added: "Unfortunately they are all different kinds and will require balls of a different calibre." The major also reported having received tents of a poor quality, axes that would not hold an edge, and mis-marked shipping boxes.

Shaking his head in disbelief, St. Clair said: "Quartermaster Hodgdon just arrived---please inform

* "Ouabache Adventure" by Allen Johnson, Dayton, OH (1991)

him of your findings." Turning to Jason, St. Clair commented: "As you are aware, we sorely need every carpenter, artificer, gunsmith, and blacksmith that we can enlist and I was delighted to hear the major say you are strongly considering joining my expedition. As I have said, I can offer you a commission if you are interested in a career in the army."

"Thank you sir--thank you for your confidence. Although I have been thinking about your suggestion I accompany the expedition as a ferrier, I have not given any serious thought to a career in the army-- my bride would not favor that I am certain. But, I do intend to talk with her tonight about both of us going along with the expedition and staking out a claim in that river bottom land up north my friend down in Kentucky talks about."

Jason paused--was he talking too much? Throwing caution to the wind, he quickly added: "By the way sir, as I mentioned to Major Ferguson, Benjamin Van Cleve met a friend of mine down in Kentucky the other day and he told him to tell me he was coming up here next week. Hank hopes to obtain work as a woodsman or wagon driver and go along too. He is a mighty fine man sir--and a good worker."

St. Clair glanced at Major Ferguson as he said with a smile: "We will need all of the able-bodied souls we can muster to cut our way through the wilderness." Looking back at Jason, St. Clair added: "The horse-master will need wagon drivers all right but you tell you friend to talk with Major Ferguson first. As for you young man, I shall be anxious to hear you have decided to accompany my expedition as a ferrier--we need you!"

That evening Jason broached the subject to his wife who calmly remarked: "I was expecting this-- a woman learns to know what her husband is thinking and you are an open book Jason dear!"

Although Jason had dismissed it from his mind as his wife's desire to distance herself from where she had lost their child, he recalled that Mary had

mentioned moving downstream to North Bend or Louis-
ville--and back to Baltimore on one occasion. But
this night Jason only grinned as he said:

"You probably heard Hank talking about joining
the expedition. Be rather nice if we could travel
together if we decide to go---you notice I said IF!
Of course, Sarah and the children are not going."

"I have always thought Sarah was an unusually
intelligent woman," said Mary with an impish smile.

"There you go throwing cold water on my plan,"
said Jason. "This might be our golden opportunity
to get some rich bottom land!"

"So it is a <u>golden</u> opportunity now is it? You
do have a way with the words Jason." Before Jason
could say anything she added: "But seriously, I do
not really care to live here and you may be right--
we would certainly have the protection of the army.
Shall I start packing in the morning?"

"Whoa! Not so fast!" replied Jason. "But with
settlers arriving every day, we should not have any
difficulty selling our place. And Sam Blackburn, a
pioneer settler here, told me he might know a buyer
if we decided to move."

"Oh," said Mary with faked surprise, "Then you
have been talking about moving?"

Caught off guard, but recovering very quickly,
he replied: "Well, St. Clair has asked me to consider joining his expedition and others have heard
him. The word gets around--you know how it is."

"Yes dear, I know how it is--a wife is usually
the last to hear about her husband's plans."

"Now that is not fair Mary--you know very well
I always talk with you about any plans I have."

"You are right Jason," said Mary. Her feigned
frown faded into a mischievous smile as she added:
"We always talk about the plans you <u>have</u> made. But
let us not quarrel---I agree with you. Just let me
know when we are moving!"

St. Clair glanced at the threatening sky as he
rode toward the Ludlow Station encampment the next

morning. Half-aloud he muttered: "September 8th! Another week or ten days and we must move out!"

There was a note of fall in the air on the 9th of September as Jason watched Major Heart, Captain Shaylor, and Lieutenant Bradley lead their men into Fort Washington. The fall of 1791 was to be a bitter disappointment to many settlers who had, only a few months before, shouldered their seed bags anticipating the rewards of the earth in September and October. There were some beans and pumpkins but a major portion of the ribboned rows of corn in July were victims of a blight. What little corn escaped the blight was soon harvested by wilderness predators--squirrels, raccoons, and deer feasted on the tender crops. An artificer working on an artillery wagon remarked to Jason: "A damn squirrel feasted on my corn--tonight I'll be feasting on him!"

Avoiding thoughts about the loss of her child, Mary spent much of her time collecting a miscellaneous collection of herb medicines, spices, catnip, sage, tansey, boneset, penny-royal, fennel seeds for seasoning, and a strong-smelling bitter-tasting plant called wormwood said to be an aphrodisiac. Gathered in season, and shared by women as needed, this made up the settler's materia medica.

St. Clair awakened September 10th at the field encampment and found evidence of a light frost--the first of the season. Riding north along Mill Creek the previous day he had seen two wedges of arguing geese winging south---a sure-fire sign cold weather was not far away.

The last of the white, crystalline coating had not totally vanished under the morning sun when St. Clair watched his army pass in review. He knew his army's training was woefully insufficient but the time for procrastination must soon end. He recalled a remark Major John Palsgrave Wyllys had made a year ago while waiting for General Harmar's army to march: "Its time to fish or cut bait!"

Back at Fort Washington on September 13th, St.

Clair read Secretary Knox's communique dated August 18th pertaining to the alleged defective gunpowder. Advised of the manufacturer's tests, Major Ferguson again declared his tests at Fort Pitt had indicated the powder he tested was defective.

On Thursday, September 15th, St. Clair watched Major Heart, Captain Shaylor, Lieutenant Bradley, leave Fort Washington headed for the Ludlow Station encampment. And as he watched, Major Ferguson told him Jason Evenstar had decided to accompany the expedition as a blacksmith.

"And that friend of his?" inquired St. Clair.

"Hank Weiser--a stout fellow that one. He arrived yesterday from Maysville and I engaged him as a carpenter and wagon driver." With a big grin the major added: "I understand Hank caught a ride on a flatboat coming downstream and met a settler who is interested in settling here. Jason said he planned to talk with the settler last evening."

Indeed the fortuitous meeting with the settler proved advantageous for both parties--the newcomer had a fine pair of oxen and a Conestoga wagon that would be of use for Jason's intended travel. Thus, in practically no time, the two men shook hands and a "trade" was consummated. Elated by his good fortune, and accompanied by Hank, Jason rushed home to tell his wife. Seated by the fireplace nonchalantly staring at the pot of bean soup simmering above the flames, Mary glanced up at Hank and her husband as Jason exclaimed:

"Well, you can start packing---we are going to join St. Clair's expedition!"

Devoid of any enthusiasm, Mary replied: "That is nice Jason. I have been expecting we would go." Looking intently at Hank, she added: "It certainly is unfortunate Sarah is going to miss this golden opportunity Hank."

Jason's frown foretold his intention to rebuke his wife's sardonic remark but Hank, unaware of the implication of her comment, said with a smile:

"You got that right Mary. But me and maw figured she ought to stay with the kids--them going to
school and crops to bring in you know." Blissfully
unaware of what fate had in store for him, Hank optimistically added: "Maw and the kids will have an
opportunity to eyeball the country up north when we
head back up that way next spring."

Late the following day, September 16th, at the
field encampment, Colonel Winthrop Sargent informed
St. Clair: "Today the board of inquiry exonerated
General Harmar. They concluded his conduct was ir-
reproachable and his campaign plans were judicious
as well as calculated."

The adjutant general also informed St. Clair a
messenger had reported Major Hamtramck's detachment
had reached the banks of the Great Miami River the
previous afternoon without incident. Clasping his
hands together, St. Clair smiled and said:

"That's good news! Tell Colonel Darke I want
to see him as soon as he rides into camp tonight."

Using an organization chart the administrative
minded adjutant general had prepared, that evening
St. Clair briefed his officers and said they would
"move out" the following morning.

"Colonel Darke will take the point," St. Clair
explained. "Our line of march will be similar to
that of Colonel Bouquet during his march to relieve
the besieged people of western Pennsylvania."

The march plan St. Clair outlined required the
scouts to scour the advance with a party of riflemen in front of the main body. Woodsmen would cut
two parallel swaths and build necessary roads and
bridges. The troops, artillery, wagons, ox teams,
and cattle were to move in two columns. The camp
followers would be followed by a rear guard. Without the two columns, at 300 feet, the cavalry would
march. St. Clair concluded by saying:

"And without the cavalry, scouts and riflemen
will advance. Outriders will insure against a surprise attack! Any questions?"

Seated beside a campfire at the mouth of the Auglaize the same night, Little Turtle's eyes swept across the faces of representatives of the Ottawas, Eels, Chippewas, Potawatomies, and the other Indian factions seated by the fire. Tarhe the Crane, Blue Jacket, Buckongahelas, and Chief Pipe (White Loon) were there. Feelings among some discordant tribes were laid aside--the enemy of all was the white man who had proposed to "eradicate" them. Stone-faced, the elderly Little Turtle watched nods of agreement as he declared: "The white man must be driven back beyond the Ohio.!"

Seated beside the Miami chief, and urging them to continue harassing the white invaders, a British officer promised supplies and ammunition to Little Turtle and his friends in the event of an attack on them by the army Tecumseh reported was being formed six miles north of the white man's hated fort along the Ohio. Still smarting from their defeat in the Revolutionary War, the British hoped to hasten the collapse of what the British officer referred to as "that unstable republic!"

Little Turtle concluded the conference saying: "Apekonit will give each of you a bundle of sticks. Throw one away each morning and when they are gone, bring your warriors to Kekionga."

Early on the morning of September 17th Colonel Sargent reported 700 regulars and 690 levies ready to march from the Ludlow Station encampment where the army had been engaged in training for the past six weeks. And now this morning as St. Clair rode through the encampment he carefully eyed the assembled troops, artillery wagons, supply wagons, and a host of civilian camp followers who intended to accompany the expedition--land hungry settlers, wives and children, soldier's girl friends, enterprising entrepreneurs, and prostitutes who chose to ignore St. Clair's admonishment against such travel. With a last word of warning to some who watched him ride by, St. Clair signaled Colonel Darke to "move out!"

The path blazed by Major Hamtramck followed an old Indian trail requiring time consuming hard work to expand the narrow pathway through the tall trees and underbrush. George Adams, a Revolutionary War veteran and now a scout for St. Clair, was a knowledgeable woodsman but he had never set foot in the wilderness through which the army planned to march to reach the Miami villages at Kekionga.

As the army began to move, the wilderness soon echoed with the dull thud of axes, the shouting and cursing of perspiring men, and orders by artillery and infantry officers. Bogging down time and time again, the light cannons--recommended for use after Harmar's campaign and called "grasshoppers"--slowed the march. Adding to the problems of clearing the wilderness road was the lack of tools requisitioned months before. Berating the quartermaster for providing the army only one grindstone and far too few axes, Major Ziegler declared bitterly: "For want of axes, two watch while one works!"

As the army hacked and clawed its way through the wilderness, accompanied by the noise of falling trees, men shouting and swearing, women yelling at their children, drums beating, horses neighing, and cattle bellowing, Tecumseh and his scouts carefully watched every move and kept Little Turtle informed.

Riding back and forth to Fort Washington, St. Clair coordinated the many facets of his responsibility as both governor and field commander. Five months before, at Pittsburgh, the far-sighted expedition commander had ordered finishing lumber for a wilderness fort designed by Major William Ferguson. These materials had arrived at North Bend and even now were being towed up the Great Miami River under the watchful eye of Joseph McMaken, a guard--he had advised St. Clair it would take three trips.

As the expedition moved north, in Cincinnati the "vindicated" Harmar talked with Ebenezer Denny. Years St. Clair's junior, Harmar adamantly declared during their conversation: "St. Clair is a victim of hurried recruiting, outdated schedules, frantic corrections, and ill-thought substitutions. He is the victim of circumstances a commander just cannot ignore!"

Out of favor with President Washington and the War Department, Harmar's suggestion that St. Clair employ oxen instead of pack horses had been ignored in planning the 1791 expedition. Speaking somewhat paternally, the thirty-eight year old Josiah Harmar told Denny paternally: "Remember son, there's only about twelve inches between a pat on the back and a kick in the rump!"

Although General Harmar expressed astonishment that St. Clair would hazard soldiers under the conditions he faced, and indicated he had little hope for the success of the expedition, nevertheless he felt his successor would profit by Denny's service and encouraged him to join the expedition. Before they parted that night Denny assured the general he would join St. Clair's expedition.

Harmar's recommendation concerning use of oxen had not escaped Jason's attention--he had worked at Fort Washington with many who had been with Harmar the previous year and spoke of the merits of these slow and stolid members of the bovine family. Thus it was that Jason and Mary started north on Monday, September 19th, in their Conestoga pulled by oxen. Casually indifferent to what was happening, "Molly" walked along behind the Conestoga chewing her cud. Riding a horse he had purchased in Cincinnati, Hank leisurely accompanied Jason's wagon keeping a sharp lookout along the wilderness swath. Behind them in a wagon loaded with his belongings was John Finley, a preacher's son from Bourbon County, Kentucky. A stone's throw back of him Ezra Axton and his family trudged along beside two heavily laden horse-drawn wagons--eleven year old Nathaniel drove one team of horses. The Evenstars, Axtons, Hank, and John were destined to become good friends as they laboriously made their way north along the wilderness road.

Moving north slowly, beyond Ludlow Station two or three groups of soldiers on foot passed by them. Although many shouted words of encouragement, there were those who derided their undertaking. In spite of the catcalls--which were quickly squelched when the offender caught sight of Hank--their occasional presence was comforting to those who traveled this wilderness road. And, on one occasion, the appearance of a small contingent of troops was fortuitous when Jason's Conestoga became mired down in the mud and he needed help. The young men cheerfully helped to free the Conestoga from the sticky morass and then continued on their way. Later that afternoon, Jason saw three officers riding north and he recognized one as being General St. Clair.

Three days out of Cincinnati, through an opening in the trees, Jason and Mary looked out across the carpet of red, yellow, and orange--the autumnal leaves reminded Jason of a quilt his aunt had made. The colors were in sharp contrast with the blue sky and the tranquility was broken only by an occasional raucous outcry of a crow rising triumphantly out of the multi-colored woods below. The maple tree's magnificence was awesome as its yellow blended with the sea of flame. The yellow of the hickory, soft purple of the ash, the brown flecked yellow of the beeches, glossy red and brown of the lofty oak, the red and yellow of sassafras and dogwood--autumn's parade of colors! High above them the wind gently stirred the branches and leaves slowly drifted down high lighted by shafts of golden sunlight filtering through the canopy overhead. Taking Mary's hand in his, Jason softly repeated the 121st Psalm:

"I will lift up mine eyes unto the hills, from whence cometh my help. My help cometh from the Lord which made heaven and earth."

Seated astride his horse on September 20th, at the fording place where the Columbia Bridge in Hamilton, Ohio would later span the Great Miami River, St. Clair said this was to be the site of his first

wilderness fort. Privy to St. Clair's intent, the
surrounding wilderness already echoed to the sounds
of crosscut saws and axes wielded by woodsmen under
the direction of Major Ferguson and Major Rudolph.
The virgin timber was cleared 300 yards away from
the planned stockade and oxen were employed to drag
the large, heavy, dressed timber to where whipsaws,
manned by two woodsmen, were employed to cut thick
planks for barracks, gates, and bastions. Bastions
gave the men inside a wider firing range--two had a
platform for artillery pieces. 2,000 wood picquets
(pickets)--20 feet long and 9 to 12 inches in diam-
eter--were buried close together three feet in the
earth to form "curtains" between the four bastions.
Near the top of the pickets a ribband (ribbon) was
held fast with wooden pins. For added protection,
a second row of pickets was set inside the first
with one of these placed between every two of the
others. To carry away surface water, a trench was
dug outside the curtains. The fort was one hundred
and fifty feet square. General James Wilkinson was
destined to add a picketed enclosure on the north
side the following year.

In a letter to Secretary Knox dated September
21, 1791, St. Clair reported: "We are hard at work
on the first of the chain of fortifications between
impregnable Fort Washington and the Miami villages.
When completed, I intend to name it in honor of our
distinguished and efficient financier, Secretary of
the Treasury Alexander Hamilton."

Emerging from the wilderness on September 24th
and seeing the beehive of activity along the Great
Miami, Jason and his fellow travelers were astound-
ed. They had not expected to see the progress that
had been made on the fortification that some coming
back down the wilderness road said was being built.
Already a few had decided the expedition was not to
their liking and had turned back. But Jason, Hank,
and their traveling companions were elated to catch
up with the expedition and quickly found a place to

make camp. That finished, Jason and Hank proceeded to locate Major Ferguson and offered their services as might be needed.

Erected on the first bank along the river, the bastion on the northeast corner included a raised platform enabling the artillery to scour the second bank with cannon fire. The bastion along the river side was similarly equipped to command the upstream and downstream approaches. Inside the curtains was a two-story barracks for 100 soldiers, a two-story building for provisions, an officer barracks, and a guard house. The formidable looking structure was in its final stage of construction when General Butler and Ebenezer Denny arrived September 27th.

That same day the Muster and Inspection Report prepared by Francis Mentges, Inspector of the Army, indicated "2,300 fit for duty." This Revolutionary War Colonel of the Pennsylvania Line mentioned in his report: "This is the most completely equippped force that has ever been seen in the west!"

Referring to this report in his communique to Knox that evening, St. Clair took polite exception with the part reading "completely equipped" saying: "Numbers do not always tell the complete story."

His communique finished, St. Clair listened to Adjutant General Sargent's report about "dissention in the ranks." As he explained, some of the troops were complaining about not being paid and others were dissatisfied with the rations. Several of the recruits had voiced a dislike for the military service and among the early six-month levies there was talk about their time being up. Sargent said a few company commanders had indicated this latter matter was creating a morale problem. Indicating he would "take the matter under advisement," St. Clair asked Sargent if he had heard anything from Fort Washington about the arrival of the Kentucky militia?

"Nothing sir!" replied Sargent. "Both General Butler and Ebenezer Denny said they had not arrived on the 25th as you expected."

Disregarding the bad news, St. Clair thought-fully commented: "Glad to hear Denny decided to go along with us. General Harmar spoke very highly of his service at Fort Finney. Remind me to offer him an appointment as my aide-de-camp with the pay and allowances of a major."

Sargent reminded St. Clair that General Butler would be needing an aide and had inquired regarding the availability of Lieutenant John Morgan.

"He is that regular in the First Infantry as I recall--from New Jersey. Well, if Major Hamtramck is agreeable, I will interpose no objection. Work out the details with Butler and Hamtramck."

Seated near the fire to fend off the chill of the early autumn evening on September 28th, with Mary and Hank seated on either side of him, Jason listened to John Finley say Lieutenant James Stephenson reported 58 horses had been stolen by Indians the previous night. "One of the men in his company said they had seen unmistakable tracks of Indians. One guard claims he saw an Indian west of here just before sunset but couldn't get off a shot before he disappeared in the woods. He said that redskin was wearing a blue jacket and riding a black horse with white forefeet."

Surprised by the man's comment, Jason quickly asked: "Did that black horse have a white star on its forehead?"

"He didn't say," replied Finley. With a broad smile he added: "The horse was probably heading the other way!"

Although Hank and Mary caught the humor of the remark and smiled, Jason didn't--he was thinking of Star and said: "I understand. I was just thinking that horse might have been Star."

Jason explained about the loss of Star and his neighbor's report about seeing an Indian wearing a blue jacket who was attempting to steal a horse of his. "Do you suppose that was the Shawnee War Chief folks call Blue Jacket?"

"Not likely," replied Finley. "The old chiefs leave the horse stealing to the young braves. That old war chief called Blue Jacket must be over fifty years old--my father said he heard a preacher named David Jones talk of visiting Indians along the west side of the Scioto River in 1773 and heard mention of a Blue Jacket's town northwest of there. Father also said Blue Jacket visited Lord Dunmore in 1774 before the battle at Point Pleasant so he must have been a grown man then."

"I agree," injected Ezra Axton who had quietly listened to the comments. "I've always thought the Shawnee war chief called Blue Jacket, who succeeded old Chief Moluntha in 1786, was an elderly man who would not be out stealing horses--might be his son. You probably heard about them Indians murdering the settlers near the mouth of the Scioto last March-- them ones with Thomas May, Jonathan Greathouse, and Hubbell. Well, I heard it said at Maysville one of the men in Orr's expedition that buried those poor souls, Joe Lemon, shot an Indian said by some to be Blue Jacket's son."

"I heard that too Ezra," said Finley. "Judge Christopher Wood said he saw Blue Jacket in Boone's Tavern at Maysville four years ago when he and some Shawnees were captured after they stole some horses at Strode's Station."*

Long after everone had sought the seclusion of their own sleeping place, Jason remained seated by the fire--his eyes fixed on a glowing piece of wood smoldering among the ashes. Fifty yards away, con- cealed by thick underbrush, a pair of eyes watched him--these were the eyes of a copper-skinned scout whose black horse was safely tethered not far away. High overhead a million eyes stared down at the two men from the blue velvet sky. Of different colored skins, neither understood the other and never would this side of eternity.

* Draper MSS, "Kenton Papers," 8BB 50-52-107

On Friday morning, September 30th, with troops standing at attention and camp followers looking on with mixed feelings of reverence, fear, and pride--and Indian spies in the surrounding woods watching the pomp and ceremony--the artillery roared a noisy salute and the impressive wilderness fortification was officially dedicated "Fort Hamilton." St. Clair knew how to make "points" among his peers.

But construction of this first wilderness outpost had taken longer than anticipated, there was a shortage of rations, morale among the early April six-month levies was low, and the Kentucky militia had failed to arrive as September ended. Under any other circumstances, the expedition commander might have ordered his army into "winter quarters" here--indeed, in light of future events, he should have. But such a delay had not been anticipated by anyone in approving the expedition and each communique St. Clair received urged him to "move ahead with utmost haste." Adding insult to injury, the Secretary of War's August 25th message read:

"The President laments exceedingly the unfortunate detention of your troops for which no reason sufficiently strong have been assigned."

Faced with the fact most of his six-month levy personnel would be eligible for discharge within a few weeks, and "failure" was not even in this loyal and dedicated officer's vocabularly, St. Clair gave no thought to going into winter quarters. Instead, with the dedication ceremony over and contemplating a return trip to Fort Washington, St. Clair briefed his second-in-command concerning moving forward and building the next outpost. He provided the general explicit instructions regarding the order of march, battle order, and encampment security saying there was to be no firing of firearms without permission. As he explained to Butler: "The ample availability of game is a tempting target for the men."

Then, accompanied by his newly appointed aide-de-camp, Ebenezer Denny, St. Clair mounted a horse and rode back to Fort Washington hoping to expedite movement of the Kentucky militia forward. Adjutant General Sargent had advised him a sergeant and 25 of the militiamen turned around and headed south on September 30th and the following day another 10 had taken off for home.

By his most pessimistic calculation, St. Clair had anticipated 750 of Kentucky's militia would be available for his expedition. It was disappointing when St. Clair was given Lieutenant Colonel William Oldham's report on October 3rd indicating only 350 militiamen would join the expedition. Shaking his head in frustrated disbelief, St. Clair looked at a Muster Report of Captain Presley Gray's company and that of Captain Adam Guthrie's which had been taken at the mouth of the Licking River the previous day, October 2nd.* In scanning the roster St. Clair had no reason to take special notice of such names as Benjamin Ash, Thomas Beard, William Briggs, or John McGinnis. But, as fate would decree, their mortal remains would forever be mixed with the soil along the banks of the Wabash River. Twenty of those on that roster were destined to be among the sixty who deserted St. Clair's expedition on October 31st.

An inspection of those Kentucky militiamen who gathered in front of Fort Washington on October 3rd showed a few were old, infirm, and ill-equipped for the arduous expedition--most were undisciplined and insubordinate and devoid of any respect for the so-called "army regulars."

Adding to St. Clair's frustration this day, an urgent express military dispatch from the Secretary of War dated September 1, 1791 arrived. In lengthy dialogue Knox belabored "the threatening situation on the western frontier," described the Indians as "turbulent and discontented," and urged the general to "proceed with the greatest haste." In customary fashion he closed by saying: "The president enjoins

* National Archives, RG 94:54 Box 1, Muster Roster, Oct 2, 1791

you by every principle that is sacred to stimulate your operations in the highest degree and to move as rapidly as the lateness of the season and the nature of the case will possibly admit."

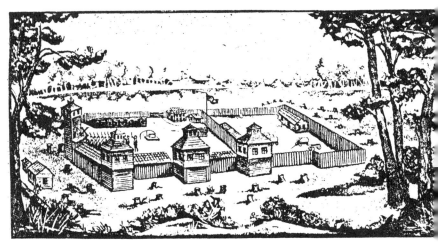

FORT HAMILTON AS ORIGINALLY BUILT.

Page 100, Vol. XIII, Ohio Arch. & His. Pubs (1904)

CHAPTER THIRTEEN

WILDERNESS ROAD

Leaving Captain John Armstrong and 20 soldiers of the First U. S. Infantry to garrison Fort Hamilton, early on Wednesday, October 4, 1791, General Butler led the 2,000 man expeditionary force across the Great Miami. Disregarding St. Clair's repeated admonishment they return to Cincinnati, about 300 camp followers tagged along. Slowly hacking their way north along the river and through the trees and thick underbrush, the woodsmen opened up two swaths 250 yards apart in accordance with St. Clair's plan of march. Followed by packhorses, bullocks, and an assortment of baggage and supply wagons, the artillery was sandwiched between battalions of infantry commanded by Majors Thomas Butler and John Clarke and Majors Henry Gaither and George M. Bedinger. A dark cloud hovered ominously on the western horizon above the hills of red and yellow as General Butler muttered to himself:

"This is the wrong time of year to be launching an attack against the Indians in this country— a wilderness area we are totally unfamiliar with."

Secretly admiring their stubborn courage, St. Clair's second-in-command cursed the persistence of the land hungry settlers, washerwomen, mistresses, harlots, wives, and children that forded the Great Miami behind the army. A shortage of rations with which to share with the camp followers had prompted a few to heed St. Clair's admonishment but most of the camp followers persisted in their undertaking.

Late in the afternoon of the first day the two column formation made camp three miles north of the fording point just north of "Two Mile Creek." This night General Butler--during St Clair's absence and contrary to his explicit instructions--decided that it would be more expedient to open a single broad-cut road 12 feet wide which would acommodate the artillery and wagons. The cavalry was ordered to march 100 yards distant on the flanks with scouts beyond them to scour the woods along the course of 343 degrees which the surveyor would lay out using a crude eight inch brass compass mounted on a Jacob Staff and a 33 foot surveyor's chain.

Included in St. Clair's dispatch to Henry Knox on October 6th was General Butler's report indicating 21 men had deserted the night of October 4th.

Meantime, north of Fort Hamilton Butler pushed across "Four Mile Creek" shortly after noon on the 5th of October. And this same day Lt. Col. William Oldham led a contingent of 350 Kentucky militiamen north from Cincinnati. Many, in true pioneer fashion, wore a leather jacket and leggings, a coonskin cap, and carried a long-barreled musket and hunting knife. Crossing the Great Miami at Fort Hamilton, Oldham slowed their advance preferring to maintain a discrete distance behind the army.

Ahead of Oldham's militia, Butler continually made his way through the ranks of toiling woodsmen, scouts, and surveyors, shouting words of encouragement. And, near sunset on the 6th of October, the army turned up the crooked "Seven Mile Creek" and encamped along this gorge near what would later be identified as the eastern edge of Milford Township in Butler County, Ohio.

From Fort Washington this same day St. Clair's communique advised Secretary Knox:

"I returned to Fort Washington on October 3rd to get the Kentucky militia who marched on the 5th. 300 more should be joining us by October 10th. We have 2,000 men not including the Kentucky militia."

In spite of this optimistic forecast, 300 more did not join the expedition.

Resuming their march early on Friday, October 7th, that night the army made camp where Camden, OH would later stand. Lieutenant Daniel Bradley noted in his diary they had marched only 16 miles in four days. And, for want of sufficient hobbles, bells, and experienced drivers, horses were reported missing. Cursing the quartermaster for his negligence, Butler ordered a runner back to Cincinnati for such equipment and personnel.

With long crimson and yellow aisles on either side leading into kaleidoscopic mazes of the underbrush and gigantic trees, on the 8th of October the woodsmen opened the wilderness road to a point east of where Fort St. Clair would be erected two years later by General James Wilkinson.

And on October 8th St. Clair, riding north to rejoin his army, dispatched an urgent message from Fort Hamilton to Israel Ludlow at Fort Washington advising he had sent 300 horses back to pick up the 90,000 rations which had been requisitioned.

The following morning, about twenty-four miles north of where St. Clair remained overnight at Fort Hamilton, those members of the expedition who were so inclined participated in Sabbath services before resuming their wearisome march at ten o'clock under fair skies. Surrounded by huge oak, walnut, beech, hickory, and ash trees, the army forged ahead deeper and deeper into the unknown wilderness country. And, as if the living trees were not problem enough to traverse, all through the forest lay thick butts of dead trees covered with moss. But on and on the army marched along the road cut by the hard-working woodsmen.

That same morning--in full uniform and carrying his left arm in a sling to ease the pain of his gout--St. Clair crossed the Great Miami and started north on one of the newly cut roads. Then noticing

the change from two parallel roads to one after he
crossed Two Mile Creek, St. Clair quickly urged his
mount forward. Nursing frustrated anger, St. Clair
halted briefly to confer with Colonel Oldham taking
strong exception with Oldham's expressed preference
for maintaining a short distance between his party
and the advancing army. Before taking his leave of
the militia commander, St. Clair strongly suggested
Oldham's men press forward and join the rest of the
expedition as soon as possible.

Having pushed ahead five miles this Sunday, at
three o'clock Butler ordered the army to make camp.
The order had hardly escaped Butler's lips when St.
Clair rode up beside him, his white horse wet with
sweat. Livid with rage, St. Clair demanded to know
why the order of march was not in keeping with his
instructions. Although Butler attempted to explain
his reasons for deviating from the orders, and the
time and effort to be gained by such a change, St.
Clair countered by saying his planning was based on
a belief that parallel roads were more advantageous
in the event of a surprise Indian attack. However,
having heard Butler's explanation, the fair-minded
St. Clair decided he would defer to his second-in-
command's change with the understanding the single
road order of march would be countermanded when the
army approached an area where the scouts indicated
there was a possibility of encountering the enemy.

But this was another "thorn" in the rift which
developed between St. Clair and Richard Butler--one
never to be healed this side of eternity. This may
have contributed to the breakdown of communications
vital to effective command--particularly in a wilderness campaign where tiny bits of intelligence can
spell the difference between victory and defeat.

Even as St. Clair admonished Butler, Tecumseh
dispatched a runner to Kekionga reporting to Little
Turtle: "The old white-haired general has rejoined
the expedition but he now carries his left arm in a
sling."

There was an ominous threat of bad weather as Major General St. Clair gave the order to march on October 10th. Resplendent with his bearskin crested leather cap with a red turban, blue coat faced and lined with buff, a buff vest and breeches, and a pair of silver stars on gold epaulettes, the "old white-haired general" was an extremely visible personage on his white horse. Spearheading the march through level country and open woods, St. Clair led the army eight miles this day before making camp at four o'clock near where Route 40 would later cross Price's Creek. Though still preferring to maintain a separate and distinct space between them and "the regulars," shortly after noon on October 10th, Oldham and his militiamen "caught up" with the army.

With Jason's Conestoga parked not far from the Kentucky militia's camp, that evening after supper Jason, Hank, and John Finley walked over hoping to get acquainted with some of them. Approaching the perimeter of the militia's camp, they were met by a somewhat surly individual who introduced himself as "Sergeant Abner Chalfin." Learning that both Hank and John Finley were from Kentucky, Chalfin became more hospitable--he was also obviously impressed by Hank's size and demeanor. Although Jason tried not to dislike Chalfin, some of his crude remarks about General St. Clair and Colonel Sargent made it quite difficult. It would come as no surprise to Jason when, only three weeks later, Chalfin and 59 of his companions would simply head back to Kentucky.

Among others they met was Private Benjamin Ash whose father, John Ash, had mentioned having talked with Hank Weiser. Ben, as he preferred to be called, told how his ten year old brother, George, had been taken by some Shawnees eleven years before and his father had heard his son had been adopted by an Indian family. Regardless, Ben still hoped to find his older brother. After telling how Star had been stolen last month, and his prayerful hope he might find his horse, Jason added with a smile:

"I just hope your brother George is not riding my black gelding when you find him!"

They also met Privates Beedy Ashby, Tom Piety, James Pursley, Jacob Ruble, Joseph Todd, and Ennis Innes—the latter being miffed that St. Clair would not honor his Kentucky commission. Before leaving, Jason talked briefly with Sergeant John Parker who expressed an interest in hearing more about the gun the blacksmith carried.

It was overcast and a disagreeable wind out of the northwest was foreboding. Autumn's colors were fast giving way to time as the wearisome march continued on October 11th at ten o'clock. Slowly the woodsmen chopped a road through the immensity laced with occasional islands of age-old trees and thick underbrush, tiny streams, and animal trails. Often a seemingly endless mat of leaves and dead grass, sometimes a foot thick, made the walking difficult. But on the expedition marched through swamps, bogs, bottoms, sloughs, marshes, sticky black dirt, clay, marl, and rich loamy dirt—on and on but ever north and west toward the Miami villages.

About noon this Tuesday the army crossed what would later be the Preble-Darke County line. Then, an hour later, St. Clair's spirits were lifted when Colonel Sargent informed him Robert Benham's supply convoy had arrived. It was good news but, one hour later, Captain Denny reported "bad news" ahead. At two o'clock, having marched but six miles, the army was forced to halt and encamp at the edge of a "wet prairie" or swamp (the headwaters of the Twin Creek Branch of the Great Miami River) northwest of where Castine, Ohio would later stand. That night one of the camp followers wrote a letter to her mother and father in Philadelphia saying: "This country is so breath-takingly old. No wonder these Indians cling so tenaciously to the hunting grounds through which the army is blazing a road. We have crossed many old and well worn paths our scouts say the Indians follow through the wilderness. These ruts are made by buffalo and other beasts of the forest and we're told they lead unerringly to streams."

The same night Captain Daniel Bradley wrote in his journal: "We are now 62 miles from Fort Washington and a better tract of land I never saw. The timber exceeds all I ever saw--white oaks from 4-6 feet through and 50 to 80 feet high. And white ash from 2 to 4 feet through and very tall." *

Although Captain Denny informed St. Clair some horses had been reported missing that morning and a scout reported finding Indian mocassin tracks along the northern perimeter of their camp, the general's communinque to Knox on October 11th optimistically stated: "In the course of this month I expect the matter of the Indians will be settled. We are now 50 miles from the Indian towns." The truth was St. Clair was more than twice that distance from Miami-town and the two Shawnee and three Delaware Indian villages located within a six mile radius of where Fort Wayne would later stand. Only 62 miles from Fort Washington, and with General Harmar's somewhat circuitous march to the Miami villages reported as approximating 170 miles, there was no way St. Clair could be only "50 miles from the Indian towns."

Never enchanted with the tiresome undertaking, most of the footsore, weary, and bedraggled levies would have sworn they had marched at least one hundred miles! And now the "wet prairie" necessitated either building a quarter-mile corduroy road across the bog or marching around the eastern edge which St. Clair ordered General Butler to explore while Lieutenant Denny was looking over the west side.

Wednesday, October 12th, was a bracing, fair fall day--there was not a cloud in the sky. Captivated by the beauty of it all, Jason and Mary stood by their Conestoga gazing out across the "obstacle" that lay in their path. Although the swamp posed a problem to the army's forward progress, the prairie

* "Biography of Captain Daniel Bradley" by F. E. Wilson (1935)

before them was beautiful. Ablaze with purple cone
flowers, golden rod, and Queen Ann's lace, wild sun
flowers raised their head from the sea of grass for
a last look at the autumn sun. 10 to 15 feet high,
and undulated by a gentle morning breeze, the grass
looked like the waves of the ocean. Here and there
were small islands of trees with their magnificent
red and yellow leaves silhouetted against the azure
sky.

Just before noon St. Clair made his decision--
they would proceed along the eastern by-pass route
Butler had explored. Having marched six miles, the
army made camp about one mile south from where St.
Clair's next fort would be erected. That afternoon
they had encountered a well-worn Indian path which
parallelled their line of march (Route 127) and St.
Clair remarked to his other aide-de-camp, Viscount
de Malartie, "Perhaps this is a good omen!"

Winthrop Sargent was less optimistic. Pushing
his mount forward of the encampment that afternoon,
Sargent reported he almost surprised some recently
departed occupants of an Indian camp site and there
were evidences of both old and new camp sites along
the Indian trail they had encountered.

The following morning, October 13th, St. Clair
reconnoitered the high ground one mile north of the
encampment in the vicinity of streams destined to
be known as Prairie Outlet, Bridge Creek, and Mud
Creek. Pondering the fact he was now 44 miles from
Fort Hamilton and had intended to build forts every
25 miles, in spite of some adverse comments regarding his choice of this site, here in what he called
"Hills of Judea" General St. Clair decided to build
his second fort--one that he would name in honor of
the Secretary of State, Thomas Jefferson.

Morale had steadily degenerated and there were
increasing signs of discontent as the army marched
forward one mile and made camp. There was a lot of
talk among the troops about four young men from the
First Regiment of Levies that started back down the

wilderness swath toward Cincinnati the previous day after declaring their six months of compulsory levy service was over! There was also a rumor that Oldham was having difficulty in keeping his militiamen from "just heading back home to harvest the crops." Although naturally concerned about such rumors, St. Clair was also disturbed by the fact the militiamen from Kentucky seemed determined not to have a thing to do with the army and pitched their tents to the rear of the main camp as far as possible.

As word spread regarding the name selected for the new fort, a dejected levy from Virginia bitterly said: "Old St. Clair sure knows which apples to polish! But he can kiss my ass tomorrow--me and my troops are getting discharged and heading back down the road! He can take his fort and shove it!"

The site St. Clair picked for the new fort was only six miles south of where General Anthony Wayne would build Fort Greene Ville three years later but this night Jason felt a little shiver of excitement as he pondered the fact this fort would be the most advanced outpost in the entire Northwest Territory! In his headquarters tent, St. Clair was pondering a different fact---his army was marching only four to six miles a day and this gave the Indians plenty of time to organize a counter-offensive. Thoughtfully the gray-haired general recalled Washington's farewell admonishment: "Beware of a surprise!"

Far across the ocean in Prussia the same night in 1791 a boy of only eleven was studying about the royal family of Hohenzollern that ruled the Empire. Frederick the Great believed in the principle that "might makes right" and had built a huge army based on discipline and authority---a policy of universal military training had been instituted. The boy who studied was Karl Von Clausewitz and was destined to become a well known writer on military science. It was Clausewitz who would later advocate: "Surprise is a tactic for the aggressor!" Marching northwest at a snail's pace, St. Clair could not have had any illusions about "surprising" the Indians.

There was a great deal of excitement on Friday morning, October 14th---a deer ran through the camp knocking down tents and upsetting stacked guns and kettles of water. Although a boisterous recruit-- one who appeared to enjoy arousing the anger of his company commander by wearing a long black and white feather in the crown of his cap--threatened to kill the frightened deer but was dissuaded from doing so when reminded there was a penalty of 100 lashes on anyone's bare back for the indiscriminate shooting of wild animals.

In advising St. Clair early this same day that this new fort would be erected at 40° 4' 22", Major Ferguson reported 200 men were now working but more manpower would be needed if the commander wanted to expedite construction. The following morning every able-bodied soldier was pressed into service. But, unfortunately--and just when he needed all the man- power he could muster--Colonel Sargent informed St. Clair several squad leaders of the six-month levies had requested their men be discharged today because their time of service expired on October 15th. St. Clair had no choice and instructed Sargent to "take appropriate action to discharge those so eligible." That Saturday afternoon several squads of six-month levies started south along the wilderness road.

That evening Major Ferguson reported: "I have 1,381 men building four block houses, barracks, the curtains, storage magazine, a bullock pen, digging a well, making a windlass for raising and lowering supplies to the fort, and putting up some privies."

The "three holer" was the soldier's favorite place to rest during the dawn to dusk workday. And if looking for someone, the privy was generally the first place to check. Caught "resting," one of the better educated recruits from Maryland explained he had paused to "cogitate" when Colonel Sargent asked him the reason for his delay in reporting as order- ed. It was one of the few times Jason ever saw the adjutant general at a loss for words.

Charged with insubordination, one of the six-month levies from Virginia was assigned to a detail building one of these useful edifices. Bitterly he complained: "Don't seem right I gotta help build a damn outhouse for them Kentuckians to sit on their rear end and spit tobacco juice all over the walls. You just wait--twenty-one more days and I'm headin' for God's country!"

The youthful recalcitrant was closer to "God's country" than he could possibly know. Three weeks later his mortal remains would lay on the banks of the Wabash River near the lifeless body of Captain James Bradford--the artillery officer from Pennsylvania who had imposed the punishment.

Construction of Fort Jefferson was hampered by the same delays that plagued Fort Hamilton. A case in point being the work detail of 200 men with only 80 axes and one saw. There was, however, an ample supply of spades and mattocks so work on a well and an 80 foot tunnel connecting the magazine pit and a blockhouse progressed satisfactorily. The overall effort was encumbered by a shortage of rations, the controversy concerning the levy personnel's term of service, general discontent, and inclement weather after October 15th.

Adding to these frustrating difficulties, both St. Clair and Butler now began to show evidences of being ill as rain fell continually on the 16th and 17th of October. The tiring efforts of leadership, irregular eating and sleeping, and exposure to the elements, were starting to take their toll. It was only natural their temperaments would suffer and those close to them often caught the brunt of unintentional curt remarks--the frustrations of command cause a physical drain on both energy and patience. The regular officers showed understanding and bit their tongue in silence and the contractors gritted their teeth in passive acquiescence. The Kentucky militia grimaced, muttered colorful expletives, and threatened to "head for home!"

Privy to one such explosive use of expletives, and criticism of St. Clair's delay to build another of "his damn forts," Jason later asked Colonel Sargent about the "status" of the Kentucky militia in the military establishment and why they were never involved in work details. Sargent replied: "Well, the militia is an independent volunteer body never enrolled in the army's general roster for duty."

Given leave to hunt on the 17th of October despite the dreary weather, several of the militiamen took off through the woods west of the encampment. A few hours later they returned carrying one of the men saying he had been shot through the hip by some Indian who got away.

That same day, as overcast skies unleashed intermittent rain, Private William May decided he was tired of "short rations." Caught trying to escape, this First Infantry regular was pardoned but given extra detail. He was destined to be taken prisoner by Mingo Indians the next year and his life spared by the intervention of Simon Girty. While serving as a spy for General Wayne in 1793, May would help locate cannons in December left along the banks of the Wabash two years earlier. But in the summer of 1794 William May's luck would run out when he was captured by Indians and he would be executed on the 19th of August.

Although the rain stopped on October 18th, low hanging clouds signaled the possibility of more to come. Standing near a brass three-pounder, some of the artillerymen listened as Captain Bradford tried to explain how the quartermaster's inept purchasing resulted in the shipment of four-pound shot with a three-pound cannon. Two six-month levies standing not far away listened and then one exclaimed:

"Some of us won't have to worry about that--my time will be up in twenty days Captain!"

He didn't know how prophetic his comment was-- but his "time" would really be up in only 17 days!

The "date of expiration" of the levy's term of compulsory military service hung like the sword of Damocles over General St. Clair's head--soon all of the six-month levies would be gone. Each day now a party of "discharged" levies started back down the wilderness road diminishing his army. Just talking about the "date" their term of service expired sort of helped to ease the frustration of being far from home, tired, and thinking about "mom's cooking" on a half-filled stomach.

Although 240 bullocks of 300 pounds weight and 6,000 pounds of flour arrived on October 18th, provisions were still scarce. As Sargent informed St. Clair: "This is our whole stock of provisions, and the daily issues, including women and retainers, is 2700 rations per diem. Our provisions are just not sufficient to permit the issue of full rations--the troops will get only one half of their allowance of bread. This shortage of rations is causing discontent among the men."

After voicing some choice adjectives regarding the quartermaster and contractors whose failures were jeopardizing his campaign, St. Clair summoned Captain Robert Benham, Superintendent of the Horse Department, and instructed him to send 300 baggage horses and 50 of the contractor's horses back down to Fort Hamilton and bring back flour and supplies. Although St. Clair requested Colonel Oldham to send a detachment of his militiamen to escort the supply train, he declined.   Under the circumstances, and believing an armed escort was advisable, St. Clair ordered Captain Faulkner and his company of levies to perform this duty.

Benjamin Van Cleve waited impatiently as Jason repaired a shoe on his horse's back foot. Hired by his uncle, Captain Benham, young Benjamin worked as a pack horseman for fifteen dollars a month. While Van Cleve talked with Jason about heading back down the road to Fort Hamilton, Major Rudolph approached carrying a broken spade which he said needed a good blacksmith's attention. Rudolph also said Ferguson had advised St. Clair this morning the anticipated height of the fort had been attained.

Filling his clay pipe with "Kentucky green," a disgruntled pack horseman standing nearby exclaimed bitterly as Van Cleve joined him: "You know Van, I've shoveled it, and I've lived in it, but I'm not about to take much more of this crap. I'm gonna go back to Hambleton but I might not come back!"

On October 20th Sargent penned in his journal: "Troops placed on one-quarter rations—our stock of supplies is almost expended. St. Clair dispatched a courier to Fort Washington with orders to use all means available to procure and forward the urgently needed supplies."

While St. Clair wrestled with his problems, on Thursday morning, October 21st, General Butler came to his headquarters tent asking:

"Would the general entertain a proposal?"

St. Clair eyed the Irish officer carefully and grimaced painfully as he replied:

"And what would that be General Butler?"

Without hesitation Butler succinctly said:

"Would the general permit me to select a thousand men for a rapid march to the Miami villages before the elements are at a disfavor to us?"

Richard Butler, eldest of Thomas Butler's five sons, was born in Ireland—two of his brothers were also born there and two in Pennsylvania. All five had been officers in the Pennsylvania Line during the Revolutionary War and served with distinction. Well liked by his men, General Butler had discussed his bold plan with several officers and had received favorable endorsement despite the risk involved. But now he didn't have to wait long for St. Clair's cool response:

"General Butler, my campaign will continue as planned and approved!"

That such a bold plan might have been successful, no one would ever know—St. Clair rejected the

proposal and the breach in their relations widened.
Later a few "Monday-morning-quarterbacks" would say
he should have approved this radical departure from
the plan to build a chain of forts from Fort Washington to the Miami villages---a plan submitted and
approved by Washington and so ordered by the Secretary of War. And Arthur St. Clair was a loyal and
dedicated officer who followed orders!

That night "nature" itself took a swipe at St.
Clair's undertaking--a heavy frost and cold weather
which left one-half inch of ice in outside vessels.
Light frosts had previously jeopardized the supply
of forage but now it would be necessary to assign a
guard to escort the horses and cattle to such grass
as might be found available. Men were also detailed to gather prairie grass for the animals. While
thus engaged, and with game plentiful and tempting,
some levies disobediently discharged their firearms
courting punishment of 100 lashes.

Dated October 21st, St. Clair wrote to General
Harmar saying in part: "Sickness and desertion have
reduced the ranks of my force. I have no idea of
the numbers that oppose us but I feel we have a
sufficient force. We have gone 69 miles without
Indians looking at us, nor stealing a horse."

This was in conflict with what Lt. Stephenson
wrote in his journal in late September and mentioned in the post-campaign investigation. The "stolen
horses" might have been taken by disgruntled souls
who returned to Cincinnati or never reported to St.
Clair. But he did err in stating the Indians were
not "looking" at them---they were! In fact, every
move he made was reported to Little Turtle.

Still saddled with his responsibilities as the
governor of the Northwest Territory, on October 21,
1791 St. Clair approved a military escort of a sergeant and 15 troops to protect Thomas Hutchins and
his party who planned to survey the land purchased
by the Ohio Company of Associates and that included
in the Symmes Purchase. The Board of Treasury was

delinquent in providing an advisement regarding the controversy over the eastern boundary of the Symmes Purchase and John Symmes continued his written and verbal attacks against St. Clair's exercise of discretionary powers authorized the governor under the provisions of the Ordinance of 1787. The rancor by Symmes was a continual thorn in St. Clair's side.

Putting aside a map of the Territory Northwest of the Ohio River prepared by Thomas Hutchins, St. Clair turned his attention to Captain Nicholas Hannah, a levy officer from Alexandria, Virginia, who reported discharging ten levies from Virginia that morning. "Sir," said the captain, "As I was telling Colonel Sargent, this matter of the levies' date of enlistment continues to be a problem in determining the expiration of their term of service." And this would continue to be a bone of contention when, on November 12th, 1791, one of the levies who survived the forthcoming surprise attack was court-martialed at Fort Washington. At these proceedings he would object to St. Clair's arbitrary decision the "date of enlistment" was the date the man arrived at Fort Washington, not the date he signed the muster roll. Protesting such decision, the levy would say: "The impropriety of annexing such a condition to the enlistment is without precedence!"

The matter was one which many levies had asked about at Fort Pitt and one which was now the topic of much heated discussion. As one levy declared:

"My damn term of enlistment started the day I signed that muster roll, not the day I reached some 'rendevouz point!' Hell, it ain't my fault that I had to wait at Fort Pitt for thirty days--I oughta get credit for that time!"

Another dscouraged levy injected: "I'm sorta like that John Symmes fellar I heard about down at Cincinnati who was ticked off about old St. Clair's discretionary power out here in this country---he's got the final word on everything!"

A levy from Trenton shrugged his shoulders and

exclaimed bitterly: "Hell man, I thought this damn campaign would be over before the leaves fell!"

Shoeing a horse nearby, Jason had to bite his tongue to keep from saying: "So did St. Clair!"

In a loud voice, a tall lean levy emphatically remarked: "Well, it better end pretty damn soon-- way I got it figured my time is up November 4th!"

Unfortunately, his words were prophetic.

But now, with October already three weeks old, the administrative faux pas regarding determination of a levy's date of enlistment was not St. Clair's only frustration. The shortage of rations, morale, disagreeable weather, and sickness were all matters of deep concern. Plagued by a recurrent attack of gout, St. Clair rode slowly through camp on Friday, October 21st, with Lieutenant Denny. The commander could not help but overhear the men's "bitching" as he paused to watch a fatigue detail laboring in the eight foot square excavation which was to be twenty five feet deep and lined with logs. Intended to be a storage area, it would have a magazine on top and a tunnel connecting it to the central area. It was hard work and inclement weather and the one-quarter rations did nothing for the men's morale.

Among the camp followers St. Clair experienced everything from polite condemnation to verbal abuse by wives and prostitutes. Some of the harlots had headed back down the road with the baggage train as word spread that the military payroll had failed to arrive. Although Colonel Sargent had expressed his happiness in seeing the harlots leave, the adjutant general's elation was not shared by all. As one of the levies who had experienced his first "intimacy" only two months before declared:

"Them ladies can't live on credit! Us fellars only get three dollars a month and ain't even paid that. You can't blame Ella Mae for heading back to Cincinnati where she can see an occasional oblong!"

The "oblong" he referred to was a three dollar government note but they were in short supply---the "wheels" of government bureaucracy turned slowly in Philadelphia and St. Clair's sorely needed payroll had been delayed. In spite of urgent dispatches by St. Clair to Secretary Knox requesting cooperation in getting the payroll forwarded, it would be early December before it was dispatched and be January of 1792 before it arrived at Fort Washington. Many of those who awaited their earned pay in October would not be in the pay line in January--their mortal remains would lie in the snow along the banks of the Wabash 29 miles north of Fort Jefferson.

Although physically and mentally exhausted by his loss of sleep and painful gout, that night St. Clair discussed with Sargent and a few of his field grade officers the open comments he heard among the levies and militia about "deserting." Despite the waning discipline and growing insubordination among the levies and Kentucky militia, it was a tribute to his officer's respect for him that they carried on in the face of such adversities. Trying hard to allay St. Clair's concern, Sargent said: "Soldiers are always bitching and moaning! Perhaps supplies reported by the courier today as coming up the road will permit us to increase the rations--that should stop some of the belly-aching!"

To himself St. Clair rationalized: "The deeper the army gets into this country, the less likely the men will desert--some will probably want to re-enlist rather than head back down the road!"

With morale at a dangerously low ebb, early on Saturday morning, October 22nd, Colonel Sargent announced some beef and one-half pound of flour would be authorized for daily use. On the heels of this announcement, Colonel Oldham informed St. Clair 20 of his militiamen had taken off for home during the night and several more had left that morning. But the ones reported missing returned about noon that day with a Kentucky militia officer from Lexington named Ellis who was escorting 60 militiamen forward to join Oldham's contingent. Ellis said several in his original party had left him at Fort Washington and gone back to Kentucky. Ellis added: "Some have been apprehended and jailed but it is unlikely they will remain incarcerated long."

While Ellis was talking with Colonel Oldham, a small drove of cattle was driven into camp followed by two brigade of horses carrying 18,000 pounds of flour. And St. Clair's spirits received a "shot in the arm" when Major Ferguson reported the construction detail had been reduced to 60 men and thought the final touches could be completed the next day. But the "good news" was soon overshadowed when the results of three court-martial proceedings were put on St. Clair's desk with a recommendation that he not interfere with the sentences in order that all of the men be properly impressed. The sentences of "execution by hanging" were scheduled for sunrise the following morning. Although St. Clair had the discretionary power to commute the death sentences, after review of the specifications and findings, he approved the judgment of the court.

Sunday, October 23rd, was a somber day--one no member of the expedition would forget. Suffering from painful gout, and unable to take any food the past 24 hours, St. Clair had not slept a wink. But he was not alone--there were many in the encampment who faced the new day without sleeping. For three young men it was to be their last sunrise this side of eternity. Adjudged appropriate in the interest of "justice," considered necessary to try and put a halt to the rash of desertions, and hoping it would foster better discipline, as a drum roll echoed ominously across the parade ground and the sun peeked over the horizon, the court-martial sentences were carried out in front of the assembled troops. Two artillerymen had tried to desert declaring they intended to join the Indians---an infantry levy tried to shoot his captain. Another levy had planned to desert but he changed his mind at the last minute and informed his company commander of the plan--the "snitch" was given 100 lashes after the hanging.

This sobering early morning spectacle dug deep into the fibre of everyone including St. Clair himself--the final authority in such matters northwest of the Ohio River in 1791. As if the troops needed further admonishment, the Articles Of War were read to the assembled troops.

Having received word a number of supply wagons would be arriving in camp this Sabbath morning, the adjutant general had obtained St. Clair's approval to increase the ration. Seemingly unbefitting the moment, immediately after the Articles Of War were read, Colonel Sargent announced that everyone would now be authorized a full ration. Remembering the hangings and flogging they had just witnessed, it was difficult to appreciate the increase.

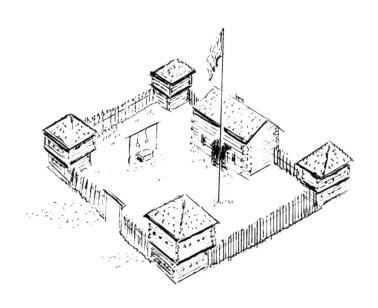

CHAPTER FOURTEEN

A BUCKSKIN MAP

With the grim Sabbath spectacle still haunting everyone's thoughts, and leaving Captain Shaylor in command of Fort Jefferson, the following morning at nine o'clock the army headed on north following the old Indian trail they had come upon east of the so-called "wet prairie." With the rain becoming heavy that afternoon, an early encampment was ordered by St. Clair on a plain skirting the bluffs of a river later to be called "Greene Ville Creek" and a small tributary destined to be named "Mud Creek." At the confluence of these two streams, and about half-way between the Ohio River and the Miami villages, was an old Indian fording place.

Still suffering from the same malady which had plagued him the past several days, and made worse by the bone-chilling rain that had started shortly after two o'clock, St. Clair wrote in his journal:

"October 24, 1791. Left Fort Jefferson garrisoned with Captain Joseph Shaylor in command, Lieutenant Bradley, and 120 men including those unable to stand the rigors of march. Left two cannons. Marched six miles and encamped on good ground at an old Indian fording place. So ill today I had great difficulty in keeping up with the army."

His aide, Ebenezer Denny, penned in his diary:

"We made six miles today and made camp along a handsome creek. St. Clair is not well."

Colonel Sargent's journal this night indicated "We are now 74 miles from Fort Washington." In his

442

post-battle memoirs the adjutant general would say:
"Major George M. Bedinger's indisposition compelled
him to quit the army immediately after its advance
from Fort Jefferson."*

According to the post-expedition investigation
by a congressional committee, on October 24th, 1791
"the army consisted of 1,770 non coms and privates
fit for duty but had no more than a three days supply of flour."

Mary Evenstar sought the "comfort" of her Conestoga early this rainy night. Discouraged by the
day-to-day "living" in their Conestoga, the hanging
spectacle the day before had left her depressed and
in tears most of the time. Although Mary had said
nothing to Jason, she thought she might be pregnant
again. Pensively listening to the rain pelting the
canvas overhead, she recalled a remark she had made
back in Turkey Foot about having her child in some
lean-to in the wilderness.

Beside the Conestoga, partially sheltered from
the cold rain by a piece of canvas stretched overhead, Jason worked by lantern light shoeing a horse
for Ensign Glenn. Not far away soldiers cursed the
quartermaster for providing poor quality tents that
leaked like a sieve and made sleeping difficult, if
not impossible. They were destined to endure five
days of cold, rainy, and overcast weather.

Ironically, it was here General Anthony Wayne
would heed the advice of his officers and scouts
two years later. With winter approaching, he would
decide to go into "winter quarters." Recalling the
demands placed on his predecessor, and St. Clair's
tragic defeat, the campaign commander in 1793 would
not be intimidated by "pressure" from anyone or enticed by "bait" the Indians tempted him with. Even
when Little Turtle would wipe out a 20 wagon supply
convoy near Fort St. Clair on October 17th in 1793,
Wayne would not be drawn into a wilderness battle.

* Pg 266, Ohio Arch. & Hist. Soc. Pubs (OAAHSP) Vol 33, 1925

The wilderness outpost Wayme built in October of 1793 would be named "Fort Greene Ville" in honor of his friend during the Revolutionary War, General Nathaniel Greene. From here, on December 23, 1793, "Dandy" Wayne--so nicknamed because of his critical attention to dress--would send a detachment, led by Major Henry Burbeck, 23 miles northwest where they would build a fort after burying 600 human skulls and bones they found in the snow along the banks of the Wabash. These would be the mortal remains of a majority of those who camped with St. Clair's army October 24th, 1791.

In late December of 1793 Wayne would consider naming the outpost on the banks of the Wabash "Fort Restitution" but would decide on a more appropriate name for this previously lost, but recovered, site. In the orders assigning Captain Alexander Gibson as the first commander of the new outpost--the deepest penetration into the Northwest Territory's "Indian country" in 1793--Wayne called it "Fort Recovery!"

Ignoring Chief Little Turtle's admonishment in 1794 that "The Americans are now led by a chief who never sleeps. There is something whispers to me it would be prudent to listen to his offers of peace," and urged on by British Colonel Richard England at Detroit when he learned the Indians had "fired" the Miami chief and would follow "Blue Jacket," on June 30th, 1794 the Shawnee War Chief would lead 1,000 warriors in an unsuccessful two day assault against Fort Recovery. Although the Indians would kill 50 Americans, and steal 300 horses in the attack, Fort Recovery would hold and "break the back" of the red man's resistance to the white man's encroachment--- on August 20th, 1794 Wayne would watch the Indians wave the white truce flag at Fallen Timbers.

But in October of 1791 there was confidence in Little Turtle and Tecumseh's intelligence gathering system which provided reports of St. Clair's march. And, in late October, Chief Me-she-kin-no-quah, the 39 year old chief of the Miamis had everyone's ear

as he outlined his plan to "surprise" the army that
dared march against them with a declared intent to
"extirpate the Indians."   Listening impassively to
his briefing was Chief Catahecassa, or Black Hoof,
an elderly Shawnee chief more than 51 years of age;
Tarhe "The Crane," the 49 year old Grand Sachem of
the Wyandots; Buckongahelas or Deer Chaser, chief
of the Delawares; Chief Chaubeenee, the Potawatomi
Indian's youthful sachem; Chief Au-goosh-away, the
Ottawa sachem; Apekonit, or "carrot top," an adopted son of Little Turtle whose red hair had prompted
his Indian name; Wasegoboah, the husband of Little
Turtle's sister, Tecumsapease; and the Shawnee War
Chief whose Indian name, "Wey-ya-pier-sen-wah," was
said to mean "one who wears a blue jacket."

Standing near Blue Jacket was a white man who
wore a long, dirty red coat--it was Simon Girty, or
"The White Savage" as some called him. His awesome
appearance prompted mixed feelings of respect and
fear. He had sunken gray eyes, heavy eyebrows, a
flat nose, tobacco stained teeth, and a forbidding
facial expression. Around his head he wore a silk
handkerchief pulled low over one eyebrow to conceal
an ugly scar--it was a tomahawk wound given him by
Captain Joseph Brant when Girty made a disparaging
remark more than a decade before.

As Little Turtle listened to runners say other
sachems were ready to join him along the trail when
he marched against the white invader, seventy-five
miles southwest sickness and rainy weather prompted
St. Clair to "sit tight" on October 25th. With the
cold rain pelting the camp, and making life miserable for the hungry soldiers whose only shelter was
a leaky "quartermaster issue" tent, in his journal
that evening Colonel Sargent wrote:

"Inclement weather. Some clothing, and 10,000
pounds of flour arrived today. A party of Virginia
levies was discharged."

Long, gray curtains of cold and dismal drench-
ing rain greeted early risers on Wednesday, October

26th. Considering the inclement weather, and waiting for supplies said to be coming up the road, St.
Clair decided he would not march today. An express
message from Hodgdon this morning indicated 13,000
pounds of flour would arrive October 27th. Hodgdon
also said the horses ordered back on the 18th had
been sent on to Fort Washington where supplies were
"precariously short." In the courier's pouch today
was a communique from the Secretary of War advising
St. Clair of the "dire necessity of proceeding with
unequivocal haste!" The message left the commander
little room for discretion.

Faced with the urgent need for more supplies,
St. Clair immediately ordered some pack horses and
a 20 man escort back to Fort Hamilton. That afternoon a reconnaissance party returned to camp saying
they had encountered five Indians about 15 miles in
advance of the camp. As one scout declared: "Those
red-skins escaped but they left their blankets and
tomahawks!" Hearing this, St. Clair ordered Oldham
and his militiamen to cross the creek and make camp
about a half mile in advance of the main camp.

That night Sargent wrote in his journal: "The
Virginia battalion is melting down fast. Darke discharged 13 men today. The whole battalion may soon
follow their example."

The following morning, October 27th, St. Clair
reviewed with his staff officers their predicament.
His foot swollen, and in severe pain, the commander
detailed what they were painfully aware of---winter
was fast approaching, the roads were becoming worse
each day, the army was a long way from their supply
base, morale was low, and the supply of forage was
almost exhausted. It served no purpose to dwell on
the fact that thirty days ago this land around them
would have provided excellent forage. Or, for that
matter, the fact that whereas St. Clair had planned
to leave Fort Washington in early July with 4,128
troops, this morning the adjutant general reported
"1,700 effectives present or accounted for!" There

was no need to say the strength figure included the disgruntled levies who clamored: "My time is up!"

The uninspiring meeting having ended this damp and dreary Thursday morning, the commander received a report from Quartermaster Reynolds indicating the last available ration of flour had been issued. He added: "There will be no bread tomorrow!"

Colonel Sargent summed up the situation in his journal that evening writing: "Sickness, shortage of provisions, and open rebellion, coupled with the damp, cold, and cloudy weather, plague our march."

A realist, Ebenezer Denny penned in his diary: "October 27 - The season is so far advanced it will be impractical to continue the campaign. We expect flour tomorrow which will enable us to move forward a few marches, beyond that, our prospects are very gloomy."

Unable to sleep, and listening to the driving rain shake the canvas of the Conestoga, Mary moved close to Jason as a wolf howled in the nearby woods and the scream of a panther stabbed the night air. Jason was awake and patted Mary gently on her back side saying softly: "Go to sleep. You would howl too if you were out in that rain." Although always the optimist, during their conversation this afternoon Mary perceived what she felt was a "chink" in Jason's determination to continue this undertaking. Pondering the thought tomorrow might be the day she would share her "secret" with Jason, Mary fell into the arms of Morpheus.

Just before dark today the long-expected Chief Piomingo and 20 of his Chickasaw warriors showed up and declared to St. Clair their long-standing deep-rooted animosity toward all of the Indians north of the Ohio, particularly the Kickapoos. In trying to lift St. Clair's spirits this evening, George Adams told him two of the volunteers, George and William Colbert, who accompanied the Chickasaws from Fort Washington, "were of Scottish descent!" Plagued by his gout, St. Clair failed miserably in his attempt to appreciate the humor of Adams' remark.

Morning arrived on October 28th accompanied by a brief shower of snow and hail. Then, just before noon, the clouds parted and the sun appeared. Cold as it was, it was better than the rain and everyone felt better. As if taking their cue from the sun, a short time later 74 pack horses arrived carrying 12,000 pounds of flour. Weakened by their lack of sufficient forage, the pack horses could only carry 162 pounds. Some warm clothing arrived too but the shipment did not include the urgently needed woolen overalls and socks that were requisitioned---a note from Hodgdon indicated these "were on the way."

Although the 12,000 pounds of flour was only a four days supply at full rations, St. Clair hoped this was a harbinger of better things to come. The "good news" about full rations and some warm clothing swept through the camp like wildfire and, with word circulating that more supplies were now on the way, General St. Clair was not surprised when Major Hamtramck came to his headquarters tent and said 40 of the six-month levies discharged that day had enlisted in the regular army.

But his elation was short lived---Major Butler came to his tent that afternoon saying two privates of his battalion had been fired on by Indians about three miles from camp. Although one of the levies had been killed, the other did manage to return to camp but was seriously wounded. Later that afternoon two of Colonel Oldham's militiamen were attack by Indians in the forward area and only one made it back to camp--he reported his comrade had probably been taken prisoner. Still later, just after nine o'clock that night, a sentry put the entire camp in a state of alarm when he reported seeing an Indian near the perimeter of the camp. Recalling Washington's farewell admonishment, St. Clair ordered the troops to be under arms at the drum's first tap the following morning. Also remembering how Washington often prayed at Valley Forge, St. Clair kneeled and prayed this Friday night, the 28th of October.

Early the following morning a bridge was built across the rivulet in front of camp and a fatigue party of 120 men with a militia escort was ordered across the creek to start opening a road the survey party indicated would closely parallel the Indian trail which now snaked off through the woods northwest. St. Clair also requested Chief Piomingo and his warriors, along with Captain Richard Sparks and four riflemen, to reconnoiter the area ahead of the army to determine if there was an enemy threat, the strength and location of such a threat if there be one, and to capture an Indian for interrogation if any could be found.

Then, and since most of the baggage horses had been detailed to the quartermaster for transport of supplies, St. Clair ordered a three-day ration of flour be issued in order to make horses available to carry baggage. At three o'clock that afternoon the fatigue party returned to camp.

Agreeable to St. Clair's orders, the following morning, October 30th, Captain William Powers and a detail of the militiamen crossed the creek at nine o'clock and took the "point." With a fatigue party of 130 woodsmen opening a single road on a heading approximating 340 degrees, and leaving behind their quartermaster tents which had proved of little use in rainy weather, the army marched away from what Ebenezer Denny called "a very handsome encampment."

With only minimal information about the region through which they marched, St. Clair's army pushed deeper into the Indian country. Watching St. Clair riding northwest this Sabbath, Jason could not help but marvel that the old veteran was able to keep up with the army—but he did! Late in the afternoon, having marched almost eight miles, the army camped on high ground just east of where Captain Powers said there was a large, deep peat bog. Two and one half miles south of what was destined to be called the Stillwater River, this camp site would later be

named Camp Sulphur Springs by St. Clair's military
successor. Typical of the many stories which would
later circulate concerning this wet and soggy marsh
area--a place where the C.C.C. & St. Louis Railroad
would cross Route 49 in the 20th century--was one
saying a large brass cannon became mired in the bog
and was left there in 1791.   Such a loss was never
reported to, or by, St. Clair and Sargent's journal
for October 30th only stated: "Encamped on a small
run of poor water 81 miles from Fort Washingon."

     But trains and automobiles were unheard of as
St. Clair listened to Sargent say a large number of
baggage horses were coming up the road and would be
arriving the next day. He had hardly finished with
his report when Colonel Oldham walked into the tent
declaring there was great dissatisfaction among his
men. "They are annoyed by the delays and impatient
to get back to their homes." Although one-third of
his militiamen had expressed their determination to
go home, Oldham assured St. Clair he had prevailed
upon them to stay. But even as he was talking with
St. Clair, between 60 and 70 of his militiamen were
loudly venting their discontent and swearing to not
only "head home" but to intercept the supply convoy
reported to be coming up the road.

     In the early morning hours on October 31st, as
gale force winds and a cold driving rain raked the
camp site, occasional flashes of lightning revealed
60 sneaky figures "going over the hill!" Some were
leading horses! The "desertions" really came as no
surprise--many of the missing men at roll call had
been threatening to "go home." But it was discouraging for Colonel Oldham when Captain Presley Gray,
Captain Adam Guthrie, and the other officers of his
command reported the names of the sixty missing men
which included Sergeant Abner Chalfin and Privates
Thomas Hatfield, Philip Friggs, John Drew, Nicholas
Moore, Jeremiah Sturgin, Solomon Serring, Willford
Haydon, Benjamin Lasly, Philip Strange, David Mead,
Jeremiah Paine, Joseph Tibbes, Dennis Smith, Garvis

Houghman, John Samuels, Mason Woots, John Stilwell, Joseph Stilwell, and John Stilwill, Sr.*

Understandably dejected, the militia commander dutifully went to Colonel Sargent's tent and handed him a list of the sixty missing men. Glancing over the hastily written list, Sargent noticed the names of John Stillwell, Sr. and John Stillwill and said: "Like father, like son I suppose!" Without waiting for a reply, Sargent arose from his chair and added bluntly: "I am certain General St. Clair will want to see this. I presume you have an explanation!"

Although some future writers would indicate it was "300 men" who deserted, suffice the 60 that did "desert" that morning posed a serious threat to St. Clair's urgently needed supplies. And, faced with the decision of dispatching military protection for the critically needed supplies at the peril of re- ducing the strength of his "effectives," St. Clair never hesitated--he ordered Major Hamtramck and 300 men of the First Infantry, "the cream of his army," in quick pursuit back toward Fort Jefferson. Faced with retreat, or bringing up provisions to ease the food shortage predicament, he acted with dispatch. Later St. Clair would state he instructed Hamtramck to march only 25 miles, or until he met the supply convoy. In his letter to General Harmar on October 31st, 1791 St. Clair stated: "Specific orders were given him (Major J. Hamtramck) to send a sufficient guard back with the first provision convoy and to return with the second to rejoin the army."

Regardless of Hamtramck's "instructions," 300 "regulars" of the First Infantry would not be along the banks of the Wabash River a few days later. In his late-evening retrospection on November 4th, St. Clair would say Hamtramck's decision to proceed be- yond the "25 miles" limit was probably a fortuitous one in light of what happened.

* "Muster Rolls, Record Group, Records of the Adjutant General's Office, Entry 54, Box 1

But that was four eventful days in the future
as word about the "desertion," a possible threat to
the resupply effort, and non-receipt of the payroll
swept the camp like a prairie fire with the flames
fanned by complaints about short rations, back pay,
and the levies' concern about their term of enlistment. As one levy declared bitterly:

"Major Gaither says my enlistment didn't start
until I got to Fort Washington. That's a bunch of
crap! I've been gone from home six months and I've
a good mind to go home just like them damn Kentucky
militiamen did!"

But he didn't--he remembered the three men who
had been hanged at Fort Jefferson. Unfortunately,
he would also be dead before the week ended. Now a
pock-marked levy from Maryland vented his feelings:

"Yeah, them damn Kentuckians take off and that
colonel says, 'Oh, they just went home!' Hell, you
let one of us do that and the old general will sure
as hell call it 'desertion.' You can't win in this
damn army!"

A levy who was cleaning his gun remarked: "I
don't want to win, I just want to break even!"

One hundred and fifty years later, on November
5th, 1949, the Secretary of Defense, Louis Johnson,
would stress the importance of "morale" as he spoke
to the American Legion Convention in Indianapolis,
Indiana. As Secretary Johnson would declare: "The
incident at Fort Recovery on November 4th, 1791 was
both suggestive and significant! Morale was a big
factor in General St. Clair's defeat and the victorious campaign of General Anthony Wayne."

But on October 31st, 1791, St. Clair's spirits
were lifted as 212 horses--each carrying 155 pounds
of flour--arrived. Richard Benham reported he left
1,200 pounds of flour at Fort Jefferson, had met 50
disgruntled militiamen who gave him no trouble, and
added: "The First Infantry was in quick pursuit of
those deserters!" In his conversation with Captain
Denny, young Benjamin Van Cleve had nothing but the

highest praise for Captain William Faulkner, Lieutenant Huston, and their 30-rifle military escort.

Standing near Colonel Sargent and watching the the flour being unloaded, Jason and Hank heard the adjutant general mutter: "32,000 pounds of flour at seven cents a pound, that's $2,240. Now if we only had some of that eight cents a pound beef! We have an adequate supply of whisky but that's a poor substitute for good victuals!" That evening he penned in his journal: "We are deprived of 300 effectives, the best in the service."

Deciding to wait for Major Hamtramck's return, and the arrival of the second convoy of provisions, St. Clair ordered all heavy, unnecessary equipment be deposited here behind an embankment in order to lighten the load on the weakened pack horses. That finished, St. Clair spent the rest of the afternoon preparing a record for Secretary Knox of happenings since October 21st—his illness had precluded entry of such information in his journal. In his express dispatch to Henry Knox dated November 1, 1791, St. Clair stated:

"Since the 22nd of October I have been plagued with repeated attacks of a bilious colic, rheumatic asthma, and gout in my arm and hand. Now my stomach is relieved and the cough, which had become excessive, is gone."

He also mentioned having received equipment of an inferior quality supplied by the quartermaster. Recalling General Butler's often expressed comments about having an "in" with Knox, St. Clair included in this letter: "General Butler is displeased with my decision against his proposal to take a force of of soldiers and proceed on to Miamitown alone. It was my considered judgment this would be an unwise action and would not provide for building intervening fortifications as planned."

He concluded this November 1st communique saying: "The utmost harmony has prevailed through the army during the campaign so far."

Apparently Richard Butler was not held in such high favor by Henry Knox as he thought. In response to St. Clair's November 1st communique--and as yet unaware of the adversity the army had suffered--the Secretary's letter of December 2, 1791 to St. Clair would indicate James Wilkinson had been appointed a Lieutenant Colonel and was to be Commandant of the 2nd Infantry Regiment; the duties of the Adjutant General were to be given Lieutenant Colonel Francis Mentges; and would provide for dismissal of General Richard Butler and terminatiion of the service of the Pennsylvania levies. The irony of this letter was Secretary Knox's closing remark:

"I hope by now you are back at Fort Washington and crowned with success!"

But on Tuesday, the 1st of November, 81 miles north of Cincinnati a party of discharged Virginia levies noisily prepared to head down the wilderness road. Shoeing Captain Alexander Trueman's horse, Jason paused for a moment and looked at the levies as the cavalry officer from Maryland said bitterly: "I'm sorry to see them go. With the First Infantry gone, we now have less than fourteen hundred men!"

Standing nearby, Captain Van Swearingen glanced at the exuberant levies and nodded. The 30 year old officer, son of Thomas Swearingen IV and Mary Morgan, had led 88 levies from Winchester, Virginia to Fort Washington after making out his will August 4th, 1791 in Berkeley County, Virginia. His uncle, "Indian " Van (1742-1793), a son of "Thomas of the Ferry" Swearingen, witnessed his will.* The captain owned a plantation in Berkeley County that had been willed to him by his father who died February 20th, 1786. Having spent more than a month escorting his party of levies west, he was well aware of how most of them felt about this wilderness undertaking.

* Francis B. Heitman's "Historical Register of Officers of the Continental Army" (1914) erroneously combined the captain's Service Record with those of "Indian" Van Swearingen Pg 529

Thoughtfully eyeing the levies who now started south on the wilderness road shouting and waving at those whose "time" had not expired, Van Swearingen remarked: "I tell you one thing, Major Bedinger is getting pretty well fed up with the way things are going. I wouldn't be surprised if he didn't resign his commission!"

Having finished shoeing Trueman's horse, Jason looked at Captain Swearingen and said:

"Begging the captain's pardon, there is something I have been meaning to ask you. Would your given name be Marmaduke?"

"Heavens no," replied the captain. "My given name is Van and I'm the only Swearingen in the army that I know of. Why do you ask?"

Jason explained about the old codger he met in Pennsylvania and what he had said about a Marmaduke Swearingen who was captured. The captain listened carefully and then said:

"Marmaduke huh? That'd be a distant cousin of mine--younger than me. He's a son of John and Kate Swearingen. They moved out to western Pennsylvania back when relations between Virginia and her northern neighbor were strained. John was one of those Swearingens who signed a petition to create a new state called 'Westsylvania'--Pennsylvania called it an act of treason! But regardless of the settler's feelings concerning that disputed area, the common enemy was the Indians. John had a lot of land, and a flock of kids! Let's see, there was Daniel, the oldest, Elizabeth, John, Van, Drucilla, Sarah--she is about my age and married Charles Larsh in 1781-- Marmaduke, Joseph, Charles, Isaac Stull, Samuel, Andrew, and the youngest, Thomas." *

* Labeled "History's Biggest Hoax" by George Swetman (PITTSBURGH PRESS, Oct 8, 1972, the HORN PAPERS by W.F. Horn (HERALD PRESS Scottdale, PA 1945) erroneously refer to "Vance" and "Steele" as brothers of Marmaduke, and sons of James and Eliza Swerangen of Staunton, Virginia on page 309.

With a smile Captain Van Swearingen continued:
"Van, Marmaduke's older brother, married Susannah
Greathouse in Westmoreland County eleven years ago.
Charles, four years younger than Marmaduke, married
Nancy Pottenger in 1788. As you can easily see, we
Swearingens are a prolific bunch---well, all except
me! As General Butler said this summer, 'Ragweeds
and Swearingens are going to take this country!'"

The smile on the captain's face faded as Jason
asked: "Did the Indians capture Marmaduke?"

"Good question Mr. Evenstar! And I must admit
I don't know--and I don't know anyone in the family
who does. Some say Duke always had a fancy to live
with the Indians and he may have just wandered off.
Seems doubtful the Indians would have adopted him
at his age but who knows for sure.* Then too, some
folks have mixed up Marmaduke's disappearance with
that of another Swearingen's capture."

A quizzical look on Jason's face prompted the
captain to quickly add: "I also have an uncle who
is called "Indian" Van Swearingen. As a matter of
fact, he and his wife, Eleanor, and their daughter,
Drucilla, witnessed my will just before I came out
here. His son, Thomas Swearingen, was captured by
Indians west of Fort Pitt four years ago this past
September." **

---

* "Marmaduke Swearingen, when about 17 years old, was
captured by the Shawnee Indians some time during the
Revolutionary War." (Pg 19, FAMILY REGISTER OF GERRET
van SWERINGEN AND DESCENDANTS." 2nd Ed., 1894). John
Swearingen's Will, signed August 3, 1784, and proven
September 3, 1784 in Fayette County, PA includes: "I
will that if my son Marmonduke Sweringen have one year
of my Negrow fellow Herry then to return to my wife."
(Pg 19-20, Book A, Wills of Fayette County, PA).

** "Six Men Named Van Swearingen" (1992) by Louise F.
Johnson, Round Rock, TX 78664-3222

"Excuse me Van," said Captain Trueman, "I hate to interrupt your genealogical dissertation but we are due at General St. Clair's tent in five minutes and I suggest we not be late. Scuttlebut has it he plans to march in the morning."

"Provided we can get him on a horse," said Van Swearingen with a mischievous smile. "Let's go!"

That afternoon while Hank and Jason were talking about this undertaking and the number of levies who had left the army, Jason said abruptly: "Hank, I have a problem! My wife is worried sick over the way the army is shrinking. She's been sick to her stomach the past few mornings and talks about wanting to turn around and head back down the road."

Hank cradled his chin between his index finger and thumb and scratched his beard slowly before he drawled: "Well, she's right about the army shrinking! And I gotta admit this thing is taking a mite longer than I figured. Been more than seven weeks since I left home and Sarah's sure to be wondering where I am. Glancing at the western sky he added: "Its gittin' mighty late to be going any further up north. Might be better to come back up next spring and look for some land."

Jason nodded. He had been giving some thought to the same thing. His wife had not only mentioned wanting to return to Cincinnati, she suggested they consider going back to Baltimore. And, in spite of what the Viscount de Malartie, St. Clair's aide-de-camp, said concerning St. Clair having confided the army was only 50 miles from Miamitown, Jason could not reconcile that with what the surveyor told him about being 81 miles from Fort Washignton when Hank had heard veterans of General Harmar's campaign say they marched 170 miles to the Miami villages. They said they marched 65 miles northeast before heading northwest, but even such a circuitous routing could not be shortened to 131 miles by a direct route—no way! Hank was not a mathematician or a geographer, but admitted he had a funny feeling about following the army through a wilderness region no one had the slightest knowledge of. As Hank quipped: "A feller could get killed doing this!"

Malartie, the Frenchman who had volunteered to join the 1791 expedition, had a copy of the "Map of British and French Dominons in America" (1755) that John Mitchell made in England. It was the same map used at the peace conference in 1783 to mark boundaries but it was of little use for this wilderness undertaking.   St. Clair's primary knowledge of the wilderness region through which his army marched in 1791 was based on a map provided by Thomas Hutchins and one which had been made by Abel Buell in 1785. Unfortunately, none of the maps indicated his route of march would cross the headwaters of the Wabash.

Figuring Major Hamtramck could easily catch up with the relatively slow-moving army, on Wednesday morning, November 2nd, under leaden skies and with snow flakes heralding the coming winter, St. Clair gave the order to march from a supine position--the expedition commander was carried from the camp on a litter. In accordance with a reconnaissance report by Captain Powers, a few degrees change to the west in the line of march would parallel the old Indian trail and "will bring the army to a big bend in the river ahead which then flows north."

Seeing St. Clair being carried on a litter, an insolent young Kentucky militiaman jerked his thumb toward the general declaring sarcastically: "Would you look at that old gray-haired bastard! He just lays there on his back watching the birds and leads us deeper and deeper into this damn wilderness that is full of red niggers!"

Although being carried, St. Clair was thinking about his army---an army sadly depleted until Major Hamtramck returned with the army's only "seasoned" regulars. Unfortunately the war veterans that were recruited had been drilled in mass tactics used in European warfare--not wilderness fighting. Most of the recruits in the Second Infantry had been taken

from the streets, alleys, and jails of Philadelphia
and Baltimore and needed more training. A few were
old and infirm and were having difficulty enduring
the exposure and hardships of the march. The ranks
of the inexperienced six-month levies were being
drained by the day by day expiration of their terms
of service. St. Clair flinched from a stab of pain
and muttered:

"The one saving grace in my army are officers
like Colonel Gibson, Major Heart, Captain Kirkwood,
Captain Piatt, Captain Doyle, Captain Ford, Captain
Cribbs, and Captain Van Swearingen. Given enough
time, they could whip these men into shape."

But "time" was not St. Clair's ally and now he
frowned as his thoughts turned to Oldham's militiamen. "One good man out of every three I would say.
I must speak again with Colonel Oldham about their
insubordination!"

Jostled by the men who carried his litter, St.
Clair gritted his teeth and silently endured the
painful ordeal as events of the past flashed across
his mind. As if it had been yesterday, he recalled
how he had surrendered Fort Ticonderoga to General
Burgoyne. Although court-martialed in September of
1778 and acquitted of any failure of leadership, he
still carried the scars of this single "black mark"
against an otherwise spotless record of service and
prayed for the opportunity to atone for this "failure." This old "wound" may have been instrumental
in the aging veteran's decision not to approve Butler's proposal which would have left St. Clair behind. Submitting to the humility of being carried
by litter, St. Clair consoled himself with a single
thought--his solemn promise to President Washington
to end the hostilities in the Northwest Territory!

In the bone-chilling weather it was impossible
for the troops to enjoy their midday meal Wdnesday,
November 2nd, on the north bank of a small river at
a place St. Clair's successor would later call Camp
Stillwater noting in his journal this stream was 86

miles from Fort Washington. But everyone ate their
ration hungrily casting furtive looks back down the
road---pack horses had brought flour and surely the
sugar and salt and other supplies could not be very
far behind. A rumor circulating indicated a Mister
Ernest or Wells had confided to a pack horseman on
October 31st that there was 24 days of flour, 14 of
whisky, 19 of salt, 27 of soap, 8 of candles, and 6
of beef in the commissary magazine at Fort Hamilton
but there were not enough pack horses to bring the
provisions forward. In his post-expedition report,
Samuel Hodgdon stated "most needed rations remained
in the magazine at Fort Hamilton." Only 350 of the
urgently needed pack horses had been procured.

When Jason optimistically advised his wife the
army had sufficient flour on hand to last until the
7th day of November, Mary merely said saucily: "Man
doth not live by bread only you know!"

Jason offered no reply--he was well acquainted
with the 3rd verse, 8th chapter of Deuteronomy.

Mary was more concerned with what had happened
to one of the camp followers, a woman, who had disappeared that morning. Although the guard had been
doubled on each flank that morning, it was now said
a rifleman had been found dead in the woods--he had
been scalped! Courageous as Mary tried to appear,
Jason knew his wife was scared to death.

Forging on northwest that afternoon the horse-
play of the older troops subsided and no longer did
anyone hear "there's an Indian behind that tree" or
"lookout for that red nigger!" And no more did the
soldiers wander away from the line of march gathering walnuts and hickory nuts. Whereas there was an
occasional imitation of the sounds of crows, owls,
and various animals--or false warnings which scared
the unseasoned levies and rattled the nerves of all
the camp followers--this afternoon an atmosphere of
apprehension prevailed.

Shortly following the midday halt, and topping
the brow of a little rise, the black earth became a

sea of ankle-deep muck making walking tiresome and bogging down wagons in what would later be known as Black Leech Woods. Exhausted after seven miles of wearisome marching, late in the afternoon the army encamped on the banks of what would later be called the Mississinewa. It was a small river that flowed west and emptied into the Wabash but St. Clair was unaware of this on November 2nd, 1791. And most of the weary souls who camped this night on the banks of the wilderness stream would never see the little crossroads settlement that was destined to blossom, and die, on the hill ahead--a settlement that would be called "Rose Hill."

Aggreeable to Colonel Oldham's request to camp separately, St. Clair ordered the Kentucky militia across the river. Crossing the stream on the eastern fringe of the army's camp area, and pausing to allow his horse to drink, one of the militiamen saw Hank Weiser a short way upstream obtaining a bucket of water. Dismounting, the militiaman struck up a conversation with Hank:

"Seems to me I've laid eyes on you somewhere," said the militiaman. "Ever been down southwest of Lexington? Bardstown maybe?"

"That I have," replied Hank. "Friend of mine and I was down that way this summer. You happen to know a settler down there by the name of Ash?"

"Sure," said the militiaman. "That's where I saw you. Old man Ash was telling you about his son that was taken by the Indians! His other boy, Ben, is with us here! Ben's dead set on finding George. Thinks he might be with that nest of Indian thieves up around Little Turtle's Town."

Hank listened carefully--he had heard the same story before. Being a good listener, Hank endeared himself to the talkative militiaman who now glanced around to make certain no one could hear his voice and said in a low voice:

"Notice anything peculiar about this stream?"

Hank looked at the stream, glanced to the left

461

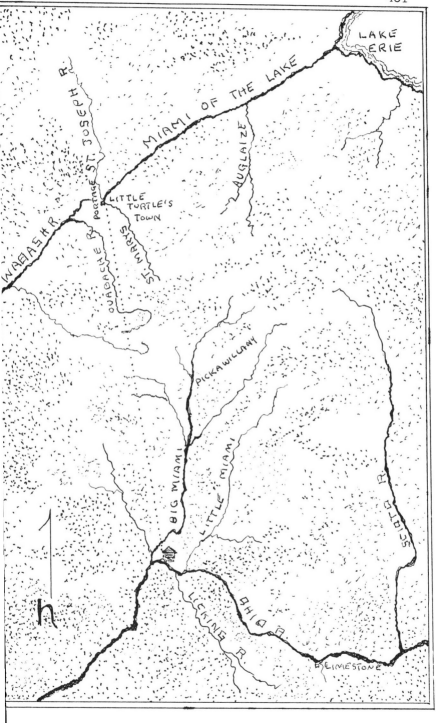

and right, and then eyed the militiaman cautiously
as he replied: "Nope---you see one wilderness crik
and you've seen 'em all!"

With a secretive smile the militiaman confided
in a low voice: "See, this one flows west!"

"So?" Obviously the stream flowed toward the
setting sun but Hank did not catch the significance
of the river's course. With Hank's face reflecting
complete puzzlement, the militiaman surreptitiously
glanced around to see if anyone was watching. Satisfied no one could see him, he pulled a yellowish-
gray piece of buckskin from his coat and, unfolding
it, he pointed to what was a map declaring:

"See, this is the first river we have crossed
that flows west!"

Hank studied the map which had been made using
what appeared to be red and blue berry juice. Hank
was still trying to comprehend the meaning of the
buckskin map when the militiaman remarked:

"The other streams we have crossed since Fort
Hamilton have all flowed east but this one flows in
the direction of the setting sun. Only a few miles
ahead we cross the headwaters of the Ouabache River
which flows east a little way and then doubles back
and this Indian trail crosses it again." Pointing
to a spot on the map he added: "The Ouabache flows
west at that fording place and then turns north."

"Hold on there--ease up a bit. You got me all
addled!" Hank rested the barrel of his gun against
the crook of his left arm, thoughtfully scratched
the side of his head, and continued: "What's this
Ouabache River? And where did you get that map?"

"Ouabache? That's what early French explorers
called the Wabash my father says. It's the French
spelling of an Indian word meaning 'white' he told
me." Pointing to the map the militiaman continued:
"See, it snakes around north and west and flows into the 'Wabash.' I got this map from some thieving
redskin along the Licking southwest of Limestone--
said he got it from a trapper." With a smile that

needed no explanation, the militiaman added: "That red-skinned horse-thief didn't need it anymore!"

Tracing the meandering course of the westward flowing river on the map, and then pointing toward the stream at their feet, the militiaman said: "The way I figure, we're here along this Indian trail!"

Although crude, if correct the army was a long way from the Miami villages. Hank remembered Major Ferguson saying earlier that day that St. Clair was of the opinion they were nearing their destination. Glancing up from the map, Hank instinctively said:

"Has the general seen this? Colonel Oldham?"

"Hell no," replied the militiaman adamantly. My cousin Innes wanted to join the army but old St. Clair refused to recognize his officer's commission in the Kentucky militia. Well, if my kinfolk ain't good enough for his army, St. Clair can do his own navigating. And besides, St. Clair sent that Chief Piomingo forward to scout the area so that Indian's probably found that fording place on the Ouabache by now. I'd sure be obliged if you wasn't to tell anyone about this map."

Hank said nothing--he had not asked to see the map.   Later that evening, seated by the fire, Hank shared this disclosure with Jason.   Staring at the orange flames licking freshly cut wood, Jason pondered what Hank had just said---intuitively both he and Hank had felt they were some distance from the Miami villages. Jason's thoughts were suddenly interrupted when from out of the darkness across the stream he heard what appeared to be the sound of a violin.

Indeed, seated on a stump near the fire in the Kentucky militia's camp area, John McGinnis cradled an old violin beneath his bearded chin and "sawed" on his out-of-tune fiddle. Moments later the sound of a harmonica was heard. Although their "harmony" left something to be desired, it helped to lift the spirits of some that night--to others it was just a reminder of happier days.

Never taking his eyes off the fire, Jason listened for a while and then shook his head slowly as he muttered: "It is almost sinful what that fellar is doing with that violin!"

Sensing Jason's obvious disapproval of the way someone was "murdering" a fiddle, Hank switched his chew to the other cheek, let fly a stream of brownish fluid into the fire, and never cracked a smile as he said dryly: "Pretty bad, ain't it! I might not let that fellar back across the Ohio!" Said in jest, he had no way of knowing tonight was the last time that militiaman would ever play his violin—48 hours later his lifeless desecrated body and broken violin would lie along the banks of a little stream his comrade-in arm's buckskin map indicated was the "Ouabache."

A short distance from where Jason and Hank sat watching their fire, a number of tired and footsore soldiers huddled around their campfire like kittens trying to cozy up to a warm brick. A bone-chilling wind whipped through the ghost-like wilderness sentinels that rimmed the encampment but the cold that gripped most this night was one fire didn't remove. And their meager meal had done nothing to raise the spirits of the uneasy troops who had heard varying stories about one of their military comrades being killed and the hysterical scream of the female camp follower who had disappeared that morning. With a gnawing feeling in the pit of his stomach, Private Thomas Irwin, a young artillery wagoner, glanced at twenty-one year old Samuel McDowell and remarked:

"Cook says we ain't to worry Sam—he won't run out of soup. Every time he hands out a tin of soup he puts in a tin of water!"

Regardless of his intent, the comment produced only a few half-hearted laughs and this remark by a recruit with peach fuzz on his face:

"Funny! Very funny! My belly button is playing tunes on my back bone and you're cracking jokes about our rations!"

Standing close to the fire and briskly rubbing his weather-beaten hands together, a crusty recruit bitterly complained: "Gettin' so you can't believe nobody any more! That damn recruiting officer promised me I'd get four pairs of shoes, socks, pants, coat, blanket, a daily ration of a pound of meat or fish, a pound and a half of flour or bread, salt, vinegar, soap, candles, a half pint of whiskey, and three dollars a month. Now here I am in the middle of nowhere with a cold ass, a hungry gut, and that damn prissy adjutant general promising, 'provisions and the pay roll are on the way!' Well, I'll tell you now, them supplies and pay roll better catch up with us pretty quick or I'll be on my way back down the road and that Colonel Sargent can take his damn three dollars a month and shove it up his ass!"

With a loud, coarse burst of laughter, another recruit with a silly looking feather in his cap exclaimed: "I'm with you Walt--and if it's as big as he thinks it is, he can get the whole damn pay roll up his ass too!"

Neither the supply convoy or the pay roll were destined to "catch up" with the army and neither of the two recruits were destined to go back down the wilderness road--only two days later their lifeless bodies would be covered with a blanket of snow just eight miles north of where they "bitched" tonight.

A quarrelsome soldier called Max now remarked: "This damn army life ain't what it's cracked up to be. And the further we get in this woods, the more of them red niggers we're bound to find."

They didn't have to find them---from carefully selected observation places in the woods the Indian spies watched every move the army made. Anticipating the army would maintain a line of march closely paralleling the old Indian trail, Little Turtle had seized the initiative and was leading his warriors southeast a discrete distance west of the trail and avoiding observation by scouts St. Clair might send to scour the advance area. And, leaving nothing to

chance, the crafty Little Turtle had dispatched his
second-in-command, Blue Jacket, to take a firsthand
look at the white man's army his spies reported was
marching against the Miami villages. Having agreed
to rejoin Little Turtle "north of the fording place
on the mother waters of the Ouabache," tonight Blue
Jacket had tied his black gelding to a tree east of
the army's encampment and carefully wormed his way
forward to a spot where he lay hidden in the underbrush. The Shawnee chief knew he could easily pick
off one or two of the soldiers around the campfire
and disappear in the wilderness but he would wait--
tonight he would watch and listen!

Oblivious to the fact they were being watched,
the boisterous soldier called Max exclaimed loudly:

"I 'spose you heard some redskin made off with
one of them women camp followers this morning--that
one with the black hair and big tits!"

As the laughter subsided he added: "Some red-
skinned bastard's got someone nice to keep him warm
tonight!"

Josiah Whiting, a native of Boston, smiled and
said with a straight face: "By the way Max, do you
know why the eastern Indians wear feathers in their
headband?"

"No," replied Max quizzically. "Why?"

"To keep their wigwam!"

A chorus of laughter was still echoing through
the surrounding trees when the sound of gunfire was
heard and everyone quickly dropped to the ground or
sought refuge behind a log. When no more shooting
was heard, the soldiers again sought the comfort of
the fire. Folding the toe of a worn sock back, and
pushing his foot into a well worn muddy shoe, Max
was still smarting from being a victim of Whiting's
question. And, with a flurry of comments about the
shooting fading, Max vented his suppressed humiliation as he glanced angrily at Whiting and sneered:

"All right smart ass, you got any idea how far
it is to them Miami villages we're heading for?"

Carefully avoiding being drawn into any verbal fisticuffs, Whiting thoughtfully replied: "Well, I heard my company commander, Captain Phelon, talking with Lieutenant Greaton and he said Captain Purdy's of the opinion St. Clair doesn't even know how far it is. He said the general thought we should reach the Miami-of-the-lake (Maumee) in a day or so."

A young recruit from Virginia eagerly contributed: "Last Sunday I was talking with one of them Kentucky militiamen and he said he'd seen an Indian map that showed we ain't even halfway there."

Max eyed the young recruit carefully and said: "Why would he tell YOU something like that?"

Slightly intimidated by the boisterous query, the recruit replied: "I knew him back in Virginia--his folks lived not far from us near Shepherdstown. He said the owner of that map got it from some redskin he caught. Said the map shows this old Indian trail we have been following and it leads right to them Miami Indian villages."

Still probing, Max queried sarcastically: "Did he say how far it was to them villages?"

A hush fell over the group and everyone waited anxiously for the young private's answer. Savoring the attention, he proudly replied: "He told me last Sunday we had more than seventy miles to go."

Max pondered this revelation a moment and then ended a string of vulgarities saying: "Christ! We marched eight miles today so that means we got more than sixty miles to go! And with this damn weather colder than a well digger's ass in January too!"

With the stillness of the cold early November night broken only by the sound of a violin and harmonica, St. Clair sat in his tent and thought about the breach that had developed, and widened, between General Butler and himself. In the dispatch he had just finished, St. Clair advised Secretary Knox the army was nearing their objective. In truth he was almost sixty miles from Miamitown as the crow flies and St. Clair was an earthbound creature. Not only was he earthbound, on November 2nd, 1791 he did not know exactly where he was--a tactical blunder for a field commander.

But Little Turtle knew where his adversary was this night. And, only forty yards from St. Clair's tent, a blue-jacketed Indian--cold and with only a strip of jerked venison to satisfy his pang of hunger--intently watched several artillerymen who were huddled close together around a fire near a cannon. 25 miles northwest from where Blue Jacket lay carefully counting the army's artillery pieces, Little Turtle's warriors didn't have the "luxury" of campfires--the wise old Miami chief had said there were to be no fires this night which might warn of their presence. Although Little Turtle had no cannon to impede his warrior's movement through the woods and across streams, the army's artillery was of concern to him. Encamped this night south of the St.Mary's River, and only 18 miles northwest of the Ouabache fording place, the Miami chief talked with Apekonit about his plan to quiet the white man's artillery.

Meantime, this same day, November 2nd, 1791, a young ensign reported for duty at Fort Washington-- he had received a presidential appointment the 30th of September after attending Hampden-Sidney College from 1787 to 1790. Born February 9th, 1773, he was the son of a man who had signed the Declaration of Independence and served as governor of Virginia for two years. Ensign William Henry Harrison, the son of Benjamin and Elizabeth Bassett Harrison, said he was "chagrined and dejected" at not being with St. Clair on his military campaign against the Indians. Chagrined perhaps, but probably fortunate!

Although missing the 1791 expedition, William Henry Harrison would be with General Anthony Wayne three years later when they returned victorious to Fort Greene Ville after seeing the enemy raise the truce flag at the Battle of Fallen Timbers.

CHAPTER FIFTEEN

BANKS OF THE OUABACHE

Long before first light on Thursday, November 3rd, Hank arose and threw some wood on the fire--he hadn't been able to sleep much. Now seated near the fire, he searched the flames for answers to his quandary. Half aloud he muttered: "If that map is right, we must be a long way from the Miami-of-the-lake river bottom land and winter's comin' on fast. Maybe we ought to go on back and have a try at this thing next spring."

"Talking to yourself so early in the morning?" It was Jason and Hank replied:

"Yep! No harm talking to yourself I've heard. It's when you start getting answers that you're in trouble maw says."

"My uncle used to talk to himself," said Jason with a smile. "Said he enjoyed talking with a man who had good sense!"

"If you men had good sense we would be heading back down that trail to Cincinnati!" It was Mary's voice.

"Top of the morning to you Mary," said Hank as he glanced up to where Jason's wife was peering out from the front end of the Conestoga. "And there is something in what you say--Jason and me was talking about that last night."

Although Mary had decided the time had come to share with Jason the fact she was pregnant, she had fallen asleep last evening waiting for him to join her. This morning she awakened fully determined to tell him but, unfortunately, this intention was put in abeyance when Captain Snowden came by asking her husband to repair his horse's loose shoe. And that done, Jason began preparing to "move out" and Mary didn't have an opportunity to talk with him.

After crossing the small creek and topping the little rise in their path this morning, through the partially naked trees Jason could see the terrain ahead was fairly flat. But, on the western horizon an ominous dark cloud served as a harbinger of bad weather that afternoon or night.

Two hours later the forward progress slowed as word was passed the woodsmen were building a bridge across another little creek in their line of march. Having walked ahead to take a first-hand look, Hank returned and engaged Jason in quiet conversation:

"Like that map shows, that crik up there flows east!" Hank referred to a little wilderness stream whose waters had cut a gully ten feet wide and four feet deep through years of uninhibited flow. There was only a minimal amount of water in the creek but the gully did impede the forward movement of supply and artillery wagons. "If that map is right, we're gonna find that Ouabache or whatever you call it up ahead a few miles."

Jason studied Hank's face as he pondered something he had overheard that morning while repairing the loose shoe on Captain Snowden's horse. "Hank, I heard someone say this morning a scout had reported there is a pretty good sized river about four miles ahead which St. Clair says is the St. Mary's River! Either that map or St. Clair is wrong!"

Dead serious, Hank remarked: "Let's just ride easy in the saddle this afternoon and get a look at that river. Van Cleve told me there's some baggage horses heading back down the trail tomorrow morning and we could tag along with them if we're a mind to do so. I'll nose around a little more up ahead and talk to you after bit."

As Hank disappeared around Ezra Axton's wagon, Jason turned and made a slight adjustment to the U-shaped part of the yoke on his lead oxen. The yoke needed no attention but it gave Jason time to think about his alternatives. He was thus occupied when pack horse master Darius C. Orcut walked by saying:

"A little nippy this morning! Had hoped for a long Indian summer but them clouds in the west sure look like we might get a little snow tonight." He had mentioned on several occasions that his wife of one year, Sally McHenry, was anxiously waiting for him in Cincinnati and now added: "Shore be good to git back to Cincinnati!"

Mary overheard the last remark and muttered to herself: "Amen!"

Soon thereafter Hank came back saying a bridge across the wilderness stream was completed and the wagons again began to move. As the "point" of the expeditionary column reached what would years later be the intersection of Fox Road and State Route 49, General Butler sent word to St. Clair recommending encampment on the high ground immediately northwest of the line of march. Butler had decided this site would be less favorable to an enemy attack than one along a river two miles ahead. In spite of the re-commendation, and having performed a reconnaissance of the advance area in company with Colonel Darke, Colonel Oldham, Major Ferguson, and Ebenezer Denny, St. Clair ordered the march would continue forward to the banks of the river which he estimated to be twelve yards wide and erroneously believed was the St. Mary's. Seated proudly astride his white horse on the banks of what Indians called "the Ouabache," St. Clair confidently told his officers:

"We are now only fifteen miles from the Miami villages. Because of the protection afforded us by the embankments of this Pickaway Fork of the Omee, we will encamp here. First thing in the morning I want to throw up a light earthwork---Major Ferguson and I will discuss the details tonight. As soon as

Major Hamtramck and the First Infantry arrives, I
want to be ready to march against Miamitown. It is
a day's forced march at the best. I am thinking of
leaving the traveling forges, anvil, and the men's
knapsacks here--leave everything which is not absolutely necessary to our intent and purpose!"

With respect for General St. Clair's knowledge
and experience as a surveyor, Ebenezer Denny didn't
take exception with the commander's estimate of the
river's width although he himself estimated, and so
advised officials in Philadelphia six weeks later,
the stream approximated 20 yards in width. And, as
circumstances would later reveal, St. Clair was in
error concerning both the identity of the river and
the distance to the Miami villages. The encampment
was but one mile east of where the Ohio and Indiana
line would be established years later and 50 miles
distant from the junction of the St. Joseph and St.
Mary's which spawned the Maumee--the spot where St.
Clair hoped to find Little Turtle and his "nest" of
troublesome Indians.

As the officers talked and the army moved forward, some Indians across the river melted into the
lengthening shadows of late afternoon---one wearing
a blue jacket rode a beautiful black gelding with a
white star on its forehead. Examining the plethora
of hoof tracks and moccasin prints along the river,
Oldham was of the opinion these had been made by an
Indian observation party. But, as he said:

"These are the first ones that have been about
us since I joined the expedtion. All the others we
have noticed were hunters!"

After examining the tracks, St. Clair ordered
several small parties of riflemen into the forward
area across the river but they soon returned saying
they had found nothing. With darkness approaching,
they had not traveled far.

Discouraged, disheartened, and exhausted, the
army reached the river about four o-clock with sunset only 35 minutes away. Crossing a bridge over a

little ravine which would later be known as "Bloody Run," and still later as the "Buck Ditch," the army was encamped in two lines 70 yards apart. Although customarily St. Clair would have ordered some sort of a defense thrown up regardless of the soldier's fatigue, for some unexplained reason this Thursday afternoon it was not done. In spite of the fact it was completely out of character for St.Clair to put off erecton of a vital earthwork defense, in an orderly manner on what the Sargent called "a handsome piece of rising ground with a stream forty feet in front," the army made camp on November 3rd in 1791. As Sargent's diary reported:

"Camp was ordered on the banks of a stream St. Clair said was the Pickaway Fork which empties into the Omee at the Miami villages. Here are an immense number of old and new Indian camps, and it appears to have been a place of their general resort."

Although prudent consideration of Washington's farewell admonishment should have prompted St.Clair to a more defensive action, he did order the troops to sleep on their arms this night and ordered Colonel Oldham's militia to cross the shallow river and low bottom land and make their camp a quarter of a mile in advance of the main army camp. The general also ordered Oldham to perform a reconnaissance of the area in advance of the forward camp. It was an order which was not obeyed to the extent intended. Even as the Kentucky militia waded through the tall dead grass, swale, and cattails in the marshy river bottom to the high ground beyond and bedded down in the open woods, several Indians silently fled into the dense wilderness. After his late evening visit to the militia's camp, Sargent told St. Clair:

"The militia campsite is better than ours!"

During a post-battle interview Colonel Sargent would tell a board of inquiry: "The militia's position was a defensible one. For four hundred yards in front the woods was open and afforded the enemy no cover."

474

Censured later for failure to reconnoiter the
area in advance of the Kentucky militia's position,
a fortunate survivor would defend Oldham's reported
indifference to an enemy threat declaring St. Clair
himself had expressed a belief the Indians were not
watching the army's movement with a view to attack
and his optimism may have provoked over-confidence.
Summarizing his defense of Oldham, he said:

"All the militia, including the colonel, were
suffering from their tiresome eight mile march that
day. The bitter cold damp night air and occasional
snow flurries caused extreme discomfort that night
among militiamen who hadn't anticipated such a long
campaign. Under such circumstances, it is possible
the men's alertness to danger may have been numbed
and any reconnaissance that was undertaken was done
with minimum effort."

The members of the Kentucky militia contingent
were not the only ones who had endured the tiresome
march November 3rd--nor were they the only ones who
suffered from the bone-chilling weather that night.
Indeed, it was a tribute to the endurance of those
brave souls of St. Clair's army that they were able
to perform the myriad of tasks necessary to prepare
the encampment that night.

The main camp fronted on the river and extended 300 to 400 yards in length. The right wing, or
front line--not 25 yards from the river in places--
included infantry units under Majors Thomas Butler,
John Clarke, and Joseph Patterson. Three six-pound
brass cannons and one three-pound cannon were sandwiched in between Butler and Clarke's battalions by
Lt. Colonel John Gibson with Captain Mahlon Ford in
command. 70 yards behind and parallel to the front
line, the left wing--or second line--included Major
Henry Gaither's battalion, the battalion Major Bedinger had commanded, the Second U. S. Infantry, and
Captain James Bradford's company of artillery which
was located between Gaither's battalion and the one
Bedinger had left.

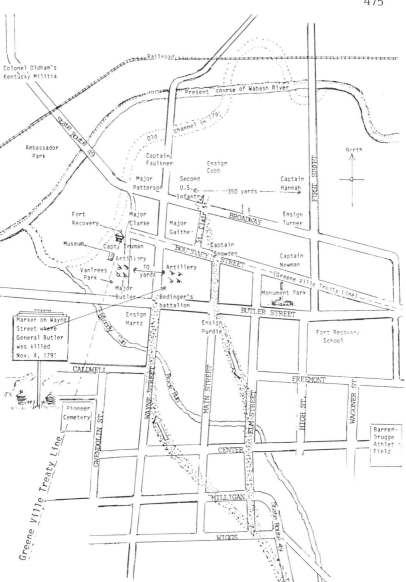

St. Clair's encampment November 3-4, 1791
where Fort Recovery, Ohio stands in 1994

The steep river bank west of the front line provided a measure of protection and riflemen under Captain Faulkner, located next to Major Patterson's battalion, augmented this natural guard. A company of riflemen was also positioned in between the two lines at either end of the encampment. The cavalry and pickets were located on the flank of each wing with Captain Trueman in command of one company and Captain Snowden commanding the other. Troops under Ensigns David Cobb, Jr., Martz, and Purdie guarded the outer flanks of the two lines with Cobb nearest the river on the north side and the other two units fronted on a narrow cut that emptied into the river southwest of Butler's battalion. 350 yards to the rear of--and parallel to--the second line, Captains Newman and Hannah, and Ensign Turner, commanded the troops of the rear guard.

The sketch included herein on page 475 is the author's conclusions based upon research, knowledge of past and current topography, and the army's line of march (330 degrees) on November 3rd intended to bring the army to a crossing one-half mile upstream from the "bend in the river" reported to St. Clair by Captain William Powers. Location of the cannons probably accounts for the fact that some of the artillery pieces were later found in the nearby ditch called "Bloody Run."

With the steep banks of the river on the north and west side of the main encampment, St. Clair may have envisioned himself positioned in front of his headquarters tent facing the south when he prepared his post-battle summary on November 9th, 1791:

"The right wing composed of Butler's, Clarke's and Patterson's battalions, commanded by Major General Butler, formed the first line; and the left wing, consisting of Bedinger's and Garther's (sic) battalions, and the Second Regiment commanded by Lieutenant Colonel Darke, formed the second line."

To say it was a "planned" encampment would not be right--to some extent the troops just dropped in their tracks thoroughly exhausted by the eight mile march. Unfortunately the camp was laid out to the advantage of the wilderness enemy and the watching Indians made careful note of this as they patiently waited among the silent sentinels of the woods.

Interspersed among the various army units were the persistent camp follower's wagons, tents, lean-tos, baggage, and animals. Although Sargent called them "excess baggage," most now accepted these camp followers as members of the expedition "family" and treated them accordingly. But today an undefinable air of uneasiness had silently infiltered the ranks of both the military and camp followers. You could see it in people's eyes and sense it in their talk.

In speaking with St. Clair, Colonel Darke reminded him there had been repeated signs of hostile Indians in their vicinity since leaving Fort Jefferson and several scalps had been taken. St. Clair countered by pointing out this only happened when a careless person had wandered too far from the line of march. He was mindful there had been increasing reports of Indian sightings, and occasional gunfire had been heard around the perimeter, but St. Clair attributed it to the nervousness of the guards. In a similar manner the general did his best to allay the concern of other officers who politely pointed out the moccasin prints and hoof marks in the area where they were now camped.

Although St. Clair took judicious note of such concern, and ordered ammunition be issued each man, with calloused disregard for safety that comes when unseasoned troops characteristically laid their gun aside and went about building fires to provide some warmth for their hungry bodies. There was a gnawing fear they couldn't shake among the few who had some experience fighting Indians but unfortunately there were only a few such men. The increasing number of shooting and scalping reports had convinced most of the seasoned officers, and a few veteran non coms, they were being watched and efforts to placate them

fell on deaf ears. And although a few did maintain
a sharp vigil, and urged their tired comrades to do
the same, for most of the levies and green recruits
the fatigue and numbing cold was a compelling force
and the warmth of a campfire was more inviting than
paying attention to talk about a threat of danger.

A foul-mouthed awkward lanky private---one who
claimed he was from Maysville and had been with the
Harmar expedition last fall after drifting down the
river to Cincinnati and enlisting in the army--made
several caustic remarks about the length of time it
was taking St. Clair to march an army to Miamitown.
Obtaining little reaction from the cold and hungry
troops huddled around the fire, the private bitterly remarked:

"If it warn't fer that old squaw bitch of mine
wantin' to git back up thar to Little Turtle's town
to see her kin, ah'd damn quick say kiss ass to St.
Clair and git me and my old lady back down the road
and upstream to Maysville. Hell, ah shouldn't have
fetched that squaw back in the first place!"

Nearby a Revolutionary War veteran started his
own fire with flint and steel and then proceeded to
toast his feet as the flames danced in the bitterly
cold night air. When several other young men moved
in close to his fire, the veteran infantryman tried
to raise the spirits of his youthful comrades telling them about that winter at Valley Forge when he
and his comrades huddled together "with nothing but
a candle to keep us warm!" Feigning sobriety, but
with a twinkle in his eye, he added:

"It got so blessed cold one night the candlelight froze and we couldn't blow it out!"

It was almost that cold on November 3rd, 1791
as Doctor Edward Grasson went about the encampment
administering to the sick as best he could with his
limited supply of medicine. The sick were given a
a tiny bit of mutton or an ounce or two of grog--an
unsweetened mixture of water and spirits.   Medical
supplies were almost non-existent and the ceaseless

vomiting of some was repulsive and made others ill. Among the remaining camp followers the doctor found a few sick children and he treated them the best he could under the circumstances. The ranks of these camp followers had diminished since they left Fort Hamilton but many of the wives and children of the soldiers, civilian volunteers, contractors, and the Kentucky militia had tenaciously tagged along praying "the breadwinner" of their family would be able to stake out a property claim in the Miamitown area after the Indians were subdued. For most it was a "dream" that would never come true.

But now on this cold and disagreeable night as the doctor made his way through the camp and passed a camp follower's tent, he heard a man reading from the 5th Chapter of Matthew: "Blessed are the pure in heart: for they shall see God."

Nearby, in another tent, Grasson heard a woman and child reciting the 23rd Psalm: "Yea, though I walk through the valley of the shadow of death, I will fear no evil, for Thou art with me....."

Passing St. Clair's tent Grasson overheard his aide, Viscount Malartie, advise the general: "Sir, there is no provender for the commander's horse!"

Moments later, and approaching downwind from where Jason and Hank stood talking with Captain Van Swearingen and Major Ziegler beside a fire next to Benjamin Van Cleve's horseman's tent, or "marquee" as it was called, the doctor caught a whiff of the strong smell of horses nearby who were stomping the ground nervously--they had sensed something upwind. Little Turtle was no fool, he had purposely ordered his "cold camp" be located upwind from St. Clair's camp near where Isaac Raus would plat tiny Monterey in November of 1849 and Ralph Jutte's Roadside Market would blossom in the middle of the 20th Century along Route 49 north of Fort Recovery.

As Van Cleve had informed Jason and Hank a few minutes earlier, he was preparing to leave the next morning with his uncle--they were heading back down the wilderness road for urgently needed provisions. Greeting those standing near the fire, Grasson held his chapped hands close to the flames and silently cursed the bone-chilling gusts of wind that carried a few flakes of snow. In taking their leave of the men around the fire, Jason and Hank called to young Van Cleve saying they would see him in the morning. Those around the fire this night never dreamed they would be involved in the chaotic nightmare that lay ahead less than ten hours.

After bidding Hank goodnight, and climbing into his Conestoga, Jason faced his wife saying:

"I have something to tell you!"

Without hesitation Mary injected quickly:

"And I have something to tell you Mister Evenstar!"

Somewhat taken aback by his wife's abruptness, Jason's chin dropped. Even in the dim candlelight Jason could see the tears in his wife's eyes and he said: "All right dear--you first. What is it that you wish to tell me."

Mary took a deep breath, dabbed at a tear with her handkerchief, and said in a choking voice what she had wanted to say for so long:

"You probably do not remember what I said back in Turkey Foot about having a child in some lean-to way out in the middle of nowhere. Well, my beloved husband, it appears that will be my lot in life!"

Jason stared at Mary for a few moments before the full meaning of what his wife had said filtered through what he had planned to tell her. Suddenly his face lighted up and he exclaimed:

"You mean...ah, you mean....are you telling me you are with child? Our child? Are you sure?"

"Yes dear," said Mary calmly. "We are going to have a baby!" Pausing briefly she quipped: "Wait, allow me to put that another way Jason, I am going to have a baby!" She emphasized the "I."

Jason didn't need to be hit with a hammer--he caught his wife's sarcastic inference and remarked:

"I got the message dear---and it is wonderful! Now, may I tell you what I wanted to say before you interrupted me...with your wonderful news that is." Smiling mischievously he continued: "What I wanted to say was Hank thinks we probably should return to Cincinnati and come back up this way next spring or summer." As a frown crossed his wife's face, Jason quickly added: "Provided of course we are still of the mind to stake out some land north of here. How about that?"

The smile of relief on Mary's face bespoke her reply and she quickly remarked: "I think Hank is a very smart man! When do we go?"

"Tomorrow morning," replied Jason. "There are some baggage horses going back down the road and we can tag along with them."

Mary was elated and for the first time in more than a month she knew she would sleep soundly this night. Not only were they going back down the road to Cincinnati, Mary was thinking it would certainly be nice if they continued on south to Lexington and then crossed the mountain road east which she heard led to Baltimore. Mary had had more than enough of Jason's talk about slaying dragons in the Northwest Territory. As she kissed Jason and said goodnight, Mary stifled a snicker as she thought to herself:

"You can work with my father and chase dragons to your heart's content in the business world!"

Hearing his wife's stifled laugh, Jason turned to her and said: "What is so funny?"

"Nothing Jason," replied Mary. "Go to sleep."

Less than fifty yards from Jason's Conestoga, Colonel Gibson was showing some levies how to dress a raccoon he had caught when Captain Jacob Slough, an officer from Pennsylvania, joined them. Calling the colonel to one side, Slough volunteered to lead a party of two subalterns and 23 soldiers to thwart any attempt by Indians to steal their horses during the night. Gibson referred the request to General

482

Butler who approved the reconnaissance effort. Before the contingent was paraded at ten o'clock, the general gave Slough a glass of wine and advised him to exercise extreme caution in the undertaking. He also ordered Slough to report to Colonel Oldham before passing beyond the militia encampment. Still fully clothed and ready for action, Oldham suggested Slough and his guide, George Adams, forget their mission saying:

"I expect the army will be attack in the morning and your party might be cut off!"

But since the captain's orders had been issued by General Butler, he obtained the password from a picket guard and inched forward through the unknown woods about a mile northwest of the main camp. Now Slough divided his men into two parties and ordered them to lie quietly, close to the ground and about 40 yards apart, concealed in the underbrush on each side of a well-worn Indian trail they had followed. With Lieutenant Cummings in charge of the troops on one side, and Slough with the remainder of his contingent hiding in the underbrush on the other side, they waited. They didn't have to wait long!

Suddenly Slough gulped as through the darkness a sliver of moonlight revealed six or seven Indians stealthily making their way down the trail toward the army's encampment. A heartbeat or so later the deathly silence was broken as seven or eight troops opened fire from both sides of the trail. When the Indians had hastily retreated--one possibly wounded but all escaping--Slough whispered the order to reload and remain quietly in hiding.

Although Captain Slough had served in the Revolutionary war, he obviously did not agree with the "Instructions In Respect To War" written by Captain Ewald of the Hessian Jager Corps which stated: "If an officer by night stumbles on the enemy, let him give a volley and charge with the bayonet, without troubling himself as to the strength of his opponent." The captain must have missed that page!

Fifteen minutes later Slough saw another large party of Indians coming down the trail--probably in search of them. But this time the troops remained quiet and held their breath as the Indians passed a few feet from where they were hidden. With the men getting uneasy about their advance position, Slough ordered a return to the militia encampment and they retreated by a circuitous route with fixed bayonets and carefully listening for any sign of Indians. A few times they thought they heard a movement in the surrounding woods but saw nothing and the return to the militia's advance camp was without incident.

Slough reported their experience to Oldham who listened carefully and once again indicated he felt the Indians would probably attack the next morning. Although it was now midnight, the colonel suggested Slough report his experience to St. Clair.

Cautiously leading his party back across the river bottom to the main camp, Slough found General Butler's tent dark. With an understandable respect for the senior officer's privacy, Slough sought out Colonel Gibson and requested the colonel accompany him to Butler's tent. Although Gibson declined the request, he did urge the captain to make his report to Butler at once. Thus, it was one o'clock in the morning when Slough awakened Butler and related his experience. After listening to the reconnaissance report, being advised of what the militia commander had said, and hearing Slough's expressed conviction they could expect an attack by Indians in the morning, Butler suggested Captain Slough get some sleep and not disturb St. Clair with the report.

Perhaps General Butler thought it might not be advisable to disturb the ailing old general at this late hour. Maybe he decided it was more prudent to relay the report to St. Clair the following morning after breakfast--a breakfast Butler would not have.

While Captain Slough and his party were reconnoitering the advance area, St. Clair limped around his tent supported by a crutch--he could not sleep.

MAP OF THE STATE OF OHIO (1804)
by Rufus Putnam
Collections of the Ohio Historical Society

He was pondering the condemnation he received after surrendering the "impregnable" Fort Ticonderoga to General John Burgoyne in 1777. Although exonerated in September of 1778, and unanimously acquitted by courts-martial, this "stain" on an otherwise honorable record of service to his adopted country was a source of ingrained frustration. For 14 years St. Clair had labored hard to eradicate this "blot" on his dedicated service and tonight he felt supremely confident "victory" was within his grasp. "Perhaps vindication is near at hand," he thought.

Forgotten this night was his intention to construct forts every 25 or 30 miles enroute to Little Turtle's wilderness refuge. This night he was only 29 miles from Fort Jefferson but the old war horse smelled victory--a victory that would put an end to the Indian problem that plagued his administration. In the absence of accurate maps of the area through which his army now marched, St. Clair had no reason not to rely on Major Heart's counsel which supported his belief the Miami villages were not more than 20 miles away. Wilderness-wise Heart had been with General Harmar only one year before and should have known the estimate was wrong. St. Clair's army had marched only 98 miles whereas Harmar's expedition--although marching by a slightly circuitous route--had traveled more than 170 miles to reach the Miami villages. 24 year old George Adams, army scout and veteran of Harmar's campaign took no exception with Major Heart's counsel. *

In the distance St. Clair heard several shots fired in rapid succession and he stepped out of his tent into the bitter-cold night air. The sword he wore at his side rattled and clanked as he drew his greatcoat close around his shoulders. Staring into the darkness across the river from which direction

* Map of the State of Ohio by Rufus Putnam (page 484) dated January 1804 still did not indicate the headwaters of the Wabash River on whose banks St. Clair camped Nov. 3, 1791

486

the shots seemed to come, he pondered the fact the
surrounding woods were ideal for a surprise attack.
Cupping his ear and listening for more shots--shots
that never came--St. Clair wished their late afternoon arrival had permitted the army and opportunity
to throw up an earthwork before dark but took some
consolation knowing Major Ferguson had been ordered
to do this first thing in the morning.

Remembering the many occasions at Valley Forge
when Washington had sought communion with God and
the general's inspiration guided his troops through
many difficulties, on this fateful night St. Clair
looked up at the threatening snow clouds and then
kneeled by his campfire and silently prayed for the
same divine guidance and early arrival of his sorely needed supplies. Painfully he then arose, stared intently into the darkness across the river, and
then limped into his tent. A chilling gust of wind
sent sparks from his campfire whirling upward where
they silently expired as they mixed with occasional
snow flakes.

In the stillness of this early November night
there were many--soldiers and civilians alike--who
prayed. Some openly wept not knowing that for many
this was to be their last night of cold and hunger;
their last night of fear and privation; their last
night this side of immortality.*

In the same cold and deathly quiet surrounding
woods this night, the Indians watched...and waited.

---

* "On November 3, 1791 St. Clair camped at Fort Recovery with
1400 soldiers where they slept a fitful sleep." (Page 15,
HEROES AND HEROINES OF THE FORT DEARBORN MASSACRE (1896) by
N. Simmons, Journal Pub. Co., Lawrence, Kansas

CHAPTER SIXTEEN

COLD CAMP

Marching south and east along the banks of the St. Marys River, Little Turtle had led his warriors away from the Miami villages. And now, late in the afternoon on November 3rd, 1791, the sly and crafty Miami chief ordered his "cold camp" be located two miles north and west of the Ouabache fording place. As Little Turtle told his followers:

"The fire of our hate for the white invader is enough to keep us warm tonight."

One of his warriors who was present that night later said the confederated force was "close to one thousand!"

Used and abused by fur-traders, provisioned by the shrewd British, hated by Kentuckians, and feared by white settlers, the Miami and Shawnee Indians were a formidable foe. Since early spring in 1791 tension had been mounting between the white man and the Indians. Like the drawing back of a mighty war bow, in the summer the "arrow" had been fitted and now the war bow was fully taut. For several weeks the Indians had drilled along the east side of the St. Marys aided and provisioned by British officers from Detroit. Among the warriors now assembled and ready for a surprise attack against the hated white man were those from Miami, Shawnee, Delaware, Wyandot, Chippewa, Potawatomi, and Ottawa septs. A few Mohawks and ten Iroquois had also answered the call by Little Turtle.

Through the half-naked trees a few snow flakes floated down and a biting chill gusted through the Indian's camp when the mournful cry of a wolf echoed through the surrounding woods. As if the lonely wail signaled the start of a war council, a copper-colored man stood up. Six eagle feathers were attached to the lock of hair over his right ear with the quills pointing up and the plumes laying across his shoulder. As all eyes now focused on this man silhouetted against the deeping shadows, a hushed silence blanketed the low and indistinct murmuring.

Buckongahelas, Tarhe the Crane, Tecumseh, Blue Jacket, and other Indian personages had watched the thirty-nine year old Me-she-kin-nogh-gah rise from their midst--this dark complected man's Indian name meant "wise, with a soul of fire." A picture of health and strength, he was the tribal chief of the Miami Indians. Crafty in council, and on a battle-field, the sun of Indian glory would set with this man known far and wide as "Little Turtle." Normally a man of great wit, humor, and vivacity--and the son of an Indian chief--he had gained great respect among the tribes. Looking out over the Indians who strained to see him in the gathering darkness, his eyes burned with vengeful hate as he permitted his gaze to move slowly from the right to left and then back to the right again. There was an aura of confidence, defiance, and unbridled hate in the air on November 3rd in 1791 and this night Little Turtle's stoical bearing mirrored it as he raised his arms, palms forward, and spoke in a language his warriors could understand:

"These are the banks of the Ouabache where the prints of my ancestors are to be seen everywhere. My forefathers kindled the first fire at Detroit in the days when they walked in peace along the rivers and through the woods. But now the white man gives us beads and trinkets, fills us with whisky, and we smoke the green weed that brings strange dreams and makes us weak. Now the white man drives his stakes in the land and builds his forts. Now I say to you my brothers, the white man must never be allowed to plant his corn in the Ohio country!"

The Miami chief paused as a shaft of moonlight filtered through the canopy of snow clouds overhead revealing deeply etched lines in his face that made him look older. Those seated at his feet could see the hate which smoldered in his eyes and there was no mistaking the all-consuming contempt and vengeance in his vigorous voice as he now uttered three words:

"I show you!"

Word quickly circulated that Little Turtle now held over his head a white wampum belt in his right hand and his left hand, raised aloft—palm forward, admonished all to maintain quiet. Regardless, the excited murmuring among the warriors signaled their opposition to the belt which signified peace, prosperity, and "burying of the hatchet!"

When only the gusting of the winds through the half-naked trees could be heard, Little Turtle let the belt fall to the ground. Moments later a wave of suppressed excitement permeated the silence when word passed that Little Turtle was now holding high over his head a black wampum belt---the "war belt."

As the murmuring died down, in measured speech Little Turtle told his listeners:

"Our friend Tecumseh, son of Chief Pucksinwah, has kept me and the one who wears the blue jacket advised of the white general's preparations to come against us. From his hiding place at the doorstep of the enemy he has used his eyes and ears well and told us where the white man is weak and strong."

Turning his head slightly he acknowledged the presence of Tecumseh seated nearby and then added:

"From the hills close to the white man's fort along the Ohio Tecumseh has seen the white soldiers arrive and watched them unloading supplies. He has walked the streets of Cincinnati with our enemy and entered the white man's fort wearing the clothes of the hated Long Knives!"

A murmur of respect and admiration was heard. Little Turtle waited with ingrained patience until all was quiet--then he spoke again:

"Tecumseh has watched our enemy drill his soldiers and heard it said the white general expected three thousand men would be ready to march against us before the full moon in July. But the soldiers have not come and the supplies St. Clair waited for are still sitting on the dock at Pittsburgh--or at the bottom of the Ohio!"

Little Turtle permitted the warriors to savor the thought of the scalps they had taken along the Ohio and the many boats they had sent to the bottom of that river. Then he continued:

"It was Tecumseh who said we should attack the army in the woods before more soldiers and supplies arrive. This afternoon he and Blue Jacket rejoined us saying St. Clair's army, weak and ill-equipped, would probably make camp tonight near the old fording place along the Ouabache."

A murmur of expectancy swept the audience like wildfire but it quieted when the speaker continued:

"When the first traders and trappers came to our villages they were greeted as friends. Now the white man pushes deeper and deeper into this land where we have lived in peace. The white man drives stakes in the ground, cuts down the trees to build his cabins, and kills the deer and buffalo. In his craving to divide the land the white man cuts roads through the wilderness and builds his ugly forts!"

A ripple of suppressed fury swept through the audience. When all was quiet again, Little Turtle went on with his commentary:

"Some of you well remember the fort the white man built where the Kanawha empties into the Ohio-- he called it Fort Randolph. In the summer of 1778 Cornstalk went to that fort under a flag of truce-- he wanted to talk with Captain Arbuckle. He had no weapons and took with him his son, Elinipsico, and

Chief Red Hawk. And what happened?   They were put
in the white man's jail and then murdered!"

As a wave of hateful vengeance circulated thru
the assembly of warriors, Little Turtle raised his
hand and said in a guttural voice:

"Defenseless, and under a flag of truce, they
were killed in cold blood by Captain John Hall!"

He said nothing about the Indian's retaliatory
raid September 18, 1778 on Fort Boonesborough. But
then of course Colonel Bowman had led an attack on
Black Fish's village in July of 1779.   Roused into
a frenzied state of alarm, frustration, and hate,
the red-skinned wilderness natives struck back time
and time again in the only manner they knew--agents
of the British like Simon Girty and Alexander McKee
"kept the pot boiling."   Back and forth across the
Ohio the Indians and white settlers traded "blows."

In 1783 England had signed a treaty that ceded
to the United States the land northwest of the Ohio
where the Indians lived--but the Indians were not a
party to that treaty! For years Indians had watched the French and British--and now a "young upstart
of thirteen fires" as Tecumseh called the fledgling
republic--divide by treaties the land where Indians
lived. The Treaty of Paris in 1763 which ended the
French and Indian Wars; the Treaty of Fort Stanwix
dated October 22, 1784; the Treaty of Fort McIntosh
inked January 21st, 1785; the treaty signed at Fort
Finney in January of 1786; and treaties arranged by
St. Clair and signed at Fort Harmar in 1789.   Each
served to limit the Indian's "domain."

There was also some misunderstanding among the
tribes regarding the provisions of the treaties. A
number of sachems complained the signatories to the
treaties did not represent their tribe. As for the
wording of some treaties, one Indian observed:

"Did not the one you call 'the Great Father in
Philadelphia' say he himself did not understand the
provisions of the treaty he signed after he was defeated at Fort Necessity?"

These were the words of a young Indian warrior
Little Turtle had praised this night--a warrior who
had learned the white man's language from a boy his
own age who had been captured by a Shawnee raiding
party and adopted by his family. And now, in 1791,
this young man was not only a competent spy, he was
becoming a very capable orator as Little Turtle was
about to learn when he ended his "pep talk" saying:

"And now I say to you my brothers, tonight the
weary blue coats sleep with empty bellies and argue
among themselves nearby along the banks of the Ouabache. Tonight many have left the camp of the old
gray-haired general who is sick and grows weary of
the march. Tonight we are all indebted to the one
who has kept me well informed about the white man's
army--and tomorrow we will repay that debt with the
scalps of those who march against us. My brothers,
I would have you hear the counsel of Tecumseh!"

A wave of feverish excitement coursed through
the assembly as word passed saying "Tecumtha" stood
before them.* Standing five feet ten, there was an
aura of strength in this 23 year old Shawnee's perfectly proportioned muscular bearing.   Destined to
become known far and wide as "Tecumseh," the Indian
name for this son of Pucksinwah and Methotasa meant
"The Shooting Star." He had shoulder-length glossy
black hair and wore a two feathered headpiece. Although his facial features were hidden by the gaudy

*   Although Emilius O. Randall, a prominent Ohio historian, in
his TECUMSEH, THE SHAWNEE CHIEF (OAAHSP, Vol. XV, 1906), says
Tecumseh was concealed on the banks of Nettles Creek watching
St. Clair march north from Fort Jefferson (pg 442), and was not
at St. Clair's defeat (pg 444), research by others, including
Dr. William H. Van Hoose's TECUMSEH, AN INDIAN MOSES, 1984 (pg
68), indicates he was present. Located just west of present-
day Urbana, Ohio, Nettles Creek is 45 miles east of St. Clair's
line of march. Randall probably referred to Harmar's line of
march in 1790 which followed the trace made by General Clark in
October of 1782.

red, yellow, and black war paint, those near to him could see the hate in his hazel eyes. Attired in a knee-length buckskin frock with beaded edging along the hem, he wore buffalo-hide beaded moccasins

Around Tecumseh's neck hung a rock he had been given when a boy. Grooved and carried on a length of rawhide since then, it would be around his neck when he was laid to rest in Canadian soil along the Thames River October 5, 1813. The eventful life of Tecumseh would be at an end and so would the War of 1812...the British Union Jack would never again fly over the forts in the Northwest Territory. But all that was 22 years in the future in November of 1791 as a hush now fell over the assembly---the warriors sensed Tecumseh's keen eyes must be sweeping across their midst. They had heard of this man's seething hate for the white man and, during that moment when a shaft of moonlight bored through the dark clouds overhead, those near him saw the all-consuming hate in Tecumseh's eyes as he began:

"Little Turtle spoke of the white man's hunger and he speaks the truth! My brothers, the one many of you called 'Gunshot,' spoke wisely of the white man's hunger before he died. With his dying breath he said: 'The white man is a monster who is always hungry--and what he eats is land!'"

A young warrior whispered to his painted companion: "Indians give white man land--Indians fill white man's mouth with dirt!"

Hunger pangs gripped the warrior's insides but it only served to whet his appetite for the white man's scalps. As he waited for Tecumseh to speak, Tecumseh was recalling something his older brother once said: "When the white man wins a battle with us, he calls it 'a victory.' When they lose, it is called 'a massacre!'" Tecumseh's caustic voice now proclaimed:

"Hungry for this land where we live, the white man makes roads through the woods, builds his ugly forts, and drives stakes in the ground to divide up this land where we live in peace. Tomorrow we will teach this white invader a lesson he will not soon forget!"

Like his older brother, Tecumseh was a capable orator. And, although living his youthful years in the shadows of his two older brothers, Tecumseh's loquacious younger brother was to become a skilled, eloquent speaker too. Named Lawlewasikaw, and then taking the name Tenskwatwa ("the open door"), this one-eyed Indian was destined to become widely known as "The Prophet" after a solar eclipse would prompt the opportunist to boast he could "bring night at noon!" He would derive his prophetic insight over-hearing men from the east coast discussing plans at Vincennes to observe this phenomenon of astronomy. Given to weeping and trembling while addressing his superstitious and awe-stricken audience, his wildly insane oratory would prove to be his downfall---and that of Tecumseh too for all practical purposes.

Tecumseh was destined to become a leader among all Indian tribes after a treaty conference at Fort Greene Ville in 1795---a 55 day conference he would refuse to attend. A future historian would say of the Treaty of Greene Ville:

"By that treaty in 1795 the United States paid about one cent for every six acres of land."

Although the inevitable curtain of time would drop on the part Tecumseh played on the wilderness stage, in 1791 his name was already being mentioned with respect around camp fires. During the ensuing two decades Tecumseh's travels would prompt talk of his great strength, ferocity, bravery, leadership, and oratorical ability. On August 15, 1810 he was destined to have the temerity to call William Henry Harrison "a liar" and prompt this future president to draw his sword from its scabbard. Having been a member of General Wayne's Legion at Fallen Timbers in 1794, Harrison was well acquainted with Tecumseh and his reputation. As hatred burned in Tecumseh's eyes, and Potawatomie Chief Winnemace at Harrison's

side drew his pistol, an infantry officer standing
nearby drew his dagger. The tension would finally
be broken when the tall and gaunt governor of the
Indiana Territory would drop his sword and firmly
suggest Tecumseh withdraw. Negotiations under such
circumstances would be impossible. Harrison wisely
decided he would "watch" this Tecumseh and bide his
time. His time did come!

Although relatively small in some respects,the
Battle of Tippecanoe on November 7, 1811 would send
Tecumseh's dream crashing to the earth. Six months
earlier he would have more than a thousand warriors
on the Tippecanoe River and have thousands more "on
call." But The Prophet's ill-advised seizure of a
piroque of salt on June 19, 1811 would provide the
governor of the Indiana Territory with the incident
he waited for. With the Secretary of War's tacit
approval for an attack against "the banditti under
The Prophet," and while Tecumseh was on a "recruiting trip" in the south, nine hundred soldiers would
attack the Indians at Tippacanoe. Ironically, only
approximately 20% of the more than 175 who died on
the battlefield were Indians but after that battle
the warriors would return to their villages and the
"seeds of defeat" would spread.

After the death knell of Tecumseh's grand plan
to unite the Indians "crashed," he was destined to
meet General William Harrison again in 1813 along
the Thames River in Ontario. And when that meeting
was over, Tecumseh--as well as the Indian's hopes--
would be dead. A historian would later note: "Had
Tecumseh's ambitious plan succeeded, the history of
the Territory Northwest of the Ohio would have been
written differently."

But all that was in the future as Tecumseh now
stood before an assembly of warriors in November of
1791 and offered an intelligence summary that would
have gladdened the heart of any field commander:

"Tonight the white general's soldiers sleep in
their tracks where they dropped from fatigue. Only

a few small fires have been built to keep them warm but they sleep with empty bellies. No breast work of logs was thrown up this afternoon as the general usually does. The wagons were brought to a halt as in the line of march and not formed as a protection from attack."

From somewhere far off everyone heard the single shot but not an eye moved from where Tecumseh stood bathed by a sliver of moonlight that filtered through the snow clouds above--his brows were drawn together in a frown and the hate in the young man's eyes was unreal. Now Tecumseh raised his war club over his head and whispered in a guttural voice:

"We attack at first light! Let's all remember how the white man murdered Chief Cornstalk!"

The murmur that coursed through the assembly was unmistakeable--everyone had clung to Tecumseh's words and now their lust for "the play" was like a gorge in each person's throat all but choking them. The adulation they felt for Tecumseh was overwhelming and could be felt by everyone in spite of the silence wherein it was proclaimed. Although he had praised the great spirit for their good fortune in finding the white army on the banks of the Wabash-- privately Tecumseh lauded his own initiative. In Tecumseh's mind were thoughts of an army of fifty thousand Indians--not tribes but a union that would enable them to force the white man from this land.

It took a lot of self restraint by the painted warriors to not let go with a war whoop. Even the Shawnee war chief who wore a blue jacket felt prone to do so. But, like everyone else this night, such a venting of pent up emotion must be saved for the first light. Now as Tecumseh took his seat beside Little Turtle, Blue Jacket felt a vice like grip on his arm and he turned toward his co-leader in this undertaking. Little Turtle nodded and Blue Jacket heard him speak firmly:

"And now Wey-a-pier-sen-waw, we would hear your counsel!"

Only the hoot of a lonely owl was heard as the blue-jacketed chief rose to his feet. The muscular and finely proportioned Shawnee chief stood looking over the assembly without saying a word...there was no hurry. Standing six feet tall, he was an imposing figure. Bold, strong, implacable, intelligent, and cunning were just a few of the adjectives used to describe this Indian who had earned the respect of Little Turtle and other sachems. A thick braid of hair hung down behind his left ear imprisoned at the end by a silver cylinder. From his ears dangled large round flattened silver earings and a big silver bracelet encircled his wrist. His buckskin leggings were decorated with hand-painted porcupine quills in geometric designs and knee-high moccasins were trimmed with beads.

Blue Jacket's eyes had grown accustomed to the darkness as the curtain of night had fallen and now he could see the look of expectancy on those seated cross-legged near him. As with Tecumseh, a little shaft of moonlight momentarily revealed his painted face and his black, pin hole eyes now gleamed like those of a dog in the glare of the moon. As a dark cloud suddenly swept the vision from the warrior's sight, Blue Jacket began:

"My brothers, I am Wey-a-pier-sen-waw and I am Shawnee! It fills my heart with great pride to sit beside the chief of the Miamis. At the first light tomorrow morning we will attack the army that dares to cut down trees and build their ugly forts in the woods where we live. Like Me-she-kin-nogh-quah did last year when the leaves were red and yellow, and his brave warriors sent the white general and his soldiers running back to their big fort on the Ohio River like scared squaws, tomorrow we will put St. Clair's army to rout!"

He paused as a wave of murmuring swept through the assembly. They had plenty of time before first light so he permitted the wave of excitement to run its course before he continued:

"Before our Shawnee Chief Catahecassa--the one some call Black Hoof--the Shawanese were wisely led by Chief Black Fish who took the white man's lead bird in the hip socket and died as the leaves were falling in 1779. It was Black Fish who said to us: 'It is not the number of warriors we have but their unyielding spirit that makes the difference in battle!' Now I say to you, it is that same spirit in those gathered here tonight that will enable us to overcome the white man's army that sleeps nearby!"

Blue Jacket raised his silver-tipped tomahawk in silent anger and a spirit of defiance as he said softly but meaningfully:

"We attack at first light so we can see and do not kill each other! We will take many scalps before the sun sets again!"

As Blue Jacket concluded and took his seat beside Little Turtle, Tecumseh nodded his approval. He was thinking about the year of 1779 Blue Jacket mentioned. On March 21st in 1779 the leader of the Delaware Rabbit Clan, Chief Running Fox, counseled his followers after George Rogers Clark had captured the British fort at Vincennes:

"Now we must leave this country--the white man has deep roots in the soil of the land north of the Ohio and their hold will be impossible to destroy. They will overrun this country!"

In the darkness no one could see the look of utter contempt on Tecumseh's face as he thought to himself: "Running Fox would feel different were he sitting in this war council tonight!"

His thought process was now interrupted as the Miami chief turned to Apekonit asking him to summon "Tarhe, The Crane" to share his counsel with them. Called "The Crane" because of his tall, graceful, and slender build, the Wyandot's tribal chief was known far and wide for both his physical endurance and a willingness to get along with the white man. This would be particularly true after the Treaty of Fort Greene Ville. Tarhe also had a reputation for being merciful to his captives and many belligerent Indians had rejected his counsel and leadership on occasion. But this night it was Little Turtle who decided they would hear Tarhe's counsel.

Seated beside Tarhe was his second-in-command, "Roundhead," and he listened carefully as Apekonit relayed the summons. Slowly the Wyandot chief rose to his feet and murmurs of resentment swept through the assembly as word passed that the Wyandot chief now stood before them. He knew some considered him less militant than his Wyandot predecessors who had formed an alliance with the Shawanese on the Scioto River boasting: "The Wyandot Indian is never taken alive!" It had been this alliance of former years that gained for them an unenviable reputation among the white men as being: "First for war and last for peace!"

This Wyandot leader's willingness to listen to what others had to say was destined to gain for him great respect during the Treaty of Greene Ville ne- gotiations and General Wayne would accord Tarhe The Crane the privilege of being given a duplicate copy of the treaty for safe-keeping among the Indians. The treaty would consist of two sheets of parchment as big as a door and be signed by 80 Indian chiefs and by General Wayne and his staff. By the treaty the Indians would receive a $9,500 annuity and one sixth of a cent per acre for the land surrendered to the United States---land which was to be divided among twelve tribes.

Seated beside Little Turtle, Tecumseh eyed the Wyandot chief with mixed emotions--four years later he would tell Tarhe The Crane what he could do with the Treaty of Greene Ville. Now, in early November of 1791, he watched Little Turtle rise to his feet, raise his hand--palm forward--and say:

"My brothers, the Wyandot warriors journeyed a great distance to join us and now we will listen to the counsel of their chief, Tarhe The Crane!"

Even in the semi-darkness Tarhe the Crane saw

the imperceptible nod by Little Turtle as a hushed silence blanketed the assembly. Then Tarhe began:

"Tonight I have heard my brothers speak of the all consuming hate that burns in their hearts for white men who drive their wood stakes in the mother earth to divide this land into what they call 'property.' I say to you now what I have told the white man--the earth belongs to everyone and no one has a right to divide it! The Great Spirit does not want it to be divided! For many moons I have asked the Great Spirit to bring a peace to those in this land who have different colored skin but my prayers have gone unanswered and a treaty seems as far away as the moon that does not light our way this night."

From the snow clouds an ever increasing number of snow flakes now fell through the tree branches and many Indians pulled blankets close around their shoulders as they listened to The Crane:

"With the first light my Wyandot warriors will join you against those who violate this land. But I tell you, as I have told my warriors, there is no courage, no bravery, no strength in torturing those unable to defend themselves--such acts do not prove our superiority! My heart has been heavy with revulsion and shame by some of my brother's actions-- we all lower ourselves to something beneath animals when we torture our enemy! The white man deserves death--but the death of a man!"

The Wyandots were a branch of the Huron nation trained to die for the honor of their tribe and to consider submission to the enemy the lowest form of degradation. They had once lived near the Georgian Bay in Canada until 1648 when their ancient and relentless foe, the Iroquois, almost succeeded in exterminating them. Thwarted in their move westward by the Sioux, the Wyandots migrated to the western end of Lake Erie about 1701 and then to the region south of the Sandusky River in 1749. Here they were instrumental in erecting the first Catholic Church in the region that was to become "Ohio" and Father

Armond de la Richardie was their spiritual leader.

Tarhe pledged his allegiance to Little Turtle in 1791 out of desperation and frustration with the many abortive peace overtures; the senseless murder of Chief Logan's family; the unbelievable slaughter of Delaware Christians at Gnadenhutten; the killing of Chief Cornstalk; and the wanton destruction of the Indian's food supply by General Harmar's troops the year before. These were acts by the white man Tarhe did not understand! But it would be this man who in 1795 would be a supporter of the peace offer by the United States in open and bitter opposition to the young Shawnee Little Turtle had praised this night and now listened out of respect for the Miami chief.

Based on the Treaty of Fort McIntosh signed on January 21, 1785, the Treaty of Greene Ville would declare that all of the north-western land in what would become Ohio would be exclusively Indian land forever. Ungraced with the knowledge and education of the white negotiators, the legalistic term "in perpetuum" would be explained and understood by the Indians as meaning: "As long as the trees grow and the rivers run."

Clear and simple as it would sound, in 1795 it would be Tecumseh who would counsel "caveat emptor" to Tarhe and the Indians who "bought" the promises of the white man. The unique situation provided by the Treaty of Greene Ville was to last only a short time and on July 4, 1805 the United States government would initiate its first diplomatic thrust for more property in "the promised land! The Treaty of Fort Industry would be inked as an embittered Chief Tecumseh glowered and exclaim: "Did I not tell you it would be so!"

In the ensuing years the white man would dismember and separate the Wyandot's "domain." And by 1817 the Treaty of the Maumee Rapids would reduce the Indian land to only nine reservations...a tenth would be graciously added in 1818 by the Treaty of

St. Marys. But then in 1827 the reservations would
be divided up among the individual Indian families
with 160 acres apportioned to the majority--more to
large families. The "common bond" would be gone!

But even in this "end" there would be one more
restriction--the government decreed none of the apportioned land could be "divided up" and sold.   It
would be the brutal murder of Chief Sum-mum-de-wat
in 1841 that would convince the Wyandots they could
not live in "peace" with the white man. So in 1842
they would reluctantly accept the U.S. Government's
offer of a "home in the west" and Chief Jacques was
destined to lead his Wyandots to Kansas--their last
claims to Ohio land would be extinguished.   Unfortunately, this would not be the last sad chapter in
the Wyandot's history. Later they would once again
be uprooted and moved to Oklahoma.

But the sun would shine for many years on the
Wyandots after November of 1791 and Tarhe The Crane
would be mercifully spared much of the humiliation
and discomfort of his people's moving problems--his
mortal remains would be put to rest in November of
1818 along the banks of the Sandusky River in Crane
Town, Ohio as his second wife, Virginia born "Aunt
Sally" Frost, looked on.

Now, on this bitter cold night in early November of 1791, Tecumseh was not "buying" any of Chief
Tarhe's veiled hopes or admonishment about "mercy"
for the white invader--there had been enough "talk"
and it had not stopped the encroachment. Instinctively Tecumseh touched his war club and then his
hand closed around the scalping knife hanging from
his belt.   Before the sun would set again his war
club would summarily end the lives of many who now
shivered on the opposite side of the Ouabache River
a short distance south of the Indian's "cold camp."
Tecumseh was relishing the thought of cleaving some
white man's skull when Tarhe again began to speak:

"I would remind all of my brothers our fathers
and their fathers before them always prayed to our

Great Father for strength to win."

The normally mild-mannered and gentle Wyandot chief raised his face toward the sky where a little break in the inky darkness above provided a glimpse of the moon and bathed Tecumseh's face briefly as he added fervently: "Let us pray our Great Father will be with us tomorrow."

When Tarhe The Crane had taken his seat again, Little Turtle arose from his cross-legged position and stepped forward among the warriors. With palms upturned and face uplifted, the Miami chief's voice carried out over the hushed assembly:

"Never have these eyes beheld such an army of brave warriors so determined to crush the white man who invades the land where we live and carries away our women and children. I listened with sadness as Tecumseh spoke of Cornstalk and his capture by the white soldiers. Now I tell you that even as we are gathered together tonight my daughter, Wanagapeth, wife of Apekonit who is as my own son, is now held prisoner at Fort Washington by the general who now camps across the Ouabache and dares to lead an army against us!"

A startled gasp swept through the audience and word quickly passed saying Little Turtle had turned to look upon his adopted son, William Wells, whose name was changed to "Apekonit" after he willingly submitted to the Indian ritual of having the white blood washed from his body. His red hair prompted the name whose English translation was "carrot top" and he had married Wanagapeth, the Indian name for "Sweet Breeze." Now tonight Apekonit felt an over-whelming sense of sadness as Little Turtle said:

"Like Tarhe, I too have long dreamed of living in peace with the white man who comes to this land and inflames our warriors with hate and makes them cry out for revenge! Like Blue Jacket and Tecumseh there is a great hate in my bosom tonight. But the promise of many scalps and fine horses that will be ours before the sun sets again does not bring great joy as I think of my daughter being held a prisoner by the white general who makes his camp across the Ouabache tonight!"

The hushed stillness was broken by the murmurs that spread through the assembly as word passed indicating Apekonit had stepped to the side of Little Turtle who now added:

"My son, Apekonit, also carries this burden in his bosom. The white man has burned our villages, scoured our fields, destroyed our food, girdled our trees, and devastated our orchards. Now the white man holds my daughter in his prison while he marches to kill us!"

Apekonit glanced at Little Turtle and recalled he too had been taken prisoner when 11 years of age by Gaviahatte, a Wea chief called "The Porcupine." Later Gaviahatte gave the boy to Little Turtle who adopted him as his son. As a boy, his being white proved a big help when he was used as a willing decoy to lure boat travelers on the Ohio to the shore where those who hoped to help a stranded youth were robbed and killed. Tonight Apekonit also recalled that only two months before he learned his younger brother was Colonel Samuel Wells who marched with General Charles Scott in August of 1791 and, at the mouth of the Tippacanoe, it was this party that had taken prisoner his wife, Wanagapeth.

It had been a real surprise when the brothers faced each other September 1st---the Piankashaw and Wea sub-tribes of the Miami nation desired to talk about "peace" and Apekonit served as an interpreter when they met with American soldiers escorting prisoners to Fort Washington. Apekonit was not aware his wife was among the prisoners. In a subsequent meeting with Colonel Wells, Apekonit was told about their brothers Hayden, Jonathan, and Carty--and the colonel said he himself had married and now he and his wife Mary had a daughter, Rebekah. The family news tugged at Apekonit's heart strings but he remained loyal to Little Turtle.

And, until the day when he would face Little
Turtle and declare his intent to return to his people and fight against the Indians if necessary, he
remained faithful to his red-skinned brothers. On
this bitterly cold night in early November of 1791
Apekonit knew where his allegiance lay.

In the summer of 1792 William Wells would tell
General Rufus Putnam where the cannons left by St.
Clair's army along the banks of the Wabash had been
secreted. Three years later he would become chief
of General Wayne's "spies." Two other victims of
Indian kidnappings, Henry and Christopher Miller,
would also leave their red-skinned brothers and become scouts and interpreters for General Wayne. In
the summer of 1795 all would be at Fort GreeneVille
with the victorious white soldiers.

A grandson of Little Turtle, Wayne Wells, was
destined to graduate from West Point in 1821 but by
then his father, William Wells, would have died in
a massacre at Fort Dearborn on August 12, 1812--the
Indians would never forget Apekonit's "about face"
after being adopted and he would suffer the "death"
accorded such turncoats.

Now, on November 3, 1791, Apekonit's recollection of his brothers was broken as Little Turtle's
voice pierced the hushed silence:

"Now we rest in order that our bodies will be
strong for the play tomorrow. Confidence must fill
our empty bellies tonight! Thoughts of the scalps
we will take will be a fever that heats our blood.
You know the signals Blue Jacket and I have agreed
on and at first light we attack! Together we will
drive from this country the monstrous white dragon
that seeks to devour us! Oh Great Spirit, protect
us and guide us in the play tomorrow!"

Twenty-two year old Apekonit felt a strong arm
encircle his shoulder--it was Blue Jacket. Seeing
the two men embrace, Tecumseh thought to himself:

"I am not convinced all of the white blood has
been washed out of Apekonit! Little Turtle and his

adopted son are close but I feel we will someday no longer have Apekonit at our campfire---his knowledge of our ways will be used against us!"

Tecumseh had no way of knowing how prophetic his intuition was. Williams Wells was destined to receive $2,000 for 23 months of service to the U.S. Government from September 1793 to August 1795. For a wound received while in service, he would receive a lifetime pension of $20 per month. And, in 1808, Congress would grant him a pre-emptive right to 300 acres of choice land near Fort Wayne. But that was years in the future as Apekonit now waited with his comrades to "surprise " St. Clair's army.

Standing close to Little Turtle this night was an Indian sympathizer. In his long red coat he had quietly listened to the orations by various Indian personages. Simon Girty was the only British agent present this early November night---Matthew Elliott and Alexander McKee were elsewhere.

The British had liberally supported the attack with clothing, guns, ammunition, axes, and hatchets but preferred to maintain a low profile insofar as personnel were concerned. They remembered Governor St. Clair's letter to Major Murray, Commandant of Fort Detroit, in September of 1790 assuring him the Americans had no intention of attacking the British interests---they also remembered the plundering and looting of John Kinzie's trading post in October of 1790. Now, in spite of the Indian's "victory" over General Harmar and the passage of one year's time, the British were carefully avoiding a face-to-face confrontation with the Americans at this time.

Their agent, Simon Girty, had had a long asso- ciation with the Indians. His family was captured in 1756 by French led Indians who seized and burned Fort Granville on the banks of the Juniata River in Pennsylvania. After his step-father, John Turner, had been tortured to death, Simon and his brothers, 13 year old James and 11 year old George, had been adopted---James by Shawanese, George by Delawares, and Simon by the Senecas.   Released in 1759 by the Indians, Simon Girty was employed as an interpreter at Fort Pitt under British agent Alexander McKee. Small wonder Simon Girty found his allegiance tied closely to the interests of the British and Indians with whom he had associated so long.

And now, on this early November night, the man many called "a deserter and renegade" recalled how on June 7th in 1782 he warned Colonel William Crawford about the Indian's avowed vengeance after the senseless murder of the Moravian Indians at Gnadenhutten and the "surprise" that awaited him.   Later Simon Girty helplessly watched the Indians torture and burn Crawford at the stake along the Tymochtee River.   Although Girty had offered money to obtain Crawford's release, he himself was almost tied to a stake for suggesting such a thing.   Still fresh in their minds was how he had helped Simon Kenton, his "blood brother," who later had forsaken the Indian adoption pledge.

Girty was very familiar with the Indian's vengeance and would never forget his inability to help William Crawford.   But how could he save a man who led an army in 1782 that posted signs reading: "No Indian heathen, Christian, man, boy, or girl should be spared!"

In the "diaper years" of this nation's history many claimed Indians slayed from an utter depravity of the heart and not just a retaliation against the wrong doer.   But many of the sachems, and warriors, who now waited for "the play" on November 3rd, 1791 wondered if the proclamation on those signs carried by Colonel William Crawford's followers represented a different attitude than the one they were accused of.

Standing beside Simon Girty this night was the grotesquely painted sachem known as "Black Eagle." Pulling a buffalo robe around him, a shiver coursed through his muscular body---it was as much the hate that possessed his body as the cold.   Although his

body ached with the pangs of hunger, and his pouch
contained a strip of dried meat and a some parched
corn, he would not touch these tonight. Beside him
lay his war club made from the skin of an ox tail
which had been softened and split so a round, fist-
sized rock could be sewn into one end and the other
end sewn around a short length of strong stick. As
it had dried, the hide stretched tightly around the
stone and handle leaving a limber section of hide
about eight inches long separating them. The makeshift mace was very effective and this night Black
Eagle savored the thought of smashing a white man's
skull with his war club. Such thoughts helped ward
off the raw winds that brought an icy chill to the
very marrow of his bones.

It was difficult for some people to understand
the uncontrolled hatred of what they referred to as
"the savage mind"---a human being who had witnessed
the utter devastation of the wilderness in which he
lived, hunted, and fished the quiet streams flowing
through untouched virgin forests devoid of property
stakes. Admittedly many of these pagan inhabitants
of the Northwest Territory had massacred the "white
invader" and even bashed out the brains of children
against trees. But the red-skinned natives did not
understand the encroacher either--the white invader
who drove his "property stakes" in the land, built
forts in the woods, bludgeoned to death the Indian
Christians, murdered Chief Logan's daughter without
cause, and killed in cold blood the Shawanese chief
who entered the white man's fort carrying a flag of
truce. It was a time without understanding on both
sides and in early November of 1791 unbridled hate
filled the hearts of the Indians who waited in the
darkness north of St. Clair's encampment.

But it wasn't so dark that Black Eagle did not
see the silent expression of intent by Shemento, or
"Black Snake" as some called him, who gesticulated
his vengeful hate by drawing an index finger across
his throat. Black Eagle's lips tightened as he now

lifted his war club in silent agreement.

It was a common thought among white people the Indians, by their very nature, could never live in peace. A white personage in Philadelphia declared:

"Even among their own kind, Indians are seldom calm for long. It is their nature to be warlike!"

Little Turtle had heard this during talks with the British at Detroit and told his tribal sachems:

"Far across the great waters toward the rising sun, wars in Europe between the white soldiers are legend. Are we any different?"

And around their campfires the Indians talked about the many treaties "negotiated" with the white man. Well respected in 1791, Little Turtle said:

"Treaties with the white man are difficult to understand sometimes---there is a language barrier. But was not the man called 'The Father of the Thirteen Fires' once criticized when he signed a treaty with the French he did not understand? Are we any different?"

Treaties were often not understood by either party and were, unfortunately, easily broken---the effects of the whiskey soon wore off, the beads and presents were soon forgotten, and the settler's desire for land was without end in the eyes of those who watched their wilderness "domain" shrink. And so the settlers felled trees by day with their guns at their sides and watched for the Indians who lay in wait for an opportunity to "get even!"

At breakfast on November 3rd, 1791, Washington had inquired of the portly and pompous Secretary of War as to the progress of St. Clair's expedition. It was generally agreed early that year the government had no choice but to dispatch a military force to "subdue" the Indians and establish a strong military presence at the head of the Maumee River. In typical language Knox had said: "The Indians must be removed, absorbed, or extirpated!"

The president had eyed the secretary carefully and said: "Let's not be pedantic Henry!"

But now, as the rays of the autumn sun filtered through a leafless tree just outside his office
window, Knox carefully examined St. Clair's report
dated September 21, 1791.   With a smile he noticed
work had started on the first of the line of forts
and it would be called "Fort Hamilton." Henry Knox
knew the Secretary of Treasury would be elated. He
also knew the president would be pleased with this
progress so the former bookseller began to prepare
"his report" for Washington.   Reviewing the draft,
he lined out "extirpate" and inserted "root out."

A century and a half later "extirpation" of a
people would bring almost universal condemnation of
a German paper hanger. Descendants of many who had
applauded Henry Knox's declaration regarding extirpation of the Indians in the Ohio country would cry
out in righteous indignation against the fiend who
would advocate extirpation of some people who could
trace their descent from Abraham, Issac, and Jacob.

Progenitors of some who would cry out against
the German Chancellor's inhumanity in the 20th century would, in the 19th century, proclaim: "A time
soon will be coming when white laborers will all be
be crowded out by a pestiferous class of ignorant
blacks and we will have a reign of crime and want!"
And, in 1850--by a two-thirds majority vote of the
Constitutional Convention--a senator from Ohio was
destined to present a memorial to the U. S. Senate
requesting the federal government establish a line
of steamers between the United States and Liberia
on the ground of giving impulse to colonization of
blacks in Africa. The memorial would read:

"We should use all honorable means to induce
the free blacks to emigrate to Africa!"

Although the Indians were not privy to the education of many white men who came to the Northwest
Territory, they were not stupid. They had heard at
Fort Detroit about the white man's avowed intent to
"extirpate" them. At Detroit Apekonit also heard
the British Commandant, Richard G. England, was not

favorably impressed with Blue Jacket and had said:

"I have not the highest opinion of either his zeal or abilities.!"* Now, on this tension-filled early November night in 1791, Apekonit had mixed emotions as he looked at Blue Jacket and thought to himself:

"Tomorrow my father and you will lead us as we do unto the white invader what he would do unto us! But so be it! Caesar would be proud of you tonight Blue Jacket!"

In the cold cheerless late autumn darkness the red-head did not see the momentary cloud of sadness that crossed Blue Jacket's face--he well remembered the proud black runaway slave who became a Shawnee warrior and was killed at Fort Boonesborough during the Indian's attack on that settlement in September of 1778. As young warriors Caesar and Blue Jacket had been friendly antagonists but each proved his worth in their youthful years never thinking of the difference in the color of their skins.

Six years after Apekonit and Blue Jacket talked this November night in 1791, Little Turtle would visit Philadelphia and talk with Francis Volney, a French philosopher and traveler. While speaking of the color of one's skin, Little Turtle would say:

"I have seen Spaniards in Louisiana and found no difference of color between them and me--and why should there be any? In them, as in us, it is the work of the 'Father of Colors,' the sun that burns us. Indian means 'indigine' or one sprung from the soil."

---

* Referred to as "a white man turned Indian" by some 19th and 20th century writers whose narratives are either self-serving, repetitious, or sensational drivel devoid of supporting facts, many credible researchers believe "old" chief Blue Jacket was of Indian parentage. Contrary to what some have written, the author found no proof to support the story that Marmaduke, son of John and Catherine (Stull) Swearingen, became the Shawnee War Chief, co-leader of the attack on St. Clair's army in 1791

Another tribal sachem, one who was destined to visit with President Adams nine years later, was in Little Turtle's "cold camp" on November 3rd. Buckongehelas, chief of the Delawares, would later talk with Colonel Israel Ludlow and his wife, Charlotte, in Cincinnati. Called "Deer Chaser" by some, Buckongehelas would call Mrs. Ludlow "La-na-pak-wa" and profess his religious belief telling her:

"Me know Jesus--me love Jesus. Me old and soon lay down but me shall meet Jesus."

But this fateful night in 1791 Buckongehelas' face was set in expressionless lines and his hate-filled eyes were cold and steely---they matched the ominous dark snow clouds above. He was thinking about how Colonel Williamson's soldiers had shown no mercy as they murdered the Indians at Gnadenhutten. Tomorrow his warriors would do the same. Surrounded by Delaware warriors, Buckongahelas now pulled a small silver box from the doeskin pouch he carried. As he had told Chief Teteboxti, the old king of the Delawares:

"Me got little box from The Silver Man who has store at Miamitown."

Using a greasy substance from the box, he now began applying to his face and exposed skin his war paint--a mixture of black soot and water.

The Delawares were a branch of the Lenni-Lenope (The People) tribes of Algonquin stock who had been pushed out of the verdant fields along the Delaware River by their neighbors to the north, the Iroquois Indians, and moved west about 1740 to the Muskingum Valley northwest of the Ohio River. The French had called this tribe "the wolves" or Loups. They were given their "white name" by the white man in honor of the then governor of Virginia, Thomas West, third baron of Del La Warr. The senseless killing of the Indians at Gnadenhutten had brought the frustrated Delaware's vengeful hate to a boiling point! They were done talking and Buckongehelas, Little Turtle, and Blue Jacket formed an alliance against the army led by St. Clair vowing to: "Fight unto death!"

Sheltered from the bitter wind by the trunk of a huge oak tree, Chief A-goosh-a-way of the Ottawas sat motionless beside "Whingy Pooshies," a Delaware sachem his British friends called "Big Cat." With a blanket draped tightly around his shoulders, the Ottawa chief's face was impassive as he listened to the short and brawny "Big Cat" talk with the young and muscular Thu-pe-ne-bu, son of Potawatomie Chief Anaquiba from along the St. Joseph River. Although hungry, the trio would not touch the jerky or pemican in their pouches. When "Big Cat" mentioned the treaty talks with St. Clair at Fort Harmar, Thu-pe-ne-bu, not yet twenty-one years of age, echoed the words of his hero, Tecumseh, who had said:

"White man's talk is like bird that flies!"

Conspicuous by the absence of any great number in November of 1791, the Potawatomies were destined to appear en masse for the Treaty of Greene Ville negotiations. Although Chief Thu-pe-ne-bu would be there, and would sign the treaty in 1795, he would follow the guidance of Tecumseh as long as his hero trod the wilderness paths. He would be awe-struck when Tecumseh correctly prophesized the two-thirty in the morning earthquake on December 16, 1811 that would center around the confluence of the Ohio and "Lord of all waters," the muddy Mississippi.

Crouching with their feet drawn close to their body, two Shawnee warriors listened to Apekonit and Blue Jacket talk. Only the occasional lonely hoot of an owl had been heard when, close to midnight, a dozen shots echoed through the woods. The one with an ugly scar on his left cheek remarked:

"Those were close!"

"White man's guns," said the other Indian confidently. "Our warriors would not shoot tonight."

He was right.

Unable to sleep, and seated by the fire enjoying a fresh chew of tobacco, Hank Weiser heard the volley of shots and thought: "Them shots came from across the river—Kentucky militia probably! Never know what they may be up to." Listening carefully, but hearing no more shooting, Hank stretched, yawned, and muttered to himself: "Time I get my beauty sleep! Sure be good to get back home and see Sarah and the kids!"

Infrequent shots had been heard all evening as the flank and rear guards took pot shots at real or imaginary Indians who appeared around the periphery of St. Clair's encampment. Plagued by his painful gout, and unable to sleep, St. Clair heard the gunfire across the river about midnight and stepped to the opening of his tent. Hearing no more shots, he lay down consoling himself with the thought that he was a short distance from what Little Turtle said was: "That glorious gate through which all the good words of our chiefs pass from east to the west and from the north to the south!

Regardless of the lack of detailed information on maps St. Clair carried--and it is understandable he might have mistaken the headwaters of the Wabash for the St. Mary's River--failing to know precisely where his army was in the wilderness was a tactical error by St. Clair who now found himself ringed on all sides by infrequent but disconcerting sounds of gunfire. Thus, with the snowflakes now falling in an ever increasing amount as the night wore on, St. Clair was closer to the gates of eternity than the gates of the Miami villages---but St. Clair did not know that on Thursday night, November 3rd, 1791.

And only two miles north of where the general lay, Little Turtle had also heard the staccato gunfire but his stoic countenance did not change---his warriors had been told not to fire their guns under any circumstances. The lead balls of the frightened soldiers had harmlessly buried in the trees and fallen logs where the scouting party quickly took refuge. Even as the white soldiers passed near the spot where the warriors lay hidden in the shadow of the thick underbrush, the Indians never moved. the soldiers faded into the snowy darkness back toward the river and then all was deathly quiet--but still the Indians lay still for a long time.

Soon after the war council ended Little Turtle sent Apekonit to summon the son of the Mohawk chief who had been unable to join the war party, Captain Joseph Brant (Thayendanega). Apekonit located the young man standing by a horse that nuzzled his hand affectionately--the black gelding had a white right forefoot and a little white patch in the middle of its forehead that resembled a star. Like his well-known father, the youthful warrior wore a bear claw necklace and a single feather headpiece. When told the black gelding belonged to Blue Jacket, Captain Brant's son remarked:

"Chief Blue Jacket knows his horses! I wonder where he got such a beautiful creature?"

While stroking the gelding before Apekonit put in his appearance, this son of Captain Joseph Brant had been thinking about his 51 year old father who was busy back home cultivating peace overtures and could not attend. As a boy his father had attended Doctor Eleazar Wheelock's Indian School (Dartmouth College in later years) and had been asked by Henry Knox to promote peace proposals. Although Thayendanega could not join Little Turtle's undertaking, he did send his son and some Mohawk warriors of the Six Nations confederacy.* As his son was preparing to leave, Captain Joseph Brant had said:

"St. Clair has always treated me fairly in our dealings---it is unfortunate he marches against the Miamis and Shawanese while I talk of peace. *

Years later, in his "Memoirs of Early Pioneer Settlers of Ohio" (1854), Arthur Hildreth would relate how, as a young man, Joseph Brant embraced the

---

* The personal memoirs of Benjamin Van Cleve indicate he was instructed by Henry Knox on June 23, 1792 to deliver two fine horses to Captain Joseph Brant at the City Tavern in New York

teachings of Freemasonry. Now in early November of
1791 Joseph Brant's son recalled a story his father
had told him about the party of 500 Indians and 200
Tories who had attack the Cherry Valley settlement
northwest of Albany in 1778 and Col. William Stacey
from Massachusetts, a Freemason, had been captured
in the murderous assault. As Stacey was being prepared for burning at the stake, the doomed man gave
the Masonic "distress" sign and Brant, true to his
oath of allegiance, responded and saved his Masonic
brother's life.   At Marietta in 1789 Captain Brant
had seen Colonel Stacey and only last January heard
his son, John Stacey, had been murdered and another
son, Philemon, had been taken prisoner and died in
captivity following what the white man called "The
Big Bottom Massacre."   With mixed emotions Captain
Brant's son pondered the fact tomorrow he must face
his father's Masonic brother, Arthur St. Clair.

A story that circulated years later would say
Captain Joseph Brant was captivated by St. Clair's
daughter and asked for her hand in marriage at Fort
Harmar in 1789. Although a request for the hand of
a white woman by an Indian sometimes provoked great
indignation, the governor merely politely refused.
There were some who felt the Indian's marriage was
motivated by greed and the bride was "bought" like
a bow and arrow--she was a warrior's property. The
white man was superior in intellect and employed a
more sensible arrangement in "civilized "marriages,
the "dowery." It was the job of the warrior to obtain the meat and fish for their subsistence and to
fight when the occasion required...his "squaw" performed all the "drudgery." The white man performed
the same chores as a warrior but his wife only had
to wash dishes and clothing, cook, sew, mend, bear
and care for the children, and "enjoy" the endless
hours of lonely privation in her windowless cabin--
she could also hoe in the field if the weather was
favorable. But no "drudgery!" Women were also not
required to walk behind their man's horse when they

traveled-- well, most of the time anyway.

There were a number of Indian women in Little Turtle's "cold camp" this night--they had conributed nothing to the oratory but squatted around the perimeter of the camp listening. Most wore a loose fitting buckskin pullover garmet that came down below their knees. Around their shoulders they held a blanket tightly to ward off the bitter cold night air. Wearing mocassins, they had walked many miles this November day giving no thought to the "rights" that would be espoused by proponents of NOW and ERA two hundred years later.

Close to where Blue Jacket stood talking with Apekonit, Jonathan Alder listened carefully to each word. Born in New Jersey on September 17th, 1773, like William Wells, Alder had also been captured by Indians when only seven years of age and was adopted by Succohanos, a Mingo chief. Now 18, Alder had volunteered to help Little Turtle. He was destined to remain with the Indians until 1795.

Intently watching the two white youths who had had their "white blood" washed out, an Indian with a hideous scar on his left cheek thought about the young white blacksmith who had saved his life near Cincinnati--Tecumseh had said he was with the white general. It was unfortunate, and would be in the coming years, that many felt the Indians were without feelings of love, compassion, and humor. Many white people called them "stupid, illiterate, backward savages" and traders and settlers were quick to take advantage of them. The fact was the Indian loved, pitied, and perpetrated pranks--and was capable of hate just like the white man.

Near where Little Turtle sat cross-legged engaged in individual conferences with various tribal chiefs, Wingenmund, White Loon, Blackbeard, and the sachems of the Pawnee and Seneca septs talked with the chief of the Ottawas, Egushawa--an Indian chief destined to sign the Treaty of Greene Ville.

But a "treaty" with the white invader was four

518

years in the future and "peace" was the last thing
on any Indian's mind this November night in 1791 as
they waited! Indians had remarkable patience when
necessary--some would spend their lifetime making a
stone tomahawk and not finish it. Their singleness
of purpose, self-control, and self-restraint was i-
deally tailored for wilderness warfare. Now, cold
and uncomfortable--but warmed by their intense hate
for the white man's army that marched north with an
avowed intent to "extirpate" them--Little Turtle's
followers waited in the darkness for "first light"
not more than two miles north of where St. Clair's
army was encamped.

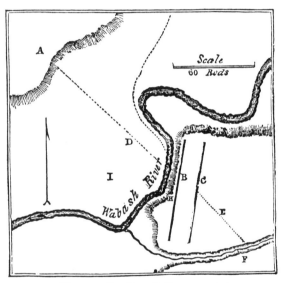

PLAN OF ST. CLAIR'S BATTLE-FIELD.

"References - A. High ground, on which the militia were encamped at
the commencement of the action. B.C. Encampment of the main army.
D. Retreat of the militia at the beginning of the battle. E. St.
Clair's trace, on which the army retreated. F. Place where General
Butler and other officers were buried. G. Trail to Girty's Town,
on the river St. Mary's, at what is now the village of St. Mary's.
H. Site of Fort Recovery, built by Wayne, the line of Darke and
Mercer runs within a few rods of the site of the fort. I. Place
where a brass cannon was found buried in 1830; it is on the bottom
where the Indians were three times driven to the highland with the
bayonet." Pg 228, HOWE'S HISTORICAL COLLECTIONS OF OHIO Vol 2 1896

CHAPTER SEVENTEEN

" THE PLAY "

"Jason, are you asleep?"

"I was--but I am awake now!"

Mary had been unable to sleep much since hearing the staccato gunfire about midnight and she had passed the past five hours thinking about Jason and her starting back down the wilderness road. With Jason now awake, Mary said: I think Hank is up--he put some wood on the fire a while ago."

Jason pulled his wife close to him and kissed her. Although Mary appreciated Jason's amorous intentions, she wriggled out of his embrace saying:

"Jason! Now you stop that!" Trying very hard to be stern, she added: "Dear husband, we have far too much to do this morning for that. And besides, Hank is probably waiting for you."

"But Hank doesn't have Sarah with him! He has nothing else to do!"

Realizing he could not change his wife's mind, Jason added: "All right Mary, you get some sleep-- I will see what Hank is up to."

The first chill gray of dawn had not outlined the surrounding trees on Friday, November 4th, when Jason emerged from his Conestoga. From the nearby woods he heard what sounded like a rooster crowing. To himself Jason thought it must be that one he had seen among the camp followers last week--he did not know the bird had provided the wife and children of its owner with sorely needed food several days ago.

Little Turtle heard the "crowing" of a rooster too but he recognized it as one of the pre-arranged signals he and Blue Jacket had agreed on. As Jason walked over to where Hank was standing close to the fire, his friend said: "Mornin' Jason! Looks like we got a skiff of snow last night."

Although there had been some snow, it was more like a heavy hoarfrost that whitened the ground, tree limbs, and underbrush. Hank had already made some of his "bark tea" and offered Jason some as he said with a smile: "It ain't the best, but it sure will warm yer innards! By the way, did you hear a rooster crow a minute ago? I didn't know there was one within miles of here."

There wasn't!

Now, not far from where Jason sat sipping what tasted like sassafras tea, a husky voice filled the crisp pre-dawn air as the first sergeant of the 2nd U. S. Infantry bellowed:

"All right men, drop your cocks and grab your socks!"

After having performed this perfunctory chore, the "first soldier" as he was called, poked a stick in the smoldering campfire and soon it was blazing brightly. Several of the soldiers now edged close to the fire massaging their cold hands together and uttering mixed expletives. Unable to sleep, one of the young recruits had been writing a letter to his mother when the drum summoned him to roll call. He hastily scribbled "wish I were home" and placed the letter in his pocket as he headed for the military formation. It would never be posted.

Colonel Sargent returned from a pre-dawn visit to the militia camp and reported to St. Clair: "The militia excepted, today we have 1380 troops present or accounted for including the officers and 80 of their servants. The militia's strength is 290 non coms and privates and 29 officers."

And in the Kentucky militia's camp across the river, Private John Burnes faced another breakfast of "short rations" and exclaimed: "Keerist! What I wouldn't give for a slab of side meat and a couple fresh eggs! Bet them regulars ain't up yet!"

He was wrong. St. Clair had been adamant all soldiers must be up and around before daybreak and November 4th was to be no exception. This day was, however, the birthday of a young ensign in Captain Swearingen's company and his fellow officers had a "little surprise" planned for him. Little Turtle had a "big surprise" planned for everyone this day!

In front of the horseman's marquee wherein Van Cleve was preparing to leave at sunup, Officers Mc-Nickle and John Crawford, and Privates Thomas Irwin and Samuel McDowell, enjoyed the heat from a roaring fire. Not far away Major Thomas Butler talked with George Adams about last night's reconnaissance mission. Having already saddled his uncle's horse, Benjamin Van Cleve put some letters in his pouch he had promised to post at Cincinnati. Then he walked out of the marquee saying:

"Morning gentlemen! It's right nippy out this morning--fire sure feels good! I sure hope General St. Clair's gout is better--must be mighty painful. My uncle said he informed the general we might have lost that last load of flour if it had not been for Captain Faulkner and Lieutenant Huston who escorted us down to Fort Hamilton and back. Those soldiers in the captain's company are mighty fine troops!"

He had no way of knowing the Lieutenant Huston he mentioned was destined to fight a duel with Captain Bradshaw at Fort Greene Ville in February of 1794 and both would die of their wounds.

As the troops were now being mustered for roll call in the pre-dawn darkness, St. Clair glanced at the book he held and noted sunrise would be at six-thirty-three and sunset at four fifty-four...it was to be a long day! The general fervently prayed the sorely needed supply train would arrive this day so everyone could be put back on "full rations" and there would be some provender for the animals.

A short distance away Jason and Hank were busy preparing to head back down the wilderness road and Mary hummed as she optimistically used the last of their corn meal to make some corn pone and sorghum molasses for their breakfast. Mary thought to herself: "We can certainly obtain some food from that supply train Jason said was coming up the road."

"Hear that Jason?"

"Sounded like a wild turkey," Jason replied.

"At this hour of the morning?" said Hank.

They had no way of knowing it was Blue Jacket signaling to Little Turtle that his warriors were in place and ready for the attack.

And so, at six-thirty on November 4th in 1791, while campfires were blazing merrily and the first inkling of pre-dawn light was filtering through the trees, the crisp morning air was suddenly rent with what sounded like a thousand cowbells, the staccato sound of gunfire, and the unmistakeable blood curdling war whoops of vengeful Indians. With maniacal screams only blood thirsty savages are capable of, the pre-dawn air errupted and gunfire was heard on all sides of the encampment. From the surrounding woods hundreds of garishly painted Indians swooped upon the Kentucky militia with such fury most fled in wild alarm. With energy born of fathomless hate and vengeful intent, the Indians waded through the panic-stricken militia with tomahawks and war clubs flailing.

Colonel Sargent would later enter in his journal: "The fury was preceded by about 5 minutes by the Indian's yelling, the first I had ever heard. The resistance of the militia deserves not the name of defense...it should be branded as the most ignominious flight."

A post-battle account said Robert Bradshaw saw an Indian and fired the first shot. William Keenan fired at an Indian and then threw his gun aside and ran toward the river. Some of the seasoned militia tried to raise their guns but were hindered by the slashing tomahawks around them. In the midst of an early morning call of nature, Stephen Littell heard the very first war whoop and dove headlong from his squatting position into the nearby underbrush--then he quickly wormed his way into a hollow log whose end was fortunately hidden under the thick branches and dead leaves of a huge uprooted sycamore tree. Paralyzed with fright, Littell prayed as he heard Lieutenant William Briggs yell:

"Take cover men! Take cover!"

For many militiamen the order was too late and even this terror-stricken command was followed by a look of frantic astonishment on Briggs' face as he pitched forward and lay dead--a tomahawk was buried in the lieutenant's skull. Leaping, writhing, and screaming, the crazed red horde swarmed through the Kentucky militia's camp killing their startled vic- tims as they went and then just disappearing in the morning haze and shifting clouds of gunsmoke. Dis- organized, and massed so closely they couldn't keep out of each other's way as they scrambled to locate their gun, the highly touted "wilderness-wise" Ken- tucky militia was literally caught "in the jaws of death" and most never had a chance to fire a single shot before his head was cleaved by some vindictive Indian who wielded his tomahawk, war club, gun, and knife with the vehemence of a depraved mad man.

Officers Montgomery and Leman were killed very early in the attack and Doctor J.S. Gano,* himself wounded, ignored the onslaught around him and tend- ed the wounds of Captain Madison, Lieutenants Owen and Stagner, Private Todd, and others.

With an unending supply of energy prompted by his hate for the white man, Tecumseh waded into the one-sided battle swinging his war club and taking a deadly toll. Swinging his war club with grace and speed, there was still a look of total disbelief on the face of many such as Dan Smith when their head

* Howe, Vol II (1898) pg 226

was split open as if it were an over-ripe pumpkin.
From his inert grasp Smith dropped his prized maple
silver-inlaid pipe tomahawk which he had taken from
the body of a dead Indian during the Battle of Blue
Licks in 1782--engraved on the glistening blade was
"James Stephenson." Pausing only to seize the pipe
tomahawk, Tecumseh continued his murderous attack.

The early morning surprise attack was colossal
and the undisciplined militia never had a fighting
chance as wave after wave of the screaming warriors
ran through the advance camp with a desperate fury.
A half-hour after the attack began, Colonel Oldham
fired a pistol at point-blank range and killed the
Indian who attack him but was felled immediately by
another hideously painted Indian who looped his arm
around the colonel's neck and simultaneously buried
a knife in his back. Then, with lightning speed and
a bloodcurdling yell, the warrior's tomahawk almost
severed Oldham's head from his body as he fell. In
Sargent's post-battle memoirs he declared: "Colonel
Oldham deserved a better command than he had." *

Born in Virginia, and destined to be governor
of Kentucky (1816-1819), Captain George Madison was
wounded but escaped the scalping knife when a young
private in Captain Presley Gray's company shot the
Indian at close range. With a look of surprise on
his painted face, the Indian stumbled and fell into
the militiaman's arms. Allowing the lifeless form
to fall to the ground, the effusive militiaman drew
his knife and began cutting the warrior's queue--it
was the last thing he ever did. Unseen, a warrior
stepped from behind a tree swinging a huge club and
and crushed the young man's skull as if it were an
egg shell. The Indian then pulled his own scalping
knife from his belt and the cold steel did the rest
of the grisly job. The one who had reached for the
queue never saw the blood-spattered Indian who ended his life.

* Pg 267, OAAHSP, Vol. 33 (1925)

Paralyzed by the murderous frenzy, many of the demoralized and panic stricken militia merely stood and looked at the Indians who came leaping from all sides into the militia's camp. The militiaman who had showed Hank the buckskin map fought bravely and might have done more damage but he took a bullet in the throat as he was frantically trying to reload. As the sickening mixture of blood and tobacco juice gushed from his mouth, his wounded comrade-in-arms, Private Thomas Baird, shot the warrior who was preparing to "lift" his friend's scalp. Moments later Baird joined his comrade in eternity.

Seeing a screaming warrior bring his tomahawk down crushing Adam Troyer's skull, Private McGinnis quickly fired his gun at the warrior but he missed. Now threatened with death himself, he threw his gun at the Indian and then raced through the tall grass and cattails in the river bottom.*

In wild confusion the undisciplined militiamen swarmed back across the river into the main camp as the Indians, wielding their war clubs with maniacal fury, downed victim after victim in brutal hand-to-hand combat or close pursuit of the militiamen who threw down their guns and ran for their lives. The thud of war clubs, the frenzied screams of the warriors as well as their quarry, and the overpowering din, was beyond description. Then, in quick order, the waters of the Wabash literally erupted as blood thirsty Indians followed the militia closely brandishing tomahawks and braining the terrified troops with stone axes and gunstocks. The ferocity of the attack and disorganized retreat quickly threw the entire camp into disorder and chaotic rout.

On the brow of the river bank overlooking the bottom land, attempts to utilize the cannons proved

* Genealogical research by Robert D. Von Tress, Dallas, TX indicates Troyer's sister, Mary Elizabeth, married Jacob May. Her sister, Christena, married William Von Tress, Robert's progenitor. Pg 911, HISTORY OF KENTUCKY (1885)

to be futile. Not only was it impossible to lay an effective barrage in the lower terrain, Apekonit's warriors were doing a good job of "taking out" the artillery as Little Turtle had instructed. Colonel George Gibson was wounded early in the assault on the artillery. But even as he was being carried to the center of the main camp by Private Thomas Irwin and Ensign Bines, Gibson shouted:

"Show no fear men! True Virginians don't show fear! Stand your ground and fight! Better to die ten thousand deaths than let those red savages take the field."

Destined to die of his wounds at Fort Jefferson the following month, of this man Sargent would write in his memoirs: "Colonel Gibson, dangerously wounded, had not, that I know of, an opportunity to display much military ability."*

As the artillerymen tried desperately to ready their pieces for firing, Captain Mahlon Ford barked orders to the troops who were casting frantic looks at the horde of painted Indians swarming across the shallow river and wading into Major Thomas Butler's infantry battalion. Small but feisty, Captain Ford was breathing fire like the oldest warhorse as he shouted words of encouragement to his artillerymen. Suddenly, and without warning, a party of screaming warriors rushed forward from the brow of the river bank trying to spike the cannons. Although Captain James Bradford and his troops managed to thwart the attempt, he was mortally wounded. Startled by the fury of the charge, Lieutenant Burgess stood dumbfounded looking at Bradford who slumped over one of the cannons—he had taken a ball in the temple and blood spurted from the hole in a pulsating geyser. An Indian's tomahawk killed Burgess moments later.

Mislabeled kegs and defective powder added to the confusion and artillerymen soon began to desert their pieces as the Indian marksmen mowed them down with deadly accuracy. A shrewd military tactician, Little Turtle had instructed Apekonit: "Take three hundred warriors and concentrate on the artillery!" The artillery was silenced less than one hour after the attack began.

With the cannons in the front line now silent, some of the Indians moved about removing scalps as the fighting raged all around them. Private Irwin, one of the few surviving artillerymen, wrote in his diary later: "The battle reminded me of a furious thunderstorm that comes up quickly and rapidly, and soon disappears leaving havoc and destruction in its path."

Twirling his grisly trophy around, and sending blood from it flying, an Indian uttered an unearthly victory cry as he ran through the camp close to where Jason and three other men lay behind an overturned wagon. Shortly after the attack started, it was Hank who suggested his wagon be overturned and used as a bulwark against the Indians. Assisted by John Finley, Jason and Hank turned the wagon on its side and leaned it against the tree beside Jason's Conestoga. Among their earthly possessions in the Conestoga, Jason's terrified wife took refuge under a tarpaulin. As the blood-spattered Indian came abreast of where the three men lay, he stopped and gave them a menacing look. Then tucking the grisly scalp beneath his belt, he reached for the tomahawk hanging at his side and took one step toward them. But that was as close as he ever got--the ball from Hank's gun hit the warrior between his eyes and he fell forward dead.

A little shaken by the incident, Jason heard a familiar voice calling his name. He turned quickly and saw the adjutant general leaning against an old elm tree holding his left elbow in his right hand and blood oozing from between his fingers. Signaling with his left hand that he wanted help, Colonel Sargent exclaimed:

"I've taken a ball Jason! Help me get over to

Doctor Grasson's tent."

It was not a request--it was a command. Jason stared at Sargent for a split second as he thought: "The colonel called me by my first name!"

It was one hell of a time to be thinking about such a trivial matter but Jason could not help but recall how the pompous colonel had always insisted on formality and required the use of one's rank in all conversations. To the colonel he now said:

"Let me put a tourniquet on that arm and then I will help you over to the doctor's tent."

The zing of a ball passing close prompted Sargent to duck nervously and Jason thought: "That is a useless gesture sir! You'll never hear the ball that has your name on it!"

Having quickly applied a tourniquet, Jason now helped Sargent to the tent where Doctor Grasson was providing medical service as best he could with the limited supplies he had. Although destined to stay on the battlefield, he attended the wounded as much as possible. One poor soldier had taken a gun shot in his stomach and part of his intestines protruded through a gaping hole in his belly. Sargent took a look at the soldier's stomach and threw up.

Emboldened by their success among the Kentucky militia, the Indians swarmed through Major Butler's battalion and into the one commanded by Major John Clarke. Although Clarke had his thigh bone broken by a bullet, he led a spirited charge on his horse. But in spite of Clarke's courageous leadership, and that of Captain Richard Sparks whose insistent encouragement repeatedly rallied his men for a while, their brave efforts proved to be of no consequence as wave after wave of the screaming Indians pushed across the shallow river and up the banks into the main camp. Winthrop Sargent's later account of the battle read:

"Determined to enter the main camp the Indians followed close on the heels of the militia and the smart fire from the first line met the enemy. This hot fire scarcely slowed the vicious onslaught and the withering return fire caused panic. In a few minutes the soldiers were engaged in every quarter. Killing off the perimeter guards, the Indians then approached close to the lines firing from behind trees. They advanced from one tree, log, or stump, to another under cover of the smoke of our fire. The artillery and musketry made a tremendous noise but did little executions. The Indians seemed to brave everything. It was difficult, if not impossible, to know where to direct your fire."

At the first sound of the blood curdling war whoops and gunfire that echoed through the pre-dawn air, the ailing St. Clair had mounted his horse as quickly as his painful condition would permit and rode up and down the line shouting to his officers to prepare for an attack. Such a warning scarcely needed vocal expression as the militiamen soon came bounding up the river embankment closely pursued by the hideously painted warriors wielding their tomahawks and knives in a murderous onslaught.

St. Clair ordered his aide to secure a strong box which contained some military papers and a very small sum of cash. The military payroll, reported "on the way" from Philadelphia, was not destined to arrive at Fort Washington until January—two months later. St. Clair's personal cash funds were meager and he had spent much of it, and incurred personal indebtedness, in his sincere efforts to satisfy all government obligations. His aide soon found a hole in a white oak tree near Major Gaither's battalion and secreted the strong box noting only the hollow had housed raccoons and other wild life for years.

An imposing figure on his white mount, General St. Clair soon became a target for the Indians who had been instructed by Little Turtle to "kill the officers who lead the white soldiers." One of the Indians now raced through the shallow waters of the partially ice encrusted river and quickly made his way to the brow of the river bank. With a complete

530

disregard for his own personal safety, the warrior
ran upstream a short distance, dropped to one knee,
and took aim at an officer on a big white horse who
was shouting words of encouragement to the frightened troops. Fortunately, for St. Clair, his horse
reared just as the warrior's gun flashed--his mount
was not as lucky and it fell dead. Thrown off his
horse, St. Clair scrambled away from the dead beast
as quickly as his painful condition would allow and
sought cover by a cannon where several lifeless men
stared at him with unseeing eyes. Quickly ordering
an ensign to find him another mount, St. Clair now
eyed a wounded militia officer limping toward him.
With the harsh, bitter gun smoke burning his eyes,
the officer managed a half- hearted salute saying:
"Lieutenant Stagner sir."
The lieutenant had taken a ball in his arm and
was being helped by Joseph Todd,* a twenty-two year
old private in Captain George Madison's company who
had also been wounded--he had been shot in the left
wrist. Along with several other wounded men, they
had escaped across the river but now blood covered
Stagner's breeches and the red sap of life dripped
from the fingers of his left hand which hung limply
at his side--the fear he felt was stronger than his
shame and tears rolled down his cheeks as he said:
"As I told Colonel Gibson, they killed Colonel
Oldham and took his scalp sir! Those savages killed most of our men--we never had a chance!"
St. Clair was well acquainted with the misery,
suffering, and death of battle--he could understand
the officer's terror but he said firmly:
"Get a hold of yourself lieutenant! Private,
get the lieutenant over to the doctor's tent! Have
the doctor take a look at your hand too!
Suddenly catching a glimpse of General Richard

* A descendant of Joseph Todd (1769-1837), Terry L. Todd,
Batavia,, IL located his progenitor's pension records
in the National Archives, Old War Indian File #25886

Butler through the smoke, St. Clair called him over and exclaimed:

"General Butler! The advance party has given away--the right wing must hold!"

Without hesitation Butler confidently replied:

"And it will sir!"

Twenty minutes later General Butler was wounded--ten minutes more and he was dead! Although he had been propped against a saddle beside a tree and was suffering terribly, the general had insisted on giving orders and shouting words of encouragement to his men as Doctor Edward Grasson tried to dress his wound. Brandishing his tomahawk, and screaming like a maniac, a jubilant Indian had quickly dashed out of the smoke and buried his weapon in the brave man's skull. But even as the tomahawk was descending, Butler had fired his pistol and the Indian had fallen dead at his side. Both had faced their last earthly adversary.

Chief Cornplanter was destined to later return to Butler's widow the general's Society of the Cincinnati medal which had been removed from the brave officer's lifeless body by an Indian. Although he would assure Mrs. Butler the general's body had not been scalped or mutilated, another gruesome story would say Butler's heart had been divided among the warriors in customary fashion--the heart of one who was so courageous would make them brave and strong. Regardless of such stories, suffice to say the most decent thing done that day for the mortal remains of those who fell along the Wabash was the curtain of pure white snow that was lowered that night over the frightful scene of man's inhumanity to man.

With the "battle" less than two hours old, and the dismal morning light filtering through the age-old trees, hundreds now lay dead and dying near the lifeless body of Richard Butler--and still the carnage continued. But, as Chief Cornstalk once said:

"It is easy for hot blood to flow when the war eagle screams!"

And so, with the adrenalin of combat now flowing freely in St. Clair's veins, not far from where Butler lay dead the white-haired general led a party of hastily assembled troops against some Indians Lieutenant Henry De Butts reported were creeping up a little ravine ("Bloody Run") and threatening the army's left flank. Although the Indians fell back at first, minutes later they stormed the left flank with such determined vigor it prompted St. Clair to fall back.

Captain Van Swearingen* and Ensign Brooks, two brave and fearless officers, attempted to organize a counter-offensive on the left flank but they were killed. Then, with their arms and leggings covered with blood and screaming like depraved savages, the Indians followed the retreating troops cleaving the skulls of their quarry. One Indian with zigzagging red and white lines painted on his chest deftly cut off the head of his victim and then impaled it on a spear he carried. Witnessing the inhuman savagery, Officer John Cummings threw his gun to his shoulder and put a ball through the warriors's heart. A few moments later Cummings received a fatal blow from a warrior's war club and fell dead in his tracks.

In charge of the outposts around the perimeter of the encampment, Ensign Cobb and Ensign Mortz had been killed during the early minutes of the attack and Ensign Turner was reported killed or missing in action and probably taken prisoner. Captain Newman was wounded and retreated to the center of camp but was later killed. Using reconnaissance information provided by Tecumseh, Little Turtle had ordered the early eliminaton of St. Clair's outpost guards.

In a post-battle account, Ebenezer Denny would say: "Our left flank, probably from the nature of

* Contrary to some accounts, including that of this author in BANKS OF THE WABASH (1986), this officer's given name was "Van." He was a distant cousin of Marmaduke Swearingen and not his brother. National Archives Records.

the ground, gave way first and the Indians got possession of that part of the camp. But, it being
clear ground, they were exposed and soon repulsed."

With the naueous thud of war clubs, screams of
both Indians and their quarry, shouting of officers
and noncoms, and snorting of the frightened horses,
the overpowering din was beyond description. While
trying to raise a flag during the fray, Lieutenant
Hooper was killed.

Fighting with the courage of Spartans, and in
the face of unbelievable carnage, Lieutenant Edward
Spear and his cannoneers attempted to organize some
resistance but their efforts were futile and, along
with other artillerymen, the lieutenant was killed.
The six brass and two iron cannons were never used
effectively--only two were ever fired. Efforts to
use the cannons had been thwarted when two of five
kegs of gun powder were found to contain sand. One
contained powder of an inferior grade that wouldn't
even fire. In advising St. Clair the artillery had
been "wiped out," Captain Mahlon Ford said Ensign
Bartholomew Shaumburgh, a regular of the U.S. First
Infantry who had attached himself to the artillery
after Major Hamtramck left, was the only officer in
the artillery, other than himself, who had escaped
the scalping knife. In his post-battle memoirs the
adjutant general applauded Shaumburgh's performance
during the attack. But now St. Clair asked Ford:

"And Major Ferguson?"

Shaking his head slowly, Captain Ford replied:

"The major was mortally wounded in the early
fire-- Officers Morehead and Thompson were with him
at the time and they were badly wounded sir!"

Two hours after the "battle" began, implements
of death and the dead and dying lay everywhere--but
still the vengeful warriors continued the murderous
attack without respect to age or sex. The smoke of
gunfire lay heavily about Private John McGinnis as
he seized a bayoneted gun from a lifeless soldier's

inert grasp and aimed it at one of the two warriors
who bore down on him. The militiaman still grieved
over the loss of his friend, Revolutionary War veteran Adam Troyer. With frenzied anger born of fear
and frustration, McGinnis yelled:

"I'll get one of you red niggers!"

But he didn't. Even as he charged the Indians
with intended bullet and bayonet, one of his adver-
saries ripped the gun from his grasp and the other
hit him with a war club splitting his head open and
splattering the grinning warriors with a sickening,
thick grayish-red substance. The confiscated rifle
had not fired--it still held some of that "inferior
grade" powder the soldiers complained about.

Nearby a gawky young levy from Delaware pulled
the trigger of his gun loaded with the same powder
and a heart-sickening "click" was the only reward
for the surprised youth whose seventeenth birthday
was the next day, November 5th. Now he kneeled on
his knees defenseless. With his unfired gun at his
side, and tears turning the dirt on his boyish face
into muddy tracks, the thud of his heart drown the
screams around him. Although tears now blurred his
vision, he made no sound--his eyes did his pleading
as he prayed. With a horrible grimace and fiendish
war whoop, the hideously painted figure before him
brought his tomahawk down with a dreadful blow that
split the levy's skull wide open.

With the Indians storming the left flank, Captain Truman and his cavalry dragoons waded into the
warriors with their long-bladed swords flashing and
firing their long-barreled pistols at close range.
Although the Indians initially scurried back across
the ravine at the south edge of the main camp, they
soon came back again against the spent muskets and
pistols keeping a sharp eye open for the cavalry's
swords. The abortive charge did not last long and
the spent dragoons fell back when Captain Alexander
Truman (Trueman), himself a seasoned veteran of the
Revolutionary War, was wounded and had to retreat.

Not only were military troops caught up in the slaughter, civilian contractors and camp followers alike were indiscriminately slain as Indians leaped from one victim to another--men,women, and children were killed in cold blood as the screaming warriors reaped their vengeance. Soon after the first shot was heard Robert Bonham (Benham) took a ball in his elbow. A captain in the Revolutionary War, and now employed as a horseman by Hodgdon, Bonham was later killed in the hand-to-hand combat around him. Daniel Bonham, a young man raised by Captain Bonham, was also wounded early in the attack. Shot through the hips, he was unable to walk. With great effort Benjamin Van Cleve got Daniel on a horse and pointed the scared youth, and equally frightened beast, toward the center of the camp. But in spite of all subsequent efforts to assist the lad, he was---like Captain Bonham---destined to remain on the banks of the Ouabache.

Actually, with guns being fired at point-blank range by friend and foe alike, war clubs and tomahawks being wielded with amazing rapidity and taking a heavy toll, and scalping knives glistening in the early morning light, it was difficult to avoid a death blow.

Men--civilians and military--literally ran in circles. Wives, children, washerwomen, and harlots were indiscriminately killed--some of the women ran aimlessly and some stood slack-jawed paralyzed with fear watching death approach. One future historian would estimate 197 of approximately 200 such camp followers were murdered this fateful day. Cut down if they tried to run, slaughtered if they faltered, officers, soldiers, wagoners, contractors, and camp followers alike fell in the crimson slush along the banks of the Wabash this early November day.

Trying to fend off an attack by three warriors who attack his Conestoga, Ezra Axton was killed and his wife was repeatedly stabbed as she attempted to protect her three children. Only Nathaniel escaped the Indian's scalping knife when he leaped from the Conestoga and hid behind a huge log.   Crying as if his heart would break, and babbling incoherently, a few minutes later he stumbled into the interval between Hank's overturned wagon and Jason's Conestoga where they had taken refuge.   Admonishing Nathaniel to "stay down," Hank tried hard to console the boy while Jason kept a sharp eye peeled for Indians.

Suddenly through the smoke Jason saw Viscount Malartie trying to help St. Clair mount a spirited brown horse that moved nervously about straining at the rein.   Throwing caution to the wind, Jason took off running and helped get St. Clair in the saddle. Then, without any hesitation, the general urged the horse forward and began urging his officers and men not to panic and make every shot count. Making his way back to where Hank lay all set to reprimand him for unnecessarily exposing himself to danger, Jason could hear St. Clair shouting:

"Hold your fire! Steady now...aim well! Make every shot count!"

In spite of the general's age and infirmities, and danger of constant exposure to repeated attacks from all sides, St. Clair rode up and down the line calling out orders and shouting words of encouragement.   Some, like Ensign Maxwell Bhines (Bines) of the cavalry, Captain Patrick Phelon of the 2nd U.S. Infantry, and Lieutenant Boyd of the 1st Regiment of Levies fell mortally wounded even as he watched. Seasoned officers, recruits, levies, pack-horsemen and camp followers were dropping everywhere the old general looked—he would have cried if he had time! But he didn't so he cursed the Indians, shouted orders, and moved among his troops with disregard for his own safety. There were several bullet holes in his great coat when a ball hit his second horse and it fell dead. Uttering mixed expletives, St. Clair recovered the sword he dropped when he fell off the horse and limped away looking for another mount.

As the carnage and looting continued, and more

and more of the grotesque and mutilated bodies lit-
tered the battlefield, Ensign John Whistler murmured a prayer his wife and children had not come with
him as they had discussed. Even as he now surveyed
the mangled "trophies" of the Indian's bloodthirsty
revenge, Whistler took a tomahawk blow on his arm.
In a quick counter-movement, he whirled around and
ripped open the belly of a startled warrior who had
stumbled over the body of a dead soldier who lay in
his path. The Indian fell face down and the ensign
buried his bayonet in the warrior's back.

Moments later another ensign knocked an Indian
down with the butt of his gun and then pushed the
bayonet on his weapon into his victim's chest until
the barrel was flush with the garishly painted skin
of the Indian. Momentarily stunned by the spurt of
the crimson fluid that sprayed his leggings, Ensign
Chase froze in his tracks staring down at the gory
mess at his feet. Standing there spellbound by his
own aggressive action, he was hit by a tomahawk and
moments later his bloody scalp hung from the belt
of an Indian who had a hideous scar on his face.

With the unbelievable melee raging all around,
a wounded officer addressed St. Clair:

"General. Captain Brockman, First Regiment of
Levies sir!"

St. Clair looked intently at the young officer
who had blood flowing down the side of his cheek.

"Yes captain, what is it? You are wounded."

"Just a little nick--I'll be all right sir."

The captain now looked down at the hand he had
wiped across his face--it was covered with blood.

"I was lucky I guess. But I am afraid we are
taking an awful drubbing sir! Captain Swearingen,
Captain Bradford, Lieutenant Spear, Lieutenant Mc-
Math--they are all dead sir!"

"And Colonel Darke?"

"He has been wounded," replied Brockman. "But
he was still giving orders and encouraging the men
to fight when he ordered me to give you this report

of the officers who have been killed."

"Thank you captain.   Now help me find a mount and then tell Colonel Darke I want to see him."

Brockman quickly located a bay mare and helped St. Clair into the saddle. But even as he did, two Indians raced out of the woods and headed for them. Quickly Brockman raised his pistol and sent a ball through the forehead of the first screaming Indian and then dodged as the other one swung his war club at him. The warrior made no move toward St. Clair. Now a shot rang out close to Brockman's ear and the Indian in front of him clutched his chest and blood oozed from between his fingers--a look of disbelief crossed the Indian's face as he took a step forward toward the captain and then fell to his knees--in a continued motion the warrior lunged forward and lay still on the ground. Brockman turned and saw Lieutenant Read (Reed) holding a smoking gun.

"Good work lieutenant!" shouted St. Clair.

And with that the general slapped his horse on the side and rode toward Major Gaither's battalion. He had not gone far until an Indian leaped from behind a huge tree and tried to grab the reins of St. Clair's horse. With a celerity of action men half his age would have envied, St. Clair's sword severed the Indian's arm from his body. In a lightning-swift follow-up movement, his second slash cut his adversary's throat and the mortally wounded warrior sank into eternal rest.

Although Colonel Sargent would later say Major Henry Gaither "attempted no extraordinary exertion" during the battle, an officer in his battalion, and veteran of the last war, Captain Benjamin Price led his company in a spirited charge but the brave captain was mortally wounded. Then, as men floundered in a shocked state of disbelief, the warriors raced through the breach braining everyone in their path with their tomahawk and war clubs. Occasionally a screaming Indian would pause long enough to rip off a scalp before leaping on to his next victim. Some were still alive when their scalp was taken and any plea of "mercy" went unheeded.

As Colonel Sargent's account of the battle was to reflect, men were not the only ones that fought the Indians that day:

"Even the women exerted themselves this day, and drove out the skulking militia and fugitives of other corps from under wagons and hiding places by firebrands and the usual weapons of their sex. We lost about 30 of them, many of whom were inhumanly butchered, with every indecent and aggravated circumstance of cruelty that can be imagined, three only making their escape." *

One of the camp followers, reported as "having her way with the soldiers," stood by an overturned wagon clutching some clothing she had grabbed when the onslaught overran where she had rolled up in a buffalo robe and slept. Using a sword he had taken from the body of a dead officer, and yelling like a demented savage, an Indian unceremoniously cut off her head--in her lifeless grasp she held two pieces of silver and five oblongs.

Nearby another woman stood defenseless in the shelter of a Conestoga holding the hand of her son. With the fingers of her other hand she touched the gaping gash in the child's head--it was spongy with coagulation. The lad whimpered and the poor woman screamed hysterically for mercy as an Indian with a hideous grin swung his tomahawk and struck her with a smashing blow across the face. As she slumped to the ground and loosened her hold on the boy's hand, he fell to his knees. Feeling a flood of warmth as her sphincter muscle failed, unseeing eyes searched the blackness for her son----a merciful void settled over her from which she never returned.

His lustful vengeance still not satisfied, the Indian kicked the child in the face. The lad's incessant cries for help stopped abruptly as his head

* Pg 268-269, OAAHSP, Vol. 33 (1925)

crashed against a wagon wheel. With seeming unconcern for the din of the battle, the warrior removed
their scalps. Laughing insanely, the blood-thirsty
heathen then slit the woman's throat and threw back
her dress exposing her crotch. Picking up a frozen
clod, he put it between the woman's legs, gave it a
vicious kick, and exclaimed:

"White woman want land? Me give her some!"

The Indian laughed hideously—it was to be his
last. Ensign Wilson had just rounded the corner of
the Conestoga and seen the Indian kick the sprawled
figure. Using the butt of his gun, Wilson knocked
the Indian down and quickly pushed his bayonet into
the warrior's chest. Somewhat startled by his own
aggressive action, the normally mild-mannered young
man now respectfully pulled the woman's dress over
her naked legs, kicked the dead warrior in disgust,
and was walking away when another Indian hit him in
the head with a tomahawk and ripped off his scalp.

Through the gun smoke Officer McNickle saw the
Indian taking Wilson's scalp and, taking a page out
of the Indian's book on wilderness warfare tactics,
he waited behind a tree for the killer to pass. As
the Indian now passed twirling his bloody "trophy,"
McNickles hands closed around the warrior's throat
in a death grip. Although the Indian struggled and
kicked violently for a few moments, McNickle never
loosened his grip until there was no more movement.
Only then did he allow the lifeless body to sink to
the ground. Thoroughly shaken by the life or death
struggle he had just "won," the officer was staring
at the bloody scalp beside the Indian he had killed
when a tomahawk ended his life.

Astride a horse that insisted on trying to get
the bit in its teeth, St. Clair saw Colonel William
Darke approaching and heard him say:

"You wanted to see me general?"

"Indeed I do," replied St. Clair. "I want you
to make a charge with part of the second line. Use
your swords and bayonets! Fixed steel is the only

thing those infernal savages feel!

With Major Jonathan Heart and his brave troops following closely, Colonel Darke led 350 soldiers--mostly troops of the Second U. S. Infantry--against the Indians. But despite the spirit with which the effort was undertaken, and the initial success of a bayonet charge, after the warriors were driven back 300 yards they regained the initiative and launched a devastating counter-attack. The resultant withdrawal only served to cause more chaos in the main camp. Repeated attempts were initiated on the left flank to drive the Indians back but the unseasoned troops were just no equal to the infuriated Indians who fought on their "home field" and their hit-and-run, hide-in-the-woods tactics kept the entire camp in a constant state of alarm and confusion.

Seizing a sword from her dead husband's hand, a half-crazed woman chased a soldier out from under a wagon tearfully exclaiming:

"Get out from under there and fight like a man you yellow-bellied laggard!

A soldier with a feather stuck in the crown of his hat reluctantly emerged from his hiding place, ran a dozen yards, and was preparing to crawl under another wagon when an Indian stepped from behind a tree and sunk a tomahawk in his skull---the vicious blow cut the feather in half. Quickly removing the blood-covered tomahawk and hat, the warrior glanced at the bloody hat and stem of the feather, threw it aside, and proceeded to rip off his victim's scalp.

Pausing briefly behind the silent artillery on the right wing, Captain Doyle's eyes were misty as they swept over the lifeless bodies of several poor souls who had been draped across the cannons to aid further desecration. Shaking his head sadly, Doyle saw an Indian pick up a powder keg and start toward the brow of the river. Taking quick aim, he sent a ball through the keg--nothing happened! Doyle then exclaimed:

"That lousy damn quartermaster!"

542

Left behind with the baggage detail when Major
Hamtramck departed, Captain Doyle reloaded and then
fired a ball through the head of an Indian who was
removing the shoes of a dead soldier. Five minutes
earlier Sargent had told him Indians had broken into the army's cache of liquor. His arm in a sling,
the adjutant general had exclaimed:
"Maybe those murderous heathens will get drunk
and fall in the river and drown!"
Having reloaded his gun, Doyle walked forward
to where he could better see the Indians across the
river who had crowded around what he saw was a keg
of whiskey. Close by an Indian was cutting off the
testes of a corpse impaled to a tree with a spear.
Doyle put a bullet through the Indian's heart.
Partly hidden by heavy smoke, a party of 25 or
30 Indians were stealthily making their way through
the silent cannons in the second line when seen by
a veteran of the Revolutionary War, Captain William
Piatt.*   This charter member of the Society of the
Cincinnati had just shouted to his men::
"Keep those guns primed and ready! Make every
shot count!   Corporal, get that wounded man behind
that wagon over there."
Seeing the Indians, in a voice that showed his
own disbelief, he called to Ensign Reaves saying:
"My God Reaves! There's hundreds of them red-
skinned devils!"
These were his last words--he never heard the
ensign's frantic warning before he took a murderous
tomahawk blow behind his left ear.
"Lookout captain--right behind you!"
According to a post-battle account written by
Jacob Fowler--a relative of Piatt, a veteran of the
Revolutionary War, and one who was there that fate-
ful day--the blow that Piatt received did not kill
him and he helped to guard the survivor's retreat.
Unfortunately, Captain Piatt and Ensign Reaves were

* Progenitor of genealogist/historian Roy Nichols, Columbus,OH

both destined to remain on the banks of the Wabash.

With dead and dying bodies everywhere, and the Indian's slashing corpses and driving sharpened oak stakes through some who were still alive, at eight forty-five Captain Robert Kirkwood exclaimed:

"My God Likens, look over there!"

Although wounded, Lieutenant Likens painfully turned and saw a woman waving a white cloth--in her left arm she held a crying infant wrapped in a blue blanket. In front of her stood an Indian threatening to strike her with his raised tomahawk. All of a sudden the Indian threw his weapon on the ground, snatched the baby from its mother's arm, and bashed the infant's head against a tree ending its crying.

Even as the infant's head exploded against the tree, Kirkwood shot the Indian. As another warrior now lunged at Kirkwood, the brave captain threw his gun aside and drew his sword from its scabbard. As he lifted the sword against the Indian, he was hit by a flying tomahawk. Fatally wounded, and now on his knees, the captain swung wildly with his sword until he fell forward on his face and lay still. A few moments later Likens was also dead.

Using his gun as a makeshift crutch, Adjutant Inslee Anderson* from Delaware stood rooted against a tree. His right leg was a mangled piece of flesh and his right arm had been severed below the elbow. Captain Erkuries Beatty from Trenton (NJ) had put a tourniquet around his arm to stem the flow of blood but the loss of his life sap had made the adjutant from the Second Regiment of Levies lightheaded and he was unable to help Kirkwood and Likens who fell nearby. In his state of delirium, he thought about his wife who had died back home, his two fine sons, James and Joseph, and his brother, Enoch. Watching the Indian now savagely rip off the captain's scalp

* Progenitor of Evylene Anderson Canup, Marietta, GA; Luther Allen Johnson, Owosso, MI; Jackie Ann Johnson Clift; and Jeanne Lynn Clift Guild, Sugar Land, TX.

and drive a sharp hickory stake through Lieutenant
Likens' heart, Anderson threw up. Moments later he
joined his wife, Elizabeth nee Inslee, in eternity.

At the rear of the second line Ensign William
Balch from Massachusetts, and five troops from the
Second U. S. Infantry, were suddenly assaulted by a
party of fifteen screaming Indians who raced out of
the trees and thick underbrush east of the encampment. Although the intrepid officer quickly raised
his pistol and took aim, a ball sent it spinning to
the ground before he could squeeze the trigger. In
a lightning fast movement, Balch drew his sword and
shouted words of encouragement to his troops as he
met the Indian charge head-on. Sorely outnumbered,
and then immobilized by fear as Balch fell mortally
wounded, the five soldiers were quickly wrestled to
the ground where they were bludgeoned to death and
scalped.

Near the center of the encampment a levy with
yellowish-brown hair and blue eyes walked aimlessly
through the smoke in a paralyzed daze. Although he
had taken a bullet in his chest, still he staggered
on with blood running down from the corners of his
mouth. Suddenly a pair of Indians rushed up behind
the mortally wounded levy and one buried a tomahawk
in his neck severing his spine. As he fell forward
on his face, and his body jerked spasmodically, the
two heathens fought savagely for the levy's scalp--
the long, blond hair would be a prize trophy.

In the relatively close confines of the battle
area--where deliberate acts of wanton cruelty were
now on permanent parade--Captain Slough stood with
Cheniah Covalt surveying the carnage and remembered
his midnight report to General Butler. He wondered
if his report had reached St. Clair--it had not. A
letter from Captain Buntin to St. Clair in February
of 1792 following a trip to the banks of the Wabash
with General Wilkinson's burying party would read:

"In the former part of this letter I mentioned
the camp occupied by the enemy the night before the

545

action. Had Colonel Oldham been able to have com-
plied with your orders that evening, things at this
day might have worn a different aspect. Some distance in advance of the ground occupied by the militia, they found a large camp not less than three-
fourths of a mile long, which was supposed to be
that of the Indians the night before the action."

Trying hard to rally his troops, but with the
adrenalin that flows from the hope of a victory now
ebbing, St. Clair sat astride his horse staring at
the carnage and thinking there must be 3000 Indians
in the surrounding wilderness. 120 years after the
surprise attack, an account* written by S.A.D. (his
initials) Whipple would report "2000 savages attack
the expedition." George Ash, a white youth who was
taken prisoner, adopted by the Shawnee Indians, and
present that fateful day, would say in 1829:

"Eight hundred fifty warriors went out to meet
St. Clair and on the way we were joined by about 50
Kickapoos."

But regardless of the precise number on Little
Turtle's "team," suffice to say after two hours and
a half of their determined assault the dead and dying along the banks of the Wabash was grim evidence
of the Indian's hate and fiendish depravity. Seated on his horse, St. Clair gave a fleeting thought
to a September day in 1788 at Monmouth, New Jersey
when General Charles Lee had let a possible victory
turn into a rout. With profanity that would make a
sailor blush, General Washington had thundered onto
the battlefield encouraging the soldiers and turned
the tide.

But that was Washington, and such good fortune
was not to be St. Clair's this early November morning. And now, as St. Clair was pondering President
Washington's farewell admonishment, his third mount
was hit by a bullet and two Indians nearby eyed the
fallen general with murderous anticipation. As one

* "Old Fort Recovery" by Whipple (1911)

Indian raised a silver-tipped tomahawk with obvious
intent, the other pulled a scalping knife from his
belt and started toward St. Clair who lay prostrate
with his left leg pinned under the horse. His eyes
now swept up from blood-stained moccasins past the
garishly painted chest and met the smoldering stare
of an Indian who surely intended to finish him off.
As a nauseous feeling of helplessness swept through
his body, the old general sucked in his breath and
prayed. One heart-stopping second later he heard a
guttural exclamation by one of the Indians.

With this utterance by the warrior holding the
bloody tomahawk, the Indians turned and disappeared
into the smoke. After painfully extracting his leg
from beneath the horse, he limped away toward where
his tent had stood. As he hobbled along, St. Clair
pondered the fact his life had been spared for some
unexplained reason. Suddenly he remembered---those
guttural Indian words he had heard meant "no kill!"
But then he scratched his head and wondered why his
life had been spared? He didn't have the answer.

His thoughts now quickly turned to the officer
who approached him inquiring if he could be of any
assistance. Moments later Captain Nicholas Hannah,
a levy officer from Alexandria, Virginia dropped a
gun he was holding as a bullet grazed his shoulder.

"Wow!" he exclaimed. "That was close general.
Where on earth did all of these Indians come from?"

Near the center of the second line an officer
of the Second U. S. Infantry thought the same thing
when he saw a party of Indians sneaking through the
trees between his regiment and Maj. Henry Gaither's
battalion. Fixing his bayonet, and grabbing a car-
touche, Captain John Cribbs* led a spirited charge
against the warriors with Lieutenant McRae covering
his right flank. Although Cribbs and his followers
fought bravely, they never had a chance. Suddenly,

* Progenitor of Ruth E. Cribbs, Steubenville, OH and
  Mildred G. DeWeerd, Pennville, IN

"ST. CLAIR'S DEFEAT"

Oil painting by Robert V. Van Trees in Fort Recovery Public Library

from behind a log, an Indian put a ball through the
captain's temple and he fell forward into the arms
of a grinning warrior--moments later his scalp hung
from the Indian's belt. With their fearless leader
now dead, the weapons of his disheartened men were
of little consequence against the ferocious enemy.

On Cribb's right flank Lieutenant McRae raised
his sword and charged the screaming Indians followed closely by his troops. Lunging and parrying, he
dropped the first two Indians he met but was wounded by a bullet and carried back towards the center
of the camp. Discouraged by the loss of Lieutenant
McRae, and faced with the overwhelming carnage all
around them, those who could walk or run retreated.
As they fell back, the bloodthirsty warriors took a
heavy toll. When one warrior's flying tomahawk hit
a soldier in the back and he fell mortally wounded,
he quickly ripped off his victim's scalp. Not content with just killing the soldier, the Indian then
repeatedly slashed the lifeless body with a knife.
While trying to halt this senseless, brutal action,
Ensign Purdie was killed by a tomahawk blow.

Literally caught in the middle as the warriors
pursued their quarry with murderous intent, a young
settler pleaded for mercy. Ignoring his pleas, and
uttering a war whoop, a jubilant Indian ran a spear
through his body, cut off his head, stuffed dirt in
the mouth, and exclaimed sarcastically:

"White man want land? Me give him land!"

This inhumane savagery referred to the fervent
efforts of white men to settle the wilderness land
Little Turtle was talking about when he adamantly
declared: "The white man will never plant his corn
beyond the Ohio!" At fifteen minutes after nine on
Friday morning, November 4th, 1791, it looked as if
the Miami chief's declamation might become a fact!

Captain Tipton, a member of the First Regiment
of Levies--and destined to die this day--remembered
the story his father had told him about how George
Washington had been accorded the "honors of war" at

Fort Necessity and thus spared total anihilation of his command by the wilderness enemy. Surveying the carnage before him, Tipton wondered why St. Clair was not being accorded this special privilege today when defeat was so obvious.

Even as he contemplated the impossible, nearby an officer of the Second U. S. Infantry, Lieutenant Richard Greaton, paused and took refuge behind Hank Weiser's overturned wagon. He was a veteran of the Revolutionary War wherein he became acquainted with Hank. Noticing the blood on Greaton's sleeve, Hank inquired about his wound and the officer replied:

"Some Indian tried to do me in! He did get my friend, Pat Phelon--he's from Massachusetts too you know. Small consolation but one of our troops sent that redskin to his happy hunting grounds! Indians got Ensign Balch too. We have really been taking a beating in the Second!"

One post-battle account would indicate 101 of 219 enlisted men in the Second U. S. Infantry Regiment were KIA (killed in action) and another 50 had been reported MIA (missing in action). 7 officers were also KIA. Greaton also told Hank:

"The general is talking with Colonel Darke and Major Clarke--something must be cooking! I better get my rump back to my outfit. Keep your gun handy and your powder dry Hank--and stay ready in case we have to run for it!"

Moments earlier St. Clair had made up his mind that further resistance was useless. Pondering his limited alternatives, he was aware of the perils of retreat--certain death was the penalty for everyone should such an undertaking fail. He also knew that removal of the cannons, gun carriages, and supply wagons would not be possible--there were only a few horses left to pull them anyway. The tents and all the baggage must be left behind. And, unfortunately, the wounded who were unable to travel would be abandoned--a tough choice for a field commander but one that had to be made.

600 miles east the president had just finished a breakfast meeting with Secretary of State Thomas Jefferson and the Secretary of War, Henry Knox. It was an enjoyable meeting but the president had been restless—he had a premonition something was wrong. As the two gentlemen were departing, the president suddenly remembered that terrible day in 1755 when Indians had swarmed out of the wilderness attacking General Braddock's army. In a flash his mind turned to his farewell admonishment to his friend, St. Clair: "Beware of a surprise attack!"

And now just before nine thirty on November 4, 1791 St. Clair also recalled that farewell warning. But now it was too late and he had made up his mind he must save the members of his expedition who were still alive and could join in a retreat back toward Fort Washington. Turning to William Darke he said:

"Colonel, I want you to take some of your men who are still of the spirit and condition to assist you and regain the road to the south by which we marched here yesterday."

Without hesitation Darke replied: "Yes sir!" Equally as old as St. Clair, and having served with distinction in the Revolutionary War, Colonel Darke gave a fleeting thought to that day in 1755 when he had been with Braddock surrounded by the wilderness enemy. Dismissing that frightful thought from his mind, with coolness and dispatch born of his years of military experience, Darke promptly organized a company of volunteers and explained their mission. That done, Darke ordered: "Fix bayonets men!"

Having given Darke his orders, St. Clair turned to Major Clarke and ordered the wounded officer to prepare to cover the rear of the retreat. Like Darke, this fine officer immediately went about his way selecting troops from a group of volunteers and then briefed them regarding their assignment as the "rear guard" for a retreat. Aided by Private John Harbeson, Major Clarke painfully mounted his horse and waited for the signal to go into action.

Feigning a charge designed to turn the enemy's right flank, from behind and to the immediate right of the Second U.S. Infantry Regiment, Darke led his task force in tight formation through the woods toward the "escape" road. With life itself at stake, and under the strong stimulant of fear, every nerve and muscle in their tired bodies was steeled to its utmost tension as they braved the fusillade of war clubs, tomahawks, spears, scalping knives, and guns with bayonets taken from dead soldiers. Every man knew the forfeit should he lose the race. With energy born of renewed hope, and swords and bayonets flashing as they ran, the spirited offensive caught the Indians by surprise and they gave way. With an "escape hole" open, the drums sounded "retreat!"

On the heels of this "wedge" of brave men, and closer than the hands of a clock at noon, the disheartened fled from an enemy that sought the blood of everyone and took no prisoners. As word of this "escape hole" swept through the camp like wildfire, anyone who could run, walk, crawl, or ride a horse, followed the "wedge" which had opened up their only possibility of staying alive. Although he had been wounded, General Butler's aide-de-camp, Lieutenant John Morgan from New Jersey was fortunate--he had a horse when the drums sounded "retreat!" Urging his mount forward through the trees at breakneck speed, Morgan made a determined dash for the "escape road" as surprised Indians fell back without resistance.

Then, with a complete disregard for everything other than saving their own life, the disorganized stampede of humanity rushed south on the newly cut wilderness road like the bulls running through the streets during the fiesta of San Fermin in Pamplona (Spain).

Minutes earlier Jason had watched Lieutenant Greaton leave the interval between Hank's wagon and his Conestoga. Then, peering out from the opposite end of where he and Hank had taken shelter, Jason's heart almost stopped when he saw an Indian wearing

a blue jacket riding toward him on a black horse--
it was Star! Ignoring Hank's quick admonishment to
"stay down," Jason dropped his gun and sprinted toward the horse and rider shouting:

"That's my horse you thieving Indian! Get off
my horse!"

Any recognition the horse might have had was
lost as the rider pulled up the rein sharply, eyed
the defenseless white man running toward him, and
quickly pulled a knife from his belt with his right
hand. Then, as Jason reached for the horse's rein,
the Indian grabbed his horse's mane with his left
hand and, in a lightning fast fluid movement, swung
under the horse's neck and came up with a slashing
blow that ripped Jason's body open from his crotch
to his throat.

Mary heard her husband's voice and was peeking
out from behind the canvas flap of their Conestoga
when Jason sank to his knees and then fell sideways
mortally wounded. Giving no thought to her safety,
and screaming hysterically, Mary jumped down from
the Conestoga and ran over to where her husband lay
bleeding profusely.

Blue Jacket intended to scalp the one who had
reached for the rein of the horse he had stolen in
Cincinnati, but as he turned quickly to insure his
horse was still there, a scar-faced Indian grabbed
his arm saying in Shawanese: "He is my friend!"

Although a little taken aback by the audacity
of a warrior who would interfere with the intent of
a war chief, Blue Jacket knew the warrior was very
brave...he could deal with him later. And besides,
there were plenty of scalps to be had this morning.
Giving the scar-faced warrior a scornful look, Blue
Jacket jumped on the black gelding and disappeared
in the smoke.

Meantime, Mary reached Jason's prostrate body
and, dropping to her knees, she cradled his head in
her arms as she moaned:

"Please God...please don't let him die!"

Mortally wounded, Jason looked up into Mary's tearful eyes and gasped:

"Oh Mary what have I done. I love you so much dear. I'm sorry. I am so sor........"

Jason's voice trailed off and he went limp in Mary's arms--he had chased his last dragon!

At this exact moment the warrior with the scar on his cheek shifted his eyes from those of the war chief to where Mary kneeled holding the head of her dead husband and crying hysterically. And while he looked--and a split-second before he could stop the murderous move--another Indian leaped from behind a tree and buried his tomahawk in Mary's skull. Now, as he watched, Mary slumped over beside Jason's already lifeless body.

Stepping forward quickly intending to stay the knife of the Indian who had killed the woman he had called his "friend," he was too late--blood spurted from a hole in the head of the Indian who was still holding a blood-stained scalping knife in his hand. With a look of surprise frozen on his painted face, the Indian dropped his knife and fell to the ground beside where Jason and Mary lay near the scar-faced warrior's feet. Knowing his two "friends" were beyond mortal help, the Indian glanced at the ring of smoke hanging over Hank's overturned wagon and then took eight or ten steps backward. Now he cautiously watched Hank approach the place where Jason and Mary lay.

As Jason had run toward the Indian in the blue jacket seated astride a black horse, Hank had taken quick aim with his gun and pulled the trigger but a heart-sickening "click" was all he heard. A nauseous feeling swept through his body and he grabbed Jason's gun but it was too late---his friend lay on the ground and Mary was in his line of sight. Moving quickly to the end of the overturned wagon for a clear shot, his attention shifted from the Indian mounting the black horse to another warrior who had suddenly appeared out of the smoke and now held his

raised tomahawk above Mary's head. As the tomahawk
was descending, Hank fired his gun. Unfortunately,
the ball from Hank's gun that hit the Indian in the
temple was a split-second too late and the descending tomahawk stuck in Mary's skull.

Keeping a sharp eye on the scar-faced warrior,
Hank quickly reloaded the gun Jason had treasured.
Then, and never taking his eyes off the scar-faced
warrior who stood motionless not far from where his
friends lay, Hank cautiously moved over to Mary and
Jason's lifeless bodies. Glancing down, Hank slowly shook his head as Mary's eyes stared unseeingly
at him and the sickening crimson substance from her
head mixed with the life sap of her husband.

Feeling someone touching his hand, Hank looked
down into the sad and tear-filled eyes of Nathaniel
Axton standing at his side. As tears now welled up
in Hank's eyes, and he quickly wiped them away with
the back of his hand, suddenly he heard what seemed
to be a lot of extra commotion and guns firing just
to the north of him where the Second U. S. Infantry
was located. Instinctively Hank looked over at the
place where the scar-faced Indian had stood--he was
gone. Momentarily stunned by all that had happened
the past minute or so, Hank's eyes had just shifted
from Nathaniel to where his friends lay in an ever-
widening pool of blood when he heard drums sounding
"retreat" and someone shout:

"Head for the trace boys! Run for you lives!"

Hank instantly recognized the voice as that of
his Revolutionary War friend, Jacob Fowler. Only a
couple of minutes before Lieutenant Greaton stopped
at his wagon, Hank had been talking with the wilderness wise veteran and recalled him prophesizing:

"We may have to make a run for it Hank!"

Grabbing Nathaniel's hand, and telling the boy
to "run like hell son," Hank headed for the Second
U.S. Infantry Regiment--he anticipated any "escape"
effort would probably be initiated by that regular
army organization.

With the rising sun now filtering through the
trees like threads of burnished gold, and clouds of
smoke hanging like a veil of death over the camp,
through the haze Hank suddenly caught sight of the
flashing swords and bayonets of Darke's volunteers.
Urging Nathaniel to run as fast as his legs would
carry him, Hank and the boy joined those who closely followed the "flying wedge" through the trees to
the wilderness road. A silver-haired descendant of
this boy* would visit Fort Recovery, Ohio 194 years
later and share with museum personnel (Mrs. Evelyn
Muhlenkamp, Barbara Meiring, & Richard Meiring) the
story of how the cold, hungry, and heart-broken boy
had been overtaken by a young woman on a horse who
offered to let him ride between her and a child behind her she said was her daughter. Arriving safely in Cincinnati, the woman took care of Nathaniel
Axton until he was grown.

Others who wanted to flee that day were not as
fortunate as Nathaniel. Some of the wounded pleaded in vain for a ride. Others merely asked someone
for a loaded gun and loaded pistol declaring: "I'll
get one of them Indians before they get me!"

But those who could ride, run, walk, or crawl,
soldiers and civilians alike, were motivated by one
dominant need--survival! Most of the soldiers discarded their spent guns---a few thoughtfully bashed
their gun against a tree so it could not be used a-
gain. Forgetting their comrades were right behind,
some thoughtlessly jabbed bayonets in the ground in
hopes a pursuing Indian would fall on it.

It was the opinion of one officer who was present that fateful day the conduct of the army after
quitting camp was disgraceful. But considering the
unmatched carnage the survivors had just witnessed,
it would be difficult to fully appreciate the feelings of those who sought to escape--they just threw
away any impediments and ran like scared rabbits.

* Mrs. Mattie Chase, Carrollton, Kentucky

Left along the retreat path were powder horns, guns, gun slings, pistols, cartridge boxes, company books, red and brown painted knapsacks, steel yards (scales), canteens, axes, axe slings, camp kettles, buff and black waist belts, quivers, drums, fifes, wooden bowls, wooden buckets, bayonets, scabbards, shovels, blankets, hammers, screwdrivers...anything to lighten the person of those who fled what only minutes ago seemed certain death. In spite of the cold weather, and upon hearing shots not far behind him, Benjamin Van Cleve took off his shoes in order to run faster. Later, along with a wounded ensign, Bartholomew Schaumburgh, Van Cleve trotted all the way to the Stillwater Creek crossing saying little but remembering much about what lay behind them.

Racing wildly down the wilderness road a tall, red haired woman stumbled over a discarded powder horn and would surely have fallen had not a soldier instinctively caught her. Then, as they rushed on, she hysterically related how her baby had been murdered right in front of her eyes. Although she had managed to save her flaming scalp, she would never forget this fateful day. In a 19th century graphic account of her flight, one writer would portray her as: "Red headed Nance, the oriflamme which soldiers followed back to Fort Jefferson!"

Another writer would relate:

"Like a frightened gazelle, Catherine Miller ran ahead of the fleeing troops, with her long hair streaming behind her!"

Regardless of the verbiage used to portray her flight, suffice to say both women and men ran for their lives this day and some woman gained an ill-sought place in history when her flight was likened to the ancient five-pointed red silk royal standard of France...the "oriflamme" which soldiers followed away from the bloody banks of the Wabash in 1791.

Stumbling along the wilderness road with tears streaming down his face, Corporal Mott could hardly believe what he had seen. Minutes before the drums beat "retreat," Mott had found his wife dead among the camp followers--her body savagely mutilated and her scalp ripped off. Swallowing convulsively, and urged on by Cheniah Covalt, Thomas Irwin and Samuel McDowell, Mott hurried on down the wilderness road.

Coming abreast of where a man, woman, and boy were talking with two wounded soldiers on a horse, the four men heard the man encouraging the woman to keep moving and pleading with the two blood-covered soldiers to permit the boy to ride with them. Only pausing for a moment, McDowell helped the boy mount between the two soldiers and then continued on down the road. McDowell would return on this road three months later with Colonel Wilkinson, and again in December of 1793 with Major Henry Burbeck, to help bury the mortal remains of the more than 900 dead and dying left behind this day. He was destined to return in 1838 with his wife, Mary nee Studebaker, and son, John, and purchase 200 acres of land north of Fort Recovery in Section 5 of Recovery Township. Before Samuel McDowell (1770-1847) would be buried in the Pioneer Cemetery at Fort Recovery, he would visit Kentucky during the autumn years of his life and chance to meet in Georgetown the small boy--now a man--whose life he helped to save this day.

As Cheniah Covalt hurried along the wilderness road, a sobering thought flashed across his mind-- of all the brave men who had left Covalt's Station to join General St. Clair's expedition, he would be the only one to return.

Although he himself was wounded, Sgt. Whistler had helped seriously wounded Colonel George Gibson mount an old horse. Already weakened from the want of provender, and now burdened by the weight of two men, the animal reluctantly responded to Whistler's constant urging as they wormed their way along the wilderness road. Although the two men would reach

* Progenitor of James J. Wagner, Lafayette, IN and Sherry K. Hunt, Greenville, OH

Fort Jefferson just before sundown, the colonel was
destined to die there of his wounds December 13th.

And while the survivors were fleeing for their
lives, St. Clair remained on the battlefield urging
everyone, except Major Clarke's party of rear guard
volunteers, to head for the "escape hole" opened up
by Colonel Darke's spirited charge. As the last of
those who could leave the battlefield ran, or rode,
toward the wilderness road, St. Clair ordered Major
Clarke's volunteers to initiate a rear guard action
to halt or delay the advance of Indians who pursued
the fleeing horde.

With energy born of prayerful hope, and heroic
dedication to the protection of those who fled for
their lives, Clarke's brave volunteers closed ranks
and met the Indians head-on. Fighting with swords,
pistols, guns, and bayonets in hand-to-hand combat,
the volunteers fought the Indians as shouting, cursing, and gunfire blended with screams, war whoops,
thud of tomahawks, and the clashing of steel swords
and bayonets filled the air. Firing at close range
and then falling back a few steps as they reloaded,
they were afforded a measure of protection as their
comrades swung swords and lunged at the enemy with
bayonets. Using rifle butts and bayonets, Clarke's
men thrust, parried, and dodged in the face-to-face
combat. Raising his sword to fend off an attack by
a warrior, Lieutenant McMath was hit by a bullet--
he was already dead when he fell against the blood-
stained bayonet held by the Indian.

Although Captain Slough was wounded, he was in
the thick of the rear guard action and saw McMath
fall. Quickly raising his sword, Slough put an end
to the warrior's intent to take McMath's scalp. As
the warrior fell to the ground dead, Captain Slough
heard Major Clarke summon him to his side.

Standing near the rear of those engaged in the
rear guard action, and watching the tail end of the
survivors rushing down the retreat road, St. Clair
said to Ebenezer Denny:

"I want you to push forward with all haste and cause a short halt in front so those in the rear can catch up. We will all fare better if we remain close. Advise me of any attack."

It would be almost two hours before Lieutenant Denny would get to the front and enjoin Lieutenants Morgan and Sedam to spread out the troops and fill the road to slow the stampede. Selected by General Butler as his aide, Morgan was capable but a little headstrong at times. One of the first to reach the "retreat road" opened by Darke's troops, Morgan now seized this opportunity to vent some of his pent up bitterness declaring:

"A more vigorous commander would have been able to effect a better security against a surprise attack!"

In answering questions posed by the committee appointed to investigate the "surprise attack," St. Clair would be adamant:

"The army was not surprised! We were prepared for action! We maintained the conflict with order and firmness. Three hundred of the undisciplined advance party gave way at the instant of the onset. Beaten we were—not surprised!"

During the unveiling ceremony of a monument at Fort Recovery, Ohio over the mortal remains of many who made the supreme sacrifice on November 4, 1791, General J. Warren Kiefer would counter criticism of St. Clair on July 1, 1913 saying:

"That there was a surprise attack is not even well established. We are too often prone to attribute defeat in any cause to the misconduct or neglect of friends, and rarely to the superior skill and energy of the opposition. The defeat must be attributed, not to the character of the attack alone, but to the active skill and bravery by which the Indians were led." *

Having vented his bitterness, Morgan joined in

* Pg 435-453 OAAHSP Vol. XXII (1913)

the effort to slow the nervous and impatient crowd that insisted on moving ahead as fast as possible. All too well they remembered the carnage that lay a short distance behind and everyone kept a sharp eye on the woods flanking the wilderness road fearful a bloodthirsty warrior would attack them any moment. And spurred on by occasional gunfire behind them, or the frightened scream of someone who had fallen behind, the survivors resisted any and all efforts to deter their forward progress.

Meantime, having dispatched Denny forward, St. Clair turned his attention to the fierce rear guard action before him and was shouting encouragement to the troops when he heard Captain Slough say:

"Sir, Major Clarke advises the rear guard cannot hold their present position much longer. The men's strength and resolve are ebbing!"

With further procrastination pointless, and in response to repeated suggestions he "hit the road," the disheartened general was assisted in mounting a decrepit horse by his aide, Malartie, and a wounded lieutenant. Although the lieutenant then ordered a frightened levy to lead the old pack horse, and St. Clair was indeed a "sitting target," he was forced to wait as the pack horse--with seeming unconcern--stretched out its hind legs and answered "nature's call." Only then did the decrepit old animal yield to the pressure of the soldier's impatient tugging. Slapping the old horse on the rump, the lieutenant shouted: "Hang on sir!"

"Thank you lieutenant" said the general. "And now young man, you look to your own safety."

St. Clair was fortunate--he was astride one of the few horses still available. Three horses had been shot from under him and eight bullets had gone through his clothing. Pulling his bullet-pierced coarse coat tightly around his shoulders, St. Clair disappeared among the terror-stricken survivors and the dead and dying along the retreat road.

Although nothing could detract from the heroic

offensive led by Colonel Darke, or the "rear guard" action led by Major Clarke, moments before the rear guard sprung into action Little Turtle had surveyed the battlefield from a point of vantage on the brow of the Ouabache. Seated astride a brown and white horse, an austere look of satisfaction crossed the face of the Miami chief as he looked at the silent cannons. Seated nearby on his black gelding, Blue Jacket relished the thought the white man would now know the Indians were "invinceable!" Standing next to the Shawnee war chief with his blood-covered war club at his side, Tecumseh pondered the thought of a force of thirty-five thousand warriors who would never need to fight what he called "the land hungry white invaders." He was destined to travel far and wide extolling the virtues of his plan for the "unification" of all Indians---a plan that would never materialize. Nearby Buckongehelas tucked a bloody scalp under his belt and savagely kicked the lifeless body of an artilleryman at his feet. With his own blood-stained tomahawk hanging at his side, and his leggings spattered with blood, Tarhe the Crane stared at the carnage before him and silently prayed Manitou, the Great Spirit, would now bring peace to this land where the Indians lived.

But "peace" was several years in the future on Friday morning, November 4, 1791 as Little Turtle's eyes swept the scene of man's inhumanity to man--mute evidence "the play" this morning had given the Indians a great "victory." To Blue Jacket he said:

"Soon the word must be passed. The singing of the lead birds must stop now. Our warriors must be satisfied with the scalps they have taken. Now the killing must cease!"

Little Turtle's proclamation, coupled with the Indian's avarice, probably as much as anything else prevented the total annihilation of everyone in St. Clair's expedition. Stragglers, and the sick and wounded who could not "keep up," were either killed and scalped or subjected to indescribable inhumane treatment. Although years later a writer would say "the Indians pursued the survivors all the way to Fort Washington," the fact is only a few engaged in chasing the fleeing survivors and "the chase" ended after no more than two or three miles. Most of the Indians were tired of "the play" and stayed on the battlefield taking scalps from the dead and dying, removing fecal-stained clothing, and fighting among themselves as the greedy warriors stripped the dead and wounded and wagons of loot while others engaged in inhumane desecration of lifeless bodies and torturing those still alive. As James H. Perkins related in his "Annals of the West" in 1846:

"Those unfortunate men who fell in the enemy's hands, with life, were used with the greatest torture---having their limbs torn off; and the women have been treated with the utmost cruelty, having stakes as thick as a person's arm drove through their bodies."

With St. Clair's army now in full retreat, the Indian women swarmed over the battlefield like bees in a field of new clover. Casually they went about taking scalps and removing blood and fecal-stained clothing from the dead and dying. Years later an Indian woman who was there said:

"Oh, my arm was weary that night from scalping white men!"

As the Indians loaded their plunder on horses, it was painfully obvious the cannons were too heavy to be easily transported. Accordingly, the cannons were removed from their carriages and either hidden or thrown in the creek (Bloody Run). Later events indicated they had anticipated retrieving them at a later date. Apekonit supervised the hiding of the cannons and later would tell Rufus Putnam where the artillery pieces had been hidden--but then he would be using his white man's name, William Wells.

John Brickell, a white boy who was captured by Indians and adopted by a Delaware chief called "Big Cat," was present this day. Later he would say he

saw no prisoners taken on November 4, 1791.   Among
Big Cat's plunder of guns, axes, and clothing, was
a marquee which the Delaware chief said would "make
good home for family of Whingy Pooshies!"

A post-battle report would indicate the army's
loss as including 316 pack horses and harness;   39
artillery horses, an unspecified number of private
and dragoon horses; 4 ox teams, 2 baggage wagons;
3 brass three pounders; 2 pieces of iron ordinance;
2 traveling forges; 384 common & 11 horseman tents
and marquees; 1200 muskets & bayonets; 163 felling
axes; 89 spades; 88 mattocks; 2 medicine chests;
all of the blankets; and the greater portion of the
pistols and swords carried by the military.   The
loss would be estimated by a quartermaster officer
at $34,000--another would say $32,810.* But in none
of the detailed accounts would there be any mention
of a missing paymaster's box which would excite the
imagination of some treasure hunters years later.

And years later a writer would say the Indians
lost 150 warriors in this "battle" but other credible accounts would estimate their casualties at 66
to 69 killed. In keeping with the Indian's custom
of concealing their dead, in order to deceive their
adversary, Little Turtle ordered their dead wrapped
in tent canvas shrouds and loaded on the captured
horses.   Then, as the victorious war party prepared
to leave with their loot, the warriors raised their
guns and fired an ear-splitting salvo to their dead
comrades. With the sun low in the western sky, and
leaving behind more than 900 mutilated bodies along
the Ouabache, the Indians rode north. Gloating and
glutted with spoils of victory, Little Turtle headed back to the Miami villages.

Twenty miles away, and headed in the opposite
direction, the tail-end of the survivors cringed in
fear as they heard the volley of gunfire and quickened their steps toward Fort Jefferson.   Ahead the

* Pg 423, OAAHSP, Vol. XXII (1913) indicates $33,000

first of the survivors met the First U. S. Regiment
eight miles north of Fort Jefferson and heard Major
Hamtramck say they had heard the cannons when still
a mile south of Fort Jefferson. Upon hearing some
say the army has been totally destroyed, Hamtramck
dispatched Lieutenant Kersey and a detachment forward to obtain more information and led the rest of
the regiment back to Fort Jefferson to insure the
security of that wilderness outpost. Later Colonel
Darke, whose son had been mortally wounded, accused
Major Hamtramck of cowardice saying he should have
led his troops forward and attack the Indians. Although Darke had him arrested, he was acquitted.

Near sunset Captain Shaylor watched the first
survivors drag into Fort Jefferson and ordered his
garrison to prepare for an attack. Arriving shortly after sunset, St. Clair told Hamtramck:

"It was terrible, simply dreadful! Your desire
to have been present is laudable, and no one appre-
ciates it more than I, although I sincerely doubt
whether you would have succeeded in doing more than
increase the death roll. I have looked upon human
slaughter but this reign of terror and bloodshed is
the most disastrous of all battles I have ever witnessed. My heart is sad and almost broken!"

Calling together the adjutant general, Colonel
Darke, Majors Gaither, Hamtramck, Ziegler, and Captain Shaylor, St. Clair took the initiative saying:

"Even with the First Regiment here the situation is dire. I want Colonel Darke to select some
men and push on immediately toward Fort Hamilton to
obtain sorely needed provisions. Officers Truman
and Sedam will accompany him."

Obviously too small for all of the survivors,
and with the shortage of provisions at Fort Jefferson making the situation even more acute, St. Clair
decided the sick and wounded would stay at the fort
and the rest of the survivors would push ahead. He
had concluded they might meet the supply convoy and
it was prudent he return to Fort Washington as soon

as possible. On the heels of Darke's departure at
ten o'clock, St. Clair's tired and hungry followers
continued on south in the cold and darkness.

Twenty-nine miles north of Fort Jefferson, and
shortly after the last Indian had left that macabre
scene of massacre, a lone figure slipped stealthily
away from the hollow tree where he had taken refuge
ten hours earlier. In the deathly silence he could
still hear the sound of war whoops, guns going off,
and the heart-breaking screams of the tortured and
dying. Already shocked and dazed by the day's har-
rowing experience, and now carefully making his way
through the bloody sylvan morgue, in the gathering
darkness he saw some among the mutilated bodies he
recognized. Choking down his urge to vomit, in the
cheerless light of the dying sun the lonely figure
cautiously followed the footsteps of the other survivors who had disappeared down the wilderness road
long ago. Stephen Littell was also gone before the
nocturnal visit of wolves and other wilderness pre-
dators that came to gormandize on human flesh.

That night a blanket of snow was gently spread
over the mutilated bodies and the barren branches
of the silent trees along the Wabash dropped tears
of pity on more than 900 pioneers whose earthly
hopes and dreams had ended---among the silent forms
lay Jason and Mary Evenstar. The wind that night,
and every night thereafter, would sing a solemn re-
quiem anew for the unsepulchered dead whose mortal
remains would blend with the hallowed ground where
Fort Recovery would be erected in December of 1793.

FORT RECOVERY

Scraping away the snow, and burying the mortal remains of those not buried in a common grave in early February of 1792, a detachment led by Major Henry Burbeck built a fort in late December of 1793 and named it FORT RECOVERY. According to THE ST. CLAIR AND WAYNE TRAILS (1989) by Toni T. Seiler, Sec'y-Treas., The Darke County Historical Society, Greenville, Ohio, the fort was about 150 feet by 350 feet with blockhouses twenty feet square. A one-third size replica (above photo) was built in 1936.

EPILOGUE

It came as no surprise to the disheartened St. Clair when he arrived in Cincinnati on Tuesday, the 8th of November in 1791, and found condemnation had replaced the elation that accompanied his departure a month earlier. Word of the massacre had preceded his arrival and the enormity of the debacle was the primary topic of conversation everywhere he turned. Momentarily laying aside the mountain of paperwork attendant his responsibility as governor, St. Clair prepared his report for the Secretary of War which he dated November 9, 1791:

"Sir: Yesterday afternoon the remains of the army under my command got back to this place. I have now the painful task to give you an account of a warm and unfortunate action as almost any that has been fought, in which every corps was engaged and worsted, except the First Regiment that had been dispatched upon a service I had the honor to inform you of in my last dispatch, and had not joined me."

After providing a candid account of the fierce engagement, St. Clair added a postscript:

"P.S. Some orders that had been given to Colonel Oldham over night and which were of much consequence, were not executed; and some very material intelligence was communicated by Captain Slough to General Butler, in the course of the night before the action, which was never imparted to me, nor did I hear of it until my arrival here."

Distressed over the death of his son, Captain

566868

Darke, during the November 4th battle--and incensed
by Major Hamtramck's refusal to proceed forward and
attack the Indians on November 4th, Colonel Darke's
scathing letter of November 9th to the President of
the United States said in part:

"I don't know what St. Clair intends to do but
I know the Indians are weakened and I would venture
my life if the Indians have not moved the cannons.
Time is of the essence and a violent push with one
hundred brave men................."

At Fort Washington Major Henry Gaither showed
Winthrop Sargent the ring, watch, and sword which
had been given him by General Butler before he was
killed. The sword was engraved: "No me sacque sin
razon----no me embaines sin honor." Gaither said he
was told the inscription meant: "Draw me not without just cause, sheath me not without honor." With
tears in his eyes he added:

"The general was a fine officer--a brave man!"

Arriving back in Cincinnati tired and depressed on Wednesday, November 9th, Darius Orcutt, Jacob
Fowler, and Hank Weiser were standing on the upper
level of the bank overlooking the Ohio bidding each
other farewell when Ebenezer Denny walked by saying
he was going upstream. Asked about the whereabouts
of Captain Samuel Newman, a regular from the Second
U. S. Infantry Regiment, Denny replied sadly:

"He was killed during the retreat--took a ball
in the back and fell off his horse I heard."

Watching Lieutenant Denny making his way down
the bank toward the river, Hank caught sight of a
familiar figure--it was Tom May. Excusing himself,
Hank walked over and said to Tom:

"Well, I see you're back again!"

Tom glanced at Hank and exclaimed:

"Hank, my God--what happened to you?"

Hank had paused along the retreat road to help
a seriously wounded soldier and the arm of his coat
and trousers were covered with blood. Busy staying
alive the past five days, Hank had given no thought

to his appearance. Not taking his eyes off the old pilot, Hank merely replied:

"I'm not hurt Tom. I'm all right."

When he offered no further explanation the old pilot broke the awkward silence saying:

"I brought another ark and three families down the river--just tied up. Rube told me the army had had a fight with the Indians but he didn't have any details. Said he thought you and Jason had gone up north with St. Clair's expedition."

The distress in Hank's bloodshot eyes prompted Tom to quickly add with a note of alarm:

"Have you seen Jason and Mary?"

Tears welled up in Hank's eyes as he replied:

"They're both dead Tom--Indians killed both of them. I.." Hank paused. Understandably shaken by the carnage he had seen, Hank shook his head slowly and continued almost apologetically: "It happened so fast Tom...and there wasn't a damn thing I could do! And to make matters worse, I had to leave them laying on the banks of some wilderness river a hundred miles north of here. That's awful!"

Tom said nothing--there was really nothing for him to say. He couldn't say "I understand"--no one could really understand the feelings of anyone who had survived the three hours of living "hell" Hank had been through or how he felt regarding having to leave his two friends. At last Hank added:

"It was either run or stand and be killed Tom! And poor Mary, she didn't have a chance. As for my friend Jason, well, he put up a good fight against the dragon out here, I will say that!"!"

Tom wiped a tear from his cheek with the back of his weather-beaten hand and thoughtfully said:

"I just remembered something you said you told Jason at the foot of the Laurels on your way out to this country Hank, 'sometimes the dragon wins!'"

Hank rubbed his chin, spit, and said:

"Yeah, I said that all right. By the way Tom, why don't you come down and stay a spell with Sarah and me and the kids? We'd sure like to have you."

As Hank and Tom walked down to the ark and Tom introduced the settlers to his friend, Denny headed up the swollen and ice-clogged river on November 9, 1791. Normally a four week trip, inclement weather and the treacherous river slowed his travel and he did not reach Philadelphia until December 19, 1791. Meantime, and upon being advised by a courier Denny had not reached Wheeling until November 29th, Major Ziegler was left in command at Fort Washington and St. Clair departed for Philadelphia December 8th on horseback. His overland route took him to Lexington and Crab Orchard in Kentucky, to Abingdon in southwestern Virginia, northeast through the Blue Ridge mountains to Roanoke, and on to Hagerstown and Lancaster. Following his 750 mile trip, he arrived at Philadelphia in mid-January to "face the music!"

Six days before Denny arrived in Philadelphia, on December 13, 1791 the MARYLAND JOURNAL reported an express had arrived on December 12th from the District of Kentucky telling of St. Clair's defeat. Arriving in Philadelphia December 19th, 1791 Denny had delivered St. Clair's message to Secretary Knox who immediately passed the tragic news to President Washington. Shocked and angry when he was advised of the "defeat," a widely circulated anecdote indicates Washington, in the presence of Colonel Tobias Lear, his secretary, angrily exclaimed:

"Its all over! St. Clair's defeated--routed--the officers nearly all killed and men by the hundreds! Yes, here on this very spot I took leave of him; I wished him success and honor. 'You have your instructions' I said, 'from the Secretary of War! I had a strict eye to them and I will add but one word...beware of a surprise! You know how Indians fight us!' He went off with that as my last solemn warning thrown in his ears. And yet, to suffer that army to be cut to pieces...hacked, butchered, and tomahawked, by a surprise--the very thing I guarded him against!"

Thrusting his hands in the air, he added:
"Oh God! Oh God! He is worse than a murderer!
How can he answer for it to his country! The blood
of the slain is upon him--the curse of the widows
and orphans--the curse of heaven!"

Moments later Washington, a fair and just man,
reportedly said to his secretary:

"This must not go beyond this room. I looked
hastily through the dispatches---saw the whole disaster but not the particulars." Soberly he added:
"I will hear St. Clair without prejudice. He shall
have justice!"

News of the massacre created a wave of depression from the infant government offices on the east
coast to the windowless cabins on the western frontier. And, in "finger-pointing" discussions of the
disaster, St. Clair was condemned everywhere. The
December 24th edition of the COLUMBIAN CENTINEL reported Major Jonathan Heart, one of Connecticut's
finest officers, had been killed in the debacle and
the topic on the tongues of concerned citizens was:

"Is Arthur St. Clair a rugged individualist or
a blundering misfit?

Although St. Clair requested trial by a court-
martial, there were not a sufficient number of senior officers available to serve on such a board and
his request was denied. Subsequently, on March 27,
1792 a resolution was introduced into the House of
Representatives requesting the president institute
an inquiry into the debacle. Seven representatives
were selected by President Washington to serve on a
committee--the first congressional investigation in
the history of this nation.

Although it took a long time, and the pompous
Henry Knox and Samuel Hodgdon tried to overturn St.
Clair's initial acquittal, a subsequent re-examina-
tion of the original findings resulted in unanimous
agreement confirming the findings and stating:

"The committee conceive it but justice to the
commander-in-chief, to say that, in their opinion,

the failure of the late expedition can, in no respect, be imputed to his conduct either at any time before or during the action, but that, as his conduct, in all preparatory arrangements was marked with peculiar ability and zeal, so his conduct during the action furnished strong testimony of his coolness and intrepidity."

Although the acquittal was gratifying, and St. Clair returned to Cincinnati where he continued to serve as governor, his "defeat" hung over his head like the sword of Damocles and he never escaped the veil of censorship that plagued his administration until he was summarily removed from office November 22nd, 1802 by President Thomas Jefferson. Returning to Pennsylvania, the tired old veteran lived on Chestnut Ridge west of Ligonier and died August 31, 1818. Having devoted his life and personal fortune to his adopted country in "fighting" the wilderness "dragon," it is a sad commentary on this country's respect for dedicated service that a pioneer leader and public servant like St. Clair should have lived penniless in the autumn years of his life and died in abject poverty being remembered by posterity for his "defeat."

Since there was only one Major General authorized for the U. S. Army in 1792, and Washington had picked Anthony Wayne to be the commander-in- chief, despite his old friend and comrade-in-arms's objection, the president insisted St. Clair resign his commission. Although it was not a popular appointment in Virginia where Governor Lee had been one of the nominees, Washington said:

"He (Wayne) has many good points as an officer and it is hoped that time, reflection, good advice, and above all a due sense of the importance of the trust which is committed to him, will correct his foibles, or cast a shade over them."

A "boy soldier" and veteran of the recent war, Wayne's blind obedience and leadership had earned him Washington's confidence on September 11th, 1777 in the Battle of Brandywine. Indicative of Wayne's respect for Washington was his reported declaration to his superior as they contemplated an attack on a promontory on the Hudson River called Stony Point:

"If your excellency will plan it, I will undertake to storm hell!"

Wayne's "daring bayonet attack" against Stony Point on July 15th, 1779 brought him conspicuously before the eyes of his country and he had been breveted a Major General in 1783. Knowing he had this officer's unquestioned respect, Washington was also confident Wayne wouldn't yield to the "unreasonable and ungenerous goading" the board of inquiry said St. Clair was subjected to. Properly admonished by Washington to not repeat the failures of his predecessor, the bold and confident Wayne headed west.

Called "Dandy" behind his back because of his disciplined manner of dress, Wayne was instrumental in the reorganization of the military. Proceeding to Fort Pitt in June of 1792, in early September he issued an order declaring each of his "Sub Legions" would wear distinctive colorful uniform markings to "develop esprit-de-corp." Later, on December 27th, the president announced that in the future the army was to be called "The Legion."

During the Great Indian Council in October of 1792 along the Miami-of-the-lake, British officials warned the over-confident Indians about a general who gathered soldiers while others stalled for time with their "peace offers" and pointed out the white man's avowed intent to "extirpate" the red man from the Northwest Territory. They also pointed out how the white man was "partioning" the land north of Cincinnati which was now called "Hamilton County."

As the white man talked of "peace," the Indian scouts told Little Turtle an army was being formed 20 miles northwest of Fort Pitt at a place called "Legionville." And, in April of 1793 they reported the general some called "Mad Anthony" had led 2,600 soldiers down the Ohio to a place below Cincinnati

574

he called "Hobson's Choice." Wayne wanted nothing
to do with St. Clair who watched the "Legion" drift
by Fort Washington. In June Little Turtle was told
"Mad Anthony Wayne" had enlisted the services of an
Indian fighter who now wore a major's uniform--they
knew him as Simon Kenton.

As the ground troops engaged in field training
on the north side of the Ohio, across the river the
mounted troops engaged in mock warfare. Wayne also
smoked the calumet with old Chief Cornplanter who
had been advised by Rev. Heckewelder, a missionary,
there were now more than 3,220 white people living
north of the Ohio excluding the military who trained on the Indian's "doorstep" with obvious intent.
Recalling Lord Dunmore's Treaty signed in 1771, the
chief hopefully remarked to Wayne:

"My mind is on that river, may that water ever
continue to remain the boundary of lasting peace
between the red man and his paleface brother."

But a treaty signed in 1771 was the last thing
Cornplanter's "paleface brother" had in mind as he
prepared to march north. On October 7, 1793 Wayne
led his Legion to a point beyond Fort Jefferson and
erected a fort he named in honor of General Nathaniel Greene who some said was "the man who saved the
south during the Revolutionary War." Here, at Fort
Greene Ville, Wayne went into winter quarters--the
general did not intend to suffer another "Surprise
at Paoli's Tavern" as he had in 1777.

Advised by his scouts of the "Legion" that now
moved ever closer, and the erection of yet another
of the white man's hated forts as they "negotiated"
a peace, Little Turtle could feel the hot breath of
"his dragon" and he counseled his Miami followers:

"We have beaten the enemy twice under separate
commanders. We cannot expect the same good fortune
always. The Americans are now led by a chief who
never sleeps. There is something whispers to me it
would be prudent to listen to his offers of peace."

But flushed with the warrior's success against

Harmar, and the overwhelming defeat of St. Clair's army, Blue Jacket's Shawnee warriors watched every move made by the general some called "Mad Anthony" and the Shawnees called "Kitcha Shemagna." Just as Tecumseh had predicted, Apekonit switched his allegiance and now helped Wayne in his campaign against the Indians. "Turncoat" William Wells was destined to meet "his dragon" at Fort Dearborn on August 15, 1812 and be killed by Potawatomi Chief Blackbird.

Refusing to be enticed into a winter conflict, Wayne dispatched Major Burbeck on December 23, 1793 northwest to the snow covered site of St. Clair's defeat where, during a five day period starting on Christmas day, a fort was erected. Although Wayne had considered naming it "Fort Restitution," he decided "Fort Recovery" would be a more fitting name. the "American Gazetteer" of 1798 said of this fort:

"RECOVERY, FORT, in the Northwest Territory, is situated on a branch of the Wabash River, about 23 miles from Greenville and 98 miles north by west of Cincinnati. It consists of two blockhouses and barracks with curtains, and contains sixty men."

As Tecumseh's spy-scouts informed Blue Jacket, in the spring of 1794 Captain Alexander Gibson, the commander of Fort Recovery, added a second story to the corner bastions of the wilderness outpost which was only 55 miles from the Miami villages and 65 miles from the mouth of the Auglaize where most of the Shawnee Indians now lived. In spite of Little Turtle's sage warning, and reluctance to attack the "dragon" which had reared its "ugly head" on the site of the Indian's 1791 victory against the white man, on June 30, 1794 he and Blue Jacket led 2,000 over-confident warriors in a fierce two-day assault against Fort Recovery during which Major McMahon, Captain Hartshorn, Lieutenant Craig, nineteen other officers, and 120 non coms and privates were slain. Repulsed in their British-aided attack, on July 1st the frustrated and dejected Indians picked up their dead and withdrew. The inability to shoot at their enemy from every side violated a cardinal rule of wilderness warfare. Although Little Turtle learned the "dragon" sometimes wins, and "resigned" as the Indian's leader, Blue Jacket was not convinced and picked up the gauntlet.

But not only had the soldiers at Fort Recovery repulsed the British-aided Indian's attack, for all practical purposes this "battle" was the beginning of the end of the red man's resistance to the white man's invasion of what had been their "domain." On July 28th (1794) General Wayne led his legion north from Fort Greene Ville and built "Fort Defiance" at the mouth of the Auglaize River declaring:

"I defy the British, the Indians, and all the devils in hell to take it!"

Reinforced by 1,500 Kentucky militiamen led by General Scott--but now under the flamboyant Wayne's command--at the Battle of Fallen Timbers on August 20th in 1794 the well-trained and well-supplied Legion defeated the Indians two miles from where the British had erected Fort Miami. Demoralized by the defeat, the Shawnees, Wyandots, Ottawas, Delawares, Miamis, Weas, and Chippewas then found the doors of Major William Campbell's nearby Fort Miami closed. Trading paper insults, but no bullets, the British literally "threw the Indians to the wolves."

Offering to negotiate peace with the Indians, Wayne marched up the Maumee and built a fort at the junction of the St. Marys and St. Joseph rivers in October which he named "Fort Wayne." Leaving John Hamtramck, now a colonel, in charge, he returned to Fort Greene Ville erecting several wilderness forts along the way. Taking judicious note of the number of the white man's forts that had now been erected, as early as November 3, 1794 the Indians began making peace overtures despite the British efforts to pour oil on the flames of the red man's indecision. Finally the "council of fires" was lighted at Fort Greene Ville on June 16, 1795 and Indians began to arrive bearing white flags and indicating they were ready to negotiate a peace agreement. It cost the Government about ten cents a day to feed the 1,130 Indian conferees who feasted on army beans, bread, molasses, and liberal rations of whiskey. With respect to Article 3 of the proposed treaty boundary line on the west, Wayne eloquently explained:

"You all know Fort Recovery, as well as the mouth of the Kentucky River. They are two points which will ever be remembered, not only by the present, but by our children's children, to the end of time."

On August 3rd, 1795 the Treaty of Greene Ville was finalized and signed by Wayne on behalf of the United States and 80 sachems of the Wyandots, Shawanese, Delawares, Ottawas, Chippewas, Potawatomies, Miamies, Eel Rivers, Weas, Kickapoos, Piankeshaws, and Kaskaskias. Signing the treaty, a chief said:

"We have buried the hatchet--you may depend on our sincerity." As an afterthought he added: "We cannot but be sincere, as your forts will be planted thick among us!"

Alleged to have fought in more battles against the white man than any other living person in 1795, the Shawnee Chief Black Hoof was present at General Harmar's and General St. Clair's defeat, fought at Fort Recovery in 1794, and was present when the Indians led by War Chief Blue Jacket were defeated at Fallen Timbers. One of the last to arrive for the signing of the treaty, once Black Hoof had signed, he never again fought against the Americans.

In the Garst House Museum at Greenville, Ohio hangs Howard Chandler Christy's oil painting of the "Signing of the Treaty of Greene Ville." Looking at the painting depicting Little Turtle holding a belt of wampum in his outstretched arms, the viewer can almost hear him saying what he did after signing the treaty:

"I am the last to sign this treaty. I promise I will be the last to break it."

Although Little Turtle died near Fort Wayne on

578

July 14, 1812, and the exact location of his mortal
remains is questionable, a monument 20 miles northeast of Fort Wayne was erected in his memory.   In
his "The Western Indian in the Revolution," Wallace
Notestein said: "The historian may tell its facts,
but the poet can ever tell its truth."   Thus it was
that Calvin M. Young said of the red man:

> *"Behind the hills he passed from sight,*
> *A sunken, fallen star,*
> *Until his voice is faintly heard*
> *Still calling from afar."* *

Tecumseh would neither attend the negotiations
or sign the Treaty of Greene Ville and was destined
to stir up a lot of hate and discontent before he
faced the "supreme dragon" along the Thames during
the War of 1812...and lose! As he would tell Chief
Roundhead, the infamous Delaware "executioner," in
1801 along the White River near where Winchester,
Indiana would stand years later:
"I will ride far and vist many. We will build
a single unified body of 50,000 warriors. If at all
possible, we will avoid war, but if it comes to war
we will not turn aside.   We will have a village of
Indians--not Shawnee, Miami, Potawatomie, Delaware,
Wyandot, or Cherokee. However, it will take ten or
twelve years!"
Regardless of who fired the coup de grace that
ended Tecumseh's colorful life, a Sauk chief named
Black Hawk is reported to have carried the lifeless
body of the Shawnee figure from the field of battle
along the Thames River in Canada east of Detroit as
darkness closed on the slaughter and the red man's
last hope of driving the white invader from his beloved land--the vast Territory of the United States
Northwest of the River Ohio whose Great Seal bears
the Latin phrase: "Meloriem Lapsa Locavit."

* Pg 107, OAAHSP Vol XXIII (1914)

In seeing this seal for the first time in 1936 above the east entrance of Ohio State University's Thompson Library at Columbus, and having absolutely no knowledge of Latin, the writer vividly remembers the words of another viewer who was providing his parents a "scholarly" interpretation of the phrase:
"It has something to do with a better taking the place of the fallen!"

Undoubtedly St. Clair envisioned a better land emerging from the virgin wilderness territory where he served as governor. In spite of the fact he did outlive his military successor, Little Turtle, Blue Jacket, and Tecumseh, his tenure as governor of the Northwest Territory was plagued with difficulties after the 1791 debacle. Some future writers would praise the controversial St. Clair declaring he was a self-sacrificing patriot—others would brand him as opinionated, a poor administrator, and an inept soldier. Although General John Watts de Peyster in his evaluation* of St. Clair in 1886 decried him as a politician and administrator, he praised him as a military man. In commenting on his acquiescence to "unreasonable and ungenerous goading which contributed to the 632 killed and 234 wounded of the 1400 effectives," De Peyster was of the opinion "obeying graceless and senseless orders is folly."

A poor politician? St. Clair held the highest office in this country in 1887! An inept soldier? He was appointed a major general during the Revolutionary War and was held in high respect by a military leader who became president of the U.S.A. And a poor administrator? For fifteen years St. Clair was the principal administrator of a vast territory far removed from the "seat" of a fledgling nation, devoid of readily available legal counsel, and with the troublesome Indians nipping at his posterior! In their OHIO HISTORY SKETCHES (1903), authors F.B. Pearson and J.D. Harlor declared:

* MAGAZINE OF AMERICAN HISTORY, Vol XV (February 1886)

"At the head of the long roll of Ohio's great
men it is fitting there should stand the name of
Arthur St. Clair, the friend and companion of Washington and Lafayette."

A lot of water has gone down the Wabash since
that ill-fated early November day in 1791, and the
silent sentinels that witnessed the carnage are all
gone. But yet today a lucky person, such as Larry
Keller, still finds an arrowhead, a tomahawk, or a
rare ceremonial "thunderbird stone" in the hallowed
soil around Fort Recovery. And, among the caring
citizens of the village whose motto boasts "a proud
past and a promising future," there are many like
Jim Zehringer, Nancy Knapke, Bob Freemyer, and Adam
Beach who are never too busy to take time out from
their work to pause and talk about the history of a
community that stands where so many brave pioneers
made the supreme sacrifice.

Today, far removed from the pace and turmoil
of city life, along some sylvan trail near historic
Fort Recovery one can occasionally hear what sounds
like the scraping of a bow across violin strings---
the mournful sound of Jason's violin echoing eerily
through the trees in the ethereal stillness.

A P P E N D I X

Although the author had intended to compile for inclusion herein a detailed "Military Personnel Organization Chart," fragmentary and conflicting data made this an impracticable task at this time. However, an alphabetical list of military and civilian personnel associated with St. Clair's expedition---excluding the Kentucky Militia which is presented on a separate roster---is offered below:

Legend: First U.S. Infantry (1US); Second U.S. Infantry (2US); 1st Regiment of Levies (1RL); 2nd Regiment of Levies (2RL); Cavalry (CAV); Artillery Corps (ARC); Wounded (W); Date of rank (DOR; and military personnel killed in action (KIA):

Adams, George - b VA 1767, d 28Nov1832 Fifer, 8 PA Reg. Rev War m Elizabeth Ellis 26Jun1796 Army scout with St. Clair as Captain or Civ?

Adams, Michael - Corporal

Addison, - Captain? Present at St. Clair's defeat?

Allison, Richard - Fr PA Surgeon, 1st Inf. DOR 29Sep1791 Disch. 1Nov1796 Present?

Anderson, Inslee - KIA Ensign or Lt, 2RL, Adj. Fr DE m Miss McDonough before 1791 2 sons

Armstrong, John - Fr Phila PA Captain, 1US At Fort Hamilton Nov 4, 1791

Ashton, Joseph - Fr NY Captain, 1US with Major Hamtramck 4Nov1791

Axton, Ezra P. - Civ. with wife 7 3 sons 11 yr old Nathaniel only survivor

Balch, William - KIA Ensign, 2US Aptd 4Mar1791

Bayley, - Captain, wounded. d at Ft. Jeff. per Wilson, "Fort Jefferson" Pg 25

Beatty, Erkuries - Fr PA Captain, DOR 29Sep1791 1US Surgeon? Left.Trenton NJ 23Jun1791

Beatty, - KIA? Ensign 2RL

Bedinger, George - 1756-1843 Fr VA. Rev War Off. Levy EN CO, Quit Army 25 Oct1791

Benham, Daniel - Civ. pack horseman, raised by uncle Richard Shot in hip Killed 4Nov

Benham, Richard - (Robert?) Rev War Captain. Apt horsemaster by QM Hodgdon Killed 4Nov

Bhines, Maxwell - KIA Ensign Bines rptd KIA Cavalry Cornet Bhines rptd wounded

Bird, Ross - Ensign, 1US Fr PA

Bissell, Russell - Aptd Lt 2US 4Mar1791 Arvd Ft. Wash. 21Oct1791

Boyde, Samuel - KIA (Boyd?) Lt 1US Surgeon? KIA per KY Gazette

Bradley, Daniel - Lt fr CT 2US Remained at Fort Jefferson Oct 1791

Bradford, James - KIA Fr PA Rev War Off Captain, AR Arvd Ludlow' Sta 6Sep1791

Brenham, Thoms - Captain with convoy on trail 30Oct1791 Benham, Bonham?

Britt, Daniel - Ensign fr PA 1US DOR 29Sep1791

Brooks, - KIA Ensign 1RL

Brockman, Joseph - KIA (Brock?) Fr VA Captain, Reg Army or 1RL Led 82 men to Ft Pitt

Brown, Charles? - Maj Brown rptd in KY GAZETTE, Vol V #9 12Nov1791 as KIA KY Militia?

Burgess, - KIA Lt, Adjutant 1US

Buell, John H. - Fr CT ?2US or 2RL (a Capt. Russell Buell arvd Ft. Wash. 21Oct1791)

Buchanan, Wm - Captain, wounded

Buntin, Robert - Captain ? Aptd QM by St Clair 20Aug1791 Feb. 1792 ltr to St. Clair

Burnham, John - Major 2US fr MA At St. Clair's defeat?

Butler, Edward M - Captain, 1RL W b 1762, youngest of Butler's with St. Clair

Butler, Richard - KIA Major General, Second-In-Command

Butler, Thomas - Major, fr PA 1RL Bn Commander Wounded

Butts,   – KIA Officers Butts KIA? (See DeButts and Duberts)
Call, Richard   – Major, 1US? fr VA
Carmichael, John   – Aptd Surgeon, 2US 11Apr1792   At Fort Jefferson 4Nov1791
Carberry, Henry   – Captain fr MD ?
Chase,   – KIA Ensign, 1RL Surg Mate
Clay, James   – Ensign, 1US fr GA Aptd LT 28Dec1791 1US
Cobb, David Jr   – KIA Ensign fr MA
Covalt, Cheniah   – Civilian (?) with expedition. Lived at Covalt's Station
Craig, Isaac   – Lt. 1US Not at St. Clair's defeat but KIA 30June1794 at Fort Recovery
Crawford, John   Lt. 2RL Adjutant   Wounded 4Nov1791
Cribbs, John   – KIA 2RL (Krebs, Crebbs) b 11Jan1755 Pvt 8th PA Con., Rev War
Cummings, John   – KIA? fr PA Adjutant, Levies   Lt. Cummings dismissed 7Feb1794
Cushing, Thomas   – Captain fr MA, 2US   At Fort Pitt 4Nov1791 Aptd General 2Jul1812
Darke, Joseph   – KIA Captain (Col. Darke's son) Maj Clarke's Bn   Wounded?
Darke, William   – Lt Col, 1RL d 20Nov1801 Wounded 4Nov1791
Davidson, Wm   – Lt. fr MD Levy officer d 3Sep1822
DeButts, Henry   – Lt. fr MD wounded (See Butts)
Denny, Ebenezer   – Lt. 1US fr Carlisle, PA Detailed fr 1US as St. Clair's aide 30Sep17..
                           Promoted to Capt., DOR 30Sep91 with pay & allow. as Major
Diven, William   – Lt. fr PA Discharged 1Jun1802
Donahae, William   – Captain from PA?
Doughty, John   – Major, Reg. fr NJ   Declined apt as LtCol 2US
Doyle, Thomas   – KIA Captain 1US fr PA Officer Doyle reported KIA—same man? Remaine..
                           with St. Clair as OIC of baggage detachment?
Duberts,   – Lt. ? (Butts or De Butts?)
Duer, William   – Contractor after 3Jan1791. (Theodosius Fowler former contractor).
Dunn, William   – Horsemaster
Earnest, Robert   – Employed by Wm Duer
Elliott, John   – Surgeon, 1US? Apt Surgeon, 2US 4Mar1791
Faulkner, Wm   – (Falconer?) Captain, Levies fr PA Had company of riflemen
Ferguson, Wm   – KIA Major, Commandant, ARC
Fike,   – Major (or Pike?) arvd Ft Wash 22Jun1791
Finley, John   – Civilian, preacher's son fr Bourbon Co., KY per R. Banta, pg 190
Ford, Mahlon   – Captain, ARC fr NJ Wounded Died 12Jun1820   Officer Ford KIA?
Fowler, Jacob   – Major b 1764 Surveyor Rev War Vet Relative of Capt Wm Piatt fr NJ
Gaines, Bernard   – Ensign, 1US from VA DOR 4Mar1791
Gaither, Henry   – Major, Comdr, Bn of MD Levies. Reptd KIA 4Nov1791 but died 22Jun1811
Gano(e), John S   – Capt., Surgeon Aptd Major in 1792   KY Militia in 1791?
Gibson, George   – Lt Col, 2RL Arvd Ft. Wash. 8Sep1791 with Clarke & Gaither's Bn's
                           Wounded 4 Nov. & died at Ft. Jeff. 12 or 13Dec1791
Gihon,   – In Horse Dept. said Sargent
Glenn, James   – Ensign fr VA arvd Ft Wash with Col Darke. Aptd Lt. in Horse Dept.
Gough, Joseph   – Lt ?
Greaton, Richard   – Lt 2US fr MA DOR 4Mar1791 Rev War Vet Wounded 4Nov1791
Grasson, Edward   – KIA (Grayson or Grassen?) Surgeon, 1RL
Greathouse,   – Lt. Wounded 4Nov1791
Gregg, Aaron   – Ensign fr VA d 12Oct1804
Guthrie, Adam   – Capt. Wounded. Led 23 men to Ft Pitt. Had company of men fr Nelson C..
                           Kentucky District. Promoted 9Jul1792 to Major 2US   KY Militia 179..
Harbeson, John   – Private, Major Clarke's battalion
Hamtramck, John   – Comdr., Maj, 1US DOR 29Sep1789 French Canadian fr NY
Hannah, Nicholas   – Captain, 1RL Levy officer fr Alexandria, VA, d 11Oct1794
                           On right rear flank of army 4Nov1791
Harrison, Wm H.   – Ensign fr VA, DOR 16Aug1791, 1US   At Cincinnati 4 Nov1791
Hartshorn, Asa   – (David?) Lt., 1US fr CT, DOR 4Mar1791 KIA 30Jun1794 at Ft Recovery
Hayward, Nathan   – Surgeon's Mate fr MA Present 4Nov1791?

rt, Jonathan   – KIA Major, 2nd US fr CT Rev War Vet Arvd Ft. Wash 10Sep1791

h, John   – Lt, 2US fr VA DOR 12Jul1791 Aptd Capt. 21Feb1793 Escorted Treaty of
                  Greene Ville signatories to Philadelphia in 1796

gdon, Samuel   – Lt Col fr PA Quartermaster General Rev War Vet, Commissary of Stores

per, (John?)   – KIA Lt. Fr Bourbon County, Kentucky District?

din,   – Captain or civilian, Deputy to Quartermaster General

hes, Francis   – Lt fr SC Present 4Nov1791?

hes, Thomas   – Capt. fr VA, 2US Not present 4Nov1791 Aptd Maj 1st Sub Legion 3Mar1793

t, John   – Chaplain DOR 4Mar1791

ton,   – Lt Present 4Nov1791?

in, Thomas   – Pvt, ARC wagoner See OAAHSP Vol X, pg 380 d 30Oct1847 Bur Mt Pleasant
                  Cem. north of Monroe, OH

fers, John   – Lt, 1US fr CT DOR 22Oct1790

ifer, Daniel   – Sgt Major in 1791 Fr PA Aptd Lt 7Mar1792 (Daniel St. Thomas Jenifer)

so,   – KIA Lt, 2RL In General Butler's command

r, Joseph   – Captain, 2RL?

sey, William   – Lt., 1US fr NJ Dor 4Jun1791

gsbury, Jacob   – Lt fr CT, 2US Rev War Vet CO of 1st Sub Legion at Ft Wayne 22Oct1794

kwood, Robert   – KIA Capt., 2US fr DE Rev War Vet Led 67 men to Ft Pitt in 1791

ch,   – Major in 2US

ens,   – KIA Lt. (Lekon, Lukens, Licking)

tle,   – KIA Lt Little, Lytle, Lysle, or Lyle? Wounded, not KIA?

le,   – Lt In St. Clair's defeat per Richard M. Lytle, Cedar Rapids, IA (1992)

vis, Thomas   – Lt. or Capt. fr VA Levy Officer (or William Lewis, d 17Jan1825)

kwood,Benjamin– Ensign 1US or Levy Off. "From Ohio in 1791?" d 29July 1807.

artie,   – Viscount de, former Capt. in guard of King Louis XVI. St. Clair's
                  volunteer aide-de-camp fr Gallipolis colony. Wounded, rtd to France

ks, Hastings   – Ensign, 1US DOR 16Aug1791

tin, Thomas   – Lt 1RL fr GA DOR 3Jun1790 d 18Jan1819 Present 4Nov1791?

tz or Mortz,   – KIA Ensign (Marks?)

, William   – Ensign? A deserter, pardoned 23Oct1791

arthur, Duncan – With A. McGuffey, ran 30 miles to warn St. Clair says RUST (pg 390)

lure, William – From Cincinnati per Jacob Fowler and KY GAZETTE

rea, Wm A.   – Lt in Horse Dept. fr PA or NJ Aptd Col. 1824 & d 1832 (See Rhea)

roskey,   – Doctor in Gen. Butler's command. At Carlisle, PA in 1793

onough, Micah   – Ensign 2US Dismissed from service 29Dec1793

owell, Samuel   – Enlisted man in Butler's Regiment per Howe, Vol II (1896) Pg 228

rath,   – KIA? Lt

uffey, Alex.   – Scout Alexander, father of Wm Holmes McGuffey who arvd York, PA 1771

ane, Daniel   – Lt fr MD in ARC Resigned 2Apr1793

ath,   – KIA Lt (M'Math?) 1US

ickel,   – KIA Ensign fr CT (Lt McMichel or McMichael?)

herson, Mark   – Lt, 1RL fr MD

Rhea,   – See Rhea

lcher, Jacob   – Lt 1US fr PA Resigned 13Dec1793

ller, Catherine– Survivor

ller, Edward   – Lt, 2US fr CT DOR 27Aug1791 Present 4Nov1791?

lls, John   – Capt., 2US On recruiting duty 4Nov1791 Died 8Jul1796

ntford, Joseph – Capt 1US fr NC DOR 3Jun1790 (Mumford) Led 50 men NC to Ft Wash in 1791

ntfort, Henry – Ensign, 1US fr GA Resigned 11Jul1794 (See Montford, Joseph)

orehead,   – KIA Ensign Officer Morehead wounded per one account

rgan, John   – Ensign, 1US fr NJ Lt., DOR 4Nov1791 Brig. Major, Gen. Butler's aide
                  Wounded. Rptd KIA. Cashiered out of service 31Dec1793

rgan, Rawleigh – Lt headed back to Ft. Wash 3 Nov with discharged levies

rris, Staats   – Lt ARC fr NY DOR 26Jul1791 d 1Jun1802 Presen 4Nov1791?

tt,   – Corporal in Artillery. Wife killed in the battle 4Nov1791

Mumford, Joseph – Captain, 1US fr NC DOR 3Jun1790   Led 50 men fr NC in 1791
Nance,   – Survivor "Red headed" Nance, the "oriflamme" survivors followed—Nan
Newman, Samuel – KIA during retreat, Captain, 2US fr MA or CT
Nicoll, Abimael – Lt, ARC fr NY Present 4Nov1791?

O'Neil, John   – Irish artilleryman, deserted 17-20Oct and hanged 23Oct1791 (See Wade)
Orcutt, Darius C – Civilian fr Cincinnati
Paine,   – Ensign?
Pasteur, Thomas – Lt, 1US fr NC d 29Jul1806
Patterson, Joseph– Major fr NJ BN commander
Patterson, Rob't – Colonel 1754-1827 fr Lexington, KY Not at St. Clair's defeat
Peters, William – Lt, 1US fr NY discharged 1Jun1802
Phelon, Patrick – KIA Capt., 2US fr MA Aptd Capt. 4Mar1791
Phillips, Joseph – Surgeon's Mate?
Piamingo, Chief – Leader of 22 Chickasaws with St. Clair but not in the battle
Piatt, William – KIA Capt, Rev War Vet fr NJ Charter member, Soc. of the Cincinnati
Pike, Zebulon   – Capt, Rev War Officer fr NJ Arvd Ft. Wash 22Jun1791   d 27Jul1834
Platt, John   – Lt fr DE detailed as QM fr 2US On convoy duty, not in 4Nov battle
Polhemus,   – Ensign? In 4Nov battle?
Pope,   – Ensign, 1RL KIA? With Capt. Slough on 3Nov1791 recce mission
Porter, Moses   – Lt, ARC At Fort Wayne Oct 22, 1794 d 14Apr1822 In 4 Nov battle?
Powers, William – Capt., levy officer led 78 men to Ft Pitt in 1791
Pratt, John   – Capt, 1US fr CT Resigned 5Dec1793
Price, Benjamin – Lt, levy off. fr MD Wounded   Discharged 1Nov1796
Prior, Abner   – Lt, 1US fr NY DOR 3Jun1790 d 5Dec1800
Purdie,   – KIA Ensign?
Purdy, Robert? – Capt., 2RL Resigned fr Army 30Sep1803 Reported KIA 4Nov1791?
Read or Reed,   – Lt, 2RL reptd KIA but wounded. Comdr, 3rd Sub Legion at Ft Wayne 17
Reaves (Reeves), – KIA Ensign 1RL
Reynolds,   – KIA Ensign QM Reynolds rptd KIA
Rhea, James?   – Major, Comdr Bn of Levies Aptd Capt Reg Army 4Mar1791   Thomas Rhea?
                   Comdr of Fort Industry in 1794 (? Major John Rhea, Kentucky Militia
Rudolph, Michael – Captain 1US fr GA DOR 3Jun1790 Present at battle 4Nov1791
Sample (Semple), – KIA Colonel QM in T. Butler's Bn according to one report
Sargent,Winthrop – Colonel, Adjutant General (b1755 d1820) Wounded 4Nov1791
Scott, John M. – Surg. Mate 1US fr NJ DOR 29Sep1789
Sedam, Cornelius – (Sedham, Snydam) Lt, 1RL DOR 22Oct1790 Rev War Officer d 10May1823
Shaylor, Joseph – Capt., 2US fr CT DOR 4Mar1791 Left as OIC at Ft Jefferson 24Oct179
Shomburg, B.   – Ensign Bartholomew Schaumburgh, 1US at 4Nov1791 battle, atchd to ARC
Simmons,   – Captain re St. Clair's Papers
Slough, Jacob   – Capt fr PA in Butler's 1st Bn of Levies Led 69 men to Ft Pitt
                   Wounded 4Nov1791 Wounded at Fallen Timbers 1794   d 27Jan1738
Smith, John   – Capt fr NY 1US Rev War Officer Rptd KIA Aptd Maj 28Dec179   d 181
Smith, Pike?   – KIA Capt, 2RL
Snowden,Jonathan – Capt, Reg US Army Commanded 30 horsemen Led 101 men to Ft Pitt in 1
Sparks, Richard – Captain, Levy Officer Led 83 men to Ft Pitt in 1791 At Ft Wayne 17
Spear, Edward   – KIA Lt, ARC
St Clair, Arthur – Major General Congress. Inquiry chaired by Mr. Giles fr VA ("He bea
                   bushes in Kentucky for militia Sept 20-27 and rejoined army Oct 4th"
Stephenson,James – Lt.   Lt. John Stevenson in Kentucky Militia)
Strong, David   – Capt. fr CT US
Swearengin, Van – KIA Capt, 1RL, Bedinger's BN fr Winchester, VA Led 88 men to Ft Pi
Sullivan,John Jr – Ensign, 2US fr NH DOR 2Jul1791 Not present 4Nov1791 d 1796
Thomas, Richard – Capt. 1RL fr PA
Thompson, James – Sergeant in Capt. Carberry's company
Thompson, John – Ensign fr CT 2RL Listed as MIA? (See Robert Thompson)
Thompson, Robert – Lt 2RL fr PA DOR 4Jan1791 Wounded Officer Thompson rptd KIA & MIA

Thorpe, John   - Captain? QM Supt. of Artificers (Tharp?)
Tillinghast,John - Lt (Joseph?) fr RI Apt Lt 4Nov1791 2nd Infantry Aptd Capt 22Jan1793
                    Probably at Fort Jefferson on 4Nov1791
Tipton,   - KIA Captain (See KY GAZETTE Vol V No 9 12Nov1791)
Tisdale, Elijah   - Surg. Mate, aptd 4Mar1791 fr NC Resigned 31Dec1797 Present 4Nov1791?
Trescott, Lemuel - Major 1US fr MA DOR 4Mar1791 Resigned 28Dec1791
Truman, Alexander - (Trueman) Capt., Horse Dept fr MD DOR 3Jun1790 in 1US Rev War Vet
                    Found dead and scalped 20Apr1792 along Miami River on recce trip
Turner, Edward D - Ensign fr MA 2US DOR 4Mar1791 Apt Lt 13Jul1792 & Capt in 1793
Turner, Samuel B - Ensign Turner reptd KIA but taken POW
Vance, Samuel   - Lt.?
Van Cleve, Benj. - Packman (See Benjamin Van Cleve's Memoirs)
Wade, John   - Artilleryman, deserted 17-20Oct1791, headed for Detroit. Hanged 23Oct
Wade, John   - Ensign fr PA, 1US DOR 4Mar1791 "An Irishman" Resigned 14Jan1802
Ward,   - KIA Ensign, QM
Warren, Winslow   - KIA Lt., 2RL DOR 4Mar1791 fr MA Detailed fr Capt Kirkood's company as
                    Adjutant of 2RL
Whistler, John   - Sgt., 1RL fr MD. Wounded. Aptd Ensign 1793 & Captain in 1794
Whiting, Josiah   - Soldier fr Boston at St. Clair's defeat. Shoemaker later at Belpre, OH
Wilkinson, James - Lt Col, fr Md, aptd Commandant, 2US 22Oct1791 Not at St. Clair's defeat
                    Aptd Brig Gen 5Mar1792 (b in Benedict, MD, d in Mexico 28Dec1825)
Will, George   - Sergeant fr DE at Fort Washington on 4Nov1791 reportedly
Wilson,   - KIA, Ensign 1RL
Woodhouse, James - Surg. Mate?
Zeigler, David   - Major, 1US b Heidelberg, Germany 1749, d 24Sep1811 m 22Feb1789 widow
                    Lucy Sheffield who owned 4 shares of the Ohio Company stock

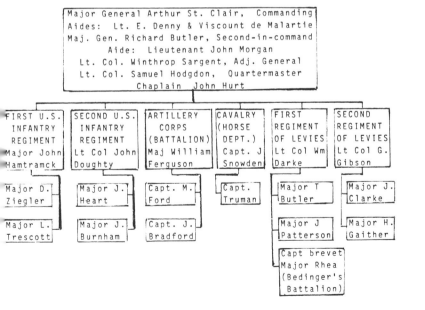

Young Street, Fort Recovery, Ohio

K E N T U C K Y   M I L I T I A

According to Washington Irving (pgs 214 & 215 of "Burton's Historical Collection"), Colonel Oldham's command included 319 troops of which 6 officers and 38 non coms and privates were KIA and 5 officers and 29 non coms and privates were wounded November 4th, 1791. Page 260 of Vol. XXXIII (1924) of the OAAHSP indicates Oldham led 290 non coms and privates and 29 officers, and 6 officers of the Kentucky Militia were KIA. Using information from numerous sources, including muster rolls of October 2 and November 11, 1791 (Record Group 94, Records of the Adj. General's Office, Entry Box 54, Box 1) provided by Stuart L. Butler, Military Reference Branch, national Archives Washington, D.C., the following roster was compiled:

Oldham, William	Lt. Colonel	KIA Commander
Adair, John	Major	Present 4Nov1791?
Brown, Charles	Major	Aide or second-in-command to Oldham?
Lemon (or Leman),	Major	KIA (Captain ?)
Montgomery,	Major	KIA (Captain ?)
Rhea, John	Major	? Capt. brevet Major or in 2RL US Army?
Chrystie,	Major	Brigade Major
Gray, Presley	Captain	Company Comdr.
Guthrie, Adam	Captain	Wounded, US Army?
Hickman,	Captain	
Madison, George	Captain	Wounded
Smith, Dan	Captain	
Tipton,	Captain,	KIA in US Army?
Briggs, William	Lieutenant	KIA
Hooper,	Lieutenant	KIA
Owens,	Lieutenant	W
Stagher (or Stagner),	Lieutenant	
Stevenson, John	Lieutenant	
Spencer, Thomas	Ensign	Wounded
Walters,	Ensign	Wounded
Nicholas, George	Officer	
Chalfin, Abner	Sergeant	Deserted 31Oct1791
McCasland, John M.	Sergean	(Castling ?)
Neal, Spencer	Sergeant	
Parker, John	Sergeant	Wounded
Shaw, William	Sergeant	

Ash, Benjamin	Private	KIA
Ashby, Beedy	Private	Wounded
Baird/Beard, Thomas	Private	KIA (Beard ?)
Barker, William	Private	
Bradshaw, Robert	Private	Militia ranger
Burnes, John	Private	Butcher, Frankfort, KY
Burnett,	Private	Later a Kentucky judge
Dougherty, Michael	Private	
Drew, John	Private	Deserted 31Oct1791
Friggs, Philip	Private	Deserted 31Oct1791
Gray, David	Private	
Hall, John	Private	
Hatfield, Thomas	Private	Deserted 31Oct1791
Haydon, Willford	Private	Deserted 31Oct1791
Heavenhill, Oliver	Private	
Hougham, Garvis	Private	Deserted 31Oct1791
Innes/Ennis,	Private	Fr Danville, KY
Kennan/Kenman, Wm	Private	b 1772 d 1827
Lasly/Lesley,Benjamin	Private	Deserted 31Oct1791
Littel/Little,Stephen	Private	
Lowrey/Lowry, Thomas	Private	
McGinnis, John	Private	KIA
Mead, David	Private	Deserted 31Oct1791
Moore, Nicholas	Private	Deserted 31Oct1791
Murphy, Arthur	Private	
Paine/Peyne, Jeremiah	Private	Deserted 31Oct1791
Paine/Peyne, Jonathan	Private	Deserted 31Oct1791
Piety, Thomas	Private	Wounded
Pursley, James	Private	
Ray, Joseph	Private	Present 4Nov1791?
Riley, Caleb	Private	Present 4Nov1791?
Ruble, Jacob	Private	Wounded
Samuels, John	Private	Deserted 31Oct1791
Serring, Solomon	Private	Deserted 31Oct1791
Shields, James	Private	
Smith, Dennis	Private	Deserted 31Oct1791
Spencer, Spear	Private	
Stilwill, John Sr	Private	Deserted 31Oct1791
Stilwell, Joseph	Private	Deserted 31Oct1791
Stilwell, John	Private	Deserted 31Oct1791
Strange, Philip	Private	Deserted 31Oct1791
Sturgin, Jeremiah	Private	Deserted 31Oct1791
Tibbes, Joseph	Private	Deserted 31Oct1791
Truble, Jacob	Private	Wounded
Todd, Joseph	Private	W Pension File #25886
Troyer/Thayer, Adam	Private	KIA
Woots, Mason	Private	Deserted 31Oct1791

BIBLIOGRAPHY

Aiken, Jane – "A Narrative Of The Campaign Against The Indians Under The
Command Of Major General Arthur St. Clair" (1812) Philadelphia

Albert, George Dallas – "Pennsylvania, Frontier Forts" Vol II (1918) Harrisburg

Alvord, Clarence Walworth and Bidgood Lee – "The First Exploration Of The Trans-
Allegheny Region By Virginians 1650-1674" (1912) Arthur H.
Clark & Co., Cleveland, OH

Antrim, Joshua – "History Of Champaign & Logan Counties" (1872) Bellefontaine

Armstrong, William Jackson – "Tecumseh, Shawnee Chief 1768-1813" (1913)

Atwater, – "History Of Ohio"

Bailey, Kenneth P. – "The Ohio Company" (1939)

Banta, R. E. – "The Ohio" (1949)

Barrett, Jay A. – "Evaluation Of The Ordinance Of 1787"

Beals, Ellis – "Arthur St. Clair" (1891) THE WESTERN PENNSYLVANIA HISTORICAL
MAGAZINE, April and July 1929

Bennett, John – "Blue Jacket, War Chief Of The Shawnees" (1943) Ross Co., OH
Historical Society

Bliss, Eugene F. – "Diary Of David Zeisberger, A Moravian Missionary Among The
Indians" 2 Vol (1885) Robert Clarke & Co., Cincinnati, OH

Bluejacket, George – "A Story Of The Shawanoes" (Oct. 29, 1829) Waupaughkonetha

Boyd, T. – "Simon Girty (1741-1818), The White Savage" (1928) Minton,
Balch, & Co., New York

Brant & Fuller – "History Of The Upper Ohio" Vol I (1890) Madison, WI

Brice, Wallace – "History Of Fort Wayne" (1868) Fort Wayne, IN

Burnett, Jacob – "Notes On The Northwest Territory" (1847) Derby, Brandley, & Co
Cincinnati, OH

Butterfield, Consul W. – "History Of The Girtys" (1890) Clarke & Co., Cincinnati

Carter, Clarence E. – "The Territorial Papers Of The U.S. Northwest Territory"
Vol III (1934) Washington, D.C.

Chase, Salmon Portland – "Ohio Laws" Vol I (1833) Corey & Fairbanks, Cincinnati

Cleaves, Freeman – "Old Tippecanoe, William Henry Harrison And His Times" (1939)

Clift, G. Glenn – "History Of Maysville & Mason County" Vol I (1936) Lexington

Colerick, E. Fenwick – "Adventures Of Pioneer Children" (1888)

Cone, Mary – "Life Of Rufus Putnam" (1886)

Cowen, Benjamin R. (General) – "The Conquest Of The Indians" (1905)

Darlington, William – "Christopher Gist's Journal" (1893) Weldin & Co. Pittsburgh

De Hass, Wills – "History Of The Early Settlement & Indian Wars Of West Virginia"
(1851) Wheeling Reprint, 1960 McClain Print. Co., Phila.

De Peyster, John Watts (General) "MAGAZINE OF AMERICAN HISTORY" Vol. XV (1886)

Denny, Ebenezer – "Military Journal Of Ebenezer Denny" (1860) Phila. Published by
Historial Society of Pennsylvania. J. B. Lippincot & Co.

Dills, R. S. – "History Of Greene County, Ohio" (1881)

Dillon, John G. W. – "The Kentucky Rifle" (1959)

Downes, Randolph C. – "Frontier Ohio 1788-1803" (1935)
"Council Fires On The Upper Ohio" (1940) Pittsburgh

Drake, Benjamin – "Tecumseh Shawnee Chief" (1841)
"Life of Tecumseh" 91858) Cincinnati

Draper, Lyman C. – MSS Wisconsin Historical Society Library, Madison, WI

Eggleston, Edward et al – "Tecumseh And The Shawnee Prophet" (1906) New York City

English, Wm Hayden - "Conquest Of The Country Northwest Of The River Ohio 1778-
              1783" (1896) The Bowen Merrill Co.
Evans, Nelson W. - "History Of Scioto County" (1903)
Farrand, Max   - "Fathers Of The Constitution" (1921) Yale Univ Press, New York
Finley, James B. - "Life Among The Indians" (1857)
Fowler,   - "Kentucky Pioneers And Their Descendants"
Franklin,   - "History Of Fayette County, Pennsylvania" (1882)
Furlong, Patrick J. - "The Investigation Of General Arthur St. Clair 1792-1793"
              (In St. Clair folder, KY Hist. Soc., Frankfort, KY)
Frazer, Ida Hedrick - "Fort Recovery, An Historical Sketch" (1948) Fort Recovery
Galbreath, Charles B. - "History Of Ohio" (1925) American Hist. Soc., Chicago
Ganoe, Wm Addleman (Colonel) - "History Of The U. S. Army" (1942) D. Appleton Co
Graham, W. R. (Colonel) - "Second Infantry Regiment"
Hale, John P. - "Trans-Allegheny Pioneers" (1886) Cincinnati, OH
Hall, Robert H. (Lt Col) - "Roster Of The Army Of The U.S., Jan. 1, 1792 (1887)
              Omaha, NE
Harmar, Josiah (General) - "Harmar Papers" Wm L. Clements Library, Univ. of Mich.
              Ann Arbor, MI   ("Outpost On The Wabash 1787-1791")
Harvey, Henry - "History Of The Shawnee Indians, 1681 To 1854" (1855) Cincinnati
Hatch, Wm S. - "History Of The War Of 1812 In The Northwest" (1812) Cincinnati
Heitman, Francis B. - "Historical Register & Dictionary Of The U. S. Army 1789-
              1889" Vol. 1 (1890)
Helderman, Leonard C. - "Danger On The Wabash" INDIANA MAGAZINE OF HISTORY,
              Vol. 34, No. 4 (December 1938)
Hildreth, Samuel P. - "Lives Of The Early Settlers Of Ohio" (1849) Cincinnati, OH
Hill, Leonard U. - Story re Geo. Ash in PIQUA DAILY CALL, Piqua, OH Feb. 21, 1951
Hinsdale, Burke A. - "The Old Northwest" (1888) T. Mac Coun New York City
Horn, William F. - "The Horn Papers: 1765-1795" " 3 Vol. (1945) Greene County
              Historical Society, Waynesburgh, PA
Howe, Henry   - "Historical Collections Of Ohio" (1847 Ed); (1857 Ed); Vol. II
              (1896), St. Clair battle site map, page 228; and Vol. I (1898)
Howells, Wm Dean - "Stories Of Ohio" (1897) American Book Co., Cincinnati & NY
Humphrey, Marshall - "History Of Kentucky" (1824) Frankfort, KY
Irelan, Mrs. Helen Moore - "St. Clair's Massacre" (1943) Booklet, Fort Recovery
Irving, Washington - "Life Of George Washington" 4 Vol (1832)
              "Burton Historical Collection" Detroit Public Library
Jackson, Helen Hunt - "A Century Of Dishonor, A Sketch Of The U. S. Government's
              Dealings With Some Of The Indian Tribes" (1881) New York
Jacobs, James R. - "Beginning Of The U.S. Army 1783-1812" (1947) Princeton, NJ
Johnson, Allan L. - "Ouabache Adventure" (1991) Creative Enterprises, Dayton, OH
Jones, A. E.   - "The Early Days Of Cincinnati" (1888)
Jones, David (Rev) - "A Journal Of Two Visits Made To Some Indians On The West
              Side Of The River Ohio 1772-1773" Burlington, Isaac Collins,
              Printer MDCCLXXIV Reprint 1971, Arno Press
Katzenberger, George A. - "Biography Of Major David Ziegler" (1912)
              "Major George Adams, 1767-1832" (1937)
Kellogg, Louise Phelps - "Frontier Retreat On The Upper Ohio 1779-1781" Edited by
              Kellogg (1917) Wisconsin Hist Society Collection
Kercheval, Samuel - "History Of The Valley Of Virginia" (1833); 2nd Ed 1850;
              3rd Ed 1902; and 4th Ed 1925

King, Rufus   -   "First Fruits Of The Ordinance Of 1787" (1888) Houghton,
                      Mifflin, & Co., Boston and New York
Lossing, Benson J. - "New History Of The U.S. From The Discovery Of The
                      American Continent To The Present Time" (1889)
Lowrie, Walter & Mathew St. Clair (Editors) - "American State Papers" (Class II
                      "Indian Affairs," Class V "Military Affairs," Vol. I)
                      Published by Gales and Seatim (1832) Washington, D.C.
MacDonald, William - "Ordinance Of 1787" (1898) Macmillan Co., New York
McBride, James   - "Pioneer Biography" 2 Vol 1869, 1871 R. Clarke, Cincinnati
McClain, G. Lee (Adjutant General) - "Military History Of Kentucky" (July 1939)
Miller, Francis W. - "Cincinnati Beginnings"
Newton, J.H. et al - "History Of The Panhandle, West Virginia" (1879)
Niles, Wm Ogden   - "Tippecanoe Text Book" (1840) Baltimore and Philadelphia
Palmer, Frederick - "Clark Of The Ohio" (1929) Dodd, Mead, & Co., New York
Pearson, F.B. & J. D. Harlor - "Ohio History Sketches" (1903) Press of Fred J.
                      Heer, Columbus, OH
Pease, Theodore C. - "The Frontier State 1818-1848" (1922) McClurg, Chicago, IL
Perkins, James H. - "Annals Of The West" (1846)
Perrin, Wm H. & J. W. Battle - "History Of Logan County, OH" (1880) Chicago
                      "Kentucky, History Of The State" (1885)
Perry, Robert E.   - "Treaty City" (copyright 1945) Bradford, OH
Quaife, Milo Milton - "Captivity Of O. M. Spencer" (1917)
                      "The Conquest Of Illinois By George Rogers Clark, 1752-
                      1818" (1920) Lakeside Press, R. R. Donnelly & Sons
Quinn, Robert Wilson - "The Kinkade Family 1756-1873"
Robinson, George F. - "History Of Greene County, OH" (1902) Clarke, Chicago
Rohr, Martha E.   - "Historical Sketch Of Fort Recovery" (1941) Ft. Recovery
Roosevelt, Theodore - "Winning Of The West" 5 Vol (1889) New York
Rust, Orton G. - "History Of West Central Ohio" (1934) 3 Vol. Springfield, OH
Ryan, Danniel J. & E. O. Randall - "History Of Ohio, The Rise And Progress Of An
                      American State" (1912) New York City
Sanders, Daniel C.   - "History of the Indian War" (1828) Richmond
Schoolcraft, Henry   - "History, Conditions, & Prospect Of The Indian Tribes Of
                      The United States" (1847) 4 Vol. Philadelphia
Seiler, Toni T.   - "St. Clair & Wayne Trails" (1989) Darke Co., OH Hist. Soc.
Shanks, J.P.C. (General) - "St. Clair's Defeat" (Speech at Fort Recovery, OH
                      published in the CINCINNATI ENQUIRER, October 17, 1891)
Shaw, Frederick B. (Colonel) - "140 Years Of Service In Peace And War" (1930)
                      Strathmore Press, Detroit, MI
Sibley, William - "The French 500" (1933) Gallia Co. Hist. Soc., Gallipolis, OH
Simmons, N. - "Heroes And Heroines Of The Fort Dearborn Massacre" (1896) Journal
                      Publishing Company, Lawrence, KS
Sipe, C. Hale   - "Indian Wars Of Pennsylvania"
Slocum, Charles E.   - "History of the Maumee River Basin" (1905) Toledo & Indpls
Smith, William Henry - "Life And Public Services Of Arthur St. Clair" Vol I & II
                      (1882) Robert Clarke & Co., Cincinnati, OH
Stephenson, John (Lt) - "Orderly Book Kept By Lt Stephenson While Serving In The
                      West, 1791-1794" Manuscript Div., Library of Congress
Strickler, Henry M. - "Massanhutten, Settled By The Pennsylvania Pilgrim" (1924)
Stuart, John   - "Memoirs of Indian Wars" (1833) Richmond

Stone, William L. - "Life Of Joseph Brant - Thayendanega" (1838) 2 Vol A. Blake
           "The Life And Times Of Sa-Gu-Te-Wat-Ha or Red Jacket" (1886)
           Albany, New York
Sweringen, Henry H. - "Family Register Of Gerret van Sweringen And Descendants"
           First Edition 1884, Second Edition 1894
Taylor, Edward L. (Colonel) - "Monuments To Historical Indian Chiefs" (1903)
Thwaites, Reuben G. - "Daniel Boone" (1903) New York
           "How G. R. Clark Won The Northwest" (1904) McClurg, Chicago
           "Early Western Travels 1748-1846" Edited (1904) Cleveland
           "Revolution On The Upper Ohio 1775-1777" (1908) Edited by
           Thwaites & Kellogg. Wisconsin Historical Society, Madison
Trumbull, Henry   - "History Of Indian Wars" (1846) Boston
Tucker, Glenn   - "Tecumseh: A Vision Of Glory" (1956) Bobb-Merrill, Publishers
Turner, Frederick - "The Frontier In American History" (1926) H. Holt, New York
Van Cleve, Benjamin - "Memoirs Of Benjamin Van Cleve, 1773-1821" MS in Dayton,
           OH Public Library. Also pub. in OAAHSP, Vol XVII (1908)
Van Hoose, William - "Tecumseh, An Indian Moses" (1984) Daring Books, Canton, OH
Van Trees, Robert V - "Fort Recovery, Scene Of Bloody Massacre" FORT WAYNE
           JOURNAL GAZETTE, Section E, May 29, 1955
           "Banks Of The Wabash" (1986) Apollo Books, Winona, MN
           "Ordinance Of Freedom" (1987) 2nd Ed. Prinit Press, Dublin
Viele, Teresa G.   - "Following The Drum: A Glimpse Of Frontier Life" (1858)
           Philadelphia 2nd Ed 1864
Van Tassel, Charles - "Story Of The Maumee Valley, Toledo, And The Sandusky
           Region" Vol II (1929) S. J. Clarke & Co., Chicago
Wallace, Paul A.W. - "30,000 Miles With John Heckewelder" (1958) Pittsburgh
Walter, Ellen Bodine - "The Early Van Swearingens" (Dec 1950) Pg 9-18 MAGAZINE OF
           THE JEFFERSON CO. HIST. SOC., Vol XVI, Charlestown, WV
Weigle, Luther A. - "The Pageant Of America" (1928) Yale U. Press, New Haven, CT
Whipple, S.A.D.   - "Arthur St. Clair Of Old Fort Recovery" (1911) Broadway Pub.
           Company, New York City
Williams, H.Z.   - "History Of Washington County, OH 1788-1881" H.Z. Williams
           and brothers, publishers (1881) Philadelphia
Willshire, Consul - "History Of The Girtys" (1890) R. Clarke & Co., Cincinnati
Wilson, Frazer Ells - "Treaty of Greenville" (1894) Correspondent Press, Piqua
           "The Peace Of Mad Anthony" (1907) C.R. Kemble, Printer
           "Journal of Captain Daniel Bradley" (1935) F. Jobes & Sons
           "Advancing The Ohio Frontier" (1937) Brown
           "Arthur St. Clair" (1944) Garrett & Massie, Richmond
           "Around The Council Fire" (1945)
           "Fort Jefferson" (1950)
Wilson, Wm Edward   - "The Wabash" (1940)
Witherell, B.F.H.   - "Reminiscences Of The Northwest" (1857) Wisconsin State
           Historical Society Collections, Vol III Madison, WI
Withers, Alexander - "Chronicles Of Border Warfare" (1831) R. Clarke, Cincinnati
           Reprint by McClain Print. Co., Parsons, WV (1961) Edit. &
           Pub. in 1895 by R. G. Thwaites. Reprint 1970, Parsons, WV
Young, Bennett H. (Colonel) "Battle Of Blue Licks: A Sequel To The Siege Of
           Bryant's Station" (1897) Filson Club Pubs., Louisville, KY
Young, Calvin M.   - "Little Turtle" (1917) Greenville, OH

OHIO ARCHAELOGICAL AND HISTORICAL SOCIETY PUBLICATIONS (OAAHSP)

Vol II (1888) – Photo, Marietta & Fort Harmar, Pg 16
Vol IV (1895) – "Beginnings Of The Ohio Co. etc." by Major E.C. Dawes Pg 1–29
Vol VIII (1900 – "St. Clair's Defeat" Pg 373–396 (List of KIA Pg 395)
                "Fort Loramie & Pickawillany" by Prof. R. McFarland Pg 479–486
Vol X (1902) – "St. Clair's Defeat" Frazer E. Wilson Pg 378–380 (Eye witness
                account by Thomas Irwin, Butler Co., OH)
Vol XII (1903) – "Clark's Conquest Of The Old Northwest" by E. O. Randall Pg 67
                Pg 145–159 Signatures On Treaty of Fort Greene Ville
Vol XIII (1904) – "History Of Fort Hamilton" by W.C. Miller Pg 97–111
Vol XIV (1905) – "Harris-Tarhe Peace Conference" by Emil Schlup Pg 132–138
                "Simon Kenton" by R. W. McFarland
                "Daniel Boon (sic)" by Wm A. Galloway Pg 263–277
                "First Newspaper Of Northwest Territory" by Galbreath" Pg 332
Vol XV (1906) – "Sinclaire's Defeat" (Poem) Pg 376
                "Tecumseh, The Shawnee Chief" by E. O. Randall Pg 418–498
Vol XVI (1907) – "Major Gen. Arthur St. Clair" by Hon. Albert Douglas Pg 455–476
                "Anne Sargent Bailey" by Mrs. James R. Hopley Pg 340–347
                "Western Indians In The Revolution" by Wallace Notestein Pg 269
Vol XVII (1908) – "Rivalry Between Early Ohio And Kentucky Settlers" Pg 30–35
                "Monument At Fort Jefferson" Pg 112–131
                "Old Fort Sandoski Of 1745" by Lucky Elliot Keeler Pg 357–430
Vol XVIII(1909) – "Me-she-kun-nogh-quah, Or Little Turtle" by N.B.C. Love Pg 115
Vol XIX (1910) – "Harmar's Campaign" Pg 393–396 (Letter by Thomas Irwin)
Vol XX (1911) – "Logan, The Mingo Chief 171–1780" by Pg 137–175
Vol XXI (1912) – "Survey Of The Seven Ranges" Pg 466
                "Major David Ziegler" by George A. Katzenberger Pg 127–173
Vol XXII (1913) – "Unveiling Fort Recovery Monument" Pg 419–454
                "Major George Adams" by Katzenberger Pg 533–542 (Map of
                St. Clair's battlefield on page 525)
Vol XXIII(1914) – "The Birthplace Of Little Turtle" by Calvin Young Pg 105–149
Vol XXV (1916) – "Editorialana" by E. O. Randall Pg 540
Vol XXVI (1917) – "Flat Boating On The Ohio River" by Rev. Isaac F. King Pg 78
                "Silver Mines Of Ohio Indians" by Prof. Roy S. King Pg 116
                "Mac-O-Chee Valley" by Karen Jane Gaumer, Urbana, OH Pg 455–469
Vol XXVII(1919) – "The Indian In Ohio" by H. C. Shetrone, Assistant Curator,
                OAAHS, Pg 274–508 (St. Clair's campaign, pg 416–419)
Vol XXIX (1920) – "Celoron's Journal" edited by Rev. A. A. Lambing
                "Father Bonnecamp's Journal, 1749" Pg 335–396
                "De Celoron's Exposition To The Ohio In 1749" by O. H. Marshall
Vol XXXIII(1924)– "Winthrop Sargent" by Charles Sprague Pg 224–236
                "Winthrop Sargent's Diary While With St. Clair" Pg 237–282
Vol XXXIV(1925) – "Tecumseh And His Descendants" by Chas Galbreath Pg 143–153
                (Tecumseh properly called Tikamthi or Tecumtha, pg 148)
Vol # 94 (1985) – "Meliorem Lapsa Locavit" by Edgar C. Reinke Pg 68–74

REGISTER – "Register Of The Army Of The U.S. From Jan 1, 1792" (May 887)
REGISTER – "Historical Register Of Commissioned Officers Of The Second U.S.
            Infantry From Its Organization March 4, 1791" Regimental Press.
            Fort Logan, Colorado (1905)

A proud past . . .
a promising future

FORT RECOVERY-OHIO

1794 BICENTENNIAL 1994

Fort Recovery
Bicentennial Logo
designed by: Colleen Vaughn